JAMES HERBERT

JAMES HERBERT

The Rats
Fluke
The Dark

GUILD PUBLISHING LONDON

This omnibus edition first published 1988 by
Guild Publishing
by arrangement with New English Library

The Rats © 1974 by James Herbert
Fluke © 1977 by James Herbert
The Dark © 1980 by James Herbert

CN 2496

Typeset by Colset (Private) Ltd, Singapore.
Printed and Bound in Great Britain by
Mackays of Chatham PLC, Chatham, Kent

CONTENTS

THE RATS

Prologue

The old house had been empty for more than a year. It stood, detached and faded, next to a disused canal, away from the road, screened by foliage gone wild. No one went there, nobody showed much interest anymore. A few windows had been shattered by the neighbourhood kids, but even they lost interest when nothing more than silence responded to the crash of broken glass. In fact, the only interest that had ever been shown by others was on the day they took the old woman away.

They knew she'd been living alone since her husband had died, never went out, and was only rarely seen peering from behind lace curtains. She never parted the curtains, just gazed through them, so only a hazy, spectral form could be seen by anyone interested enough to look. Her groceries were delivered every week and left on the back step. Powered milk was included amongst them. The local grocer said the old woman's bank paid her bills regularly every three months with never any queries as to the contents of his delivery. Which suited him. He'd been given a list at the beginning for a regular order, but if he forgot to include a pound of butter or two pounds of sugar now and again, no one noticed – no one complained.

Still, he was curious. He used to see her occasionally when her husband was alive, but even then she didn't have much to say. They were a couple of queer old birds, her and her old man. Never going out, never having company. But well off because they'd been abroad for years and since their return the husband never seemed to work. Then the old boy had died. The grocer wasn't sure of what but it had been a recurrence of some tropical disease he'd caught whilst abroad. The old woman was never seen after that, but the grocer had heard her. Nothing much, just the scraping of chairs or a door closing. He'd once heard her shouting at someone, but never discovered who.

People had begun to wonder about her. Some heard wailing coming from the house one night. Laughter another. Finally, complete silence for over a month.

It was only when the grocer found his previous week's delivery still on the doorstep that he reluctantly reported the matter to the police. Reluctantly, because he feared the worst and hated to see a nice little, regular order come to an end.

Anyway, it turned out she wasn't dead. A policeman was sent to investigate and then an ambulance arrived and took her away. She wasn't dead, just a lunatic. As far as the grocer was concerned she might just as well have passed on because that was the end of his little number. It had been too good at last.

So the house was empty. Nobody came, nobody went, nobody really bothered. In a year it was barely visible from the road. The undergrowth was tall, the bushes thick and the trees hid the upper storey. Eventually, people were hardly aware it existed.

Chapter One

Henry Guilfoyle was slowly drinking himself to death. He'd started six years ago, at the age of forty. He'd been a successful salesman for a Midland paper company and was ready to become area manager. The trouble was, he'd fallen in love late in life. And unfortunately, he'd fallen for one of his junior salesmen. He'd trained young Francis for five weeks, taking him on his business journeys up and down the country. At first he wasn't sure if the boy had the same inclinations as himself but as he grew to know him, the shyness, and the quiet loneliness of his protegé seemed slowly to dissolve that incredible gap he'd always felt with other men.

Why Francis had decided to become a salesman he'd never discovered. He wasn't the type. Guilfoyle could hold his own in the company of any group of men. He could be the typical bluff salesman; the dirty jokes, the sly wink, the back slapping, the professionalism of his trade hiding any imperfections in his maleness. He was a good actor.

Francis was different. It seemed the shadow of his homosexuality dampened his natural spirits, guilt tainting his moods. But he wanted to prove himself, to be accepted, and he had chosen a career that would make him forget his own personality by reflecting that of others.

The third week they'd stayed in a small hotel in Bradford. Only double rooms were available, so they shared one with single beds. They'd been drinking most of the afternoon with a client, after lunch, taking him to the usual local strip club. Guilfoyle had watched Francis in the darkened basement called a club because it had a bar and a membership fee.

The boy had watched the girls all right, but not with the exaggerated look of lust shown on the face of their client – and on himself, of course. And when the final sequinned garment of the

11

girl had been thrown aside, he slapped the boy's thigh, under the table with skilful heartiness, letting his hand linger, just for a moment, but long enough for their eyes to meet. And then he knew – oh, that glorious moment when he really knew.

There had been signs after the first week of course. Little test Guilfoyle had set. Nothing daring, nothing that could cause even slight embarrassment if rebuffed. But he'd been right. He knew. He'd seen the smile in the boy's eyes, no surprise, not even apprehension, and certainly not alarm.

The rest of the afternoon passed with a dreamlike quality. His heart beat wildly every time he looked at the boy. But still he acted superbly. His vulgar, and ugly – most definitely ugly – client never suspected. They were men, in a man's world, leering at big breasted, deformed women. The boy was a bit green of course, but they'd shown him how real men acted when they were confronted by naked thighs and fleshy tits. Guilfoyle emptied his glass of Scotch, threw back his head, and laughed.

When they got back to the hotel – the hotel Guilfoyle had chosen for special reasons – the boy was sick. He wasn't used to drink, but Guilfoyle had plied him with whisky all afternoon. Now he began to have regrets. Perhaps he'd overdone it. Francis had been sick in the cab on the way back from the club, and then again in their room, in the sink. Guilfoyle had ordered black coffee and poured three cups into the half-conscious boy. There was a mess on the boy's coat and shirt so Guilfoyle tenderly took them off and scrubbed the worst spots in hot water.

Then Francis began to cry.

He was sitting on his bed, head in his hands, his pale shoulders shuddering convulsively. A lock of fair hair fell over his long, thin fingers. Guilfoyle sat next to him and put his arm over the boy's shoulder. The boy's head leaned into Guilfoyle's chest, and then he was cradling him in his arms.

They stayed like that for a long time, the older man rocking the younger one back and forth like a five-year-old until the sobbing faded into an occasional whimper.

Guilfoyle slowly undressed Francis and put him into the bed. He gazed at him for a while then undressed himself. He got in beside the boy and closed his eyes.

Guilfoyle would never forget that night. They'd made love and the boy had surprised him. He wasn't the innocent he had seemed. Nevertheless, Guilfoyle had fallen in love. He knew the

12

dangers. He'd heard the stories of middle-aged men and young boys, knew their vulnerability. But he was happy. For the first time, after making love to another man, he felt clean. Purged was the feeling of guilt, gone was the feeling of self-contempt, disgust. He felt free – and alive, more alive than he'd ever been.

They'd gone back to their company after collecting a fair-sized order from their client in Bradford, and all had gone well for a while.

Guilfoyle expected to be area manager in a few weeks, large orders were coming in, and he saw Francis every day and most evenings.

Then, slowly at first, thing began to change. The younger lads seemed to be losing their respect for him. Nothing much, just a few cheeky back-answers to him. HIs older colleagues didn't seem to have too much to say to him anymore. They didn't avoid him exactly, but when in his company their conversation was always slightly strained. He put it down to the fact that he was soon to be manager and they didn't know quite how to treat him.

But then he caught some of the typists smirking behind his back at each other. Old Miss Robson, the office spinster, wouldn't even speak to him.

Finally, that fateful day. It was just after lunch, he'd returned from the local office pub where a table was always reserved for him when he was in town, and had gone into the staff toilet. He went into a cubicle, took his trousers down, sat and began to think about a new business venture he had in mind once he was area manager.

Then he glanced at the back of the door. He froze. It was covered with graffiti. All about him. Evidently, after the first one, it had developed into a game, for marks had been awarded to each one. The crude drawings were all of him (he assumed), and Francis, unmistakably Francis, because of the long hair that fell across his forehead and the gaunt features, cartoon drawings making his love ridiculous. Ugly drawings.

Blood rushed to his head, tears filled his eyes. How could they? How could they destroy their precious love like this? Dirty little minds, coming in here, scratching on the door, sniggering.

He sat there for half an hour, quietly weeping. He finally realised how ridiculous, how pathetic he looked; a middle-aged man in love with a young boy, sitting in a toilet with his trousers round his ankles, crying over words and drawings that understood nothing of his life.

He went home – he couldn't face returning to the office and the smirks of his so-called friends. He drank a bottle of Scotch.

That was the beginning of his deterioration. He went back to work next day but now it was different. He was aware. He saw a jibe in every remark made.

He went home again that lunch time, buying a fresh bottle of Scotch on the way.

After two weeks he began to get a grip on himself but suddenly Francis left. He hadn't said goodbye, just left a brief note saying he was sorry but couldn't stand the persecution from the people he worked with any longer.

He went to the boy's home but a hysterical scene with Francis's mother made him realise it was finished. Her threat of involving the law convinced him of this. Francis was very young.

His downhill plunge was rapid after this. He lost his chance of promotion, and was never quite sure if it was because of his reputation or the fact he was rarely sober now. Probably both.

He resigned and moved down to London, to lose himself in the quagmire of countless other disillusioned people. So for six years he hadn't worked much, but had drunk steadily till his money ran out. He was thrown out of lodgings more times than he could remember. He did odd jobs now and then in the markets, mostly Spitalfields, pushing barrows, loading lorries. With the few pence he made from this he bought cheap booze. He slept rough. At one time he'd been able to fulfil his sexual needs in dusty old cinemas, sitting next to men of his own kind. Only twice had he been threatened, once very quietly, with menace, the other time with much shouting and fist-waving, all eyes in the cinema centred on his shame.

But now he was too unkempt for even that. His clothes reeked, his body smelt of grime picked up in the market and the sheds where he slept. Any desire left in his body had been burned out by the cheaply concocted alcohol he now drank.

All he cared for now was saving up his meagre earnings to buy more oblivion.

Guilfoyle had worked hard that week. He'd conquered his craving for drink so that he could buy a complete bottle of cheap gin that Saturday. How he had survived, he never knew, but somehow he'd managed, the mental picture of a full bottle of gin ever-present in his mind. Now, as he shuffled along the dark streets by the docks, he drank until his head spun and his steps became more unsteady.

14

He climbed through a crumbling window of a house the slum-clearance people hadn't yet cleared. Staggering over rubble, he made his way to the back of the house to be out of the way of any lights shone in by policemen with nothing better to do.

He sat down in the corner of what must have once been the kitchen. Before the bottle was completely empty, he fell into a drunken stupor.

Hours later, Guilfoyle woke with a start. His befogged mind had registered something, but he didn't know what. He'd drained the rest of the gin before he felt the sharp pain in his left hand. As he jerked the hand up to his mouth, he heard something scuttle away. He threw the bottle after the sound when he tasted blood on the back of his hand. It began to throb and the taste of his own sticky blood made him retch.

He rolled on to his side as the gin began to pump from his body and laid there while his body shook.

Suddenly, he felt the pain again in his outstretched left hand. He shrieked when he realised something was gnawing at the tendons. He tried to get to his feet but only stumbled and fell heavily, bruising the side of his face. As he lifted his hand to his face again he felt something warm clinging to it. Something heavy.

He tried to shake it away, but by now it had a firm grip. He pulled at the body with his other hand and felt brittle hair. Through his panic he understood what held him in this monstrous grip. It was a rat. But it was big. Very big. It could have been mistaken for a small dog, but there was no growling, no long legs to kick his body. Only what seemed to be razor-edged claws, frantically beating on his lower arm.

He tried to gain his feet again as he felt more pain in his leg. He screamed.

The blinding pain seemed to run up his leg to his very testicles. More teeth sank into his thigh.

As he stood he felt tiny feet running up the length of his body. He actually felt hot, fetid breath as he looked down to see what could climb a man's body with such speed. Huge teeth that were meant for his throat sank into his cheek and tore away a huge flap.

His body poured blood now as he threshed around. Once he thought he'd found the door, but something heavy leapt up on to his back and pulled him forward on to the floor again.

15

Rats! His mind screamed the words. Rats eating me alive!
God, God help me.

Flesh was ripped away from the back of his neck. He couldn't
rise now for the sheer weight of writhing, furry vermin feeding
from his body, drinking his blood.

Shivers ran along his spine, to his shocked brain. The dim
shadows seemed to float before him, then a redness ran across his
vision. It was the redness of unbelievable pain. He couldn't see
any more – the rats had already eaten his eyes.

Then, he felt nothing, just a spreading sweetness over his
body. He died with no thoughts on his mind, not even of his
beloved, almost forgotten, Francis. Just sweetness, not even
pain. He was beyond that.

The rats had had their fill of his body, but were still hungry. So
they searched. Searched for more food of the same kind.

They had tasted their first human blood.

Chapter Two

Here we go again, thought Harris as he trudged down the dusty road to St Michaels.

Another bloody week teaching those little sods. Teaching art to little bastards whose best work is on lavatory walls. Jesus Christ!

He felt the same every Monday. The first three lessons in the morning were the worst. Around lunchtime his mood would gradually warm towards his pupils; there were one or two bright sparks amongst that crowd of scruffs. Thomas had brains. Barney had talent, and Keogh – well, Keogh had cunning. He'd never be a banker or an accountant, but he'd make money all right. Maybe not honest money, but he'd do well for himself.

Harris wondered what made one boy stand out amongst others. Keogh wasn't actually clever in academic terms. He didn't look much. Not big built, not slight. But at fourteen he had that cocky self-assurance that made him just that bit different from the rest. Hard up-bringing perhaps. But then, most of the kids in this place had tough home lives. What could you expect when they lived in dockland, fathers either working in factories or in the docks themselves, most of the mothers working as well, so that when the kids got home from school it was to an empty house. Then, when the parents got home, they had no time for them. Still, things were a lot worse in his day. Dockers earned good money these days, so did factory workers. A lot more than he earned as a teacher. The biggest division between working class and middle class nowadays was accent.

He'd come from the same area; the East End had no mystery for him. He remembered when he was at art school, telling some student friends about where he lived. 'How colourful', one girl had exclaimed. Colourful! Well, that was one way of describing it. At thirty-two he was back, teaching little facsimiles of his former self. They'd tried to give him a rough time at first, the little bastards, because art, to them, was playtime, and anyone who taught it was queer anyway. But he'd given them the treatment. He'd come down on them so hard, they were scared to whisper in his presence. Sort out the leaders, that was the trick; give them a hard time, show them up.

You didn't have to use their language exactly, but you could use their style. A good sharp clout now and again worked wonders. Because he was young, he had to show he could be a hard nut too. It was pathetic really. The times he'd had to suppress laughter when one of the little villains had tried to stare him out. He'd finally begun to win their respect, so he'd softened up a little, not too much – they'd have taken advantage – but just enough to get them to loosen up a bit.

Keogh was the only enigma. He knew he could get through to the boy, they both knew it – but Keogh would laugh at him with his eyes just at that last moment before mutual understanding was reached, and he'd know he'd lost again.

Harris wondered if it was worth it. He had his choice of schools to teach in but he wanted to help his own kind. No, he wasn't that noble. This was his home ground. He was in his element here. Besides, they paid more for teachers in 'underprivileged' areas. Still, Barney showed promise. Maybe if he talked to the boy's parents they'd let him go on to art school . . .

His thoughts were interrupted as he heard the school bell. Going through the gates he heard the clatter of running footsteps behind him.

Two giggling girls, both in short skirts, both with bouncing breasts, both about fourteen years old, flounced past.

'Anyway, the crumpet's good.' Harris smiled to himself.

He was halfway through the first lesson when Keogh walked in. He wore his usual uniform of short-sleeved, check shirt, braces holding his trousers at half-mast, showing the full length of his heavy boots.

'Good morning, Keogh,' said Harris.

'Morning.' Arrogant.

'Nice of you to join us.'

Silence.

'Well, what's your story this time?' asked Harris. 'Trouble with your back? Couldn't get off it?'

A couple of titters from some of the girls made Harris immediately regret his sarcasm. This was no way to break down Keogh's aloofness.

Still silence.

Oh God, Harris thought, he's in a mood. Christ, in my day, the kids were scared of the teachers being in a bad mood. Now, here am I hoping I don't upset *him* too much.

Then he noticed the boy's hand. He had a grubby handkerchief wrapped around it but blood was seeping through.

'Been in a fight?' Harris asked mildly.

'No.'

'What then?' Harder.

'I've been bitten,' Keogh grudgingly replied.

'By what?'

Keogh looked at his feet, trying to hide the redness creeping over his face.

'By a bloody rat,' he said.

19

Chapter Three

Karen Blakely shrieked with glee as the dog joyfully licked her nose. Only a year old, she was fascinated by this vibrant, four-legged creature who never tired of playing with her – unless it was time for its food. She grabbed its tail with her pudgy, little hands and pulled with all her tiny might.

The mongrel yelped with obvious relish and leapt around facing the girl again, plying her face with its juicy tongue, causing more delighted giggles and shrieks.

'Shane!' Karen's mother shouted at the excited dog as she came into the room. 'You mustn't lick the baby. How many more times must I tell you?'

The dog looked sheepishly at Karen's mother, tongue hanging out, panting with exhilaration. When it saw its water-bowl being filled at the sink it trotted over and began to lap furiously.

'Now, Karen, we'll just have a nice cup of tea and then we'll go out and get the shopping,' Paula Blakely said, smiling at her daughter, who was now pulling at the dog's leg. The dog and the little girl had both arrived about the same time; Karen prematurely, Shane as a present from Paula's husband, Mike. It was supposed to keep her occupied while waiting for the birth of their first child, but on the same day she'd gone into labour and had been rushed off to the hospital. It had taken twelve hours though for the baby to emerge, and the pain had been enough to discourage her from wanting any more. But she loved that child, more, she thought, than she loved Mike. Maybe because she was the only thing that really belonged to her. Perhaps not quite that. It was more because Karen was something she had produced, she had introduced into the world.

Looking at the gleeful baby, Paula smiled. Or was it just that she was so lovable? Paula and Mike hadn't wanted Karen so soon, they couldn't really afford her. They'd been lucky to get a place so quickly, dingy though it was. It was in a bad area, too near the docks, but they'd lived in Poplar most of their lives anyway, so it didn't make much difference. And it certainly wasn't a slum! Paula made sure of that. Other houses in the street may have been neglected by their tenants, but hers was spotless. Soon, when they'd saved enough money, they'd move out to Barking or Ilford, not too far from Mike's job at the garage, he was doing too well there to leave, but to a better class area, where you didn't have to keep a dog or a cat just to keep the mice down.

The whistle on the kettle began to shrill, interrupting her reverie. She turned it off and reached into the cupboard for the tea tin. She swore when she found it was empty. Mike drank coffee in the mornings but she had never liked its slightly bitter taste. She'd been reared on cups of tea as a child, the teapot in her house rarely being cold.

She looked at Karen for a moment. Would she be all right for a few seconds while she popped next door and borrowed some tea? Yes, she was preoccupied with Shane, watching him now slurp from his food bowl. She wouldn't be long, the baby couldn't get in too much mischief in the few seconds it would take her.

Taking a cup from the cupboard, she quickly slipped out of the room, leaving the door open, hoping Karen wouldn't even notice she was gone.

The baby happily watched the little mongrel gobble his food. She even tried some on the end of her finger, but spat it out when she discovered it wasn't to her taste.

Suddenly, the dog froze. The hairs on its back stood on end. It snarled at something moving in the doorway. The cellar door, which was in the hall next to the kitchen door, was slightly ajar, and a black shape scurried from it.

Shane bounded towards it, picked it up by its neck and shook it vigorously. A high-pitched squeal broke from the rat. Instantly, another appeared and leapt at the dog's throat, sinking its razor-sharp incisors deep. The infuriated dog spun around in a circle, trying to shake it off but still not letting the first rat go. Then another was on the dog's back, clutching with its claw-like feet, biting hard and ripping skin. Shane howled with pain and shock as more black creatures poured into the room.

The baby began to cry with horror as she saw her beloved playmate being hurt by the foul-smelling creatures.

More rats came into the small kitchen but these were different.

21

These were bigger, moving more cautiously, ignoring the violent struggle with the dog. They saw the crying baby, the bowl of dog food by her side. They slid forward, sniffing the air as they went. The food disappeared rapidly. They turned to the tiny figure.

The dying dog seemed to sense the child's danger, and jumped away from its attackers, three rodents still clinging to its body. It fell upon one huge rat which was already biting into the baby's leg. Shane threw the monster high into the air with its last remaining strength and turned to face the others. The little dog lasted a few seconds more, fighting with frenzied desperation, and then its body was torn to pieces under a black, writhing mass.

When Paula Blakely rushed into the room, she screamed in horror and utter panic. The scene didn't quite register in her brain. All she saw was a room teeming with bestial, furry shapes, tearing at something bloody. And then a small white shape. A tiny hand quivering above the mass of black.

'Karen,' she screamed.

She ran into the room, kicking, screaming, her blind panic giving her added strength and speed. She clutched at the arm and pulled. The little body came up but with two of the monsters clinging. Paula beat at them as she made for the door, her own legs already covered in blood from the bites she'd received. The two rats fell away, not from the blows, but because the soft flesh of the child separated from her body.

Paula ran from the house with her dead baby, screaming holding the bloody body to her breast.

The rats finished eating the dog, then scurried back into the cellar, the larger ones first.

Chapter Four

Harris took Keogh to the London Hospital to have the boy's hand seen to. He needed a chance like this to get on more friendly terms with his pupil, and as he had a free period for the next hour, he decided to take the boy himself. Already, on the way to the hospital he seemed more relaxed towards the teacher. When they got there, they were told to wait in the busy casualty department.

'Well, Keogh, how did it happen?' asked Harris.

'I was late, so I took the short cut by the canal,' Keogh replied.

'Yes, I know it,' Harris said.

The boy raised his eyebrows, but went on. 'It was just under the bridge, you know, where the old lock-keeper's house is. Well, there was a dead cat, see, and these two rats dragging it along. Christ, you should have seen the size of them, Mr Harris. Looked as big as the cat itself. Anyway, they weren't eating it, just sort of dragging it along, you know. So I slung a brick at them.' He paused, studying his bloody handkerchief. 'Well, instead of running off, they just turned and looked at me. I'd hit one, but he didn't seem bothered. Then, fuck me – oh sorry, they came at me. So I ran, didn't I. Not before one had taken a bite out of me hand, though. I kicked him into the canal and jumped over the wall and ran. But the funny thing is, when I looked back, there's this other rat, sitting on the top of the wall, watching me. He must have run right up it after me. Anyway, I didn't hang around, I cleared out.'

Harris smiled at the thought of rats big as a cat. Probably it had been a kitten anyway, and Keogh's nimble mind had done the rest. But that canal wall was high, he remembered it from when he was a kid, and even Keogh would have a job getting over it. But a rat? He knew some could climb, some species were arboreal, but to scale a six foot high brick wall? That took some doing.

Just then, all eyes in the casualty department turned as a hysterical woman, clutching a bloody bundle, was half carried in by two

23

ambulance men. A nurse dashed forward and tried to take the small shape from her, but she held on to it fiercely, her sobs racking her whole body.

It was then that Harris realised what she was holding. It was a baby. But by the look of its blood-soaked body, it couldn't possibly still be alive. Oh, the poor little sod, thought Harris. A doctor came along and tried to soothe the distraught woman, speaking quietly and calmly, making no attempt to relieve her of her burden. Then, with his arm around her, and the nurse on the other side, he led her away.

Everyone in the room appeared shaken by the drama. There was silence for a few seconds then everyone began to talk at once, although their voices were hushed. Harris turned to Keogh whose face was drained of blood and his knees trembled visibly.

Not as tough as you pretend, thought Harris, but he said nothing to the boy.

It was a while before they got in to see the doctor, who was very young, much younger than Harris. When doctors and policemen look like boys, old age *must* be creeping in, mused Harris.

'Right, let's have a look,' the doctor said, beginning to unwind the makeshift bandage from Keogh's hand. 'Nasty,' he examined the large teethmarks. 'What did it?'

'Rat,' answered Harris, for Keogh.

'More rats?' The doctor began to clean the wound, causing Keogh to flinch involuntarily.

'What do you mean?' asked Harris.

'Oh, that woman brought in earlier. Her baby had been attacked by rats. Dreadful state.' The doctor dabbed ointment on to the wound and began to bandage the hand. 'Dead of course, had no chance really. The woman's in a state of shock, blames herself for the whole thing. We had to put her out just to treat her own wounds.'

Harris found it hard to speak for a few moments. Anything nasty happening to kids always affected him this way; he'd seen too many of them mistreated to be unaffected by their misfortunes.

He said, 'But surely it's unusual for a rat to attack a human being? I mean, I know they can attack very small babies, and even fully-grown men when cornered, but this is different. When they chased the boy here, they could have got away. But they didn't choose to. They attacked instead.'

24

'Yes, I know,' said the doctor, taking a syringe from a tray. 'Just a quick jab now and you're done,' he smiled at Keogh. 'But as I understand it from the ambulance men they killed the family's dog to get at the child. Tore it to shreds according to the neighbours who went in afterwards. There was no sign of them though, just a few half-eaten carcasses, presumably killed by the dog, and gnawed at by their canibalistic chums. The cellar door was half open, but nobody ventured down there. That's a job for the police, I suppose.'

He placed the syringe in a jar. 'There we are. Come back tomorrow and we'll see how it's getting on, all right?' He turned to Harris. 'The whole business is very strange. We've always had a few cases of rat bites and even some diseases from them, this being that sort of area, but nothing like this. It's quite incredible. Let's hope they're just isolated incidents and nothing more.'

As they left the hospital, Harris noticed Keogh was still trembling.

'What's the matter? Did it shake you up?' he asked kindly.

'Nah, it wasn't that. I just don't feel so good that's all.' Keogh wiped his good hand across his brow.

Skiving? wondered Harris. No, he did seem a bit white and he couldn't fake the perspiration on his forehead. Perhaps it was the after-effects of the injection.

'Okay, you run along home, and take the day off tomorrow if you still feel the same. But make sure you go back to the hospital to get you hand looked at.' Harris knew he wouldn't see Keogh tomorrow now, he'd never miss the opportunity of a day away from school. Ah well, he'd been the same as a boy. A chance for a day off couldn't be ignored.

'Cheers,' said Keogh, and disappeared around a corner.

On the way back to the school, Harris thought about the rat incidents and the possible implications. He'd seen plenty of the disgusting creatures when he was a boy. He remembered the time years ago when he and his family had sat down to the Sunday lunch and their cat had appeared at the open window, carrying a dead rat in its jaw. They'd laughed at the idea of the cat bringing home its own Sunday lunch as they all jumped up and shooed it away. Another time, one of the neighbours had claimed she was chased down the street by a rat. Her husband had come out with a poker and had run after it, but it had disappeared into one of the bombed houses.

25

Harris thought they were a thing of the past now, which showed how out of touch you could get living in the top flat of a house in King's Cross. He supposed they existed just as much, but sanitation experts had driven them literally right underground. Lots of companies had sprung up and made quite a profit out of their extermination. Still, he supposed there wasn't too much to it, it was just that both incidents had happened on the same day. This wasn't the 14th century!

Chapter Five

The old warriors used to gather every night on one of the few remaining bomb-sites left in the East End of London. It was an old churchyard, just off the busy main road of Whitechapel and quite near Aldgate East underground station. It was thick with shrubbery and littered with open tombs. A single tower was the only remains of the once majestic church. That night six of them had gathered, safe in the knowledge that they couldn't be seen from the road. All were slowly destroying their insides by their incessant drinking of methylated spirits. All had reached the depths of despair, had given up the will to exist with the rest of the world. They rarely spoke to one another, their tormented minds were too occupied with their own misfortunes to concern themselves with anybody else's.

Among them was a woman, although barely discernible from the men in their shapeless rags. Mary Kelly was forty-nine, but she looked twenty years older. She cursed the others, cursed herself and most of all, she cursed God. The same God she had worshipped half her life in Ireland. As a child, she'd often gone to Mass three times on a Sunday and once every day of the week. She'd even gone into a convent at fifteen, but the solemn, solitary life had not suited her vivacious, although very religious, personality. Returning to her home town of Longford, she soon found life too dull for her natural exuberance. Her priest had tried to dissuade her from leaving, but one day, in the confessional, she'd told him something that had made him wonder if it wouldn't be best for her to go. Best for the boys in the town anyway.

The old priest wondered how any child so deeply religious could have developed such a sinful lust for sex. He finally decided he'd have more chance of saving her wayward soul if she remained in the town under his surveillance, so he visited her parents and persuaded them to make her stay. They had six other

27

younger children to support, so at first they weren't too eager to retain this extra mouth, but of course the parish priest had great influence over his flock. However, the following Saturday, Mary confessed an even greater sin, this time concerning his young, newly-appointed priest.

She left the following Monday to the relief of the old Father, whose ageing mind could no longer cope with the complexities of this promiscuous saint. Young father Aloysius had denied the whole affair on being directly, and rather gruffly questioned, and the old priest had been left in an even more confused state of mind. Surely, a girl so young and obviously devout could never make up such lies? But then again, if she were so devout to God as her record had shown, how could she be so incited by the evils of the flesh? His only answer was to pray for her soul and offer up a Mass to save her from eternal damnation.

Mary went to Dublin and got a job as a barmaid in a bar just off O'Connell Street. She met many men of course in her working hours and resisted none that made advances towards her.

After a while, not because of her growing reputation, but because the landlord's wife had discovered her and the landlord himself behind the barrels in the cellar, she had been dismissed. She next found employment in the canteen of a local brewery where the men soon found she was easy game. The only thing that puzzled them and caused much joking amongst them was the fact that she insisted on saying three Hail Mary's before climbing into bed with them. On her knees beside the bed, eyes closed, hands clasped tightly together like a child. They would have laughed even more if they'd known the reason for the prayers.

The first Hail Mary was to ask that she wouldn't fall pregnant, the second that she wouldn't get 'poxed', and the third that she would have an orgasm. She'd only learned about orgasms from her friends at the canteen and realised something had been missing all these years. Her craving for sex had never been satisfied and without knowing why, she had always sought more and more. It had always been enjoyable, but now she knew it could be glorious she was determined to experience it. She still attended Mass every Sunday and received Holy Communion every first Friday of the month. Soon, she began to go to church two or three evenings a week, to say the Rosary for the attainment of her sexual goal. It never once occurred to her that there was anything wrong in this. God had meant people to enjoy sex, otherwise he wouldn't have given them this wonderful gift. Hadn't she, as a child, watched her parents making love so many times without their knowing she was wide awake in the dark of their only bedroom, listening to their happy sighs and her mother crying out for Jesus Christ before the final lapse into silence followed by heavy contented snores.

The regular visits to church soon came to the attention of the priest, Father Mahar, who enlisted her aid in the various jobs done by women around God's house. She enjoyed changing the flowers and dusting the altar pieces and holy statues, hoping the small sacrifice of her time would not go unnoticed by God.

She began to help in jumble sales, she visited the old and the sick, she even joined the choir. Father Mahar was more than impressed by his new parishioner and began to make enquiries about her. He learnt that she worked at the brewery where several of his young male churchgoers were also employed. When he asked them about Mary he was surprised by their smirks and guarded answers. Then, one day, a Mrs Malone came to see him. He knew her and her husband by sight, they were regular churchgoers, but he hadn't actually spoken to them. They were both young, about thirty-fivish, and seemed good, hard-working people. But on this wet Tuesday morning, Mrs Malone wore a worried expression, giving her otherwise attractive face hard lines that all too soon would be permanent anyway.

'Ah, its Mrs . . .?'

'Malone, Father.'

'Yes, Mrs Malone. Is there something I can do for you?' The priest's voice was soft, gentle because he could always sense the approaching hysteria in the women who came to see him outside church-going hours.

Margaret Malone's voice trembled slightly as she answered. 'It's me Tom, Father. He's . . .' Suddenly, the floodgates were open. She searched in her handbag for a handkerchief.

So soon, thought the priest. How long had this been building up for her to break down so soon in front of me? They could usually get half the story out before the deluge of tears interrupted. He sighed in resignation. He'd heard it so many times before. Tom was being unfaithful or had lost interest in her body, or had taken to beating her every Friday night after a few jars in the pub. How could he comfort these poor creatures, make them

29

realise all things pass, that praying to God at least helped them to withstand the trials of this life.

'Come, now, Mrs Malone. Let's sit and you can tell me in your own time.' He took her arm and led her to a pew at the back of the church. An old woman, wearing a black shawl over her thin, hunched shoulders, lighting yet another candle for the soul or her wayward husband, dead these last six years, paid them no heed. Hadn't she seen it so often before? Hadn't she sat in the same pew, with a different priest so many years ago, pouring out her troubles to her understanding, yet wholly impotent priest?

Margaret Malone at last managed to control her shaking body. 'Oh, Father, it's me Tom, he's found another woman.'

Father Mahar patted her shoulder and sighed as he waited for the tears to stop again.

'It's a woman at the brewery, Father,' she finally went on, her long red hair now damp with her own tears. 'It's been going on for weeks. Every Tuesdays and Thursdays he sees her. He said he went to the pub at first, but Deirdre Finnegan told me she'd seen them together, lots of times. And when I asked him about it, he just laughed and said at least she was a better . . .' She stopped, remembering she was talking to a priest.

'But he doesn't care, Father. That's what hurts. He doesn't care that I know. He doesn't care about the children. He's obsessed with her. I don't know what to do, Father. What can I do?'

'Now first you mustn't upset yourself, Mrs Malone,' the priest tried to console. 'Most men go through this sort of phase at some time or other. It doesn't really mean anything. You'll see, he'll come back to you, and it will be as strong as before. Have courage.'

He paused. Now he must be practical. 'Do you know the other woman's name? Maybe I can speak to her.'

He wasn't quite sure he heard the name correctly through the sobs. It sounded like Mary Kelly.

Father Mahar was stunned. It was Saturday evening, the hour for confession was over, and now he sat alone in his sacristy. Mary Kelly had come to her weekly confession and when she'd finished relating her usual short list of venial sins, he'd asked her about Tom Malone. She hadn't even tried to deny it but spoke quite openly about their affair and when he asked the reason she hadn't confessed it before she asked why she should have to. There was nothing wrong in it, was there?

The priest couldn't believe his ears. The poor child really didn't know there was any sin involved, that what she had done was quite innocent. It was when he questioned her further that he began to doubt her sanity.

She told him of all her other affairs, why she attended church so regularly, and why she prayed so fervently.

All as though it were the most natural thing in the world. And when she asked if it would be possible for him to say a special Mass that she might achieve this wonderful orgasm she'd heard about, he was too shocked to make any reply at all.

He needed time to think, so he asked her to leave but to return in the morning before services. What could he do? She obviously needed medical help as well as spiritual, but how could a doctor cure a girl who was so completely amoral, and how could a priest cure a girl who could not comprehend the difference between right and wrong?

He prayed most of that night, prayed for guidance that he might save this young innocent from her literally soul-destroying fate. The next morning he patiently tried to explain to her why the things she did, and the things she prayed for, were wrong. Not wrong if she found one man whom she could love and eventually marry, make love to achieve a sanctifying union and have children, but wrong if she were to give her precious body to any man who wanted it, just to satisfy this greedy lust within her, and so destroying the spirit of the Holy Ghost who dwelt inside her. God loved her and wanted her to be happy, but she must respect this wonderful gift he had given her, and keep it only for marriage.

She laughed, not out of defiance, but because she genuinely thought the priest was being silly. Her brain had put up a mental block that refused to accept sex as wrong in any way. Where once she had listened to his every word with reverence, she now treated him as though he were the child, and he couldn't be serious in what he was saying.

He went on, explaining about the diseases she could contract, the homes she would break up, how it could only lead to unhappiness for herself – but it was hopeless. It wasn't like talking to another person for she was still the sweet, pure young girl he'd come to know – it was as though one section of her brain had closed a door and refused to let any argument enter.

31

Eventually, he had to suggest that she should see a doctor with him, a good friend of his, who would just talk to her, and between them they would help her back on to the right path. She agreed, although she thought it a silly idea, but if it would please him, then she'd go along. An appointment was made for the following Wednesday, but Father Mahar never saw Mary Kelly again.

Mary moved to another part of Dublin and went back to being a barmaid, her life going on in the same pattern as before. She found a new church to attend but this time she was more wary about becoming too familiar to the priest.

And then, she finally met the man who could fulfil her needs, and, surprisingly enough, she met him in church. Timothy Patrick was an immense man in every way. He had the usual Irishman's ruddy glow, wiry, fair hair, huge hands and ears that stood at right angles from his head. His appetite, not just for food, but for life, was as enormous as his bulk. He was also a good man, not piously religious, but honest and reliable.

As soon as they laid eyes on one another, when he was taking the collection plate round during Mass, instinct told them that here at last was someone who could match their own vitality. He waited for her outside the church, as she knew he would, and walked her to her lodging house. They saw each other every evening after that and on the seventh he took her to a hotel and they made love.

For him, it was the most deeply satisfying act of love he'd ever experienced; for her, it was all her prayers answered. He had laughed when she prayed beside the bed before they made love, but was moved when afterwards she said a complete Rosary in gratitude, understanding this was in some way a compliment to him.

When Mary first saw his size, she was frightened, but she also felt a tingle of excitement run through her. It was in exact proportion to his personality. Enormous. At first he was gentle, more gentle than any other man she had been with, but at her urging, he had become wild, thrusting himself into her with tremendous force, his great hands never still, crushing her breasts, shoulders and thighs. And she fought back with all her might, never allowing him to be dominant, biting, clawing, until she cried for relief from her frenzy. And then relief came, flooding her whole body, making her taut limbs liquid. She wept as he soothed her brow with tender fingers, smiling, talking, staying inside her.

It was then she'd said her Rosary while he waited quietly, his eyes never leaving her bowed head. As soon as she had finished she had laughed and leapt straight back on to the bed, where they made love many more times that night.

They saw each other every day, making love whenever they were alone, their mutual desire never diminishing, always demanding. Finally, Timothy announced his intention to go to England to find better-paid employment and he asked Mary to go with him.

Marriage wasn't mentioned but she eagerly agreed to go and within three weeks they were living together in North London. He found work on a building site and she went back to work as a barmaid. Her faith in God was stronger than it had ever been and she thanked him constantly, in church, at home or even on the bus on her way to work. She cherished her new found love and knew no other man would ever be able to fulfil her the way Timothy did, but she never once tried to push him into marriage.

When war broke out, he enlisted in the army despite her protests. Although she was really proud of him and his action, she dreaded their being apart, for although she knew no other man could satiate her as he did, and no other man could love her as he did, she wondered if she would be strong enough to resist seeking sexual satisfaction elsewhere. Timothy left and within four days she received a letter from him asking her to marry him as soon as he got leave. Then she knew she could wait.

But Timothy died three weeks later, crushed by a tank one night while out on manoeuvres. Nobody knew how it had happened; they had just found his body the next morning, the whole of his magnificent torso squashed flat in a field half a mile away from his unit. Nobody knew how he got there or why he was there, but he'd gone on record as being one of the army's first war casualties. Weeks later, one of his friends from basic training had come to see Mary and told her that Timothy had smuggled a flask of whisky out with him to 'keep out the terrible cold' and had wandered off on his own that night. The soldier thought the army had found the smashed bottle with the body and had tried to cover up the matter for both Timothy's sake and the army's.

It was then that Mary had lost faith in God. To give her so much and then to obliterate it with one cruel stroke was too much for her simple mind to take. She began to hate God almost as much as she had once loved him. They caught her on her third attempt to burn down a Catholic church. She was put into an asylum but release after two months as a model patient. On her second day of freedom she had cost a priest the hearing on his left side when she'd thrust a knife into his ear through the wooden mesh-work of a confessional. She was declared insane and sent back to the asylum. The war was over by the time she was released and she came back into a world that was too busy licking its own wounds to worry about hers.

Her decline was inevitable. She still craved for satisfaction and sought it in the only way possible, but this time she did it as a living. She began to drink heavily and soon the many men began to bore her. None could live up to her Timothy. She began to mock her clients in their futile attempts to arouse her, and laughed at their pathetic little organs. One night, a burly man, proud of his manhood broke her nose when she derided him. She began losing money, for some men refused to pay her after her demoralising sarcasm, but still she could not refrain from her derisive comments on their performance in bed. She became known to the police as a harasser of priests; she would follow a priest for miles, either cursing him or offering him her body, until the poor man had no alternative but to go into the nearest police station.

She was put away again and again but she always behaved like a model patient and was soon released. She finally contracted gonorrhoea, and in the early stages, when she knew she had it, she took great delight in passing it on to the men she slept with. She soon found herself out on the street when her landlord fell victim to her ridicule *and* her disease. Her looks had faded, her appearance was shabby, her mind failed to grasp reality any more. She went to live with a group of Pakistani immigrants in Brick Lane and stayed there for several years, being used by all the men either collectively or singly, but eventually they tired of her and threw her out. She went back one night, months later, and poured paraffin through the grating into the basement of their dilapidated house, set a whole box of matches alight and threw it in. One fireman and five of the Pakistanis died in the fire that burnt the house to the ground, but nobody suspected Mary of having caused it.

She was found one day, half-dead, on a bomb-site. It took months of hospital treatment to cure her of all her ailments and where the doctors left off the Salvation Army took over. They

34

found her a place to live, bought her new clothes and got her a job in a laundry – they felt sure they could save her from herself.

And they almost did. She worked hard, her maltreated body began to regain some of its former vigour, her mind closed another door, this time to memories. But as she grew healthier, so her body began to demand gratification. Unfortunately, the only personal contact she had with men now was the Salvation Army officer who visited her twice a week at her basement flat. When she tried to seduce him he made the mistake of calling her to look to God. Suddenly, she thought of the joy that had been snatched away by Him after all her devotion to His church. When she'd found her reward, her Timothy, He had taken it away, even his servants, the priests, had tried to prevent her from finding this happiness, and now this other man of God, this so-called 'soldier' of God was trying to deny her, hiding behind *Him*, using *His* name, reminding her of *His* treachery.

The Salvation Army officer fled when her hysterical ravings grew into physical violence. Mary left the flat and roamed the streets offering her body to every man she came across, abusing and cursing them as they refused, some jeering, most frightened by her lunatic ranting. She finally had to find her solace in a bottle of Johnnie Walker, bought with her meagre savings from her job in the laundry.

That night an ambulance was called to a public convenience at the Angel, Islington, where the attendant had found a woman lying unconscious in one of the cubicles. She had thought the woman was just drunk at first, the smell of alcohol was overpowering, but then she'd noticed the blood seeping from between the woman's legs. It took a doctor two hours to remove all the fragments of glass from Mary's vagina. She'd sought consolation from the whisky bottle in more than one way.

Mary Kelly looked around at her five companions. Her ravaged face contorted with contempt for them. Dirty, dried-up old men. Not one of them a real man. Not one would pass their bottle around. Well, tonight she had had her own bottle, and it wasn't meths. It was good Scotch. It had only taken three days to get enough money to buy the half-bottle. And it had been easy money to get for she'd gone to the West End, to the cinema and theatre queues and just stood in front of people, staring at their faces, one hand outstretched ready to receive money, the other hand

35

scratching. Scratching her hair, her arm-pits, her breasts – it was when her hand began travelling towards her crotch that they usually coughed up.

So here she was amongst the grave-stones and the rubble of the bombed church. It had taken years of wretchedness, torments to both mind and body to bring her to this point. But she was amongst her own kind, crushed by life itself. She unscrewed the top and raised the bottle to her lips with a wavering hand.

'What's that you're drinking, Mary?' came a voice from the darkness.

'Fuck off,' Mary knew this would happen, that the others would see her booze and beg for some, just a little drop, one swig, but she couldn't resist the impulse to come here tonight and gloat, to make men plead with her. She knew that they'd even make love to her for just a drop then she could mock them even more. The old men would forget her filth and she'd forget theirs, and they'd desperately try to get a hard-on with their ridiculously wasted pricks so they could fuck her and earn their drink. But they'd never managed it, and she would just laugh and enjoy the misery on their loathsome faces.

'Ah, come on, Mary, what's that you're drinking?' A figure crawled forward towards her.

'None of your business, scum,' Mary said, her vice still heavy with Irish, after so many years.

Other heads lifted themselves from their stupor and turned towards her. The figure came nearer. Two rheumy, yellow eyes gazed at the bottle she now held with two hands.

'Come on, Mary, it's me – Myer.' The eyes took on a crafty look as they realised it was nearly a full bottle of Scotch. 'I know what you like, Mary, gimme a drop, and I'll do it for you.'

'You,' Mary jeered. 'You, I remember last time. You couldn't even find it, could you?' Mary began to giggle, her shoulders jerking with the effort. 'You!'

The old man began to snigger, too. 'That's right, Mary, but it'll be different this time, you see.' Grimy fingers began to fumble at his trousers.

Mary laughed now, rocking backwards and forwards, drinking freely from the bottle.

'Just a minute, Mary, I'll soon have it.' Myer was laughing, stopping now and then as a concentrated frown swept over his face. 'Don't drink it all, Mary.' His puzzled look turned into a

36

smile of triumph as he finally produced the object of his search.

Mary's laughter reached a hysterical pitch as she pointed at his limp penis.

'You couldn't fuck a polo mint with that, you daft old sod,' she cried.

Just then, a hand grabbed at the neck of the bottle.

'Give us that, bitch,' a man loomed over her, his face almost hidden behind wild, curly hair and beard. But the hand had no strength and Mary was invigorated with the Scotch and the laughter. She pulled it back, crouching over it, clutching it between her thighs. The bearded man struck weakly at the back of her neck, but Mary laughed even more.

Old Myer tried to grope between her knees to reach the bottle but she clasped it tightly. 'Just one, Mary, just one,' he pleaded.

The other man suddenly kicked her, then grabbed her matted hair, pulling her head back, screaming obscenities. She struck out with one hand knocking him on to his back, but Myer made a lunge at the bottle. He doubled up in pain as a bony knee hit his groin.

The three other old warriors crouched and watched, slowly edging forward, eyes never leaving the bottle. The bearded man struggled to his feet and came staggering towards her, like a degenerate bull in rage, but she clawed at his eyes, drawing blood, sending him to his knees. She turned to face the other three and they drew back in fear.

'Bastards!' she shouted at them. She turned her back on all of them, Myer on all fours, tears streaming from his eyes, still pleading, the bearded man rubbing at his eyes, the three on the ground cringing. She sucked noisily at the bottle, then grabbed at her skirt, missed and grabbed again, hoisted it to her waist, and waved her bare arse at their faces. Then she disappeared into the bushes and all they could hear was her mocking laughter.

She stopped by an old tomb, still giggling and muttering to herself. Men, she thought, all the same. All weak, every one of them. She'd enjoyed herself tonight, she'd made fools of them all. She thought of Myer and his tiny prick, like a little white worm in the moonlight. Pathetic. She'd never known any man who – no, there had been someone. Now who had that been? Years ago . . . she drank from the bottle and tried to recollect who it was that she'd once loved, who was it that had once given her something? But what? What had she been given? She couldn't remember.

The rock struck her exposed throat as her head tilted far back to drink from the bottle. She fell forward and the bearded tramp pulled it from her grasp. He drank deeply, while the others kicked the moaning form on the ground. Myer took the bottle next and greedily gulped at the fiery liquid only releasing it to another when the burning in his throat caused him to splutter and choke. The man with the hairy face swayed from side to side and looked at Mary's writhing body. He knew this bitch, seen her laughing at his friends before, even laughed at *him* once when he'd tried to do her a favour. He picked up a large brick and brought it down hard on her face.

He grabbed the bottle off a thin little man who'd only just got it into his possession, and drank. They all sat round in a circle, only a few feet from Mary's still body, finished off the Scotch and then returned to their meths.

Mary Kelly wasn't quite dead, but she was close to it. Her skull had been fractured by the brick, and was bleeding profusely. Two ribs were broken and her throat had a deep gash in it. She had lain in the dirt for a long while, her life-spirit slowly ebbing away, and in a short while she would be dead. All that moved were her lips which seemed to be saying some soundless prayer, over and over again, and her fingers that tried to count to ten endlessly.

Quite nearby lay the slumped bodies of her five companions, huddled together in disturbed slumber.

The first rat approached her cautiously, the smell of blood over-coming any fear, but never blurring its cunning. It was much larger than the other rats that followed it, and darker in colour. When it was a few feet away from Mary it stopped, its hind-quarters bunching up, its whole body tensed and quivering.

Suddenly it leapt at the open wound in her throat, sinking its huge incisors deep and drawing out the blood with violent spasms of its powerful body. Mary tried to stir, but she was too weak from blood already lost, the rat now biting deep into her vocal chords. Her body shook, but suddenly another furry form buried half its head into the matted hair over the wound in her skull. Her back arched as her nerve-ends tautened and she fell forward again. Another rat pulled at her ear. Suddenly, her whole body was covered, teeming with squealing creatures as more scurried from the darkness, the smell of blood much stronger than it had been before. So Mary Kelly's unfortunate life ended. The priests had never managed to save her soul, but then it had never really been lost. Only her mind.

38

The rats drained her body of blood and gnawed her flesh until not much more than bones and pieces of skin remained. It didn't take long, for there were many of them. So many, that not all had been fully-gorged. Their hunger for human flesh had been merely inflamed – they wanted more. There were several larger rats amongst them now, and those began to move towards the five human shapes sleeping nearby.

There was no caution now as they swarmed over the bodies. Two men had no chance, for their eyes were torn from their heads as they slept. They crawled blindly around amidst the carnage that was taking place, rats clinging to their bloody flesh.

The bearded man had risen to his feet, pulling a wriggling body from his face and tearing mostly hair from his cheek in the process. But as he stood, one of the larger rats leapt at his groin, pulling away his genitals with one mighty twist of its body. The tramp screamed and fell to his knees, thrusting his hands between his legs as if to stop the flow of blood, but he was immediately engulfed and toppled over by a wave of black, bristling bodies.

Another dishevelled figure buried his head in his hands and rolled himself into a ball, his frail body rocked with sobs and pleadings. The rats bit off his fingers and attacked the back of his neck as well as his exposed behind. He stayed in his foetal position as the rats ate him, still half-alive.

Myer ran. He ran faster than he'd ever run before and he almost made it. But in the dark, and in his panic, he ran into a gravestone. He somersaulted over it, landing on his back. At once, the rats were upon him, their razor-sharp teeth soon tearing his feeble old body to shreds.

Outside the ruin, on the main road, a crowd had gathered. They'd heard the screams and the commotion but none dare enter the dark churchyard. They couldn't see through the foliage, but they knew the type that made those old bomb-sites their homes and were not too anxious to investigate.

Eventually two policemen arrived, closely followed by a squad car. A powerful searchlight was directed into the undergrowth, and three policemen with torches went in.

They emerged again three minutes later, all deathly pale. One went to the side of the road and vomited.

Chapter Six

Harris woke with a start and automatically reached for the shrilling alarm. The ringing always shocked him when it caught him unawares. Lately, he'd got into the habit of waking just a few minutes before the alarm went off, waiting for the first explosive ring, and shutting it off immediately with a fast-moving hand. Then he'd doze for twenty minutes or so.

But this morning, it had caught him in a deep dream. He tried to remember what it had been about. Something to do with teeth. Sharp teeth. Tearing.

Bloody hell, he thought, it was rats. Thousands of them. He'd looked out his window, he remembered, it was night-time, and there below him were thousands of rats, all perfectly still, just staring up at him in the moonlight. Thousands of wicked-looking eyes. Then they'd surged forward, crashing through the front door, scurrying up the stairs. Thank God for the alarm.

He turned over with a groan and put his arm around the curled-up figure lying next to him.

'Morning, Jude.' The girl curled up into a tighter ball, murmuring softly.

Harris ran his tongue down her naked back, making her squirm with pleasure. He put his hand between her arms and drawn-up thighs and lightly stroked her smooth stomach. She languidly turned around to face him, stretching her arms and legs as she did so.

'Hello,' she said as she kissed him.

He drew her close and they both stretched against each other.

'It's late,' he said.

'Not that late.'

'Oh yes it is.' He ran his fingers along the inside of her thighs, teasing her. 'Didn't you have enough last night?'

'No.' She began to kiss his eyelids.

40

'Well, I did.' He laughed as he whipped back the covers.

'Now get out in that kitchen and rattle those pots and pans.'

'Pig.'

He watched her as she slipped on her dressing gown and disappeared into the kitchen. As the sound of cupboards being opened and closed, water filling the kettle and Radio One music came through to him, he lay thinking of Judy.

They had lived together for six or seven months now and their love seemed to grow stronger by the day. She was a dress designer, a good one too, and they'd met at a mutual friend's party. They'd slept together that first night, but she hadn't let him make love to her. He'd tried of course, but she'd gently discouraged him, and to his amazement the next morning, he was glad she had. Weeks later, when they realised they were both in love with each other, he'd asked why she'd let him stay the first night but hadn't let him make love. She couldn't explain because she didn't really understand herself. Not the fact that they hadn't made love, but that she'd let him sleep with her. She'd never slept with anyone before, and although she'd been engaged for two years, her love-making had been confined to touching only.

It was just that she'd felt something 'stir' inside her that night. She'd almost felt sorry for him in a strange way. He appeared on the surface to be self-sufficient, confident, but underneath he was the proverbial 'little-boy-lost'. He'd smiled and said that was his usual trick with women but she'd nodded and replied:

'Yes, that was quite apparent. But even underneath that, there really was a little lost soul running around. You, Harris, are a man of many layers.'

He'd been impressed. Flattered that anyone should be interested enough to try and 'suss' him out like that. She'd gone on to explain that she couldn't let him go that night, that she wanted to be close to him, but she couldn't let the final barrier down until she was sure of him. And herself.

A few months later they rented a flat in the King's Cross area and moved in together. They'd talked about marriage and decided it wasn't important just yet. They would live together for at least a year and then decide. Either for – or against.

Sometimes, usually when he was alone, the old hardness would come creeping over him, and he'd say to himself: 'Harris, you're on to a good thing here, son.' But when he was with Judy, walking, holding hands, making love, tenderness would sweep away any harshness from his feelings.

Judy's voice from the kitchen interrupted his thoughts.

'Okay, lazy, breakfast's almost ready.' He leapt out of bed, shrugged on an old blue bathrobe and went into the toilet on the landing. Then he went down to the front door to collect the paper. When he returned, he kissed Judy's neck and sat down at the small table.

'Good thing you called me when you did, I thought my bladder was going to burst.'

Judy placed bacon and tomatoes before him and sat down to her hard-boiled egg. He hated eggs first thing in the morning.

He unfolded the *Mirror* to look at the headlines. He usually read the paper on the bus on the way to school – he loved to leave it around the staff-room, to the disapproval of his colleagues who thought any newspaper other than *The Times* or the *Guardian* were comic books – but he always glanced at the headlines at breakfast.

'Christ, listen to this,' he mumbled through a mouthful of bread. 'Six tramps eaten alive by rats. Late last night, police were called to a bomb-site in Stepney after passers-by had heard screams and the sounds of violent struggle coming from the ruins of the old St Anne's churchyard. On investigation, the police officers discovered the remains of six bodies, apparently killed by rats, a few of which were still feeding on the corpses. The area was immediately cordoned off, and police, wearing protective clothing and assisted by a leading pest extermination company, combed the ruins for the rats' lair but were unable to discover any trace of the vermin. Earlier in the day, Karen Blakely, aged thirteen months, and her dog, were attacked and killed by rats in their home. The girl's mother, Paula Blakely, is still in hospital under sedation and is now said to be seriously ill. An inquiry committee will be set up to . . .'

Harris finished reading the article in silence and Judy came round and leaned over his shoulder.

'It's awful.' She shuddered and pressed close to him. 'How can that sort of thing happen in this day and age?'

'I know there's still some terrible slums left, but I didn't realise that they were bad enough to breed anything like this.' He shook his head in puzzlement. 'That must be the woman I saw in hospital yesterday. And Keogh. He said he saw two enormous rats.

42

Perhaps he wasn't exaggerating after all. What the hell's happening?'

They both got dressed and left the flat. As they were both going in opposite directions, Harris to the East End, Judy to the big department store for which she 'created' fashions in the West End, they kissed goodbye in the street and went their separate ways.

On the bus Harris pondered on the question of rats and wondered if the three incidents were connected. Was it just coincidence or were they tied up in some way? Could it have been the same rats or were they different groups? He decided he'd question Keogh further about his two rats when he remembered the boy wouldn't be in that day. Well, never mind, tomorrow would do.

But there wasn't a tomorrow for Keogh. When Harris reached the school he was called into the principal's office and told that the boy had been rushed to hospital the previous night with a severe fever and was at that moment in a critical condition. The hospital had rung and asked if anyone else had been with him when he'd been bitten by the rat? And could the teacher who had brought him to the hospital yesterday come along to see them?

'Yes, I'll just get my class organised and I'll go over right away,' Harris said to the worried-looking Mr Norton.

'No, I've seen to that,' said the headmaster. 'You get going now. They insisted it was urgent. Try not to be too long.'

Harris left the school and made towards the hospital at a brisk pace. When he arrived he began to explain who he was but the receptionist had been expecting him and immediately took him to an office near the rear of the building where he was asked to wait. He had barely sat down when the door opened and three men strode in.

'Ah, you're the boy's teacher?' enquired the first man, walking around to the desk. His portly figure lowered itself into a chair with a weary slump and his tired eyes barely flickered towards Harris. He waved his hand at the two others before Harris could reply. 'Doctor Strackley' – the doctor nodded – 'and Mr Foskins from the Ministry of Health.' Foskins stretched a hand towards the teacher who shook it. 'And my name is Tunstall, I'm the Hospital Group Secretary.' The man behind the desk finished his introductions glancing through a sheaf of papers. He stopped at one in particular, seemingly studying it closely, but at the same time asking, 'Your name?'

43

'Harris. How is Keogh?'

Tunstall looked up from his document. 'You haven't been told?' Harris froze at the tone of the group secretary's voice.

'I'm afraid he died during the night.'

Harris shook his head in disbelief. 'But it was only yesterday that he was bitten.'

'Yes, we know, Mr Harris,' the doctor stepped forward and leaned on the desk, his eyes looking intently at the stunned teacher. 'That's why we asked you to come along. You brought the boy here yesterday. Perhaps you could tell us how and where he received the bite?'

'But you can't die just from a bite. And in one day?' Harris shook his head at the three men, ignoring the doctor's question.

Tunstall spoke up, putting the papers finally to one side. 'No, it seems impossible, doesn't it? A post mortem is already being carried out to see if Keogh was suffering from any other illness at the time. We thought possibly the bite may have acted as some kind of catalyst for a hidden disease carried by the boy. But we've virtually discounted that theory now, although we're still checking it out. You see, a woman was brought in yesterday too – you may have read about it in the papers; her child was killed by rats – and she was herself attacked by them in an attempt to save her daughter. She died two hours ago.'

'But that means anyone who comes in contact with the rats and gets bitten by one . . .' before Harris could finish, Foskins interrupted.

'Yes, Mr Harris. Once a person has been bitten, they have about twenty-four hours to live. That's why it's essential to learn as much as possible about these particular rats. They're obviously an unknown species, unknown to us in England anyway. From what we've heard, their sheer size is quite extraordinary . . .'

'We want to know everything the boy told you of the incident,' said Tunstall impatiently.

'Yes, of course,' Harris nodded. 'But how did they die? What did they die of?' He looked at each of the three men in turn. The room filled with an uneasy silence.

Finally, the doctor cleared his throat and looked at the group secretary. 'I think it's only fair that we take Mr Harris into our confidence. I think we can trust him to be discreet, and he may be able to help us if he knows this area well.'

'I was born here. I know most of this region – and I know exactly where Keogh saw his rats.'

'Very well,' sighed Tunstall. 'But understand, you must not repeat anything said in this room to anybody. We're not sure what we're up against yet, and until we are, we must treat it with the utmost discretion. We don't want people to panic over something that may only be a rare occurrence.'

'Like six tramps being eaten alive,' interjected Harris.

'Yes, yes, Mr Harris, we know it's a bit frightening,' said Foskins quickly. 'But we don't want people panicking do we? I mean, the first thing to suffer would be the docks, wouldn't it? Heaven knows, the dockers don't need much excuse to stay away from work so just think of what this sort of scare could do. And if foodstuff were left to rot in the warehouses and ships, what then? The whole waterfront would be infested within a few days. Vicious circle, Mr Harris, vicious circle.'

The teacher remained silent.

'Look, we'll probably overcome this problem before anything else occurs,' Tunstall leaned forward, pointing a finger at Harris. 'Now your help isn't essential, but if you do want to assist us you must agree to silence.'

What brought that on wondered Harris. He must be really worried. 'All right,' he shrugged. 'I just want to know how Keogh and the woman died.'

'Of course,' smiled Doctor Strackley, trying to break the icy atmosphere. 'The deaths were caused by an infection introduced by the bite of the rat into the bloodstream. The usual disease caused by the vermin is called Weil's Disease, Leptrospirosis or Spirochoetal Jaundice. We only have about ten or eleven cases of this a year in this country – it's that rare. The organism that causes it, Leptospira Ictero-haemorrhagae, is carried by rats and conveyed to man in their urine, either through the skin or alimentary tract. It's an occupational hazard to workers in sewers. Incubation period is from seven to thirteen days; onset of the disease is abrupt fever, muscular pains, loss of appetite and vomiting. The feverish stage lasts several days before jaundice appears and the patient becomes prostrate. Temperature usually declines in about ten days but relapses tend to occur. We often treat the disease by penicillin and other antibiotics but we do have a special serum for it. Trouble is, it's rarely diagnosed as Weil's Disease in time to use it.

'Right, so that's the disease we know about. Now, the incredible thing about last night's two cases is that the whole process

45

happened within twenty-four hours.' He paused, as if for effect. 'There are other differences too.'

He looked at Tunstall, silently seeking permission to carry on. Tunstall nodded.

'The fever strikes within five or six hours. Jaundice sets in immediately. The victim rapidly loses all his senses – sight goes first. The body goes into a coma, occasionally being racked by violent spasms. then, the most horrible thing happens. The skin – by now completely yellow – becomes taut. It becomes thinner as it stretches over the bone structure. It turns to a fine tissue. Finally, it begins to tear. Gaping holes appear all over the body. The poor victim dies a terribly painful death, which even our strongest drugs seem only to ease a little.'

The three men remained silent as the knowledge sought entry into Harris's numbed brain.

'Poor Keogh,' he finally said.

'Yes, and God help anybody else who gets bitten,' said Tunstall, almost impatiently. 'Now, before anything else happens, we're getting the Ratkill people in. They're a good company and very discreet. They're investigating the bomb-site and the woman's home this morning and if you can tell us where the boy was bitten, we'll get them to have a look around that area too.'

Harris told them about the old canal that Keogh had been using as a short cut. 'Look, let me take some of the exterminators down there, I can show them the exact spot.'

'Yes,' said Foskins, 'we're going along to the churchyard now to see how they're getting on. You can come along and then take some of their chaps off to the canal.'

'I'll have to ring the school first.'

'All right, but not a word to anyone about this. Just say the hospital needs you for a statement. Now when you do go back to your school we'd like you to ask your pupils if they've seen any rats recently, and if so, where. Also, if they're bitten by anything – anything at all – they're to go straight to the hospital. If you can tell this without frightening them, we'd appreciate it.'

'It would take more than that to frighten my bunch,' smiled Harris.

'I think it was around here,' Harris told the one Ratkill man he'd been allowed to take away from the chaotic and gruesome churchyard scene. He and the rodent exterminator, a quiet little man whose thin, pointed face, Harris mused, was not far off resembling the creature he was paid to obliterate, were now standing before a high brick wall.

'The canal's on the other side,' said Harris. 'If we walk down a bit, we'll come to railings, and unless it has changed now, there'll be a few openings.'

As they walked the little man, whose name was Albert Ferris, lost some of his reserve and slight wariness of Harris's profession and began to talk to the teacher.

'I've never seen anything like that place this morning, you know. I've been at this game for fifteen years and never seen anything like it. Blood, and bits of bodies, all over the place. Terrible. But no rats. None dead, you know. Those poor old buggers couldn't have known what hit them. Mind you, they were probably all well gone on that stuff they drink, all well boozed. But all the same, you'd have thought at least one of them would have got out of it. Or killed some of the rats anyway.' He shook his head. 'Beats me.'

'I've never heard of rats actually attacking people for food before,' said Harris, to keep the man talking. He was determined to learn as much as possible about the situation. He didn't know why, but the uneasiness he felt went deeper than the natural abhorrence of the shocking tragedy.

'No, they don't as a rule,' Ferris replied. 'Not in this country anyway. You see rats are very, very cautious. They can live on practically anything and they certainly wouldn't attack just for flesh, you know. Corpses, yes. They'd eat corpses. But attack a man just for food? No. But, what puzzled us this morning was some of the spoors we found. Twice as large as normal rats' droppings. We've sent them off to the lab to have them analysed, but what they obviously suggest is very large rats. And now, if London's started breeding a colony of bigger-than-average rats – and you know how fast they breed – well, I reckon we're in for a lot of bother. And if they're attacking people . . .' He shook his head again.

'Just how fast do they breed, in fact?' asked the teacher.

'The female can have from five to eight litters a year, with anything from four to twelve in a litter. Then the randy buggers are at it again after a couple of hours. I don't much fancy mobs of them big ones roaming around.'

Nor did Harris.

They came to the railings and found an opening.

'Look,' Harris said to Ferris, 'you know we're only looking for signs of these creatures – we don't actually want to catch any.'

'Don't worry, mate. I'm not going to tangle with them.'

Assured he was on no crusade mission with the little man, Harris led the way through the gap. They slowly began to walk back towards the starting point of the wall, keeping a wary eye for any small movement.

Ferris was the first to see them. He'd been scrutinising the far bank, looking for any dark holes, groups of droppings, anything at all, when his gaze fell upon three moving objects in the dark waters. Against the dark brown muddy canal water could be seen three small, black heads gliding in the opposite direction to which they were walking.

'Look,' he pointed excitedly. 'Three of them.'

Harris looked across to where Ferris was pointing. He saw the three black shapes instantly, their perfect triangular formation causing smooth water-trails behind them.

'All right, let's follow them.'

'They seem to know where they're going!' Harris called back to the little rat-killer, who was having a hard time keeping up with him.

Suddenly, the dark creatures emerged from the water and scurried up the bank. For the first time, the two men could see the whole of their bodies.

'Christ, they're enormous,' exclaimed Harris.

'I've never seen any that size before,' Ferris said, open-mouthed. 'We'd better keep clear of them for the moment, mate. We don't want to, er, excite them.'

'We'll have to try to follow them,' said Harris firmly. 'This may lead us to their lair.'

As he spoke, the leading rat stopped and turned his head towards them. The other two froze and did the same.

Harris would never forget the horror he felt under the gaze of the three pairs of sharp, wicked-looking eyes. It wasn't just their size, or natural repulsion of vermin that numbed him. It was because they didn't run, or try to hide. There was no sign of panic. Just three still bodies, malevolently watching the two men, as though deciding whether to swim across to them or go on their way. Harris knew if there was any hint of the foul creatures making towards them, he would not hesitate to run as fast as his legs would carry him. He guessed when Ferris' hand gripped his arm that the rat-killer had the same idea.

But the rats suddenly turned and disappeared through a hole in the old wooden fence that protected that side of the canal from public property.

'Thank Gawd for that.' Ferris exhaled a deep mouthful of air. And then, when he'd recovered slightly; 'What's over there?'

Harris thought for a moment, trying to recollect the surrounding area. 'Well, there's a bit of wasteland – we can see the undergrowth from here – and then there's . . .' He scratched his cheek and pondered. 'Oh, no. Flats. There's blocks of flats behind the waste. Fortunately most of the kids will be at school although some may be coming home for dinner around this time. My guess is that the rats are making for the big rubbish bins that belong to the flats. We'll have to get around there fast, just in case.'

As he was about to run along the iron fence on their side of the canal to find an opening, his eyes caught more movement in the water. This time coming from the opposite direction of the first three, he saw a bigger group of black shapes gliding through the water. He registered at least seven before he began running after Ferris, whose reaction to the fearsome pack was immediate.

As he ran, Harris glanced back to see the furry, wet bodies scurrying through the same hole in the fence that the other three had used.

When the two shaken men reached the road once again, Harris pulled the little exterminator to a halt.

'Look, get on to the police,' he said, his lungs gasping for air. 'Get them to contact your people and get them over here as fast as possible. I'm going around to the flats, you follow when you've phoned. There's a small road bridge across the canal not far in that direction, so follow me as fast as possible, for Christ's sake. I don't want to come up against that lot on my own!'

'Look, mate, rats are my business,' Ferris answered back fiercely. 'You go get the police. I'll find out where they're going to and I'll know how to handle them when I do. I'm no hero, but it's bloody commonsense, ain't it?'

Without waiting for a reply, the little man set off at a jogging pace.

Who's arguing? thought Harris to himself and began to look around for a phone box.

*　　*　　*

The rats sped swiftly through the undergrowth, joined now by groups of the smaller variety. They reached another wooden fence that separated the council tenements from the wasteland. They flowed under through its many gaps and made towards the large waste-disposal bunkers that stood at the bottom of each block of flats. Food and litter of all kinds were emptied down the chutes from all floors of the block by its residents into a huge round bin that was cleared by the council's sanitation department each week. Many a family pet was buried in this way when their lives ended either by accident or from old age. Potato peelings, egg-shells, stale food, paper, anything that could fit into the chute was disposed of in this way, and allowed to mix and rot for a week before being emptied into and then churned up by the grinding dust-cart. By the end of the week the smell was always abominable and residents warned their young to stay away from the rotting doors of the bunkers.

It was the first time a large group of rats had visited the site during the day. Usually there were too many children laughing, screaming, fighting, making noise because of the sheer delight of making noise, for the people-shy beasts. The night was their ally.

But now they had a new boldness. Led by the bigger, blacker rats, a species that had suddenly appeared amongst them, to dominate and intimidate, they had found a new courage. Or at least, a new driving force.

So far unseen they sped along the walls of the buildings in single file until they reached a bunker where many nights before, they had gnawed holes in the doors to provide access for their ever-hungry bodies. They hurriedly passed through and then into the holes, again made by themselves, beneath the vast cylinder of rub-bish, and so into the heap itself, gnawing, eating anything that could be chewed.

The big rats were the first to know it was there. Somebody had deposited their weekend joint into the chute. Perhaps it had been rotten, perhaps a husband, tired of being chastised for not being home from the pub on time for his Sunday lunch had thrown the whole joint away in a fit of rage. But there it was, and the rats' lust for meat was aroused to a frightening degree.

The smaller rats tried to get at the meat, but were instantly killed and then devoured by their superiors.

Ferris heard the squeals of the lesser rats as he ran past the bun-ker. He stopped dead and listened intently, his sharp little face

50

turned to one side. Then he realised where the noise was coming from. Slowly, and very quietly he walked towards the seemingly solid doors. The smell of stale food assured him of the worst. He spotted the holes at the bottom of the doors and carefully got down on one knee. He listened again. Silence, now. He cautiously lowered his head towards the larger of the black holes and tried to peer into the darkness. Nothing moved. He was down on both knees now, his right ear almost touching the ground.

The huge rat flew out at him without warning and bit deep into the flesh of his cheek. Ferris screamed and fell back, beating wildly at the creature on his face. With all his strength he pulled the rat away from him, tearing a gaping hole in his cheek, but he couldn't hold the powerful, wriggling body and it fell upon him once more. The other rodents came streaming through the holes at the little man, whose screaming had started to bring people to their doors and windows.

When the residents saw the white overalled figure on the floor, surrounded and covered with dark, furry bodies, they could not quite believe what was happening. Some, once they realised, slammed their doors, and for some reason bolted them, as though they thought the strange creatures could pick locks. Others – they were mostly women, their husbands being at work – screamed or fainted. Some who had phones, rang for the police. Many just stared in horror-struck silence. One old pensioner, a stout but active woman, ran forward brandishing a broom above her head. She brought it down heavily on the nearest bodies to her, these being the smaller rats on the outer fringes of the circle around the struggling man. As they scattered, a larger rat stopped its gorging and turned a menacing eye towards her.

The first phone box Harris found had been wrecked by vandals. Knowing other boxes in the area would probably have been tampered with, he decided to waste no more time but to try the nearest shop or pub. He found a tobacconists and hastily asked the proprietor permission to phone for the police. The shopkeeper was a trifle wary at first but the teacher's earnestness convinced him that the young man was on the level.

When the call was made and directions given, Harris thanked the tobacconist and left the shop at a run. He soon reached the spot where he and Ferris had split up and headed in the direction that the little rat-exterminator had gone. He crossed the canal

51

bridge and saw the council flats before him. He heard the commotion seconds before he came upon the ghastly scene. As he ran into the grounds and turned a corner he saw an old lady, furiously waving a broom in the air, being dragged to the ground by several large rats. Harris was frozen to the spot until her pitiful cries for help spurred him forward, only too aware of the lethal disease the rat-bites carried, but knowing he couldn't just stand by and watch the old lady be torn to pieces. Fortunately for Harris, a group of workmen from a nearby building-site had heard the screams, and were now advancing on the rats armed with picks, shovels, anything that had come to hand in their rush to the buildings.

Again the large rat that had observed the old pensioner now looked up and furtively studied the approaching men. The other, bigger rats, also stopped their frenzied attack.

This did not deter the workmen. They advanced, shouting and waving their assorted weapons.

Suddenly, as though in one body, the rats turned and fled, leaving their smaller companions to the merciless onslaught of the enraged men.

Harris backed up against the wall as he saw the creatures fleeing in his direction. They scurried past him one actually running over his shoe, causing him to shudder involuntarily. Another stopped before him, eyed him coolly for a fraction of a second, and then sped on its way. Harris almost collapsed with relief as the last horrifying shape disappeared beneath the fence of the wasteground. It looked as though two of the workmen were about to climb the fence to follow them, but Harris managed to find his voice in time to stop them.

As they walked back the teacher was able to turn his gaze back towards the carnage the rats had caused. The old lady was on the ground, her chest heaving in sharp, uneven movement, covered in blood, still feebly holding on to the broom. It was only then that Harris saw the shredded, blood-stained overalls of little Ferris. It was only the now barely recognisable uniform with its 'Ratkill' logo emblazoned on the chest that made him realise it was the little rat exterminator, for the crumpled body no longer had a face.

'Get an ambulance, quickly,' Harris said weakly to one of the workmen, knowing already it was too late for the old woman.

'There's one on the way,' one of her neighbours came forward. The others now began to slowly emerge from their homes and

52

tentatively walked towards the bodies, keeping a wary eye on the fence.

'What were they?' someone asked.

'Rats, weren't they,' another replied.

'What – that size?' the first person again.

'Big as dogs.'

'Come on, let's go after them,' the workman who had been prepared to climb the fence growled. 'We can't have things like them running around.'

'No,' said Harris. He couldn't tell them about the fatal disease the vermin carried, but he had to stop them from trying to do battle with them. 'The police are on their way, and the people from Ratkill too, better let them deal with them.'

'Time we wait for the law, the bleeders'll have disappeared. I'm going now. Who else is coming?'

Harris caught him by the arm as he began to march towards the fence. As he angrily swung around, two police cars roared into the estate and came to a screeching halt beside the group of stricken people.

Foskins emerged from the second car and strode directly towards Harris, his eyes never leaving the two figures on the ground.

As a Ratkill van arrived, he pulled the teacher to one side so the gathering crowd would be unable to hear their conversation.

'Well, Mr Harris, what happened?'

The teacher briefly told him of the events just past. He felt full of pity for the little rat-faced Ferris whose sense of duty towards his job had led to his untimely death. It could have been Harris, himself, lying there if Ferris hadn't insisted on following the rats himself.

'We'll get a search party down there immediately,' Foskins told him. 'They'll go through the fence and down the canal. We'll send out patrols along the canal and cordon the area off.'

'Look, these canals run for miles. How can you possibly cordon them off?' Harris was slightly irritated by Foskins' calm, authoritatively calm, voice. 'And in any case, how are you going to cordon off all the sewers that run beneath this area?'

'That, Mr Harris,' said Foskins coldly, 'is *our* problem.'

Chapter Seven

Harris was in no mood to go back to the school that afternoon. He walked for a while through the streets of his childhood, coming upon long-forgotten alleys; a tobacconist where he bought his first packet of 'Domino' cigarettes; Linda Crossley's house, a girl who had one night, when they were teenagers, let he and six of his mates have it off with her at the back of their local youth club – and was forever after known as '7-up'; bomb-sites, still untouched by building developments; stunted posts, once used to tie horses to, in his day to play leap-frog and today – well, not many horses around any more – and when was the last time he'd seen kids playing leap-frog? Finally, he caught a bus and returned to the flat. He made himself some tea and sat in his only armchair, still depressed by the morning's event. Keogh, the woman and her baby, those poor old down-and outs. Ferris and the old lady. Civilised London. Swinging London. Dirty bloody London!

For all its modernity, its high standard of living, it could still breed obnoxious, disease-carrying vermin of the like he'd seen today. And their size! What had caused this mutation? And their cunning. Twice that day, one of the big, black rats had just stood and stared at him (had it been the same one each time? Christ!) not cowering, nor preparing to attack, but just surveying him, seemingly studying him, inscrutable.

How many more people would they kill before they were put down? And where had they come from? What made then so much more intelligent than their smaller counterparts? Well, why should he worry. It was the problem of the bloody authorities. But what disgusted him more? The vermin them-selves – or the fact that it could only happen in East London? Not Hampstead or Kensington, but Poplar. Was it the old preju-dices against the middle and upper classes, the councils that took

54

the working-class from their slums and put them into tall, remote concrete towers, telling them they'd never been better off, but never realising that forty homes in a block of flats became forty separate cells for people, communication between them confined to conversations in the lift, was it this that really angered him? That these same councils could allow the filth that could produce vermin such as the black rats. He remembered the anger he'd felt at the time a new 'ultra-modern' flat had collapsed when by some miracle only nine people had been killed. His resentment had been directed not only at the architects who had designed the 'block' construction, but at the council who had approved its design. He remembered the rumours that had spread afterwards, the favourite being the one about the safe-breaker who had kept gelignite in his flat, and it had been this that had exploded and forced out one of the concrete slabs, causing the walls down one side to topple like a pack of cards. Then it had been the gas leak, which had, in fact, been proved as the cause. But the point was it was the construction itself that had made a minor disaster into a major one. And the construction had been a cheaper means of building – a cheaper way of cramming thirty or forty families into the smallest square footage possible. This is what embittered Harris. The incompetence of 'authority'.

Then he had to smile at himself. He was still a student at heart, a rebel against the powers that be. As a teacher, he was directly under the control of a government body and was often exasperated by 'committee' decisions, but he knew there were fair-minded men and women who really did care amongst the committee members, who fought hard to get the right decisions. He'd heard many stories of individuals who had fought the government ban on free milk for kids, for instance. Of men and women, including teachers, who had all but lost their jobs because of their opposition.

No, it was no good becoming over-wrought with authority, for he knew too well that apathy existed on all levels. The gasman who neglected to fix a leaky pipe. The mechanic who failed to tighten a screw. The driver who drove at fifty miles an hour in the fog. The milkman who left one pint instead of two. It was a matter of degree. Wasn't that what Original Sin was supposed to be all about? We're all to blame. He fell asleep.

At a quarter-past-six, he was awakened by the front door being slammed and footsteps racing up the stairs.

'Hello, Jude,' he said as she bustled in, red-faced and breathless.

'Hello, lazy.' She kissed his nose. 'Have you seen the paper yet?' She unfolded a *Standard* and showed him the headlines proclaiming more killings by rats.

'Yes, I know. I was there.' He told her of the day's events, his voice hard, emotionless.

'Oh, love, it's horrible. Those poor people. And you. It must have been terrible for you.' She touched his cheek, knowing his anger covered up deeper feelings.

'I'm just sick of it, Jude. For people to die senselessly like that in this day and age. It's crazy.'

'All right, darling. They'll soon put a stop to it. It's not like the old days, when things like this got out of hand.'

'That's not the point though. It should never have happened in the first place.'

Suddenly Harris relaxed, his natural defence when events became too much to take. He reached a certain point, and knowing there was nothing he could do about the situation, his mind walked away from it.

He smiled at Judy. 'Let's get away from it at the weekend, eh? Let's go and see your silly aunt at Walton. The fresh air will do us both good.'

'Okay,' Judy's arms encircled his neck and she squeezed it hard.

'What's for dinner?' he asked.

The rest of the week, as far as the rats were concerned, was quiet. There had been a public outcry, the usual campaigns from the press to clean up London. Angry debates on television by politicians and councillors, and even a statement from the Prime Minister. Large areas of dockland were sealed off and rat-exterminators sent in. The dockers themselves came out on strike for two days until they had been convinced that no trace of rats could be found. Canals leading to the docks were searched by police and soldiers, but nothing larger than the usual rodents were found, and not many of these either. Reports of large, black rats being seen came in regularly, but on investigation it usually turned out to be a dog or cat. Children were escorted to and from schools by parents if any quiet street were on the journey. Bombsites and playgrounds became unusually still. Pet shops all over

London did a booming trade in cats and dogs. Poisons were laid by the experts, but the victims were always mice or the usual smaller rat.

Not one large, black rat was found.

People soon began to lose interest, as other news hit the headlines. Stories of rape, robbery, and arson, political and non-political, took over as conversation points. Although the search still went on, chemicals laid to poison the rats, and still nothing was found, no deaths occurred, the matter was considered to have been dealt with. Foskins was still uneasy, and made sure his department was following the matter right through to the end; the end being the extinction of any vermin likely to cause damage to persons or property. It soon became apparent, however, that it would be a virtually impossible task unless more government aid was given, but as the outcry dwindled, so did talk of money from the exchequer's purse.

Chapter Eight

On Friday evening, Harris and Judy drove down to Walton in their battered old Hillman Minx. Judy's aunt made a great fuss of them when they arrived and proved herself to be not as silly as Harris believed by showing them into a quaint, but comfortable room with a double bed. She left them as they unpacked their one case, all three of them smiling inanely at each other.

'Well, well, good old Aunt Hazel,' grinned Harris as Judy flopped on to the ancient quilt, whooping with glee.

'She always was my favourite aunt,' she giggled, as Harris stretched beside her.

She smacked his exploring hands. 'Come on, let's unpack and go down before she regrets giving us a room together because of lack of company.'

When they went downstairs, Judy's aunt had opened a bottle of sherry. She poured them a drink and bade them sit down on a soft, flower-patterned sofa, seating herself in an armchair opposite them. As she chattered on, questioning them about their jobs, gossiping about her neighbours, reliving the times she'd had with Judy's mother, Harris felt himself relaxing.

His arm found its way around Judy's shoulders, her fingers found his. He laughed at the silliest topics of Aunt Hazel, losing himself in the charm and the enclosed world of village life. He found himself deeply interested in the vicar's jumble sale tomorrow morning; the widow next door's fancy-man; the donkey-derby held last week. He found himself laughing not at the old aunt, but with her, envying the uncomplicated life she led.

At half-past ten, she suggested that the young couple should go for a brief stroll before going to bed, the exercise would make them sleep better. They walked arm in arm through the quiet village, both sensing the feeling of peace within each other.

'Deep breaths,' said Harris, taking in a huge lungful of air.

They both took several more exaggerated deep breaths, faces raised towards the million visible stars, finally bursting into laughter at their own earnest efforts. They walked on, the stillness around them mellowing their already soft mood. 'Maybe I could get a position in a school outside London,' mused Harris. 'In a village like this. Or maybe even open a post office. What do you think?'

Judy smiled back at him, knowing how he loved to dream like this. He was a city person basically, although often he told her how he disliked it. 'All right, and I'll open a little dress shop, you know, all tweeds and woollies. But I don't know what the vicar would say about us living together. He'd probably think I was a scarlet woman.'

'Well, we could humour him and get married.'

They stopped walking and Judy turned round to face him, 'You make any more offers like that, Harris, and I'll make you stick to them.'

When they returned to Aunt Hazel's, they found hot toast and drinking chocolate waiting for them. The old aunt fluttered around in a long dressing gown, still chattering on about anything that came into her head, then bade them goodnight and disappeared up the stairs.

'She lovely,' grinned Harris, sipping his hot chocolate. 'She'd drive me mad, but she's lovely.'

When they finally went upstairs, they discovered a hot-water bottle tucked into the bed and a fire alight in the hearth. Harris couldn't stop smiling as they undressed. It was a long time since either of them had been spoilt and it was nice now that they were being spoilt together.

He climbed in beside Judy and drew her warm body towards him. 'I wish we could stay longer. I'm going to hate going back.'

'Let's enjoy what we've got, darling. We've got the whole weekend.' Judy's sensitive fingers glided down his back causing him to shiver. They crept, round to his thigh and then up.

'Judy, Judy, Judy,' Cary Grant voice. 'What would the vicar say?'

The next day they were awakened by a careful tap on the door. Aunt Hazel entered with a tray of tea and biscuits and the morning paper for Harris. They thanked her trying to keep themselves covered up as she bustled about the room, drawing the curtains, retrieving the cast-out hot-water bottle. As she rambled on with her inexhaustible comments on the weather, the neighbours and the state of Mrs Green's cabbage patch, Judy began pinching Harris' naked bottom beneath the blankets. Trying hard not to yelp, he grabbed her wrist and sat on her hand. Then he began plucking at the small mound of hair between her thighs.

When Judy could no longer refrain from crying out loud, she had to explain to her surprised aunt, between fits of laughter, that she had cramp in her foot. Aunt Hazel's hand shot beneath the bedclothes, grabbed Judy's foot and began rubbing vigorously. By this time, Harris was choking with glee and had to hide behind his trembling newspaper.

At ten, they dressed and went down to breakfast. The aunt asked them what they were going to do with themselves all day, suggesting they might like to come along to the jumble-sale. They excused themselves by saying they wanted to drive into Stratford to have a look around, and would probably stay there for lunch. After warning them to be careful of the roads, she perched a jaunty straw hat on her head, grabbed her shopping basket and waved her goodbyes, turning at the garden gate to wave at them again. They washed the dishes and while Judy remade their bed, Harris cleared the grate downstairs and a new fire was laid. Although he couldn't imagine why the old girl would want a fire in this weather, he had to admit it made a welcoming sight in the evening.

Eventually, they climbed into their car and drove towards Stratford, singing at the top of their voices as they made their way along the country lanes.

As soon as Harris had trouble in finding a parking space he began to regret their visit to the old town of Stratford. It was flooded with people, cars and coaches. He'd never been there before and had expected to find quaint, olde-worlde, oak-beamed houses in cobbled streets. Angry with himself for his naïvete, for not realising a tourist-attraction centre like this must surely be spoiled by commercialism he finally found a back street park in. Walking towards the Royal Shakespeare Theatre he saw that many of the streets had managed to retain their old charm, after all, but it was the throngs of people, multi-racial accents, that destroyed any hope of atmosphere. And the nearer the theatre they got, so the noisier the streets became.

A thin, sallow-looking round-shouldered man in an open-necked, short-sleeved, floppy shirt, camera hanging on his flat chest: 'Are you coomin',: Ilda?'

The droning reply, from a plump, bespectacled woman emerging from a shop doorway, clutching a dozen Stratford-on-Avon postcards. 'Wait, oop, wait, oop.'

An obvious Yank, short-cropped hair, checked jacket, inevitable camera: 'Will ya look at that, Immogene. Quick, while I take a shot.'

Immogene posing self-consciously before an oaked-beamed shop with a thatched roof, licking an ice cream, magnified eyes peering through blue-tinted butterfly glasses: 'Wilya' hurry up, Mervyn, I feel stupid.'

They arrived at the Theatre, a heavy depressing building, and found it closed.

'Let's take a boat down the river,' Judy suggested tentatively sensing Harris' disappointment. But the river itself was swarming with punts, canoes and row-boats.

'Let's have a drink.' Harris turned towards the nearest pub, passing windows full of people devouring Wimpies and sausage, egg and chips. They entered a dark bar, all wood and stone floors. The barmaids were wearing period costumes and smiling cheerfully as they coped with the crowds. This is more like it, he thought, ordering a pint of Brown, a red wine and two ham and tomato sandwiches, and took the wine over to Judy who was sitting on a bench seat at an old oak table and returned for the beer. Sitting next to her, he squeezed her hand to show her his mood was no reflection on her.

'This isn't so bad, is it?' He turned to study a large square timber coming from the floor and supporting the low ceiling. He reached out to let his fingers run along the deep grain.

Plastic. 'Shit!'

As they left the pub, it began to drizzle with rain. Although it was a fairly light shower, shop doorways became crowded with people. Plastic macs appeared and were draped over heads and shoulders. Harris and Judy were bumped by tourists running for cover.

'Let's go, Jude,' said Harris, taking her arm firmly and leading her into the road. They quickly walked back to the car, both fighting the feeling of claustrophobia. They sat in the car and caught their breath. Harris was halfway through a cigarette when

61

the sun came out and the rain stopped. People emerged from their shelters, laughing and calling to one another. A coach pulled up on the opposite side of the road and unloaded a stream of sightseers, all stretching and yawning, and looking for the toilets.

'Look at those women,' the teacher said in amazement. 'They all look the same. They're all fat, and they're all wearing glasses. I don't believe it!'

Judy burst into laughter. He was right. They *did* all look alike. For some reason, he felt better. At least he saw the joke of his shattered illusion of Shakespeare's birth-place. He drove out of the crowded town, heading into the country.

As they left the town behind he felt a deep sense of relief. He could breathe again. He didn't fully understand why the crowds had affected him so much. He'd had a feeling of revulsion towards the people, not as individuals, but en masse. Strangely enough, it had been slightly akin to the revulsion he'd felt towards the rats. As though they were a threat.

'Jude, I'm not becoming a headcase am I?'

'No, darling. You just came into contact with too many people at the wrong time and in the wrong place. The point of coming here was to get away from it all and we ran slam-bang right into the middle of it again.'

The quieter the roads became, the freer he felt. Ahead they spotted a high-curving hill, the top crowned with trees and culti- vated fields below, its shades ranging from the brightest yellow to the deepest green. Sheep grazed on the wilder middle slopes.

'Fancy a climb?' Harris asked Judy.

'Okay.'

He pulled over on to a grassy verge and locked the car. They climbed a fence and skirted around the edges of the field, Judy explaining the difference between wheat, corn and barley, Harris enjoying his ignorance.

Watched by the sheep they climbed over a gate, the hill now becoming much steeper. As they got nearer the top, the exertion began to tell and they laughingly clung to each other, occasion- ally pulling the other down. Finally they reached the trees and found a path leading through them to the summit. Here was a plateau of still more fields, stretching across to the downward slopes and shading into woods again.

Lying back on the grassy slope, the rested, taking in the

surrounding hills, the tiny houses , the grey lines that were roads. A slight breeze stirred the otherwise warm air.

'Better now?' Judy asked.

'Yes.'

'Deep breaths.'

He reached for her. 'It's so quiet. No people. It somehow puts everything into its right perspective.'

A sheep, lost from its flock scampered past them. Once past, it turned and bleated at them, then ran off.

'And you,' shouted Harris.

He turned to Judy and kissed her, first softly, small tender kisses, just touching her lips – then hard, urgent. His hand crept to her small, round breast beneath the jumper.

'Harris, someone might come,' she warned.

'Up here,' he scoffed. 'You're joking. Who'd be silly enough to climb all the way up here?'

He pulled at the zipper of her trousers. She kissed his face, his neck, her love for him stirring her desire, pushing her body towards him in rhythmic motion. He tugged at the trousers, her body lifting to help him, then ran his fingers lightly over her smooth thighs. He bowed down to kiss them, his tongue creating thin moist trails along each limb. His hand began to stroke the fine material of her panties – then between her thighs.

She moaned with pleasure and reached for him, loosening his clothes, setting him free. His hand crept slowly between her filmsy panties and soft skin, finding her private silky hair, then down, between her thighs, his fingers becoming wet from her. He pulled the panties gently down her long legs and lay them to one side with her now discarded trousers. He half-sat, gazing down at her, taking pleasure from the sight of her naked thighs against the rich green grass.

She pulled him down to her. 'Darling.' she whispered, not really caring, 'someone might see us.'

'Not up here. Nobody can see us up here.'

He moved into her, very gently, and very slowly. Then they clung to each other, her legs slightly bent, feet flat against the slope. He began to move back and forth inside her, their passion, as so often, equally matched. She thrust up at him, both now losing themselves in the sweetness of physical love.

But as their motions became more frantic, so his toes and knees began to lose their grip on the grassy slope. He began to slip down. He wriggled forward again grabbing tufts of grass to pull himself up. But as soon as they resumed he began to slip down again, this time losing her. He wasn't amused as she was.

'We'll have to turn around,' he said, struggling back inside her. They carefully inched their way round, anti-clockwise, desperately trying to keep together, now both laughing at the ridiculous spectacle they must have made. 'I can feel the blood rushing to my head,' she giggled.

'I won't tell you where it's rushing to in me,' he groaned, trying hard not to topple forward over the body. He held on to the grass, pushing against it now, the strain on his arms becoming more intense as their bodies sped towards their crescendos. She writhed under him, a couple of times nearly sending him over her and rolling down the hill. They reached their climax, Harris almost with relief, and, still together, let themselves slide languidly down to a few feet, bodies turning.

They rested for a few minutes, their bodies relishing the warm sun, enjoying the light breeze on their nakedness.

'I love you, darling,' Judy said.

'Good, because I love you.'

Reluctantly, they dressed, and Harris lit a cigarette. Judy settled back against him and they both studied the cobalt sky.

A voice broke through their tranquil thoughts.

'Susan, don't go too far, poppet!'

They both sat up and turned their heads towards the sound. A young girl of about seven came skipping over the brow of the hill, closely followed by a man and a woman who wondered why the young couple sitting on the hillside had burst into laughter.

Chapter Nine

Dave Moodie lounged against the wall of the dingy Underground platform, occasionally tilting his head back and drinking from a carton of milk. I'm pissed off with this lark, he told himself, peering into the gloom of the colourless station. Seeing the same girl, three times a week, for two months now, was a bit strong. Pictures Wednesday, club Saturday, telly Sunday; and now she wanted him to cut out his Friday night football. Some chance! It wasn't as though they were even engaged, but Gerry was becoming more and more possessive, laying down the law about his friends, finding fault in his clothes, picking him up on his language. And all this performance; running to catch his last train, racing down those treacherous steps of Shadwell tube, a couple of times missing one and nearly breaking an ankle. He wouldn't mind but he'd spent the whole evening groping and trying to get her worked up but getting nowhere, and then, when it was time to go, she'd suddenly turn on and start getting fruity. His mates had told him she was a P.T., prick-teaser, but he hadn't believed them, in fact, he'd even belted one of them.

'Maybe I'll give her the shove next week,' he said to himself, voicing his thought for extra assurance. He began to whistle. But it was funny how he looked forward to seeing her by the time Wednesday came around. He stopped whistling. She always looked good, always dressed smart. Her mother got on his nerves, but he rarely saw her. Her father was a lazy old bastard too. Not like his mum and dad. He got on well with his own parents. He always had a freshly-ironed shirt for Saturday night, always a good hot dinner waiting for him after work, and the old man could always be tapped for a quid or two towards the end of the week. He supposed his being an only child had a lot to do with it. After his older brother had been knocked down and killed by a car seven years ago, his parents had seemed to turn all their affection on to him. He didn't mind – he liked them.

He could always bring his mates round for a party, his father would always chip in for the beer, his mother would always dance with the boys. The old man would even chat up the birds. No, they weren't like Gerry's parents. Miserable old sods.

His thoughts were interrupted by footsteps descending the long flight of stairs. A coloured station-worker came into view and walked towards the other end of the platform, entering a door marked 'private'.

Dave's thoughts returned to his present situation. Where's the bloody train? For once he'd got down there early only to be left hanging around in the gloom. Gerry would always come to the door with him to say goodnight, her passion becoming stronger as his thoughts of missing the last train became stronger. She'd finally let him go and wait at the door till he was out of sight.

He'd nonchalantly turn and wave back at her two or three times and she'd blow kisses but as soon as he turned the corner, he was off like a shot, his lungs soon sore with the sudden exertion of running. He invariably arrived at the station with a painful stitch in his side, dashed through the barrier without paying, took the stairs two or three at a time, and was usually just in time to leap through the closing doors of the train. It was good thing Gerry never heard his curses if he wasn't in time. It meant a long walk home down the trouble-filled Commercial Road. There was nearly always a mob on some street corner, or a 'perve' lingering in a doorway. Dave wasn't chicken but it *was* a drag.

Something moving caught his eye. A dark shape was moving along between the tracks. he walked to the edge of the platform and peered down the track into the gloom. Nothing. Then he noticed the shape had stopped. Realising it must be a rat, he threw the empty milk carton to see if he could make it scamper back into the darkness of the tunnel, but it merely shrank beneath the electric rail. The boy looked up sharply as he heard noises coming from the dense black cave of the tunnel. It sounded like the rush of air, but not the sound caused by an approaching train. He glanced nervously back at the form lurking in beneath the track and up again as the noise grew louder. As he did, hundreds, it seemed, of small black bodies came pouring from the tunnel, some between the tracks, others up the ramp and along the platform.

He turned and ran even before he realised they were rats, much larger than normal, and much faster. He reached the stairs, a long, black river of vermin almost at his heels, and flew up them, three at a time. He slipped once, but quickly regained his balance, grasping at the hand-rail by the side, pulling at it to gain momentum. But a rat had raced ahead of him, and his next step was on its back, causing Dave to stumble once more. As his hand went to steady himself, sharp teeth snapped at his fingers. He shouted in fear, kicking out wildly, sending two of the bristling bodies back down over the backs of their companions. He lurched onwards, now weighed down by rats that had attached themselves to his clothes and his flesh. He fell again, hitting the bridge of his nose on the sharp corner of a step, causing blood to spill down his face and on to his white long-collared shirt.

He kicked and screamed but they pulled him back down the stairs, rolling to the bottom with him, ripping his body, shaking him as though he were a toy doll. His screams echoed through the old station. He half rose and before his senses blacked out completely he cried for his mother.

Errol Johnson pulled the door marked 'private' open and rushed out. He'd heard the screams and assumed someone had fallen down the long stairway to the platform. He knew it would happen some day – those stairs were too badly lit. If he ever became station-master, if coloureds ever became station-masters he'd clean it up and make it a respectable station. Just because it wasn't used by many people didn't mean it should be badly kept.

He stopped dead at the spectacle before him, his mouth hanging wide.

Millions of rats swarming all over the station. And big ones, like those he'd seen in his own country, but even bigger. His mind didn't even stop to evaluate. He ran, without looking back. There was only one place for him to go, the stairs being cut off by a struggling mass of vermin. Without hesitation, he ran down the ramp and into the dark womb of the tunnel. His fear drove him straight into the approaching train, mercifully killing before he was aware of death's presence.

The driver, who was braking anyway, slammed them on even harder, pitching his few passengers forward in their seats. As he emerged from the tunnel, the train's wheels screeching in high-pitched protest, the scene before him caused him to react instinctively, thereby saving the lives of his passengers and himself. He released the brakes and drove on.

67

The rats became still and glared at the huge intruding monster. Those beneath the tracks crouched low as it rumbled over them, the squealing from its wheels freezing them.

The passengers stared down through the window, horror-struck, wondering if the train had found its way down to the corridors of hell. One fell back as a dark furry body hurtled itself at him only to bounce off the window and back on to the plat-form. As the train began to gather speed, more of the creatures leapt at the windows, some falling between the train and the platform to be sliced by the grinding wheels. A rat broke through the window of one carriage and immediately attacked its solitary passenger. The man was strong and managed to pull the frenzied creature from his throat. It tore at his hands with teeth and claws, causing him to shout out in pain, but he still held its neck and body. His terror gave him added strength and speed; he threw it to the floor and brought his heavy boot swiftly down on its head, crushing its skull. He picked up the limp body, amazed at its size, and threw it through the broken window into the black tunnel that the train was now in. He sank into his seat, shock spreading through his body, not knowing that within twenty-four hours he would be dead.

The station-master choked on his tea as he heard screams coming from the stairs. He spluttered as he tried to regain his breath. Not another fight. Why was it that his station always attracted hooligans on weekends? Especially Saturday nights. Underground stations always attracted trouble on Saturday nights from the yobbos and drunks, but Sundays usually weren't too bad. He hoped that daft ape Errol wasn't involved. Always interfering. Making suggestions about how to run the place. Helping drunks instead of booting them out. Where did he think it was – Charing Cross?

Shadwell suited the station-master. It was quiet compared to most stations and that suited him fine. Of course it was dirty, but what could you do with an old dump like this? Anyway, it helped keep the people away.

When he'd recovered his composure, he slipped his jacket on and stepped out from the ticket office. Without rushing he ambled towards the top of the stairs to Platform One.

'What's going on down there?' he bellowed, squinting as he tried to see through the dim lights. He heard one cry of what sounded like, 'Mum' and saw one black, thrashing shape. He moved cautiously down a few steps and stopped again. 'Come on, who is it?'

The black shape seemed to break up into little shapes that began mounting the stairs towards him. He heard a train grinding to a halt downstairs, and then suddenly, for some unknown reason, the whine of it picking up speed again and carrying on through the station without stopping. Then he heard the squeaks that sounded like hundreds of mice. He realised that the creatures were coming up the stairs towards him. Not mice – but rats. Horrible big rats. Black, ugly.

He moved surprisingly fast for a man of his bulk. He cleared the few stairs he'd descended in two bounds and headed for the ticket office, slamming the door behind him. He leaned back against it for a couple of seconds, fighting for breath and giving his heartbeats a chance to slow down. He made for the phone and with trembling fingers dialled emergency.

'Police. Hurry! Police? This is Shadwell Underground, Stationmaster Green speak . . .' He looked up as he heard a scuttling noise. Staring across at him from the ticket-office pay window was a huge, black, evil-looking rat.

He dropped the phone and ran to the back of the office. The windows were barred, preventing any escape. He looked around in desperation, his gross figure shaking with fear. He saw the cupboard set back in the wall, where brooms and buckets were kept for the cleaners, pulled it open and pushed himself inside, closing the door behind. He crouched, half sitting, whimpering, wetness spreading between his thighs, in the darkness, scarcely daring to breathe. That scream! It must have been Errol or someone waiting for a train. They'd got him and now they were coming for him! The driver of the train hadn't stopped. He'd seen them and driven on. And there's no one else on the station. Mother-of-God, what's that? Gnawing. Scraping. They're in the office. They're trying to eat their way through the cupboard door!

Chapter Ten

Eight-thirty. The Monday morning rush was in full swing. The passengers on the underground train read their morning papers or novels; slept or dozed; chatted or thought; stood or sat. Some even laughed occasionally. Accountant clerks rubbed shoulders with financial directors; typists with models; tea-ladies with executives; filing clerks with computers programmers; black with white. The men stared boldly or secretly at the girls' legs; the girls stared back or pretended not to notice. Minds filled with the coming week; minds reflecting on the weekend past; minds almost blank.

Jenny Cooper sat reading the problems page of a woman's magazine, occasionally smiling at the ridiculous situations some girls seemed to get themselves into. She scoffed at some of the answers too. Flicking over the page, not really interested in the words before her, her thoughts returned to the previous Saturday night and the party she'd gone to. She was impatient to get to work to tell her friends about the fabulous boy who'd taken her home – especially Marion, who always had hundreds of blokes and never let the other girls forget it. Jenny considered herself to be a little bit plain; her eyes were too small and too close together, her nose just a fraction too long. Her legs were good though; long, not too thin and not too fat. Her hair always looked nice. Nice curls, nice soft colour. And her face *was* quite attractive if she didn't smile too broadly. Anyway, this boy really fancied her – he'd told her. She'd had boyfriends but none of them up to Marion's usual standard. She'd liked them but always felt slightly ashamed of them when they'd taken her out. But this one was different. He was just as good-looking as any of Marion's, in fact, better than a lot of them. And he'd asked her out again! Tonight. Pictures. She couldn't wait to show him off to her friends – she'd make Marion green.

Violet Melray, sitting next to Jenny, read her historical romance. She always became so engrossed in romantic fiction, always knowing exactly how the heroine felt in every situation, suffering with her, experiencing her disappointments, her happiness. She sighed inwardly as the hero, having lost his wealth, his wife (who had been so wicked and conniving), and his right arm in a hunting accident, now returned to the woman he really loved, the heroine, so soft, so pure, so willing to have him back in her arms and comfort him in his grief, ready to sacrifice everything for him, this man who had betrayed her trust and who now needed her so much. Violet remembered how romantic George had been. In their courting days, he'd given her flowers, small gifts, little poems. How thoughtful he'd always been. But now, sixteen years and three kids later, he was more inclined to pat her back than tickle her chin. He was a good man though, very straight, but very soft.

He'd been a good husband to her and a good father to the children, ever faithful, ever patient. Their love had mellowed over the years, not really fading as most couple's seemed to. But if only he wasn't so sensible. Every problem was tackled with logic rather than emotion; and emotion was carefully measured, never just let loose. If only once he would surprise her. Do something startling. Not have an affair – but perhaps flash his eyes at another woman. Or have a flutter on the horses. Or come home drunk. Or punch his brother Albert on the nose. But no, she wouldn't really change him. It wasn't his fault that she had urges now and again for a bit of romantic adventure, a bit of glamour. At forty-two, she should have got over her wilder impulses for adventure. Now, with the kids at school and able to look after themselves, her only outlet was her part-time job in an insurance office. The men were pretty stodgy but some of the girls were a laugh. It kept her busy for most of the day anyway and she had enough to do when the kids got home from school and George from work. She reminded herself to go into Smith's at lunch-time for a new book.

Henry Sutton clung to his strap as the train lurched round a bend in the tunnel. He tried to read his folded paper but every time he attempted to open it out to turn a page, he nearly lost his balance. Eventually, he gave it up as a bad job and looked down at the woman sitting in front of him reading a book and wondered when it would be her station. No, she'd stay on for a while

71

yet; the book-readers always had long journeys. The young girl next to her. No. Works in an office, won't get off until we reach the City or the West End, and it's only Stepney Green next stop. Over the years of rush-hour travel, Henry had become an expert on where people lived. It didn't work so well in the mornings – he rarely got a seat – but in the evenings, he would position himself in front of a person most likely to get off fairly soon. For instance: the scruffier the person, the sooner they reached their destination; coloured people never went further than West Ham; well-dressed people often changed at Mile End for the Central Line. Twenty years as a solicitor's clerk, mundane but comfortable, had taught him a lot about people too. Life proceeded at a steady, regular pace; not very exciting – the odd interesting scandal – but one day pretty much like another. No cases of murder, rape or blackmail – mainly divorce, embezzlement, or house purchasing. Steady stuff. Mostly monotonous, often dull. Secure. He was glad he wasn't married and able to lead his own life without worrying about children, schools, neighbours, H.P., holidays. Not that he really ever got up to much on his own. He believed in keeping himself to himself and not getting involved in other people's problems. He had enough of that at work, although he never became emotionally involved. The church choir was the only social outlet he enjoyed, meeting once a week to rehearse, and Sunday morning singing his heart out, the only form of exhibitionism he allowed himself.

He raised his glasses and rubbed the bridge of his nose. Mondays were neither depressing nor exhilarating for Henry Sutton; one day was much the same as any other.

The train suddenly gave a lurch and screeched to a halt, throwing the surprised solicitor's clerk on to the laps of Violet Melray and Jenny Cooper.

'Oh, excuse me,' he stuttered, his face reddening as he pulled himself up again. Other passengers were in the same predicament and were now picking themselves up, some laughing, others tutting angrily.

'Here we go,' a voice was heard to say. 'Another twenty-minute delay.' He was wrong. They sat or stood for forty minutes in a state of agitation, trying to hear the shouted conversation between the driver and the guard over their intercom. Henry Sutton, Violet Melray and Jenny Cooper were in the first carriage so they could hear the driver's replies to the guard's questions quite plainly. He'd seen something on the line, not quite

72

sure what, but it had been quite large, so he'd jammed on his brakes and cut his power. Having decided that whatever it was, man or animal, it must have been killed by the train and there wasn't much he could do about it now, so the obvious thing to do was to go on and send a crew back from the next station. The only trouble now was that he couldn't get any juice. No power. It could be that whatever he'd run over had done some damage to the train although he doubted it. A faulty cable maybe? He'd actually heard of rats chewing through cables.

The driver, or 'motor-man' as he was officially called, had been on to central control and they'd advised him to sit tight for a while until they located and repaired the fault. But it was the smell of smoke that decided him upon his course of action. The passengers became aware of the smoke at the same time and began to stir apprehensively.

The next station, Stepney Green, wasn't very far, so he would get them off the train and up the tunnel. With so many passengers it would be dangerous, but it would be better than have them panic in the confined spaces of the carriages. Already he could hear excited voices coming from the carriage next door. He told the guard of his intentions then opened the connecting door, to be confronted by anxious-faces.

'It's all right,' he reassured them with false confidence. 'Slight hitch, that's all. We're going to go along the tunnel to the next stop – it isn't far and the rails won't be live.'

'But something's burning,' a concerned-looking business-man informed him gruffly.

'That's all right, sir. No cause for alarm. We'll soon put that right.' He made his way forward to the end of the carriage. 'I'm just going to inform the rest of the passengers and then I'll be back to lead you through the tunnel.' He disappeared into the adjoining compartment leaving the dismayed commuters in an uneasy silence.

A few minutes later, they heard a scream followed by shouts of alarm. The connecting door burst open and passengers spilled in, pushing and shoving their way through the crowded carriage. The smell of burning followed close behind. The hysteria spread like the fire that caused it.

Henry Sutton was once again thrown upon the two female travellers before him.

'Oh dear, oh dear,' he murmured, his glasses skimming to the end of his nose. This time, the crush of people prevented him from disentangling himself from the frightened women. They were forced to stay locked together as men and women pushed by them, terrified now by the billowing smoke that began to fill the train. Scuffles broke out as men found their escape impeded by others. All the way down the tube train doors were being forced open and passengers were jumping down into the dark tunnel, some knocking themselves senseless against the wall and being crushed by others landing on top of them.

Violet gasped for breath beneath the prostrate solicitor's clerk, while Jenny struggled to get free.

'I'm terribly sorry, ladies,' he apologised, helpless to move. 'If – if we keep calm, I'm sure the crush will ease soon and then we'll be able to make our way off the train. I don't think the fire will spread this way for a while. We've plenty of time.' Strangely enough, Henry felt extremely calm. For one whose life had had so little adventure he marvelled at his own composure. He'd often wondered whether he'd be brave in time of crisis and now, as people panicked, and pushed, and screamed all around him, he'd surprised himself by his own lack of fear. He felt quite pleased.

By now, the carriage was becoming less crowded as the people used the side-doors to escape the choking smoke.

'Ah, now I think I can stand.' Henry got to his feet and reached down to pull the woman and the girl to theirs. 'I think we should stick together, ladies. When we get into the tunnel we'll hold hands and feel our way along the wall. I'll lead, come along.'

He led the two white-faced passengers towards the front of the carriage. Suddenly the screaming reached a new pitch. In the gloom of the tunnel, lit by the lights of the train, they could see struggling figures. There were so many faces out there that they couldn't comprehend exactly what was happening. Henry caught a glimpse of one man, still wearing a bowler-hat, disappearing from view beneath the window with something black against his face. As they neared the open door of the driver's compartment, they saw that people were struggling to get back on the train but were being blocked by those still trying to get off.

Henry and his two female companions reached the small darkened driver's compartment.

'Now let me see,' he said, half to himself, 'there should be a

74

torch or a lantern somewhere here – ah, just the job.' He reached down for a long rubber-covered torch tucked away in one corner. A sudden scraping noise made him turn towards the driver's open door. Something black was crouched there. He switched on the torch and shone a beam of light towards it. Jenny screamed as it reflected on two shining, evil-looking eyes. Instantly, without realising his actions, Henry lashed out with his foot, catching the rat's head and knocking it back into the tunnel.

'It's one of those black rats that the papers were on about!' Violet cried in horror. Jenny burst into tears, burying her head into the older woman's shoulder. Henry shone the torch down into the darkness and was dumb-struck at the scene before him. In the confined space of the tunnel, men and women were running, fighting, cowering as hundreds of black rats rampaged amongst them, leaping and tearing, their bloodlust stirring them into a frenzy. He quickly closed the door and then looked back into the carriage. He saw that the rats had entered the train and were now attacking the passengers who hadn't managed to get off or had scrambled back on. He slammed the compartment door shut and switched off his torch.

He was trembling slightly but managed to control the tremor in his voice. 'I think, our best bet is to sit tight for a while, ladies.'

They all jumped as something fell against the door. Jenny began to moan loudly, her whole body shaking fitfully. Violet did her best to comfort her. 'It's all right, dear. They can't get in here,' she soothed.

'But you must keep quiet,' Henry said, placing a hand kindly on her shoulder. 'They mustn't hear us. I think I broke that devil's neck, so he won't try to get in. I suggest we all crouch down on the floor and keep as still as possible.' He helped lower the sobbing girl to a sitting position and took one more glance out of the window. He wished he hadn't. His mind registered a mental picture he knew he would never forget for as long as – he quickly pushed the thought of life and death from his mind. Below him was part of a nightmare. A scene from hell. He saw bloody-covered limbs; torn faces; ripped bodies. A man stood almost opposite him, against the wall, stiff and straight, his eyes lifelessly staring, it seemed, into his own, while three or four rats gorged themselves on his bare legs. A fat woman, completely naked cried pitifully as she beat at two rats clinging to her ample breasts. A young boy of about eighteen was trying to climb to the top of the train by pushing his feet against the wall and slowly levering himself up. A huge rat ran up the side of the wall and landed on his lap, causing the boy to fall back to the ground. Screams pervaded the air. Cries for help beat into his brain. All in the half-gloom, against the blackness of the tunnel, as though the whole event was taking place in black limbo. And everywhere scurrying, furry black creatures, running up the walls, launching themselves into the air, only stopping when their victims' struggles ceased, and then eating and drinking.

Henry sank to his knees and weakly crossed himself.

He jumped when a hand touched his shoulder. 'What should we do?' Violet asked him, trying to see his face in the darkness. He made an effort to push the horrible scene from his mind.

'We'll wait for a while – see what happens. They're bound to send someone down the tunnel to investigate. Shouldn't be too long.' He reached out for Violet's hand and patted it softly. He began to secretly enjoy the woman's dependence on him. In the past, he'd always been a little shy of the opposite sex, but now, amidst the chaos, he was finding a new side to his timid nature. Sense of pride in himself began to quell the fear inside.

Abruptly, the screaming ceased. They didn't move for a few seconds, their ears straining for the slightest sound. And then they heard moaning. It started with one long low moan and developed into several more. Soon the whole tunnel echoed with cries of misery, wailing voices, calls for help. But there were no more screams. The strident urgency had gone from the voices. It was as though the mutilated people – those left alive – knew that nothing more could happen to them. The horror had been perpetrated, now they could only live or die.

Henry raised himself and looked through the window. He could see one or two bodies nearby, but the blackness concealed anything else.

'I think they've gone.' He turned back to the woman and girl. 'There doesn't seem to be any sign of them.'

Violet got to her knees and peered out. 'But – but what's that glow. There's a red glow coming from somewhere.'

Henry leapt to his feet. 'Of course. The fire! It's spreading, and probably frightened off the rats. We'll have to get out.'

'No,' cried Jenny. 'We can't go out there. They'll be waiting!'

'And we can't stay here,' he told her, not unkindly. 'Look, I think they've gone now, frightened by the fire. I'll go out and look first and find out. Then I'll come back for you.'

'Don't leave us.' Violet clutched at his arm. He smiled at her, his face now visible in the red glow. She was a fine-looking woman, he thought. Probably married. Kids too. Wouldn't look at me twice at a more normal time. Pity.

'All right. We'll go together.'

'No, no, I'm not going out there.' Jenny crouched back against the opposite corner.

'You must, my dear. You'll suffocate here before very long.' The smoke had begun to get heavier. 'It'll be safe now – you'll see.' He reached out for her and forced her to her feet, Violet helping him. 'When we get out, I don't want either of you to look round,' he told them. 'Just hold on to me and look straight ahead. And please trust me.'

Cautiously opening the door he shone his torch along the tunnel, although he hardly needed it now because of the glow from the fire somewhere back along the train. Bodies were strewn all along the track as far as he could see, some amongst them still moving, some crawling up the tunnel, away from the carriage, others lying perfectly still. He thought he saw small shapes moving against them but wasn't sure whether it wasn't the flickering light deceiving his eyes.

'Come along, ladies. Remember what I said and keep your eyes straight ahead – we mustn't stop for anything – or anybody.' Normally a compassionate man, he knew it would be fatal to try and help any of the injured. They would have to be rescued later.

He climbed down and reached up to help the young girl, who was shaking uncontrollably. He talked to her softly, coaxing her, trying to soothe her distraught nerves. Violet smiled down at him, frightened, but placing her life in this kind little man's hands. They went forward, bending to escape the smokey upper air. Henry first, the girl next with her face against his back, Violet following up close behind, her arms around Jenny.

They stumbled forward, trying to ignore the moans, the feeble cries for help. Henry felt a hand weakly grasp his trousers but it fell away at his next step. He knew he couldn't stop, the lives of the woman and the girl depended on him. He would come back with the rescuers. His duty now was to get the three of them out, to warn the people at the station ahead. He heard a squeal and felt something soft squirm beneath his feet. Shining the torch down he discovered a rat glaring up at him. He saw others all round – but these were different from others he'd seen. They were smaller. Normal. Hideous – but normal. He kicked out at it and it scampered away as another dashed forward and bit into Henry's trouser leg.

Fortunately, it only tore into the material and he was able to bring his leg up swiftly against the wall, causing the rat to lose its grip and fall to the ground. He brought his foot down hard on its back and was shocked to hear the crunch of small bones breaking.

Jenny screamed.

'It's all right, it's all right,' he said quickly. 'They're ordinary rats. They're dangerous, but nothing like the big ones. They'll probably be more frightened of us than we are of them.'

Through her fear, Violet felt admiration well up inside her for the little man. She'd hardly noticed him on the train, of course. He was the type you didn't really see. Just a face. The sort of man you would never speculate about – just wouldn't arouse the interest. But now, down here in this frightful place, how brave he was. Rescuing her from this carnage. Her *and* the girl of course. But how brave!

When Henry had killed the rat, Jenny had been forced to look around her. The sight caused her to retch. She sagged against the wall, wanting to collapse but being held by the woman behind her. Why wouldn't the man let them get back on the train where they'd been safe? She tried to stagger back but Henry caught her arm.

'This way, dear. It won't take long.'

As they stumbled on, they saw rats feeding on the corpses of men and women – people who had set out to work, thinking it would be the usual Monday, minds filled with small worries and small joys, never expecting to die that day. Never expecting to die at any time in such a gruesome way. The three went on, choking with the smoke, now and again falling to be picked up by the others, moving all the time, finally leaving the dead or maimed behind. Suddenly, Henry stopped, causing Jenny and Violet to bump into him.

'What is it?' asked the older woman anxiously.

'Just ahead. There's something there. I saw a gleam.' He followed a silver rail with his torch-beam until it fell upon four black objects. Four giant rats. Waiting for them. Lurking in the dark, waiting for them. Neither party moved for a few frozen seconds, then the human trio began to slowly back away. The rats just stared. Henry heard Violet gasp behind him and her grip tightened on his arm. 'Behind us. There's more,' she managed to say.

He whirled around and saw them. Two. Advancing stealthily towards them. He realised they were trapped. Now the four in front had begun to move forward, taking tiny crouching steps, the back muscles tensing, ready to spring. Perhaps I could make it on my own, he thought. Jump over the ones ahead and keep running. The girl and the woman would never make it – but on my own there might be a chance.

'Against the wall, ladies.' He pushed them back, shutting out thoughts of escape from his mind. 'Keep behind and if they try to get past me, kick out, hard as you can.' He took off his jacket and wrapped it round his arm keeping the light from the torch on the rats now gathered before him. The girl hid her face against the wall, the woman began to weep for her children.

One rat moved forward, its chill gaze never leaving Henry's eyes.

A light flashed from ahead in the tunnel. They heard voices. Footsteps. More lights. The whole tunnel lit up as the footsteps and voices grew louder.

The rats and the three people looked towards the sounds, neither group stirring. Scuffling noises brought Henry's eyes back to the rats in time to see them disappear towards the burning train. All except one. The one that had been closest was still there, studying the man. Not moving, seemingly unafraid. The solicitor's clerk felt icy cold as though his very soul was being scrutinised. He became paralysed with fear. Almost contemptuously, the large rat turned it head towards the approaching men, looked once again at Henry, and then fled.

'Over here, over here,' Henry called.

Soon they were surrounded by uniformed men; police and underground staff. As Henry told them of the apalling events, they stared in disbelief.

'Come along, sir. Rats couldn't – and wouldn't – attack a whole train-load of people,' a police sergeant said, shaking his head. 'Giant or not, they couldn't get into a train. Perhaps it's the fumes, sir. They've made you a bit muddled.'

Violet Melray pushed roughly past the little clerk and shouted angrily. 'Well go and bloody look then!' and turned back, taking his hand into hers, said more softly, 'Thank you. Thank you for helping us.'

Henry blushed and dropped his gaze.

'Er, yes, well,' the sergeant said, 'we'll go on. Two of my men will take you on to the station.'

'No,' Henry said. 'I'll come back to the train with you. You'll need all the help you can get.' He looked at the woman still clutching his hand. 'Goodbye. I'll see you again.'

Before he could pull his hand away, she stepped forward and kissed his cheek.

'Goodbye,' she whispered.

Chapter Eleven

Harris felt happy as he walked into the noisy classroom. The weekend had done him the world of good. Must do it more often. Fresh air, open spaces. Green. Can't beat it.

'All right, you lot, shut up!' he barked above the din. 'Scalley, sit down and blow your nose. Thomas, away from the window, back to your seat. Maureen, put your mirror away now. Right. All had a good weekend? That's enough! Let's call the register.'

The pupils sensed he was in a good mood and knew they could get away with a little more cheek than usual. This morning, anyway.

'Only two absentees. Not bad for a Monday morning. Yes, Carlos, what is it? Toilet? But you've only just got in. Go on then, you'll never concentrate if you don't.'

Carlos, a thin dark-skinned boy, thanked-him-sir, and left the room, a smirk on his face when his back was to the teacher.

'Carol, give out the paper – Shelagh, give out the pencils. We're going to draw some animals today,' Harris told the class.

'Can I draw a pig, sir?' a boy at the back asked.

'Why a pig, Morris?'

'I can copy tubby Toomey, sir.'

The offended fat boy swivelled round in his chair as the class erupted into laughter and swore at his tormentor.

'Come out here, Morris,' Harris said, firm-mouthed. The boy slouched to the front of the class. 'Any good at drawing monkeys, Morris?'

'No, sir.'

'Well try copying from a mirror,' Harris told him knowing the class expected and enjoyed his bringing-down of a loud-mouth, even though any one of them could be next. Feeble, Harris thought, but not bad for a Monday morning. 'Right, get on with it. Any animal you like, but I don't want any to look like me.

81

When you've finished, we'll choose the best one, then I'll explain why it's the best one. Remember your light and shade.' He walked up and down the aisles, talking to them individually, giving answers, posing questions. He came to a boy named Barney, small for his fourteen years, but very bright, good at drawing but still needing to learn the techniques of painting. He was especially good with pen and ink, a skill he'd taught himself by copying comic books. Harris looked over the boy's shoulder and stared at the picture taking form.

'What made you draw a rat, Barney?' he asked.

'Dunno, sir,' Barney said, sucking the end of his pen, then adding, 'Saw one the other day. Big one, like Keogh saw . . .' His voice trailed off as he rememebered his classmate who was now dead. The rest of the class became silent at the mention of Keogh's name.

'Whereabouts?' asked the teacher.

'By the canal. Tomlins Terrace.'

'Did you see where it went?'

'It jumped over a wall and disappeared into the bushes.'

'What bushes? There isn't a park down there.'

'Where the lock-keeper used to live. It's like a jungle now the canal's been shut down.'

Harris vaguely remembered the old house that stood well back from the road, where, as a kid, he used to go to watch the barges passing through the lock. The lock-keeper liked the kids to watch him work provided they weren't cheeky, and used to encourage them to come. Funny, he'd forgotten all about the place. He'd been down Tomlins Terrace a few times recently and hadn't remembered the house had been there. It must have been because of the 'jungle' in front.

'Did you tell the police?' he asked the boy.

'Nah.' Barney turned his attention back to his drawing adding a few more strokes to his strikingly evil-looking rat.

Might have known, Harris thought to himself. Kids around this area don't get involved with the law through choice.

At that moment, Carlos burst into the room in a state of extreme agitation.

'Sir, sir, in the playground! There's one of them things!' He gesticulated towards the window, his eyes wide, smiling in his excitement.

The whole class rushed as one towards the windows.

82

'Back to your seats!' Harris roared, and strode quickly to a window. He drew in a sharp breath at what he saw.

There wasn't 'one of them things' but several. As he watched, more joined the first bunch. Huge black rats. *The* rats. They crouched in the playground, staring at the school building. More, then more.

'Close all windows,' he ordered, quietly. 'Johnson, Barney, Smith; go round to all the other classrooms and ask the teachers to close all windows. Scalley, go to the Headmaster's study and ask him to look out of his window – no, I'd better go.' If a boy went, the Headmaster would probably think it was some kind of prank, and valuable seconds would be wasted. 'I don't want anybody to move from this room. And no noise. Cutts, you're in charge.' The tallest boy in the class stood up. The boys were excited now, the girls becoming more and more nervous.

He hurried out of the room and made towards the Principal's study. As he walked down the corridor, several of the teacher's heads popped out of various doors.

'What's going on?' he was asked nervously by Ainsley, one of the old-timers of the school.

He told him quickly and hurried on. There was a strange hush throughout the school, a hush that could be entirely ruined if only one girl became hysterical.

Barney dashed from one of the classrooms.

Harris caught his arm and told him: 'Steady, Barney. Take it slowly and calmly. Don't frighten the girls. We don't want panic, do we?'

'No, sir,' was the breathless reply.

As Harris approached the stairs leading up to the next floor and the Headmaster's study, he looked down the short flight to the main doors. Naturally, they were open.

He crept slowly down, his hand on the rail to steady himself. As he reached the bottom, he heard a soft noise on the stone steps outside. Springing quietly to the side of the double-doors he glanced out, ready to slam both sides shut instantaneously. On the wider top step he saw a small boy looking back into the playground where about thirty of the rodents had now gathered.

Jesus Christ, Harris thought in horror. He must have walked right past them!

He stepped outside and swiftly scooping the small boy up, dashed back into the building. He dumped him on the floor without ceremony and turned back to close the doors. The rats hadn't stirred. He shut the heavy doors quickly but quietly and bolted them, then breathed out for the first time in nearly two minutes.

'There's animals in the playground, sir,' the seven-year-old boy told him with wide eyes, but no trace of fear. 'What are they? What are they doing there, sir?'

Ignoring the question because he didn't know what to tell him, Harris picked the boy up and raced back up the stairs. Putting him down at the top he told him to run along to his classroom. He heard the murmur of voices as teachers began to gather in the corridor. He ran up the next flight of stairs, three at a time, and almost collided with the Headmaster as he emerged from his office.

'Please phone the police, Mr Norton.' Harris said urgently. 'I'm afraid we've got trouble.'

'I already have, Mr Harris. Have you seen what's in the playground?'

'Yes – that's the trouble I mean. They're the giant ones, the killers.'

They went back into the study and looked out of the window. The rats had multiplied it seemed to a couple of hundred.

'The playground's black with them,' the young teacher said in disbelief.

'What do they want?' The Headmaster looked at Harris as though he would know.

'The children,' said Harris.

'It won't take the police long to get here – but what they'll do about the situation is another matter. Let's make sure every door and window is shut tight. All the children must go up to the top floor and barricade themselves in. I still don't quite believe it's happening but let's not waste any time on pondering over the situation.' The Headmaster strode briskly to the door.

'Now you check every possible opening, Mr Harris, I'll get the staff organised.'

Harris followed the gaunt figure of the Headmaster down the stairs where the buzz of conversation was beginning to build up. He heard him clap his hands and order silence. Harris brushed past the throng of teachers, looking into every room, making sure all the windows were firmly closed.

Thank God all the lower windows had iron grilles over them to prevent broken window panes from boisterously kicked footballs. Good.

All seemed tight. Now the staffroom.

As he entered he saw one of the windows was open, and because it faced the narrow passage between the building and the outer wall, it had no grille to protect it. And on the floor before it, sat one of the creatures.

How it had scaled the wall was something Harris would never know, but there it was, as though it were a scouting party for the others. It looked to and fro, sniffing the air, its pointed nose twitching. It saw Harris and rose on its haunches. It stood at least two feet from the ground. The teacher stepped inside and slammed the door behind him. He had to close that window.

This particular rat spent no time studying its victim – it sprang forward, straight off its haunches and into the air, aiming itself for Harris's throat. But the teacher was just as fast. He reached for a chair even as the creature's muscles tensed for the leap and swung it before him. The chair struck the rat's body in midjump, like a cricket bat meeting a ball, and threw it to one side, the wood splintering.

The rat landed on its feet and sprang towards Harris again, who brought the chair crashing down on its back. It was stunned for a few seconds, but still not severely hurt. However, it had gained the teacher time enough to reach for the heavy poker lying in the hearth of the unlit fire. He brought it down viciously, more in hate than fear, on the rat's thin skull with a sickening thud. Then again. And again. He turned towards the window in time to see another claw its way on to the sill. Without hesitation, he lashed out with the poker, knocking the rat back down into the narrow passage-way below. He pulled the window shut and leaned against it, gasping for breath and trying to control his trembling knees. The window was a type with fine wire mesh set in the glass to prevent it shattering.

'It *should* hold them,' he said aloud.

Then he went to the staffroom door, took the key from the inside, stepped out and locked it. But not before taking a close look at the creature lying on the threadbare carpet.

Its body must have been at least two feet long, its tail another nine or ten inches. The bristly fur wasn't exactly black, but very dark brown, with lots of black speckles mottling it. Its head was larger in proportion to the ordinary rodent's and its incisors were long and pointed. Its half-lidded eyes had the lifeless glaze of the dead, but its partially-covered teeth seemed to grin wickedly. Even in death, the body seemed deadly, as though the disease it bore could be passed on by mere touch.

Once outside in the hall, Harris saw that the children were being herded towards the stairs.

'Are you all right, Mr Harris?' the Headmaster came striding towards him.

'Yes. I've killed one of the monsters.' Harris realised he still held the blood-stained poker.

'Good man. Well, the place is sealed off and the police will soon be here, so I don't think we've anything to worry about,' the Headmaster said reassuringly, his smile disappearing instantly at Harris's next remark: 'What about the basement?'

They both turned towards the cellar stairs and broke into a run as they neared them. They stopped at the top and peered down into the gloom.

'I think we'll be all right,' said the Headmaster. 'Mr Jenkins, the caretaker, will probably be down there checking the boiler. It always takes him a while to get it going on Monday mornings. Heaven knows, I've complained about the cold water on Mondays enough . . .' he broke off, slightly annoyed at the young teacher who had carried on down apparently not listening to a word he was saying.

Harris approached the door of the basement with some caution, pressed his ear to it, and listened. He shushed the Headmaster with a finger to his mouth as the older man reached him.

'Oh, come along, man,' the Headmaster pushed by him impatiently, and grasping the handle, swinging the door open wide. 'Jenkins, are you . . .' his words choked off at the sight that met his eyes.

Black, scurrying creatures, swarming all around the basement. A small, high window, level with the playground outside, was wide open, and in poured more and more of the furry beasts, a constant stream of vermin.

And they were feeding on something on the floor. All Harris and the Headmaster were able to see was a single boot, protruding from the writhing mass of bodies. The teacher pulled his Principal back from the open doorway as several dark shapes dashed foreward. He grabbed the handle and pulled hard but two of the rats slithered through, a third being trapped by its

86

shoulder. He kicked at it three times before it fell back into the basement. He whirled around to see the other two scampering up the stairs. The Headmaster was on his knees staring after them.

'My God, they're enormous,' was all he could utter.

'If they reach the children . . .' Harris began to say.

'I'll stop them, I'll stop them, Harris, you cover that door. Block it with anything you can find. It's extremely heavy, but we want to be sure!' The distressed Headmaster was regathering his wits. 'When you've done that, come straight upstairs.'

'Right, but don't let them bite you!' Harris shouted after the ascending figure. 'Their bite's fatal. Keep them away from you.'

He looked around for something big to block the door with. The store-room was on his right. He opened it and carefully looked in. No windows, so it should be all right. He switched on the light. Tables, chairs, blackboards. Good. He pulled out a heavy table and turned it on its side, then pulled it along to the basement door. He upended it and was pleased to discover that it completely covered the door. He pushed it flush against it and went back to the store-room. He noticed an old radiator leaning against the wall and dragged it out, making a loud grating noise on the floor. He leaned it against the upturned table and went back for some chairs.

Just then, he heard a scream from upstairs. He picked up the discarded poker and raced upstairs.

The Headmaster was on the floor of the corridor, struggling with the two hideous rats. Mercifully, the door at the end of the corridor had been closed, and the children had all escaped to the floor above. The Headmaster had one of the rats by the throat and was fighting to keep it from his face. The other was boring a hole in his side.

'Help me, help me!' he implored Harris, turning his head to see the teacher.

Sickened, knowing his Principal was already dead, Harris ran forward and brought the poker down with all his might on one of the rats. It squealed, high-pitched, an octave above a frightened child's, and withdrew its teeth from the struggling man's side. Its back was broken, but it made an attempt to crawl towards Harris. He brought his foot down on its head and crushed it. He couldn't hit the second rat for fear of hurting the Headmaster, so he dropped the poker and reached for it with his hands. He grabbed it near its shoulders and lifted, taking care not to let its snapping teeth touch his body. Unfortunately, the Headmaster was too frightened to loose his grip on the squirming rodent.

'Let go, let go!' Harris shouted, now lifting the man with the rat.

But the Headmaster was too crazed with terror to hear. The teacher braced his foot against the Headmaster's chest and pushed him back to the floor, staggering back as the grip was released and falling, but still holding the rat high. Its weight and its strength were tremendous, and he felt his jacket and shirt being torn to shreds by the clawing feet. Holding it from behind, he raised himself to one knee and pushed it against the floor. He saw the Headmaster crawling away from him, his eyes never leaving the squirming monster in his grasp, backing away towards the wall, trying to push himself into it. In the background, Harris could hear the sound of police sirens. Where the hell have they been? What am I going to do with this?

He looked around desperately. The thing was slipping from his grip. He wouldn't be able to hold on much longer. And one bite from those teeth, even if he killed the bloody thing, one bite and he'd die later. 3c had an aquarium. That was the answer. He'd drown it. But all the doors were bloody shut. He could never hold on with one hand.

'Mr Norton,' he shouted. 'The door to 3c! Open it, quick, I can't hold on much longer!'

The Headmaster shook his head, dully, never taking his gaze from the rat.

'Open that fucking door!' Harris screamed.

The elder man at last tore his eyes away from the rat and looked at the red-faced teacher. He nodded slowly and began to crawl towards 3c's classroom.

'Hurry, hurry,' Harris shouted.

In what seemed an eternity, the Headmaster reached the door and lifted a shaky, blood-soaked hand towards the handle. The blood made his hand too slippery to turn it and he had to reach up with his other. At last, the door opened.

Harris dragged the rat along the ground, his fingers aching, trying to squeeze the life out of the wriggling body, but not having the strength or the grip. The rat dug its claws into the wooden floor, forcing him to hold its head and shoulders slightly off the floor. The small head snapped from side to side, endeavouring to sink its teeth into the man's flesh. But Harris was careful, so very careful. When he got to the door, the Headmaster uttered a small cry and kicked out, catching his leg and almost causing him to lose his grip.

'Get out of the way,' he said slowly, through clenched teeth. 'Get out of the fucking way!' Louder.

The Headmaster scrambled aside and Harris was in. He saw the tank on the window-sill. He moved towards it. When he came to the teacher's desk at the head of the class, he swung the rat up on to it, using all his strength, but never loosening his grip. Then he pushed the desk forward with his body towards the aquarium, holding the rat's head against the table, his body being raked by the creature's hind-legs.

At last, the desk butted against the window-sill. He raised one leg and crawled on top of it, then dragged the rat towards the tank full of water.

He rested before he made the final effort. Gathering all his strength, sweat streaming from his face, he raised himself and the rat and plunged the writhing body into the water.

The tank seemed to explode. Water and fish cascaded over him but he held on grimly pushing its head down to the deep bottom, ignoring the pain in his chest and arms. He began to wonder if there would be enough water left in the tank to drown the rat, or whether its flying limbs would crack the glass sides. But gradually, the struggles became weaker, the twists of its body more feeble, the jerk of its head less violent. Finally, there was no movement at all. But Harris still held it there. Just to be sure.

He looked up, through the window. Several police cars had arrived, and many blue-uniformed men stood outside the front gate, not knowing what to do.

He finally released the dead body and wearily climbed off the table. His clothes were torn, and blood covered his shirt-front, but he was fairly sure he hadn't been bitten. He walked back to the Headmaster, who was still sitting in the doorway with his head in his hands.

'It's all right now, sir. The police are here. They'll soon clear them.' Harris knelt down beside the trembling man.

'It was horrible,' the Headmaster said, raising his head from his hands. 'Frightful. Those foul creatures were waiting for me. They weren't running away at all. They were at the top waiting for me.'

Harris didn't know what to say. How could you comfort

someone you knew was going to die within twenty-four hours?

'Let's go upstairs, sir. We'll be safer there.' He helped the Headmaster to his feet. They walked down the corridor towards the door leading to the stairs.

When Harris tried to open it, he found it was locked.

'Come on, they can't turn bloody door-knobs, you know!' he shouted, banging on the door with his fist.

They heard the sound of footsteps and then bolts drawn back.

'I'm so sorry, we didn't realise anybody else was still down here,'Ainsley apologised, his bald head peeping round the door. 'Oh, dear, is everything all right?' he asked, anxiously looking at their bloodied clothes.

They half-carried the Headmaster through, closing the door behind them.

'Are the children okay?' Harris asked.

'The girls are beginning to get a bit hysterical, but the boys still have plenty of swagger in them,' replied Ainsley, catching his breath under the weight of the Headmaster.

'They'll need it,' muttered Harris.

They took the injured Headmaster to his study and laid him in his armchair.

'I'll be all right now. Go and see to the children.' His face was pale, and Harris wondered if it was imagination or could he actually detect a tinge of yellow in the injured man's face? And did the skin really look tight or was it just the stiffness of pain?

'Mr Ainsley will treat your cuts, sir,' he said. 'I'll go and find out what's happening.'

He left the study, feeling pity for the man he'd never liked, but had at least respected. The sight of him grovelling on the floor like a frightened child would stay in his mind for a long time.

He entered a classroom full of teachers and children and all heads turned towards him. He noticed the door to the adjoining room was open and anxious faces peering in. He beckoned the teachers to gather round him.

'The Headmaster's been injured,' he said quietly, so the children wouldn't hear. 'I think we'll be safe enough up here, but we'll barricade the doors just in case the rats get up the stairs. Get all the girls in one corner and away from the windows. The bigger boys can help push the desks and chairs against the door.'

Grimble, a beak-nosed, sparrow of a man, pushed forward. 'Really, as Deputy-Head, I . . .' he began.

90

'We've no time for internal politics now, Grimble,' Harris snapped, making some of the younger teachers hide smiles of pleasure behind their hands. Grimble was well-known and disliked for his conniving and petty ways. He turned away, huffily.

Harris went over to a window and opened it. He saw many police cars, among them a van-load of dogs. Some of the police were donning protective clothing. Two fire-engines rounded the corner at the end of the road, their frantic sirens adding to the noise. Crowds had gathered in the narrow street.

Below, he saw that the number of rats had thinned out considerably. Then he discovered why. They were disappearing two or three abreast through the small ground-level window to the boiler-room. Others were making for the narrow passageway at the side of the building. He assumed the staffroom window was their target.

He heard screaming behind him. Turning, he found one of the girls had become hysterical and was sitting at a desk while some of her classmates and one of the women teachers tried to comfort her.

A voice hailed him through a loudspeaker, sounding mechanical, inhuman: 'Are you all right up there? Is anybody injured?'

Harris cupped his hands around his mouth and shouted: 'Yes, we're okay so far. One man injured though!'

'Right. Well, barricade yourselves in. We don't know what the rats are up to yet, but they may try to reach you.'

Of course they'll try to bloody reach us, Harris thought to himself. What does he think they're here for? A school outing? He fumed impatiently as the policeman turned and waved his arms at the squad cars, instructing them to clear the way for the fire-engines.

He turned back to the school and raised the loudspeaker again: 'We're going to set the dogs on them first, and while they're occupied we'll try to reach you with ladders from the fire-engines.' He obviously knew of the lethal bite of the vermin and wasn't going to risk his men against them.

'No!' Harris shouted back. 'You'll never get all these children down those ladders. And your dogs won't last five minutes against those rats!'

'Do not panic up there. I repeat: do not panic. The experts will soon be here.'

Harris swore under his breath as the voice droned on: 'We

believe they are bringing gas to deal with the problem. Please keep calm. They will not be very long.'

The teacher groaned aloud. How long would it take those monsters to gnaw their way through a door? They weren't ordinary rats; they had intelligence, system. It would only take one of those monsters to get through to create havoc amongst these kids.

'Listen,' he called out again. 'The hoses! Flood the basement! Flood the lower classrooms! At least it'll panic them!'

He saw the policeman, whom he assumed was a Chief-Inspector conferring with a fireman. The firemen suddenly burst into activity, and began unwinding the long, thick hoses. Meanwhile the dogs were yelping excitedly, straining at their leashes, eager to tackle the black creatures. Two burst loose and streaked across the playground towards the thronging rats. The first, a hefty Alsatian, picked up one of the rats by the neck, shook it violently, and threw it into the air. The second dog, a massive Doberman leapt into the thick of the furry mass, snapping its huge jaws in all directions.

But they were soon covered by the rodents, being pulled down, their coats covered in blood. Several times they rose, but always they were dragged back to the ground. The other dogs were turned loose, about ten of them, and they flew into the mêlée. One actually trampled over the backs of the rats and scrambled through the small basement window.

Harris, watching from above, shuddered at the thought of its fate.

Although the dogs were brave, they were no match for the vast number of giant rats. Soon they were either lying on the ground being torn apart or trying to hobble back to their grief-stricken trainers. The men themselves had to be ordered back by their Chief-Inspector. He alone amongst them knew the risk involved, of the deadly disease carried by the vermin, and had no intention of allowing his men to lay down their lives until it was entirely essential for the sake of the children.

Suddenly, the hoses came into action. They swept through the playground, icy torrents of water, clearing a path clean through the rats, tossing them against the brick wall of the school building. They scampered in all directions, scambling over each others backs, fighting amongst themselves to get away. The blood from the dogs was soon washed away by the steady flow of water.

A jet was aimed at the basement window, pushing several rats inside but preventing any more from entering.

The children, who had by now crowded round the windows, cheered at the sight of the disrupted vermin. As the rats began to disperse, most running towards the coal bunkers, another jet of water was directed at the downstairs windows. The crash of glass as it showered into the classrooms brought grins of delight to many of the pupils.

Harris turned away from the window and walked across the room, gently pushing his way through the throng of children.

'Where's the Headmaster?' he asked Grimble.

'You should know. He was with you,' was the curt reply.

'Pull some of these desks back. He must still be in his study with Ainsley.'

The desks were pulled back allowing him just enough room to open the door and slip through.

'I'm going to see if they're okay, then I'll check the doors in the corridor,' he said. 'Push the barricade back after me. If I come back fast and bang on the door, tell them to get those ladders up here. But don't open the door – I'll go into the Headmaster's study and get away from that window.'

He closed the door behind him and heard the grating of the desks being pushed against it. He noticed the door of the Headmaster's room was wide open. Hurrying to it he breathed a sigh of relief when he found old Ainsley still fussing over the injured Principal.

'He – he seems fine now, Harris,' Ainsley said, mopping the Headmaster's face with a wet flannel.

'Good. I'm going to check all the doors now and I want you to shut this one after me. Stay here, and if there's more trouble . . .' he paused, not bothering to explain what he meant by 'more trouble', but letting the silence do it for him. 'If there's more trouble, go to the window and call to the firemen. They'll get a ladder up to you.' He didn't suggest they join the others in the classrooms – the sight of the blood-soaked Headmaster would frighten them too much. Up to now, the children had been remarkably controlled, but the sight of blood could easily push them over the edge.

He closed the door and walked quickly to the stairs. He opened the door fractionally and peeped through. All clear. Good. He went through, closed it, and crept down the stairs. Water was seeping underneath the door at the bottom. He opened it cautiously. The corridor was empty of life. One of the dead rats that had attacked the Headmaster lay in the water. For a moment, Harris thought he saw it move, but realised its body was merely being stirred by the surging water.

He splashed down the corridor, remembering to close the door behind him but opening all the classroom doors to allow the water to flow more freely. He passed the staffroom and thought he heard noises. The basement was the more urgent problem at the moment. That was where he'd seen most of the rats disappear. He had to make sure the door was still firm, maybe shove some more furniture against it. He could come back and deal with the staffroom door later.

He descended the stairs to the basement, taking care not to slip in the gushing water. He suspected more fire-engines had arrived and the forces outside were using more hoses to completely flood the lower floors.

He reached the bottom and waded towards the door. He could hear frantic scraping, scratching. He leaned forward to listen more intently above the noise of the swirling water. Yes, they were trying to scrape their way through the door. He eased the desk back slightly to see what damage they'd done. Christ, cracks were beginning to appear already. He could hear them gnawing at the wood now. Dropping the desk back he plodded to the storeroom. He looked around. Just the thing, heavy drapes. Old curtains that had been used in the school hall. He dragged them down from the shelf where they'd laid for the best part of a year, ready to be used for the next end-of-term prize-giving. They were heavy, but one would be enough for his purpose.

He left them draped over a bench, to prevent them getting wet and thus heavier, and went to a stack of blackboards. They were of the old type – they had to be used with easels – and took two. Carrying them outside, he leaned them against the wall. Then he pulled the radiator and the desk back away from the basement door.

He saw bulges in the wood where the rats had nearly eaten their way through. God, they must have strength in those jaws! Quickly he went back to the storeroom and gathered up the curtain. He hurried back in time to see the wood beginning to splinter.

Almost in a panic, he stuffed the material in the crack beneath

94

the door, folding it to make as many layers as possible. He grabbed the blackboards and slid them up against the door, as close to the bottom as the curtain would allow. Then he pushed the table up against the door, and the radiator against that, re-enforcing the barricade with chairs and boxes – anything he could find from the storeroom.

At last satisfied, he leaned back against the wall and regained his breath. He thought he could hear squeals from inside but wasn't sure if it was his mind playing tricks on him.

By now he was knee-deep in water. He waded to the stairs and climbed up. As he gained the top step he heard a cracking noise coming from the staffroom door. He saw a long black pointed head emerging, still gnawing at the surrounding wood. He stood frozen to the spot. Would it never end? He looked around desperately and caught sight of the heavy poker he'd used before, still lying in the corridor, almost hidden by the streaming water. He sprang forward, slipped in the wet and fell headlong. Glancing back, he saw the rat's shoulders emerge from the widening hole. Frantically, he stumbled forward on all fours, snatched for the poker and got to his feet, using the wall to steady himself.

It was almost as though the rat knew of his intention as it redoubled its attempt to escape from the splintered wood. Most of its body was out, only its heavy flanks holding it captive.

Harris ran forward, this time taking care not to fall. Without pause, he brought the weapon down upon the twisting skull. Amazingly, it missed as the rat pulled its head to one side, and crashed against the door-frame. The rat bared its large, sharp teeth at the teacher, snapping at him, its eyes glaring venomously. But with some fear in them, Harris noticed, almost with satisfaction. What's happened to its inscrutability now? It's scared. Of me! He cried out in blood-lust, bringing the poker down hard upon the thin skull. It split wide open and substance flowed out, the whole body stiffening and then going limp.

Harris felt sick. Killing even monstrosities like this held no pleasure, no triumph. He backed away, knowing the body now blocking the exit for the other rats wouldn't last long. It would either be pushed through or its hind-quarters eaten away.

Even as he walked backwards, he saw the body jerking, as though being tugged from behind. Suddenly, half its body dropped from the hole. That's all it took, he thought. Less than half-a-minute to chew away its hind-quarters! Another black

95

shape began to push its way through. Harris turned and ran, first throwing the poker back at the door, more in frustration than in panic. It missed the rat and clattered to the floor.

The rat was through, another taking its place immediately as it dashed towards the retreating teacher.

The door opened slowly because of the presure from the few inches of water at its base and Harris barely made it in time. As he slipped through and pulled it shut behind him, he heard the heavy thud of the rat's body crashing into the other side. Clawing noises soon followed. There was nothing on the stairs that he could jam against the door. He raced up the stairs and through to the next floor, slamming the door shut behind him. He burst into the Headmaster's study, giving Ainsley a fright. The Headmaster still seemed to be in a state of shock.

Harris ran to the window and leaned out. Ladders from the fire-engines had alreay been extended to the adjacent classroom windows and firemen were about to clamber in.

'Over here!' he cried. 'Bring one over here – with a hose.'

One of the firemen looked across at him. 'The hoses are being used below, sir,' he said, then added, 'Don't worry. We'll get to you in a moment, sir. Soon as we've seen to the children.'

'Get a hose up here quickly!' he shouted impatiently. 'We've got to stop the bloody things getting up the stairs!'

Without further argument, the firemen began to descend.

'Mr Harris, there is no need for one to lose one's temper.' Grimble's head was sticking out from a nearby classroom window. 'If we all remain calm . . .'

'Shit!'

Grimble's head disappeared abruptly. Harris smiled to himself. At least he was getting *some* satisfaction from today. He looked down to see the fireman talking to his superiors, pointing out his window. He saw them nod and the firemen run over to where two others were controlling a hose. The steaming jet of water died and the heavy hose was man-handled towards the base of the long ladder. The first fireman mounted the steps carrying the metal hose point over his shoulder, his colleagues paying it out as he ascended.

Harris noticed a white van bearing the name of 'Ratkill' had arrived. Men in white overalls were unloading several long silver cylinders. He assumed it was some sort of gas. The whole street was blocked now by police cars, fire-engines, ambulances, and the crowds were being held back by a cordon of policemen at both ends. He saw anxious parents, the women crying, pleading with the police to be let through.

As the fireman neared the top of the ladder, it was swung over towards Harris's window.

'Good,' he said, helping the man into the room.

'Which way is it?' the fireman asked looking round, ignoring Ainsley and the Headmaster.

'Straight through. Follow me,' said Harris, pulling more of the hose through the window. He noted more uniformed figures were climbing up.

They both carried the hose through into the corridor.

'Just a minute,' said the teacher, halting in front of the door to the stairs. 'Let's just check first.' He wondered if he would ever be able to open a door confidently again as he peeped through the merest crack. He opened it wide when he saw it was safe. They went down to the bend in the stairs and looked at the closed door below. The fireman looked at Harris as he heard the clawing noise coming from it.

'My Gawd, is that them?' he asked.

'Yes,' said Harris. 'It's them. Gnawing their way through. It won't take them long either – they've got teeth like electric saws.'

'Well, the place seems to be filling up with water all right,' said the fireman, removing his helmet and scratching his head.

Harris nodded. There were three or four inches of water at least at the foot of the stairs. 'The basement must be completely flooded by now. Up to the windows anyway, and the jet from the hoses must be preventing any rats from getting out.'

They heard footsteps behind them. Three policemen, one a sergeant and two more firemen were coming down to join them.

Harris gestured to them to stay where they were. 'The rats are trying to break through the door. If one of your men stands at the window, another by the study door and another at the top of the stairs, we can signal back for the right moment for the water to be turned on.'

'The only trouble is, we'll only be able to use half-power, because of the bends,' said the fireman at his side. 'If we use full power, the force will try to straighten the hose out.'

'Let's try and make all the curves fairly rounded then,' said the sergeant. 'No sharp turns.'

They formed the hose in a series of curving arcs around the various corners.

'The force will throw it against the right hand wall, so I'll stand there and hold it off. Harry, you get on the other side,' said the fireman at the teacher's side.

The sergeant ordered the other fireman back to the window upstairs, and his two men into strategic positions along the way.

'Right. Let the bleeders come,' he said.

They waited in silence, watching tiny cracks grow larger in the door below.

'Get ready up there!' the first fireman bellowed. 'It's unbelievable. Solid wood.'

'Yes, and this is the second time this morning,' commented the burly sergeant.

'What do you mean?' Harris asked.

'They attacked a train-load of people in the rush-hour. We don't know the strength of it yet, but it seems it was a massacre. Didn't believe it, myself, 'till I saw this lot.'

'A train-load of people? They attacked a train?' Harris stared incredulously at the policeman. 'I don't believe it.'

'Oh, it's true enough,' replied the sergeant. 'As I said, we don't know all the facts yet. It could have been exaggerated. But we were called out last night as well, to Shadwell. Three people dead. We found what was left of the station-master – which wasn't much – inside a cupboard. The door had been cracked open. They were going to try and hush it up for a while, but you can't keep something like *this* quiet.'

They heard the splinter of wood and a hole appeared in the door, spreading upwards as a large chunk was dislodged.

'Right!' shouted the fireman.

'Right, right, right,' came the echoes from the other men.

A rat began to wriggle through the hole.

The lifeless hose stiffened as it filled with water and the fireman released the jet immediately, aiming it directly at the squirming creature. It hit the door a fraction of a second too late. The rat scrambled free just in time, its hind-quarters being knocked aside by the powerful liquid jet. The fireman aimed low, throwing it back against the wall.

'The door. Concentrate on the door. Don't let any more get through,' shouted Harris, but it was already too late. With lightning speed, another rat had leapt through the exposed hole. The fireman returned his jet to the door, completely covering the hole, and in fact, making it bigger by pushing the loose pieces inwards. The two free rats half-ran, half-swam towards the stairs.

'I'll deal with them,' roared the sergeant, snatching one of the firemen's small axes from his belt. He advanced towards the approaching rats taking care to keep out of the path of the cascading water. To gain him more time, the fireman lowered his aim for a split second, sending the two creatures sprawling back against the opposite wall.

The policeman jumped the last two steps and landed with a splash, brandishing the axe above his head. He slipped, but lashed out at one of them as he did, managing to cut deep into its back. Once again, the child-like squeal of the injured monster. Without waiting to do further damage, he turned on the second rat, but only hitting it a glancing blow with the flat of the axe. It fell back, twisted round, and launched itself at the big man's legs. The policeman cried out as the vicious teeth sank into his knee. He hit sideways at the tenacious beast, wary of cutting his own leg with his bloodied weapon, trying to dislodge it. In desperation, he fell to one knee, pushed the rat flat against the ground, and brought the axe down with all his might. He almost cut the black-furred body in half.

The other injured rat tried to make it to the stairs but Harris ran forward and kicked it back as it mounted the first step. The policeman chopped its head off with one stroke. Then he prised the jaws of the rat still clinging to his knee loose. He limped up the side of the steps, cursing loudly.

The fireman who had been stationed at the window came running down. 'They've just brought the cylinders of gas into the playground. They're going to feed it into the windows. They said it's harmless to humans providing you don't get too much of it, but lethal to vermin – cover your faces with wet handkerchiefs to stop yourselves choking on it.'

'Tell them to pour gas into the window around the side of the building. It's the staff-room window – they may try to get back out that way!' Harris shouted above the noise of gushing water.

'Right!' The fireman raced back up the stairs.

'Think you can hold them?' Harris asked the man with the hose.

'No problem. Even if the door bursts open under the pressure, we can keep them off the stairs until the gas gets them!'

Harris helped the sergeant with his torn knee up to the second floor. As he limped along, the policeman said: 'I've been told these bites can be dangerous. Didn't the kid who died from one last week come from this school?'

'Yes, he did. His name was Keogh.'

'That's right. He must have been pretty badly bitten, wasn't he?'

'I don't know,' Harris lied.

He took him into the Headmaster's study and sat him on a straight-backed chair.

'Oh dear. Have you been wounded too?' Ainsley asked querulously, reaching for the medicine box.

'Only the one bite, sir. Nothing much. Just stings a bit,' the policeman told him.

Harris went along to the next-door classroom and rapped on the door.

'It's all right,' he called out. 'Let me in.'

He heard the grating of furniture being dragged back and the door was opened to him. The room was completely full now with teachers, pupils, policemen and firemen.

He raised his hand for the children to be quiet. 'Everything's under control now. The stairs are being blocked by water, and gas – harmless to us – is being pumped into the classrooms downstairs. We should be able to leave fairly soon.'

'Thank you very much for your appraisal of the situation, Mr Harris,' Grimble said acidly. 'I'm sure the Chief-Inspector can take charge now. With your permission, of course.'

There's one rat the gas won't destroy, Harris thought.

The rats in the school were slowly exterminated. The ones not drowned in the basement were finished off by the gas. The others on the ground-floor scurried around, swimming through the rising water, frantically looking for a means of escape. They climbed on top of radiators, gnawed through doors into classrooms and tried to escape through the windows only to be stopped by the meshwork grill fixed to the outside frames. They jumped on to desk-tops, cupboards, anything above ground level, to escape the torrent of water. Then gas seeped through and one by one, convulsing violently, rearing up on their hind legs, they finally dropped, some into the water, others sprawling on the tops that might have saved them from drowning.

Many tried again and again to crawl through the hole in the door at the end of the corridor, but were beaten back by the powerful jet of water. Their panic caused a madness in them. They fought amongst themselves, whenever they collided or whenever more than one tried to reach the same point of safety. Then a pack would single out one particular rat for no apparent reason, and attack it, killing it in a matter of seconds because no resistance was offered. Then the pack would pick on one of its own members and destroy it. Thus the numbers were depleted.

Soon, they were all dead.

Chapter Twelve

It became known as 'Black Monday' for Londoners. Reports came in at regular intervals all day long; reports of deaths and injuries. The Underground tragedy was the major disaster, the school had almost been the second. Deaths occurred in bizarre ways: the man who went to get his car out and found his garage full of the vermin; the baby left in his pram in the morning sun, laughing at the black creatures, to be dragged out and killed; the priest saying his morning devotions, alone in his church; the two electricians rewiring an old house for new tenants; a pensioner, living in the top of a new council building, opening her front door to take in her milk; the dustman who took off a dustbin lid to find two creatures lurking inside.

There were miraculous escapes too; a postman delivering letters to a basement flat turned to find three sets of evil-looking eyes staring at him from a coal bunker – the rats made no attempt to attack him as he stumbled backwards up the stone steps; a gang of dockers were trapped by rats in a dockside shed – they escaped by climbing stacked crates, through the skylight and across the roof; a milkman warded off two black rats by throwing milk bottles at them; a housewife found her hall filled with the creatures – she ran upstairs and jumped from a bedroom window into the street.

But perhaps the most fantastic escape of all was the newspaper boy, on his early-morning round, who took a short cut across debris to find himself in the midst of thirty or forty giant rats. Amazingly cool for a fourteen-year-old boy, he calmly walked through them, taking great care not to tread on any. For no apparent reason, they let him pass without harm. The boy would never have been believed save for the fact he was seen from the road by two men on their way to work. There was no explanation for the phenomenon, no logical reason.

People in Stepney, where most of the incidents occurred, were in a state of fear – and anger. They blamed the local authorities for the whole situation, insisting that proper sanitation for the area had never been maintained to its full and proper extent. Old bomb-sites had been neglected since the war; houses that were condemned for years still remained standing; garbage from markets and rubbish dumps were never cleared soon enough. All breeding places for filth – all sanctuaries for vermin. The local councils blamed the government, implying that the investigation carried out by the Department of Health was not thorough; that not enough money had been allotted to the task of destroying the pests; that too little time and labour had been allowed on the project; that not enough care had been taken to ensure the total extinction of the vermin. The government ordered a public inquiry in which the ultimate responsibility was laid squarely and irrevocably on the shoulders of Foskins, the Under-Secretary of State.

He accepted responsibility and resigned, knowing it was expected of him. The Ratkill organisation came in for stiff criticism too. They were accused of negligence and publicly reprimanded by the government but claimed they were dealing with an unknown and unpredictable species of rodent. They asked to be given another chance to tackle the menacing problem and were informed that virtually every pest-control organisation in the country was in fact to be brought in to deal with the situation, and all were to work strictly in conjunction with each other.

It became a political issue, the Labour Party claiming the Conservatives, the party in power, never *really* cared about the living conditions of the working-class people and had neglected to clear slums, allowed filth to pile up in the streets and had never implemented proposed plans (proposed by Labour when they were in office) for a completely new network of sewers to cope with London's vast waste problem. The Conservatives replied that the living conditions of London's working class had not suddenly degenerated when their party had taken over Parliamentary power, but had been allowed to deteriorate by the previous Labour Government. They quoted statistics of huge new development areas, not just in London's East End, but in every poorer section of the city. Pollution, they said, was being rescinded dramatically.

All eastern regions of the city's Underground were temporarily shut down until a full purge of all tunnels had been completed. However, most people declined to use any section of the Tube system and rush hours became chaotic. Dockers came out on strike, refusing to work in dockside areas where the menace seemed strongest. Dustmen refused to risk their lives clearing rubbish that could contain the deadly vermin. Troops were called in to deal with the problem – rubbish could not be allowed to accumulate at such a precarious time. The municipal workers who maintained the sewers naturally resisted any persuasion to continue their work.

When news of the deaths from the disease carried by the rats became known, matters became even more critical.

People living in the East London boroughs demanded immediate evacuation. The government urged them to remain calm – the situation was firmly under control. Parents refused to send their children to school. The war-time measure of child evacuation came into being once more and the children were shunted off to all parts of the country. Poisons were laid in cellars, gardens and dustbins, killing small rats, mice and many household pets. Restaurants were mistrusted and not used. Many butchers decided to close up shop for a while – the thought of being amongst all that raw meat proved to be too uncomfortable. Any job that entailed working beneath ground was turned down. Any job that involved night-work was refused.

The attacks continued and more people died from injuries or disease, or both.

Although the pest-control companies were meant to be working together on counter measures against the apparent rat invasion, each tried to out-do the other in finding the solution. Poisons proved fairly ineffectual for the rats seemed to feed mainly on human or animal flesh. Sodium Fluoroacetate and Fluoracetamide were used after the normal poisons, Zinc Phosphide and Arsenious Oxide, had failed, but these too seemed to have little effect.

Gas, as had been proved in the attack on the school, was the effective answer, but the rats had to be caught in a confined space. It was poured into sewers and basemenets of old buildings but when teams of men wearing protective clothing were sent down to investigate the results, they found many dead normal-sized rats but only a small number of dead giant rats.

*　　*　　*

Harris was staring out of the window of his flat when the phone rang. He'd been gazing at the small private park set in the square, surrounded by tall, terraced houses, magnificent in their Regency days but slightly dilapidated now. The teacher was waiting to be assigned to another school now that St Michael's and others in that area had been shut down until matters were improved. His mind always became more relaxed when he studied the peaceful little park, and after the ordeal in the school, his taut nerves needed all the relaxation they could get.

He answered the phone, its shrill cry stirring up the tension again.

'Hello, Mr Harris? Foskins here.'

After this initial surprise, Harris answered. 'Hello, Foskins. What can I . . .?'

'We wondered if you could help us in a small way, old chap?'

'Well, of course, I . . .'

'Just a few questions some of our boys would like to ask you. Nothing much, shouldn't take long. You see, it turns out that you're one of the very few people that have had actual contact with these killer rats and lived. If you could come along this afternoon . . .?'

'Right. But I thought you'd been . . .'

'Dismissed? On the surface, I have, old boy, had to be. Public demand. But I'm afraid the Ministry rather needs me at this particular time, so don't believe everything you read in the papers. Now, here's the address I want you to come to . . .'

He was greeted by Foskins himself when he arrived at the adddress he'd been given. It had turned out to be Poplar Town Hall, a natural enough base for operations, he supposed. Foskins led him to a large assembly room, the walls covered with enlarged maps of the area, diagrams of the Underground and sewage networks, blow-ups of the giant rats themselves vivisected as well as whole, even photographs of their spoors.

The room was a hive of activity but Foskins took him over to a group of men gathered round a table in quiet, unexcited discussion.

'Gentlemen, this is Mr Harris, the teacher I told you of,' Foskins introduced him. 'This is our team of experts. Researchers from the major pest-control companies, biologists, sanitation experts from our own department – even a couple of chemical warfare chaps!'

He nodded hello.

'Let me just briefly bring you up to date and then we'll put some questions to you,' said Foskins. 'We've examined these monsters

105

thoroughly and haven't really found anything unusual about them apart from their size of course and their slightly larger brain. Their teeth are bigger, but only in proportion to their body. Their ears, which seem peculiarly long at first because of their nakedness, are also in exact proportion to their body. But the Black rats normally have longer ears than the brown species. Which brings us to an interesting point.' He paused, indicating that Harris should take a seat, then went on: 'The Brown rat seems to have vanished from London. Since the Brown rat is unable to climb as well as the Black, over the years it has had less chance to survive in the city. Whereas the Black rat is able to scale walls and leap across rooftops, the Brown has found it increasingly harder to gain access into premises that have barriers against them. For years, the two species have been battling for superiority and now it appears that the Black have won. We've found no trace of the Brown, not even its spoors which are quite different from those of the Black.'

'It's natural to assume that the introduction of the freak giant Black rats tipped the balance,' interrupted one of the group of men.

'Yes, rather like a small country acquiring the Hydrogen bomb,' continued Foskins. 'Well, it seems they completely vanquished the Brown rat. One of our younger members,' he looked at the man who had just spoken, 'came up with the idea of bringing back multitudes of the Brown to do battle with the Black, giving them the advantage of numbers. Needless to say, we have no intention of turning East London into a battleground for vermin. The consequences could have been disastrous.'

The young researcher turned a deep red and studied his fingernails intently.

'So this is the villain we face.' Foskins held up a photograph of a large, but dead, rat. *Rattus rattus*. Black rat. Or Ship rat. There are some of the species known to be this size in tropical countries. We think a member, or members of that species came over in a ship and bred with our own common variety. Because of the difficulties involved, we suspect they were brought over secretly. The zoos claim no knowledge of such an undertaking and as the whole idea would be illegal anyway, we don't expect an individual to come forward to admit it.'

'Now what we want from you, Mr Harris, is information,' said another member of the committee. 'Anything at all that might tell us more about these creatures. You see, we haven't managed to capture any alive yet and you are the one person that has had close contact with them on more than one occasion and lived. We don't know anything of their behaviour pattern, where they go after they've attacked, why sometimes they won't attack at all, and what's caused their hunger for human flesh. The slightest peculiarity you may have noticed could be of invaluable help to us.'

Harris told them of his experiences with the rats; about Keogh, one of their first victims, and how they had chased the boy along the canal, scaling a six-foot wall but letting him escape; the episode with Ferris, the little man from Ratkill, and of their first sighting of the vermin, swimming in a kind of formation; how one had stopped on the opposite bank of the canal to study him, suddenly disappearing through the fence.

'Did you frighten it, is that what made it go?' he was asked.

'No, no. It wasn't fear. It seemed to raise its head, as though it had suddenly heard something, almost as if it had been called. But I heard nothing.'

One of the researchers spoke up. 'They do have an acute sense of hearing, as do many animals or mammals. Rats can locate their offspring in a field of corn by its high-pitched whistle. Nothing unusual. In fact, my company is working on a method of rooting out rats from buildings by the use of ultrasonic sound beams. It's in its early stages as yet, but it certainly seems to work.'

'Well, maybe that was it. But it *is* unusual the way they study you. It's happened more than once, almost as if they're reading your mind. It's uncanny.' He went on to tell them of the battle in the school, relating every detail he could remember. When he'd concluded there was silence around the table.

'Sorry, it's not much help to you,' he said, feeling he'd left something out, his mind groping unclearly towards it.

'On the contrary, Mr Harris,' smiled Foskins, 'it's been quite useful. Now if you leave us to digest the information you've given us . . .'

The young researcher whom Foskins had caused to blush earlier sprang to his feet excitedly. 'Infect them,' he cried.

All eyes turned towards him.

'Look, we can't poison them because they only want human or animal flesh. But we could infect them.'

'How exactly?' asked the sceptical Foskins.

'We inject a group of animals – dogs, cats – what about Brown rats? – with a virus, something highly infectious, deadly to rats – our bio-chemists could easily come up with one – set them loose at certain points that Mr Harris could show us – that section of the canal, for instance – the infected animals are attacked by the Black rats, they themselves are infected, they spread it amongst their own kind. They destroy themselves!'

There was silence for a few moments.

'It could infect people. It could cause an epidemic,' someone ventured.

'Not if we used the right virus.'

'It could kill all the animals in and around London.'

'It's worth the risk, isn't it?'

More silence.

Then Foskins said: 'You know, it might just work.'

The young researcher beamed a smile of gratitude.

'Yes, it might,' one of the scientists leaned forward enthusiastically. 'They're too bloody clever to be baited with poison – or they're immune to it. But if we could infect them . . .'

'Not with rats though,' said another, the idea, perhaps out of desperation, beginning to catch fire. 'Too much of a risk with other rats. Too unpredictable.'

'All right, dogs then. Pups, to make it easier for the rats.'

Harris's mind rebelled at the idea of feeding young pups to vermin.

'Why not just infect raw meat?' he suggested.

'No, the virus would have to exist on living flesh.'

'But how do we know what virus? We haven't got a live giant rat in captivity. How do we know which virus would kill it?' asked Foskins.

'I have a pretty good idea already,' said a bio-chemist. 'We can test it on the normal Black rat – and hope it will work on its larger brother.'

The debate continued, arguments flared, solutions found. Harris felt quite flattered to be involved in the centre of the operation, but his mind still nagged him about something forgotten.

'Very well,' Foskins finally drew the discussion to its noisy conclusion. 'It shouldn't take more than a few days to find the right virus. Although it must be tested thoroughly – I needn't

108

stress how thoroughly – we should be ready to put the plan into action by the middle of next week. In the meantime, Mr Harris and I, together with the Borough surveyor will work to find the most suitable locations for deploying the infected dogs. Mr Harris was brought up in this area, I might add, so I presume knows most of the likely places the rats might use as lairs. You will all carry on with your usual activities of laying poisons, using gas or anything else you may think of, and we'll assemble every morning at eight-thirty to see how things are going. Are there any questions? No? Good. Let's get on with it then.' He turned to Harris, and said quietly, 'Join me for a drink, Mr Harris.'

They crossed the road from the Town Hall and entered a pub just opening its doors for the early evening rush. Their eyes adjusted to the gloom reluctantly after the bright sunshine of late afternoon. 'What will you have?' Foskins asked, reaching for his wallet.

'Keg.'

'Pint of Keg and a gin and tonic, please.'

They found a quiet corner and relaxed into imitation leather seats.

'Cheers,' said Foskins.

'Good health,' replied Harris.

They drank in silence for a few moments.

'I'm surprised,' said Harris.

'At what?'

'That you're still running things.'

'Ah, that. As I explained over the telephone, Mr Harris, the public wanted somebody's head, I was in charge, I was the only choice.' He smiled thinly, his eyes examining the rim of his glass. 'A scapegoat always has to be found – it's the way things are.' He quickly shrugged off his dejected mood, and smiled at the teacher. 'But I'm too good at m'job for them to do without me and they – indefinable they – are well aware of it. You see, the only mistake I made last time was in underestimating the foe. A bad mistake, I grant you. It certainly had serious consequences. But under the circumstances, it was a natural error, don't you agree? I mean, it's not the sort of thing that happens every day, is it?'

'I suppose not.' Harris took a long drink, feeling Foskins' eyes on him.

'You were rather harsh on me yourself, last time we met,' Foskins said.

It suddenly dawned on Harris why he had become involved in the operation. He wasn't really that necessary – he'd hardly call his help invaluable. Foskins had been mistreated by the public. Mistreated and unappreciated. They'd yelled for his blood and his superiors had given it to them. On the surface, anyway. And he himself had scorned him. So Harris, in a symbolic way, represented the public. He was Foskins' actual contact with the people who had derided him. And now he was going to prove them wrong. Through him. Showing he was still in command, and very, very able.

Good *luck*! thought Harris.

'Well, it seems we've had quite a breakthrough today.' Foskins settled back in his seat, a broad smile on his face. 'Don't know why we didn't think of it before. Like another drink?'

'Let me,' said Harris, draining his glass and rising to his feet. 'Same again?'

He brought the drinks back to the table, catching the other man deep in thought. Foskins looked up at him, almost as though he were a stranger.

'Thank you,' he said. 'Well, I think we've cracked it now, don't you? Yes, things will soon be back to normal. You'll be back at your school, I'll be re-instated – not publicly, of course, or perhaps moved to another department. Not dishonourably though.' He sipped his gin. 'Tell me, what makes you teach in the East End? There are more pleasant places aren't there?'

'Home ground.'

'Oh, so you live here still?'

'No, I've got a flat near King's Cross.'

'Married? Must be.'

'No, not really.'

'I see. I used to be.'

Foskins took a large gulp from his drink, his mind drifting away again. Harris began to get slightly irritated by the melancholy turn the conversation kept taking.

'Do you think they'll come up with the right virus in time?' he asked, changing the subject.

'Oh, yes. No problem. Those boys could come up with a way to make fleas catch German Measles. Time is the important factor. Do you know how fast these bloody rats breed? Five to eight times a year. And their offspring can breed within three months. You're a teacher, you work it out; if we don't kill the

110

bloody things soon, they'll over-run the whole city. Have another drink?'

'No, I've got to go,' said Harris. 'Someone waiting.'

'Yes, yes, of course.' Dejected once again. 'Well, see you bright and early tomorrow then, eh?' More brightly.

'You want me to come along then?'

'Why, yes. You're involved now, old chap. Don't worry about your people. I'll clear it with them. As a matter of fact, I already have. Sure you won't have another? Right. I'll see you tomorrow.'

Harris left the pub with relief. He wasn't quite sure why he disliked Foskins – perhaps it was his unpredictable moods. One minute bright, hearty, efficient, the next – well, 'hang-dog' was the only expression that sprang readily to mind. Harris couldn't wait to get home to Judy.

Foskins stared moodily into his glass. Mustn't stay here too long, I suppose, he thought to himself. Wouldn't do to have any of his staff pop in from across the road and catch him drinking by himself. Wouldn't look good, especially just now.

He wondered about the young teacher. Probably living with a girl – didn't look queer. Sure of himself, self-contained. Young. Might be useful in this exercise, though. Not essential of course, but at least the teacher would learn just how difficult it was to organise a project like this. The experience would do him a lot of good – only wish *more* people had some idea of the difficulties involved, then perhaps they wouldn't be so ready to cry for blood at the first crisis. They'll soon see I'm not ready for the shelf just yet.

He ordered another drink – just a quick one, he told himself – and returned to his seat.

Funny how things turn out, he brooded. Always having to prove yourself to others. To some it comes easy, they're born with the gift, but for the others it requires constant, hard work, not relaxing for a minute, never revealing your weakness to those who'd be only too pleased to turn it to their own advantage. That's how it's always been with me. Work, leadership – they've never come easily. Always the struggle a well-guarded secret. If only they knew of the night hours spent in sheer slog, sheer tedious grind, to keep up with the work output. Not just keep up, but to be ahead of.

But Rosemary had found out. She had to of course – she was

111

my wife. Any other woman would have offered consolation, but not Rosemary. She grew bored with the nights spent plodding through paperwork. And when she discovered that prowess in bed was also a task that didn't come naturally to me – well, the disillusionment was too great. If we'd had children I suppose she'd have had something to occupy her, but she even blamed me for that. Nevertheless, it lasted for fifteen years so she must have felt some love for me. Even though I knew she was having the odd affair, it didn't really matter as long as she was discreet. Even her jibes in front of friends, and colleagues, I could have survived by ridiculing her in return in that false-hearty way. But when her affairs became much more frequent and much less discreet – and worst of all, much less discriminating, then it had to be brought to an end. But she jumped the gun by ending it first, walking out, running off with a bloody travel agent! A travel agent! Did my best to hush things up, but word always gets around, so there was nothing left but to work even harder, to become more successful, anything to cover the shame of being left high and dry by an unfaithful wife. And the double-shame of having been cuckolded by her and a damn travel agent! How could you retain your dignity after that? But I managed it, worked myself up into this position. Yes, there was the affair of the rats that had done some damage to my esteem, but my superiors wouldn't let me go, would they? No, they know my true worth. Public be damned. And when this little episode is over, they'll all acknowledge my worth. The fact of the matter is, the more power you have, the easier it is to find solutions to any problems. You merely surround yourself with the right people, the right brains – they come up with the answers and you take the glory. The hard part was to gain that position of authority, but once you had it, the rest was easy.

I'll just have one more drink and then perhaps I'll go along to the club, tell the boys all is going well, drop a few hints about our idea, not too much, in case it doesn't work, but enough to let them know old Foskins has done it again. Feel better now, no point in going home to an empty house just yet. The boys'll be pleased to see me, I should think.

He drained his glass and walked out into the still bright sunshine.

Harris reported at eighty-thirty every morning to the daily Town Hall meetings. He worked out with Foskins and the Borough surveyors ten key locations that they considered to be likely rat-infested spots. By the end of the week, the bio-chemists had come up with the correct virus.

They laughed at the teacher's admiration for their speed. 'That wasn't the problem,' they told him. 'You see, we've had the virus itself for many years. In fact, we inherited it from the Germans after the war. They'd been working on a way of killing off all our livestock by infection without harming the population and they had actually come up with the answer. Fortunately, for us, the war ended before they had time to use it and it's been a well-kept secret, along with a few other nasty little items, ever since. The hard part – and this has taken the time – was to find an antidote to contain it. We don't relish the idea of wiping out all animal life in the country. Well, we've found the antitoxin and it will be a simple matter to introduce it into our animals, either by injection or mixing it with their food or water. It's already being produced in bulk, and, just as a safeguard, we're working on another serum in case the first fails. As a safeguard, we must stress. We see absolutely no reason for the first to let us down.'

Foskins congratulated them on their fine work and they set a time to put the plan into action.

'Very well, gentlemen,' concluded the minister. 'On Tuesday morning, at six, we'll plant the first infected puppies. We'll go on to nine other locations throughout the morning, all key points, and leave the unfortunate but expendable animals to their fate. Any questions?'

'Yes,' said Harris, raising his hand but quickly dropping it realising he was emulating his absent pupils. 'What happens, when we're planting the pups, if we become the victims of the rats?'

'Everyone is to wear protective clothing, Mr Harris. It's standard procedure on any operation like this. I think you'll find the suits adequate even if uncomfortable.' Foskins looked around at the faces. 'Any more questions?'

'Yes,' said Harris.

'Mr Harris?'

'What if it doesn't work.'

'If what doesn't work?'

'The idea.'

'Then God help us, Mr Harris.'

*　　*　　*

113

The grey dawn cast a mist over the old canal. Not even a bird disturbed the chill morning silence. The dirty waters stirred occasionally in the slight dawn breeze, sending small ripples lapping lazily at the stone sides of the man-made river.

The silence was broken by a tiny yelp. Along the bank came five men looking like visitors from another planet. They were covered from head to foot in a heavy, plastic-like material and wearing helmets with large glass visors. Two of the men carried a large basket. The lid bounced now and again as if the occupants of the container were striving to get free. One of the men motioned towards a spot by the side of the canal and the basket was placed on the ground.

'This should do for the first lot,' said Harris, sweating inside his heavy suit. He lifted the glass visor so the others could hear him more clearly.

'This is where we saw the rats last time. They were swimming along the canal up to this point. Then they climbed out and disappeared through that hole over there.' He pointed towards the other bank.

The basket was opened and three small dogs were lifted out. Harris fondled one of them affectionately. Poor little bleeder, he thought.

The young researcher, introduced to the teacher after their first meeting at the Town Hall as Stephen Howard, lifted his visor and wiped his brow with a gloved hand. 'Well, let's chain two down and let the other wander,' he said. 'That way, the rats are bound to get them.'

Harris watched as a metal stake was driven into the hard path that ran alongside the muddy canal and two of the pups were chained to it.

'All right, little'n, off you go.' He placed the pup he was holding on the ground and gave it a gentle shove, but it pushed back against his hand, licking it and looking up at him.

'Go on, boy, it's for Queen and country.'

The pup squatted on its haunches and looked up at him. 'Oh Christ,' muttered Harris, 'it's going to be more difficult than I thought.'

Howard reached into the basket and brought out some raw meat. 'This should tempt him. It's meant as rat bait, but I don't see why these little blighters shouldn't enjoy a last meal. I'll entice him along to the bridge and leave him there with enough to

114

feast on. Here boy, come on.' He bumped the meat against the pup's nose and trailed it along tantalisingly just above its snapping jaws.

'Don't go too far!' shouted Harris, as the strangely-clad figure disappeared underneath the bridge. He and the others began to scatter more raw meat around the two remaining puppies, feeding them a little to keep them happy.

They looked up at the sound of running feet to see Howard coming towards them, waving his arms excitedly. At first, they couldn't understand his shouts, but as he pointed back towards the bridge they realised why he was making such haste to get away from it.

In the gloom under the bridge they saw several black-shaped creatures surrounding the pup, which had begun to whine piteously. Harris made as if to move towards it, but a restraining hand was placed on his arm. He nodded, seeing the sense of it. What did it matter if a pup lost its life when countless people were to be saved because of it? But it was a horrible way for the poor little mite to go.

Suddenly they saw a line of rats break out from the dark interior of the bridge and streak out after the lumbering researcher. The leading rat swiftly caught up with the suit-clumsy figure and leapt at the plodding legs. It clung to the material of the suit but its razor-sharp teeth failed to penetrate. Howard continued to run, dragging the persistent creature along with him.

'Your visor,' shouted Harris. 'Close your visor!'

Howard heard him and snapped the glass protection shut. He stumbled as another rat attached itself to his other leg, but managed to keep on his feet. The group of men looked on in horror as another scaled his back and perched on his shoulder, snapping at his head covering. He went down heavily, one arm splashing into the canal water. He raised himself to his knees, rats swarming all over him now. He tried in vain to brush them off, but they clung to his body like giant leeches.

Harris saw what he feared most - a tear beginning to appear in the tough material. He ran forward, the three other men following. Reaching Howard, he began pulling at the rats which were now tearing at the cloth in frenzy, oblivious to the blows being dealt them. Harris kicked two into the canal, hoping they were stunned enough to drown, and ignoring the clinging creatures, he dragged the researcher to his feet and pulled him along the canal bank.

All the men were fighting for their own lives now as more of the rodents poured over them. They staggered on, back towards the gap in the fence that would allow them to escape from the death-trap canal. Some of the pressure was taken off them as they passed the two howling pups and the littered raw meat, for the rats pounced on the easier prey with relish.

'Back to the vans!' Harris heard a muffled shout. 'We've got the gas cylinders there!'

They kept going, the way easier now for most of the rats were converging on the animal flesh. Helping one another, they reached the gap and climbed through. Abruptly, the rats still clinging dropped to the ground as if they sensed the danger to themselves once outside the boundary to the canal. Harris lunged at one before it could escape, ignoring the revulsion within him caused by the squirming creature. He held on to its neck with one hand, its back legs with the other and lifted it high into the air.

'Here's a live specimen for you!' he cried, struggling to keep his grasp.

'Good man,' shouted Howard and dashed forward to help the teacher. The giant rat was immensely strong and struggled fiercely in their arms, but the two men held on grimly. The other rats, which had not fled, but had remained on the other side of the gap, suddenly came through and began to attack the two men.

The other three kicked and pulled at the vermin, trying to beat them off but it soon became apparent that their efforts would be wasted unless they had more help. Their companions in the nearby vans started their engines and roared towards them, screeching to a halt by the side of the mêlée. The back doors of the walk-through vans were flung open and the struggling men began to clamber in, the rats clinging to them and leaping into the two vehicles. The noise was deafening to Harris, even through the protection of the helmet; the pups in their baskets barking furiously, the vermin squealing in their peculiar high-pitched fashion, the shouts and cries of the men. He realised the driver of the van he'd made for wasn't wearing his helmet or gloves. He shouted at the man to cover his head and hands but the driver failed to hear above the clamour. Two men were inside the first van now and were swiftly unpacking the gas tanks, kicking at the rats as they leapt into the interior. Harris and Howard climbed in holding their captive between them, ignoring the pain of bites that did not penetrate, but squeezed their flesh in excruciating pinches. The van began to move forward, the rats chasing it and trying to leap through the open back doors, some making it, others being kicked back on to the road. The doors were slammed shut, jamming in the middle on the body of a rat which fell out again with the help of a sharp kick from one of the men.

The gas in one of the cylinders was released to deal with the vermin left inside the van and still persisting in their attack.

'Not this one!' ordered Howard. 'Find something to put it in. We want it alive!'

A metal box of tools had its contents emptied and the frenzied rat was placed roughly inside. The lid clicked firmly shut. The van's sudden swerving caused them to look anxiously at the driver. He was trying to shake off one of the black beasts from his exposed hand. A jet of gas was aimed at the rat and soon it flopped to the floor at the feet of the driver, whose arm now hung limply at his side. He kept driving, moaning with the pain, but steering with his right hand only. The gas was aimed around the large interior of the vehicle, dealing death within seconds to the vicious rats.

'Not too much gas!' shouted Howard. 'We don't want to kill off the dogs as well!'

As the last rat staggered drunkenly then stiffened and died, the men removed their protective helmets and looked towards the injured driver, knowing he was doomed.

'The other van is close behind,' said Howard, peering through the back door window. 'We're far away enough now,' he called to the driver, 'so let's pull up and we'll deal with your wound.' He looked across at Harris shaking his head in despair.

The van pulled over to the kerbside, the other stopping close behind. The doors were opened and the men wearily climbed out, glad to breathe the fresh morning air after the acrid fumes of the gas. Harris, feeling sick and slightly dizzy, leaned against the side of the van.

'Too much of that gas can kill a man,' Howard told him, 'especially in a confined space like that. It was lucky we were wearing the helmets. The driver has just blacked out, not from his wound I suspect, but because of the gas – and *he* was near an open window.'

117

'Does the poor sod know he'll die?' asked Harris, his mind still fuzzy.

'Everyone knows about the disease now, Mr Harris. He was aware of the risk, he should have protected himself.'

'Well maybe you haven't been too lucky either,' said Harris, pointing at the rip in Howard's suit.

The researcher paled and put his hand to the hole. 'I don't think I've been bitten,' he said, 'but I'm bruised all over from their teeth. Oh Christ.' He fumbled at the zip in the grey suit and managed to pull it down haltingly. To his relief, he found the clothes he wore underneath undamaged. With a deep sigh, he too leaned against the side of the van.

After a while, he said, 'Let's take this poor blighter to the hospital, not that it'll do him much good, and then get on with the rounds. Only this time I'm going to get us more protection from Foskins. I mean, this is only the first location. I hope you've chosen some safe places for us, Harris, in the next nine.'

Harris smiled thinly at him. 'Are there any safe places around here any more?'

They suffered attacks from the vermin on three other occasions that day. Harris returned to the flat in the evening completely exhausted, both mentally and physically, his nerves almost numbed by the terrors the operation had held. He sank into an armchair and told Judy of the day's events. 'The canal was about the worst. It shook us up pretty badly, especially the driver being hurt, so after that we were a bit more cautious. From there we went to the dock area – I've never seen the streets so deserted – left the bait and got out fast.' He carefully avoided mentioning the pups, not wanting to upset her, knowing her love of animals.

'But at one spot, we stopped the vans at the entrance of an alley leading to the river, got out and carried the bait to the end of it. We dumped it and turned round to make our way back and found our exit cut off by the bastards. They were streaming from a basement grid. We didn't stop to think – Howard was off like a shot, right through them, and we all followed en masse, kicking and stomping, thanking God for protective suits. We bundled into the vans and got away fast.

'It's funny, but sitting there in the Town Hall, making plans, hearing all the reports, even my own first-hand experiences of the rats – we didn't realise just how bad the situation was. It took today's events to really being it home. In the morning, the streets were practically deserted, and later on, people were only travelling around in groups or in cars and vans.

'Anyway, after that we met up with our escort promised by Foskins. He'd brought the army into it. Two truckloads of troops armed with water-cannon, flame-throwers, gas – the whole bloody works. It certainly made us feel a bit better.'

'You should have started out with them,' interrupted Judy, cross not with Harris but at Foskins, who was in control.

'Yes, I know,' said Harris, 'but we've done it all along. We've underestimated them. Despite all the reports, we've just thought of them as highly dangerous pests, not as the overwhelming force that they seem to be becoming. Even after the train massacre and the attack on the school we didn't expect to meet up with so many of them in one day. True, I'd chosen the most likely places – I had to if our part was to be effective – but even I wasn't prepared for the number of times we came face to face with them. I tell you, Jude, if this doesn't work, that whole area will have to be razed to the ground.'

Judy shuddered. 'What if it's too late? You told me how fast they breed. What if they spread all over London?'

Harris was silent for a while, then he said: 'Goodbye London.'

'Oh, darling, let's go now. You've done all you can, you've helped them as much as possible. You said yourself you're not really necessary, you're just there for Foskins' ego. Well let them get on with it. Let's go before it gets worse.'

'Come on, Jude, you know we can't. Where would we go?'

'Aunt Hazel's for a while. You could be transferred to a local school and I wouldn't mind working in a shop for a while. With all the schools overflowing with evacuated kids they're crying out for more teachers to come out of London.'

'No, love. I couldn't leave now. You see, as we drove on today, dressed in those ridiculous space-suits, escorted by soldiers armed to the teeth, and I took them all to places I knew, places familiar to me, places that had been part of my life, I knew I had to see it through. If you like – and I know it may sound silly – it was *my* patch. The men with me were strangers to it. As far as Foskins and his ministry are concerned it could be a foreign land. Oh, I'm not saying I love the area or it's in my blood. Nothing daft like that. But I do feel some responsibility towards it – like

119

it's my old school and it's being demolished by age. See?'

'Yes, I see.' Judy smiled at him, holding his hand to her cheek.

'You dope.'

He shrugged, smiling to himself.

'Any more incidents today?' she asked.

'Yes. In a children's schoolground we saw a score of them attacking a dog, so we drove in and went straight through them, dropping the bait without stopping.' Into his mind crowded the terrible sight of his companions dropping the pups from the vans into the midst of the rats, something he'd been unable to take part in. 'Later we went into a bombed-out church and discovered the flesh-cleaned bones of two people. Who they were and how long they'd been there we couldn't tell; the skeletons were too clean to have been there too long and there wasn't a trace of clothing. The strange thing was that they were locked in a tight embrace – like lovers. We began to unload the bait when we heard a scream. One of our men had a rat clinging to his neck and was running around like a madman. Fortunately, his suit saved him from serious injury, but his fear was contagious. We all made for the exit. Two men went to the attacked man's aid but soon found they had their own problems. The three of them ran from the opening, rats clinging to their bodies and as soon as they were clear, the water-cannon were directed at the gap to stop anything else coming through. The soldiers helped the three men get free of the rats by using their bayonets. The army wanted to till the place with gas, but Howard wouldn't let them. It was the one time we wanted the rats to live, so they could spread the virus.

'After that episode, we didn't have too much trouble although we still made contact with them. We'd learned to be cautious and kept as close to the vans as possible, leaping inside at the first hint of risk. None of us were very brave, I'm afraid. We were too aware of the consequences.'

'I don't want a dead hero, Harris,' said Judy.

'Believe me, you won't get one.'

'So what happens now?'

'We wait. We wait to see if the virus takes effect and if it does, then it shouldn't take long for it to spread. They reckon within a couple of weeks we'll know one way or another.'

120

'And if it doesn't work, what then?'

'Well it wouldn't be just the East End's problem anymore. They couldn't possibly contain the rats in that area. They'd spread throughout London. And if that happens, I don't want to be around.'

Chapter Thirteen

The rats came out on to the streets to die. It was as though having spent their lives scuttling around in the semi-darkness they wished to breathe the fresh air of the upper world before they perished. They littered the streets, their corpses bloated in the sun, at first causing great alarm to the people who lived in the area. The alarm gave way to relief as the people realised the vermin were dying, the crisis was passing. The diseased corpses were gathered up in bulk and loaded into lorries and taken to incinerators where they were reduced to harmless dust. It had taken only two days for the first signs of the virus' effect but it escalated rapidly in the week that followed. There were still attacks on people but they were far less numerous than before. And then a remarkable side-effect of the virus was discovered.

A soldier was bitten by a rat he'd assumed to be dead because of its prone position. He shot it and reported to the hospital where he expected to die. It was extremely critical for three days but he managed to pull through, his survival being attributed to a reaction on the disease carried by the rat from the virus infecting it. The deadly germ had been weakened considerably.

Others bitten by the rats were not quite so fortunate. Some died in the usual twenty-four hours, others lingered on the edge for anything up to a week. Not enough people were bitten to allow any assumptions to be made, but the fact that one person had survived and others had lasted for almost a week was definitely encouraging. Tests were tried on animals but instead of dying from the disease caused by the rats, they died from the man-made virus introduced into the rodents.

After three weeks, the danger from the vermin was thought to be virtually over although only approximately two thousand bodies were found. It was assumed that the rest of the rats' population was dying or dead below ground.

Life began slowly to return to normal. Plans were made to begin a massive clean-up operation on East London's older districts. Houses were to be pulled down, wastelands to either be utilised for building or flattened into concrete playgrounds or car-parks. The dockside areas would be renovated into modern open-plan blocks. Disused basements would be forever sealed, sewers and drains thoroughly cleansed or rebuilt. It would cost millions but a sharp lesson had been learnt. Stepney and Poplar would eventually become fashionable areas and their history of slums forgotten.

Foskins was completely exonerated of any blame for initial mistakes and reinstated publicly to his former postion. He was congratulated personally by the Prime Minister and passed on the compliments to the team that had helped him accomplish his critical task. At a press conference he praised the specialists whose painstaking endeavours coupled with their dynamic ingenuity had finally begun to defeat this fearsome mutant creature and the deadly disease it carried, whilst subtly implying all credit really belonged to him, as originator and organiser of the project.

They still held daily meetings in the town hall to discuss the progress of the operation but the urgency was no longer felt amongst the members. A serum was derived from the virus to be used as an antidote for the rat-bites which made the disease non-mortal although now such cases were becoming much less frequent anyway.

The danger had passed. So everyone thought.

Chapter Fourteen

Judy was in the bath, enjoying its cocoon warmth, when she heard the phone ring. Harris's muffled voice came through the half-open bathroom door as it was answered. She idly wondered who the caller was. After a few moments of one-sided conversation she heard the click of the receiver being replaced and footsteps crossing the lounge towards the bath-room. Harris came in with a wry smile on his face.

'That was Foskins,' he said, sitting on the edge of the toilet.

'Ringing on a Sunday morning? He must miss you.'

'Hardly. He's given me the sack.'

'What? Why?'

'My services are no longer needed. "Thank you for your extremely valuable assistance, old boy, but the worst is now over and I think it would be unfair to you to take up any more of your valuable time." '

'The old bastard.'

'No, not really, I couldn't have done any more. To tell you the truth it's a bit of a relief; I've felt a bit useless the last couple of weeks.'

'Yes, but to get rid of you now, just when it's nearly all over.'

'Well, he's proved his point hasn't he? He doesn't need me to show off to now – he's got the whole of the public. Anyway, the kids will be coming back in a few weeks and then it'll be back to the old routine.'

'Hm, I suppose so.' Judy settled further down into the water. 'But I still think he's an old bastard.'

Harris laughed, flickering water gently into her face. 'He's invited us to "a small social gathering" next Tuesday evening.'

'What?' Judy sat up again. 'I don't believe it!'

'He knows he's a swine and he can't really cope with it. That's probably his weakness – he's only half-bastard.' He dipped his

124

hand into the soapy water and trailed his finger along Judy's thigh. 'He's doing the dirty on me but he still wants me to love him.'

'I see. And do you?'

'It's not really important, is it? I feel sorry for him, in a way, but I don't care one way or the other about our little commit-tee – I'm glad to be out of it. Now the worst is over, I've got better things to do.' He stroked the inside of her thigh, her legs parting slightly to allow him access.

'And are we going to his little social gathering?'

'Why not? It'll fill an evening.'

Judy murmured in soft appreciation as his hand reached the top of her legs.

'What will you do till the school re-opens?' she asked.

He pulled gently at her small mound of hair, almost pre-occupied with his own thoughts. 'I might just have a look round the area; see how things are being cleaned up. Might even do a bit of painting.'

'I could get a few days off.'

'Aunt Hazel's?'

'Yes, please.' She began to squirm in the water and Harris wondered if the 'Yes, please' was an affirmation to his question or an encouragement to his exploring fingers.

'Harris,' she said.

'Yes?'

'Isn't it time for your bath?'

He began to unbutton his shirt.

Foskins greeted them warmly when they arrived at his home the following Tuesday.

'Hello, old boy. Ah, this must be Judy. Do come in.'

Half-plastered already, thought Harris, catching Judy's eye and winking.

'Most of my guests have arrived,' said Foskins in an over-loud voice. 'Bathroom's upstairs to the left, bedroom to the right.'

Judy disappeared up the stairs to attend her make-up and Harris followed Foskins into a room full of chatting people. He saw Howard amongst one of the groups, his face flushed with the glory of the previous week's events. 'Hello, Harris!' he called, waving a glass-filled hand and spilling some of its contents on a young woman next to him. 'Come and meet everybody.'

Harris walked over, Foskins leading him by the arm, taking a Scotch from the waiter with a tray full of assorted drinks on the way. Howard introduced him to his group with an air of camaraderie he'd never shown in their working relationship.

'Oh, you're the teacher who saved all those little children at the school, aren't you?' the girl standing next to Howard said excitedly.

'With the help of half London's police force and fire brigade,' smiled Harris.

'Now, my boy, mustn't be modest,' said Foskins, placing his hand on the teacher's shoulder and shaking it heartily.

'Fiona adores heroes,' Howard laughed, putting a possessive arm around her waist.

'Come along, you must meet everybody,' Foskins tugged him away from the group. They were joined by Judy as they made their circuit of the room, smiling, shaking hands and being congratulated. After his third Scotch, Harris' mood began to mellow towards the Under-Secretary as he watched him laughing and bantering with his fellow ministers, accepting their praise with mock modesty at one moment and skilful braggartism the next. He noticed Howard standing to one side, glaring at Foskins, taking no notice of the chattering Fiona at his side.

His thoughts were interrupted by Judy whispering in his ear. 'So this is the jet-set?'

'It could have been worse,' he smiled down at her. 'At least the booze is flowing smoothly.'

'Old Foskins is certainly bathing in the glory.'

'Of course. What do you think the party's for? You can't blame him though.'

'Harris, for a belligerent man you're very easy-going.'

He laughed, putting an arm around her shoulder and pulling her to him. 'All right, he made a mistake once, but he soon made up for it.'

'Yes, with the help of you and all the others!' Judy said indignantly.

'She's quite right you know, Harris!' Howard had crossed the room to join them, Fiona at his heels. 'He's busy taking all the credit – very modestly, I grant you – when after all, it was *my* idea.'

'Yes,' agreed Fiona, breathlessly.

'And by the way,' he added maliciously. 'I'm sorry to see you're no longer part of the team.'

Harris grinned at the researcher, refusing to be drawn out.

'What does it matter? It's all over now, anyway,' he said, looking around for the waiter and his tray.

'Yes, and we're all going back eventually to our obscure little jobs while he . . .'

'Look, if you don't like it, don't tell me about it, tell him.' Harris deftly grabbed a Scotch from the passing tray.

'Right,' said Howard. 'I bloody will!' and marched towards Foskins.

'Harris, you're evil,' Judy admonished the smiling teacher.

'Oh dear, he's going to create a scene,' wailed Fiona.

Just as Howard reached the jovial Foskins, the telephone rang in the hall and the Under-Secretary excused himself from his group, leaving the researcher standing open-mouthed and flat-footed.

Harris suppressed his mirth as he watched the researcher gather his wits and stride after him.

Two minutes later, Howard came back into the room ashen-faced. He rejoined them, slowly shaking his head, a look of disbelief on his face.

'Darling, what's the matter, what's happened?' asked Fiona, worriedly.

He looked at each of them in turn, not really seeing their faces. 'That phone call,' he started to say. 'It was from our operations room.'

They waited in impatient silence.

'There's been another attack. Another massacre – in North London.'

Chapter Fifteen

Stephen Abbott sat in the darkened cinema and stole a quick glance at his girlfriend's face, illuminated by the cinemascope screen. He was bored with the film, partly because the big, craggy cowboy on the screen was now too old to act like superman, and partly because he wasn't wearing his glasses. Vikki didn't know he wore glasses sometimes and he thought it might spoil their relationship if she did. She'd probably go off him too if she ever found out about his two false front teeth; he had to be so careful in their 'snogging' sessions that her probing tongue didn't dislodge the plate. She was very fussy. And she deserved to be, with her looks! Best looking bird in the club.

He had another problem too – he wanted to go to the toilet. He wasn't desperate yet, but the thought of not being able to go was steadily making it worse. And he couldn't go because he didn't have his glasses and without them he'd never find his way back to the seat. It had happened to him once before; he'd wandered up and down the aisle in the dark until his embarrassed girlfriend had waved to him. And that was the last time he'd dated her.

He shifted uncomfortably in his seat. His arm reached around her shoulders and she snuggled against him, one of her hands resting on his thigh. The area under her hand became the centre of his feelings until the weight caused stirrings elsewhere. He kissed her cheek softly and then her lips hard as she turned her head towards him, her fingers increasing the pressure on his leg. Well, he'd bided his time for two weeks now so as not to spoil things; maybe now was the time to make his move. His heart thumping, his head filled with concentrated love and the desire to urinate overpowered by a stronger desire, he put his free hand on her wrist and stroked the silky material of her blouse. He drew his trembling and cautious fingers to the centre buttons and poked a finger through an opening, giddy at the feel of the warm flesh of her tummy. After a few moments of making circling motions with his exploratory finger and waiting for the rebuttal, he withdrew it and moved his hand upwards towards her breasts. He found the gentle swelling and cupped it tremblingly. Her restraining hand rested on his and weakly, without conviction, tried to pull it away. Instead he moved it along and slid it inside the opening of her blouse, getting it stuck between the buttons.

He wriggled it loose and undid one of them, hearing her gasp as his hand reached inside again for her.

My first one, he thought. My first proper good-looking bird! After all those fat ones, skinny ones, ones with big noses, ones with big teeth – at last a good-looking one! Ooh, I'm in love. Wait till I tell the boys she lets me have a feel!

His hand crept inside her lacy bra and felt her hard little nipple, squeezing it between his fingers, pressing it as though it were a button.

Suddenly she screamed and leapt to her feet, pulling his arm up with her.

'I didn't mean anything,' he began to bluster, his face reddening as people turned to look at them.

'Something bit me!' Vikki cried. 'There's something there on the floor! It bit my leg!'

He looked downward but failed to see anything in the dark. He bent down, more to escape the accusing eyes of the cinema crowd than to discover the offending 'something'.

'There's nothing there,' he said miserably.

'There is, there is!' She began to cry, backing away on to the lap of the person sitting next to her. Someone in the next row flicked on a lighter and leaned over the back of his seat with it, holding a small flame towards the floor.

A large dark shape scuttled underneath the seat.

As Vikki screamed, a woman behind in the next row leapt to her feet and screamed also. Then pandemonium broke loose throughout the theatre. People jumped up and kicked out at or leapt away from something at their feet.

'Rats!' a terror-stricken voice echoed around the cinema, the cry being taken up by others equally frightened.

Vikki began to pound her feet hysterically up and down on the floor, as though contact with it would make her more vulnerable to the vermin. Stephen grabbed her shoulders and tried to calm her just as the house-lights came on. Then the terror really took grip as the people saw the horror between the seats. Rats were flowing down the aisles, branching off through the rows of seats, pouring over the tops; leaping on to the panicking crowd. Women and men screamed as they fought each other to get free of seats, blocked in on either side by stumbling bodies. The exit doors became jammed, people falling over one another in their bids to escape the death behind them. The big cowboy in the film began his final shoot-out with the villains.

Stephen pulled a rat from Vikki's hair and hurled it away from him, his hands torn by the creature's gnashing teeth. He grabbed her arm and pulled her along the row, pushing at the people ahead of him. Inexplicably, the house-light dimmed and finally faded leaving the confused scene lit only by the light reflected from the huge screen. Something was biting into the boy's leg and he tried to kick it against the back of a seat, but because of lack of space the rat was able to hang on. He bent down to pull it away and his hands were nipped at by another rat. In desperation, he sat on top of a seat back and painfully raised his leg on to the back of the seat in front, lifting the great black rat with it. Vikki ran from him and stumbled over a man in his last death struggles with three rats. She fell heavily, and was immediately engulfed in bristling bodies, her screams unheard amongst the screams of others.

Stephen grabbed the rat's throat with his hands and squeezed with all his strength but still it clung to him. He felt another as it landed on his back and bit into his coat which he quickly shed without thinking, dropping it and the rat into the row behind him. A man in front saw his plight and bravely grabbed at the rat clinging to his leg and pulled. Abruptly, the creature released its grip and turned on the man, biting into his face.

He went down screaming in agony.

The boy looked over the seats and saw there was nothing he could do to save his rescuer. He looked around but seeing no clear line of exit, he jumped up on to the back of a seat and carefully began to walk along the rows, using peoples' shoulders where he could, but mostly depending on luck to keep his balance. He slipped a few times but managed to spring upright again, the fear inside him giving him the extra strength he needed to keep going. The holocaust around him became unreal. It was a nightmare, the strange light from the screen heightening the unearthly effect.

A man in front lifted a rat above his head and threw it away from him, hitting the boy with its long body and causing him to slip between the rows again. He landed heavily on his back and lay there stunned for a few moments. Someone stumbled and fell across him, struggling with something in his arms. The rat was pushed into Stephen's chest causing him to shout out in anguish. He beat at both rodent and man with his fists, cursing and crying at the same time. The weight was lifted from him as the man regained his feet and staggered on, the rat still clinging to his arms, another around his shoulders, chewing at his neck.

The boy got to his feet and climbed on to the seats again, continuing his hazardous journey across the sea of helpless people. Many were in the aisles now, their panic pressing them together in the confined space, preventing the use of speed as a means of escape. The doors were blocked with scrambling bodies and those that managed to get through were being chased into the foyer by the vermin.

An elderly couple near him clung together in a last desperate embrace, the vermin biting at their legs and buttocks, finally bringing them down to their knees.

Another man sat rigid in his seat, eyes still on the screen as though watching the film, hands clenching the seat-arms. A rat sat on his lap gnawing a hole into his stomach.

A group of teenage boys had formed a circle, back to back, and were slowly making their way up the aisle, kicking out at the vermin with their heavy boots. Unfortunately they could get no further than the thronging mass of people around the exit.

The people in the balcony above were no better off; they only had two exits of retreat and rats were pouring through these. They were forced back by the bodies of others and many were toppling over the rail into the theatre below.

Stephen went on, sobbing with fright, and at last reached the front stalls. It was comparatively empty of people and vermin, the sides and the exits of the cinema now being the main points of disorder. He leapt on to the floor and headed towards the stage. He managed to get one leg on to it, quickly finding his feet again. A stream of black, furry bodies emerged from the curtains at one side making straight towards him. He turned to run in the opposite direction but slipped in his own blood from the torn leg. The vermin were on him in an instant, smothering his body with their own foul-smelling forms, biting into him, pushing each other aside to get at his flesh. His arms beat at them growing weaker and weaker at every effort until he finally lay them across his face for protection, allowing the creatures to gorge themselves on his body.

Raising one arm from his eyes, he stared up uncomprehendingly at the huge coloured screen above him. His eyes read the words, and his voice spoke them faintly, but his brain did not understand. He whispered 'The End.'

George Fox had worked at the zoo for twenty-odd years now. Unlike many of his comrades he had a deep regard for the animals in his care; he worried when one of his lions was unwell, pampered his pet gazelle when it was off its food and once even spent a sleepless night at the side of a dying snake. When hooligans had broken into his bird-house and for no other reason than sheer bloodlust had slaughtered thirty of his exotically coloured winged friends, he'd broken down and cried for three days. He had a deep sympathy and understanding of his animals, big or small, ferocious or docile. Even when a monkey had bitten off half his ear a few years back he hadn't reprimanded it, but gently put it down, ignoring the pain, and quietly left the cage clasping a blood-soaked handkerchief to his injured part.

And tonight, he felt the zoo was restless. There was a stillness in the air, a quietness unnatural to London's large animal estate – but the animals weren't sleeping. As he made his rounds he noticed the beasts prowling to and fro in their cages, the monkeys huddled together staring out nervously into the night, the birds silently blinking on their perches. Only the lunatic laugh of the hyena disturbed the uneasy silence.

'Easy now, Sara,' he soothingly reassured his favourite cheetah in the large cat-house. 'Nothing to be nervous of.'

Suddenly, the screeching of birds broke through the night. Sounds like the aviary, he told himself, making for the door and running towards the tunnel that led under the public road to the canal where the fantastic bird sanctuary stood. He was joined by another keeper at the entrance of the underground passage.

'What's up, George?' the man gasped.

'Don't know yet, Bill. Something disturbed the birds, sounds like they're going mad.'

They plunged into the dark tunnel using their torches for added light. As they emerged on the other side they heard a squeal from the giraffe section. To their horror they saw one of the graceful creatures racing round its enclosure with large black creatures clinging to its trembling body. It plunged into the water acting as a moat around its paddock and thrashed about crazedly.

'Oh my Gawd – what is it?' asked Bill, unsure of what he'd seen in the night light.

'I'll tell you what it is,' cried George. 'It's those bloody rats. The ones that are supposed to have been exterminated – the giant rats!' He took several steps towards the helpless animal but then turned back to Bill. 'Back to the office, quick. Get on the phone to the police – tell them it's an attack on the zoo by the rats! Tell them we need every available help we can get! Hurry!'

He ran towards the giraffe again, knowing there was nothing he could do for the poor creature, but going on anyway. He turned as he heard a human scream coming from the tunnel and saw Bill emerge, swarming with black shapes and what must have been blood gushing from his head. He saw him go down, half rise and slump forward again.

'God Almighty,' he breathed. He had to get to the telephone. There was another ticket office in this section but would mean passing the rat-filled tunnel and crossing the bridge over the canal. And the canal must have been where they came from. Those bastards said they'd cleared out the rats, they were all dead or dying. But the vermin are killing my animals. My poor animals!

He moaned aloud, not knowing what to do. Finally, he decided on a plan of action, trying to ignore the cries from the rat-besieged animals in that section. He ran towards the fence protecting the zoo from the dividing road and scrambled over it in hurried clumsiness. He fell over on to the other side and as he sprawled there he saw the lights of an approaching car. Scrambling to his feet, he ran into the road, waving his arms frantically. At first it seemed as though the car was going to drive on, but the driver must have seen his uniform in the glare of his headlights. It screeched to a halt causing George to jump to one side to avoid being hit.

The excited keeper was shouting instructions even as the driver was winding the window down. At the uncomprehending look on the motorist's face, George began again: 'Call the police, tell them rats, hundreds of them, are attacking the zoo. If they don't get here soon, the bastards will slaughter my animals! Move, man, move!'

As the car sped off a horrifying thought struck George. When the police and the soldiers got there, the only weapon they'd be able to use would be gas. And gas would be just as lethal to his animals as it would be to the vermin. He cried out in despair and ran across the road to the main entrance of the zoo. Climbing the turnstile, he saw the figures of two other keepers on night duty approaching him at a run.

'Is that you, George?' one of them shouted, shining a torch into his face.

'Yes, it's me,' he answered, shielding his eyes with his arm.

'Get out, George, come on. The whole place is swarming with rats! Those giant ones. They're after the animals.'

'No, we've got to let them out, turn them loose – we can't let them be slaughtered.'

'Not bloody likely, we're getting out, there's nothing we can do. And you're coming with us!' So saying, he grabbed the old keeper's arm and tried to pull him back towards the turnstile. George struck out blindly, knocking the torch from his colleague's grasp and ran off towards the main office.

'Leave him, Joe,' the other man said. 'We'll only get ourselves killed chasing him. Let's get out of here.'

Reluctantly, the first man shook his head and climbed the turnstile into the street.

George ran, his lungs bursting, ignoring the dark shapes that were streaming from the tunnel, and tore up the short flight of steps that led to the office where all the keys to the cages were kept. By now, the zoo had erupted into an explosion of sound. Roars, shrieks, squawks, bellows – all combined to create tumultuous pandemonium. He snatched as many key bunches from their racks as he could carry, knowing exactly which belonged to each section, and ran from the office.

He stopped aghast at the sight of the mighty gorilla, the old man of the zoo, recapturing its ancient primitive majesty, pulling the rats apart with its great hand, crushing their bones with its immense strength, tossing them away like limp rags. But even its might had to succumb to the unlimited number of razor-toothed vermin. They swarmed over the gorilla, enraged by its strength, and brought it crashing to the floor where it still fought bravely on.

George watched the impressive creature's death-struggle in fascinated silence but movements around his legs brought him to his senses. Looking down, he saw the wretched-looking dark bodies flowing past him, inexplicably ignoring him. In a rage, he

134

kicked out at them, but still they sped on, eager to fill themselves on the trapped animals.

The keeper ran with them, unlocking cages and swinging their doors open wide as he went. Many of the unfortunate animals merely crouched at the rear of their abodes whilst others saw their chance for freedom and hurled themselves through the open doors. The birds were the luckiest – they could take to the air. But for the other creatures, their only means of escape was speed. The prouder ones stayed to fight and killed many of the vermin before they themselves fell, but the majority chose to flee. When they reached the outer fences of the zoo, they threw themselves at it, going mad with the frustration of being trapped. Some managed to clear it – the apes or the more fleet-footed – but the others either cringed against it or raced around its perimeter.

The old keeper found himself at the big cat-house. Still he hadn't been attacked by the vermin; his mind never questioned it, he was too distressed over the plight of his beloved animals to worry about his own safety. The roars were deafening as he ran for the iron cages, the cats snarling both in fear and defiance. He reached the lions and unhesitatingly unlocked the metal doors.

'Come on, Sheik, come on Sheba,' he called to them softly, urging them to come out. He raced along, unlocking all the cages, oblivious to the danger. The lion sprang forward with an angry roar as it saw several dark shapes coming through the doors of the cat house. It tore them into shreds, tossing them into the air with its jaws, ripping their bodies with its claws. As more poured in, the other cats joined with the lion in the slaughter of the vermin; the tiger, the leopard, the panther, the puma, the jaguar, and the cougar – all joined in the fight against the common foe. Only the cheetah remained in its cage.

'Come on now, Sara, you must come out,' pleaded George, but the cautious animal merely snarled from the back of the cage, baring its teeth, raising a claw.

'Please, Sara, there's a good girl. There's nothing to be afraid of. You've got to come out.' In desperation, he began to scramble into the cage. 'Come on, girl, it's only old George. I've come to help you.'

He slowly advanced on the cheetah, hand outstretched. talking soothingly all the time. The animal crouched away, snarling more ferociously.

'It's me, Sara, George. Only old George.'

The cat sprang at the old keeper and within seconds reduced him to a bloodied carcass, dragging the dead body around its cage in triumph.

Then it sprang from the cage and streaked towards the fight between cat and rodent, but instead of attacking the rodents, it leapt upon the back of the panther, sinking its teeth into its shoulder. Still the vermin poured in and the battle between might and multitude continued to its bitter end.

Chapter Sixteen

Harris drove through the clutter of military and police vehicles that jammed Whitehall. He was waved down several times by the police and asked to show his pass. When he did, they briskly waved him on, saluting curtly. He threaded his way through to the granite-grey Ministry of Defence building, now the operation's headquarters. The drive through the deserted streets had been eerie to say the least; the only times he'd experienced anything like it had been in the pre-dawn hours, returning from a late-night celebration, when London's concrete canyons seemed virtually devoid of life and the noises of traffic and people were something unreal, hard even to imagine. But even then, there had usually been the sight of another lonely car or perhaps a man on his bike returning from night work. But today there had been nothing. He hadn't even seen any army scout cars that he knew were patrolling the streets, checking that the city was empty, that no unauthorised person remained. For the past two days, there had been a lot of trouble with looters – scavengers who saw the chance of a lifetime to fill their pockets without hindrance. They had been wrong; security had never been tighter. To be in London now, without authorisation, meant immediate arrest and the whole area was concentrated with police and army personnel with the express task of enforcing the government ban.

'Will it work, darling?' Judy interrupted his thoughts.

He turned towards her, smiling tightly, unable to hide his unease. 'It's got to, hasn't it?' he said. Stopping to allow an army lorry to pull out from a row of other brown vehicles all filled with soldiers wearing heavy protective suits and each carrying gas masks balanced on their knees, he reached out and squeezed her hand. As part of the newly reorganised 'action committee' he'd been able to use some influence to keep Judy with him instead of being shipped off to the country for five days. Not that he'd wanted her to stay; the danger involved today (and possibly the next couple of days) to anyone still in the city could be great. The whole operation was unpredictable to a certain extent. But she'd insisted on staying with him and he had managed to get her dispensation from the ban, having her conscripted into the large administration organisation necessary for 'Operation Extirpate'.

'Operation Extirpate', as it was named was based on a simple plan put forward by Harris, and the idea that had placed him back on the committee. It was the sort of inspiration that could only have come from someone not used to or bogged down by the intricacies of a scientific mind, so bold and uncomplicated was its concept. After the initial shock of the rats' counter-attack, the members of the original team had sunk into a state of confusion and despair; the vermin had swiftly become immune to the virus although the disease they carried had been considerably weakened. But they, themselves, had become stronger, almost as if they had a burning desire for revenge, and they wreaked havoc, not just in East London, but all over the city, leaving a trail of bloody slaughter wherever they emerged from their lairs. There had been many attacks that fateful Tuesday night; a cinema, a hospital, an old people's home – even a public house. The animals in London zoo had suffered a terribly vicious onslaught, many escaping to the surrounding park and those that couldn't be captured had to be shot. There had been mass individual attacks, people alone having no chance against the overwhelming vermin. Reports had come in throughout the night of destruction and bloodshed.

An emergency meeting was held between the committee and government officials. Foskins didn't attend – he had been dismissed from office by the P.M. instantly the news broke and wasn't seen again in the hectic days that followed. New members were added to the original team but the new plan had been devised before the change had had time to take effect.

When Harris had thought of the idea, he'd blurted it out almost immediately without giving himself time to think. If he had, he reflected later, he would probably have held his tongue with the notion that it was too simple, too broad in concept, and that if it had any merit, then one of the shrewder, more scientific members of the team would have produced it.

The idea, stemming from a previous team meeting, was bascially this: as gas was the only proven method of destroying the vermin, they had to be lured into the open for the gas to be

138

effected upon them; this could be achieved by the use of ultra-sonic sound beams set up at strategic points all over the city sending out sound-waves to the widest area possible, luring the rats into the open where the gas could be used. To Harris' amazement, the idea was agreed on in principle with only slight reservations; a few refinements to be thrashed out. London would have to be evacuated. It was drastic, but then the consequences would be fatal if the necessary steps were not taken. Londoners would have to leave their homes and migrate to the surrounding countryside if they were to escape the effect of the vast quantity of gas that had to be used. Evacuation was essential anyway to avoid the attacks from the rats. Safety could not be guaranteed any more. Huge enclosures would be built in the parks, as many as possible in the time, and the transmitters placed inside where the high-frequency sound waves would be sent out. The right pitch could easily be found by testing captive black rats. Once inside the enclosures, the entrances would be blocked and the deadly gas poured in. Because of the danger to anyone on the ground, helicopters would be used to hover over the enclosures to drop the gas into them, and ground troops would stand by outside in heavily-armoured trucks armed with water-cannons, flame throwers and more gas. The building of the compounds and the complete evacuation of London (save for those people vital to the running of the city's essential services) would have to be achieved within six days at the most – otherwise the risk of the fast multiplying rodents completely overrunning the city would be too great. It was no time to ponder over the very existence of the vermin; their size, their strength, where they'd originated from, how their numbers had grown despite the virus, why they were so much more cunning than the smaller of their species (what gave them the instinct to lie low while the infection was taking effect on their companions). All these questions would have to be answered later. For now it was a question of survival.

That day – the plan had to be created, devised and put into action throughout the night – the city was declared to be in a state of emergency. The inhabitants were informed they were to be evacuated in sections, although thousands left without any urging at all on hearing of the night's events; village halls, churches, schools – all public buildings – were to be used as temporary shelters; huge marquees and tents were to be erected in fields; people were asked to stay with relatives if they had any in other parts of the country; an order was made known that looters would be shot on sight; any unauthorised person found in London after the sixth day would be arrested (it was known that all the people living in the city would never be cleared but at least the emergency laws would keep them indoors and hopefully away from harm).

Mercifully, the area south of the river had not been affected as yet, but it was decided to clear the inner boundaries of the sprawling suburbs as an extra precaution.

Many people protested; they didn't want to leave their homes, *they* weren't afraid of the vermin. But they were given no choice – if they wouldn't leave peacefully, then they were forced, there being no time for politeness or argument. The period of exile would be two weeks from the day of the first gas onslaught. Time would be needed to ensure that every last rodent was exterminated; the sewers would be completely and utterly filled with gas; basements, tunnels, ruins – any possible place that could harbour the vermin would be cleared and thoroughly cleansed.

Whether the shame and the disgrace in the eyes of the world would ever be erased was another matter.

The barricades around the parks went up in remarkably swift time, their use being more to confine the gas in a more concentrated area than to contain the rats. The roads out of London were jammed with cars and coaches, and trains ran non-stop services into the neighbouring provinces. Troops poured in to patrol the streets and to train for the emergency. More protective clothing was mass-produced in a very short time for the police and army. Any public demonstration was quickly broken up and dealt with, peacefully if possible.

At first, it looked as though the city would never be ready for the oncoming battle but micraculously – and mostly due to the co-operation, caused by fear, of the public – on the fifth day the stage was almost set. Last minute conferences were held, revisions to existing plans made, final instructions to helicopter crews and the army given, and then the long vigil through the empty night, waiting for the dawn and the deciding climax it would bring.

Harris and Judy had laid awake most of the night, making love, talking – trying to push thoughts of the on-coming day's events from their minds. They'd finally fallen into fitful sleep as the grey dawn forced the night darkness aside, the sun slowly rising upon a strangely still city.

140

When they awoke, their tiredness evaporated instantly as thoughts of the day flooded their minds. Judy cooked a breakfast which was left almost untouched and they made ready to go out into the deserted streets. As they opened their front door they saw a black rat scurry across the road into the small square park opposite. They hurried to their car and drove off, Harris glancing into his rear-view mirror, almost expecting to see the road behind him filled with vermin.

They finally reached the Ministry of Defence building, parked beside a shining Rolls Royce, and made their way into the gloomy entrance showing their passes. On their way down the endless corridors to their respective operations rooms they encountered a beaming Howard.

'Good morning! All set for the big day?' he clapped his hands together enthusiastically.

'Ready enough,' smiled the teacher.

'I've been here all night. Spent a few hours on a camp bed. Everything's set for the big operation.'

'Good.'

'I'd better get to my room,' said Judy. 'Locating sewer entrances from those old maps and positioning them on new streets maps isn't my idea of fun, but if it all helps the cause . . .'

They all turned at once as a familiar figure came striding towards them from the other end of the corridor, waving his arm at them. As the figure drew nearer they realised with shock that it was Foskins. Tieless, badly in need of a shave, but with an excited look in his eyes.

'Good Lord, what are you doing here?' asked Howard, looking incredulously at the ex-Under-Secretary.

'I've been around since last Tuesday,' he said, the excitement giving way to a look of bitterness. He pulled at his open shirt collar and buttoned his jacket. 'Before our last, er, unsuccessful operation, I ordered a search through records of anyone entering the country within the past two to three years who'd come from a tropical zone.'

'You mean the sort of country that would breed this type of rat – or at least something like it?' said Howard.

'Exactly. But unfortunately, because we thought the virus operation would be so successful, it was rather pushed aside. I – I must admit, I forgot all about it in the excitement that followed.'

There was a slightly embarassed silence which Harris broke:
'So?
'So, after my dismissal, I gathered the information I'd asked for and began sifting through it myself.'
'Why?' asked Howard coldly.
'Because, well . . .'
'Never mind,' Harris cut in, glancing at Howard disdainfully. 'What did you find?'
'There were many entries from the tropics, of course, but only a few that fit the bill for our purposes. I made enquiries – I still have friends in Civil Service departments – and came up with one man.'
His hand shook as he held up a piece of paper.
'This man. Professor William Bartlett Schiller – zoologist. He'd spent several years in New Guinea and the surrounding islands apparently investigating report of mutant animals seen by the locals. Its seems quite feasible, for an island in that area had been used for a nuclear test and some of the inhabitants had been affected by radiation. Of course, it was all hushed up, but somehow Schiller got wind of it and decided to do some investigating.'
'All right,' said Howard impatiently. 'But what makes you think this professor had anything to do with the rats?'
'Well obviously the fact that he'd been in New Guinea *and* he'd been involved in the study of abnormalities in animals.' In his irritation, Foskins almost became the man he'd once been – been in public anyway.
'Added to that', he continued, 'he took up residence in London. Near the docks. In a house by a canal.'
'The Canal!' Harris exclaimed. 'Of course I've been trying to remember. In the beginning, that's where the rats were seen, Keogh saw them. I saw them! Near the old lock-keeper's house. I used to play there when I was a kid but they closed the canal down and the lock-keeper moved on. I bet it was his house the professor took over.'
'This is the address', said Foskins, thrusting the piece of paper at him.
'That's it.'
'Oh, come now,' broke in Howard. 'What does it matter how? So this lunatic professor smuggled in one of his mutant species and took it to his home to study . . .'
'And allowed it to breed . . .'

142

'Yes, allowed it to breed. But that knowledge doesn't help matters now; the operation goes on as planned. Maybe later we can investigate . . .'

'But why not now?'

'Because, Mr Foskins, there are too many more important thing to contend with today. Or haven't you heard of "Operation Extirpate"?'

'Yes, of course I have, but if you're going to root them out . . .'

'I've got no more time for this sort of discussion, Mr Foskins, so if you'll excuse me . . .'

'You bloody fool! You soon sank into the background when your last idea didn't work.'

'Huh! you were busy taking all the credit for it – I didn't see why you shouldn't take all the blame.'

Foskins paled and then his whole body seemed to lose its tautness.

'Y-yes, you're right. I accept the blame – but I implore you, learn by my mistakes.'

'It isn't important just now, don't you understand? Good God, man, we can make all the investigations we like after, don't you see, but today, we're going to wipe them out.' He turned towards Harris, who had failingly tried to keep from sympathising with the ex-Under-Secretary. 'Are you coming, Harris? We've plenty to do.'

'Right.' He touched Foskins' arm. 'It'll be looked into, don't worry.' And I'll make sure he at least gets some credit for it, he thought.

They strode off towards the big operations room, leaving Judy standing alone with the distressed man.

All thoughts of Foskins were pushed from their minds as they entered the bustling operations room. In the centre was a huge map of London, with shaded green areas illustrating the parks and dead red lights indicating the positions of the transmitters. When they came into operation, the red lights would come on. The position of the helicopters was shown by yellow arrows and the troop vehicles by blue. The room was crowded with people, most of them having a function, but many were there as onlookers. Harris noticed the Prime Minister discussing last-minute details with the Chief of Staff. One side of the room was devoted to radio and television equipment; the transmitters would be operated from here, instructions sent out to the troops and helicopters, everything monitored by cameras aboard the helicopters and those set up in the strret. The whole event was to be televised nationwide, and relayed by satellite to other countries. The P.M. felt his presence was vital, not to the operation itself, but to his political career. To be seen at the head of such a vast life-saving exercise such as this – and seen all over the world – was a bonus few other leaders had shared. He disappeared into the adjoining room to be interviewed by the television networks.

Harris had barely begun to study the vast glass map when he saw Judy at the door talking excitedly to an army sergeant whose job it was to prevent intruders, pointing towards him. He went over.

'What's the matter, Jude?'

'Foskins. He's gone off to that house by himself.'

'To do what?'

'I don't know. He just said he had to do something – something that would make amends – maybe he could find the nest.'

'Oh, Christ. He'll get himself killed!' He went out into the hall, taking Judy by the arm.

'What are you going to do?' she asked anxiously, suspecting what he had in mind.

'I'll have to go after him.'

'No. No, please don't, Harris'.

'Don't worry, Jude. I'll beat him to the house – he'll have to find his way there, I can go straight to it. At least I can stop him going in.'

'But the sound-beams – they're due to start any minute now.'

'That's all right. It'll make it safer. The rats will just head straight for the parks.'

'You don't know, they might attack you.'

'I'll be safe in the car. I've got a gas-mask and a protective suit, remember – standard equipment.'

'Please don't.'

He held her to him. 'I love you, Jude.' He kissed her forehead. 'But I'm going.'

Chapter Seventeen

Harris drove recklessly, knowing there was no chance of meeting other traffic. He was stopped once by an army scout car and had to waste valuable minutes showing his pass and explaining his mission. The officer in charge regretted not being able to accompany him but he had his own duties to carry out. He wished him luck and waved him on.

As he drove through the city, the office blocks towering over him on either side, the feeling of being utterly alone became almost overpowering. He wanted to turn back, to be amongst people again, to feel the security of numbers, but he forced himself to go on, knowing he had to prevent Foskins from entering the house.

As he reached Aldgate he saw the first of the rodents. They were running along the side of the road, a heavy black stream of bristling bodies. They were joined by others from buildings, flowing into the main stream, jostling and climbing over each others backs.

He turned his head sharply at the sound of crashing glass and saw the front window of a J. Lyons restaurant cave in as rats poured through it. They were all headed in the same direction and Harris guessed it was towards the park near the Tower of London where one of the transmitters was located. On he went, aware of the gradual build-up in the numbers of the creatures, but all mercifully ignoring the speeding car. As he turned into Commercial Road he brought the car to a screeching halt. It seemed as though there was a huge moving carpet stretching before him – the broad road was wholly filled with black vermin, creating an undulating cover over the road.

His heart froze at the sight. They were coming mostly from a side street and disappearing into another on the opposite side of the main road. The whole dark mass seemed to be about fifty

145

yards wide, without a single break in its length. Should he turn back, find another route? Or would other roads be similarly filled? And how much time would it cost him to find another way around? Should he drive straight through them? What if the car stalled and he was trapped in the middle of the flow? If they attacked, his protective suit would hardly withstand their onslaught. His instinct told him to turn around, to get back to the protection of the military, but as he looked through his rear window he saw other streams of rats, pouring from streets and buildings, like molten lava pouring from a volcano, forming tributaries around obstacles and joining again to form major streams. He realised the way back would be just as hazardous.

Something landed on his bonnet with a thump causing him to swing round to the front again. One of the giant rats was staring at him through the windscreen, its evil face almost level with his own, the distance between them only two feet, a thin sheet of glass his only protection.

It gunned him into action. He thrust the gear-lever into first and revved the engine, slipping the clutch to build up power. He moved forward, slowly at first, then eased his foot up gently to gather speed. The rat slithered across the bonnet trying to retain its grip with its long claws but the smooth surface of the car soon defeated it and it slid back on to the road.

Harris kept his foot firmly down on the accelerator, telling himself it would be just like driving through a flood-washed road and the trick was to keep going, slowly but steadily. The car reached the edge of the stream and plunged into the surging bodies. It began to bump as it went over them, the crunch of bones and squashed bodies nauseating the teacher who could only force his eyes on the road ahead and will his foot to stay on the pedal. The rats seemed oblivious to the car, making no attempt to escape its crushing wheels. Several leapt across the bonnet and roof – one jumped at the side window, cracking but not breaking it. Twice the car slid on the wet blood its wheel were soaked in and Harris had to fight to keep it in a straight line, praying he wouldn't stall the engine.

He felt a thump on the roof above his head, then a pointed head appeared at the top of the windscreen, its nose twitching from side to side, the tips of its claws spread flat against the glass.

Harris pushed himself back against his seat in sheer frightened reaction, almost allowing his foot to slip from the accelerator

146

pedal but automatically dipping his clutch to avoid stalling. The creature flopped on to the bonnet, mainly because of the car's jolt, and turned to face the man inside.

It seemed even bigger than the usual giant rat and Harris wondered why it wasn't affected by the sound waves as much as the others. He quickly recovered his wits and drove on, trying to ignore the monster glaring evilly at him through the glass. The sharp squeals of the rats trapped between his tyres strengthened his hate for them and this spurred him on.

Sunddenly the rat on the bonnet lunged at the windscreen, baring its teeth and using them to try and shatter the glass. The glass held, but the teacher know it wouldn't stand up to too much pressure. With relief, he realised he was almost through the black writhing mass and he began to gather speed. The rat lunged again causing a large jagged scratch to appear across the windscreen. At last the car broke through the vermin river and Harris immediately pushed it into second then third gear. He knew he had to shake the monster off quickly before the glass shattered and he began to turn the wheel jerkily from side to side hoping to dislodge his unwelcome passenger.

But he was too late.

The rat took a final desperate lunge at the windscreen almost as though it knew it was its last chance and the whole of Harris's vision became cloudy white as the glass shattered into a myriad of tiny cracks.

Harris found himself staring directly into the face of the rat. Its head had broken through and it struggled to enlarge the hole to accommodate the rest of its powerful body. It bared its bloodied incisors at the teacher, its eyes glaring and bulbous because of the restraining glass that pulled its skin back at the neck. Harris knew it would be matter of seconds before the glass gave and the creature plunged through on to his exposed face. He jammed on the brakes, knowing and fearing what he had to do next. As the car came to a skidding halt he pulled on the heavy gloves of his protective suit and opened the door on his side. He jumped out and ran around to the front of the car, grabbing at the loathsome body and pulling with all his strength. The sudden cold air on his face made him realise how exposed his head and face were and the panic gave him even more speed and strength. He pulled the rat free, the glass cutting into its neck as it thrashed from side to side.

147

He held it above his head and threw it towards the other side of the car, its weight taking him by surprise and weakening his throw. The rat's body brushed the edge of the bonnet and rolled on to the ground with stunning force but it was on its feet immediately and tearing back underneath the car towards the teacher. Harris move fast but hadn't expected the rat to come from beneath the car.

As he jumped in and began to pull the door shut he felt an excruciating pain in his leg and he looked down and saw the rat clinging to a spot just above his ankle, the tough material of the suit saving him from serious injury. He tried to shake it off but it clung relentlessly increasing the pressure, trying to climb into the car.

Harris beat at it with his fist but to no avail. Bringing his foot back inside but resting it on the very edge, he grabbed at the door-handle with both hands and slammed the door shut with all his strength. The rat gave out a piercing shriek and loosened the grip on his leg. Its neck was trapped between the door and frame but it still thrashed around wildly, its eyes glazed from its mouth frothing. He pulled the door tighter, slipped a hand through the narrow crack for a firmer grip, and squeezed the life from the rat.

When its struggles ceased, he opened the door just enough for the body to flop on to the ground and quickly closed it tight. He sat there shaking for a few moments, feeling no relief because he knew he had to go on. It was only the sound of the roaring engine that brought him fully to his senses. His foot was resting on the accelerator pedal and because he purposely had not turned the ignition off, the engine was racing madly. He eased his foot off, made the hole in the windscreen larger, and engaged first gear, driving slowly at first then picking up speed as he remembered his mission.

He saw many more of the giant rodents, unhesitatingly driving through them without even reducing speed when they blocked the road. At least the idea of the ultrasonic sound waves seemed to be working, he thought. It had flushed the vermin from their nests. Maybe there was some truth in the story of the Pied Piper of Hamelin after all. Maybe his pipes were tuned in to the rats' frequency as well.

He looked up through the side window at the sound of a helicopter. It's up to those boys now, he told himself. And their gas.

He turned off from Commercial Road and drove towards the disused canal, the rats now seeming to diminish in numbers. When he reached the street that ran alongside the old canal, it was deserted of any rodent life at all. He spotted a car halfway down the street and assumed Foskins had beaten him to it. He stopped at the place where he knew the house to be hidden behind a high wall and screened by wild foliage. Foskins must have parked his car and walked back looking for the house. He sat there for a few moments, listening for any sound, reluctant to leave the comparative safety of his vehicle. He reached for the glass-visored helmet and got out of the car. He stood there and looked both ways down and up the street. Carrying the helmet in one hand, ready to don it at the slightest cause, he moved towards the boarded-up gap in the wall where the iron gates had once stood. Two of the heavy boards had been pulled aside leaving a hole large enough for a man to get through.

Harris stuck his head through cautiously and shouted. 'Foskins! Foskins, are your there?'

Silence. Compelete, utterly lonely, silence.

The teacher took one more look up and down the street, put on the helmet, hating the clammy, claustrophobia it caused him, and stepped through the hole. He pushed his way through the undergrowth, along the path that had once existed, viewing everything remotely through the glass visor. He reached the old familiar house and stood at its closed front door. Taking off the helmet, he called out again: 'Foskins, are you there?'

He banged on the door but the house remained silent. Hell, I'll have to go in, he thought. At least, if there were any rats, they'll have all cleared out by now.

He peered through the broken window but could see nothing through the gloom, the surrounding trees and undergrowth preventing a lot of the light from penetrating into the interior of the house. Returning to his car, he brought out a torch from the glove compartment then went back to the house. He shone the light through the window and saw nothing but two old mildewed armchairs and a heavy wooden sideboard. He drew back at the stench that wasn't due entirely to the must of age. He tried to open the front door but it was firmly locked. He then went round towards the back.

What must have been at one time the kitchen overlooked the muddy canal and its door was slightly ajar. He pushed it open

149

gently, its creak the only sound that broke the uneasy silence.

He went in.

The smell that assailed his nostrils was even stronger than before and he quickly replaced his helmet in the hope that it would act as a mask. The kitchen still had crockery in its sink, now dusty with time, cobwebs hung across the windows and from the corners of the small room; ashes, still lying in the fireplace, uncleared from its last fire. Whoever had lived here had left in a hurry.

Harris opened a door and went into a dark hall, switching on his torch although he was still able to see enough without it. He stopped outside a door that, as a child, when the lock-keeper had let him and his friends visit, he'd never been allowed to enter. Not that there had been any mystery on the other side, but because the lock-keeper had said it was a private room, a room used for rest and reading the Sunday papers. He didn't understand why, but the unknown room presented him with deep apprehension, fear looming up inside his very soul. Nervously he turned the handle and pushed against the door, slowly at first but then swiftly and firmly, letting go so that it crashed against the wall.

It was almost completely dark, the dusty lace curtains across the window no longer allowing light to pass through its fine mesh. He shone the torch around the walls, searching and dreading what he might find. It seemed to have been converted into a study; a round globe stood in one corner, a blackboard in another; on the walls were drawings of animals, bone structures, variations of species; a long bookcase, crammed with huge volumes; a desk piled with maps and drawings.

Harris flashed the light back to the blackboard. The chalk drawing on its surface, faded and difficult to distinguish in the poor light seemed to be of a – he removed his helmet for better vision and moved closer. The thin pointed head, the long body, heavy haunches, slender tail – yes, it was unmistakeably a rat. And yet – it was hard to see in the poor light – there appeared to something odd about it.

A noise from somewhere downstairs abruptly broke his thoughts.

'Foskins, it that you? he shouted.

For a moment, there was silence, but then he heard another sound. A faint scuffling noise. He hurried back to the door and called Foskins' name again. Silence and then a dull thump coming, it seemed, from the back of the house. Below.

He edged quietly down the hall, one hand on the wall to steady himself. Opposite the kitchen was another door he hadn't noticed before, but now he remembered it from his childhood. It was the door to the cellar and it wasn't quite closed.

He pushed it wide and shone the torch down the steep flight of stairs but was only able to see a small area at the bottom.

'Foskins?'

He took a tentative step down and almost retched at the nauseating smell. He saw that the bottom of the door had been chewed away. If the zoologist had brought mutant rats into the country, this must have been where he'd kept them, Harris told himself, allowing them to breed – encouraging them. But what had happened to him? Killed by his own monsters? And once he was dead, there would have been nothing to control their rapid growth in numbers. But the cellar must be empty now – the sound-beams would have cleared them out. But what of the rat on his car? It didn't seem affected by them. Perhaps there were others like it. Turn back, or go on?

He'd come this far, it would be an utter waste not to continue his search. He descended the stairs.

As he reached the bottom, he saw there was a faint light shaft coming from some point ahead. He trailed his torch along the ground towards it and discovered many white objects littered around the floor. With a gasp he recognised them as bones – many resembling human bones. If this *had* been a rat's nest, they must have dragged their human victims down here, to gorge themselves in safety, or perhaps to feed their young.

He flashed the torch from side to side and discovered cages set around the room, their meshwork of wire torn away, their bottoms filled with straw and more white objects. He played his beam back towards the small shaft of light and then realised where it came from. It was another torch, the kind kept on key-rings, giving out a weak pinpoint of light, enough to allow a person to find a keyhole in the dark. It was lying next to a body and with dread in his heart, Harris directed his torch over it.

The lifeless eyes of Foskins stared brightly towards the ceiling. He was hard to recognise for his nose had gone and one cheek was flapped open wide, but Harris instinctively knew it was the ex-under-Secretary. The lower half of his face was covered in

151

blood and there was something moving at his crimson, open throat. A black rat was feeding on him, drinking the red liquid with greedy gulping motions. It stopped as the light was shone fully on it, two evil slanted eyes, yellow and malevolent, glaring directly at the bright torch.

As Harris took an involuntary step back, the broad beam took in the rest of the mutilated corpse. The clothes were in shreds, an arm seemed to be almost torn from the body. On the exposed chest, a hole gaped where the heart had once been. Another rat lay half across the corpse's body, its head buried into the lifeless man's intestines, oblivious in its greed to the presence of another human. In his other hand, Foskins held an axe in a death-grip, its head buried into the skull of another giant rat. Another of the vermin lay dead nearby.

It was as though the whole scene was frozen in Harris's mind, as if his eyes had acted as a camera lens and had snapped the macabre scene into timeless immobility. Although he couldn't have stood there for more than two seconds, it seemed like an age, like a void in time that couldn't be measured in hours or minutes.

Dimly, through his shock, something else registered in his mind. Something lurked in the far corner. Bloated and pale. Indefinable.

The paralysing catalepsy was suddenly broken as the rat at Foskins's throat broke loose and leapt towards the light.

Harris stumbled backwards, tripping over bones, landing flat on his back. He lost his grip on the torch and it went skidding along the floor, fortunately not breaking. As he lay there slightly stunned, he realised he was not wearing his protective helmet, and it, too, was lost from his grasp. He felt heavy paws clambering along his body, towards his exposed face. He managed to catch the rat by its throat as it was about to sink its teeth into his flesh. The fetid breath from the creature's jaws, inches from Harris's face, struck even more terror into his mind. The rat appeared to be even larger and heavier than the giant species, similar to the one on his car. He rolled over desperately, his feet kicking out and landing a lucky blow on the head of the other approaching rat.

Pushing the pointed head against the ground, he beat at it with his free fist, but the rat's claws raked at his body, pounding in furious ryhthm, preventing him from using his weight to pin it down. It snapped at the heavy-gloved hand as it descended again and caught the material between its teeth. Harris felt something land on his back and a sharp pain as his head was yanked back by his hair. He rolled over again, trying to crush the rat on his back but losing grip on the other to do so. The trick worked but he felt his hair tear at the roots as he got to one knee.

The first rat jumped up at his face but he managed to turn his head just in time and felt a searing pain as the razor-like incisors cut along his cheek. With his right hand he helped the rat in its flight with a hard shove at its haunches sending it sailing over his shoulder to crash into one of the scattered cages. He made a move towards the axe he remembered seeing in Foskin's dead hand, stretching on all fours, becoming like the creatures he was fighting.

As he reached for the axe, lit by the eerie light from his lost torch, he discovered his hand was bare – exposed to the slashing teeth and claws of the vermin. He almost drew it back towards him, to protect it with his body, but his balance depended on his gloved hand. He stretched his arm again to reach the weapon his life depended on, but sharp teeth clamped down on his hand, shaking it furiously.

With a scream he scrambled to his feet, drawing the hand with him. The rat fell back to the ground, two of his fingers between its jaws.

Incredibly, he felt no pain, his mind too numbed by terror and shock for the message to reach his brain. He staggered towards the door, intent on escape, no longer caring about Foskins, no longer concerned with the defeat of the vermin, only wanting to be free of the nightmare. He was knocked to the ground by one of the rats landing on his shoulder. He fell onto a cage and rolled over behind it, dislodging the rat as he went. The desire to cower, to lie down and die swept through his frenzied mind but with a roar, a scream, a cry of rage – he never knew which – he regained his feet, grabbing for the rat as he did so. He caught it by its hind legs and pulled it off the ground. The other rat had jumped at his thigh and Harris felt it biting through the material of the protective suit. As the blood flowed warmly and freely down his leg, he knew the teeth had penetrated the heavy cloth. It added to his fury, giving him extra strength – not a madman's strength, for his mind was now cool and calculating, ignorant of the pain – but the strength of a man refusing to be beaten by an inferior and loathsome creature.

153

He twisted his body, dragging the rat in his hands with him, ignoring the one at his thigh. He lifted the struggling creature as high as he could, then swung it against the wall with all his might. The stunned creature emitted a high-pitched squeal, not unlike the scream of a child, but still twisted and turned in his grip. He swung again, this time grunting with satisfaction at the sound of crunching bones as the thin skull hit the concrete. He tossed it away from him, as far as he could, not knowing if it still lived.

Reaching down, he pulled at the rat at his thigh, but now the pain became unbearable. He lifted the writhing body and staggered towards the lifeless figure of Foskins. He sank to his knees, almost passing out with the effort and pain, but managed to crawl desperately on. But he could not endure the pain in his leg much longer. With one final supreme effort, he reached for the corpse and collapsed against it. His weight forced the rat to release him but it immediately launched itself into another attack. Harris rolled on his back, drew his knees up, and kicked out with both feet. The blow sent the rat scuttling across the room, giving him time to get to his knees.

He grabbed for the axe and pulled its head from the dead rat. To his horror. Foskins's hand still held grimly on to the handle. He grasped the wrist with his injured left hand and wrenched the weapon free with his right. Turning sharply, he was just in time to meet the charging black beast, its jaws frothing with blood and foam, its eyes bulging with hate. He brought the axe down to meet its flying attack, the blade cleaving right through its pointed skull. It landed in a heap before him, dead already, but twitching violently. He had decapitated it.

Harris sank down, his forehead almost touching the ground but a slithering sound brought him to his senses. Looking up, he saw the other rat, the one he'd tossed from him, the one whose skull he thought he'd fractured against the wall, crawling towards him. It was badly injured, almost dead, but still it found the strength and hate to move towards him, leaving a wet trail of blood in its wake.

He crawled towards it and the rat raised its loathsome head and bared its teeth, a sound like a snarl rising from its throat. Harris realised its back was broken, but still it kept coming, determined to destroy him.

When they were no more than two feet apart he raised himself to his knees, lifting the axe high above his head with both hands.

154

The back haunches of the rat quivered as it tried to summon strength to leap, a feat it could never accomplish. The teacher brought the axe crashing down against the back of its neck, shattering its spine at the top, severing its arteries.

The exhausted teacher collapsed in a heap.

He didn't know how long he'd lain there. It could have been five minutes, it could have been five hours. He removed his gloved hand and examined his watch. It was impossible to judge accurately for he had no time-table of the horrifying events that had preceded his collapse. The pain in his hand was excruciating now, overpowering the throb of his thigh. His whole body ached and his cheek was sticky with blood. A sharp pain brought his good hand to his ear and he discovered with shock his ear-lobe was missing.

'Jesus Christ,' he muttered. But he was alive and a lightness filled his whole being. The shots I've had will prevent any disease, he reassured himself. All I need to do is get out of this bloody hole.

He sat up and his hand brushed against the dead Foskins. Poor sod, he thought. He must have put up quite a struggle to kill two of the rats. Well, he discovered the nest all right; this must have been where they originally bred, the home-lair.

A sound made his body stiff. The fear came flooding back. Oh, God, he thought, isn't it over yet? He looked hurriedly round for the axe, found it still buried in the dead body of the rat, and retrieved it with a tug.

The sound was like a whimper, a strange mewing noise. It came from the far corner.

Suddenly, Harris's mind flashed back to the moment he'd discovered Foskins's corpse. The photograph his brain had taken. The pale, bloated image he'd seen in the gloom.

Now there were small scuffling noises.

He crawled desperately for the fallen torch, mercifully still working, but its beam gradually growing dimmer. Am I strong enough to defend myself against another attack? he asked himself. He doubted it. His intention was to retrieve the torch and then get up the stairs and out into the street as quickly as possible.

But as he reached the torch and no attack came, he became curious. He shone the light in the direction of the noises. Something was there, something white or grey, moving slightly. Two

155

eyes were reflecting back at him. Small eyes. Luminous. He moved slowly towards them.

As he drew nearer, his whole body trembled, repulsed at what he saw. He stopped when he was five feet from it, resisting the urge to run, forcing himself to look.

On the straw before him, tucked into the farthest corner, surrounded by human bones, lay the most obnoxious creature he had ever seen, either in dreams or in life. In some ways, it resembled a rat, a huge rat, bigger, much bigger than the others. Its head was pointed, its body long, though obese, and he could see a long, thick tail curling forward, from behind. But there the resemblance ended.

Its whole body seemed to pulse spasmodically; it was almost hairless, a few grey threads clinging sparsely; it was completely white, or perhaps grey-pink, impossible to tell in the poor light, and its veins showed through obscenely, throbbing in time with the body movement. It reminded Harris of a huge, dismembered, bloodshot eye. He swallowed hard to stop the rising sickness.

He looked into the sightless eyes. There were no pupils, just yellow, gleaming slits. The head waved from side to side, seemingly sniffing the air, the only way it could locate him. The stench from the creature was foul, putrid – almost poisonous. A shape at the side of its large head puzzled Harris. Resisting his revulsion, he took a step closer, realising the creature was crippled by its own obesity.

The lump was almost as big as the head next to it and it, too, waved to and fro in the air. He peered closer, holding the torch nearer to it and saw what looked like – a mouth!

God! It had two heads!

Harris staggered back with a cry of horror. The second head had no eyes at all, but it had a mouth and stumps of teeth. No ears – but a pointed nose that twitched and sniffed.

The obscene creature's mewing became louder as it thrashed ponderously around in its straw crib. But it was unable to move. It sensed the danger and it knew it was helpless. The giant rats Harris and Foskins had fought had been its guards. Guards to the king. But now they were dead, and it was unprotected. Vulnerable.

With a sob, Harris raised the axe and stumbled towards the monster, frightened but knowing he had to kill it, knowing he couldn't leave it to the authorities, knowing they would keep it

156

alive to study its strangeness, its rarity, knowing he would never sleep peacefully again unless it were dead. And if it were to die – he must be its executioner.

He lunged forward and the sightless creature tried to back away. But its gluttony and reliance on its subject creatures defeated it. It was too heavy, it was too old, it was too helpless.

The body popped like a huge balloon filled with dark red blood. Harris became drenched in the thick, sticky fluid, but he hacked away at the pulsating flesh, in a rage he'd never felt before.

'For the people who've died because of you!' he screamed at the dying creature. 'For the good, for the bastards, for the innocent – for the rats like yourself!' He hacked at the heads, killing the two brains that had dominated its fellow creatures.

'And for me! So that I know that filth like you can always be erased!'

He plunged the axe deep into the creature's sagging back in one final thrust, then he sank to his knees and wept.

Soon he wiped his eyes and got to his feet. Taking one last look at the heap of obscene flesh, he turned and staggered from the cellar glancing at Foskins's body as he passed, feeling drained of emotion.

He wearily climbed the stairs and walked through the kitchen into the open sunlight. He stood at the edge of the canal for a few moments, seeing gas clouds drifting through the bright blue sky, secure in the knowledge that the gas would be fulfilling its deadly purpose. He breathed deeply, trying to lose the pungent cellar odour from his nostrils. He winced at the pain in his hand and examined the stumps of his fingers. His heart suddenly ached for Judy. And for people. He wanted to be back amongst them.

He turned and walked back down the path, his body no longer trembling, warmed by the sun. He stepped through the gap and into the street, climbed tiredly into his car and drove away from the old house.

Epilogue

The rat had been trapped in the basement for five days. It had crawled into a dark corner behind a row of shelves to give birth to its litter and when it had tried to follow the sound that had buzzed through its head, it had found the way blocked by a heavy iron door. The sound had continued for five long days, almost driving the mother-rat and its tiny offspring mad with its incessant, monotonous pitch. But they had found food in abundance in the basement, for the owners had ignored the government warning to leave all doors open so that every building would be cleared. They knew that when the city's population returned from their short exile, food would be scarce for the first few days, and their shop would be ready to cash in on the shortage. The rat and its litter gorged themselves on the food, for the young ones seemed only to need their mother's milk for the first three days then finding greater replenishment in the food around them. They grew larger and sturdier day by day, already dark brown, almost black hairs beginning to grow on their bodies. Except for one. Only a few white hairs sprouted on its pink, almost white body. It seemed to dominate the others which brought it food and kept its body warm with their own. A curious lump seemed to be growing on its broad lop-sided shoulder, next to its head.

Patiently, they waited for the people to return.

FLUKE

PART ONE

Chatper One

The warmth from the sun beat against my eyelids, soft persuasion to open them. Noises crept into my ears then burst through to my consciousness, confusing sounds, a gabble broken by strident pitches.

Cautiously, almost unwillingly, I half opened my eyes, the sleep in them sticky, a soft moist glue. Through the blur I saw a dark furry body, big as me. It heaved rhythmically up and down, up and down, in a contented sleep. My mouth opened wide as a yawn escaped and my eyes suddenly snapped fully open. Other bodies lay around me, blacks and greys – mixtures of both – some of the coats short and straight, others tufty and curly. A flash of white leapt over me and I felt sharp teeth nip at my ear. I pulled away with a whimper. Where was I? Who was I? *What* was I?

Smells came to my nostrils, unpleasant at first and then strangely pleasing. I wrinkled my nose, breathing in the fumes, powerful odours that somehow made me secure. I wriggled my body closer to the other warm bodies, away from the energetic white pest that finally gave up and bounded towards the surrounding wire. He stood up on his hind legs, resting his paws on the top of the wiring, his rump and stubby tail waggling excitedly. A huge pallid hand reached down and he was lifted away out of sight.

I whimpered again, this time with shock. The hand – so big, so strong! And the smells emanating from it – so alien. Frightening, yet . . . interesting. I tried to snuggle further into the packed lumps of sluggish fur, seeking a contact I didn't understand. Why was I surrounded by these monster animals and why did I feel so akin to them?

The sleep had left me now and my body quivered with awareness. I was in some sort of pen - it looked very large to me - the floor of which was covered in straw. The wiring around us was high, much higher than me, and my companions were dogs. I don't think I really felt fear at that moment; probably just confusion. I remember my breath coming out in short panting gasps and I think I urinated a little, just a trickle. I know I tried to burrow even further between two plump bodies, with two of which I felt some association, some common bond. Now I can guess it was because we were related, but at the time I reacted to instinct alone.

I peeped around me, keeping my head low, my jaw firmly tucked into the straw. Everything was so muted, the colours barely distinguishable apart from their varying tones, only hues of greys and muddy browns. Yet I saw the colours in my mind's eye because I had known them before . . . before . . .

Before?

In my bewildered state even the question, let alone the answer, evaded me.

But now colours were already beginning to filter through, a legacy left to me, a gift that separated me from my fellow creatures. The soft greys turned to light browns, the denser greys to darker browns. The blacks remained black, but deeper. The rainbows flew at me, filling my head with a dazzling variegation, blinding in its intensity. The blacks were no longer black, but blue, indigo, hundreds of shades of browns. The colours hurt my eyes and I was forced to close them. Yet the sun still stung through and the colours still exploded before me. And then the spectrum took its proper order, the colours found their correct balance; the flashes became subdued, the tones began to relate to each other. I opened my eyes and the brief monochrome world had vanished and been replaced by a rich, moving canvas where each colour belonged to itself yet interlocked and shared with its opposites. Even today, I still delight in everything I see, new, surprising colours revealing themselves without warning, seeming to be borne freshly before me only for me to realise they'd always been there but that I'd never really looked. The colours are more muted now, but still fresher and more interesting than they'd been in the past. I suppose it's something to do with the world being bigger to me; being closer to the ground somehow makes me closer to nature.

Having passed through this curious stage I neither understood nor appreciated, I began to be a little more adventurous in my

164

exploration. I lifted my head from the straw and stretched my neck upwards. Faces passed by, looking down at me, funny tender smiles on them. At that time, they all looked the same to me; I couldn't tell male and female apart, nor one individual from another. Nor did I know what they were exactly. Strangely enough, I could tell the difference between the smaller giants right from the start, not just from the elders, but as individuals. Several looked down at me, laughing and making strange noises with their mouths, peering expectantly at the taller ones behind. Above these giants I could see enormous grey-brick buildings stretching far into the sky – and the sky itself seemed so blue, so deep and so clear. Sky is the purest thing I've ever known, whether it's the cold azure of dawn, the striking cobalt of day, or the deepest silver-perforated blackness of night. On the darkest day, when the sky is masked by sullen clouds, the tiniest patch of blue makes my heart jump a little. It seemed then as if I were seeing sky for the first time, and in a way I was – through different eyes.

I gazed rapturously at the blue ceiling for several moments until the rays of the sun made my eyes mist over, causing me to blink rapidly. It was then I realised what I was. I wasn't shocked, for my new brain was still functioning mainly as it should and memories were still lying dormant within it. I accepted what I was; only later did I question my new beginning. But at that time, I thought it was perfectly normal to be a dog.

Chapter Two

Is it doubt I sense in you, or something more? Maybe a little fear. All I ask is that you let your mind listen, that you forget for a moment your prejudices and beliefs; when I've finished my story you can decide for yourself. There's a lot that's not clear to me yet and I know it never will be – not in this existence anyway – but I may help you to understand your life a little more. And I may help you to be less afraid.

As I looked around, my vision so different to yours, I felt the fur at the back of my neck being tugged, and suddenly the straw bed dropped away leaving my paws waggling frantically in empty air. A huge rough hand came up from beneath and the pressure was taken off the taut skin at my neck as my bottom was given support. I didn't like the smell of the hands at all, or their hardness. Each smell was separate and mostly new to me. They didn't blend together to make one complete odour; each had its own identity and combined to represent the man. It's difficult for me to explain, but as humans identify each other by assembling in their mind's eye the various features of another person – the shape of the nose, the colour of the eyes, hair, general skin tones, the set of the lips, the build of the body – we animals find it easier to assemble through our senses the various body smells. They're much more reliable, for physical features can be disguised or may change through age, but there's no disguising your own personal scent. It's a gradual build-up from everything you've done in your time and no amount of scrubbing can erase it. The food you've eaten, the clothes you've worn, the places you've visited; that's what gives us your identity, and no visual aspect is more recognisable.

I suppose the giant (I still had no concept of man at that point) who lifted me from the pen reeked of tobacco, booze, fatty foods and the aroma I've found is ever present – sex – but at the time

166

they were all new to me and, as I've said before, frightening, unpleasant, yet interesting. The only familiar smell was the doggy one, and my sensitive nose sought this out and clung to it for comfort. I could now see what seemed like millions and millions of two-legged animals shuffling backwards and forwards, their noises hurting my ears and baffling me. I was in a street-market, of course, and even in those early stages there was some recognition, some familiarity with the place. Rough, growling sounds came from somewhere close to my ear and I snapped my head round nervously. The lips of the creature that held me were moving and these were the source of the growling noises. I don't say I recognised the actual words then, but I understood the intent.

Another voice spoke on the other side of me and I was thrust forward into another pair of arms. The aroma was so different. I suppose the food and drink smells were still there, but the nicotine stench was absent. And there was so much more. You can smell kindness; it's like a fragrance. It's not that interesting, but it's reassuring. There wasn't too much of it, but compared to the hands I had just left, it was like suddenly being sprayed by the finest perfume. I began to lick the hands, for there were still traces of food on them. It's such a treat to lick a human hand or face; the sweat on every part of a human body still holds the food recently eaten and the saltiness gives it a special tang of its own. The taste is subtle and soon gone, but the delicate flavour, combined with the ticklish scratching of tongue against skin, is an exquisite pleasure every dog loves. It's not affection, you see (although after a while a familiar taste is more pleasurable than a strange one and almost becomes a show of love) but more an exercise for appreciative taste-buds.

While one hand hugged me against the friendly giant's chest, the other stroked my head and softly tickled me behind the ears. This sent me into raptures and I tried to nip his nose. He jerked his head away with a sound I could only interpret as a happy growl so I increased my efforts to reach that bulbous feature on his face. My tongue touched his chin and scratched against its roughness. This surprised me a little and I drew back, but the excitement overcame me again and I launched myself forward in a fresh attack. This time, firm hands restrained me.

The voices bartered to and fro and suddenly I was placed back in the pan. I immediately jumped up again, trying to reach the

167

friendly giant, my front paws resting on the wooden top of the wiring. A white body joined me and attempted to shoulder me out of the way. I pushed back though, realising something nice might be about to happen to me and I saw several pieces of greenish paper pass over my head to the rough red hands of my keeper. Then I was in the air again, hoisted high and hugged to the kind-smelling giant-creature's chest. I let out a little yelp of glee and tried to lick the huge face above me. I don't know if or what I suffered under the care of the other giant, but something told me it was good to get away from him; badness poured from his body. Looking down at the other bundles lying there, I felt a pang of regret; they were my brothers, my friends. Sadness swept through me as I was carried away and a vision of a much bigger dog, probably my mother, flashed into my head. I wept then and cowered into the huge creature. At the sound of my whimpers his hand began to stroke my body and soft tones came from his lips.

The crowds of two-legs were even more frightening now I was moving among them and I began to shiver with fear. Everything, everyone, was so big. I tried to snuggle my head inside a fold of the big animal's skin and he allowed me, sympathising with my fright, quietly reassuring me. Now and again I would peep out, but the noise, the flashing colours, the bustle, would soon send my head digging back deeper inside the loose skin, the beat from the broad chest having a strange calming effect on me. Soon we had left the market-place and a new, more terrifying sound roared in my ears.

My head jerked out from its hiding place and my jaw dropped open with fresh terror at the sight of the huge monsters bearing down on us, then whisking by in a whirlwind of disturbed air, seeming to miss us only by inches. They were strange animals to me, much stranger than the animal that carried me, and fearsomely devoid of any character except power and size. Their fumes were nauseating and lacked any food or sweat smells. A worse monster was to appear: brilliantly red and four times the size of the other creatures. I just had time to notice its legs were round and whirled at a tremendous rate before I leapt from my bearer's arms, spilling droplets of urine on to the grey concrete as I dashed away from the approaching beast. Shouting noises sounded from behind me, but my legs refused to stop running as I dodged between the giants who tried to block my path. A foot stretched out in front of me, but I flew over it without even breaking my stride. I veered off course as big hands reached down to grab me, leaving the pavement, throwing myself into the river of fast-moving monsters. Screeches filled my head and dark shapes loomed over me, but I kept running, my eyes focused only on what lay ahead, the advantage of my new-found wide periphery not used, my whole being concentrated on a dark hole that lay ahead of me. And then a memory stirred: *I was something else for a moment, high off the ground, and the fear inside me then was the same as the fear inside me now. Something hurled itself at me, something white and blinding. Then the light exploded into pain,* and I was a dog again, fleeing in a straight line across the paths of screeching cars and buses.

It must have been then that things were triggered off inside me: memories, feelings, instincts – I don't know what – flickered, were aroused, but were not yet exposed, uncovered. They had been woken and had begun to live, but my canine brain was not yet ready to receive them.

I entered the shop doorway I'd been heading for and skidded along the floor in an effort to prevent myself crashing into a tall thing which held brightly coloured squarish objects. It tottered dangerously as my scurrying body struck and hands clutched at it while voices were raised in alarm. I found another hole to scoot into and whipped through it, round a corner and into a nice secure dark area. I cowered there, shivering, my jaw open and my tongue hanging down like a long streak of loose liver. My stomach heaved as I drew in short, sharp panting breaths. My sanctuary didn't last long though: hands grabbed me by the scruff of the neck and rudely tugged me from the recess. Angry growls flayed at me and I was pulled along the floor, my yelps of protest ignored. My head was cuffed several times, but I don't think I felt any pain. I reached the bright doorway and tried to dig my paws into the unhelpful shiny floor. I had no desire to be back out there among those murderous creatures.

A dark shape appeared in the doorway and familiar smells came to my nostrils. I still wasn't sure of the giant but instinct told me he was all I had. He came forward and I allowed him to lift me without protest. I sought out the steadying beat of his heart again and tried to shut out the angry sounds around me. The thumping from inside his chest had a different rhythm now, slightly faster, but I still derived great comfort from it. Tempers, if not actually soothed, were checked, and I found myself out in

169

the open again, this time held more firmly, fingers digging into my soft body like iron rods. Fresh sweat glands had been aroused in my protector and new smells released; I was soon to learn that these were the smells of anger or distress. He carried me along the road, his voice scolding and misery dragged at my spirits.

Gradually, his heartbeat slowed to a more comforting pace and his grip lost its rigidity. A hand found the back of my ear again and began to stroke it, eventually calming my shaking body. Soon I had plucked up the courage to withdraw my nose from inside his jacket and look up at him. As he brought his head down I licked his nose and once again sniffed the smells of affection. His face changed in a strange way, and that was when I first began to recognise expressions and associate them with feelings. It was the start for me, the thing that set me apart from others of my kind. Maybe it *was* the shock of the roaring traffic that in some way had set off remembrances in me, shocked my system into a freakish awareness; or perhaps it would have happened in its own time anyway. At the time, though, I knew the big creatures that moved so fast on round legs were something to be feared – and for me, to be despised.

The man suddenly broke his stride and turned to his left, pushing open a heavy piece of wood and stepping through. The stale atmosphere engulfed me; the contrast between the bright sunshine outside and this cool, dim, smoke-filled cavern was awesome. The hubbub of sound was confined within walls and rebounded from them; the smells, the foul smoke, were contained and magnified, and, overriding all, came a powerful smell which filled every nook and cranny, pungent and bitter.

The man moved forward and set me down between his foot and a gigantic wooden wall, a wall he was able to lean over so that half his body disappeared from view. I peered round his legs and studied the other animals standing about the place in groups, their commotion making a rich, interesting sound, unlike the sharper, less friendly, noises of the market. Everyone seemed to be holding clear bowls of liquid in their hands which they raised to their lips and poured into their mouths. It was fascinating. I saw others sitting around the walls with the various-coloured liquids set on a sort of platform before them. Again, something familiar stirred within me but I wasn't yet ready to pursue the thoughts.

Something wet struck my head and instinctively I flinched.

Several huge pats of liquid splattered on the floor before me and I backed away against the wall. I couldn't go far, for I was surrounded by legs, rearing up like thick tree-trunks around me. But curiosity soon overcame my wariness of the wet, shiny pools. My nose twitched and I inched forward, the smell from the liquid not as unpleasant as it had originally seemed. I bobbed my nose over one pool then moved on to another. Rashly I stuck my tongue into it and lapped up the liquid. The taste was ghastly but it made me realise how thirsty I was. I quickly moved to the other puddles and licked them dry. It took about three seconds, I think, to clear that small area of drips. I gazed expectantly up at the man, but he was ignoring me, his body hunched over, head out of vision. I could hear the familiar sounds he made over the general din. I shied away as a strange hand reached down for me and patted my head. I sniffed and the smells were good; I sensed friendliness.

A roundish, yellow-brown object was shoved under my nose and against my mouth. The saltiness reached my taste-buds and released waters in them. Without further thought, I snapped at the proffered food and crunched it into gooey mash. It was crisp yet oily, full of lovely flavours; it was delicious. I swallowed three in quick succession and shuffled my hindquarters in anticipation of more, my head craning upwards, jaws half open. No more was offered me, and as the figure moved away a funny gurgling noise came from his throat. Disappointed, I studied the ground for any small crumbs that may have escaped my munching teeth. Soon, the floor around me became a very clean area. I gave a little yap at the man above me, demanding his attention. But still he ignored me, and I became a little cross. I pulled at the soft skin that hung over his hard feet (it was a little time before I realised these tall creatures wore other animal's skins and in fact *couldn't* shed their skin at will).

His hand came down and once again I was hoisted aloft. A big round face, big as my body, confronted me across a wide expanse of shiny wood. The mouth opened wide, exposing closed teeth that were subtle shades of yellow, green and blue. The smells from him made me wary but didn't alarm me at all. He reached a great fat hand towards me and I sank my teeth into the soft flesh. Although I hadn't the strength really to hurt anyone yet, the hand was jerked away in surprise then returned to give me a firm cuff on the jaw. I shouted at him and tried to nip the offending

171

hand again, but it began to weave in circles, teasing me by suddenly tapping my nose. Now a dog's nose is a sensitive area, and I began to get really angry. I shouted at him again and he roared mockingly at me, increasing his taps to a very annoying degree. My protector seemed quite happy to let this stranger irritate me, for I sensed no nervousness in him at all. Pretty soon, my whole world was focused on that moving lump of flesh and I lunged my head forward hopefully.

This time, my pointed little teeth sank into the meat and I crunched down, hard as I could. The taste wasn't much but the satisfaction was exquisite. Even though the hand was wrenched from my grasp, I had the pleasure of seeing tiny pinpricks of blood in a neat row across three fingers, and the short howl of pain excited me even more. I yapped defiantly at the creature as he shook his stinging paw in the cold air. He made as though to lunge at me and I was whisked smartly away by my giant. Once again I found myself on the floor, small and vulnerable among the massive figures around me. Curiously, the sharp roaring sound from above had a quality to it that bespoke friendliness; I was beginning to recognise the sound of laughter from the other noises these big animals made.

Still puzzled by everything that had happened to me that day, and still trembling with the excitement of it all, I spread my legs and urinated on the floor. The puddle spread beneath me and I had to shift slightly to prevent my feet getting wet. This time, although many of the sounds that reached me were of this happy nature, there were others that alarmed me terribly. I felt a blow to my flank, sharp growls, then I was dragged by my neck across the vast cavern. The sun hit my eyes, blinding me after the gloom, and the giant crouched beside me, stern sounds coming from him, his finger waving in front of my nose. I tried to bite the finger, of course, but a hard thump across my withers told me this would be the wrong thing to do. I felt utterly miserable again and my tail dropped between my legs. The giant must have sensed my dejection, because his tone softened and once again I was riding high, snug against his chest.

As he walked, a new sensation reached me. It was a fresh sound in my inner ear and I looked up in surprise. The giant's mouth had formed a curious round circle and he was blowing air through it, making an appealing, high-pitched noise. I watched him for a few seconds then called out encouragement. Abruptly

172

the noise ceased and he looked down. I sensed his pleasure and the noise continued. The whistling had a soothing effect on me and I settled down on his arm, my rump supported in the crook of his elbow, his fingers spread across my brisket, and my head against his heart. I began to feel drowsy.

It was just as well I felt tired, since the next stage in my traumatic journey was inside one of those mammoth red creatures. I realised now that the things were not living animals like the giant and me; but they were all the more disconcerting for it. However, my sleepiness overcame my fear and I half slept on his lap for most of the journey.

My next memory is that of a long drab grey road with equally grey drab houses on either side. I didn't know what houses – or roads, for that matter – were at that time, of course; to me, the world was full of strange shapes which had no identity or particular relevance. I learned fast, however, because I was unique; most animals accept rather than learn.

He stopped and pushed a wooden caging that reached as high as his waist. A section of it opened and he marched along a hard flat surface, surrounded by beautiful green fur. The multitoned greenness dazzled my eyes and I was aware that this fur was a living, breathing thing. One hand reached inside his skin and emerged with a thin-looking object. He put this into a tiny hole in the structure before him and gave it a quick twist. A rectangular shape, sharp-cornered, taller than both of us, and coloured a vivid brown (even deep brown can be vivid when you see things as I do), swung inwards and we entered my first real home as a dog.

Chapter Three

I didn't stay there long.

Those early months are a confusing blur to me. I suppose my freakish brain was trying to adjust to its new existence. I remember being placed in a basket which I refused to stay in; I remember strange white flimsy things placed on the floor all around me; I remember the lonely darkness of night.

I remember being shouted at, my nose being rubbed in foul-smelling puddles – and worse, nasty, sticky stuff, the smell of which clung to my nostrils for hours afterwards. I remember torn and mangled articles waved in front of me, the giant's companion screeching hysterically. I remember an excitingly smelly place, the mingled scents of many creatures blending into a sniffer's paradise, where an ogre in a loose, white skin stabbed me with a long, thin object, pressing it into my back and holding it there while I yelped. I remember an annoying length of dried skin being fastened round my neck, occasionally joined to a longer piece which the giant held and used to drag me along or hold me back when we were out in the open. I remember my dread of the big non-animal creatures that would chase us but lose interest and speed by with snarling roars just as it seemed they would crush us to death.

If all this sounds as though I had a miserable time as a pup then it's not quite accurate. There were lovely moments of both comfort and exhilaration. I remember cosy evenings snuggled up on my keeper's lap in front of the wispy hot thing that scorched my nose when I tried to sniff it. I remember my coat being smoothed by the giant's hand, from the top of my head to the root of my tail. I remember my first introduction to the endless green fur that lived and breathed, and smelled so fragrant, so full of life itself. I ran, jumped, rolled in its softness; I chewed, sniffed, I positively wallowed in its abundance. I remember chasing the

174

funny, sharp-eared thing who belonged to the creatures living on the other side of our wall, his fur sticking out from his body like thousands of needles, his tail ramrod straight, his mouth spitting obscenities at me. That was fun. I remember teasing my giant by grabbing one of the funny old pads he would cover his feet with, and making him run after me until he gave up in exasperation. I'd sidle up to him, place it on the ground before him, give a happy grin, then whisk it away before he had a chance to grab it. I remember the delicious scraps of food they would feed me; the food I refused to eat at first because it was so distasteful, but when hunger pains had overcome my repugnance, I'd eaten it with relish, saliva drooling from my clamping jaws. My own blanket, which I chewed and pawed until it became a tatty old thing, but which I refused to be parted from. My favourite bone, which I hid behind a bush in the little square green patch just outside our see-through wall. All these things I remember vaguely, but with nostalgic fondness.

I suppose I was a neurotic pup, but then you would be too, if you'd been through my experience. As indeed, you might.

I'm not sure just how long I stayed with the giant and his companion – I suppose it was three or four months at least. It was a doggy life for me, my human senses still dormant but ready to erupt at the slightest nudge. I'm thankful I was allowed to adapt to my new shell before the shattering knowledge burst through. The next stage wasn't far off though, and of course I was quite unprepared for it.

The reason for getting rid of me, I imagine, was because I was a pest. I know the giant liked me, even loved me in a way, for I can still remember his affection, *feel* his goodness, till this day. Those first terror-filled nights when I howled in the darkness for my brothers and sisters – my mother – he took me up to his sleeping-place. I slept on the floor beside him, much to the annoyance of his companion, and much to her even greater annoyance when she discovered the damp patches and the soft, gooey mounds scattered around the spongy floor the following morning. I think that put me on the wrong side of her from the start. The relationship between us never really developed into anything more than wariness of each other. In due fairness to her, I think the best I can say is she treated me like a dog.

Words were only sounds to me then, but I could feel the

emotion in them. I sensed, without understanding that I was a substitute for something else, and it's easy enough now to realise just what. They were, as far as I can remember, a mature couple, and they were alone. I could tell, from the noises the couple often made at each other, that the giant was full of shame and his mate full of scorn. I was confused enough as a pup and the atmosphere between them did nothing to help my emotional stability. Anyhow, as a substitute, I was no great success.

I don't know whether it was just one particular incident or an accumulation of disasters that led to my dismissal. All I know is that one day I found myself back among canine companions. My second home was a dogs' home.

And it was there that the breakthrough came.

Chapter Four

I'd been there for about a week, quite happy with my new friends, although a few were a bit rough. I was reasonably well fed (you had to fight for a fair share, though – a case of dog-eat-dog really), and quite well looked after. The big two-legged animals used to file past most days, calling down to us, making silly clucking noises, then pointing out one of us in particular. An older dog told me these creatures were called people, and it was they who governed everything; they ruled the world. When I asked what the world was, he turned away in impatient disgust and ran over to the people, sticking his nose through the wire grille in a show of homage. I soon learnt he was an old hand at the game of selection, for this wasn't his first visit to the dogs' home. I also learnt it wasn't a good thing not to be selected – eventually you would be taken away by a white-skin, and there was no mistaking the smell of death hanging over you.

The more experienced dogs told me about people: how they shed their skins at will, since it was only dead skin like the thing round my neck; how there were males and females, like us, and that they called their puppies children. If they kept repeating a sound to you, sometimes kindly, sometimes harshly, then that was probably your name. They would feed you and look after you if you were obedient. They had learned to walk on two legs a long, long time ago, and had felt superior ever since. They were a little stupid, but could be very kind.

They had the power to destroy *all* animals, even those bigger than themselves.

And it was that power, *and only that*, that made them the masters.

I discovered I was what was called a crossbreed – in other words, a mongrel. There's no class system among dogs, of course, but different breeds do have different characteristics.

For instance, a labrador retriever is gentle and intelligent, whereas a greyhound is generally skittish and somewhat neurotic; you can hardly say a word to the latter without getting a snappish reply. It's funny how the dogs knew what they were: a terrier knew it was a terrier, a spaniel it was a spaniel. However, a Scottish terrier couldn't tell it was different from an Airedale; nor would a cocker spaniel know it was different from a clumber. These differences weren't important enough to be noticed.

Another point I soon discovered was that generally the bigger the dog, the more placid he or she was. It was the little squirts who caused the most trouble. And at that time, I was a little squirt.

I'd howl for my once-a-day meal; I'd whine against the blackness of night, I'd torment the sillier dogs, I'd wrestle the friskier ones. I'd snap and snarl at anyone who displeased me and I'd get very angry and chase the long thing that curled from my rump (I never caught it and it was quite a while before I accepted I never would). Even the fleas irritated me, and if I saw one hopping about on a companion's back I'd lunge for it, nipping the other dog's flesh. This would usually create a fine din and pretty soon a white-skin would throw a cold-making liquid over our struggling bodies.

I was soon earmarked as a troublemaker, often finding myself separated from the rest in a cage of my own. This made me even more morose and irritable and pretty soon I felt very unloved. The people just didn't realise: I had problems!

The problems were of course buried deep inside me where a strange conflict was going on. I knew I was a dog; yet instincts, senses – call it intuition – told me I wasn't. The conflict erupted to the surface on a cold, dream-filled night.

I had been asleep on the fringe of a group of furry bodies that had closed their ranks on me – I wasn't very popular with the other canines by that time – and my head was full of strange images. I was tall, precariously balanced on two legs, my face level with those of the people; a female people was walking towards me, kindness radiating from her, nice sounds coming from her jaws. I seemed to know her, and I wagged my tail, the motion almost unbalancing me. She made a soft sound that was familiar to me and her jaws formed a curious round shape. Her head was only inches away from mine and coming closer, making contact. My tongue snaked out and licked her nose.

178

She pulled back, a tiny sound escaping from her. I could tell she was surprised by her sudden body smell. She became even more surprised when I started panting and wagging my tail even harder. She backed away and I followed unsteadily on my two back legs.

She began to run and now I had to drop on all fours to follow. Colours, sounds and scents cascaded into my head, and all was chaos, all was confusion. Other faces appeared before me. One was tiny, beautiful, a little female people – a child. She rubbed her head against mine, then climbed up on my back, kicking her legs against my flanks. We frolicked on the green stuff and I felt I would burst with joy. Then darkness shadowed the sky. Another face. Anger glowing from it. I disappeared and I was in a cage. In the market-place. Then I was in among other warm bodies which froze, went icy cold when the dogs opened their eyes and saw me.

Then all was total blackness.

But I was safe. I was warm. A loud, comforting thumping noise sounded close to me, almost inside me. Other, less strong sounds ticked away furiously all around. Everything, everywhere, was soft; I was encased in life-giving, life-preserving fluid. I was in my mother's womb and I was content.

Then the driving force behind me – the sudden brutal jerks of contraction. I was being forced from my safe nest, thrust down a long black tunnel into the harsh cold of the outside. I resisted. I wanted to stay. I'd known that outside before. I didn't like it. Please, please let me stay! Don't send me out. I don't want life. Death is more pleasant.

But the forces were so much stronger than me. Death had been stronger, and now life was too.

My head was pushed through first, and for a moment my small body lingered. There were others in the queue though, and they forced me through, eager in their ignorance. I shivered and my eyes refused to open: reality would find me in its own time. I felt the other glistening wet bodies around me, then a sandpaper-rough tongue cleansed the filth from me and I lay there, humble and vulnerable.

Reborn.

I screamed and the scream woke me.

My head felt as if it would explode with the new knowledge. I wasn't a dog; I was a *man*. I had existed before as a man and

179

somehow I had become trapped inside an animal's body. A dog's body. How? And why? Mercifully the answers evaded me; if they hadn't, if they had come roaring through at that point, I think I should have become insane.

My scream had woken the other dogs and now the pen was a bedlam of excited barking. They snapped and snarled at me, but I just stood there shivering, too dazed to move. I knew myself as a man, I could see myself. I could see my wife. I could see my daughter. Images rebounded around the walls of my mind, merging, splitting, rejoining, bedevilling me into a state of complete disorientation.

Suddenly the place was flooded with light. I squeezed my eyes shut to ease the pain and opened them again when I heard men's voices. A door opened and two white-skins stepped through, grumbling and shouting at the disturbed dogs.

'It's that little bugger again.' I heard one of them say. 'He's been nothing but trouble since he got here.'

A hand reached down and grabbed me roughly. My collar was used to drag me from the pen and down a long corridor of similar cages, the dogs in these now yapping furiously, adding to the uproar. I was shoved into a dark box, a kennel separated from the others to house nuisances. As the door was locked behind me I heard one of the men say, 'I think he'll have to be put down tomorrow. Nobody's going to want a mongrel like that anyway, and he's only upsetting the others.'

I didn't hear the murmured reply, for the words had struck new terror in me. I was still confused by the awful revelation, but the brutal statement had cut right through the haze. Standing there, rigid in the dark with my mind in a fever, I began to weep. What had happened to me? And why was my new life to be so short? I slumped to the floor in despair.

Soon, other instincts began to take over; my jumbled self-pitying thoughts began to take on an order. I had been a man, there was no doubt about that. My mind was that of a man's. I could understand the words the two men had spoken, not just their general meaning, but the actual words themselves. Could I speak? I tried, but only a pathetic mewing noise came from my throat. I called out to the men, but the sound was just a dog's howl. I tried to think of my previous life, but when I concentrated, the mental pictures slid away. How had I become a dog? Had they taken my brain from my human body and transplanted it into the head of a dog? Had some madman conducted a gruesome experiment and preserved a living brain from a dying body? No, that couldn't be, for I had remembered being born in my dream, born in a litter, my mother-dog washing the slime from my body with her tongue. But had that merely been an illusion? Was I really the result of a sick operation? Yet if that had been the case, surely I would be under constant surveillance in a well-equipped laboratory somewhere, my whole body wired to machines, not cast into this gloomy wooden dungeon.

There had to be an explanation, whether logical or completely insane, and I would seek out the truth of it. The mystery saved my mind, I think, for it gave me a resolve. If you like, it gave me a destiny.

The first need was for me to calm myself. It's strange now to reflect on how coldly I began to think that night, how I held the frightening – the awesome – realisation in check, but shock can do this sometimes; it can numb sensitive brain cells in a self-protective way, so that you're able to think logically and clinically.

I wouldn't force my memory to tell me all its secrets just yet – it would have been impossible anyway. I'd give it time, allow the fragments to make a whole, helping the images by searching, searching for my past.

But first I had to escape.

Chapter Five

The latch being lifted aroused me from my slumber. It had been a heavy sleep; empty; dreamless. I suppose my fatigued brain had decided to close down for the night, give itself a chance to recuperate from the shocks it had received.

I yawned and stretched my body. Then I became alert. This would be my chance. If they were to destroy me today, I must make my move while they were off-guard. When they came to take me to the death chamber, their own sensitivity to the execution they were about to carry out would make them wary. It's easy for humans to transmit their feelings to animals, you see, for their auras radiate emotions as strong as radio waves. Even insects can tune in to them. Even plants. The animal becomes sensitive to his executioner's impulses and reacts in different ways: some become placid, quiet, while others become jittery, hard to handle. A good vet or animal keeper knows this and endeavours to disguise his feelings in an effort to keep the victim calm; but they're not successful usually and that's when there's trouble. My hope was that this visit was social and not for the more ominous purpose.

A young girl of about eighteen or nineteen wearing the familiar white smock of the handlers looked in. She just had time to say 'Hello, boy' before I caught the whiff of sadness from her, then I was off like a shot. She didn't even try to grab me as I dashed by; she was either too startled or secretly pleased I was making a bid for freedom.

I skidded, trying to turn aside from the pound opposite and my toenails dug into the hard ground. My whole body was a scrambling mass of motion as I streaked around the half-covered yard, searching for a way out. The girl gave chase but in a half-hearted way as I scurried from corner to corner. I found a door to the outside world, but there was no way to get through it. I was filled with frustration at being a dog; if I'd been a man, it would have been easy to draw the bolt and step outside. (Of course, I wouldn't have been in that position then.)

I turned to growl at the girl as she approached, soft, coaxing words coming from her lips. My hair bristled and I went down on my front legs, my haunches quivering with gathering strength. The girl hesitated and her sudden doubt and wear wafted over me in waves.

We faced each other, and she felt sorry for me and I felt sorry for her. Neither of us wanted to frighten the other.

A door opened in the building at the far end of the yard and a man appeared, an angry look on his face.

'What's all the fuss, Judith? I thought I told you to bring the dog from Kennel Nine.' His expression changed to one of exasperation when he saw me crouching there. He strode forward, muttering oaths under his breath. I saw my chance – he'd left the door open behind him.

I hurtled past the girl, and the man, now half-way down the yard, spread his arms and legs as though I would jump into them. I passed underneath him and he vainly scissored his legs together, howling as his ankles cracked together. I left him hopping and flew through the open doorway, finding myself in a long, gloomy corridor, doors on either side. At the end was the door to the street, huge and formidable. Shouting from behind made me scurry down the corridor's length, desperate for a way out.

One of the doors on my left was slightly ajar, and without pausing I burst through. A woman on her knees just in the process of plugging in an electric kettle in the corner of the room stared across at me, too surprised to move. She began to rise to one knee and in panic I ran beneath a desk. My nose picked up the scent of fresh air mingled with dog fumes and, looking up, I saw an open window. A hand was reaching under the desk for me now and I could hear the woman's voice calling to me in friendly tones. I sprang forward, up on to the sill, then through the window.

Terrific. I was back in the yard.

The girl Judith saw me and called out to the man who had by now entered the building, but the yapping of the other dogs succeeded in drowning her cry. I kept running, back through the door and up behind the man chasing me.

He shouted in confusion as I scurried round him, and gave

183

chase immediately. I was sure they'd have the sense to close one of the outlets if I went through my door-window-door routine again, so I ignored the open office. I found an alternative: facing the heavy street door was a flight of stairs, broad and dark-wooded. I did a scrambled U-turn and flew up them, my little legs pumping away like piston-rods. The man began mounting the stairs behind me and his long, long legs gave him the advantage. He sprawled forward, arms reaching upwards and I felt my progress abruptly halted by an uncompromising grip on my right hind leg. I yelped in pain and tried to draw myself away and up. It was no use, I hadn't the power to escape from such a tight clutch.

The man pulled me down towards him in one strong wrench and grabbed me by the neck with his other hand. He released my leg and put his hand underneath me, lifting my body up against his chest. At least I had the satisfaction (even though it was unintentional) of peeing on him.

It was my good fortune that at that precise moment someone else decided to show up for work. Brilliant sunshine flooded into the hallway as the front door swung open and a man carrying a briefcase entered. He stared in surprise at the scene before him: the young man and the woman from the office gazing anxiously up at the dancing, cursing man who held the struggling pup away from his body, trying desperately and failing miserably to avoid the yellow stream that jetted from it.

It was just the right time to bite my captor's hand and, with a twist of my neck, I managed to do so. My jaws weren't that strong yet, but my teeth were like needle-points. They sank into his flesh and went deep – deep as I could make them. The sudden shock of pain caused the man to squawk and release his grip on me; I suppose the combination of wetness at one end and burning fire at the other offered him no other alternative. I fell to the stairs and tumbled down them, yelping with fright rather than hurt. When I reached the bottom, I staggered to my feet, gave my head a little shake, and bolted into the sunlight.

It was like bursting through a paper hoop from one dark, depressing world into a neighbouring world of brightness and hope. It must have been the taste of freedom that exalted me so, the gloom of the building I had just left contrasting with the brilliance of the sun and the exciting multifarious scents of life on the outside. I was free and the freedom lent vigour to my young

184

limbs. I fled and wasn't pursued; nothing on this earth could have caught me anyway. The taste of life was in me and questions pounded my brain.

I ran, and ran, and ran.

Chapter Six

I ran till I could run no more, shying away from passing cars, ignoring the entreaties from the bemused or curses from the startled, nothing on my mind but escape – freedom. I had streaked across roads, blind to the danger because of the worse fear of capture, and had found quieter refuge in the back-streets; yet still I did not decrease my pace, still my feet drummed on the concrete pavements. I fled into the courtyard of an ancient, red-bricked block of flats, its redness darkened by the grime, and came to a quivering body-heaving halt inside a dark stairwell. My tongue flapped uselessly below my lower jaw, my eyes bulged with still unshed fright, my body sagged with utter weariness. I had run for at least two miles without pause, and for a young pup that's quite a distance.

I sank to the cold stone floor and tried to let my muddled brain catch up with my still dancing nerves. I must have lain there, a boneless heap, for at least an hour or more, too exhausted to move, too fuddled to think, the previous elation dissipated with dispersed energy, when the sound of heavy footsteps made me jerk my head up, my ears twitching for more information. I hadn't realised until then how acute my hearing had become, and it took long, long seconds for the owner of the footsteps to come into view. An immense figure blocked out most of the light infiltrating the dark stairwell, and in silhouette I saw the round shape of an enormous woman. To say her bulk filled the whole of my vision, periphery and all, may sound an exaggeration, but that's how it seemed to me in my shrunken body. It was as though her grossness were about to envelop me, to roll over me so that I would come up again, flattened to her side, just another added layer to the multitude of other layers. I cringed and I grovelled, no defiant pride in me, no sense of manhood available to hinder my cowardice for I was no longer a man. But her words halted my rising fear.

'Hello, boy, what you doing there, then?' The voice was as

expansive as her body, booming and raspy, but the words were full of goodness and delighted surprise. She lowered her crammed shopping-bags to the floor with a grunt, then bent her vast upper structure towards me.

'Now, where've you come from, eh? Lost are you?'

Her gravelly tones suggested London, probably East or South. I backed away from the approaching hand even though my fear had been subdued by the quality of her voice; I knew once within the grip of those big, sausage-fingered hands, no amount of struggling would free me. But the lady was patient and undemanding. And the delicious aroma from those puffy fingers was overwhelming.

I sniffed small, tentative sniffs, nose-twitching sniffs, then inhaled deep lungfuls, the juices beginning to flow in my mouth. I flicked out my tongue and almost rolled my eyes in ecstasy. What this woman must have eaten! I could taste bacon, beans, tangy meat I couldn't identify, cheese, bread, butter – oh, butter – marmalade (not so nice), onions, tomatoes, another kind of meat (beef, I think) – and more, more, more. A taste of earthiness tainted everything, almost as if she had collected potatoes fresh from the ground, but it failed to sicken me as it should; instead, it heightened the deliciousness of it all. Here was a person who believed in food, who worshipped it with her hands as well as her palate; no stainless steel instruments would delay the journey from plate to munching jaws when the trip could be accomplished faster and with a heavier load by using her own living flesh to transport the goods. I could feel my devotion growing with every lick.

Only when the fat hand had been completely licked free of all its flavours did I turn my attention fully to the rest of the woman.

Dark blue eyes grinned down at me from a wide, rusty face. Rusty? Oh yes, you'd be surprised at the colours in faces if you could only see them as I did then. Red and blue veins coursed through plump, flushed cheeks, just beneath the skin. Other colours glowed from her – yellows and oranges mostly – changing hues constantly as her blood circulated beneath the surface. Brown and grey hairs stood out from her chin like tiny porcupine quills; and over the whole countenance ran deep grooves, starting at the corners of each eye and spreading down and around the cheeks, up and over the forehead, twisting and merging, crosshatching and fading to a gradual end. It was a wonderful face!

I saw all this in the gloom of the stairwell, remember, and with the light behind her. That's how powerful my new vision was and would have remained had not time organised and dulled it.

She clucked her tongue and gave a little laugh. 'You're a hungry little thing, aren't you? You know me, though, don't you? You know I'm a friend.'

I allowed her hand to ruffle the fur at the back of my neck. It was soothing. I sniffed fresh food from the shopping-bags and edged towards them, my nose twitching inquisitively.

'Oh, smell food, do you?'

I nodded. I was starving.

'Well, let's just see if there's anyone about that might have lost you.'

She straightened up and lumbered back towards the entrance and I trotted after her. We both stuck our heads out into the courtyard and looked around. It was deserted.

'Come on then, let's see what we can find.'

The old woman turned back into the gloom, hoisted her shopping-bags with a loud grunt and carried them down the short hallway behind the stairwell, calling encouragingly to me as she went. I padded after her and muscle movement in my rump told me my tail was wagging.

Placing the bags on the floor next to a badly worn green door, she produced a purse from her coat and rummaged through it until she found a key, cursing her failing eyesight. She opened the door with a hard shove and a practised twist of the key, reached again for her bags, and disappeared inside. I ambled cautiously up to the door and poked my nose round it. The musty smell that hit me was neither pleasant nor unpleasant; it told of old-age neglect.

'Come on, boy,' the woman called out, 'nothing to be frightened of. You're all right with Bella.'

Still I did not enter the room. My nervousness had not yet completely disappeared. She patted her knee in enticement, not an easy thing to do for one of her proportions, and without further thought I skipped towards her, my tail now causing the whole of my rump to vibrate.

'There's a good boy,' she rasped, and now I could understand words and not just feel them, I knew I really was a very good boy.

I forgot myself and tried to speak to her then; I think I wanted to tell her how kind she was and ask her if she knew why I was a dog. But of course I only barked.

188

'What's that, then? You hungry? Course you are! Let's see what we can find then.'

She went through a door and soon I heard the clatter of cupboards opening and closing. The deep, scratchy sound of her voice puzzled me for a few seconds, then I realised Bella was singing, an occasional word interrupting a series of monotone 'mmms' and 'laaas'.

The crackle of frying fat took my attention and the glorious smell of sausages beginning to cook sucked me into the kitchen like dust into a vacuum cleaner. I jumped up at her, resting my front paws against a broad leg, my feverishly wagging tail threatening to unbalance me. She smiled down at my excited whimpers and placed a huge hand over my head.

'Poor old thing. Won't be a minute now. I suppose you'd like them raw, wouldn't you? Well you just wait a couple of minutes and we'll share them between us. Now get down and be patient.' She gently pushed me away but the savoury smell was too much. I jumped up at the cooker and tried to see into the frying-pan.

'You'll burn yourself!' she scolded. 'Come on, let's put you out of harm's way until it's ready.' She scooped me up and lumbered over to the kitchen door where she dropped me with a soft grunt. I tried to squeeze through the narrowing gap as the door closed on me but had to withdraw when my nose was in jeopardy. I'm ashamed to say I whined and groaned and scratched at the kitchen door, my thoughts concerned only with filling my belly with those mouth-watering sausages. Questions of my bizarre existence were thrust aside, easily overwhelmed by the stronger, physical desire for food.

Finally, after what seemed an eternity of waiting, the door opened and a cheery voice called me in. I needed no second bidding; I streaked through and made a bee-line for the plate containing three powerful-smelling sausages. I yelped as the first I snapped at burnt my tongue, and the old lady chuckled at my greedy attempts to bite the sizzling meat. I'd picked one up and immediately dropped it on to the floor when it stung my mouth. I did manage to swallow a chunk but it scorched my throat painfully. Bella thought it wiser to take the sausages away from me and, annoyed, I yapped at her.

'You just be patient,' she reprimanded. 'You'll do yourself an injury with these.'

Gingerly she picked up the sausage I'd already bitten into and blew on it – long, strong puffs that defied the sizzling heat to resist it. When she was satisfied she popped the sausage into my upturned mouth. In two quick swallows it was gone and I was pleading for more. She went through the ritual again, ignoring my impatient entreaties. I appreciated the second even more, the savoury meat filling my mouth with its juices, and, I can honestly say, never had I enjoyed a meal so much in my life – lives – either as a dog or as a man.

When I had gulped down the third, the old lady turned her attention back to the frying-pan and stabbed out four more sausages with a fork, placing two each on a slice of thick bread lying on the table. She smeared them with mustard and covered them with another slice, almost tenderly, as if putting a couple of children to bed. Without bothering to cut it she opened her jaws and stuffed as much of the sausage sandwich into her mouth as possible. Her teeth clamped down and when she withdrew her hand, a huge semicircular hole had been left in the bread. I watched enviously and tried to jump up on to her lap, the sight of those huge munching jaws sending me into a frenzy of pleading. I was starving! Didn't she have any pity?

She laughed and ruffled my head, holding me at bay, keeping the sandwich well away from my snapping teeth. I was in luck, for a lump of sausage fell from the bread and I was on it in an instant. I licked my lips with pleasure as I looked up for more.

'All right, you villain. I suppose it'll do you more good than me.' Bella smiled, and with that she dropped the rest of the sandwich on to the plate on the floor.

So we feasted, me and the fat lady, happy in each other's company, both of us demolishing our piece of sausage sandwich in seconds, grinning and smacking our lips at each other when we'd done.

I was still hungry, but at least the edge had been taken off my appetite. I lapped up the water Bella gave me in a soup-bowl and licked the traces of food from her hands. I asked for more but she didn't understand. She hoisted herself to her feet and began to unpack her shopping-bag while I kept a wary eye out for any scraps that might fall to the floor. It was risky dodging between those two wonderfully stout legs, and no food fell my way, anyway, but I enjoyed the game.

Bella dropped my spotless plate into the sink and called to me to follow her. I padded after her into her front-room and scrambled up on to the musty old settee as she sank into it with a groan. I jumped up at her chest, two paws placed between two massive breasts, and licked her face in gratitude. It was a pleasing face to lick. She stroked my head and back for a little while and the strokes became slower and heavier as her breathing became slower and heavier.

It was not long after Bella had lifted those great tree-trunks on to the settee and rested her head on a cushioned arm that she was fast asleep, her snoring strangely comforting to me. I curled up my own weary body between her mountainous tummy and the back of the settee and soon I was deep in slumber too.

My awakening was fairly alarming. I heard a key in the lock and was instantly alert. I tried to stand, but my legs were wedged firmly inside the crevice between the old lady and the settee. I lifted my head and began to bark as loud as I could. This startled Bella into wakefulness and she looked around for a few moments as though she didn't know where she was.

'The door, Bella.' I told her. 'There's someone coming in!'

She didn't understand, of course, and gruffly told me to hush my barking. I was too young though, too easily excited, and my barks only got louder and more challenging.

A man staggered in and fumes of alcohol assailed me. I had been into pubs a few times with my previous master and had always found the smell of alcohol unpleasant but not disturbing. However, this had the smell of sickness.

'What the bloody 'ell's that?'

The man lurched towards us. He was fairly young, about thirty, thirty-five, prematurely balding, his face vaguely containing the same features as Bella's. His clothes were untidy but not dishevelled; he wore no shirt, just a loose-fitting sweater under his jacket. Just as Bella was broad and expansive, he was small and mean. A giant, to me, of course, but a small, mean giant.

'Haven't you been in to work again?' Bella asked, still drawing her sleepy wits together.

He ignored the question and made a grab for me, a horrible sneer distorting his lips. I growled and snapped at his hand; I didn't like him at all.

'Leave the dog alone!' Bella pushed his hand away and heaved her legs on to the floor, causing me to fall back into the space she'd just vacated.

191

'Dog? Call that a dog?' He cuffed my head with malicious playfulness. I warned him not to do it again. 'Where'd he come from? You know you're not allowed dogs in the flats.'

'Leave him be. I found him outside – starving, he was, poor little thing.'

Bella rose, towering above me and dwarfing the weasel I supposed was her son. 'You stink,' she told him, standing between us to stop his teasing. 'What about your job? You can't keep taking time off like this.'

The weasel cursed his job then his mother. 'Where's me dinner?' he asked.

'The dog's had it.'

I groaned inwardly. That should endear me to him.

'He bloody better not have!'

'I didn't know you'd be home, did I? I thought you'd gone off to work.'

'Well, I haven't, so find me something.'

I think she should have picked him up by the scruff of the neck and stuck his head in a bucket of water – she was big enough to do so – but instead she marched off into the kitchen, and soon the sounds of cupboard doors opening and closing reached our ears.

He leered down at me and I glared nervously back at him.

'Off!' he commanded, jerking his thumb away from the settee.

'Get lost,' I replied with more coolness than I actually felt.

'I said *off*!' He lunged and swept me from my comfortable perch with a strength that petrified me. I still had to learn I was only a dog, and a pretty feeble one at that. I yelped in dismay and scooted off into the kitchen, seeking protection from Bella.

'All right, boy, all right. Take no notice of him. Let's give him his dinner and he'll soon be off to sleep, don't you worry.' She busied herself preparing the weasel's meal while I kept as close to her as possible. The food odours began to arouse my palate again and suddenly I was just as hungry as before. I rested my paws against her broad flank and begged to be fed again.

'No, no. You get down now!' Her hand was more firm than before. 'You've had your dinner, it's his turn now.'

Still I persisted, but Bella ignored my whines. She began to talk to me, maybe to soothe me, or perhaps she was really talking to herself.

'Takes after his father. Never no good, but what do you do? They're flesh and blood. He could've been something, that boy, but he's wasted himself. Just like the old man, God rest him, same blood in 'em. I've done me best, God knows I've done me best. Kept him – kept 'em both – when they were out of work. They've made me old, they have, between 'em.'

The smell of cooking was making me delirious.

'He's had some nice girls too. Can't keep 'em, though. Run a mile when they find out what he's like. He'll never change. Arnold, it's nearly ready! Don't you go asleep!'

Bacon, eggs, more sausages. Oh God!

She began to butter bread at the kitchen table while I stayed rooted beneath the cooker, oblivious to the hot fat that spluttered and occasionally spat over. Bella brushed me out of the way with a leg and emptied the contents of the pan on to a plate. She put the plate on the table then clattered about for a knife and fork.

'Arnold! Your dinner's ready,' she called out. No reply. With an annoyed grunt and a determined look on her face Bella marched into the front room.

The dinner on the table beckoned to me.

It was unfortunate really that the chair previously occupied by Bella was still projecting out from the kitchen table. I clambered on to it, falling back down once but renewing my efforts with desperate eagerness, then rested my paws on the table-top. Bella could only have been out of the room for no more than a few seconds, but that's all it took for two slices of bacon and one and a half sausages to be devoured. I was saving the eggs till last.

My shriek of alarm joined Bella's shriek of dismay and the weasel's shriek of rage in a reverberating cacophony. I leapt from the chair just as the son lunged past his mother, claws outstretched to throttle mc. Fortunately Bella used her massive frame to block his path and he sprawled forward over her fleshy hip, tumbling on to the floor in a loose bundle as only drunks can.

But even Bella was cross with me. I could see those muscled forearms were going to deal out some heavy punishment, so I did my best to keep the kitcheen table between us. She stepped round her floundering son and advanced on me. I waited till she was half-way round the table, my front legs down, chin almost touching the floor, haunches high and quivering, then I shot beneath the table, heading for the oepn doorway – and straight into the arms of the weasel.

He picked me up by the neck, using two hands and squeezed as he did so, and raised himself from the floor, his demonic face only inches away from mine. My squirming body made him even more unsteady on his feet and he fell forward against the table. What was left of his dinner went flying as my back legs scrabbled for support, and his buttered bread, tomato sauce and God-knows-what-else followed suit.

'I'll kill 'im!' was all I heard before I sank my teeth into his skinny nose. (I'll bet he's still got those two rows of indents on either side of his snout today.)

'Get 'ib boff,' he cried out to his mother, and I felt huge banana hands engulf me. Bella ripped me away from him and I had the pleasure of seeing red skid-marks down the length of his nose. He clutched at it with both hands and howled, skipping on the spot in a sort of dance.

'Jesus, Jesus,' moaned Bella. 'You'll have to go now. I can't keep you now.'

She swept me out of the kitchen, shielding me with her body from her hopping son, lest he forget his pain for a moment and make a grab for me. I don't think I wanted to stay any more, so I hardly protested when the front door opened and I was dumped outside. A heavy hand descended upon me and gave me one long last stroke. 'Off you go now, go on, get away,' Bella said, not unkindly, and the door closed, leaving me alone again.

Even then, I lingered for a moment looking mournfully up at the door, but when it flew open and the weasel appeared, his nose a bloody protuberance and his body shaking with fury, I knew it wouldn't be healthy to stay any longer. So I scooted, and he scooted after me.

As an ally to speed, I think terror has it over rage; I soon left him far behind, anyway.

Blurred images again: cars, people, buildings, none of them focused, none of them very real. Only the overpowering scent from a lamp-post halted my flight. I skidded to a stop, my back legs overtaking my front legs, and executed a clumsy turnabout. I trotted back to this ambrosial column, senses keen, nose twitching inquisitively. Of all the smells that had recently come to me, this was by far the most interesting. It was dog, you see, dog in the plural. There were six or seven different personalities

194

wafting from the base of that concrete structure – not to mention a couple of human smells – and I drank them in giddily. I had sniffed trees and lamp-posts before, but now it seemed my senses were wakening afresh, or perhaps they were just heightening. I could almost *see* the dogs that had visited this towering urinal, almost *speak* to them; it was as if they'd left a recorded message for me. I could even detect the female of the species, and that, I think, has a lot to do with the dogs' interest in each other's pee: the sexual instinct, the search for a mate. The girls and the boys had left their calling cards as if to say: I've been here, this is my route; if you're interested, I may pass this way again. I was too young to be disturbed by any sexual connotation at that time, the rank yet spicy odours interesting me on a different level. They were company.

When my nose had been satiated I began to sniff my way along the pavement, oblivious to the passers-by, lost in the pursuit of intriguing trails. It was not long before sounds even more intriguing reached my ears. They were just a babble at first, like the clacking of excited geese, but as I drew nearer to their source, they took on a distinctly human quality. I quickened my pace, elation beginning to rise in me, the sounds sending out attracting waves of excitement.

Reaching a broad river of road I hesitated before dashing across and, fortunately, no dragons bore down on me. The sounds were now clamorous in my ears and, turning a corner, I fell upon their origin: an enormous expanse of running, jumping, shouting, screaming, giggling, crying, playing children. I had found a school. My tail launched into its self-motorised wagging and I sprang forward, thrusting my narrow head between the railings surrounding the playground.

A group of small girls spotted me and gleefully ran over, their hands reaching through the iron bars to pat my back. They screamed in delight as I tried to nip any fingers that tried to stroke my head; my intention wasn't to bite them, but to taste their soft flesh, to savour them. Soon, a large group of both boys and girls had formed a semicircle around my protruding head, the bigger boys pushing themselves forward through the crowd. Toffees were thrust into my eager mouth and fingers hastily withdrawn when it seemed I would swallow them too. A tiny girl with sunshine hair pushed her face close to mine and my tongue made her nose and cheek glistening wet. She didn't pull away, though, she hugged my neck.

And then fickle memories returned to taunt me. I had owned one of these! I almost thought this one was mine, she was the child who had belonged to me, but different features swam into vision. The hair was the same, a bright halo around an urchin face, but my daughter's eyes had been blue and the eyes that now smiled into mine were brown. A cry of hopefulness escaped me and the girl mistook it for one of fear. She tried to soothe me over the clamour of the other children, pleading with me not to be afraid, but my mind was paralysed with one thought. I was a man! Why was I living as a dog?

Then the paralysis wore off as the realisation slipped back into its hidden crevice and once again, in essence, I was a dog. (Although the disturbing fact that I was really a man never left me in those early months, because of the conflict of also being a dog, my humanness played a very varying degree of importance.)

My tail began its flag-waving again and I gratefully accepted more sweets. The kids fussed over me and tried to discover my name by calling out possibilities and waiting to see if I reacted to any. For the life of me I couldn't remember what I'd been called before, and the boys found nothing inscribed on my collar. Rover, King, Rex, Turdface (Turdface! What little horror threw that one in?) – I beamed at them all. Names meant nothing to me, nor do they to any dog – they recognise particular sounds. I was just happy to be among friends.

A sharp whistle shrilled through my ears and a loud moan went up from the children. Reluctantly, and only after a few sharper blasts from the whistle, they turned away and left me, my shoulders pressed hard up against the railings in an effort to follow. Sunshine Hair stayed till last and gave my neck a long, hard squeeze before departing. I woofed at them not to go, but they stood in rows with their backs to me, occasionally sneaking a look round, their shoulders jerking in suppressed giggles. Then, row by row, they filed into a miserable grey building and the door was closed behind the last one.

I stared blankly into the empty playground, distressed that I'd lost my new friends. I grinned and straightened up as little white faces appeared at upstairs windows, but these were soon joined by the older, wizened face of a teacher whose harsh, muffled voice carried across the playground, ordering the pupils to return to their seats. A boy who was slower than the rest got his ear tweaked as encouragement. I stayed there for a few more hopeful minutes, but finally, and mournfully, I tugged my head loose from the railings.

Dogs generally have happy spirits, and most emotions are sacrificed to inquisitiveness anyway, so when an old man cycled by with a shopping-bag dangling from his handlebars, I forgot my disappointment and trotted along after him. I could see a leafy sprig protruding from a hole in the base of his shopping-bag. I think it must have been rhubarb - it had a sweet tangy smell - and it looked very appetising. I soon caught up with him, for he was quite old and peddling very slowly, and before he had a chance to notice me I leapt up at the tantalising sprig. I was both lucky and unlucky.

I pulled the leaf and its stalk through the hole, but the sudden action unbalanced the cyclist and he came crashing down on top of me, machine and all. The breath was knocked from me so that my yelp of pain was only a crushed squeal. I spluttered for air and tried to apologise to the old man for bringing him down, but my words emerged as a series of wheezy grunts which he didn't understand. He flailed his arms around, trying to hit me, not even *trying* to sympathise with my hunger, cursing and groaning as if he'd been tossed by a bull on to a bed of nails. And I'd managed to break his fall too!

There was no point in my staying, he wasn't in the mood to offer me any food, so I tried to struggle free of both man and machine. A few hefty clouts from him helped me considerably and I was delighted to discover the contents of the shopping-bag had scattered along the pavement. I ignored the long red stalks whose brief taste of foliage hadn't excited me tremendously and dashed at a juicy looking red apple. My jaws clamped down on it - not an easy feat, for it was a large apple - and then I scampered out of range of angry fists and abusive language. It was fortunate his feet were tangled up in the bike frame otherwise I'm sure they'd have been used to send me on my way. At a safe distance, I turned and dropped the apple on the ground before me. I had meant to apologise again for I did feel sorry I'd caused the man to fall and hurt himself, but his purple face and shaking fist convinced me he wouldn't be pacified. So, picking up my apple, I made off, looking back once to see him being lifted to his feet by two passers-by. He seemed all right as he hobbled around testing his aged legs, so I continued on my way.

I found a reasonably quiet side-street and settled down against a wall to eat my plunder. My appetite never seemed to be satiated in those early days and those 'experts' who tell you dogs need only one meal a day are talking through their hats. Certainly a dog only *needs* one meal a day to get by, but then, so does a human. How would you feel if that's all you had? And how would you feel if you had to fast for one day a week, something the 'experts' also recommend? What's the use of a glossy coat and a damp nose if you've got a gnawing stomach? I wolfed that apple down, core and all, as if it was all I'd eaten that day. The sun beat down on me and I dozed off, forgetting my problems, drowsiness forcing me to accept what was.

One of those inevitable English summer showers aroused me and I automatically looked at my wrist to see what the time was. The sight of my thin, hairy dog's leg shocked me into reality. I trotted to my feet and shook myself, then looked around; it must have been mid-afternoon and I was hungry again.

I set off down the narrow street, investigating new smells as they came to me, chasing a beetle as it scurried across my path, calling hello to a dog being lead by a man on the other side of the street. The dog, a disdainful little corgi, ignored me and I just wasn't interested enough to make conversation. It slowly dawned on me as I trotted on that I needed a quiet safe place, somewhere I could rest and try to unscramble my jumbled thoughts. I needed food and I needed protection. Some kind of sympathy would have been welcome too.

But I didn't find it that day.

I pushed my rump back in the doorway to avoid the drizzling rain spattering against my nose and foreface. It had been an afternoon of wandering and wondering; the sun had been dimmed by the steady drizzle and the damp had made the people even more insulated. Earlier on, the streets had suddenly become crowded, overwhelming me with their congestion so that I could only cower miserably under a railway arch. After what seemed a long time, their numbers dwindled and I ventured forth again, but by now my spirits had caved in completely. My tail dropped between my legs and my eyes scarcely left the pavement in front of me. As the evening drew on and the light faded, my loneliness had increased to such an extent that I was tempted to go back to the dogs' home – the Return of the Prodigal, Lassie Comes

Home. The thought of being put to sleep – murdered, I mean – wouldn't have deterred me. I would be good, I would play the underdog to its lowest level, and the keepers would forgive me, give me another chance to prove my worthiness to be an unworthy creature, to be just another dog. I couldn't remember where the hell the dogs' home was, though.

I gazed longingly up at lighted windows, yearning for company, drinking in the inviting smells, but the rain drove me on, searching and just not finding.

The hour was late now and, apart from the occasional swish of a passing car, the streets were cold and empty. I huddled in the doorway, and my wretched spirit huddled within me. Tiredness made my eyelids droop, only hunger keeping me awake. Questions invaded my misery.

This place wasn't familiar to me, yet I knew it was London. Was I from London? No, I wasn't from London. How did I know? I just knew. I had a memory of green fields, open space; a town, but not a big town. They had formed the greater part of my life, these fields and this town. Where were they? If only I could find them. And yet I knew this city, even if this particular district was unfamiliar. Had I worked in London? I had a sudden vision of a woman, in her late fifties, plump but not large, smiling and holding her arms out, and it seemed she held them out to me, calling a name that was soundless to my ears. Her head became that of a dog's, and was just as warm, just as affectionate, just as welcoming. My two mothers vanished from my mind and were replaced by the figure of a man, a man who appeared quite normal, handsome in a featureless way, and his environment was somehow different, not part of the scene I had just envisaged.

I hated him. Was it me?

My thoughts wearily wandered on, uncontrolled, undirected: the child again, obviously mine; the girl – young woman – certainly my wife; a house; a street, a muddy lane; a town. The name of the town almost came to me; the names of the girl and the child hovered behind a tissue-thin barrier; my own name was rising from ocean depths and about to break surface. But a car swished past and the names scattered like startled fish.

I watched the car's rear lights recede into the distance, twin reflections on the soggy road diminishing with them, suddenly reinforced by brake lights, and disappearing as the vehicle turned

199

a corner (even that seemed familiar). I was alone again in an empty world and with an empty head. Then I saw the ghost.

Have you ever seen a ghost? Probably not. But have you ever seen a dog suddenly become alert, for no apparent reason, his ears cocked, his hair bristling? You'd undoubtedly think he's just heard something that's escaped your ears, somebody walking by the house, another dog barking somewhere far in the night: and many times you'd be right. But often, it's because he's aware of presence – a spirit. He won't always be alarmed, perhaps just disturbed; it depends largely on the nature of the ghost itself. It could be friendly or unfriendly.

Think I'm going a bit far now? Just wait till later.

The ghost drifted across the road towards me, a shadowy form, a wispy, vaporous figure. It didn't see me, or, if it did, it chose to ignore me, and as the shape drew nearer, I was able to distinguish a face, shoulders, and a part of a torso. The apparition seemed to be wearing a jacket, and I could certainly make out a shirt-collar and tie. Why wasn't it naked – why do astral bodies never seem to be naked? Don't ask me, I'm only a dog.

Now, I was disturbed, I admit it. There was nothing evil emanating from the spirit, I'm sure, but it was my first ghost both as a dog or as a man. My hair stood on end and my eyes widened. My mouth suddenly felt very dry. I was too frightened even to whine and the power to run had left me completely.

It had the saddest countenance I've ever seen, a face that had been made aware of the ills of mankind, had learned the first lesson in death. It passed by me, close enough to touch, and I could clearly see the rain drizzling through it. Then the spectre was gone, drifting off into the night, leaving me to wonder if my restless mind hadn't invented the whole thing. It hadn't, for I was to see many more of these wandering spirits, most with the same burden of sadness, unaware it was just a phase for them; but it was to be a long time before I discovered their meaning.

The experience drained me of what strength I had left and I fell into a deep undisturbed sleep.

Chapter Seven

Gentle nudging woke me.

I shifted my position and tried to ignore the prodding, but I was too cold to become comfortable again. My eyes opened of their own accord and I saw a big black dog hovering over me.

'Come on, squirt, don't let them find you napping there.'

I blinked my eyes furiously, now fully awake.

'Where did you get loose from, eh? Run away from home, or did they lose you on purpose?' The big dog grinned down at me.

I shivered and tottered to my feet. 'Who are you?' I asked, unable to stifle a yawn. I stretched stiff limbs, my front legs going down on the ground, my back pushing my rump into the air as far as it could go.

'Rumbo's what they call me. You got a name?'

I shook my head. 'I might have. I can't remember it, though.'

The dog regarded me silently for a few moments, then had a sniff around me.

'There's something funny about you,' he announced finally.

I gulped at the understatement. 'You don't seem like the other dogs I know either,' I said. And he wasn't, I could sense it immediately. He was somehow brighter, or un-doglike, or . . . more human.

'We're all different. Some are more dopey than others, that's all. But with you it's something else. You're definitely a dog, aren't you?'

I nearly blurted out my problems to him there and then, but he suddenly lost interest in that line of thought and directed my own on to a much more basic level. 'You hungry?' he asked.

Only ravenous, I thought, nodding my head sharply.

'Come on, then, let's go and find something.' He turned away and was off down the road at a brisk pace. I had to scamper to catch up with him.

He was a bony mongrel, about five or six years old, an amalgamation of several breeds. Imagine a Dalmatian without spots, just black all over, and without elegant lines, with turned-in toes, cow-hocked hindquarters, excessive angulation of the back legs (they stuck out backwards too far) and weak pasterns, then you'd have a fair impression of Rumbo. He certainly wasn't ugly – not to me anyway – but he wouldn't have won any prizes, either.

'Come on, pup!' he called over his shoulder. 'We don't want to be late for breakfast!'

I drew level with him and said breathlessly, 'Do you think we could stop for just a minute, I need to do something?'

'What? Oh yes, all right.' He stopped and I squatted on the ground before him. He turned away in disgust and trotted over to a nearby lamp-post, cocked his leg and relieved himself in a professional manner. 'You'll avoid accidents if you do it this way,' he called over, as I tried to shift a leg that was being threatened by a spreading puddle.

I smiled back feebly, grateful that the streets were fairly empty and no human could see me in this undignified pose. It was the first time I'd felt self-conscious about that sort of thing, a sign of the dog versus human instinct conflict that was going on inside me.

Rumbo came over and sniffed mine and I went over to the lamp-post and sniffed his. When we were both satisfied, we went on our way.

'Where are we going?' I asked him, but he ignored me, his step becoming faster, excitement tightening his movements. Then I caught the first whiff of food, and my attention was captured.

The roads were busier now, yet the noise and the bustle didn't seem to bother Rumbo at all. I stuck as close to him as possible, my shoulder occasionally bumping against his thigh. The roads still frightened me; the buses seemed like mobile blocks of flats and the cars like charging elephants. My supersensitive vision didn't help matters much, the blinding colours heightening my fears, but nothing seemed to bother Rumbo. He skilfully avoided pedestrians and used crossings to negotiate the dangerous roads, always waiting for a human to cross first, then trailing behind him, with me trying to become an extension of his body.

We reached a thunderous place where, even though it was still early morning, there were masses of people, hustling, bustling, hurrying – worrying. The noise was deafening, with men shouting, lorries hooting and hand-pulled barrows grinding along the concrete. Rich scents filled the air – the tang of many different fruits, the more earthy smell of vegetables, raw potatoes. If it hadn't been for the apparent chaos, I would have believed I'd found Heaven.

We were in a market, not a street-market, but a covered wholesale market, where restauranteurs, fruiterers, street-traders – anyone who sold fruit, veg or flowers – came to buy their stock; where growers and farmers brought their goods; where lorries arrived from the docks laden with food bought from exotic countries, and trucks departed, full to bursting point, bound for different parts of the country, or back to the docks where their contents would be loaded on to ships; where voices were surly as barter took place, as credit was extended – even as debts were paid.

A burly man, red-faced, bull-necked, wearing a dirty once-white smock, lumbered past us, pulling a barrow piled high with precariously balanced boxes, all packed with greenish-yellow bananas. He sang at the top of his voice, stopping only to swear amiably at a passing workmate, unaware that a hand of bananas was about to topple from the top of his load. As it did so I started forward, but Rumbo barked sharply.

'Don't you dare,' he warned me. 'They'd skin you alive in this place if they caught you stealing.'

Someone shouted and the man stopped his barrow, looking back round the stacked boxes to see the stray bananas. He cheerfully walked back to them and threw them high on to his load. He spotted us as he returned to the barrow's handles and stopped to give Rumbo a hearty pat on his back. I think the pat would have broken my spine. My new friend wagged his tail and tried to lick the man's hand.

'Hello, boy. Brought a friend with you today, 'ave you?' the market porter said, reaching out for me. I backed away; my young body was too tender for such rough treatment. The man chuckled and turned back to his barrow, resuming his tuneless tune.

I was puzzled by Rumbo's attitude: why had we come here if we couldn't sample the food?

'Come on,' he said, as if in answer, and we were off again, dodging round salesmen, porters and buyers, threading our way

203

through the disorder, Rumbo receiving a welcome or a friendly pat now and again. Occasionally we would be shooed on, and once we had to avoid a malicious boot aimed at us, but generally my older companion seemed to be well-known and an accepted part of the scene. Rumbo must have been working at it for quite a long time, for animals – apart from rat-catching cats – aren't generally tolerated around food-markets, particularly strays.

A new overpowering smell reached my sensitive nostrils, easily defeating the tang of mixed fruit and vegetables, and much more enticing to my grumbling tummy: the smell of frying meat. I saw where Rumbo had been heading and raced ahead, leaping up at the high counter of the mobile snack-bar. It was much too high for me, and I could do no more than rest my front paws against it and look up expectantly. I couldn't see anything because of the overhanging counter, but the smell of frying wafted down over me.

Rumbo appeared quite angry when he arrived, and said through clenched teeth, 'Get down, squirt. You'll spoil everything.'

I obeyed reluctantly, not wanting to upset my new-found friend. Rumbo paced himself back so that he would be visible to the man behind the high counter and yipped a couple of times. A skinny old head peeked over the edge of the counter and broke into a yellow-toothed smile.

''Allo, Rumbo. 'Ow yer doin' today? 'Ungry belly, eh? Let's see what we can find yer.' The head disappeared from my view so I rushed to join Rumbo, excitement at the prospect of food elating me.

'Keep still, pup. Don't make a nuisance of yourself or we'll get nothing,' he scolded.

I did my best to remain calm, but when the man behind the counter turned to face us, a juicy-looking sausage held between two fingers, it was too much for me. I jumped up and down in anticipation.

'What's this, then, brought a mate along? This ain't meals-on-wheels yer know, Rumbo, I can't start feedin' all yer mates.' The man shook his head disapprovingly at Rumbo, but nevertheless dropped the sausage between us. I made a grab for it, but my companion was quicker, snarling and gobbling at the same time – not an easy thing to do. He gulped the last morsel into his throat, smacked his thin lips with his tongue and growled. 'Don't take liberties, shrimp. You'll get your turn, just be patient.' He looked up at the man who was laughing at the pair of us. 'What about something for the pup?' Rumbo asked.

'I suppose yer want something for the pup now, do yer?' the man asked. His tired old eyes crinkled and his large hooked nose became even more hooked as his grin spread wide across his thin face. He was an interesting colour actually: yellow with deep mahogany etchings patterning his features, greasy but still somehow dry skinned, the oiliness being only on the surface. 'All right then, let's 'ave a look.' He turned away again and as he was about to find me something a voice called out, 'Cuppa tea, Bert.'

One of the porters leaned his elbows against the counter and yawned. He looked down at us and clicked his tongue in greeting. 'You wanna' watch this, Bert, you'll 'ave the inspectors after you if you 'ave too many of these 'anging about.'

Bert was filling a cup with deep brown tea from the most enormous metal teapot I'd ever seen.

'Yerse,' he agreed. 'It's usually the big one on 'is own. Brought a mate today though, probably one of 'is nippers, looks like 'im, dunnit?'

'Nah,' the porter shook his head. 'The big one's a proper mongrel. The little one's a crossbreed. Got a good bit of Labrador in 'im and . . . let's see . . . a bit of terrier. Nice little thing.'

I wagged my tail for the compliment and looked eagerly up at Bert.

'All right, all right, I know what you want. 'Er's yer sausage. Eat it and then scarper, you'll 'ave me licence.'

He threw the sausage down at me and I managed to catch it in mid-air; it burnt my tongue though and I had to drop it hastily. Rumbo was on it immediately. He bit it in half and swallowed. I pounced on the other half, but Rumbo stood back, allowing me to gulp it down. My eyes watered from the heat of it and I could feel its warmth working its way down my throat.

'Sorry, squirt, but you're here only because I brought you. You've got to learn respect.' Rumbo looked up at the snack-bar man, barked his thanks and trotted away from the stall.

I glanced at the two chuckling men, said my thanks, and chased after him.

'Where we going now, Rumbo?' I shouted.

'Keep your voice down,' he reprimanded, waiting so I could

catch up. 'The trick is not to be conspicuous in a place like this. That's why they don't mind me coming in, because I behave myself, keep out of their way and . . .' he looked meaningfully at me, seeing I was about to run after a rolling orange which had fallen from one of the display stands '. . . and I *never* take anything unless it's offered to me.'

I ignored the orange.

We left the market, accepting half a black soggy banana each on our way, and skipped along into the less cluttered streets.

'Where are we going now?' I inquired again.

'We're going to steal some food now,' he answered.

'But you just said back . . .'

'We were guests there.'

'Oh.'

We found a butcher's on a busy main road. Rumbo stopped me and peeked round the open doorway. 'We've got to be careful here, I did this place last week,' he whispered.

'Er, look, Rumbo, I don't think . . .'

He hushed me up. 'I want you to go in there over to the far corner – don't let him see you till you get there.'

'Look, I'm . . .'

'When you're there, make sure he *does* see you, then you know what to do.'

'What?'

'You know.'

'I don't know. What do you mean?'

Rumbo groaned aloud. 'Save me from stupid mutts,' he said. 'Your business, you do your business.'

'I can't. I can't go in there and do that.'

'You *can*. You're *going* to.'

'But I'm not in the mood.' The thought of the danger had put me in the mood, though.

'You'll manage,' Rumbo said smugly. He sneaked a look back inside the shop. 'Quick, now's the time! He's cutting meat on his slab. Get in there, quick!'

He bustled me in, using his powerful jaws to nip my neck as encouragement. Now, I'm sure you've never seen two dogs act this way outside a butcher's shop before, but there aren't many dogs like Rumbo and me around, just the odd few. You've seen dogs mugging kids for their ice-creams and sweets, though, and I'm sure you've caught your own dog stealing at some time or other. What you haven't seen – or perhaps noticed – is organised canine crime. Most dogs are too stupid for it, but I can assure you it does exist.

I entered the shop and slunk along under the counter where the chopping butcher couldn't see me, looking back pleadingly at my forceful partner. There was no reprieve in his dark brown eyes. Reaching the end of the counter, I cautiously looked up, the sounds of that falling chopper making my body judder with every blow. I made a dash for the corner and squatted, squeezing my bowels to make something happen. We were lucky it was still early morning and there were no customers to complicate things. After a few strained grunts, I began to have some success. Unfortunately, I'd forgotten to draw attention to myself and could have squatted there in peace for quite a long while had not Rumbo lost patience and begun yapping at me.

The butcher stayed his small meat chopper in mid-air and looked over to the doorway.

'Oh, it's you again, is it? Wait till I get hold of you,' he threatened.

He hastily placed his chopper on the corner and started making his way round towards Rumbo. That's when he saw me.

Our eyes met, his wide and disbelieving, mine wide and knowing only too well what was going to happen next.

'Oiii!' he cried, and his journey round the counter took on a new pace. I half rose, but running was a problem at that particular moment. Instead, I did a sort of undignified shuffling waddle towards the open doorway. Rumbo was already up at the counter, sorting out the nicest cut for himself while the butcher's whole attention was focused on me. The red-faced butcher had picked up a broom in the course of his journey, one of those heavy jobs used for scrubbing floors as well as sweeping. He waved it in the air before him like a knight's lance, its base aimed at my backside. There was no avoiding it and my awkward predicament didn't help matters.

Thank God the broom had a multitude of bristles, strong and hard but not as strong and hard as the handle would have been. I yelped as they cracked down on my rump, the butcher extending his arm so I was sent scuttling across the floor. I skidded and rolled but was up like a rabbit, running for the open doorway, Rumbo close on my heels, at least a pound and a half of raw steak hanging from his jaws.

207

'Oiiiii!' was all I heard from the butcher as I flew down the street, my partner-in-crime keeping pace and chuckling at his own cleverness.

Men and women hastily stepped to one side when they saw us coming and one man foolishly tried to snatch the dangling meat from Rumbo's mouth. Rumbo was too wily for that and easily avoided the grasping hand, leaving the man sprawled on hands and knees behind him. We ran on, Rumbo keeping a measured pace beside me and much amused by my panic. Finally he called out through his clenched mouth, 'This way, squirt, into the park!'

The urge to go my own way, to get away from this thief, was great, but my appetite was greater; besides, I'd earned my share of the booty. I followed him through rusted iron gates into what seemed to me to be acres and acres of lush greenery surrounded by giant foliage, but what must actually have been a fairly small city park. Rumbo disappeared into a clump of bushes and I chased after him, flopping into a panting, eyes-rolling heap on the soft soil two feet away from the spot where he'd decided to go to earth. He looked at me in a smirky was as I heaved in great lungfuls of air, nodding his head at some inner satisfaction. 'You did all right, pup,' he said. 'With a little bit of guidance you could amount to something. You're not like the other stupid dogs.'

I didn't need to be told that, but his praise pleased me all the same. Nevertheless, I growled at him. 'I could have been hurt there. I can't run as fast as you.'

'A dog can always outrun a man. He'd never have caught you.'

'He did, though,' I retorted, wriggling my rump to make sure nothing had been seriously damaged.

Rumbo grinned, 'You'll learn to take more than that in this life pup. Men are funny creatures.' He turned his attention to the meat lying between his front paws, nudging it with his nose then licking the juices on it. 'Come on, come and get your share.'

I rose to my feet and gave my body a shake. 'I've got some unfinished business first,' I said huffily, and slunk off further into the bushes. When I returned only a few moments later, Rumbo was well into the raw steak, chomping and sucking in a disgusting manner. I hurried forward lest he swallowed the lot and launched myself into the meat in an equally disgusting manner. It was a fine meal, the finest I'd had since being a dog. Perhaps the excitement of the chase, the tension of the robbery, had increased my appetite, for even Bella's sausages hadn't tasted as good.

We lay among the bushes smacking our lips with satisfaction, our mouths still full of the steak's juicy blood flavours. After a while, I turned to my new companion and asked him if he often stole food in that way.

'Steal? What's steal? A dog has to eat to live, so you take food where you find it. You can't rely on what man gives you – you'd starve if you did – so you're on the lookout all the time, ready to grab anything that comes your way.'

'Yes, but we actually went into that butcher's and stole that meat,' I insisted.

'There's no such thing as steal for us. We're only animals, you know.' He looked at me meaningfully.

I shrugged my shoulders, unwilling or too content for the moment to pursue the matter further. But all the same I wondered just how aware Rumbo was.

He suddenly jumped to his feet. 'Come on, pup, let's play!' he shouted, and was gone, streaking through the bushes out on to the open grassland. A burst of energy swept through me as though a switch had been on somewhere inside, and I dashed after the older dog, yapping joyfully, tail erect, eyes gleaming. We chased, we rolled, we wrestled, Rumbo teasing me mercilessly, showing off his skills of speed, manoeuvrability and strength, submitting to my wilder onslaughts and tossing me aside with the slightest shrug just when I began to feel his equal. I loved it.

The grass was wonderful to wallow in , to rub our backs against, to breathe in its heady fumes. I'd have been happy to have stayed there all day, but after ten minutes or so a surly park-keeper came and chased us away. We mocked him at first, taunting him by coming within easy reach then dodging just as he took a swipe at us. Rumbo was the more daring, actually leaping up and giving the man a gentle push in the back when his attention was on me. The park-keeper's angry curses made us roar with laughter, but Rumbo soon tired of the game and was off through the gates without a word, leaving me to chase after him.

'Wait for me, Rumbo!' I called out, and he slowed his pace to a trot, allowing me to draw alongside.

'Where are we going *now*?' I asked.

'We're going to have our breakfast now,' he replied.

Rumbo led me through a confusing number of side-streets until we reached an enormous corrugated-iron wall running the length of the pavement. We reached a break in it and Rumbo trotted through, his nose twitching for some familiar scent.

'Good,' he said to me. 'He's in his office. Now listen to me, pup: stay good and quiet. The Guvnor doesn't have much patience with dogs, so don't be a nuisance. If he talks to you, just wag your tail and play dumb. Don't get frisky. If he's in a bad mood – I'll give you the nod if he is – make yourself scarce. We can try again later. O.K.?'

I nodded, beginning to feel apprehensive about meeting this 'Guvnor'. Looking around, I saw we were in a vast yard filled with old broken-up and broken-down cars, all piled in precarious-looking heaps. Other, smaller heaps, were scattered around and I saw these were made up of rusted parts from the damaged cars. A weary-looking crane stood at one end and I realised we were in a breaker's yard.

Rumbo had made his way towards a dilapidated wooden hut which stood in the centre of the metal-torn domain and stood scratching at its door, occasionally giving out a moderate bark. The shiny blue Rover parked near the hut stood out like a sore thumb among the mangled wrecks around it, the bright morning sun making its bodywork gleam disdainfully.

The door of the hut swung open and the Guvnor stepped out.

''Allo Rumbo, boy!' He beamed down at my tail-wagging friend; his mood seemed good. 'You been out all night again? You're supposed to be a guard dog, you know, stop me having headaches.' He squatted in front of Rumbo and ruffled the dog's fur, slapping his flanks for extra welcome, Rumbo was good – very good; he wagged his tail and shuffled his feet, grinning up at the Guvnor all the time, but not trying to thrust himself on to him, his tongue hanging loose, occasionally flicking upwards to lick the man's face. The Guvnor was heavily built, his long leather jacket bulging tight around the shoulders. He had that fleshy-looking hardness about him, a tough nut who had become used to the good things in life – good food and good liquor. A fat cigar protruded from his mouth and it looked a part of him, like his flattened nose; he would have looked silly

210

without either. His hair, which was just beginning to thin, covered his ears and flowed over his collar at the back. A gold-sovereign ring flaunted itself from one hand while a large diamond ring outdid it on the other. He was about fortyish and had 'Villain' written all over him.

'Who's this you got with you?' The Guvnor looked over at me, surprise on his face. 'Got a little girl friend, have you?'

I bridled at his silly mistake. Fortunately, he corrected himself. 'Oh no, I can see he's just a pal. Here boy, come on.' He extended a hand towards me but I backed away, a little afraid of him.

'Get over here, squirt,' said Rumbo quietly, warning me with annoyance in his voice.

I crept forward cautiously, very uncertain of this man, for he was a strange mixture of kindness and cruelty. Generally, when you taste them, people have both these qualities but usually one is more dominant than the other. With the Guvnor, both characteristics were equally balanced, something I now know is very common in men of his kind. I licked his fingers, ready to bolt at the least sign of aggression. He stopped me as I got carried away with his delicious flavours by clamping my jaws together with a big fist.

'What's your name then, eh?' He yanked at my collar and I tried to pull away, very fearful of him now.

'It's all right, squirt, he won't hurt you if you behave yourself,' Rumbo reassured me.

'No name? No address? Someone didn't want you very much, did they?' The Guvnor let me go, giving me a playful shove towards Rumbo. He stood up and I could sense I was instantly forgotten.

'O.K., Rumbo, let's see what the missis has sent you.' The man walked round to the boot of his Rover, unlocked it and pulled out an interesting-looking plastic bag – interesting because it bulged with what our noses told us could only be food. We danced around his ankles and he held the bag aloft out of reach. 'All right, all right, take it easy. Anyone would think you hadn't eaten for a week.' Rumbo grinned at me.

The Guvnor walked round to the back of the hut to where an old plastic bowl lay and emptied the contents of the bag into it. A meaty bone, soggy cornflakes, bits of bacon fat and half a chocolate bar fell into the bowl, a rich concoction of leftovers. There were even some cold baked beans among the scraps. As a human, my stomach would have turned over; as a dog, it was a gastronomic delight. Our noses disappeared into the mixture and for a few moments our minds were concentrated solely on filling our bellies. Rumbo got the tastier morsels, of course, but I didn't do too badly.

When the bowl was spotlessly clean, my friend wandered over to another bowl which stood beneath a dripping tap. He began to lap greedily at the water and I, my stomach fit to burst, drifted over and did the same. We slumped on the ground after that, too full to move.

'Do you eat this well every day, Rumbo?' I asked.

'No, not always. It's been a good morning. The Guvnor doesn't always bring me something – there've been times he hasn't fed me for days – and it's not always easy to steal. The shop-keepers around here are a bit wary of me now.'

The Guvnor had disappeared inside the hut and I could hear music blaring from a radio.

'Have you always belonged to the Guvnor?'

'I can't remember, to tell you the truth. He's all I've known.' Rumbo became deep in thought. Finally he said, 'No, it's no good. My mind goes fuzzy when I try to think too hard. Sometimes I remember scents when I sniff certain people. They seem familiar to me. I can't remember not knowing the Guvnor, though. He's always been there.'

'Is he good to you?'

'Most of the time. Sometimes he ties me up when he wants to make sure I stay in all night, and sometimes he kicks me hard for shouting too loudly. But I can't help it. He's got some nasty friends and I just let fly at them when they come round.'

'What do they do here?'

'Talk mostly. They stay in that hut for hours, arguing and laughing. There's a few regulars who do the work around here, mess around with those heaps of junk, and things; bring new ones in. They're never very busy.'

'What does the Guvnor do?'

'You're a bit nosy aren't you, squirt?'

'Sorry. I'm just interested, that's all.'

Rumbo eyed me suspiciously for a few moments. 'You're not like other dogs, are you? You're . . . Well, you're a bit like me. Most dogs are very stupid. You're stupid, but not in the same way. Where exactly *are* you from, pup?'

I told him all I could remember and discovered I was beginning to forget my past also. I could still remember the market where I was bought, but not much more between there and the dogs' home. It's something that's happening to me more and more; I have periods of complete lucidity, then my mind can go virtually blank – my past, my origins, a vague blur. I often forget I was a man.

I didn't voice my anxiety over my human ancestry at that time because I didn't want to alarm Rumbo in any way; I needed him so I could learn how to survive as a dog. Acceptance of circumstances comes more easily to an animal, you see, and it was that animal part of me which turned away maddening thoughts.

'You were lucky to get away from the dogs' home, pup. That's the death-house for many,' Rumbo said.

'Have you ever been inside?'

'No, not me. They'll never catch me as long as I can run.'

'Rumbo, why aren't all dogs like us? I mean, why don't they talk like us, think like us?'

He shrugged. 'They just aren't.'

'Rumbo, were you ever . . . do you ever remember being . . . er, have you always been a dog?'

His head jerked up. 'What are you talking about? Of course I've always been a dog? What else could I have been?'

'Oh, nothing.' My head sank miserably down on to my paws. 'I just wondered.'

'You're a strange pup. Don't cause me any trouble here, shrimp, otherwise I'll turn you out. And stop asking silly questions.'

'Sorry, Rumbo,' I said and quickly changed the subject. 'What does the Guvnor do?' I asked again.

Rumbo's answering glare and bared teeth killed my curiosity for the moment. I decided to take a little nap, but just before I dozed off another thought struck me.

'Why don't men understand us when we talk, Rumbo?'

His voice was drowsy with sleep when he replied. 'I don't know. Sometimes the Guvnor understands me when I talk to him, but usually he just ignores me, tells me to quit yapping. Humans are just as stupid as stupid dogs sometimes. Now leave me alone, I'm tired.'

It was then that I realised we hadn't actually been communicating with words: it had been our *minds* speaking to each other.

213

All animals or insects – fish even – have a way of communication whether it's by sound, scent or body display, and I've come to learn that even the dumbest creature has some sort of mental link with his own species – as well as others. It goes far beyond physical communications: how do you explain individual grasshoppers grouping into a swarm of locusts, what makes soldier ants march, what suddenly makes the lemming decide it's time to jump in the sea? Instinct, communication by body secretions, the sense of race survival: they all play their part, but it goes deeper. I'm a dog, and I know.

But I didn't know then. I was a pup, and a confused one at that. I'd found a friend I could talk to through my mind, someone who was more like me than the other dogs I'd met; few had come close, but none were like old Rumbo. I gazed at him fondly through blurred eyes, then dozed off.

Chapter Eight

They were good, those days with Rumbo. The first morning had been enlightening and the days that followed were an education. We spent a large part of the time foraging for food, visiting the huge market most mornings (it slowly dawned on me that this was Nine Elms, the fruit and veg. market which had been yanked cruelly from the Covent Garden area to an obscure South Thames position, so I knew I was in South London, somewhere around Vauxhall) and then visiting the shops to see what we could steal. I soon learned to be as swift and cunning as Rumbo, but I never became as audacious. He would disappear into an open doorway of a house and seconds later calmly stroll out with a packet of biscuits, or a loaf, or anything he could lay his jaws on (he once emerged with a leg of lamb between his teeth but he didn't get away with that; a coloured lady came flying out and frightened old Rumbo so much with her shrieking he dropped the meat and bolted, a thrown milk bottle shattering on the pavement behind him).

Once we came across one of those pastry vans unloading its morning delivery. It was filled with trays of sweet-smelling buns and cakes, not to mention freshly baked bread. Rumbo waited until the driver had taken a large tray of pastries into the baker's then leapt into the open interior of the van. I held back, of course, coward that I am, and watched enviously as Rumbo jumped from the van with a lovely sugared bun glued to his mouth. He crouched beneath the vehicle wolfing his booty as the driver returned for another tray. When he went back into the shop, freshly laden, Rumbo was up inside the van again, gulping down the remains of the first bun while snatching a chocolate èclair from another tray. He did this three times, each time hiding beneath the van before the driver returned, swallowing as fast as he could, when the dope (me) decided to chance his arm. I waited

215

until the man was well inside the shop, scrambled up into the van (no easy task for a pup) and fussily sniffed my way along the delicious racks of confectionery. Rumbo was in and out like a shot, needless to say, but me – I had to be choosy. I had just decided upon a large, succulent-looking lemon meringue tart, torn between it and the chocolate éclair oozing cream lying beside it, when a shadow fell across the open doorway.

I yelped in fright and the man yelped in surprise. His surprise turned to menace and my fright turned to more fright. I tried to explain I was starving, that I hadn't eaten for a week, but he wasn't having any of it. He lurched forward and grabbed for my collar; I backed further into the van. The man cursed and hauled himself inside, crouching so he wouldn't hit his head on the low roof. He advanced on me and I retreated as far as I could go, which wasn't far enough. It's an unpleasant feeling when you know you're going to be hurt and, I must admit, I indulged in pity for myself to the full. Why had I allowed myself to be led on by that thief Rumbo, that crook in dog's clothing? Why had I let myself be bullied into this low life of petty thieving by this sneaky mongrel?

And then there he was, good old Rumbo, on the tail-end of the van, snarling at the delivery man's back, shouting defiantly at him. He was magnificent! The man turned in alarm, bumped his head on the roof, lost his balance and fell backwards on to the trays with their squashy contents. He slipped almost to the floor of the van, only the confined space saving him, and his elbows sunk into the creamy goodies behind him.

I dodged over his sprawled legs and leapt from the van, running even as I landed. Rumbo took his time and helped himself to one more delicacy before he jumped down after me. When we stopped, about a hundred miles later, he was smacking his lips contentedly. I panted my thanks to him and he grinned in his superior way. 'Sometimes, squirt, you're as dumb as the other mutts – maybe dumber. Still, I suppose it takes time to teach a new dog old tricks.' For some reason, he thought that was very funny and repeated it to himself over and over for the rest of that day.

Another trick of Rumbo's, using me as bait, was his diversion tactic. I would gallop up to an unsuspecting, shopping-bag-laden housewife and use all my puppy charms to make her lower her burden to the ground and pet me, maybe even offer me a titbit. If

216

she had children with her it was even easier, for she would be forced into making a fuss of me with them, or at least drag them away. When all her attention was on me – I'd be licking her face or rolling on the ground, offering my tummy to be rubbed – Rumbo would rummage through her unguarded shopping. When he found something tasty he would streak off, leaving me to make my excuses and follow at a more leisurely pace. We often got found out before he'd grabbed anything useful, but that didn't spoil the enjoyment of the game.

Taking sweets from babies was another delightful pastime. Mothers would howl and their offsprings would bawl as we scooted off with our prizes. Sudden raids on kids around ice-cream vans were always rewarding, the van's jangling jingle acting as a homing beacon for us. The coming of winter forced us to cut down on this kind of activity unfortunately, for the parks were empty and the ice-cream vans in hibernation.

Rumbo loved to taunt other dogs. He looked down on all other animals as inferiors, resenting their stupidity, especially dogs, most of whom he considered more feeble-minded than any other living creature. I don't know why he held such a prejudice against dogs; it may have been because he was ashamed of them, ashamed they didn't have his intelligence, his dignity. Oh yes, rogue that he was, Rumbo had lots of dignity. Rumbo never begged, for instance; he asked for food, or he stole it, but he never grovelled for it. Sometimes he might act out a parody of a dog begging for food or affection, but this was always for his own cynical amusement. He taught me that life took advantage of the living, and to exist – really to *exist* – you had to take advantage of life. In his opinion, dogs had let themselves become slaves to man. *He* wasn't owned by the Guvnor, he did a job of work for him by guarding the yard, thereby earning his keep, such as it was. The Guvnor understood this and their relationship was based on mutual respect. I wasn't sure the Guvnor had such finer feelings, but I kept my opinion to myself, for I was only a pupil – Rumbo was the master.

Anyway, my companion never lost a chance of telling another dog how stupid he was. Poodles were his greatest source of derision and he would laugh uncontrollably at their clipped curls. The poor old dachshund came in for a bellyful too. Rumbo didn't care whom he picked on, be it an Alsatian or a Chihuahua. However, I did once witness him go very quiet and reflective when a Dobermann passed us by.

217

He got himself, and often me, into some fine old scrapes, other dogs sensing our difference and ganging up on us. I suffered as a pup, but it certainly toughened me up. I learned to run a lot faster too. The funny thing was, Rumbo could have been leader of the pack easily, for he was strong as well as smart, a good combination for the dog world; but he was essentially a loner, he went where he wanted to go, unhampered by thoughts of others. I'm still not sure why he took up with me; I can only suppose he recognised our mutual freakishness.

He was a Romeo, too. He loved the ladies, did Rumbo, and there again, size and breed meant nothing to him. He would disappear for days, returning with a tired but smug grin on his face. When I asked where he'd been, he always said he'd tell me when I was old enough to know.

I always knew when he would be off, for a strangely exciting smell would suddenly fill the air and Rumbo would stiffen, sniff, and bolt out of the yard – with me vainly trying to follow. It would be a bitch in heat of course, somewhere in the neighbourhood, possibly a couple of miles away, but I was too young to know about such things. So I'd wait patiently for his return, moping around until he did, angry at being left behind. Still, Rumbo was always pretty easy to live with for the next few days.

Another great pastime of his was rat-catching. God, how he hated rats, that Rumbo! There were never many in the yard, he made sure of that, but occasionally the odd two or three would make a reconnoitre, looking for a fresh supply of food, I suppose, or perhaps a new breeding ground. Rumbo would always know when they were about, he had a sixth sense for it. His hairs would bristle and his lips curl back revealing yellow fan-like teeth, and he'd snarl a deep menacing animal snarl. It would frighten the life out of me. Then he'd creep forward, taking his time, and he'd mooch through the old junks, oblivious of me, a hunter stalking his prey, a killer closing in on his kill. At first, I'd stay in the background, the vile creatures terrifying me with their evil looks and their foul language, but eventually Rumbo's hate passed on to me, turning my fear into revulsion then detestation. Detestation led to anger, and anger overcame my nervousness. So we'd rout the rats together.

Mind you, they were brave, some of those rats, loathsome as they were. The sight of nice juicy puppy flesh may have had something to do with their fearlessness, and in those early days my life was often in jeopardy, and it's thanks to Rumbo that I'm still in one piece today. (Of course, he soon realised what wonderful rat-bait he possessed, and it wasn't long before he'd coaxed me into acting as such.) As the months went on, my meat became more stringy – thin I think you'd call me, despite our scavenging – and my legs longer, my jaws and teeth stronger. The rats no longer regarded me as dinner but as diner and treated me with much more respect.

We never really ate them. We'd tear them to pieces, we'd break their bones – but their flesh just wasn't to our taste, no matter how hungry we felt at the time.

Rumbo loved to taunt them when he had them cornered. They'd hiss and curse at him, threaten him, bare their cruel teeth, but he would only sneer, taunt them all the more. He would advance slowly, his eyes never leaving theirs, and the rats would back away, bunch up their hindquarters, their bodies tensed for the leap forward. They'd make their move and Rumbo would make his. Dog and rat would meet in mid-air and the ensuing fight would be almost too frenzied to follow with the eye. The outcome was always inevitable: a high-pitched squeal, a stiff-haired body flying through the air, and Rumbo pouncing triumphantly on his broken-necked opponent as it landed in a nerve-twitching heap. Meanwhile, I was left to deal with any of the unfortunate vermin's companions, and this I learned to do almost as ably – but never with quite as much relish – as Rumbo.

We almost came unstuck one day, however.

It was winter, and the mud in the yard was frost-hard. The yard itself was locked and deserted – it must have been a Sunday – and Rumbo and I were warm and snug on the back seat of a wrecked Morris 1100 which was acting as a sort of temporary bedsitter until more suitable accommodation came along (our previous lodgings, a spacious Zephyr, having been broken up completely and sold as scrap). Rumbo's head shot up first and mine was a close second; we'd heard a noise and that familiar rank smell was in the air. We crept silently from the battered car and followed our noses towards the odour's source, in among the jumble of wrecks, through the narrow alleyways of twisted metal, the rat scent drawing us on, the occasional scratching against metal making our ears twitch. We soon came upon them.

Or rather, he came upon us.

We had stopped before a turn in the path through the cars, aware that our prey lay just around the corner, the strong smell and the scratching noises our informant, and were tensing up for the rush when, suddenly he appeared before us.

He was the biggest rat I'd ever seen, more than half my size (and I'd grown considerably), his hair was brown and his incisors were long and wicked-looking. The creature was just as startled as us by the sudden confrontation and disappeared instantly, leaving us to blink our eyes in surprise. We rushed round the corner, but he was gone.

'Looking for me?' came a voice from somewhere high up. We looked around us in bewilderment then spotted the rat together. He was perched on the roof of a car and looking down at us contemptuously.

'Up here, you mangy-looking curs. Coming up to get me?' he said.

Now rats aren't generally given much to conversation, most of them just spit and swear or scowl a lot, but this was the talkingest rat I'd ever come across.

'I've heard about you two,' he went on. 'You've caused us a lot of problems. At least, so the ones who've managed to get away tell me.' (You can't catch 'em all.) 'I've been wanting to meet you both – especially you, the big one. Think you're a match for me?'

I had to admire Rumbo's nerve, for I was set to run and hide. The rat may have been smaller than me, but those teeth and claws looked as though they could do a lot of damage to tender dog-meat. However, Rumbo spoke up, not a trace of nervousness in his voice: 'Are you going to come down, mouth, or do I have to come up and get you?'

The rat actually laughed – rats don't laugh much – and settled himself into a more comfortable position. 'I'll come down, cur, but in my own time; first I want to talk.' (*Certainly* no ordinary rat this.) 'What exactly have you got against us rats, friend? I know we're loved neither by man nor animals, but you have a special dislike, haven't you? Is it because we're scavengers? But then aren't you worse? Aren't all captured animals the lowest scavengers because they live off man – as parasites? Of course, you can't even dignify your existence with the word "captured" because most of you choose that way of life, don't you? Do *you* hate us because we're free, not domesticated, not . . .' he

220

paused, grinning slyly,' . . . neutered as you are?'

Rumbo bridled at this last remark. 'I'm not neutered, rat-face, they'll never do that to me!'

'It doesn't have to be a physical thing, you know,' the rat said smugly. 'It's your mind I'm talking about.'

'I've still got a mind of my own.'

'Have you, have you?' The rat snorted. 'At least we vermin run free, no keepers for us.'

'Who the hell would want you?' Rumbo scoffed. 'You even turn on each other when things get rough.'

'That's called survival, dog. Survival.' The rat was displeased. He rose to his feet. '*You* hate us because you know we're all the same – man, animal, insect – all the same, and *you* know rats live an existence others try to hide. Isn't that so, dog?'

'No, it's not so, and *you* know that!'

There were a lot of 'you knows' flying around. Unfortunately, *I* didn't know what they were talking about.

Rumbo advanced towards the car, his coat bristling with rage. 'There's a reason for rats living the way they do, just as there's a reason for the way dogs live. And you know it!'

'Yes, and there's a reason for me to tear your throat out,' the rat spat at Rumbo.

'That'll be the day, ratface!'

They ranted at each other for another five minutes before their anger finally boiled over. And it boiled over in a strange way.

Both rat and dog went suddenly quiet as though there were nothing left to say. They glared into each other's eyes, Rumbo's brown and bulging, the rat's yellow and evil; both pairs were filled with hate. The tension between them mounted, a screaming silence, a building of venom. Then, with a squeal, the rat launched himself from the car roof.

Rumbo was ready. He leapt aside so that the vermin landed heavily on the hard earth, then struck out for the rat's neck. But the rat squirmed away and turned to meet Rumbo's charge. Teeth clashed against teeth, and claws dug into flesh.

I stood there, stunned and fearful, watching them try to tear each other to pieces. Growls, snarls and squeals came from the struggling bodies, but it was Rumbo's yelp that set me into action. I rushed forward, shouting at the top of my bark, trying to find the rage to give me the courage. There wasn't much I could do, for they were locked together in a writhing embrace, rolling over and over, flaying each other with their feet, biting, drawing blood, ripping skin. I could only lunge in whenever I caught sight of that stinking brown fur, nipping at it with bared teeth.

Quite suddenly, they drew apart, panting, beaten, but still glaring into each other's eyes. I saw that Rumbo's shoulder was badly torn and one of the rat's ears was shredded. They crouched, bodies quivering, low growling sounds at the backs of their throats. I thought perhaps they were too exhausted to carry on, but then I realised they were only regathering their strength.

They sprang at each other again and this time I sprang with them. Rumbo caught the rat by the throat and I managed to bite into one of his front legs. The taste of warm blood sickened me, but I clung to the creature with all my strength. He rolled and squirmed and snapped at us; I felt a sharp pain across my shoulders as he scythed across them with his teeth. The shock made me lose my grip of his leg and, twisting his body, the rat kicked out at me with his hind legs, sending me rolling across the frozen mud.

I rushed straight in and received a deep gash across my nose from the rodent's claws. The pain sent me back again, but I returned just as quickly. Rumbo still had the rat by the throat, endeavouring to lift him from the ground and toss him, a trick I'd seen him use to break other vermin's backs. The rat was too big, though – too heavy. At least the grip Rumbo held prevented the rat doing serious damage with those teeth; he'd cut my shoulders but could have seriously wounded me had his incisors been allowed to sink in. Such was his strength that the big rat managed to break away. He ran free, turned, and streaked back into us, twisting his head from left to right, striking at our vulnerable bodies with his vicious weapons. Rumbo cried out as he was gored along the flank. He staggered to one side and the rat, with a shout of triumph, flew at him. But in his excitement, he'd forgotten about me.

I leapt on to the rat's back, bringing him down with my weight, and biting into the top of his head, breaking a tooth against his skull. The rest was messy and unglorious: Rumbo leapt back into the fray, and between us we managed to kill the creature. The rat didn't die easily, and even to this day I have a grudging admiration for the fight he put up against two heavier opponents. When his squirming finally stopped and the last gasp left his bloody body, I felt not just exhausted but degraded too. He had had just as much right to live as we had, despicable though he was in the eyes of others, and his courage could not be denied. I think Rumbo felt the same sense of shame even though he said nothing.

He dragged the dead body out of sight beneath a car (I don't know why – a sort of burial, I suppose) and returned to lick my wounds for me.

'You did well, pup,' he said wearily between licks. His voice had a quietness to it that was unusual for him. 'He was a big brute. Different from most I've met.'

I whimpered as his tongue flicked across the gash in my nose. 'What did he mean, Rumbo, when he said we're all the same?'

'He was wrong. We're not.'

And that was all my friend had to say on the subject.

The rat incident soured me for the killing of others of the species; I'd fight them certainly, chastise them, but from then on I let them escape. Rumbo soon became aware of my reluctance to kill and grew angry with me; he still hated the creatures and slew them whenever we came in contact with them, perhaps with less relish than before, but with a cold determination.

I've no wish to dwell on our dealings with vermin, for it was an unpleasant and ugly part of my dog life, albeit a very small part; but one other incident has to be mentioned because it shows just how deep Rumbo's hate went for these unfortunate and unblessed creatures.

We came across a nest of them. It was at the far end of the yard and in a car which lay at the very bottom of a tumble of others. The vehicle's roof was crushed flat, there were no doors, and nestled among the stuffing of a torn back seat were a dozen tiny pink rats suckling from their recumbent mother. Their little bodies were still glistening and slick from their birth. The scent drew us like a magnet and we wriggled our way through the twisted junk to reach them. When I saw the babies and the alarmed parent, I prepared to retreat, to leave them in peace. But not Rumbo. He tore into them with a fury I'd never seen before.

I called out to him, pleaded with him, but he was oblivious to my cries. I ran from the place, not wanting to witness such slaughter, and flew from the yard, away from that terrible destruction.

We didn't speak for days after that; I was bewildered by Rumbo's savagery and he was puzzled by my attitude. It has, in fact, taken me a long time to come to terms with the brutality of animal life, and of course it was my very 'humanness' which hindered my progress (or regress – however you care to look at it) towards this acceptance. I think Rumbo put my sulkiness down to growing pains, for growing I certainly was. My puppy fat had almost disappeared entirely, my legs were long and strong (although my back legs were a little cow-hocked). My toenails had been kept trimmed by the constant running on hard concrete and my teeth were firm and sharp. My vision was still excellent, still vivid, unusually lucid. (Rumbo had the normal dog's eyesight: not quite as good as man's and unable to distinguish colours too well. He could see all right in the dark, though, perhaps better than me.) My appetite was extremely healthy and I had no trouble with worms, tartar on the teeth, mange, constipation, diarrhoea, irritable bladder, eczema, ear-canker, nor any other normal dog ailments. Nevertheless I did itch a lot and it was this irritation that brought Rumbo and me together again.

I had observed him scratching with more and more frequency and, I had to admit, it had become almost a full-time occupation for me, this sucking of fur and raking of skin with hind legs. When I actually saw the little yellow monsters hopping freely over my companion's back like grasshoppers on a heath, my disgust for our condition forced me to make a comment.

'Doesn't the Guvnor ever bath us, Rumbo?'

Rumbo stopped his scratching and eyed me with surprise. 'Fleas annoying you, are they, squirt?'

'Annoying me? I feel like a walking hostel for parasites.'

Rumbo grinned. 'Well you won't like the Guvnor's method of dealing with it.'

I inquired what the method was.

'Whenever he gets fed up with my scratching or can't stand the smell any more, he ties me with a drainpipe, then turns a hose on me. I try to keep out of his way when I'm particularly rancid.'

I shivered at the thought. It was mid-winter.

'There's another way,' Rumbo went on. 'It's just as cold, but at least it's more effective.'

'Anything. Anything's better than this itching.'

'Well,' he hesitated, 'I usually reserve this for warmer times, but if you insist . . .'

I took up my usual position on his left, my head level with his flank, and we trotted out of the yard. He took me to a park, a big one this, and quite a distance from our home. The park contained a pond. And when we reached it, Rumbo told me to jump in.

'Are you kidding?' I said. 'We'll freeze to death. Besides, I don't even know if I can swim.'

'Don't be daft,' Rumbo retorted. 'All dogs can swim. As for the cold, you'll find this less unpleasant than being hosed down by the Guvnor. Come on, give it a try.'

With that he plunged into the water, much to the delight of the few children and their parents who were about that wintry morning. Rumbo paddled out to the middle of the pond, swift and confident. He even ducked his head beneath the surface, something I'd never seen a dog do before. I could just imagine the panic among those fleas as they fled to the top of his head, the last refuge on a sinking island, and then their dismay as even this sunk below the waters. He swam in an arc and headed back towards me, calling out for me to join in. But I was too much of a coward.

He reached the bank and hauled himself out. Mothers dragged their offspring away, for they knew what was going to happen next. The dope (yes, me) didn't.

I was drenched with a freezing shower of water as my friend (my crafty friend) shook his whole body to rid his fur of excess moisture. I felt foolish as well as angry; I'd seen dogs do this often enough in my past life, so I shouldn't have been caught napping. Anyway, there I stood, dripping wet, as cold as if I'd plunged in myself.

'Come on, squirt, you're wet enough. You might as well go the whole way now,' Rumbo laughed.

I shivered and had to admit he was right. There was no point in not going in now. I crept towards the edge of the pond and gingerly dipped in a front paw. I pulled it out fast; the water was colder than freezing! I turned my head to tell Rumbo I'd changed my mind, I could put up with the itching for a few more months till the weather got warmer. I barely caught a glimpse of his big black body as he hurtled himself at me. With a yelp of surprise, I fell head-first into the pond, Rumbo tumbling in behind.

I came up spluttering, gasping for air, my mouth and throat, my nose, my ears, my eyes filled with choking water.

'Ooh!' I cried. 'Ooooh!' And over the sound of my splashing I could hear Rumbo laughing. I wanted to strike back at him, I wanted to drown him, but I was too busy trying to survive the cruel pond. My teeth were chattering and my breathing came in short, desperate gasps. Pretty soon – when I realised I could swim – the unpleasantness drowned instead of me and I began to enjoy this new experience. I kicked out with my back legs and paddled with my paws, just managing to keep my nose above the waterline. The effort prevented my limbs from going completely numb and I found I could use my tail as a sort of rudder.

'How d'you like, pup?' I heard Rumbo call out.

Looking about, I saw that he was back in the centre of the pond. I made towards him.

'It's g-good, Rumbo, b-but it's cold,' I replied, my anger forgotten.

'Huh! You wait till you get out!' He submerged again and came up smiling. 'Down you go, pup, put your head under or you'll never get rid of them!'

I remembered the point of the exercise and ducked my head beneath the surface. I came up coughing.

'Again, pup, again! Go right under or they'll never leave you!'

Down I went again, this time holding my breath and staying under for as long as possible. I don't know what the people on the bank thought, for it must have been a peculiar sight to see two mongrels acting like performing seals. We romped around in the water, splashing and barging into each other, thoroughly cleansing ourselves with our vigorous actions. Five minutes was enough, and by mutual consent we headed for the shore. We clambered out, deliberately drenched the human onlookers, and began a game of chase to warm ourselves up.

By the time we got home we were both laughing and giggling, feeling fresh and alive as never before – and, of course, ravenous. We found a well-wrapped packet of sandwiches that one of the Guvnor's workmen had foolishly left lying on a bench while he dismantled a broken engine, and we took them to our snug bedsitter, scoffing the lot within seconds. For once, to my surprise, we shared the food equally, Rumbo making no attempt to gobble the major portion. He grinned at me as I finished the last few crumbs and, after smacking my lips contentedly, I grinned back at him. Our differences were forgotten and Rumbo and I were friends again. There was a subtle change, however: I wasn't exactly equal to Rumbo now, but I was a little less inferior than I had been.

The pupil was beginning to catch up with the master.

Chapter Nine

So what of my feelings of being a man in a dog's body?

Well, they certainly never left me, but they didn't often play an important part in my thinking. You see, I was developing as a *dog*, and this development took up most of my time. I was always conscious of my heritage and my human instincts often took over from my canine tendencies, but my physical capabilities were those of a dog (apart from my extraordinary vision) and this governed my attitude. There were many times – nights mostly – when memories fought their way to the surface and questions, questions, questions, tussled with my mind; and there were many times when I was completely and wholly a dog, with no other thoughts but dog thoughts.

I recognised my similarity to Rumbo and I'm sure he recognised it too. The disturbing fact was that I also recognised it in the big rat. Had Rumbo? He was deliberately vague when I tackled him on our difference to others of our kind, and I was never quite sure whether he understood it or if it was just as big a mystery to him. He would shrug his shoulders and dismiss the subject with a remark such as 'Some animals are dumber than others, that's all.' But I would often find him regarding me with a thoughtful look in his eyes.

So I lived my life with Rumbo and the urge to discover the truth of my existence was held in abeyance while I learned to live that life.

Like all dogs, I was fanatically curious; nothing near me went unsniffed, nothing loose went untugged, and nothing pliable went unchewed. Rumbo would lose patience, scold me for behaving like any other stupid mutt (although he liked a good sniff and chew himself) and would generally berate me for my inquisitiveness. We had many afternoons or evenings when he did answer my questions (he had to be in a relaxed and talkative mood to do so), but when he thought too long or too deeply he would become confused and irritable. I often seemed to be about to learn something of significance – perhaps a clue to my own strange existence or a reason for our obviously more advanced development to others of our kind – when his eyes would become blank and he'd go into a long, trance-like silence. It would frighten me, for I would think I'd pushed him too far, his searching mind becoming lost within itself, unable to find the route back. On such occasions I was afraid he'd become just another dog. Then he would blink a few times, look around curiously as though surprised at his surroundings, and carry on talking, ignoring the question I'd asked. These were strange and apprehensive moments for me, so I refrained from triggering them off too frequently.

Other apprehensive moments were when we saw ghosts. It didn't happen often enough for it to become a common occurrence, but enough to be disconcerting. They would drift sadly by, a feeling more than an expression of utter loneliness about them, and some seemed to be in a state of shock, as if they had been torn brutally from their earthly bodies. Rumbo and I would freeze at the sight, but we'd never bark as other dogs might. My companion would warn them to keep away from us with a low growling, but we were of no interest to these spirits and they would drift on without even acknowledging our presence. On one occasion – it was in broad daylight – four or five ghosts, bunched tightly together, wandered through the yard like a small, drifting cloud. Rumbo had no explanation for the phenomenon and forgot about it as soon as it had passed, but it puzzled me for a long time afterwards.

The comings and goings of more mortal beings into the yard began to increase. There were normally two or three full-time overalled men working in the yard, breaking up the junks, and a steady stream of customers looking for cheap parts. Gigantic lorries (gigantic to me) would be loaded with crushed car bodies by the yard's crane, then disappear through the gates with their valuable metal. Vehicles battered beyond repair or too old and tired to run anymore were brought in and dumped unceremoniously on top of precariously balanced scrap piles. But it was a different increase in activity that aroused my curiosity.

The Guvnor began to have frequent visitors who had no

228

interest in the yard itself, but would disappear into his office and remain there for hours on end. They arrived in twos and threes and left in the same numbers. They came from different areas, mostly from Wandsworth and Kennington, but others from Stepney, Tooting, Clapham, with a few from nearby outlying counties. I knew this because I'd listened to their conversations as they waited outside the hut for the Guvnor's arrival (he was often late). One or two would even play with me, or torment me in a friendly way. Rumbo frowned upon my childishness with these men, for they never offered food nor were they relevant to our life-style (Rumbo was choosy about offering his friendship), but I, like any other pup, wanted to be loved by everyone and anyone. I didn't know what their business with the Guvnor was (I noticed they treated him with a lot of respect), nor did I care much; I was just curious because they were outsiders and I could learn more about the other places from them – not just the surrounding area, for I knew enough about that – but other parts further away. I was looking for clues, you see, clues about myself. I felt the more I discovered – or rediscovered – about the world outside, the more chance I had of solving my own riddle.

It was on one such occasion, in fact, that I earned my permanent name. Some of the workmen in the yard had taken to calling me Horace (God knows why, but it seemed to tickle them), and it was a name I detested. They used it in a mocking way and usually – unless they were offering something (which was rare) – I ignored their calls with a nose-up dignity. Even Rumbo, in moments of sarcasm, would call me Horace rather than 'squirt'. In the end, even I was beginning to get used to it.

However, the Guvnor had never bothered to give me a name – I was never important enough to him for that – and he really didn't have much cause to refer to me anyway after our initial meeting months before. I was grateful, at least, that he hadn't picked up this awful nickname from his workmen.

So this is how I got a proper and appropriate name.

A small group of the outsiders had gathered in front of the Guvnor's office – hut – and were awaiting his arrival. Rumbo was away on one of his 'bitch-in-season' jaunts and I was wandering aimlessly around the yard, sulking at being left behind again. I trotted over to the group to see if I could overhear anything of interest (or perhaps to beg for some affection). One of the younger men saw me coming and crouched low, a hand

229

outstretched, to welcome me. 'Ere, boy. Come on.'

I bounced towards him, pleased to be called. 'What's your name, then, eh?'

I didn't want to tell him I was called Horace so I kept quiet and licked his hand.

'Let's 'ave a look at you,' he said, pulling my collar round with his other hand. 'No name on this, is there? Let's see what we've got for you.' He stood up, reaching into his overcoat pocket and my tail began to wag when he produced a small green tube of sweets. He levered a sweet out and held it up for me to see. I went up on my hind legs immediately, mouth gaping for the treat to be dropped into. The man laughed and let the little round sweet fall and I caught it deftly on my tongue, crunching and gulping it down by the time my front legs touched ground again. I jumped up and put my muddy paws against him, asking politely for another; they had a nice minty flavour to them. He was a bit annoyed at the mud on his coat and pushed me down again, brushing at the marks left with his hand. 'Oh no, if you want another one, you've got to earn it. 'Eeyar', catch it.' He threw the mint high into the air and I jumped up to meet it on its downward journey, catching it smartly. The young man laughed and his bored companions began to take an interest. They had been lounging against the car they'd arrived in, a maroon Granada, stamping their feet to keep the circulation flowing, their coat collars turned up against the cold.

'Let's see 'im do it again, Lenny,' one of them said.

The one called Lenny tossed another sweet and again I caught it in mid-air.

'Do it a bit 'igher next time.'

Lenny tossed and I jumped. Success once more.

'You're a clever old thing, aren't you?' said Lenny.

I had to agree; I was feeling quite pleased with myself. As Lenny poised a mint on his thumb and index finger I prepared to repeat my performance.

''Old on, Lenny.' A different man spoke this time. 'Make it do somethin' more difficult.'

'Like what?'

The group of men thought hard for a few moments, then one spotted a couple of tin mugs standing on the hut's windowsill. 'Use them,' he said, pointing towards the mugs. 'The old ball-an'-cones trick.'

'Do leave off! It's only a bleedin' dog, you know,' Lenny protested.

'Gorn, see if it can do it.'

He shrugged and walked over to the mugs. The regular yard workers used these for their tea-breaks, but I don't think they would have offered any objection to these men using them for other purposes. In fact, I had noticed that the Guvnor's regular employees kept well away from the business acquaintances of their boss. Lenny placed the two mugs upside-down on an even piece of ground while I nuzzled him for more sweets. He pushed me away and one of the men took hold of my collar to hold me back.

Lenny levered out a little round mint again and, in exaggerated motions, showed it to me, then placed it under one of the mugs. I pulled against the restraining hand, eager to get at the sweet.

Then Lenny did a puzzling thing: he placed a hand on either mug and whirled them in circles around each other, never letting their lips come off the ground. He did it slowly, but even so it was confusing for a mere dog. He stopped and nodded for the other man to let go. I bounded forward and immediately knocked over the mug which held the strong scent of mint.

I couldn't understand the group's cries of amazement and Lenny's delight as I gulped down the sweet. I accepted Lenny's friendly thumps on the back with a wagging tail, pleased that I had pleased him.

'Aah, it was a fluke. The dog couldn't do it again,' one of the men said. He was grinning though.

'Oh yes it could. It's a clever old thing, this pup,' Lenny retorted.

'Let's 'ave some money on it, then.'

The others agreed enthusiastically. It's funny what a group of bored men will find to amuse themselves.

Once again I was held back while Lenny went through his hand-holding-mint ballet. 'All right. A oncer says 'e does it again.' I was no longer an 'it' to Lenny.

'Right.'

'You're on.'

'Suits.'

And suddenly four pound notes appeared on the ground. The four men looked at me expectantly.

Lenny went through his mug swirling again and one of the men told him to speed it up. He did, and I must admit he had a definite flair for this sort of thing: the movements were baffling to the naked eye. But not to the sensitive nose. I had knocked over the mug and swallowed the sweet within three seconds of being released.

'Fantastic! 'E's a bloody marvel.' Lenny was delighted as he scooped up the four pounds.

'I still say it was a fluke,' a disgruntled voice muttered.

'Put your money where your mouth is, Ronald, my son.'

The bets were placed again, this time one of the men dropped out. 'He's sniffin' it out, I reckon,' he grumbled. This stopped the action; they hadn't thought of that.

'Nah,' Lenny said after a few moments' thought. ''E couldn't smell it with the mug over the top.'

'I dunno, it's pretty strong – peppermint.'

'O.K., O.K. Let's see what else we've got.'

The men rummaged through their pockets but came out with their hands empty. 'Just a minute,' one of them said and turned towards the Granada. He opened the driver's door, reached across the front seat and delved into the glove compartment. He came out with a half-eaten bar of chocolate. 'Keep it in there for the kids.' he said self-consciously. 'Keep the wrapper on so it don't smell so much.' He handed it to Lenny.

My mouth watered at the sight and I had to be firmly held back.

'Fair enough. Let's do it again.' Lenny made sure the wrapping covered all the exposed end of the chocolate and placed it carefully beneath a mug. The mug had a nasty-looking grease smear on its base.

The fourth man rejoined the betting and, once more, Lenny's lightning hands went into action. Of course I made straight for the grease-smeared mug.

The chocolate was pulled from my mouth before it could be devoured, but Lenny was more generous with his praise. 'I could make a fortune with this dog,' he told the others, breaking off a tiny square of chocolate and popping it into my mouth. ''E's got brains, 'e's not as daft as 'e looks.' I bridled at this but the thought of more chocolate kept me sweet. ''Ow'd you like to come back to Edenbridge with me, eh? Connie and the kids'll love you. I could make a bomb out of some of the locals with you.'

232

'That's the Guv's dog, 'e won't let you 'ave it,' the one called Ronald said.

''E might. 'E's got two.'

'Anyway, I still say it was only luck. No dog's that clever.'

Lenny raised his eyes heavenwards. 'You wanna' see 'im do it again?'

Ronald was a bit more reluctant this time and the sound of a car pulling into the yard saved him from deciding whether to risk another pound or not. A sleek Jaguar stopped behind the Granada and the Guvnor stepped out; he changed his cars with more frequency than most people checked their tyres. He wore a heavy sheepskin coat and, of course, a fat cigar jutted comfortably from his mouth. The men greeted him with a friendliness born out of respect more than liking.

'What you lot up to?' He stuck his hands deep into his coat pockets as he swaggered his way round the Jag to the group.

'Just 'avin' a game with the dog 'ere, Guv,' said Lenny.

'Yeah, it's a clever little bugger,' said one of the others.

Lenny seemed hesitant to tell the Guvnor just how clever he thought I was; plans for me were beginning to grow in his mind, I think.

'Nah, it could never do it again, never in a thousand years,' Ronald piped up.

'Do what, Ron?' the Guvnor asked affably.

'Lenny's done 'is ball-and-cones trick and the dog's guessed right every time,' another of the men said.

'Do me a favour!' the Guvnor scoffed.

'Nah, straight,' Lenny said, the thought of making some more instant cash overriding his future money-making plans.

'It must 'ave been a fluke. Dog's ain't that bright.'

'That's what I said, Guv,' Ronald chimed in.

'Yeah, and you lost your money, didn't you, my son,' Lenny grinned.

'Ow much you made so far, Lenny?'

''Er, let's see, Guv. Eight pounds in all.'

'All right. Eight more says it don't do it again.' He had style, the Guvnor.

Lenny hesitated for only a second. He chuckled and went down to the mugs again. 'Now then, boy, I'm relyin' on you. Don't let me down.' He looked at me meaningfully. For myself, I was enjoying the game; I liked pleasing this man, I liked him

233

knowing I was no ordinary dog. I wasn't really grovelling for titbits. I was earning them.

Lenny shuffled the cups, even faster than before under the Guvnor's level gaze, but this time he'd placed the chocolate beneath the mug without the grease smear. He finished his intricate hand movements and looked up at the Guvnor. 'O.K.?' he asked.

The Guvnor nodded and Lenny looked across at me. 'O.K., boy, do your stuff.'

And at that moment Rumbo trotted into the yard.

Curiosity drew him over to the group, and when he saw me being held by the collar and the twin mugs set on the ground before me, he screwed up his brow in a puzzled frown. In an instant he had guessed a trick was being performed for the benefit of the men and I, his protégé, the mutt he had taken under his wing, the scruff in which he had tried to instil some dignity, was the star performer. Rising shame burnt my ears and I hung my head. I looked dolefully up at Rumbo, but he just stood there, his disgust apparent.

'Come on, boy,' Lenny urged. 'Get the chocolate. Come on!'

My tail drooped: I had let Rumbo down. He'd always taught me to be my own dog, never become a pet of man, never become inferior to them; and here I was, like some circus animal, performing tricks for their entertainment. I stepped towards the mugs, kicked the empty one over with a paw and trotted away in search of a dark hole in which to bury myself.

Lenny threw his hands up in the air in disgust and the Guvnor chuckled. Ronald, chortling loudly, stooped and picked up the Guvnor's winnings and handed them to him. As I disappeared round the corner of the hut, I heard the Guvnor say: 'I told you it was a fluke. Yeah – fluke. That's a good name for 'im. 'Ey, Georgie,' he called out to one of the yard workers. 'Get the pup's collar and put its name on it. Fluke! Yeah, that's good!' He was pleased with himself: the money meant nothing, but the scene had made him look good. He was making the most of it. I could still hear him chuckling as he unlocked the office door and the group of men disappeared through it.

So, I had a proper name. And like I say, it was appropriate: Fluke by name, fluke by nature.

Chapter Ten

Rumbo never mentioned that incident again. He was a little distant with me for a few days afterwards, but my final action had at least saved me some grace and, because of our need for each other (which Rumbo himself would never have admitted), we were soon back to our old relationship.

Lenny had lost interest in me, his plans for making money out of me dashed by my contrariness. Apart from a rueful grin now and again, he really didn't take much notice of me anymore when he came into the yard. The breaker called Georgie took my collar from me and returned it later. Rumbo told me there were scratch marks on the small metal nameplate and I assumed '*FLUKE*' had been inscribed there. Anyway, that was what they called me in the yard now, and so did the people who petted me in the street once they'd looked at the collar. I was thankful I was no longer known as Horace.

The winter froze on and times for Rumbo and me got leaner. We still made our daily trips to the fruit-market, but our pickings in the shopping-zones had become increasingly more hazardous. The shopkeepers now knew us by sight and would chase us away as soon as we came sniffing around: the cold weather made the housewives more guarded, less friendly. I was fast losing my puppy cuteness (I suppose I was around seven or eight months old by then), and people are less inclined to stop and stroke a gangly mongrel than a plump, furry bundle, so I had become next to useless as a decoy for Rumbo. However, the hardship made us more cunning, swifter in our attacks, and more resourceful in our methods.

A wild dash through a supermarket usually proved fruitful, provided there was a clear exit. One of us would knock stacks of cans over or generally cause a disturbance while the other would sneak in and grab the nearest edible item at hand. That was always very exciting. A romp around a school playground at lunchtime would inevitably yield a sandwich or two, or perhaps an apple or some chocolate. The pandemonium was lovely. A visit to the local street-market never failed to bring us replenishment for our greedy stomachs. The threats and curses our thieving from there caused was, nevertheless, a little alarming. Moreover, we had become too adventurous, and that led to our downfall.

One day Rumbo and I had marched boldly into a backyard, encouraged by our noses which had been enticed by delicious cooking smells. An open doorway stood before us and steam billowed out from within; we were at the back of a restaurant, at the kitchen entry. Both of us were over-confident to the point of recklessness; we had been getting away with it for too long. We ambled in.

It was a high-class restaurant, although you might never have suspected it from the state of the kitchen. I knew it was a good place because of the menu, part of which I could see steaming away on a centre table: roast duckling drippping with orange sauce. It was surrounded by other dishes, but not as mouth-watering, waiting to be carried away into the dining-room (or carried away by two hungry dogs). Apart from the chef, who had his stout back turned to us while he was busy stirring a huge cauldron of simmering soup, the kitchen was empty. Rumbo gave me a quick look, then with one bound was up on the table. I rested my front paws against the table's edge and smiled smugly. Our bellies would be full today.

Rumbo nonchalantly worked his way through the various dishes (if he had been a man, he'd have been humming) until finally he reached the duckling. He flicked out his tongue and began licking at the orange sauce. He looked back at me and I swear he rolled his eyes. My mouth was drooling by now and I was hopping from one hind foot to the other in frustration. Rumbo had a few more licks, then his jaws opened wide to grasp the entire roasted bird between them. It was at that moment the door leading to the dining-room burst open.

We stood paralysed as a waiter in a white jacket and small black bow-tie, carrying a tray full of half-empty dishes, breezed in, calling out a new order to the chef before he was even through the door. The waiter was fairly small for a man (all tall to me, you see) and wore his jet-black hair greasily slicked down. Above his

236

greasily slicked down moustache was a long, curving nose and, above that, two over-large, bulbous eyes which grew even larger and more bulbous when he saw us. His mouth dropped open to a point where it almost matched Rumbo's and the dishes on his tray slid down the incline he had unconsciously created, slipping over the edge in an avalanche. The terrible crash as they hit the tiled floor set the whole scene in motion again.

The chef whirled, clutching at his heart, the waiter screamed, (I think he was Italian), Rumbo grabbed the duckling, and I (what else?), wet myself.

Rumbo leapt from the table, slid on a slippery patch on the floor, lost the duckling, scrambled to retrieve it, yelped as the hot soup-ladle thrown by the chef skimmed across his back, grabbed the duckling again by the parson's nose end, and scurried for the exit.

The waiter threw the now empty tray at Rumbo, choked back a sob, gave chase, skidded on the same slippery patch, sprawled on his back, and managed to get his legs tangled up in dog and duckling.

The chef moved his hand from his heart to his mouth, roared with furious anguish, lumbered forward, slid on the tray which covered another slippery patch left by the skidding orange-sauce-covered duckling, landed heavily (he was very stout) on the little waiter's chest, and bellowed and kicked at dog, duckling, waiter and all.

I ran away.

Rumbo crept furtively into the yard about five minutes after I'd arrived there. He crawled through our own private entrance at the back of the yard behind a huge pile of wrecks – a one-foot high hole torn in the corrugated-iron fencing at its base – still grasping the now cold roast duckling between his jaws. The young bird looked a bit worse for wear: a *pièce de résistance* that hadn't resisted too well. Nevertheless, to two hungry mongrels it was still a gastronomic triumph, and after we'd sucked every bone clean (I warned Rumbo not to crunch the bones – too splintery, I told him) we had a good chortle over our success. The smirks were wiped from our faces a couple of days later, however.

A uniformed policeman arrived at the yard and asked one of the breakers if there were two black mongrel dogs on the

237

premises. Rumbo and I edged out of sight behind a decaying Ford Anglia and looked at each other nervously. It was obvious the shopkeepers had got together and registered a complaint to the local cop-shop; perhaps the restauranteur had instigated the action. It certainly hadn't taken the police long to track us down. We peeped from behind the old car and saw the breaker pointing nervously towards the Guvnor's office. The young policeman strolled casually over to the hut, examining the various cars parked alongside it. The Guvnor was having one of his now regular meetings with his cronies.

The plod knocked at the door and the Guvnor appeared. We watched his smiling face as he dealt with the policeman's inquiries, showing a disarming charm that had never been apparent to us before. His hands made gestures of surprise, alarm and concern; he nodded his head gravely, then shook it equally as gravely. Then he was back to smiling and smarming, his cigar never once leaving the corner of his mouth during the discourse. With one last smile of assurance from the Guvnor, the young policeman turned and strolled from the yard.

The Guvnor smiled benevolently at the policeman's back until he had disappeared through the gate: then he turned his gaze towards the rest of the yard, a look of sheer thunder on those now rock-like features. He spotted our snouts protruding from the wreck and marched towards us with stiff, determined strides.

'Run, squirt, run!' Rumbo warned me.

I wasn't quick enough. The Guvnor grabbed me before I had a chance to make a break for it. He began to flail at me with a closed fist, keeping a firm grip on my collar as he did so. I'd always felt the Guvnor had a contained cruelty about him (this didn't necessarily make him a cruel man) and now it was let loose and I was its recipient. I howled in pain, and was grateful that a dog's sensitive cells are unevenly distributed over the body otherwise some of these blows would have hurt even more.

Rumbo stood and watched from a distance, anxious for me and fearful for himself.

'Come 'ere, you!' the Guvnor bellowed, but Rumbo wasn't having any. He darted even further away. 'You wait 'till I get 'old of you,' my assailant shouted. Rumbo skipped from the yard.

The Guvnor's anger had been flushed now, but his meanness still remained. He dragged me to the back of the yard, collecting a length of rope on the way, then tied me to a wreck wedged beneath a pile of other wrecks.

'Right,' he snarled as he looped the rope around the empty window-frame of the car. 'Right!' He gave me one last wallop before he marched off, muttering something about the last thing he needed was the law snooping round. 'Right,' I heard him say as he slammed the hut door shut.

A few minutes later the door opened again and the Guvnor's cronies filed out, climbed into their various cars and drove off. After they'd gone the Guvnor appeared, roared for Rumbo and, when nothing happened went back inside. I had the feeling we wouldn't see old Rumbo for some time.

I tugged and pulled the rope, calling for the Guvnor to come back and let me loose; it was no use, he wouldn't listen. I was frightened to pull on the rope too hard because the cars towering above me looked precariously balanced; I could never figure out how the piles of cars in the yard never toppled. My calls turned into angry shouts, then piteous whining, then sorrowful whimpers and finally, much later on when the yard was deserted, sullen silence.

It was dark when my companion decided to return. I was shivering with the cold and miserable with the loneliness.

'I told you to run,' he said, coming out of the night.

I sniffed.

'He's got a terrible temper,' Rumbo went on, sniffing round me. 'Last time he tied me up, he left me for three days without any food.'

I looked at him reproachfully.

'Still, I can always bring you bits and pieces,' he added consolingly. Suddenly he looked up. 'Oh-oh. It's beginning to rain.'

A raindrop splattered against my nose.

'Not much cover here for you, is there?' he commented. 'Pity the car door's shut – you could've climbed in.'

I studied him quietly for a few moments, then looked away.

'Hungry?' he asked. 'I don't think I could find you anything this time of night.'

My head became dotted with rain-spots.

'Pity we ate that bird all in one go. We should have saved some of that.' He shook his head wistfully.

I peered under the car I was tied to and saw there wasn't enough room to squeeze beneath it. I was becoming wetter.

239

'Well, squirt,' Rumbo said with false jocularity, 'no sense in both of us getting wet. Think I'll get out of the rain.' He looked at me apologetically. I regarded him disdainfully, then turned my head away again.

''Er . . . I'll see you in the morning then,' he mumbled.

I watched him shuffle away. 'Rumbo,' I said.

He looked back at me, his eyebrows raised. 'Yes?'

'Do me a favour?'

'Yes?'

'Get neutered,' I said mildly.

'Good-night,' he replied, and trotted off to our nice warm bed.

The rain began to beat a rhythmic pattern on my body now and I curled up as small as I could, hunching my neck into my shoulders. It was going to be a long night.

Chapter Eleven

It was not only a long night but a disturbing one too. It wasn't just the discomfort of being drenched, for my fur held the moisture and formed a snug coating, keeping the worst of the chill away; but my sleep was nagged by memories.

Something had triggered the thoughts off and I didn't know what; it hid away somewhere in my mind's periphery. I saw a town – a village? I saw a house. Faces swam before me: I saw my wife, I saw my daughter. I was in a car; the human hands on the steering-wheel before me were my own. I drove through the town. I saw the angry face of a man I knew; he was also in a car and driving away from me. For some reason I followed it. It was dark. Trees, hedges, flashed by, flat and eerie in the head-lights. The car in front of me pulled in, turned into a narrow lane. I followed. It stopped; I stopped. The man I knew left his car and walked towards me. In the harsh glare from my head-lights I saw his hand was outstretched – he was holding something? I opened my door as the hand pointed towards me. Then everything became a crystal of brilliant, glittering light. And the light became dark; and I knew nothing more.

Rumbo dropped a half-eaten roll in front of me. I sniffed at it and pulled out the thin slices of ham squashed between its crusty covers with my teeth. I gulped the meat down, then licked the butter from the bread. Then I ate the bread.

'You were yelping in your sleep last night,' Rumbo told me.

I tried to remember my dreams and after a while the fragments became whole pieces.

'Rumbo, I haven't always been a dog,' I said.

Rumbo thought before he spoke, then he said, 'Don't be silly.'

'No, listen to me, Rumbo. Please. We're not the same, you and I, not like other dogs. You're aware of that. Don't you know why?'

241

Rumbo shrugged. 'We're just smarter.'

'It's more than that. We still have the feelings, the thoughts of *men*. It's not just that we're more clever than other dogs – we remember how we *were*!'

'I remember being a dog always.'

'Do you, Rumbo? Don't you ever remember walking upright. Don't you remember having hands, having fingers that you could use? Don't you remember speaking?'

'We're doing that now.'

'No, we're not – not in men's language anyway. We're thinking now, Rumbo, we're making sounds, but our words are more thoughts than those sounds. Don't you see that?'

He shrugged again and I could see the subject bothered him. 'What difference does it make? I understand you, you understand me.'

'Think, Rumbo! Use your brain! Try to remember how it was before.'

'What's the point?'

This stopped me for a moment. Then I said, 'Don't you want to know why? How?'

'No,' he replied.

'But Rumbo, there has to be a reason. There must be some purpose to this.'

'Why?'

'I don't *know* why.' There was frustration in my voice now. 'But I want to find out!'

'Listen, squirt. We're dogs. We live like dogs, we're treated like dogs. We think like dogs . . .' I shook my head at this, but he continued: '. . . and we eat like dogs. We're a little more intelligent than others, but we keep that to ourselves . . .'

'Why don't we show them we're not like the rest?' I burst out.

'We *are* like the rest, squirt. We differ only in small ways.'

'That's not true!'

'It is true; you'll find out. We could show men how clever we are – lots of animals do. They usually end up in the circus.'

'It's not the same thing! That's only animals learning tricks.'

'Did you know they're teaching a chimpanzee to talk? Is that a trick?'

'How did *you* know that?'

Rumbo looked flustered.

'It was something you knew in the past, wasn't it, Rumbo?

Not as a dog, but as a man. You read about it.'

'Read? What's read?'

'Words. Words on paper.'

'That's ridiculous, paper can't talk!'

'Nor can dogs.'

'We're talking.'

'Not in the same way as men.'

'Of course not. We're not men.'

'What are we?'

'Dogs.'

'Freaks.'

'Freaks?'

'Yes. I think we were men, then something happened and we became dogs.'

There was an odd look in Rumbo's eyes. 'I think the rain last night soaked into your brain,' he said slowly. Then he shook his body as if to shake off the conversation. 'I'm going to the park now. You could chew through the rope if you want to come.'

I slumped down on to the ground; it was obvious, as far as Rumbo was concerned, the discussion was over. 'No,' I said resignedly, 'I'll stay here till the Guvnor lets me loose. We don't want to make him any angrier.'

'Up to you,' said Rumbo and trotted off. 'I'll try and bring you something back!' he called out as he squeezed through the hole in the fence.

'Thanks,' I said to myself.

When the Guvnor turned up later that day he came over to see me. He shook his head a few times and called me a few more names. I tried to look pitiful and it must have had some effect, for he was soon untying the length of rope from my collar. He felt the dampness on my back and advised me to have a run to dry myself off. Accepting his advice, I shot out of the yard and made for the park where I knew I would find my companion. His trail was easy to follow but my progression from lamp-post to lamp-post was much more fun than just making straight for the park.

I found Rumbo sniffing round a little bitch, a skittish Yorkshire terrier, her lady owner anxiously trying to shoo my ragged friend away. Complex thoughts had gone: I couldn't understand Rumbo's interest in these silly lady dogs, but I did enjoy a good game. And this looked as though it could be a good game.

*   *   *

243

The weeks sped by – they may have been months – and I became lost in my canine world again, only occasionally being troubled by tormenting memories. Snow came, melted, was gone; winds swept in fiercely, spent their anger, and left meekly; the rain rained. The weather couldn't depress me, for I found its different moods interesting: I was experiencing things in a new way, with a different outlook; everything that happened was a *re*discovery. It was like the feeling you get after recovering from a long debilitating illness: everything is fresh and often startling; you observe with more appreciative eyes. You've known it all before, but familiarity has dulled things for you. That's the only way I can describe it.

Rumbo and I survived the worst winter could inflict comfortably enough. We had to travel further for our food, our surrounding area being a little too 'hot', but I enjoyed the excursions. We became firmer friends, since I was losing my overcharged puppy capriciousness and beginning to instigate some of our escapades rather than being led into them. Rumbo even called me Fluke now more often than squirt, for I was becoming almost as tall as him. When we weren't hunting for food or getting into mischief, Rumbo was off hunting bitches. He couldn't understand my lack of interest in the opposite sex and told me repeatedly I was old enough to feel some stirring in my loins at the scent of a ripe female body. I was puzzled myself, but really couldn't muster any inclinations whatsoever towards the female of my species; I suppose my instincts weren't yet canine enough. Apart from that small concern and the occasional sudden flashes of my past life, the times were good; but like all good times, they had to end.

And end they did one dull and drizzly day.

Rumbo and I had just returned from the fruit market and were sniffing around a new vehicle which had been brought into the yard a few days before. It was a large dark-blue Transit van, and for some reason it had been parked at the rear of the yard. The lettering on its side had been sprayed out and I'd watched one of the workers change its number-plates the previous day. Its front bumper had been removed and replaced by a much sturdier one. Parked alongside was another car – a Triumph 2000 – and the number-plates on this had also been changed. Both vehicles were screened from the rest of the yard by the piles of wrecks. It was the smell from the van which attracted us – it must have been used to transport food at some time – but my human faculties should have made me aware of what was going on. The constant meetings in the hut between the Guvnor and his flashy cronies (meetings which had become even more frequent recently); the curious affluence of the Guvnor himself; his anger at having a policeman 'snooping' around some time before: it didn't take much of a brain to figure it all out. Unfortunately, mine wasn't even much of a brain.

We heard the yard gates being unlocked and then a car was driven into the yard. Rumbo raced through the maze of junk to find out who had arrived: to our surprise it was the Guvnor himself. It was a surprise to us because he was not an early bird, usually never arriving at the yard till mid-morning. He generally left it to his employees to open up and get on with the work by themselves.

The big man ignored us as we yapped around his legs while he unlocked the door to the hut. I noticed he'd discarded his sheepskin for his old leather jacket and underneath he wore a dark-red polo-neck sweater. He was also wearing gloves, which was unusual for him. Throwing the butt of his cigar into the mud, the Guvnor entered the hut. No food for us today, then.

Rumbo and I mentally shrugged at each other and wandered off, but it wasn't long before the sound of more arrivals drew us back to the hut. A car pulled into the yard first and Lenny and another man got out, going straight into the hut, they too ignoring our wagging tails and eager expressions. Then three others arrived on foot.

A strange kind of tenseness had taken over the yard, making Rumbo and me nervous, edgy. The voices from inside the hut were muted, not the usual sounds of laughter or anger. This worried us even more.

After a short while the door opened and six men came out. The first four were now wearing dark grey smock-coats, the kind shopkeepers sometimes wear, and I saw they too were all wearing polo-necked sweaters. One man was just tugging the thick collar of his down from over his chin, suggesting that a moment before he'd been wearing it up to his ears. Lenny came out next, and although he wasn't wearing a smock he had on a polo-neck sweater. The Guvnor came out last and he still wore his leather jacket. They didn't speak as they passed, walking to the back of the yard, the nervous tension between them obvious and transferring to us, so that we became even more agitated. Lenny clucked his tongue at me and snapped his fingers in a half-hearted way, but ignored me when I bounded up to him.

We followed the six men round to the van. The back doors were opened and three of the smock-coated men climbed in, the fourth seating himself in the front. Before the Guvnor heaved his big frame into the passenger seat of the Triumph he said to the van driver: 'Right, you know what to do. Try and keep with us in the traffic, but if we get separated, you know where to meet up.' The driver nodded and the Guvnor turned away. Just before he slammed his door, he called out. 'Don't forget. You don't make your move till you see me wave my arm out the window.' The van driver thumbed up an acknowledgement.

Lenny was already in the driving seat of the Triumph and he suddenly gunned the engine. As the car crunched its way out of the yard, the big blue van following, I realised that for the first time I'd seen the Guvnor without a cigar sticking out of the corner of his mouth.

About an hour later the Triumph 2000 returned. It roared through the gates and drove straight round to the back of the yard. One of the yard's workmen ran to the gates and pushed them shut, then went back to his work as though nothing had happened.

Rumbo and I raced after the car and were just in time to see the Guvnor and Lenny clambering out. They ran round to the boot, opened it, and between them lifted out a large heavy-looking metal case. It had handles at each end and the two men used these to carry it round and into the hut. They returned to the car and pulled out four or five bulky sacks, and these too were hastily taken into the hut. The Guvnor locked the office door before they returned to the car. The men pushed us away angrily as we tried to clamber over them. There was an excited haste about them now – gone was the sullen nervousness of the morning – and this too was infecting us. A sharp whack on the nose kept me away, and Rumbo also took the hint.

'O.K., Lenny. Get shot of the motor,' the Guvnor said, taking a cigar from the inside pocket of his leather jacket. 'Don't worry about the smocks in the back – they don't matter now. You can dump it as far away as you like, but don't be drivin' around in it too long.'

246

'O.K., Guv,' Lenny said cheerfully. Before he turned on the ignition, the Guvnor poked another cigar through the open car window.

''Ere. You done well, boy. See you back 'ere Wednesday – not before!'

Lenny stuck the cigar into his mouth, grinned, put the car into gear, then moved off.

The front gate was just being opened for him by the same yard worker who'd closed it only minutes before when the police car screeched into the entrance, completely blocking Lenny's path. Doors flew open and suddenly there were blue uniforms everywhere. Another police car pulled up behind the first and more men in blue poured out.

Lenny was out of the Triumph in a flash, running for the back of the yard, his face white. The Guvnor, who was half-way back to his office when the police arrived, stood transfixed for a few seconds, then turned and bolted towards us. I can only guess that both he and Lenny intended to scale the corrugated-iron fence and make their getaway into the backstreets.

The latter didn't get as far as the former who, in the end, didn't get far at all. Lenny was brought down by a flying rugger tackle and was immediately engulfed in blue bodies. He screamed and cursed them but they wouldn't let him go.

Others gave chase to the Guvnor who had pounded past us now, throwing away his cigar as he went. The police shouted at him to stop, but he wasn't having any of it. He headed into the maze of wrecked cars.

Rumbo was both alarmed and angry. He didn't like these blue men: he didn't like them chasing his Guvnor. He growled at them and ordered them to stop. It did no good though – they weren't afraid of Rumbo. He jumped up at one and got a good grip on the policeman's sleeve, tugging and tearing at it with jerks of his body. The man went down and rolled over in the mud, taking Rumbo with him.

'No, Rumbo, no!' I cried out. 'Leave him alone! They'll hurt you!'

But Rumbo was too angry to listen. This was his territory, and the man they were after was the one he'd chosen to be his master. Another policeman kicked out at him, making him yelp in sudden pain and lose his grip on the uniform's sleeve. A stout wooden stick cracked across his nose and Rumbo staggered away

247

from the sprawling who immediately scrambled to his feet and joined in the chase after the Guvnor again.

'Are you all right?' I asked as I rushed over to Rumbo.

He moaned and his tail dropped between his legs. 'Get after them! Don't let them catch him!' He stumbled around shaking his head in a dazed way.

I dived into the alleyways separating the piles of damaged cars and pursued the pursuers. I could see the Guvnor ahead, climbing on to the bonnet of a car. He was grabbed from behind, but he kicked out with a vicious boot, knocking the unfortunate policeman on to his back. He scrambled up higher on to the roof of the car, then on to the bonnet of the car on top. If he crossed this pile of junk, it would take him close to the surrounding fence and he would be able to jump into the street below. The wreck he was climbing on to was unsteady, and it tottered precariously for a few sickening moments, nearly causing him to slither back down into the yard. He held tight and the car steadied itself. He began to climb again.

Two policemen began the ascent after the Guvnor while others headed in different directions in the hope of cutting him off. I couldn't just stand by and let them take the Guvnor; Rumbo had a loyalty to him and that meant I had too. I caught the seat of one of the climbing plod's trousers nicely with my teeth. I bit and pulled and he came tumbling down. He kicked out at me and beat me with his fists, but I was in a fury and hardly felt the blows.

Rumbo came in snarling and snapping, and the struggling policeman was forced to call on his companion for help. The dogs were tearing him to pieces, he screamed.

Well, we were being a bit rough, but we weren't savages (to tell the truth, it was a bit of a lark at that stage).

The second policeman jumped from the car bonnet into the mêlée and tried to separate man and dogs, flailing at us with his fists. This only made Rumbo more cross and he diverted his attention to the new assailant. More policemen were arriving by the second and I could see we'd stand no chance against such odds.

'It's no good, Rumbo!' I called out. 'There's too many!'

'Keep fighting, squirt,' he replied between mouthfuls of flesh and cloth. 'It's giving the Guvnor a chance to get away.'

It was no good. I felt a hand grasp my collar and I was yanked off my feet and thrown across the alleyway. I landed heavily against the boot of a car and fell to the ground badly winded. I gasped for breath and saw Rumbo receiving similar treatment. It took two policemen to deal with him, though.

By this time the Guvnor was on the roof of the second car and I could see him looking wildly around. He was being converged upon on all sides by blue uniforms and he yelled down defiantly as the police below began to climb up after him again.

'Look out!' one of them shouted. 'He's pushing the cars over!'

The policeman scrambled for safety and I saw that the Guvnor had stepped over on to the roof of the next semi-crushed car and was using a foot as a lever against the one he'd just left. It was already dangerously balanced and it didn't take much to send it toppling. The only thing was, the car the Guvnor was perched on toppled after it.

And worse, Rumbo had dashed forward again to ward off the pursuing policeman.

He couldn't have known what hit him; that was the only merciful thing about it. One minute he was crouched low, baring his teeth at the police, the next he had disappeared beneath a tumble of crushing metal.

'Rumbo!' I screamed, and dashed forward even before the crashing cars had had time to settle. 'Rumbo! Rumbo!'

I dodged around the twisted metal, trying to see beneath it, trying to find an opening to crawl through, willing my friend to be miraculously alive, refusing to accept the inevitable.

The thin stream of dark-red blood that came from beneath the cars jolted me into the truth of the situation: there was no chance at all for Rumbo.

I howled, the kind of howl you sometimes hear on an empty night from miles away; the cry of an animal at its lower point of misery. Then I wept.

The Guvnor was in agony, his arm trapped deep between the two wrecks. He was lucky, though: it could have been his whole body.

A hand took me by the collar and dragged me gently away from the metal tomb, and I felt sympathy flowing from the policeman as he led me towards the front of the yard. I was too upset to resist. Rumbo was dead, and for the moment so was my will. I heard one of the officers tell someone to get an ambulance quickly; there was an injured man back there. I saw two men in plainclothes bringing the metal case from the hut and nodding towards another man questioning Lenny. Lenny was angry now, talking belligerently as he was held from behind by two uniformed men.

'Who done it then?' he was asking. 'Who fingered us?'

'We've had our eyes on this place a long time, son,' the man before him replied. 'Ever since one of our boys spotted Ronnie Smiley's car in here awhile back. We all know what Ronnie gets up to, don't we, so we thought we'd wait awhile and let things run their course. Very interesting when we saw the stolen van coming in, then the car. Even more so when they didn't come out again – until this morning, that is.' He laughed at Lenny's obvious displeasure. 'Oh don't worry, it wasn't only that. We've had suspicions about this yard for a long time now. Wondered where your governor got his money from. Now we know, don't we?'

Lenny just looked away sullenly. The plainclothes policeman spotted me being led away.

'Funny thing is,' he remarked, 'the constable was only investigating a couple of thieving dogs when he spotted Smiley's car. Take after their master, don't they?' He nodded at the man holding firmly on to Lenny and they pushed him towards one of the police cars at the entrance to the yard. Before Lenny departed he gave me one last penetrating look that made me shiver inside.

And it was then that I knew where I was going. It pushed its way through befuddled layers and struck me physically.

I twisted my neck and snapped at the hand that held me. The startled policeman quickly drew his hand away – and I was loose. I bolted for the street and once again I was running, running, running.

But this time I had somewhere to go.

PART TWO

Chapter Twelve

How do you feel now? Is your mind still closed to my story, or are you wondering? Let me go on; there's a few hours before dawn.

My journey to Edenbridge was a long one, but strangely I knew the way as if I'd travelled that route many times before. When the town had been mentioned in the yard it had evidently planted a seed in my mind and it was a seed that suddenly grew and sprouted. I wasn't sure what the town meant to me, whether it was where my home was or if it had some other significance, but I knew it was the place to go, the place to start from. What other alternative had I anyway?

I must have run for at least an hour, narrowly avoiding being run down by uncaring traffic more than once, before I reached a piece of waste ground where I was able to grieve for my lost friend in private. Creeping under a dumped sofa, its stuffing more out than in, I sank to the ground, resting my head between my paws. I could see that trickle of blood running from beneath the rusted metal, forming a pool in a small dip in the earth and creating a miniature whirlpool, a vortex of Rumbo's life. Animals can feel grief just as deeply as any human, perhaps more so; they have limited ways of expressing their sorrow, though, and their natural optimism usually enables recovery more quickly, there's the difference. Unfortunately, I suffered both as a human *and* an animal, and it was heavy stuff.

I stayed there until long into the afternoon, afraid and bewildered once again. Only my loyal companion, hunger, roused me into movement. I forget from where I scrounged food, just as I have forgotten a great deal of that long journey, but I know I did eat and was soon moving onwards. I travelled by night through the city, preferring the empty quietness of the streets, the activity of the day making way for the quiet prowlings of night creatures. I met many prowlers – cats, other dogs, spirits (so many in the

253

streets of the city) and strange men who flitted in and out of the shadows as though light or open spaces would harm their bodies – but I avoided communication with any of them. I had a purpose and would allow nothing to distract me from it.

Through Camberwell, through Lewisham, through Bromley I went, resting during the day, hiding in derelict houses, parks or on waste ground – anywhere away from inquisitive eyes. I ate badly, for I took few risks; I didn't want to be sent back to a home, you see, not now I had an objective. I had become timid again now that Rumbo wasn't there to spur me on, to chastise me when I cowered, to threaten me when I balked and to laugh when I surprised him.

Soon I reached open country.

It rolled out before me, green and fresh under the gentle beginnings of spring. It wasn't true countryside yet, for I was only just outside the London suburbs, but after the blacks and the greys and the browns and the reds and the garishness of everything in the city, it seemed like passing through a barrier to where nature governed, and human influence played only a minor part. I was no longer afraid to travel by daylight.

The sudden strength of growing things thrilled me. Fresh green shoots thrust their way through the earth to breathe in fresh air, bulbs and tubers were sprouting and buds were breaking open on broad-leaved trees. Everywhere things were stirring, new life was being created. A vibrancy filled the air, filled my lungs and filled my limbs with its tingling life. The greens and yellows were newer, more dazzling, and the reds and oranges glowed with fire, sending out waves of energy. Everything glistened, everything shone with wetness. Everything was firm, vigorous, even the most delicate flower. It put new life into me.

I scrambled through a hedge running alongside the road, ignoring the scratchy protest of the thorny hawthorn and prickly dogrose. Two startled wrens screeched and froze as I brushed by their small huddled forms. A group of bright yellow stars flashed before me as I wormed my way through lesser celandine, plants which are the first in the queue for spring regeneration. I burst through into a field and ran like mad through its dewy wetness, twisting and rolling on to my back until my whole coat was soaked. I sucked at the grass, drinking the pure water from them, and dug holes in the soft earth to see what I could find. Beetles scuttled away from my inquisitive nose and a mole turned a blind eye. An eight-inch-long keeled slug curled its slick grey body into a ball as I sniffed at him and I quickly spat him from my mouth after a tentative taste. Cooked snails might be a delicacy for many, but raw slug isn't even fit for a dog.

My appetite soon returned, however, and I began to explore the field in search of food. I was lucky enough to find a young rabbit nibbling at the bark of a tree and unlucky enough to be unable to catch him. I cursed his speed then wondered if I could have killed the rabbit even had I caught up with him. I'd never killed for food before.

Fortunately, I found some late winter fungus among a group of trees and devoured the upturned yellow caps and stalks with relish, somehow aware that the mushrooms were not poisonous. Was this animal instinct or had I some human knowledge of fungi? The question bothered me for only a second or so, for a sleepy woodmouse shuffled lazily between my legs, his black little eyes searching the ground for snails. I felt no urge to eat or fight him, but I did give his reddish-brown back a playful tap with my paw. He stopped, looked up at me, then ambled on at the same pace, ignoring me totally. I watched him go then decided it was time to move on myself, the diversion pleasant enough but hardly profitable as far as self-discovery was concerned. I raced back across the field, scrambled through the hedge, and set off down the road again.

It wasn't long before I found myself back among shops and houses, but I kept on, pausing only once to steal an apple from a splendid display outside a fruiterer's. The road became more and more familiar to me now that the complications of the city streets were far behind, and I knew it was a route I must have taken many times before.

By the time I'd reached Keston my pads were very sore, but I kept going until I reached a small place called Leaves Green. There I rested through the cold night in a small wood, nervous of the country night noises, my unease finally driving me to seek shelter in somebody's front garden. I felt more comfortable being in range of human contact.

I didn't eat much the following day, but I won't bore you with the various misadventures that befell me in my search for sustenance; suffice to say, by the time I reached Westerham, I'd have bitten the leg off a cow.

It was at Westerham that a nasty experience was awaiting me. And this I must tell you about.

Chapter Thirteen

Church bells woke me. They had a strident Sunday morning sound that sent my thoughts racing back to other times – human times.

Awareness of my present plight dismissed the memories before they gathered pace and I stretched my aching limbs, wincing at the tenderness of my foot-pads as I pushed them against the ground. A bus shelter had been my refuge for the night, but the early morning chill had crept into my bones and seemed reluctant to leave. I yawned and my stomach grumbled for nourishment. Glancing around, I saw there were no shops in the immediate vicinity, so I trotted gingerly along the street keeping my nose high in the air, acutely receptive for the faintest waft of food smells. I soon found myself in the High Street and to my dismay realised it was indeed Sunday, for all the shops – apart from a couple of newsagents – were closed. It was a pretty dismal dog who stood shivering by the kerbside, looking first left then right, undecided, unwanted and unfed.

It was the pealing bells that gave me the idea. Small groups of people were walking briskly towards the sound, clad in Sunday best, a bightness about them that would wear off as the day wore on. Children held hands with parents or skipped along ahead of them; grannies clutched at the elbows of middle-aged offspring; sombre husbands walked stiffly alongside beaming wives. There was a fresh friendly feeling in the air, the beginning of spring enhancing the Sunday morning ritual, encouraging goodwill to all men. And maybe dogs, too.

I followed the people to their church. It was on a hill, half hidden away from the road by a screen of trees, its entrance reached by a gravelly path winding through a surrounding graveyard. A few of the people clucked their tongues at me or gave me a friendly pat as they passed by, but soon they had all disappeared into the cold, grey-stoned building. I settled down on a flat gravestone to wait.

I enjoyed the muted singing that came from the church immensely, occasionally joining in at the bits I knew. The service seemed to go on forever, and I soon became bored with the long stretches of silence between hymns so I began to explore the churchyard and was surprised at the thriving animal and insect life in this place of the dead. The unmistakable sound of the congregation rising as one body inside the church drew me away from my fascinating study of a rainbow-coloured spider's web, and I trotted back round to the enormous doorway, keeping to the damp grass which was so cool to my sore pads. I waited to one side of the porch and soon the flock came pouring out, some looking uplifted, others looking relieved now that their weekly duty was done. It was one of the uplifted members I wanted.

I soon spotted her: a little old lady, probably in her mid-sixties, round-faced, smiling constantly, knowing and known by everybody, it seemed. All lace and kindness. Perfect.

She spent several minutes chatting to the vicar, occasionally breaking off from her conversation to call hello to a passing acquaintance, giving them a little blessing with her white-gloved hand. I waited patiently until she'd ended her dialogue with the cleric then followed her as she made her way through the remaining gossiping cliques. Smiling sweetly and stopping to chat to every third or fourth person she finally drew clear of the throng and strode spritely down the gravel path. I followed, keeping a few yards behind, not ready to make my move while she still had so many distractions. We reached the road and she turned left, climbing further up the steep hill and away from the town.

'Good morning, Miss Birdle!' the people we passed called out, and she acknowledged them with a cheery wave.

Now's the time, I thought, and scampered up ahead of her. I stopped four yards ahead, turned to face her and gave her my sweetest smile.

'Woof,' I said.

Miss Birdle threw her hands up in surprise and beamed with delight. 'What a pretty dog!' she exclaimed and I wagged my rump with pride. She advanced on me and clasped my head between white-gloved hands.

'Oh, what a lovely boy!' She rubbed my back and I tried to lick

257

her face, congratulating myself on finding another Bella. 'Yes, yes, he is!' she went on.

After a few moments of unbridled affection she bade me good-bye and strode on, waving at me as she went. I bounded after her and tried to leap into her arms, slobbering and grinning and desperately trying to fawn my way into her heart and charity. I admit it: I had no shame.

Miss Birdle gently pushed me down then patted my head. 'Off you go, now, there's a good dog,' she said in her kind way.

Sorry Rumbo, but at that point I whimpered.

Not only that, I hung my head, drooped my tail and looked cow-eyed at her. I was pathetic.

It worked, for she suddenly said, 'Oh my poor dear, you're starving, that's what it is! Look at those skinny old ribs.' My chin almost touched the ground as I hammed up my performance. 'Come along then, dear, you come with me and we'll soon put you to rights. Poor little wretch!'

I was in. I tried to lick her face again in glee, but she restrained me with a surprisingly firm hand. I needed no encouragement to follow her, although she seemed to think I did, for she constantly patted her thigh and called out 'Come along now.'

She had plenty of energy, this charming old lady, and we soon reached a rusty iron gate, behind which was a muddy path leading away from the road. Tangled undergrowth lay on either side of the narrow path and there was a constant rustling of hidden life as we made our way along it. I sniffed the scent of Miss Birdle along this well-used route, not the fresh powdery smell that followed in her wake now, but a staler version of it mingled with the scent of many animals. Now and again I stopped to explore a particularly interesting odour, but her call would send me scampering onwards.

Suddenly we emerged into a clearing and a flint-walled cottage stood before us, its corners, door and window openings reinforced by cut stone. It was a beautiful scene – like walking on to a chocolate box – and in perfect character with Miss Birdle herself. Smug with my own cleverness, I trotted up to the weathered door and waited for Miss Birdle to catch up with *me*.

She pushed open the door without using a key and beckoned me to enter. In I went and was pleased to find the interior of the cottage matched the quaintness of the exterior. Ancient furniture, worn and comfortable, filled the main room in which I found myself, there being no hallway. Well-cared for ornaments were scattered around the room, one of those interesting dark-wood dressers filled with delicately painted crockery taking up a large part of one wall. I wagged my tail in approval.

'Now let's just see if you've an address on your collar, then we'll give you some food, eh?' Miss Birdle placed her handbag on a chair and leaned forward over me, reaching for the name-plate on my collar. I obligingly sat down, determined not to kill any golden geese through over-exuberance. She peered short-sightedly at the scratched lettering on the nameplate and tutted in mild annoyance at herself.

'My old eyes are getting worse,' she told me, and I smiled in sympathy. I would dearly have loved to have told her of my own peculiarly clear eyesight, of the many changing colours I could see in her face, of the blue deepness of her ageing eyes, of the sparkling colours all around us, even in her faded furniture. It was frustrating to have to keep these things to myself, and even Rumbo had been unable to understand my visual sensitivity.

She felt inside her handbag and produced a light-rimmed pair of spectacles and muttered 'That's better,' as she put them on. She still squinted through the lenses but managed to make out the name on the strip of metal.

'Fluke,' she said. 'Fluke. That's a funny name for a dog. And no address. Some people are very careless, aren't they? I haven't seen you around before, I wonder where you've come from? Bet you've run away, haven't you? Let me look at your footies . . .' She lifted a paw. 'Yes, they're sore, aren't they? You've come a long way. Been badly treated, haven't you? Thin as a rake. It isn't right.'

My hunger was making me a little impatient by now and I whimpered again, just to give her the idea.

'Yes, yes. I know what you want, don't I? Something for your tummy?' It's a pity people have to talk to animals as though they were children, but I was in a forgiving mood and willing to put up with a lot more than baby-talk. I thumped my tail on the carpet in the hope that she would take that for an affirmative to her question. 'Course you do,' she said. 'Let's get you something.'

The kitchen was tiny, and lying in a basket on the floor, fast asleep, was Victoria.

Victoria was the meanest, surliest cat I've ever come across, either before or since that time. Now these feline creatures are

259

renowned for their tetchiness, for they believe they're a race apart from other animals and well above you lot, but this monster took the prize. She sat bolt upright, her fur bristling and her tail ramrod-straight. She hissed disgustedly at me.

'Take it easy, cat,' I said anxiously. 'I'm only passing through.'

'Now you settle down, Victoria,' said Miss Birdle, equally anxious. 'This poor doggie is starving. I'm just giving him something to eat, then we'll send him on his way.'

But it's no good trying to talk sense to a cat, they just won't listen. Victoria was out of her basket in a flash, up on to the sink and through the half-open kitchen window.

'Oh dear,' sighed Miss Birdle, 'you've upset Victoria now,' and then this nice old lady gave me a hefty kick in the ribs.

I was so shocked I thought I'd imagined it, but the pain in my side told me otherwise.

'Now let's see what we've got,' Miss Birdle said thoughtfully, her index finger in the corner of her mouth as she looked up into the cupboard she'd just opened. It was as though nothing had happened and I wondered again if anything actually had. The throb in my side assured me something had.

I kept a safe distance between us after that and watched her warily when she placed a bowl of chopped liver before me. The food was delicious but marred by my sudden nervousness of the old lady I just couldn't understand what had happened. I licked the bowl clean and said thank you, very aware of my manners now. She fondled my ears and chuckled approvingly at the empty bowl.

'You *were* hungry, weren't you?' she said. 'I'll bet you're thirsty now. Let's give you some water.' She filled the same bowl with water and placed it before me again. I lapped it up greedily.

'Now you come with me and rest those poor weary legs.' I followed her back into the main room and she patted a hairy rug in front of the unlit fire. 'Rest there, nice and comfy, and I'll just light the fire for us. It's still too cold for my old bones, you know. I like the warm.' She prattled on as she put a match to the already laid fire, her words soft and comforting. I became confident again, sure that the strange incident which had taken place in the kitchen was merely a slight lapse on her part, caused by the shock of seeing her beloved pet cat leaping through the window. Or maybe she'd slipped. I dozed off as she sat in the armchair before the fire, her words lulling me into a warm feeling of security.

I woke in time for lunch, which wasn't much, she being an old lady living on her own, but she gave me a good portion of it. The cat returned and was further put out at the sight of me gobbling down food which she felt was rightfully hers. However, Miss Birdle made a big fuss of her, running into the kitchen and returning with an opened tin of cat food. She poured some of it on to a small plate and laid it before the sour-faced mog. With a menacing look at me, Victoria began to eat in that jerky cat fashion, neatly but predatorily, so unlike the clumsy, lip-smacking manner of us dogs. My portion of Miss Birdle's lunch was soon gone and I casually sauntered over to Victoria to see how she was doing, ready to help her clean her plate, should the need arise. A spiteful hiss warned me off and I decided to sit at Miss Birdle's feet, my face upturned and carefully composed into an expression of mild begging. A few tasty morsels came my way, so my fawning was not in vain. This disgusted the cat even more, of course, but her sneers didn't bother me at all.

After Miss Birdle had cleared the table and washed up, we settled in front of the fire once again. Victoria kept an aloof distance and came over to settle on the old lady's lap only after much enticement. We all dozed, I with my head resting on my benefactor's slippered feet. I felt warm and content – and more secure than ever before. Perhaps I should stay with this kind old lady and forget my quest, which might just bring me more misery. I could be happy here; the cat would be a mild annoyance but nothing to worry about. I needed some human kindness, I needed to belong to someone. I'd lost a good friend and the world was a big and lonely place for a small mongrel dog. I could always search out my other past at some future time when I learned to live as I was. I could offer Miss Birdle companionship. I could guard her home for her. I could have a permanent meal-ticket.

These thoughts ran through my head as I dozed, and I made the decision that I would stay there for as long as possible – little suspecting what lay in store for me.

Later on, Miss Birdle stirred and began to get ready to go out. 'Never miss the afternoon service, my dear,' she told me.

I nodded approvingly, but didn't stir from my cosy position. I heard the old lady bustling around upstairs for a while, then the clomp of heaving walking shoes as she descended the stairs. She

261

appeared in the doorway, resplendent in white gloves and a dark-blue straw hat. Her suit was pink and her high-necked blouse a bright emerald green. She looked dazzling.

'Come along, Fluke, time for you to go now,' she said.

My head shot up. What? Go?

'What? Go?' I said.

'Yes, time for you to go, Fluke. I can't keep you here, you belong to someone else. They may have looked after you badly, but you do belong to them. I could get into trouble by keeping you here, so I'm afraid you've got to leave.' She shook her head apologetically then, to my dismay, grabbed my collar and dragged my resisting body to the door. For an old lady she was quite strong, and my paws skidded along the wood floor as I tried to hold back. Victoria enjoyed every moment, for I could hear her snickering from her perch on the window-sill.

'Please let me stay,' I pleaded. 'Nobody owns me. I'm all alone.'

It was no use: I found myself outside on the doorstep. Miss Birdle closed the door behind us and marched down the path, calling me to follow. Having no choice, I followed.

At the gate she patted my head and gave me a little push away from her. 'Off you go now,' she urged. 'Home. Good boy, Fluke.'

I wouldn't budge. After a while she gave up and marched down the hill away from me, looking round twice to make sure I wasn't following her. I waited patiently until she was out of sight then pushed my way back through the gate and padded down the muddy path to the cottage. Victoria scowled through the window as she saw me coming and shouted at me to go away.

'Not likely,' I told her as I squatted on my haunches and prepared to wait for the old lady's return. 'I like it here. Why should you have it all to yourself?'

'Because I was here first,' Victoria said crossly. 'You've got no right.'

'Look, there's plenty for both of us,' said I, trying to be reasonable. 'We could be friends.' I shivered at the thought of being friends with this miserable specimen but was prepared to ingratiate myself for the sake of a nice secure home. 'I wouldn't get in your way,' I said in my best toadying voice. 'You could have first and biggest share of all the food' (until I was better acquainted with the old lady, I thought). 'You can have the best

262

place to sleep' (until I have wormed my way into Miss Birdle's affections), 'and you can be the head of the house, I don't mind' (until I get you alone some day and show you who the real boss is). 'Now, what do you say?'

'Get lost,' said the cat.

I gave up. She would just have to lump it.

An hour later Miss Birdle returned and when she saw me sitting there she shook her head. I gave her my most appealing smile.

'You *are* a bad boy,' she scolded, but there was no anger in her voice.

She let me go into the cottage with her and I made a big fuss of licking her heavily stockinged legs. The taste was horrible, but when I decide to smarm, there are no limits. I was sorry not to have the dignity of Rumbo, but there's nothing like insecurity to make you humble.

Well, I stayed that night. And the following night. But the third night – that's when my troubles started all over again.

At nine-thirty in the evening Miss Birdle would turn me out and I would dutifully carry out my toilet; I knew that was expected of me and had no intention of fouling things up (excuse the play on words – couldn't help it). She would let me back in after a short while and coax me into a small room at the back of the cottage which she used to store all sorts of junk. Most of it was unchewable – old picture frames, a pianoforte, an ancient unconnected gas cooker, that sort of thing. There was just enough room for me to curl up beneath the piano keyboard and here I would spend the night, quite comfortable although a little frightened at first (I cried that first night but was O.K. the second). Miss Birdle would close the door on me to keep me away from Victoria who slept in the kitchen. The cat and I were still not friends and the old lady was well aware of it.

On that third night she neglected to close the door properly; the catch didn't catch and the door was left open half an inch. It probably wouldn't have bothered me, but the sound of someone creeping around during the night aroused my curiosity. I'm a light sleeper and the soft pad of feet was enough to disturb me. I crept over to the door and eased it open with my nose; the noise was coming from the kitchen. I guessed it was Victoria mooching around and would have returned to my sleeping-place had not those two agitators, hunger and thirst, begun taunting my greedy belly. A trip to the kitchen might prove profitable.

I crept stealthily from the room and made my way through the tiny hallway into the kitchen. Miss Birdle always left a small lamp burning in the hallway (because she was nervous living on her own, I suppose) and had no trouble finding the kitchen door. It, too, was open.

Pushing my nose round it, I peered into the gloom. Two slanting green eyes startled me.

'That you, Victoria?' I asked.

'Who else would it be?' came the hissed reply.

I pushed in further. 'What are you doing?'

'None of your business. Get back to your room.'

But I saw what she was doing. She had a small wood-mouse trapped between her paws. Her claws were withdrawn so she was obviously playing a fine teasing game with the unfortunate creature. His reddish-brown back was arched in paralytic fear and his tiny black eyes shone with a trance-like glaze. He must have found his way into the cottage in search of food. The absence of house-mice (undoubtedly owing to Victoria's vigilance) would have encouraged him and he must have been too stupid (or too hungry) to have been aware of the cat's presence. Anyway, he was well and truly aware of it now, and paying nature's harsh price for carelessness.

He was too scared to speak so I spoke up for him.

'What are you going to do with him?'

'None of your business,' came the curt reply.

I made my way further into the kitchen and repeated my question. This time a wheezy snarl was the reply.

It's not an animal's nature to have much sympathy for his fellow creatures, but the plight of this defenceless little thing appealed to the other side of *my* nature; the human side.

'Let him go, Victoria,' I said quietly.

'Sure, after I've bitten his head off,' she said.

And that's what she tried to do, there and then, just to spite me.

I moved fast and had Victoria's head between my jaws before she had a chance to dodge. We spun around in the kitchen, the mouse's head in the cat's mouth, and the cat's head in mine.

Victoria was forced to drop the terrified wood-mouse before she had done any real damage and I saw with satisfaction the little creature scurry away into a dark corner and no doubt down a dark hole. Victoria squealed and pulled her head from my jaws, raking my brisket as she did so. I yelped at the stinging pain and lunged for her again – very, very angry now.

Round and round that kitchen we ran, knocking chairs over, crashing against cupboards, shouting and screaming at each other, too far gone with animal rage to concern ourselves with the noise we were making and the damage we were doing. At one point I snapped my teeth round Victoria's flailing tail and the cat skidded to a forced halt, a scream of surprise escaping her. She wheeled and drew her sharp claws across my nose and I had to let go, but her tail was now bald near the tip. I sprang forward again and she leapt upwards on to the draining-board, knocking down the pile of crockery left there to dry by Miss Birdle. It came crashing down, shattering into hundreds of pieces on the stone floor. I tried to leap on to the draining-board myself and almost succeeded, but the sight of Victoria diving head-first through a pane in the closed window amazed me so much I lost my concentration and slipped back on to the floor. I'd never seen a cat – or any animal – do *that* before!

I was still half lying there, perplexed, and a little delighted, I think, when the white-gowned figure appeared in the kitchen doorway. I froze for a second at the apparition, then realised it was only Miss Birdle. Then I froze again.

Her eyes seemed to glow in the darkness. Her white hair hung wildly down to her shoulders and the billowy night dress she wore crackled with static. Her whole body quivered with a rising fury that threatened to dismantle her frail old body. Her mouth flapped open but coherent words refused to form; she could only make a strange gargling sound. However, she did manage to reach up a trembling hand to the light switch and flick it on. The increased light suddenly made me feel very naked lying there among the smashed crockery.

I gulped once and began to apologise, ready to blame the cat for everything, but the screech that finally escaped the old lady told me words would be wasted at that particular moment. I scooted beneath the kitchen table.

It didn't afford me much protection unfortunately, for one of those dainty slippered feet found my ribs with fierce accuracy. It found my ribs a few more times before I had the sense to remove myself. Out I shot, making for the open doorway, scared silly of

265

this dear old thing. This dear old thing then threw a chair at me and I yelped as it bounced off my back. She came at me, arms and legs flailing, stunning me into submission, terrifying me with her strength. My collar was grabbed and I found myself being dragged back to the cluttered 'guest' room. I was thrown in and the door slammed shut behind me. From the other side of the heavy wood I heard language I'd been used to in the Guvnor's yard but hardly expected to hear in a quaint old cottage and from such a sweet old lady. I lay there trembling, fighting desperately to keep a grip on my bowels and bladder. I was in enough disgrace without *that*.

Another miserable night for me. I must be unique in knowing the full meaning of the expression 'a dog's life.' I know of no other animal who goes through so many highs and lows of emotion as the dog. Maybe we make trouble for ourselves; maybe we're over-sensitive; or maybe we're just stupid. Maybe we're too human.

I hardly slept. I kept expecting the door to swing open and the ancient demon to appear and deal out more punishment. But it didn't swing open; in fact, it didn't swing open for another three days.

I whined, I howled, I grew angry and barked; but nothing happened. I messed on the floor and cried because I knew it would get me into trouble. I starved and cursed the mouse who'd got me into this predicament. My throat grew sore because I had nothing to drink and I cursed the malicious cat who'd caused this situation. My limbs grew stiff because of lack of exercise and I cursed Miss Birdle for her senility. How could she change from being a charming, delicate old lady one moment into a raging monster the next? All right, I know I was to blame to some extent – her cat *had* gone head-first through the window – but was that enough reason to lock me up and starve me? Self-pity sent me into a sulk that occasionally welled up into anger, then receded into a sulk again.

On the third day the door handle rattled, twisted and the door slowly opened.

I cowered beneath the pianoforte hardly daring to look up, prepared to take a beating with as little dignity as possible.

'There, there, Fluke. What's the matter then?' She stood smiling down at me, that sweet granny smile, that gentle innocence which only belongs to the very old or the very young. I snuffled and refused to be lured out.

'Come on then, Fluke. All's forgiven.'

Oh yes, I thought, until your next brainstorm.

'Come and see what I've got for you.' She left the doorway and disappeared into the kitchen, calling my name in her enticing way. A meaty smell came my way and, tail drooped between my legs, I made my way cautiously after her. I found Miss Birdle pouring a whole tin of dogfood into a bowl on the floor.

I might be unforgiving but my stomach has a mind of its own and it insisted I go forward and eat. Which I did of course without too much inner conflict, though I kept a wary eye on the old lady all the time. The food soon went and so did the water that followed, but my nervousness took a little longer to disappear. Victoria watched me all the time from her basket in the corner, flicking her tail in a slow, regular movement of cold fury. I ignored her but was actually pleased to see she'd come to no real harm by diving through the window. (I was also pleased to see the bald dip of her tail).

I shied away when Miss Birdle reached down to me, but her calm words soothed my taut nerves and I allowed her to stroke me and soon we were friends again. And we remained friends for at least two weeks after that.

Victoria made a point of keeping out of my way and, I confess, I made a point of keeping out of hers, too. I would scamper down to the town with Miss Birdle when she went shopping and always did my best to behave myself on these occasions. The temptation to steal was almost irresistible, but resist it I did. I was reasonably well fed and the dreadful incident of my fight with Victoria was soon forgotten. Miss Birdle introduced me to all her friends (she seemed to know everybody) and I was made a great fuss of. In the afternoon I would romp in the fields behind the cottage, teasing the animals living there, inhaling the sweetness from the budding flowers, revelling in the growing warmth from the sun. Colours zoomed before me, new smells titillated my sense: life became good once more and I grew healthier. Two weeks of happiness, then that rat of a cat managed to upset everything again.

It was a sunny afternoon and Miss Birdle was in her garden at the front of the cottage tending her awakening flowerbeds. The front door was open and I trotted backwards and forwards through it, enjoying the luxury of having a home where I could come and go as I pleased. On my third or fourth trip, Victoria wandered in after me, and I should have realised something was going to happen when she slyly started a conversation with me. Being a fool and eager to make friends, I readily laid my suspicions to one side and answered her questions, settling down on the rug, prepared to have a good natter. As I said before, cats, like rats, aren't much given to conversation and I was pleased Victoria was making the effort on my behalf, thinking she had accepted me as a permanent guest and was trying to make the best of things. She asked me where I came from, if I knew any other cats, if I liked fish – all sorts of inconsequential questions. But all the time her yellow eyes were darting around the room as though looking for something. When they rested upon the huge dresser with all its fine crockery she smiled to herself. Then came the insults: What was a mangey-looking thing like me doing here, anyway? Were all dogs as stupid as me? What made me smell so? Little things like that. I blinked hard, startled by this sudden change in attitude. Had I offended her in some way?

She came closer so we were almost nose to nose, and stared intently into my eyes. 'You're a dirty, snivelling, fleabitten, worm-riddled mutt. You're a thief and a scoundrel!' Victoria looked at me with some satisfaction. 'Your mother was a jackal who coupled with a hyena. You're vulgar and you're nasty!'

Now there are many insults you can throw at a dog and get away with, but there's one we will not put up with, one word that really offends us. That's right – *dirty*! (We often are, of course, but we don't like to be told so.) I growled at her to be quiet.

She took no notice, of course, but ranted on, throwing insults not worth repeating here, but some quite ingenious for one of her limited vocabulary. Even so, I would probably have borne all these insults had she not finally spat in my face. I went for her, which is exactly what she had wanted all along.

Up into the dresser she went, spitting and howling. I tried to follow her, shouting at the top of my lungs, finding some nice insults of my own to call her. Victoria backed away along the dresser as I tried in vain to reach her and , as she moved her body backwards, so the ornamental plates which stood balanced upright on the first shelf came tumbling down.

A shadow fell across the doorway but the half-wit (that's right) carried on barking at the wailing cat. I only became fully aware of Miss Birdle's presence when the rake came down heavily on my back. I scooted for the front door, but the old lady had sprung wings on her heels and reached it before me. She slammed it shut and turned to face me, the rake clutched in her gnarled old hands like a lance, its iron-toothed end almost touching my nose. I looked up at her face and gulped loudly.

It had gone a deep purple, the tiny broken veins seeming to explode like starbursts across her skin, and her once kind eyes pressed against their sockets as though about to pop out and roll down her cheeks. I moved a fraction of a second before she did and the rake crashed into the floor only inches behind me. We did a quick circuit of the room while the cat looked on from her safe perch on the dresser, a huge smug smile on her face. On our third lap round, Miss Birdle spotted her and took a swipe at her indolent body with the rake (I suppose the frustration of not being able to catch me had something to do with it). It caught the cat a cracking blow and she shot off the dresser like a ball from a cannon and joined me in the arena. Unfortunately (more so for us), Miss Birdle's sweeping blow at Victoria had also dislodged more plates together with a few hanging cups and a small antique vase. They followed the cat but of course refused to join us in our run; they lay broken and dead where they had fallen.

The anguished scream from behind told us matters had not improved: Miss Birdle was about to run amuck! Victoria chose the narrow cave formed between the back of the settee and the wall below the front window to hide in. I pushed my way in behind her, almost climbing on to her back in my haste. It was a tight squeeze but we managed to get half-way down the semi-dark corridor. We trembled there, afraid to go further because that would lead us out again.

'It's your fault!' the cat snivelled.

Before I had a chance to protest, the long handle of the rake found my rump and I was suddenly pushed forward in a most painful and undignified way. We became a confused tussle of hairy bodies as we now struggled to reach the other end of the narrow tunel, violent pokes from the rear helping us achieve our goal. We emerged as one and the old lady dashed round to meet us.

Being the bigger target, I came in for the most abuse from the rake, but it pleases me to tell you the cat received a fair share. The chase went on for another five minutes before Victoria decided her only way out was up the chimney. So up she went and down came the soot – clouds and clouds of it. This didn't improve Miss Birdle's humour one bit, for the soot formed a fine black layer on the area around the fireplace. Now it was the old lady's habit to lay that fire every morning and light it when she settled down in the afternoon, even though the warmer weather had arrived, but for once she decided to bring her schedule forward. She lit the fire.

I gazed on in horrow as the paper flamed and the wood chips caught. Forgetting about me for the moment, Miss Birdle settled down in her armchair to wait, the rake lying across her lap in readiness. We stared at the fireplace, Miss Birdle with grim patience, I with utter dismay. The room around us was now a shambles, all cosiness gone.

The flames licked higher and the smoke rose. A spluttered cough fell down with more soot and we knew the cat was still perched there in the dark, unable to climb any further. Miss Birdle's rigid lips turned up at the corners into a rigid smile as we waited, the silence broken only by the crackling of burning wood.

A knock at the door made us both jump.

Miss Birdle's head swung round and I could see the panic in her eyes. The knock came again and a muffled voice called out, 'Miss Birdle, are you in?'

The old lady burst into action. The rake was shoved behind the settee, overturned chairs were righted, and broken crockery was swept beneath the armchair. Only the soot-blackened carpet and a slight disarray of the room gave evidence that something out of the ordinary had happened. Miss Birdle paused for a few seconds, tidied up her clothing, rearranged her personality, and went to the door.

The vicar's hand was raised to knock again and he smiled apologetically down at Miss Birdle.

'So sorry to disturb you,' he said. 'It's about the flower arrangements for Saturdays fête. We can count on your wonderful assistance again this year, can we not, Miss Birdle?'

The old lady smiled sweetly up at him. 'Why, of course, Mr Shelton. Have I ever let you down?'

The change in her was remarkable; the demon castigator had reverted back to the aged angel of innocence. She simpered and fawned over the vicar and he simpered and fawned with her; and all the while the cat roasted in the chimney.

'Now how is that little stray fellow of yours?' I heard the vicar inquire.

'Oh, he's thoroughly enjoying his stay,' Miss Birdle replied, having the nerve to turn round to me and smile. 'Come here, Fluke, and say hello to the vicar.'

I suppose I was expected to run over and lick the clergyman's hand, wagging my tail to show how pleased I was to see him, but I was still in a state of shock and could only cower behind the armchair.

'Oh, he doesn't like strangers, does he?' the vicar chuckled.

I wasn't sure if he was talking to me or Miss Birdle, for his voice had taken on that simpleton's tone people usually reserve for animals. They both gazed at me affectionately.

'No, Fluke's very shy of people,' said Miss Birdle, melting butter clogging her words.

'Have the police located his owner yet?' the vicar asked.

'Constable Hollingbery told me only yesterday that nobody had reported him missing, so I suppose whoever owned Fluke didn't really want him very much.'

They both tutted in harmony and looked at me with soul-churning sympathy.

'Never mind,' the vicar said brightly. 'He has a good home now, one I'm sure he appreciates. And I'm sure he's being a very good doggie, isn't he?' The question was aimed directly at me.

Oh yes, I thought, and the pussy is being a very good pussy, albeit a well-cooked one.

'Oh dear, Miss Birdle, the room seems to be filling with smoke. Is your chimney blocked?'

Without turning a hair, the old lady gave a little laugh and said, 'No, no, it always does that when it's first lit. It takes a while before the air begins to flow properly.'

'I should have it seen to, if I were you, mustn't spoil such a charming abode with nasty smoke, must we? I'll send my handyman around tomorrow to fix it for you. Now the Women's Guild committee meeting next Wednesday . . .' And that was when Victoria dropped from her hiding-place.

The vicar stared open-mouthed as the soot-covered, fur-smoking cat fell down into the fire, screaming and spitting with rage, leapt from the fireplace and streaked for the door. She flew past him and he could only continue to stare as the smouldering black body disappeared down the path leaving a jet-stream of trailing smoke behind. His mouth still open, the vicar turned his attention back to his elderly parishioner and raised his eyebrows.

271

'I *wondered* where Victoria had got to,' said Miss Birdle.

The cat never came back, at least not while I was still there, and I seriously doubt she ever returned. Life in the cottage went on in its crazy normal way, the incident forgotten by my benefactor as though it had never happened. Several times in the ensuing week Miss Birdle stood at her front door and called out Victoria's name, but I guess the cat was several counties away by then (I still have bad dreams of her being out there in the night, watching me, smouldering in the dark). However, Miss Birdle soon forgot about Victoria and directed all her attention towards me, but, not surprisingly, I felt I could never really trust her. I spent my time nervously waiting for the next eruption, treading very warily and learning to subdue my undisciplined spirits. It occurred to me to leave, but I must confess the lure of good food and a comfortable bed was stronger than my fear of what might happen next. In a word, I was stupid (Rumbo had been right), and even I'm amazed at just how stupid my next mistake was.

I found a nice, chewy plastic object lying on the edge of the kitchen-sink drainer one night. The kitchen was my night-time domain now that Victoria was gone and her basket had become my bed. I often had a poke around during the night or in the early hours of the morning and this time I had been lucky in finding something to play with. Not too hard, not too soft, and crunchy when I bit down firmly. No good to eat, but pretty to look at with its pink surface and little white frills around one edge. It kept me amused for hours.

When Miss Birdle came into the kitchen next morning, she showed no sign of being amused at all. Her toothless mouth opened to let the raging soundless cry escape, and when I looked into that gummy mouth, the human part of me realised what lay chewed, twisted and splintered between my paws.

'My teefth!' Miss Birdle spluttered after her wordless outcry. 'My falthe teefth!' And that old gleam came back into her eyes.

Stupid I am, yes, and stupid enough to amaze even myself, right. But there comes a time in even the most stupid dog's life when he knows exactly what he should do next. And I did it.

I went through that window just as the cat had (through the new window-pane, in fact), terror helping me achieve what I had been unable to do before (namely, getting on to that kitchen sink). The fact that Miss Birdle was reaching for the long carving knife which hung with its culinary companions on the wall convinced me this might be her worst brainstorm yet. I thought it unnecessary to wait and find out.

I went over her flowerbeds, scrambled through bushes and undergrowth and burst into the open fields beyond, a terrifying image of Miss Birdle in her long white nightdress chasing after me and brandishing the wicked carving knife keeping me going for quite some distance. It's certainly handy to have four legs when you're constantly running away.

I was a long way from that cottage before I collapsed into an exhausted heap, and had already resolved never to return. It was no way for even a dog to live. I shuddered at the thought of the schizophrenic old lady, so charming one minute, so lethal the next. Were all her friends fooled by her antique sweetness, her enchanting old maidishness? Didn't anybody see what lurked just behind that veneer, ready to be unleashed by the slightest provocation? I presumed not, for she seemed so popular and respected by her townsfolk. *Everybody* loved Miss Birdle. And Miss Birdle loved *everybody*. Who would ever guess that the endearing old lady had the slightest streak of viciousness in her? Why should anyone think such a thing? Knowing her lovable side so well, even I had difficulty in believing her kindness could turn to such violence, but I shall never trust any sweet old ladies again. How do you explain such a twist in human nature? What made her good one moment, bad the next? It's quite simple really.

She was nuts.

Chapter Fourteen

Dog's life, dogsbody, dogfight, dog-eared, dog-days, dog-end, dirty dog, mad dog, lazy dog, dog-tired, sick as a dog, dog-in-the-manger, underdog – why so many abuses of our name? You don't say hedgehog's life, or rabbit's body, or frog-in-the-manger. True, you do use certain animal names to describe a particular type of person – chicken (coward) monkey (rogue), goose (silly) – but they're only individual descriptions, you never extend the range with a particular species. Only dogs come in for this abuse. You even use various species' names in a complimentary manner: an elephant never forgets (not true), happy as a lark (not true), brave as a lion (definitely not true), wise as an owl (are you kidding?). But where are the dog compliments? And yet we're cherished by you and regarded as man's best friend. We guard you, we guide you; we can hunt with you, we can play with you. You can even race some of our breed. You use us for work and we can win you prizes. We're loyal, we trust, and we love you – even the meanest of you can be adored by your dog. So why this derogatory use of our name? Why can't you be 'as free as a dog', or 'as proud as a dog', or 'as cunning as a dog'? why should an unhappy life be a dog's life? Why should a skivvy be called a dogsbody? Why wouldn't you send *even* a dog out on a cold night? What have *we* done to deserve such blasphemy? Is it because we always seem to fall into some misfortune or other? Is it because we appear foolish? Is it because we're prone to over-excitement? Is it because we're fierce in a fight but cowardly when our master's hand is raised against us? Is it because we have dirty habits? *Is it because we're more like you than any other living creature?*

Do you recognise our misfortunes as being similar to your own, our personalities a reflection of yours but simpler? Do you pity, love and hate dogs because you see your own humanness in

274

us? Is that why you insult our name? Are you only insulting yourselves?

'A dog's life' had true meaning for me as I lay there in the grass, panting. Was my life always to follow this unlucky pattern? It was the human part of my nature coming to the fore again, you see, for not many animals philosophise in such a way (there are exceptions). Fear and that good old human characteristic, self-pity, had aroused the semi-dormant side of my personality once more and I thought in terms of man yet still with canine influence.

I shook off my misery the way dogs do and got to my feet. I had an objective which had been neglected; now was the time to continue my search. It was a beautifully fresh day and the air was filled with different scents. I was without a patron again and still without a friend but because of it I was free; free to do as I pleased and free to go where I pleased. I had only myself to answer to!

My legs broke into an unpremeditated sprint and once again I was in full flight, only this time my compulsion to run was ahead of me and not behind. I knew the direction I should take instinctively and soon found myself back on the road and heading towards the town that had sounded so familiar.

Cars swished past at frequent intervals, causing me to shy away. I was still very frightened of these mechanical monsters even after months of living in the busy city, but somehow I knew I had once driven such a vehicle myself. In another life. I came to a heavily wooded area and decided to take a small detour, knowing it would actually cut a few miles off my journey.

The wood was a fascinating place. It hummed with hidden beings which my eyes soon began to detect, and to which (surprisingly) I was able to put names. There were beetles, gnats, hoverflies, tabanad flies, mosquitoes, wasps and bees. Speckled wood and brimstone butterflies fluttered from leaf to leaf. Dormice, wood-mice and bank-voles scuttled through the undergrowth, and grey squirrels were everywhere. A woodpecker stared curiously at me from his perch and ignored my hearty good morning. A startled roe-deer leapt away as I stumbled into its hiding-place. Thousands on thousands of aphides (you might know them as blackfly or greenfly) sucked the sap from leaves and plant stems, excreting honeydew for ants and others to feed on. Birds – songthrush, chaffinch, great tit, blue tit, jays and many, many more – flew from branch to branch or dived into the undergrowth in search of food. Earthworms appeared and disappeared at my feet. I was amazed at the teeming activity and a little in awe of it, for I had never realised so much went on in these sheltered areas. The colours almost made my eyes sore with their intensity and the constant babble of animal chatter filled my head with its raucous sound. It was exhilarating and made me feel very alive.

I spent the day exploring and thoroughly enjoyed myself, seeing things through new eyes and with a completely different mental approach, for I was now part of that world and not merely a human observer. I made a few friends here and there, although I was generally ignored by this busy population of animals, insects, birds and reptiles. Their attitudes were quite unpredictable, for I had quite a pleasant chat with a venomous adder, whereas a cute-looking red squirrel I chanced upon was extremely rude. Their appearance bore no resemblance to their nature. (My conversation with the adder was strange, for snakes, of course, have only an inner ear which picks up vibrations through the skull. It made me realise again that we were communicating through thought.) I discovered snakes are a much-maligned creature for this one was a very inoffensive sort, as have been most I've come into contact with since.

For once I forgot about my belly, and allowed myself to enjoy my surroundings, sniffing out trails left or boundaries marked by various animals through their urine and anal glands. I marked my own trail from time to time, more as a 'Fluke was here' sign than a means of finding my way back. There'd be no going back for me.

I dozed in the sun in the afternoon and when I awoke I wandered down to a stream to drink. A frog sat there eating a long pink worm, scraping the earth off the shiny body with his fingers as he swallowed. He stopped for a moment and regarded me curiously, the poor worm frantically trying to work his body back out of the frog's mouth. The frog blinked twice and resumed his eating, the worm slowly disappearing like a live string of spaghetti. The worm's tail (head?) wriggled once more before leaving the land of the living, then was gone, the frog's eyes bulging even more as he gulped convulsively.

'Nice day,' I said amiably.

He blinked again and said, 'Nice enough.'

I wondered briefly how he would taste but decided he didn't look too appetising. I seem to remember from somewhere that his legs might be quite tasty, though.

'Haven't seen you around here before,' he commented.

'Just passing through,' I replied.

'Passing through? What does that mean?'

'Well . . . I'm on a journey.'

'A journey to where?'

'To a town.'

'What's a town?'

'A town. Where people live.'

'People?'

'Big things, on two legs.'

He shrugged. 'Never seen them.'

'Don't people ever pass this way?'

'Never seen them,' he repeated. 'Never seen a town, either. No towns here.'

'There's a town not too far off.'

'Can't be any such thing. Never seen one.'

'No, not here in the woods, but further away.'

'There is no other place.'

'Of course there is. The world's far bigger than just this woodland!'

'What woodland?'

'Around us,' I said, indicating with my nose. 'Beyond these nearby trees.'

'There's nothing beyond those trees. I only know those.'

'Haven't you ever gone further than this glade?'

'What for?'

'To see what else there is.'

'I know all there is.'

'You don't. There's more.'

'You're mistaken.'

'You've never seen me before, have you?'

'No.'

'Well, I come from beyond the trees.'

He puzzled over this for a minute. 'Why?' he said finally. 'Why have you come from beyond the trees?'

'Because I'm passing through. I'm on a journey.'

'A journey to where?'

'To a town.'

'What's a town?'

'Where people . . . oh, forget it!'

He did, instantly. The frog wasn't really that concerned.

I stomped away, exasperated. 'You'll never turn into a handsome prince!' I shouted over my shoulder.

'What's a handsome?' he called back.

The conversation made me ponder over the animals' point of view. This amphibian obviously thought that the world was only that which he could see. It wasn't even that there was nothing beyond, for he had never even asked himself the question. And it was that way for all animals (apart from a few of us): the world consisted of only what they knew – there was nothing else.

I spent a restless and anxious night beneath an oak tree, the sound of an owl and its mate keeping me awake for most of the night. (It surprised me to discover the 'to-whit-to-whoo' was a combination of both birds – one hooted while the other twitted.) It wasn't so much their calling to each other that bothered me, but their sudden swoops down on to vulnerable voles scurrying around in the dark below, the sudden screech culminating in the victim's squeal of terror which disturbed and frightened me. I didn't have the nerve to upset the owls, since they seemed vicious and powerful creatures, nor did I have the courage to wander around in the dark looking for a new sleeping-place. However, I did eventually fall into an uneasy sleep and the following morning I went hunting for chickens with my new friend, (I thought) – a red fox.

I awoke to the sound of yapping. It was still dark – I estimated dawn was a couple of hours away yet, and the yaps came from not too far off. Lying perfectly still, I tried to detect in which direction the yaps came from, and from whom. Were there pups in this wood? Sure that the owls were now at rest, I inched my way forward away from the trees, my senses keened, and had not gone far when I came across the fox's earth in a hollow under a projecting tree-root. A musty smell of excrement and food remains hit my nostrils and then I saw four sets of eyes gleaming out at me.

'Who's there?' someone said in a half-frightened, half-aggressive, manner.

'Don't be alarmed,' I reassured them hastily. 'It's only me.'

'Are you a dog?' I was asked, and one set of eyes detached

itself from the others. A fox skulked forward out of the gloom and I sensed rather than saw she was a she. A vixen.

'Well?' she said.

'Er, yes. Yes, I'm a dog,' I told her.

'What do you want here?' Her manner had become menacing now.

'I heard your pups. I was curious, that's all.'

She seemed to realise I was no threat and her attitude relaxed a little. 'What are you doing in these woods?' she asked. 'Dogs rarely come in here at night.'

'I'm on my way . . . somewhere.' Would she understand what a town was?

'To the houses where the big animals live?'

'Yes, to a town.'

'Do you belong to the farm?'

'The farm?'

'The farm on the other side of the woods. Over the meadows.'

Her world was larger than the frog's.

'No, I don't belong there. I'm from a big town, a city.'

'Oh.'

The vixen seemed to have lost interest now and turned back when a small voice called from the darkness.

'Mum, I'm hungry!' came the complaint.

'Be quiet! I'm going soon.'

'I'm hungry too,' I said, and I really was.

The vixen's head swung back to me. 'Then go and find yourself some food!'

'Er . . . I don't know how to in a forest.'

She looked at me incredulously. 'You can't feed yourself? You can't find yourself a rabbit, or a mouse, or a squirrel?'

'I've never had to before. I mean, I've killed rats and mice, but nothing bigger than that.'

She shook her head in wonder. 'How have you survived, then. Coddled by the big ones, I suppose – I've seen your kind with them. They even use you to hunt us!'

'Not me! I'm from the city. I've never hunted foxes.'

'Why should I believe you? How do I know you're not trying to trick me?' She showed me her pointed teeth in a grin that wasn't a grin but a threat.

'I'll go away if you like, I don't want to upset you. But perhaps me and your mate can go and find some food for all of us.'

279

'I don't have a mate any more.' She spat the words out and I could feel the anger and hurt in them.

'What happened to him?' I asked.

'Caught and killed,' was all she would say.

'Find us some food, Mum,' came the plaintive cry again.

'Well, perhaps I could help *you*,' I suggested.

'Huh!' scoffed the vixen, then her voice changed. 'There may be a way you can be used, though,' she said thoughtfully.

I stiffened to attention. 'Anything. I'm starving.'

'All right, then. You kids stay here and don't go outside! You hear?'

They heard.

'Come on, you.' The fox brushed past me.

'Where to?' I asked eagerly, following behind.

'You'll see.'

'What's your name?' I called out.

'Hush up!' she whispered fiercely, then said, 'What's a name?'

'What you're called.'

'I'm called fox. Vixen to be exact. You're called dog, aren't you?'

'No, that's what I am. Fox is what you are. I'm called Fluke.'

'That's daft. Flukes are flatworms!'

'Yes, but men called me Fluke – it's an expression.'

She shrugged off my silliness and didn't speak again till we'd walked for at least a mile and a half. Then she turned to me and said, 'We're nearly there now. You have to keep very very quiet from here on – and move very carefully.'

'Right,' I whispered, trembling with excitement.

I could see the farm stretched out before us and from the stench I guessed it was mainly a dairy farm.

'What are we going to do – kill a cow?' I asked in all seriousness, the excitement draining from me.

'Don't be daft!' the fox hissed. 'Chickens. They keep chickens here too.'

That's all right then, I thought. That could be quite interesting.

We crept towards the farm and I copied the fox's style exactly, running forward silently, stopping, listening, sniffing, then padding forward again, from bush to bush, tree to tree, then stealthily through the long grass. I noticed the wind was coming towards us, bringing lovely rich farmyard smells. We reached a huge open shed and slid easily into it. On our left were the remaining bales of last winter's barley straw, and on our right bags of fertiliser piled high. When we emerged, I stopped at a water-trough and, resting my paws on its edge, had a good tongue-lapping drink.

'Come on!' the vixen whispered impatiently. 'No time for that. It'll be dawn soon.'

I padded after her, feeling quite refreshed now, every nerve alive and dancing. The fox and I passed through the collection yard, over the feeding-troughs, by the silage pit, then past a nearly empty but pungent manure hold. I wrinkled my nose – you can have too much of a good thing – and sped after the wily fox. We could hear the cows snoring in their enormous shed, and the smell of barley managed to cover the smell of manure (although not entirely) as we went by a giant barley bin. We were soon through the yard and I could see the dark outline of a house in the moonlight ahead of us.

The fox stopped and sniffed the air. Then she listened. After a while, her body relaxed slightly and she turned to me.

'There's one of your sort here, a big ugly brute. We must be careful not to wake him – he sleeps up near the house. Now this is what we'll do. . . .' She came closer to me and I saw she was quite attractive really in a sharp-looking way. 'The chickens are over in that direction. A thin but sharp barrier keeps them in and us out. If I can get a good grip with my teeth at the bottom of the barrier, I can pull it up so we can get underneath. I've done it before – it's just a knack. Once we get in, all hell will break loose . . .' (did she understand the concept of hell or was it only my mind translating her thoughts) '. . . and when it does, we'll only have a short time to grab a hen each and make a bolt for it.'

I'm sure her eyes must have gleamed craftily in the dark, but I was too excited – or too dumb – to notice.

'Now,' the vixen went on, 'when we run for it, we must go separate ways. That will confuse the big dog and the big thing who keeps him. The two-legged thing . . .'

'Man,' I said.

'What?'

'Man. That's what he's called.'

'Like Fluke?'

'No. That's what he is. Man.'

The vixen shrugged. 'All right. Man has got a long stick that

281

screams. It kills too – I've seen it kill – so you must be careful. You had better run back this way through the yard because there's plenty of cover, and I'll go the other way across the fields at the back because I'm probably faster. O.K.?'

'Right,' I said keenly. Rumbo was probably turning over in his grave just then.

On we stalked, silently and breathlessly, and before long we'd reached the chicken-coop and its surrounding wire-mesh fence. It wasn't a particularly large coop – the farmer probably only kept chickens as a sideline, his profit coming from his cows – but it could have contained thirty to fifty hens. We heard an occasional flutter from inside, but it was obvious they hadn't detected our presence.

The vixen scuffled around at the base of the wire fencing and tried to get a grip on it with her teeth. She managed to do so and pulled upwards with all her strength. The wiring tore loose from its wooden base, but my companion was unable to keep her grip and it fell back down again, although it remained loose. There had been a rippling sound as the wire mesh tore loose and the noise had alerted the hens inside the hutch. We could hear them moving around inside. Soon they would be jabbering and screeching.

The fox tried again and this time she was more successful. The wiring sprang up and sank back only slightly when she released it.

'Quickly,' she whispered and shot through the opening. I tried to follow, but my body was bigger than the fox's and the wire cut into my back, trapping me half-way through. Meanwhile, the fox had climbed up a short run, lifted a small flap with her nose, and in a flash was inside the hutch. The screams and the thrashing sounds that came from inside paralysed me. The sudden deep barking that came from somewhere near the house made me mobile again. I struggled to get free, knowing the farmer and his 'screaming stick' would soon be down there.

The small hatch to the chicken-hutch suddenly flew open and out poured the squawking poultry, feathers and bodies flying through the air like torn pillow-cases.

Now I don't know if you know this, but hens, as do many groups of animals, have their own hierarchy. It's called the 'pecking order', and the hen who has the biggest and meanest peck is the boss, the second meanest pecker is under the first, but boss over the others, and so on all the way down the line. But now it looked as though everyone was equal.

They all ran around like lunatics and the only competition was who could fly the highest.

The fox emerged, a hen as big as her own body fluttering feebly in her grasp. She ran towards the gap where I was crouched neither in nor out.

'Move youself,' came her muffled command.

'I'm stuck!' I yelled back.

'The dog's coming, quickly!' she said, desperately pacing backwards and forwards along the side of the pen. But the dog must have been chained, for although we could hear him barking, he was still nowhere near. Then we heard the roar of the farmer as a window flew open back there at the house.

That moved me. With a terrific wrench backwards I tore myself free of the wire, scratching my back nastily as I did so. The fox, chicken and all, was through in a flash.

'You go that way!' she shouted at me, feathers spraying from her mouth.

'Right!' I agreed. And then I ran up towards the house, towards the dog, towards the farmer and his gun, while my friend flew off in the opposite direction.

I was half-way there before I stopped and said to myself, Hold on! I looked round just in time to see a fleeting black shape tearing across a field before being swallowed up by the dark line of a hedge.

I turned back as I heard the door of the house crash open and out leapt the farmer wearing vest and trousers and heavy boots. The sight of the long object he held in two hands before him nearly made me faint. The other dog was going mad now trying to get at me and I saw it was a very healthy looking mastiff. I had the feeling his stretched chain would break at any moment.

I groaned and wondered which way to run. The end of the cowshed lay to my left, outhouses to my right. Ahead was the farmer and his monster dog. There was only one way to go really, and of course the fox had taken it. I turned in my tracks and made for the open fields.

A choking kind of shout came from the farmer as he saw me and I heard him lumber out into the yard. I didn't have to look to know he was raising the gun to his shoulder. The blast told me it was a shotgun and the whistling over my ears told me the farmer wasn't a bad shot. My speed increased as my quickening heart-beat acted as a crazy metronome to my legs.

More footsteps, silence, and I waited for the second blast. I swerved as much as I could and crouched low to make myself as small a target as possible. The hens leapt into the air in horror as I passed them, no doubt thinking I had returned for second helpings.

I leapt into the air myself as my tail seemed to explode into shreds. I yelp-yelped in that rapid way dogs do when they're hurt, but kept going, relieved that I could actually keep going. The barking behind me reached a new frenzy and then I knew the mastiff had been let loose, for the sound took on a new, more excited pitch. The welcoming fields rushed forward to meet me and I scrambled under a fence and was into them, my tail on fire.

'Gorn boy!' came the shout from behind and knew the monster dog was closing up on me. The field seemed to stretch out before me in the moonlight and grow wider and longer, the hedge on the far side shrinking rather than growing. The mastiff hadn't caught up with me yet, but his heavy panting had. He'd stopped barking to save his breath and conserve his energy. He really wanted me, that dog.

I inwardly cursed myself for being so stupid and allowing myself to be used as a decoy by the fox. It made me very angry and almost caused me to turn and vent my anger on the pursuing dog. Almost, but not quite – I wasn't *that* stupid.

The mastiff seemed to be panting in my left ear now and I realised he was very close. I turned my head quickly to see just how far behind he was and immediately wished I hadn't – his grinning teeth were level with my left flank!

I swerved just as he took a snap at me and he went sailing on by, rolling over on the grass as he endeavoured to stop himself. The mastiff came racing back and I went racing on again, so he found himself running in the wrong direction once more.

Looming up ahead was the hedge and I was grateful it had stopped playing shrinking tricks on me. I dived into it and prayed I wouldn't hit a tree trunk; the mastiff plunged in right behind me. Brambles tore at us and startled birds complained of the noise, but we were through in an instant and tearing across the next field. Knowing he would soon catch up, I began my swerving tactics again. Fortunately, the mastiff wasn't too bright and he fell for my tricks every time. It was exhausting though and several times his teeth raked across my flank, but eventually even his energy seemed to be depleting. On one very successful twist he

284

had gone at least five yards beyond me, so I stopped for a breather. The mastiff stopped too and we both faced each other across the grass, our shoulders and chests heaving with the effort.

'Look,' I panted. 'Let's talk about this.'

But he had no inclination to talk at all. He was up and at me, growling as he came. So on I went.

As I ran, I picked up a scent. Foxes are usually pretty smart when it comes to covering their tracks – they'll double back, climb trees, jump into water, or mingle with sheep – but when they've got a dead chicken in their mouth, dripping blood and feathers, it's another story. She'd left a trail as strong as cat's eyes in a road.

The mastiff got a whiff of it and momentarily lost interest in me, then we both tore off down that smelly path. Through another hedge we went, and then we were in the wood, dodging round trees and heavy clumps of bushes. Startled night creatures scurried back to their homes as we crashed past, twittering and protesting at our intrusion.

I don't think the mastiff's night vision was as good as mine – probably he was a lot older – because his progress wasn't so fast, and several times I heard him cry out when he bumped into trees. I gained some distance on him and began to feel a little more confident about getting away. Then I bumped into the fox.

The hen had hampered her flight and she must have dropped it at this point and paused to retrieve it. I bore no malice – I was too frightened at what lay behind – and would probably have ignored her had I not gone straight into her crouching body. We rolled over in a struggling heap, fox, chicken and dog, but parted immediately when the mastiff joined us. He bit out at everything within reach and, fortunately for both the vixen and me, we were able to leave him there with a mouthful of chickcn, content in his catch as he shook the dead body and tried to rip it apart. The farmer would be well pleased when his guard dog returned with a mouthful of feathers and blood.

We went our separate ways, the vixen and I, she back to her cubs, me to find somewhere quiet to nurse my wounds. It was growing lighter by the minute now and I hurried to get away from the area, not sure of my directions but wanting to travel as far as possible before daybreak. I knew (how did I know?) farmers took great pains to seek out and destroy any killer dogs who plagued their livestock and this particular farmer would certainly regard me as such. My tail stung terribly now, overriding the hurt from my various other wounds, but I didn't dare stop and examine the damage. I came to a stream and swam across, enjoying the coolness on my wounds, and when I reached the other side, clambered out with reluctance. I gave myself a good shake then sped onwards, determined to get clear of the farmer's land.

The sun had risen and was gathering strength by the time I stumbled into a resting-place. I ached and I hurt, and all I could do was lay there in a dip in the ground and try to recover my strength. After a while I was able to twist my head and examine my throbbing tail. The wound wasn't half as bad as I expected; only the very tip had been damaged and much of the hair had gone from it. Victoria would have been pleased, for our tails were now a good match. The sting from the scratches on my back and flanks caused by the wire mesh and the mastiff's teeth weren't too bothersome, but irritating nonetheless. I rested my head between my paws and slept.

When I awoke, the sun was high overhead and covering my body with its warmth. My mouth and throat felt dry and my wounds were a dull throb. My stomach grumbled over the lack of food. Rousing myself, I looked around and saw I was resting in the dip of a gentle slope. A valley spread out below and other grassy hills rose up on the other side, their soft summits mounted by beech copses. I wandered down hoping to find a spring at the bottom of the hill, nibbling at certain grasses as I went. The grass – sheep's fescue it's called – wasn't too tasty, but I knew many downland animals ate it, so at least it would provide nourishment. Again, I wondered how I knew about such things: how I knew the snail I'd just pushed was a Roman snail that used calcium in the chalky downland soil to make its shell; how the bird that sang somewhere to my right was a skylark; how the butterfly that fluttered by was an Adonis blue wakened prematurely by the sudden warm weather. I had obviously taken a keen interest in the countryside in my past life and taken the trouble to learn about nature and her ways. Had I perhaps been a naturalist or a botanist? Or had it been only a hobby to me? Maybe I had been brought up in the countryside and names and habits came naturally to me. I shook my head in frustration: I had to find out *who* I had been, *what* I had been; how I had died and why I had become a dog. And I had to discover who the man was, the man in my dreams who seemed so evil, who seemed such a threat to my family. My family – the woman and the little girl – I had to find them, had to let them know I wasn't dead. Had to tell them I'd become a dog. Wasn't there someone who could help me?

There was. But I wasn't to meet him till two nights later.

Chapter Fifteen

Pay attention now because this is important. This is the point in my story where I heard a reason for my existence, why I was a dog. This is the part that may help you if you're prepared to accept it. I won't mind if you don't, it's up to you, but bear in mind what I asked of you at the beginning: keep your mind open.

I wandered on for two more days, finding the road again and relieved to find it. I was determined not to waste any more time, but to find my home and to find some answers.

Road signs were becoming more difficult to read; I had to gaze at them for a long time and concentrate hard. However, I found the right way and continued my journey, pleased to reach a town further on; it was much easier for me to get food when I was among people and shops. A few people took pity on me in my bedraggled state (although others chased me away as though I were something unclean) and gave me scraps. I spent the night with a family who took me in, and I think they had intentions of keeping me as a pet, but the following morning when they let me out to relieve myself, I ran off to the next town. I hated spurning this family's kindness, but nothing could deter me from my purpose now.

I was less successful in scrounging food in the next town, although I still ate adequately enough. The road was becoming more and more familiar and I knew I was nearing my home. My excitement grew.

When dusk fell I was between towns, so I left the roadside and entered a deep wood. Hungry (of course) and tired (naturally), I searched for a safe place to sleep. I don't know if you've ever spent the night in a wood alone, but it's very creepy. It's pitch-black for a start (no street lights), and there's a constant rustling and cracking of dry twigs as the night animals mooch around.

My night vision's good – better than yours – but even so, it was still difficult to detect much in the darkness. Eerie glowing lights set my heart racing until I investigated and discovered a couple of glow-worms going through their meeting routine. Another blue-green glow upset me until I realised it was only honey fungus growing on a decaying tree-trunk.

I could hear bats flapping around, their high-pitched squeals making me jump, and a hedgehog trundled into me and pricked my nose with its spikes. I considered going back to the roadside, but the blinding lights and roaring engines of passing cars were even more frightening.

The woods at night are almost as busy as in the daytime, except everything seems even more secretive. I adopted this secretive attitude myself and skulked around as stealthily as I could in search of a resting-place. Finally I discovered a nice soft mound of earth beneath a thick roof of foliage, just under a tree. It made a snug hiding place and I settled down for the night, a strange feeling of portentousness filling me. My instincts were right, for later that night my sleep was disturbed by the badger.

And it was the badger who explained things to me.

I had failed to fall into a comfortable sleep and lay dozing in the dark with my eyes constantly blinking open at the slightest sound. A shifting of earth behind me made me jump and twist my head round to see the cause of the disturbance. Three broad white lines appeared from a hole in the sloping ground and a twitching nose at the base of the middle stripe sniffed the air in all directions.

It stopped when it caught my scent.

'Who's there?' a voice said.

I didn't reply – I was ready to run.

The white lines widened as they emerged from the black hole. 'Funny smell,' the voice said. 'Let me see you.'

I now saw there were two shiny black eyes on either side of the middle stripe. I realised it was a badger speaking, and it was two *black* stripes running down his white head which gave him this white-striped appearance. I backed away, aware that these creatures could be fierce if alarmed or angered.

'Is it . . . is it a . . . dog? Yes, it's a dog, isn't it?' the badger guessed.

I cleared my throat, undecided whether to stay or run.

'Don't be afraid,' the badger said. 'I won't cause you any bother unless *you* mean us harm.' He waddled his great coarse-haired body out of his sett and I saw he was at least three feet long and very tall.

'Yes, I thought I recognised the smell. We don't get many dogs in here on their own. You are on your own, aren't you? You're not night-hunting with one of those cattle farmers, are you?'

Like the fox, he didn't seem to trust the dog's association with man. I found my voice and nervously assured him I wasn't.

He seemed puzzled for a moment and I felt rather than saw him regard me curiously. Whatever was going on in his mind was interrupted as another badger shuffled from the sett. I assumed this was his sow.

'What's going on? Who's this?' came a sharp voice.

'Hush now. It's only a dog and he means us no harm,' the boar told her. 'Why are you alone in the woods, friend? Are you lost?'

I was too nervous to speak up right then and the sow piped up again: 'Chase him away! He's after the babies!'

'No, no,' I managed to say. 'No, please, I'm just passing through. I'll be on my way now. Don't get upset.' I turned to trot off into the darkness.

'Just a moment,' the boar said quickly. 'Stay awhile. I want to talk to you.'

Now I was afraid to run.

'Chase him away, chase him away! I don't like him!' the sow urged.

'Be quiet!' the boar said quietly but firmly. 'You go on about your hunting. Leave a good trail for me to follow – I'll join you later.'

The sow knew better than to argue and huffed her way rudely past me, emitting a vile odour from her anal glands as a comment.

'Come closer,' the boar said when his mate had gone. 'Come where I can see you better.' His enormous body had shrunk and I realised his hair must have become erectile on seeing me and had now returned to its normal smoothness. 'Tell me why you're here. Do you belong to a man?'

I shuffled forward, ready to flee.

'No, I don't belong to anyone. I used to, but don't any more.'

'Have you been mistreated?'

'It's a lucky dog who hasn't.'

290

He nodded at this. 'It would be a fortunate animal *or* man who hasn't,' he said.

It was my turn to regard him curiously. What did *he* know of man?

The badger settled himself into a comfortable position on the ground and invited me to do the same and, after a moment's hesitation, I did.

'Tell me about yourself. Do you have a man name?' he asked.

'Fluke,' I told him, puzzled by his knowledge. He seemed very human for a badger. 'What's yours?'

The badger chuckled drily. 'Wild animals don't have names, we know who we are. It's only men who give animals names.'

'How do you know about that? About men, I mean.'

He laughed aloud then. 'I used to be one,' he said.

I sat there stunned. Had I heard right? My jaw dropped open.

The badger laughed again, and the sound of a badger laughing is enough to unnerve anyone. Fighting the urge to run I managed to stammer, 'Y-you used . . .'

'Yes. And you were too. And so were all animals.'

'But . . . but I know I *was*. I thought I was the only one! I . . .'

He stayed my words with a grin. 'Hush now. I knew you weren't like the others at my first whiff of you. I've met some who have been similar, but there's something very different about you. Calm down and let me hear your story, then *I'll* tell you a few things about yourself – about us.'

I tried to still my pounding heart and began to tell the badger about my life: my first recollections in the market, my first owner, the dog's home, the breaker's yard, the Guvnor, Rumbo, the old lady, and my episode with the sly fox. I told him where I was going, of my man memories and, as I went on, my nerves settled, although an excitement remained. It was wonderful to talk in this way, to tell someone who would listen, who understood the things I said, how I felt. The badger remained quiet throughout, nodding his head from time to time, shaking it in sympathy at others. When I had finished, I felt drained, drained yet strangely elated. It seemed as though a weight had been lifted. I was no longer alone – there was another who knew what I knew! I looked eagerly at the badger.

'Why do you want to go to this town – this Edenbridge?' he asked before I could question him.

'To see my family, of course! My wife, my daughter – to let them know I'm not dead!'

He was silent for a moment, then he said, 'But you are dead.'

The shock almost stopped my racing heart. 'I'm not. How can you say that? I'm alive – not as a man, but as a dog. I'm in a dog's body!'

'No. The man you were is dead. The man your wife and daughters knew is dead. You'd only be a dog to them.'

'Why?' I howled. 'How did I become like this? Why am I a dog?'

'A dog? You could have become any one of a multitude of creatures – it depended largely on your former life.'

I shook my body in frustration and moaned, 'I don't understand.'

'Do you believe in reincarnation, Fluke?' the badger asked.

'Reincarnation? Living again as someone else, in another time? I don't know. I don't think I do.'

'You're living proof to yourself.'

'No, there must be another explanation.'

'Such as?'

'I've no idea. But why should we come back as someone or something – *else*?'

'What would be the point of just one existence on this earth?'

'What would be the point of two?' I countered.

'Or three, or four? Man has to learn, Fluke, and he could never learn in one lifetime. Many man religions advocate this, and many accept reincarnation in the form of animals. Man has to learn from all levels.'

'Learn what?'

'Acceptance.'

'Why? Why should he learn acceptance? What for?'

'So he can go on to the next stage.'

'And what's that?'

'I don't know, I haven't reached it. It's good, I believe. I feel that.'

'So how do you know this much? What makes *you* special?'

'I've been around for a long time, Fluke. I've observed, I've learned, I've lived many lives. And I think I'm here to help those like you.'

His words were soft and strangely comforting, but I fought against them. 'Look,' I said, 'I'm confused. Are you saying I have to accept being a dog?'

'You have to accept whatever life gives you – and I mean

accept. You have to learn humility, Fluke, and that comes only with acceptance. Then will you be ready for the next level.'

'Wait a minute,' I said, taking on a new tact out of desperation. 'We *all* become animals when we die?'

He nodded. 'Nearly all. Birds, fishes, mammals, insects – there are no rules as to which species we're born into.'

'But there must be billions upon billions of living creatures in the world today. They can't all be reincarnated humans, our civilisation just hasn't been going that long.'

The badger chuckled. 'Yes, you're right. There are at least a million known animal species, over three quarters of which are insects – the more advanced of us.'

'Insects are the more advanced?' I asked in a flat tone.

'That's right. But let me answer your first point. This planet of ours is very old and it's been washed clean many times so that life can start all over again, a constant cycle of evolvement which allows us to learn a little more each time. Our civilisation, as you call it, has not been the first by any means.'

'And these . . . these people are still coming back, still . . . learning?'

'Oh yes. Much of our progress owes itself to race memory, not inspiration.'

'But no matter how long ago it all began, man evolved from animals, didn't he? How could animals have been reincarnated humans if they were here first?'

He just laughed at that.

You can imagine the state I was in by now: half of me wanted to believe him because I needed answers (and he spoke in such a soothing, matter-of-fact way), and the other half wondered if he was demented.

'You said insects were more advanced . . .' I prompted.

'Yes, they accept their lives, which are shorter and perhaps more arduous. A female fruit-fly completes her whole lifecycle in ten days, whereas a turtle, for instance, can live for three hundred years.'

'I dread to think of what the turtle has been up to in his previous life to deserve such a long penance,' I said drily.

'Penance. Yes, that's a good way of putting it,' he said thoughtfully.

I groaned inwardly and was startled when the badger laughed out loud. 'All too much for you, is it?' he said. 'Well, that's

293

understandable. But think about it: Why are certain creatures so repugnant to man? Why are they trodden on, mistreated or killed, or just plain reviled? Could these creatures have been so vile in their past lives that the malignancy lingers on? Is this their punishment for past crimes? The snake spends his life crawling on his belly, the spider is invariably crushed whenever he comes into contact with man. The worm is despised, the slug makes humans shudder. Even the poor old lobster is boiled alive. But their death comes as a blessing, a relief from their horrible existence. It's nature's way that their lives should be short, and man's instinct that makes him want to crush these creatures. It's not just abhorrence of them, you see, but compassion also, a desire to put an end to their misery. These creatures have paid their price.

'And there are many more, Fluke, many, *many* more creatures below the earth's surface. Beings that no human ever laid eyes on; bugs who live in fires near the earth's core. What evil have they done to earn such an existence? Have you ever wondered why humans think of hell as an inferno, why its direction is always 'down there'? And why do we look skywards when we speak of 'Heaven'? Do we have an instinct born in us about such things?

'Why do many fear death, while others welcome it? Do we already know it's only an enforced hibernation, that we live on in another form, that our wrongdoings have to be accounted for? No wonder those who have lived peaceful lives are less afraid.'

The badger paused at that point, either to regain his breath or to give me time to catch up with him.

'How do you explain ghosts, then? I know they exist, I've seen them – I keep seeing them,' I said. 'Why haven't they been born again as animals, or have they passed that stage? Is that the level we're reaching for? If it is, I'm not so sure I want it.'

'No, no. They haven't even reached our stage of development, I'm afraid, Fluke. They're closer to our world though than their previous one – that's why it's easier for us to see them – but they're lost, you see. That's why there's such an aura of sadness about them. Confused and lost. They find their way eventually with a little help. They get born again.'

Born again. The words struck me. Was this why my vision, the colours I could see, was so incredible? Was this why I could appreciate scents – the most delicate and the most pungent – so fully? Was it because I'd been born again yet still retained vague memories? *I had past senses to compare with the new*! A newborn baby sees freshly but quickly learns to adapt his vision, to mute colours, to organise shapes – he learns *not* to accept. That's why you're nearly blind at birth; it would be too much for you otherwise. Your brain has to sort things out first, then let you in on it gradually. My own sight was now nowhere as clear or unprejudiced as it had been when I was a young pup. Nor was my hearing. My brain which had been born with the ability to appreciate my senses was now organising them so they were acceptable to it, so they no longer dazzled it as much as before.

I shook the train of thought from my head and said, 'But why can't others remember? Why aren't they the same as men?'

'I can't answer that, Fluke. You're different and I don't know why. Perhaps you're the first of a new development. An evolvement. I've met others similar, but none quite like you. Perhaps you are only a fluke after all. I wish I knew.'

'Aren't you the same as me? Wasn't Rumbo almost? And a rat we met once, he seemed like us.'

'Yes, we're a little like you. I suppose me more so than your friend Rumbo and the rat. But you're special, Fluke. I'm special too, but in a different way, as I told you: I'm here to help. Rumbo and the rat may have been similar, but I doubt they were the same. I think perhaps you're a kind of forerunner; everything may be about to go through a change.'

'But why do I only remember fragments? Why can't I remember it all?'

'You're not supposed to remember *anything*. Many creatures carry the characteristics of their past personalities, many may even have vague memories; but they don't think as you do, not in human terms. There's a struggle going on inside you – man versus canine – but I think it will eventually resolve itself. You'll either become a dog completely, or a balance between the two will be reached. I hope it's the latter – that could mean a development for all of us is taking place. But listen to me: you'll never be a man again physically in this life.'

Despair gripped me. What had I expected? That some day, by some miracle, I might return to my old body? That I would live a normal life again? I howled into the night and wept as never before.

Finally, and with no hope in my voice, I said to the badger, 'What do I do now? How can I live like this?'

He moved closer to me and spoke very quietly. 'You accept now. Accept you're a dog, accept you are a fluke – or perhaps not a fluke. You must live as a dog now.'

'But I have to know who I was!'

'No, it won't help you. Forget your past, your family – they're nothing to do with you now.'

'They need me!'

'There's nothing you can do!'

I rose to my feet and glowered down at him. 'You don't understand. There's someone evil near them. They need protection from him. I think he killed me!'

The badger shook his head wearily. 'It doesn't matter, Fluke. You can't help any more. You *have* to forget your past, you might regret it if you go back.'

'No!' I growled. 'Maybe this is why I can remember, why I'm different. They need my help! It stayed with me when I died! I've got to go to them!'

I ran from the badger then, afraid he would make me stay, afraid to hear more, but when I was a safe distance away, I turned and called back.

'Who are you badger? What are you?'

There was no reply. And I could no longer see him in the darkness.

Chapter Sixteen

Pretty heavy stuff, right? A bit frightening? Well, it scared me. But do you see the sense of it? If there is this great goal we're all reaching for – call it perfection, happiness, ultimate peace of mind, whatever you like – then it seems right that it doesn't come easily; we have to earn it. I don't know why and I'm still not sure I believe it myself (and I'm a dog who was once a man), so I don't blame you for doubting. But, like I keep saying: keep an open mind.

I found myself in Edenbridge High Street a day or so later. I'm not sure just how long it took me to get there because, as you can imagine, my mind was in a turmoil after my meeting with the badger. I had to accept that, as a man, I was dead (if I were to believe the badger revelations), and there would be no return to normality for me. But if I were dead, then how did I die? Old age? Somehow, I doubted it. My wife seemed fairly young in my memories of her, and my daughter could have been no more than five or six. Illness? Possibly. Yet why did I feel so strongly against this mysterious man? Why was he so evil to me? Had he killed me?

I felt sure this was the answer, otherwise why should I feel such hate for him? I was determined to find the truth. First, though, I had to find my family.

The High Street was fairly busy with shoppers and delivery vans and the scene was vaguely familiar to me. I must have lived here, I told myself, or why else would I have been drawn to the little town? It wouldn't click though, it just wouldn't click.

The shoppers must have been puzzled by the thoughtful-looking mongrel who paced up and down that street, peering up at passing faces, snooping into shop doorways. I ignored all enticements, for I had more serious things on my mind than playing games.

By late afternoon I was still no better off. I just couldn't remember clearly any of the shops, pubs or people, although everything appeared too frustratingly familiar! That old teaser hunger reminded me he was still around and had no intention of letting me off the hook just because I had problems. The shopkeepers shooed me away as soon as I put my sniffing nose through their doorways, and a sudden jaw-snapping thrust at an overloaded shopping-basket earned me a sharp smack on the snout and a lot of abuse.

Not wanting to cause a fuss (I didn't want to be picked up by the police since I needed to stay around that town until something happened to restore my memory) I left the main street and wandered on to what looked like a vast council estate. Then something did click, although it wasn't particularly helpful to me: many South Londoners had been moved down to Edenbridge over the last twenty or so years, away from their slums into modern estates surrounded by good countryside. Many had taken to their new environment, while others (like Lenny, the Guvnor's man) had still yearned for their old surroundings and spent much of their time to-ing and fro-ing from the two vastly different communities. I was conscious of all this because I'd obviously lived in the town and knew of its history, but where had I lived? On one of those estates? No, it didn't click; it didn't feel right.

I followed a couple of small boys home, much to their delight, and managed to scrounge a few scraps from their scolding but kind-hearted mother. The food wasn't much but enough to keep me going for a while, and to the boys' disappointment I scampered out of their back garden and towards the High Street again.

This time I drifted down all the side-streets on one side, then all the side-streets on the other, but nothing jarred that tiny trigger in my mind which I knew would unleash a flood of memories.

Night fell and so did my spirits. Nothing had happened. I'd felt so sure that when I reached the town it would be easy to find my home, familiar things would guide me to it, but it hadn't happened. I was still in the dark mentally, and now physically.

I wandered down to the very edge of the town, passing pubs, walking across a bridge, past a big garage, a hospital – and then the buildings ran out. There was only black countryside ahead. Utterly dejected, I entered the hospital grounds, found a quiet corner in the yard at the rear of the white single-storey building, and slept.

The smell of lovely cooking awoke me the following morning and I sniffed my way over to an open window from which it wafted. Rearing up on my hind legs, I rested my paws on the window-ledge. Unfortunately, the window was too high for me to see into the room beyond, but, sticking my nose into the air, I drank in the delicious smells, then cried out in appreciation. A huge round brown head suddenly appeared above and white teeth flashed a startled welcome at me. Reds and oranges shimmered in the woman's huge face as she grinned even more broadly.

'You hungry, fellah?' she chuckled, and I wagged my tail in anticipation. 'Now don't you go away,' she told me.

The beaming head disappeared then reappeared almost instantly, the smile now threatening to split the face in half. A thin, partly burnt slice of bacon was dangled before me.

'You get this down you, honey,' she said, dropping the hot finger of meat into my open mouth.

I spat the bacon out instantly as my throat was scorched then drooled saliva on the piping meat to cool it before wolfing it down.

'Good boy,' came the woman's voice from above, then another piece of bacon plopped on to the gravel beside me. This lasted for about as long as the first and I looked up hopefully, tongue hanging out.

'You's a greedy dog!' said the coloured (multicoloured) woman, laughing. 'O.K., I get you one more, then you scat – you get me into trouble!'

The promised third slice appeared and disappeared almost as quickly, and I looked up for more. Still chuckling, the woman waggled her index finger at me and then closed the window as a final word.

It wasn't a bad start to the day and my spirits rose as I trotted round to the hospital's main entrance. Hot food in my belly and a day for discovery ahead of me! Perhaps life (or death) wasn't so bad after all. Dogs are born optimists, as I said.

I reached the entrance and turned left, heading towards the High Street again, sure it was my only chance of finding someone or something I knew.

Without thinking, I wandered into the road and screamed with fright as a green monster roared down on me. The single-decker bus screeched to a halt as I scurried to the other side of the road, tail between my legs and hair on end, and the driver hurled abuse at me, thumping his horn angrily. I cowered in a hedge and rolled my eyes at him, and with a final threatening gesture he threw his vehicle into gear again and slowly moved off.

As the row of windows went by, accusing faces glared down at me while others shook in pity. And one small pair of eyes locked into mine and held my gaze until the progess of the bus no longer allowed them to. Even then, the little girl's head craned round and pushed itself against the glass so I was visible for as long as possible.

Only when the bus had disappeared over the hump-backed bridge did I realise just whom I had been looking at and had been returning my stare. It was my daughter, Gillian, only I called her Polly because I preferred the name! I had been right! Edenbridge was my hometown! I had found them!

But I hadn't found them. The bus was gone and no memories came flooding back. I remembered the names, the minor disagreement over my daughter's, but that was all. I waited for the visions to apear, sure they would, but they didn't.

I groaned in disappointment and longing, then set off after the bus, determined to catch it, refusing to throw away such a chance encounter. As I mounted the hump of the bridge I saw the bus at a stop in the distance. Barking in my eagerness, I increased my speed and hurtled down that High Street like a bullet from a gun. It was no use, though; the bus lurched forward and continued its journey down the long road. I watched it getting smaller and smaller and my legs grew wearier and wearier until I came to a panting halt.

It was hopeless. The bus – and my child – had got away.

Two more days of anguished searching went by – searching of the town and searching of my mind – both of which proved fruitless. I had eaten regularly at the hospital, having my breakfast and evening meal there thanks to the generosity of the coloured cook, and had spent the rest of the time looking through the town and its outer fringes, but all to no avail. Then on the third day, which must have been a Saturday judging by the amount of shoppers there were around, I struck lucky.

I had been wandering up and down the High Street, trying to make myself as inconspicuous as possible (a few people had already tried to catch me now I was becoming a familiar sight around the shops), and had glanced down the small side-turning which led to the car park at the rear of the shops. There I caught a glimpse of a small familiar figure skipping alongside the much taller figure of a woman. They disappeared around a corner but I knew instantly who they were. My heart tried to escape through my throat and my knees suddenly went wobbly.

'Carol!' I gurgled. 'Carol! Polly! Wait for me! Stay there!'

The shoppers must have thought they had a mad dog amongst them, for they all froze at the sound of my barking and stared in amazement as I staggered into the small side-turning. It was like a bad dream, for the shock had turned my legs to jelly and they refused to function properly. I took a grip of myself, realising this was a chance I just could not afford to miss, and willed the power to flow through my quakey limbs. It did, but I had lost valuable seconds. I set off in pursuit of the two figures, mother and daughter, my wife and my child, and was just in time to see them climbing into a green Renault.

'Carol! Stop! It's me!'

They turned and looked in my direction, surprise then fear showing in their faces.

'Quick, Gillian,' I heard my wife say, 'get in the car and close the door!'

'No, Carol! It's me! Don't you know me?'

I was soon across the car park and yapping around the Renault, frantic for my wife to recognise me.

They both stared down at me, their fright obvious. I didn't have the sense to calm down, my emotions were running too high. Carol rolled down the window on her side and flapped a hand at me. 'Shoo, go away! Bad dog!'

'Carol, for Christ sake, it's me – Nigel!' (Nigel? I remembered that was my previous name; I think I preferred Horace.)

'Mummy, it's the poor doggy I told you about, the one that nearly got run over,' I heard my daughter say.

Then I did a quick double-take. Was this my daughter? She seemed much older than I remembered; at least two or three years older. But the woman *was* Carol, and she had called the girl Gillian. Of course it was my daughter!

I leapt up at the side of the car and pushed my nose against the bottom of the half-open window.

'Polly, it's your daddy! Don't you remember me, Polly?' I pleaded.

301

Carol smacked me on the top of the head, not viciously but defensively. Then the car's engine roared into life, the gears clunked, and the vehicle began slowly to move away.

'No!' I screamed. 'Don't leave me, Carol! Please don't leave me!'

I ran alongside the car, dangerously close, but it gathered speed and soon outpaced me. I was sobbing by now, seeing them slip through my paws like this, knowing I could never match their speed, realising they were driving from my life again. I felt like throwing myself beneath the wheels to make them stop, but common sense and my old chum, cowardice, prevented me from doing so.

'Come back, come back, come back!'

But they wouldn't.

I saw Polly's wide-eyed face as the car twisted its way round the winding road that led from the car park to the outskirts of the town, and willed her to make her mother stop the car; but it was no use, they sped away.

Many onlookers were regarding me rather nervously by now and I had the good judgement to make myself scarce before I was reported. I took off after the Renault and, as I ran, memories began to pour into me.

Soon, I remembered where I had lived.

Chapter Seventeen

Marsh Green is a tiny, one-street village just outside Edenbridge. It has a church at one end and a pub at the other, one general store in the middle and a few houses on either side. There are other houses hidden away at the back of these, one of which I stood gazing at now.

I knew this was where my wife and daughter lived – where I had once lived. My name had been Nigel Nettle (yes, I'm afraid so) and I had originally come from Tonbridge, Kent. As a boy, I'd spent a lot of time working for local farmers (hence my knowledge of the countryside and animals), but careerwise I'd turned to – of all things – plastics. I'd managed to set up a small factory in Edenbridge on the industrial estate leading to the town and had specialised in flexible packaging, branching out into other areas as the firm prospered and grew. Speaking as a dog, it all seemed very boring, but I suppose at the time the company meant a lot to me. We had moved to Marsh Green to be near the business, and I had found myself taking more and more trips up to London for business reasons (which is why the route was so familiar).

As far as I could remember, we'd been very happy: my love for Carol had never diminished with time, only grown more comfortable; Polly (Gillian) was a delight, our home was a dream, and the business was expanding rapidly, So what had happened? I had died, that's what.

How, and when (Polly seemed so much older than I remembered) I had yet to find out; but I was even more convinced my death was connected with the mysterious man who floated into view so often, yet eluded me before recognition. If he were still a threat to my family (and *that* thought still clung to me), and if he had had something to do with my death (something told me he had been the *cause* of it), then I would find a way of dealing with

303

him. Right now, though, I just wanted to be with Carol and Polly.

It was mid-afternoon, I think, and the sun was hidden behind heavy clouds. I was at the bottom of an unmade road and staring at the detached house before me. The walls of the ground floor were constructed of red brick, while the upper floor's surface was covered with red clay tiles; the doors and window-frames were painted white. A feeling of warmth spread through me and I swallowed hard.

I had to steady myself, it was no good acting the way I had in the town; they would only become frightened again. Keep yourself under control, I told myself, act like a normal dog; there'll be plenty of time to let them know who you really are once they've got used to you.

Pushing the latch of the garden gate down with a paw, I nudged my way in and trotted up the path, keeping a firm rein on trembling body and quaking nerves. I reached the front door and scratched at its surface with a paw.

Nothing happened. I tried again and still nothing happened. I knew they were in, because the Renault stood in the open garage to my left.

I woofed, quietly at first, then louder. 'Carol!' I called out. 'It's me, Carol, open the door!'

I heard footsteps inside, footsteps coming along the hall towards me. With a great effort of will, I stopped my barking and waited. The door opened slightly and a solitary eye peered through the two-inch crack.

'Mummy, it's that dog again!' Polly cried out. The crack shrunk to an inch, the eye now regarding me with both excitement and trepidation.

More footsteps sounded down the hallway, then Carol's eye appeared above my daughter's. She looked at me in amazement.

'How did *you* get here?' she said.

'I remembered where we lived, Carol. I couldn't follow the car, but I remembered. It didn't take long!' I was finding it hard to contain myself.

'Scat! Go away now, there's a good dog,' Carol urged.

I whimpered. I didn't want to go away; I'd only just found them.

'Oh Mummy, I think he's hungry,' Polly said.

'It might be dangerous, dear. We can't take chances.'

'Please,' I wailed, giving them my most beseeching look. 'I need you. Don't turn me away.'

'Look, Mummy, I think he's crying!'

And I was. Tears rolled down my cheeks.

'That's impossible,' Carol said. 'Dogs don't cry.'

But they do. In fact, I wasn't just crying, I was blubbering.

'Let him come in, please, Mummy. I'm sure he doesn't mean us any harm.' Polly pleaded.

Carol looked doubtful. 'I don't know. It doesn't look very dangerous, but you never know with dogs. They're a bit unpredictable.'

I was really snivelling by now and looking as pitiful as I could. The hardest heart would have melted and I knew my wife's heart was by no means hard.

'All right then, let it in,' she said with a sigh.

The door flew open and I flew in, crying and laughing at the same time, kissing and licking hands and legs. They were startled at first and leapt back in alarm, but soon realised I was only being friendly, 'He's lovely, Mummy!' Polly cried, and knelt on both knees to cuddle me. Fear showed on Carol's face for a second but she relaxed as I smothered Polly's face with wet kisses. It's impossible to tell you how wonderful that moment was – even now it gives me a choking feeling – but if parts of your lives closed in episodes as in a book, then that would have been the end of a chapter. Maybe the end of the book.

My wife joined my daughter on the floor, ruffling my hair with a gentle hand; and I made the mistake of trying to take her in my arms and kiss her on the lips. She screamed in horrified glee and we became a struggling heap of squirming, giggling bodies on the hallway carpet. Polly tried to pull me off and her fingers dug into my ribs, making me shriek with laughter. The harsh tickling continued when she realised she had found my vulnerable spot. The fun stopped when the first sprinkle of water jetted from me (I tried hard but I've never been on the best of terms with my bladder) and Carol leapt to her feet, caught hold of my collar and dragged me towards the door.

I found myself outside on the path again, and to convince my wife I was really quite clean I went through the exaggerated pantomime of cocking a leg (an art in itself) and sprinkling her flowerbed. She wasn't too pleased about the flowers, but understood I was trying to prove something. I waited patiently, beaming up at her, tail wagging itself into a blur, wanting desperately to hug her and tell her I still loved her, until she invited me back into the house.

'Thank you!' I barked, and shot past her legs down the hallway.

Polly chased after me, her laughter beautiful to my ears. I skidded to a halt when I reached the kitchen and my eyes drank in the room, the memories returning like old friends from an outing: the huge old back fireplace with its iron oven, a relic of the past which we decided to preserve; the round pine table, deliberately scored and scratched with initials, noughts and crosses, I LOVE YOUs and HAPPY BIRTHDAYs, and any messages we cared to mark for posterity; the antique clock which always informed us the time was a quarter to four, but did so in such an elegant way; the blue-and-yellow vase on the window-sill that looked as if it had been made up from a jigsaw, the result of my patiently piecing it together after Polly had knocked it on to the floor in her 'just-about-walking' days. There were new items around the kitchen, of course, but these seemed alien, an intrusion upon a memory. I sighed, ready to burst into tears again, but a hand grabbed my collar and interrupted my nostalgia.

'Let's just see who you belong to,' Carol said, tugging the nameplate round into view. 'Fluke? Is that your name?'

Polly cupped a hand to her mouth and tittered.

'No address? Nobody wants you, do they?' Carol said, shaking her head.

I shook my own head in agreement.

'Can we keep him?' Polly said excitedly.

'No,' was Carol's firm reply. 'We'll take it to the police station tomorrow and see if it's been reported missing?'

'But can we keep him if no one wants him?'

'I don't know, we'll have to ask Uncle Reg.'

Uncle Reg? Who was he?

Polly seemed pleased enough with that and began to run her fingers down my back. 'Can we feed Fluke, Mummy? I'm sure he's very hungry.'

'Let's see what we've got for it, then.'

Please call me him, or he, Carol, not *it*. I'm not an *it*. I prefer Fluke to *it*. I prefer *Horace* to *it*.

Carol went to a freezer, a new item in the kitchen, and looked thoughtfully into it. 'I'm sure you'd like a leg of lamb or some nice juicy steak, wouldn't you, Fluke?'

306

I nodded, licking my lips in anticipation, but she closed the freezer and said to Polly, 'Run down to the shop and buy a tin of dogfood. That should keep him happy until tomorrow.'

'Can I take Fluke with me, Mummy?' Polly jumped up and down at the prospect and I began to get excited at her excitement.

'All right, but make sure he doesn't run out into the main road.'

So off we set, my daughter and I, girl and dog, down the lane that led to the main road and the village's only shop. We played as we went and for a while I forgot I was Polly's father and became her companion. I stayed close to her skipping feet, occasionally jumping up to pull at her cardigan, licking her face anxiously once when she tripped and fell. I tried to lick her grazed knees clean, but she pushed me away and wagged a reprimanding finger. While she was buying my dinner in the grocery I stayed on my best behaviour, refusing to be tempted by the pile of within-easy-reach packets of potato crisps, 'all flavours'. We raced back down the lane and I let her beat me for most of the way, hiding behind a tree when she reached the garden gate. She looked around, bewildered, and called out my name; I remained hidden, snickering into the long grass at the base of the tree. I heard footsteps coming back down the lane and, when she drew level with my hiding-place, raced around the other side, scooting towards the gate. Polly caught side of me and gave chase, but I was an easy winner.

She reached me, giggling and breathless, and threw her arms around my neck, squeezing me tight.

We went into the house – my home – and Polly told Carol everything that had happened. Half the tin of dogfood was poured on to a plate and placed on the floor, together with a dish full of water. I buried my nose in the meat and cleared the plate. Then I cleared the dish. Then I begged for more. And more I got.

Everything was rosy. I was home, I was with my family. I had food in my belly and hope in my heart. I'd find a way of letting them know who I was, and if I couldn't . . . well, did it matter *that* much? As long as I was with them, there to protect them, there to keep the mysterious stranger at bay, my true identity wasn't that important. I wasn't worried about the police station tomorrow, for there'd be no one to claim me, and I was sure I could ingratiate myself enough for them to want to keep me. Yes, everything was rosy.

And you know how things have a habit of turning nasty for me just at their rosiest.

We'd settled down for the night (I thought). Polly was upstairs in bed, Carol was relaxed on the settee, her legs tucked up beneath her as she watched television, and I lay sprawled on the floor below her, my eyes never leaving hers. Occasionally, she would look down at me and smile, and I would smile back, breathing deep sighs of contentment. Several times I tried to tell her who I was, but she didn't seem to understand, telling me to stop grizzling. I gave up in the end and succumbed to the tiredness that had crept up on me. I couldn't sleep – I was too happy for that – but I rested and studied my wife's features with adoring eyes.

She'd aged slightly, lines at the corners of her eyes and at the base of her neck where there'd been no lines before. There was a sadness about her, but it was a well-hidden inner sadness, one you had to sense rather than see; it was obvious to me why it was there.

I wondered how she had coped without me, how Polly had accepted my death. I wondered about my own acceptance of the badger's pronouncement that I certainly was dead as a man. The lounge still contained all the cosiness I remembered so well, but the atmosphere of the whole house was very different now. Part of its personality had gone, and that was me. It's people who create atmosphere, not wood or brick, nor accessories – they only create surroundings.

I had looked around for photographs, hoping to catch a glimpse of my past image, but to my surprise had found none on display. I racked my brain to remember if ever there had been any framed photographs of myself around, but as usually happens whenever I try consciously to remember, my mind became a blank. Perhaps they had been too painful a reminder to Carol and Polly and had been put away somewhere to be taken out only when they could cope.

Whether my plastics business had been sold or was still running I had no way of knowing, but I was relieved to see my family seemed to be under no great hardship. Various household items confirmed this: the freezer in the kitchen, the new television set here in the lounge, various old items of furniture scattered about the house.

308

Carol was still as attractive as ever, despite the telltale lines; she'd never been what you might call beautiful, but her face possessed a quality that made it seem so. Her body was still an inch away from plumpness all round, as it always had been, her legs long and gracefully curved. Ironically, for the first time as a dog, I felt physical feeling stir, a hunger aroused. I wanted my wife, but she was a woman and I was a dog.

I quickly turned my thoughts towards Polly. How she'd grown! She'd lost her baby chubbiness but retained her prettiness, fair skin and darkening hair emphasising her small, delicately featured face. I was surprised and strangely moved to see her don brown-rimmed spectacles to watch television earlier on in the evening; it seemed to make her even more vulnerable somehow. I was pleased with her; she'd grown into a gentle child, with none of the petulance or awkwardness so many of her age seemed to have. And there was a special closeness between her and her mother, perhaps a closeness born out of mutual loss.

As I had noticed before, she appeared to be about seven or eight, and I pondered over the question of how long I had been dead.

Outside, the sky had dulled as night bullied its way in, and a chill had crept into the air with it, an agitator urging the night on. Carol switched on one of those long, sleek electric fires (another new item, for we'd always insisted on open fires in the past – logs and coal and flames – but maybe that romanticism had gone with me) and settled back on the settee. Headlights suddenly brightened up the room and I heard a car crunching its way down the gravelly lane. It stopped outside and the engine purred on while gates grated their way open. Carol craned her head around and looked towards the window, then turned her attention back towards the television, tidying her hair with deft fingers and smoothing her skirt over her thighs. The car became mobile again, the glare from its lights swinging around the room and then vanishing. The engine stopped, a car door slammed, and a shadowy figure walked past the window rattling fingers against the glass as it did so.

My head jerked up and I growled menacingly, following the shadow until it had gone from view.

'Shhh, Fluke! Settle down.' Carol reached forward and patted the top of my head.

I heard a key going into its latch, then footsteps in the hallway.

I was on my feet now. Carol grabbed my collar, concern showing on her face. My body stiffened as the door of the lounge began to open.

'Hello . . .' a man's voice began to say, and he entered the room, a smile on his face.

I broke loose from Carol's grip and went for him, a roar of rage and hate tearing itself from me. I recognised him.

It was the man who had killed me!

Chapter Eighteen

I leapt up, my teeth seeking his throat, but the man managed to get an arm between us. It was better than nothing so I sank my teeth into that instead.

Carol was screaming, but I paid her no heed; I wouldn't let this assassin anywhere near her. He cried out at the sudden pain and grabbed at my hair with his other hand; we fell back against the door jamb and slid to the floor. My attack was ferocious for my hate was strong, and I could smell the fear in him. I relished it.

Hands grabbed me from behind and I realised Carol was trying to tug me away, obviously afraid I would kill the man. I hung on; she didn't understand the danger she was in.

For a few snap seconds I found myself eye-to-eye with him and his face seemed so familiar. And strangely – perhaps I imagined it – there seemed to be some recognition in his eyes too. The moment soon passed and we became a frenzied heap again. Carol had her arms around my throat and was squeezing and pulling at the same time; my victim had his free hand around my nose, fingers curled into my upper jaw, and was trying to prise my grip loose. Their combined strength had its effect: I was forced to let go.

Instantly, the man slammed me in my under-belly with a clenched fist and I yelped at the pain, choking and trying to draw in breath immediately afterwards. I went straight back into the attack, but he'd had a chance to close both hands around my jaws, clamping my mouth tightly shut. I tried to rake him with my nails, but they had little effect against the suit he was wearing. Pushing myself into him was no use either; Carol's restraining arms around my neck held me back. I called out to her to let me go, but all that emerged from my clenched jaws was a muted growling noise.

'Hang on to it, Carol!' the man gasped. 'Let's get it out the door!'

Keeping one hand tight around my mouth, he grabbed my collar between Carol's arms and began to drag me into the hall. Carol helped by releasing one arm from my neck and grasping my tail. They propelled me forward and tears of frustration formed in my eyes. Why was Carol helping him?

As I was dragged towards the front door, I caught a glimpse of Polly at the top of the stairs, tears streaming down her face.

'Stay there!' Carol called out when she, too, saw her. 'Don't come down!'

'What are you doing with Fluke, Mummy?' she wailed. 'Where are you taking him?'

'It's all right, Gillian,' the man answered her between grunts. 'We've got to get it outside.'

'Why? why? What's he done?'

They ignored her for, realising I was losing, I had become frantic. I squirmed my body, twisting my neck, dug my paws into the carpet. It was no use, they were too strong.

When we reached the front door he told Carol to open it, afraid to let go himself. She did and I felt the breeze rush in and ruffle my hair. With one last desperate effort I wrenched my head free and cried out, 'Carol, it's me, Nigel! I've come back to you! Don't let him do this to me!'

But of course all she heard was a mad dog barking.

I managed to tear the sleeve of the man's coat and draw blood from his wrist before being thrust out and having the door slammed in my face.

I jumped up and down outside, throwing myself at the door and howling. Carol's voice came to me through the wood; she was trying to soothe Polly. Then I heard the man's voice. The words 'mad dog' and 'attacker' reached my ears and I realised he was speaking to someone on the phone.

'No! Don't let him, Carol! Please, it's me!' I knew he was calling the police.

And sure enough, not more than five minutes later, headlights appeared at the end of the lane and a car bumped its way towards the house. I was underneath the ground floor window by now, running backwards and forwards, screaming and ranting, while Carol, Polly and the man watched me, white-faced. To my dismay, the man had his arms around both Carol's and Polly's shoulders.

The little blue-and-white Panda car lurched to a halt and doors flew open as though it had suddenly sprouted butterfly wings. Two dark figures leapt from it, one carrying a long pole with a loop attached to it. I knew what *that* was for and decided not to give them a chance to use it. I fled into the night; but not too far into it.

Later when the police had given up thrashing around in the dark in search of me, I crept back. I'd heard voices coming from the house, car doors slam, an engine start, then tyres crunching their way back down the lane. No doubt they'd be back tomorrow to give the area a thorough going over in the daylight, but for tonight I knew I'd be safe. I'd wait for the man to come out of the house and then I'd do my best to follow him – or maybe get him there and then. No, that would be foolish – it would only frighten Carol and Polly again, and Carol would probably call the police back. Besides, the man was a little too strong for me. That would be the best bet: follow him somewhere – maybe I could even track his car's scent (even cars have their own distinct smell) – then attack him, the element of surprise on my side. It was a hare-brained scheme, but then I was a pretty hare-brained dog. So I settled down to wait. And I waited. And waited.

The shock of it hit me a few hours later: he wasn't coming out that night. His car was still in the drive so I knew he hadn't already left, and there would have been no reason for him to have gone with the police. He was staying the night!

How could you, Carol? All right, I'd obviously been cold in my grave at least a couple of years, but how could you with him? The man who had murdered me? How could you with anyone after all we'd shared? Had it meant so little that you'd forget so soon?

My howl filled the night and seconds later curtains moved in the bedroom window. My bedroom window!

How could such evil exist? He's killed me, then taken my wife! He'd pay – oh, I'd make him pay!

I ran from the house then, unable to bear the pain of looking at it, imagining what was going on inside. I crashed around in the dark, frightening night creatures, disturbing those who were sleeping, and finally fell limp and weeping into a hollow covered with brambles. There I stayed till dawn.

313

Chapter Nineteen

Have patience now, my story's nearly done.

Do you still disbelieve all I've told you? I don't blame you – I'm not sure I believe it myself. Maybe I'm a dog who's just had hallucinations. How is it you understand me, though? You *do* understand me, don't you?

How's the pain? You'll forget it later; memories of pain are always insubstantial unless you actually *feel* the pain again. How's the fear? Are you less afraid now, or more afraid? Anyway, let me go on: you're not going anywhere, and I've got all the time in the world. Where was I? Oh yes . . .

Dawn found me, full of self-pity again, confused and disappointed. But, as I keep telling you, dogs are born optimists; I decided to be constructive about my plight. First I would find out a little more about myself – like exactly when I died – and then the circumstances of my death. The first would be easy, for I had a good idea of where I would find myself. You see, now I was in familiar surroundings, memories had started to soak through. Well, perhaps not memories, but – how can I put it? – recognitions were soaking through. I was on home ground. I knew where I was. Hopefully, memories of events would soon follow.

The second part – the circumstances of my death – was more difficult, and because I felt familiar places would begin to open memory valves, a visit to my plastics factory might help.

First, though: When did I die?

The graveyard was easy to find, since I knew the location of the dominating church (although the inside wasn't too familiar to me). What was hard to locate, was my own grave. Reading had become difficult by now and many of these gravestones were poorly marked anyway. I found mine after two hours of squinting and concentrating, and was pleased to see it was still neat and tidy in appearance. I suppose to you it would seem a macabre kind of search, but I promise you, being dead is the most natural thing in the world, and it disturbed me not in the least to be mooching around for my own epitaph.

A small white cross marked my resting-place, and neatly inscribed on it were these words: 'NIGEL CLAIREMOUNT' – I'm not kidding – 'NETTLE. BELOVED HUSBAND OF CAROL, BELOVED FATHER OF GILLIAN. BORN 1943 – DIED 1975.' I'd died at the age of thirty-two, so it seemed unlikely it was from natural causes. Below this, two more words were carved out in the stone, and these made my eyes mist up. These simply said: 'NEVER FORGOTTEN.'

Oh yes? I thought bitterly.

The plastics factory was easy to locate too. In fact, as I trotted through the town, I began to remember the shops, the little restaurants, and the pubs. How I would have loved to have gone in and ordered a pint! I realised it was now Sunday, for the High Street was quiet and in the distance I could hear church bells start their guilt-provoking ringing. It was still early morning, but the thought that the pubs would not be open for a few hours yet did not lessen their attraction; I remembered I had always enjoyed my Sunday lunchtime drink.

The sight of the one-floor factory itself, almost a mile beyond the town, stirred up old feelings, a mixture of pride, excitement and anxiety. It was small, but modern and compact, and I could see a fairly substantial extension had recently been added. A long sign, itself made of plastic and which I knew lit up at night, stretching along the face of the building, read: 'NETTLE & NEWMAN – ADVANCED PLASTICS LTD.'

Nettle & Newman, I pondered. Newman? Who was Newman . . . ? Yes, you've guessed it. My killer had been my partner.

It all began to take shape, all began to fall into place; and the thing that hurt most of all was that he wasn't content just to take my business – he'd taken my wife too. I remembered him clearly now, his face – his person – clearly formed in my mind. We had started the business together, built it up from nothing, shared our failures, rejoiced together in our successes. He had the shrewder business brain (although he could be rash), but I had the greater knowledge – an almost instinctive knowledge – of plastics. It

315

seems crazy now, a silly thing to be proud of, but proud I had been of that knowledge. Plastics! You can't even eat them! We had been good partners for a time, almost like brothers, respecting each other's particular flair. It was often I, though, as smart as my partner had been, who had a hunch on business matters and, as I remember, could be very stubborn if I considered a certain direction was the right or wrong one to take. I believe it was this stubbornness which began to lead to our disagreements.

The facts of the disputes hadn't swung into focus yet, but the image of heated arguments in the later days of our partnership clung heavily to my mind. It had seemed our disagreement would lead to the breaking up of the company at one time, but then what had happened?

Obviously I'd been murdered.

Newman. Reginald Newman. Uncle Reg! That's what Carol had said to Polly when she'd asked about keeping me – 'Wait till Uncle Reg gets home'. Something like that! The creep had really crept in! Had I been aware of his intentions before I'd died? Was that why I was different? Was I like one of those unfortunate ghosts I'd seen, tied to their past existence because of some grievance, some undone thing holding them? Had I been allowed (or had my own natural stubbornness caused it?) to keep old memories in order to set things right?

I stood erect, vengeful, defiant of the odds. I would protect my own. (There's nothing worse than an idiot ennobled by revenge.)

The factory was closed for the day, but I sniffed around the outside wondering about the new extension built on to the back of the building. Business must have been good since my death.

After a while I got bored. Strange to think that an interest which had been a large part of my life should seem so uninteresting, so trivial, but I'm afraid after my initial stirring of emotions it all seemed very dull. I went off and chased some rabbits in a nearby field.

I returned to my home later on in the day and was surprised to find it empty. The car was gone from the drive and no noises came from the house. It seemed an empty shell now, just like the factory: they had both lost their meaning. Without their occupants, without my direct involvement, they were just bricks and mortar. I don't remember being conscious of this sudden impersonal attitude in me at the time, and it's only now, in times of almost complete lucidity, that I'm aware of the changes which have taken place in my personality over the years.

Starvation became my biggest concern – at least, the prevention of it – so I trotted back to the main road through the village and the ever-open grocery store. A lightning raid on the 'all-flavours' secured me a small lunch although a hasty departure from Marsh Green.

I took to the open fields when a blue-and-white patrol car slowed down and a plod stuck his head out of the window and called enticingly to me. After my attack on dear Reggie the night before, I knew the local police would be keeping a sharp lookout for me; you're not allowed to attack a member of the public unless you've been trained to do so.

A romp with a flock of longwools (sheep to you) passed a joyful hour for me until a ferocious collie appeared on the scene and chased me off. The derision from the sheep at my hasty retreat irritated me, but I saw there was no reasoning with their canine guardian: he was too subservient to man.

A cool drink in a busy little stream, a nibble at a clump of shaggy inkcaps – edible mushrooms – and a doze in the long grass filled out the rest of the afternoon.

I awoke refreshed and single-minded. I returned to the factory and began my vigil.

He showed up early next morning, much earlier than any of our – I mean his – employees. I was tucking into a young rabbit I'd found sleepy-eyed in the nearby field (sorry, but canine instinct was taking over more and more – I was quite proud of my kill, actually), when the sound of his car interrupted me. I crouched low, even though I was well hidden in the hedge dividing field from factory, and growled in a menacing, dog-like way. The sun was already strong and his feet disturbed fine sandy dust from the asphalt as he stepped from the car.

The muscles in my shoulder bunched as I readied myself to attack. I wasn't sure what I could do against a man, but hate left little room for logic. Just as I was about to launch myself forward, another car drew in from the main road and parked itself alongside Newman's. A chubby grey-suited man waved at Newman as he emerged from the car. The face was familiar, but it was only when an image of the chubby man in a white smock flashed into my mind that I remembered him to be the technical

317

manager. A good man, a little unimaginative, but conscientious and hard-working enough to make up for it.

'Scorcher again today, Mr Newman,' he said, smiling at the foe.

'No doubt of it. Same as yesterday, I reckon,' Newman replied, pulling a briefcase from the passenger seat of his car.

'You look as if you caught some of it,' the manager replied. 'In the garden, were you, yesterday?'

'Nope. Decided to get away from it all and take Carol and Gillian down to the coast.'

'I bet they appreciated that.'

Newman gave a short laugh. 'Yes, I've spent too many weekends going over paperwork lately. No fun for the wife.'

The manager nodded as he waited for Newman to open the office entrance to the factory. 'How is she now?' I heard him say.

'Oh . . . much better. Still misses him, of course, even after all this time, but then we all do. Let's go over this week's schedule while it's still quiet . . .' Their voices took on a hollow sound as they entered the building and the door closing cut them off completely.

Wife? She's married him? I was bewildered. And hurt even more. He'd really got everything!

My fury seethed and boiled throughout the day, but I stayed well hidden as the factory buzzed into activity and became a living thing. A coldness finally took over me as I waited in the shade of the hedge: I would bide my time, wait for the right moment.

Newman emerged again around midday, jacket over his arm, tie undone. There were too many factory workers around, sitting in the shade with their backs against the building, munching sandwiches, others lounging shirtless under the full blast of the sun; I stayed hidden. He climbed into his car, wound down a window, and drove off into the main road.

I gritted my teeth with frustration. I could wait, though.

The murderer returned about an hour later, but again, there was nothing I could do – still too much activity.

I slept and evening came. The workers – many of whom I now recognised – left the building, relieved to escape its exhausting heat. The office staff, consisting of two girls and an administrator, followed shortly after, and the chubby technical manager an hour after that. Newman worked on.

318

A light went on when dusk began to set in and I knew it came from our – his – office. I crept from my hiding-place and padded over to the building, gazing up at the window. I stood on my hind legs and rested my front legs against the brickwork, but even though I craned my neck till the tendons stood out I could not see into the office. The fluorescent light in the ceiling was visible, but nothing else.

I dropped to all fours and did a quick tour of the building looking for any openings. There were none.

As I completed the circuit, I saw the lone car standing where he had parked it face on to the building. And as I approached, I noticed the window on the driver's side had been left open. It had been a hot day.

The thing to do was obvious: the means to do it a little more difficult. It took four painful attempts to get the front portion of my body through that opening, and then a lot of back leg scrabbling and elbow heaving to get my tender belly over the sill. I finally piled over on to the driver's seat and lay there panting, waiting for the pain from my scraped underside to recede. Then I slid through the gap between the front seats into the back and hid there in the dark cavity on the floor, my body trembling all over.

It was at least an hour before Newman decided he'd had enough work for one day and left the office. My ears pricked up at the sound of the front door being locked and I slunk low when the car door jerked open and a briefcase came flying through on to the passenger seat. The car rocked as he climbed in and I did my best to contain my eagerness to get at him. He started the engine, clicking the light switch, and reversed the car from its parking space. A hand fell over the back seat as he reversed and the temptation to bite his fingers off was almost overpowering, but I needed something more than my own strength if I were to claim retribution.

I needed his car's speed.

He swung into the main road and sped towards the town. He had to pass through Edenbridge to reach Marsh Green and, as town and village were not too far apart, I knew I hadn't too long to make my move. There was a long straight stretch of road leading from the town before it curved to the left towards Hartfield, and a smaller road to Marsh Green joining it from the right on its apex. Most cars speeded up on the clear stretch before the bend and it seemed likely he would do the same, for the road would be fairly empty at that time of night. That was where I would go into action – even if it meant being killed myself. I'd died before; it would be easy to do so again. After all, what did I have to lose? A dog's life?

The thought of what this evil man had reduced me to made the blood rush through me again, and the anger beat against my chest. A low rumbling started way down in my throat and began to rise, molten lava full of hate, seeking an opening, gushing up the hot passage of my throat and finally bursting through to the surface with a scream, an eruption of violence.

I saw the fear in his face as he looked back over his shoulder, his eyes wide and white-filled, forgetting to take his foot off the accelerator, the car speeding on unguided. I had time to see the bend was almost upon us before I lunged forward and bit into his cheek.

He went forward, trying to avoid my slashing teeth, but I went with him, catching and tearing his ear. He screeched and I screeched and the car screeched. And we all went crashing off the road together.

My body hurtled through the windscreen and suddenly I was bathed in a blinding whiteness as I skimmed along the bonnet and into the beam of the headlights. For a split second, lasting for at least a year, I felt as if I were floating in an incandescent womb; until darkness and pain hit me as one.

Then I remembered all and knew I'd been so very, very wrong.

Chapter Twenty

Reg Newman had been a true friend. Even after my death.

The realisation hit me along with the pain as I lay there stunned and breathless in the dusty lane – the small lane rutted and stoned-filled, which ran directly on from the main road, used only by residents who lived further down its length. We'd been lucky: instead of running into the trees lining the sides of the bend, the car had plunged straight ahead into the lane, the rough bank at one side bringing it to a gut-wrenching halt.

The fragments joined; pieces merged, the jigsaw made a whole. I knew why the bad memories of Reg had lingered on after death, why my very death had confused and distorted those memories. I saw how the stupidities of life could warp the senses in the afterlife, unsettle a soul's peace. I lay there and let my mind welcome the memories, ashamed and relieved at the same time. I saw the images of my ex-partner had been only vague because he'd been connected with my death and part of me had wanted to forget why and how I had died. Because I had only myself to blame.

We'd had many disagreements in our partnership, but one or other of us had usually given way out of mutual respect for the other's special qualities: Reg's business acumen or my knowledge of plastics. Only this time it had been different. This time neither of us was prepared to back down.

The argument was one we were bound to reach at some time in our growth: level out or expand. I was for levelling out, maintaining our position in soft plastics, improving and diversifying only in certain areas. Reg was for expanding, going for hard plastics, investigating the qualities of polypropylene in this area. He maintained that eventually glass would be a thing of the past, that it would be replaced by the more durable plastic, first in the container market, then in most other areas where glass was now

321

used. Polypropylene seemed to possess most of the qualities needed: clarity, strength, the ability to withstand a variety of temperatures, and it was durable to most conditions.

We were using polythylene mainly at that time for flexible packaging such as carrier-bags, frozen food pouches and containers for garden feed produce; to change from this to hard plastics would have meant a huge investment. While I agreed with my partner about the future of plastics, I argued we were not ready to venture into that field just yet. The company would need new extruders for the raw materials to be softened and moulded, the factory itself enlarged or a complete move made to a bigger site. In addition new technical staff and engineers would be required, and transport costs would rocket because of the larger delivery bulk. It would take an investment of not less than one and a half million pounds to bring it off. And that would mean bringing in new partners, perhaps even merging with another company. The business, I argued, was fine as it was; let other companies pave the way into these new areas. It would be foolish for us to take expansion risks so soon after the oil crisis anyway. If it happened again, or if there were serious delays in bringing home North Sea oil, then many companies would be left out on a limb. Now was the time to maintain our growth, reach a good economic level, and bide our time. But Reg wouldn't have it.

He blamed my ego, my unwillingness to allow strangers into the business we had built up ourselves. He blamed my failure to see beyond the specific product I was dealing with, to see it in future business terms. He blamed my stubbornness, my lack of imagination. I scoffed and blamed his greed.

We were both wrong about each other, of course, and secretly we both knew it, but you need words to sling in arguments, and words so often exaggerate.

It all came to a head when I discovered he had already begun undercover negotiations with a hard plastics company. 'Just sounding them out', he had told me when I confronted him with my discovery (I had taken a call when Reg had been out from a director of the other company who was unaware of my resistance to my partner's plans), but I wouldn't be pacified. I had a suspicion of business 'practices' even though I had a genuine respect for Reg's flair, and now I began to be afraid that things were running too fast for me, that my technical skill was no match for business politics. Anger, spurred on by this, poured from me.

Reg had had enough: so far as he was concerned he was acting in the company's best interests, negotiating for our growth, afraid that if we didn't expand into other areas we would eventually be swallowed up by the bigger firms. It didn't worry him that we would lose much of our independence: there was no standing still in business for him, only progression or regression. And here I was holding him back, content to let the company slide into mediocrity.

He threw the telephone at me and stormed from our office.

It caught me on the shoulder and I fell back into my chair, stunned not by the blow, but by his irrational behaviour. It took a few seconds for my temper to flare again, then I tore after him.

I was just in time to see his car roar off into the main road. I yanked open the door of my own car, fumbling angrily for my keys as I did so, and jumped in. I gunned the engine as an expression of my rage and swept from the factory yard after him.

The red tail-lights from Reg's car were two tiny points far ahead and I pushed down hard on the accelerator to make them grow larger. We sped through Edenbridge, down the long stretch of straight road that followed, and round the curving bend at the end, then on into the unlit country darkness. I flashed my lights at him, commanding him to stop, wanting to get my hands on him there and then. His car pulled into a side road which would take him across country to Southborough, where he lived, and I slowed just enough to allow me to take the turn.

I jammed on my brakes when I saw he had stopped and was waiting. My car rocked to a halt and I saw him climb from his car and stride back towards me. As he drew near, his hand stretched forward, he began to say, 'Look, we're acting like a couple of ki . . .' But I ignored the look of apology on his face, his outstretched hand which was ready to take mine in a gesture of appeasement, his words that were meant to bring us both to our senses.

I threw open my door, striking his extended hand, and leapt out, hitting him squarely on the jaw all in one motion. Then I jumped back into the car, snapped it into reverse, and raced backwards into the main road again. I looked forward just in time to see him raise himself on to one elbow, his face lit up in the glare of my headlights. I saw his lips move as though calling my name, and a look of horror sweep across his features.

Then I was in the main road and engulfed in a blinding white light. I felt the car heave and heard someone screaming and through the searing pain that followed I realised I was listening to myself. And then the pain and the light and the screaming became too much and I was dead.

I was floating away, and my car was a mangled wreck, and the cab of the truck that had hit it was buckled and smashed and the driver was climbing from it, his face white and disbelieving, and Reg was crying, trying to pull me from the wreck, calling my name, and refusing to admit what my crumpled body swore to.

And then there was a blankness; and then I was reluctantly pushing myself from my new mother's womb.

I staggered to my feet, all four of them. My head was dazed and spinning, not just with the physical blow it had received, but with the facts that had been revealed to me.

Reg was not the evil man of my dreams: he had been a friend in life and a friend in death. He'd succumbed to my wishes, kept the company small; the extension was a sign that the company was still profitable and growing in the way I had wanted, for it meant no drastic development had taken place, only improvement to existing production. Had he kept it this way out of respect for me, or had his business venture merely fallen through without my added strength? There was no question in my mind; I *knew* the former was the case. And Reg, the lifelong bachelor, the man I had teased so often about his unmarried status, the friend who had admitted quite openingly there had only ever been one girl for him and I had married her, had finally taken that plunge. Not just for me, a noble act in taking care of my bereaved family, but because he had always loved Carol. He'd known her long before I had (it was he who introduced us) and our rivalry for her had been fierce until I had won, and then he had become a close friend to both of us.

Our business partnership had often been stormy, but our friendship had rarely rocked. Not until our final conflict, that is. And that was a conflict I know he regretted bitterly. As I now did.

I looked back at the car, its engine dead but the lights still blazing. Disturbed dust swirled and eddied in their beams. Blinking my eyes against the brightness, I staggered forward, out of their glare and into the surrounding darkness. My eyes quickly became used to the sudden change in light and I saw Reg's body slumped half out of the smashed windscreen across the car bonnet. He looked lifeless.

With a gasp of fear, I ran forward and jumped up at the bonnet. One of his arms dangled down the side of the car and his face, white in the moonlight, was turned towards me. I stretched forward and licked the blood from his gashed cheek and ear, begging forgiveness for what I had done, for what I had thought. Don't be dead, I prayed. Don't die uselessly as I had.

He stirred, groaned. His eyes opened and looked directly into mine. And for a moment I swear he recognised me.

His eyes widened and a softness came into them. It was as if he could read my thoughts, as if he understood what I was trying to tell him. Maybe it was only my imagination, maybe he was just in shock, but I'm sure he smiled at me and tried to stroke me with his dangling hand. His eyes suddenly lost their sharpness as consciousness slipped from him. There was little blood on him apart from the gash in his cheek and ear caused by my teeth in our struggle inside the car; my body had broken the glass of the windscreen, he had merely followed through. The steering wheel had prevented him going further and I checked to see it had done no serious damage to his body. It was of the collapsible kind and so he would have a massive bruise across his stomach the next day, but probably nothing more serious. His head must have struck the top of the windscreen frame as he'd gone through and this had caused his blackout. There was no smell of death on him.

Voices came from further down the lane as people left their houses to investigate the sound of the crash. I decided it was time for me to leave; there was nothing here for me anymore.

I stretched forward and kissed Reg on his exposed cheek. He stirred but did not regain consciousness.

Then I dropped to all fours and padded away into the night.

Chapter Twenty-One

So there you have it, old man. That's it.

Do you believe me?

Or do you think your pain is driving you mad?

Dawn is creeping up on us now, and death – for you – is creeping with it. I knew when I found you here by the roadside last night it was too late to find help for you; the cancer in your stomach had already made its claim.

How long have you walked the roads, caring for no one and no one caring for you? What did life do to make you flee from it? Well, it's over for you now; your years of wandering are done.

I wonder if you do understand all I've told you? I think your closeness to death had made our communication possible. You're in that transitive state which helps the dying receptive to many things they've closed their minds to before. Do you still think there's only blackness waiting for you? Or Hell? Heaven? If only it were that simple.

There's not much more to tell you now. I waited, hidden in the darkness, until they had pulled Reg from the car and saw he had regained consciousness again. He actually walked himself to the ambulance which had arrived by then, and I could see him twisting his head, peering into the gloom, looking for me. The people helping him must have thought he was concussed when he kept asking about the dog he'd seen.

I left the area shortly after, paying one last visit to my own grave before going. I don't quite know why I went there; perhaps in some strange way it was to pay my last respects to myself. It was the end of something for me. The end of a life, possibly.

Fresh flowers had been placed at the graveside, and I knew I had not been forgotten. The memory of the husband, the father, the friend, would dull with time, but I'd always be somewhere in a corner of their minds.

For me, it was to be different. The memories might still linger, to surface occasionally, but the emotions had changed. My emotions were fast becoming those of a dog, as though, now my search was over, a ghost had been vanquished. The ghost was my humanness. I felt free, free as any bird in the sky. Free to live as a dog. I ran for nearly a day and, when I finally dropped, the last remnants of my old self had been purged.

That all happened at least – in your terms – two years ago. Memories and old habits still visit me from time to time and I remember myself as a man. But now they only return to me in dreams. Finding you last night, tucked away in this hedge by the roadside, dying and afraid of death, stirred those hidden feelings again. Your dying, the aura that's now around you, drew those feelings out, and with the feelings came the old memories, so clear, so sharp. Perhaps you've helped me too, old man; it would never do for me to relinquish my heritage completely. What was it the badger had said? 'You're special.' Maybe he was right. Maybe everything he told me was right. Maybe I'm meant to remember. Maybe I'm here to help those like you. Maybe.

All I know is that I forget more and more what I was and become what I am.

And by and large, I enjoy what I am. I see life now from a different level: knee-level. It's surprising the difference it makes. It's like always approaching a place from the same direction, then suddenly coming from the opposite way: the familiar changes shape, looks different somehow. It's still the same, but has taken on a new perspective. Know what I mean?

I've travelled the country, swum in the sea. Nobody's ever owned me again, but many have fed me. I've talked with, ate with, and played with so many different species my head aches trying to remember them all. I've been amazed at and chuckled over the neuroses in the animal world: I've met a pig who thought he was a horse; a cow who stuttered; a bull who was bullied by a shrew he shared a field with; a duckling who thought he was ugly (and he was); a goat who thought he was Jesus; a wood-pigeon who was afraid of flying (he preferred to walk everywhere); a toad who could croak Shakespeare sonnets (and little else); an adder who kept trying to stand up; a fox who was vegetarian; and a grouse who never stopped.

I've fought a stoat (we both broke off and ran at the same time – otherwise we'd have both been slaughtered), killed an

327

attacking owl, battled with a rat-pack, and been chased by a swarm of bees. I've teased sheep and irritated horses; I've philosophised with a donkey on existentialism's possible influence on art, ethics and psychology. I've sung with birds and joked with hedgedogs.

And I've made love to seven different bitches.

Time's running out for you now; death's nearly here. I hope what I've told you has helped, I hope it's made some sense to your feverish brain. Can you smell that heavy sweetness in the air; it means I've got to go. It's a lady friend, you see. She lives on a farm three fields away and she's ready for me now. It's just a matter of getting her out of that shed, away from the jealous old farmer; but that shouldn't be too difficult for a smart dog like me.

One other thing before I go: I met Rumbo again the other day. I'd been sleeping under a tree when an acorn hit me on the nose; when I looked around I heard a voice call out 'Hello, squirt,' and there he was above me, grinning all over his little squirrel face. He showered me with a few more acorns, but when I called his name he looked blank, then scurried off. I knew it was him because the voice – thought pattern if you like – was the same; and who else would call me 'squirt'?

It made me feel good, although I had no desire to follow him. It was just good to know someone like Rumbo was around again.

Excuse me now, my lady friend's scent is really becoming too much to ignore. You don't need me anymore anyway, the next part you have to do on your own. At least, I hope I've helped. Maybe we'll bump into each other again sometime.

Good-bye.

Hope you're a dog!

The tramp tried to follow the dog with his tired old eyes as it scampered away, through the broken hedge, into the fields beyond. But the effort was too much.

His body twisted with the pain and seemed to shrivel within the rags he wore as clothes. He lay on his side, his grizzled cheek resting against the damp grass. A solitary ant, not three inches from his eye, gazed at him without expression.

The tramp's lips tried to smile but the pain would not allow it. With his last remaining strength he brought a shaking hand up, and with all the concentration he could summon he placed a finger carefully over the creature's tiny body, but the ant scurried away and hid in the forest of grass. With one last painful shudder, the old man's breath left him and took his life with it.

He died. And waited.

THE DARK

PART ONE

*. . . And God saw that the light was good:
and God separated the light from the
darkness . . .*

Genesis 1:4
(R.S.V.)

It was a bright, sunny day. Not, you might have thought, the sort of day for hunting ghosts. Nor was the house the kind of house you might expect to be haunted. But then psychic phenomena pay scant attention to time, place, or weather.

It was a nice road, but ordinary, with that mid-morning, sub-urban quietness that areas only minutes away from high streets have. The houses themselves were an odd mixture of semis and detached buildings; bright new town houses sparkled at the far end, as yet undaunted by the daily grime.

I drove slowly down the road, looking for the right house, and drew into the kerb when I saw the sign. 'Beechwood'. Unimpressive.

This was one of the detached buildings, tall, grey-bricked, Victorian. I took off my driving glasses and slipped them into the glove compartment; then I rubbed my eyes and settled back to study the house for a few moments.

The small area in front, which obviously had been a garden at one time, had been concreted over to provide an off-the-road parking space for cars; but there were no cars there. I had been told the house would be empty. The windows were opaque from the glare of the sun and for a brief, uneasy moment, it seemed the house itself was staring out at me through mirror sunglasses.

I quickly shrugged off the feeling – imagination could some-times be a hindrance in my job – and reached over to the back seat. The black case was neither large nor heavy, but it contained most of the equipment I would need. The air had a deceptive edge to it when I stepped out on to the pavement, a hint that winter would soon have its turn. A woman whose small child preferred to skip rather than walk gave me a curious look as they passed by, as though my presence in her road had broken a routine. I nod-ded but the contact made her lose interest.

After locking my car, I crossed the concrete area and climbed the five stone steps leading to the front door. There I paused, placing the case by my feet, and searched for the key. I found it and dropped it. The attached faded address card flapped loosely in the air when I retrieved the key and inserted it into the lock. For some reason I stopped and listened before I pushed the heavy door open, peering uselessly through the leaded glass of its top section. There were no sounds and no moving shadows.

I wasn't nervous, nor even apprehensive, for I saw no reason to be. I suppose my initial hesitation was simply due to caution. Empty houses had always made me so. The door swung open and, picking up my case, I stepped inside. I closed the door behind me.

The rays of the sun shone brilliantly through the leaded glass of the door and windows on either side, casting my own shadow deeply and well-defined along the hallway. A broad staircase, its ascent beginning only five feet from where I stood, disappeared into the upper portion of the house, and near the top, from the overhang of the first floor, there dangled a pair of legs.

One shoe – a man's – had fallen off and lay on its side halfway down the stairs; I could see the heel of the man's sock was worn, the pink flesh almost visible through the punctured material. The wall beside the hanging legs was scuffed and blackened as though it had been marked by the man's death-throes. I remember dropping my case and walking slowly down the hall, craning my head upwards, not wishing to mount the stairs, but strangely curious to see the rest of the corpse. I remember peering into the gloom of the stairwell and seeing the bloated face above the grotesquely stretched neck, the ridiculously small loop of plastic flex, no more than three inches in diameter, biting into his flesh as though someone had tugged at his legs to pull it tight. I remember the smell of death coming to me, subtle yet cloying, elusive but all around. It was fresh, unlike the heavy, pungent odour of stale corpses.

I backed away and stopped when I came into contact with the edge of the open doorway opposite the staircase. I turned in surprise and looked into the room; the others were in there, some lying on the floor, some sprawled in armchairs, some upright, staring, as though watching me. But they were all dead. I knew it was not just from the smell, the unseeing eyes, the mutilated bodies. I knew it from the stagnant atmosphere, the stillness of the room itself.

I pushed myself away from the door, sliding my body along the

336

wall for support, my legs suddenly weak. A movement ahead made me stop and I saw there was a small door beneath the staircase. I could only go forward towards the sun-filled front door, not daring to rush back into the depths of the house. The door under the stairs moved again, only slightly, and I realised a draught was disturbing it. I moved closer, keeping my back pressed hard against the wall, and soon I was level with the small opening, sliding past, going beyond it. And then, for some reason still unknown to me, I reached out and pulled the door open, its back slamming against the rising staircase, rebounding so it half closed again. I thought I saw movement but perhaps it was only the shadows receding from the sudden light.

There were stairs leading down to what must have been the cellar. All I could see was the blackness down there, a deep, almost solid darkness. And it was the darkness more than the corpses that made me flee from the house . . .

Chapter One

She sat at the kitchen table, lonely, brooding. She knew she had to face up to it: their life together was no good, it never would be. The idea of moving into the new town house seemed fine at the time; she thought a real home of their own would change his attitude. No more drab flats where everything mended, everything painted, was for the benefit of the landlord. A chance to build something solid, a foundation for their relationship. Marriage didn't matter to her, she'd never pressure him. But the house was right for children . . .

They had snapped up the chance of buying the place, for property prices were constantly soaring, reaching an unbelievable level, settling for a few months, then continuing their relentless upward flight. They had been hesitant about asking the agent to repeat the purchase price again, almost afraid he would realise his mistake and add on an extra three or four thousand. He had confirmed the original cost.

Richard had been a little suspicious and she had stepped in quickly with a firm offer. Whatever unseen drawbacks there might be, this was at least a new start for them. Besides, it was mostly her savings that would pay the ten per cent demanded by the building society towards the cost of the property. The existing owners had already moved out – 'Gone abroad,' said the agent – so within a month they had settled themselves in. It wasn't long before rumours reached them.

She looked down at the empty Diazepan container before her on the table, picking it up and twisting the plastic tube between her fingers. There had been seven left that morning. She had steadily cut down the valium tablets, making progress, moving away from her breakdown of six months ago, suppressing the memory, coping. But Richard hadn't changed. Her near self-destruction had only stemmed the flow briefly; his old ways had

338

soon come slinking back. His excuse was the house now, the road, the other houses. The place made him uneasy, people were unfriendly. Others were moving away – at least three families in the two months they had lived there. There was something wrong with the road.

She had felt it too, almost as soon as they had moved in, but her uneasiness had been quelled by her new hope. Things were meant to change, to become better; instead they had become worse. His drinking had always been hard to take, but bearable – his job as a rep for a finished-art studio demanded he drank with clients, anyway. The women he occasionally slept with didn't matter to her anymore – knowing his inadequacy, she doubted he even enjoyed himself. It was his resentment that had become impossible to live with.

He resented being trapped by the responsibility of owning a home, resented being in debt to a building society, resented her demands, both physical and mental, on him. He resented being the cause of her breakdown.

Now that she had finally come to bear the physical marks of his bitterness – bruising, scratchmarks – she knew it had to end, it was pointless going on. Even though they were not married, the house was in their joint names. But who would be the one to go? Would she come out with nothing after four years of torment? If he insisted, she knew she couldn't stand up to him. She smashed the empty tube down on to the kitchen table. The pills hadn't helped at all.

She stood, her chair scraping harshly against the tiled kitchen floor, and strode towards the sink. She filled the kettle, water splashing fiercely off the metal side, soaking her blouse. She swore, dumping the kettle on the gas ring. After switching on the gas she reached for her cigarettes, the packet lying open on the breadboard. She snatched one out and thrust the end into the gas flame, then quickly into her mouth, drawing her breath in sharply to make it light. Her fingers drummed against the aluminium draining-board, becoming more rigid as she tapped until it was her fist beating down, harder and harder, the sound echoing around the small kitchen. It stopped when a tear slid from her face on to her thinly covered breast, the single damp sensation more disturbing than the overall tap splatter of a few moments earlier. But one tear was all she would allow herself. She rubbed a hand roughly against her eyes, then drew in deeply on the cigarette, looking out through the window into the street below, the lights casting isolated silver pools along its length. Would he come home tonight? She was no longer sure if she even cared. She would have her coffee and go to bed; there she would decide what to do.

She lit another cigarette – the last one, she noticed with annoyance – before carrying the coffee through the kitchen towards the stairs leading to the bedroom. The town house consisted of three floors, the ground being the garage and back workroom, the second level the kitchen and lounge-dining area, the third the two bedrooms and bathroom. She paused at the top of the stairs descending to the front door: should she lock him out? Steam rose in spiralling wisps from the coffee as she pondered. Abruptly she stepped on to the top stair, her mind made up and, just as abruptly, her hand grasped tightly around the balustrade. It was dark down there.

Normally light shone in from the outside street-lamp through the reeded glass door, bathing the tiny hallway in its diffused light. Now she could only see a heavy blackness. Strange, she hadn't noticed the street-light not working from the kitchen. Twisting her body, she flicked on the switch controlling the downstairs light. Nothing happened, but sudden movement caused hot coffee to spill over on to her fingers. She gasped with shock and quickly changed the mug over to her other hand, sticking her burnt fingers into her mouth to lick the offending liquid off. The pain served to remind her of the pain she might receive if she did lock Richard out. She stepped back on to the landing and walked down the hallway, her troubled mind not noticing the bright artificial light shining through the hall window from the street-lamp outside.

Pinky Burton was still angry. The boys in the house opposite had no right to call him such names. They were nothing more than pimply-faced louts, yobbos. He couldn't understand why he had even bothered to be friendly with the younger one, the one with the long, golden locks. Golden when he bothered to wash his unruly mop, that is. Neither had any respect for their elders, not even their father. Father? God, it was little wonder the boys were so offensive with a big abrasive man like that as a father. It was hardly surprising the brute's wife had run off years ago. She obviously couldn't stand any of them.

It used to be a nice respectable road at one time, before the riff-raff moved in. He could remember when one had to have wealth to live in this road, and every family was respectable. And respected. These two gutter-snipes certainly had no respect for him. It was nonsense to suggest he would take the time and trouble to spy on them. Perhaps he had watched them sometimes as they had worked, stripped to the waist, on the older one's motor-cycle. What of it? He was interested in machinery, always had been since his RAF days. The younger one wasn't so bad at first – at least one could have a conversation with him – but the other yobbo, the sneery one, had obviously influenced his brother. How dare they suggest . . . just because a man . . . *how did they find out about that, anyway*?

Pinky turned over in bed and pulled the covers up over his ears. The road was full of nastiness. Never used to be. Nasty modern boxes they called town houses at one end, the old, bigger houses becoming dilapidated, allowed to run down; and greasy-haired louts like those two roaring up and down all night on motorbikes. Well, perhaps they were the only two, and they had one machine between them, but they still made enough noise for a dozen or more. And then there was the house further down, the big detached one – what on earth could have caused something like that? Totally unbelievable. Totally insane. Sign of the times. New – worse – atrocities every day. Made one wonder if there was any goodness at all left in the world. But nothing could match the inhumanity he had found in . . . Pinky still found it hard to form the word in his mind. Why had they sent him there? Hadn't he done enough for his country in the last war? Had it been necessary to punish him so harshly for one misdemeanour? The child had suffered no real harm. All right, so there had been other minor offences to take into account. But they *were* minor, small lapses on his part. It wasn't as if he had ever actually hurt anyone. The degradation inside that . . . place. The degenerates. The vicious, mean bullyboys. To put a man like him alongside such animals. And when he had been released after months that seemed like a thousand years, his position at the club had gone. None of the members had rallied round to support him as their bar manager. No, it was the cold shoulder, them and their bloody tweeds and afternoon golf, their bloody cocker spaniels and crusty-fannied wives. People he had known for years saying nasty, spiteful things. Thank God mother had left the house – thank God she was long dead before it all came out. The shock would have killed her. He would never have been able to afford the place on the measly sum he earned as a part-time barman. And it was humiliating to be on a 'suspect list' of sex offenders. When any crime was committed in the area that had any sexual connotations he could be sure of a police visit. Routine enquiries they always said. Well it wasn't bloody routine to him!

He turned over restlessly on to his back and stared hatefully at the light patterns on the ceiling. The nebulous shapes shivered as a breeze disturbed the leaves on the tree outside, giving the reflected light from the street-lamp a living, embryonic quality. Pinky swore at the ceiling.

The jeers, the sly insinuations, from the two louts over the road had cut deep that day. His other neighbours had always treated him with respect, had always politely acknowledged his greetings, had never pried into his affairs. But these . . . these scumbags had shouted out their obscenities for the whole world to hear, had laughed at him when his own temper had forced him to run back indoors. He did not know what he might have done if he hadn't. Well, tomorrow the police would be informed of the racket they made with their infernal machine. He was still a citizen and, as such, entitled to his rights. Just because he had made a mistake once, it didn't mean he had lost his civil rights! He bit into his lip and choked back a sob. He knew he would never venture into a police station again, not of his own volition. Those bastards, those dirty, little, long-haired bastards!

Pinky closed his eyes tightly and when he opened them, wondered why it had become so dark, why the patterns on the ceiling had disappeared.

She knelt on the bed, a small, huddled form. Susie was small for an eleven-year-old, but her eyes sometimes had a knowing look of someone way beyond her years. At other times they were completely blank. She pulled methodically at the hair of her Cindy doll, the silver strands falling on to her lap. Glass-mounted pictures of Beatrix Potter animals gazed down impassively at her from the blue walls of her little bedroom, oblivious of the sharp snap as a plastic arm was wrenched from the doll's body. The tiny limb bounced off Peter Rabbit and clattered to the floor. Susie pulled at the other arm and threw this, too,

342

across the room, towards the closed window. It fell on to her toy chest beneath the window and lay there, the hand bent back supplicatingly on its swivel-joint.

'Naughty girl, Cindy,' Susie scolded in hushed anger. 'You mustn't stare when you're at the dinner table! Mummy doesn't like it!'

The doll's expression did not change as her leg was pulled back and tugged. 'I've told you time and time again. You mustn't smirk when Uncle Jeremy tells you off! He doesn't like it – it makes him angry. It makes Mummy angry, too!' The leg came away with a sucking sound and was tossed towards the door. 'Uncle Jeremy will go away and leave Mummy if he gets cross. Then Mummy will send me away. She'll tell the doctors I've been acting bad again.' Susie drew in a deep breath at the effort of tearing the last limb free, her small body sagging into a relaxed position when her exertions were rewarded.

'There! Now you can't run away and you can't get into mischief.' Susie smiled triumphantly, but her happiness lasted only seconds. 'I hate that place, Cindy! It's nasty. And the doctors and the nurses are nasty. I don't want to go there again.' Her eyes became tearful, then her face suddenly screwed itself up into an expression of spiteful anger. 'He's not my uncle, anyway. He just wants cuddles from Mummy. He hates me and he hates my Dad! Why doesn't Daddy come back, Cindy? Why does he hate me too? I wouldn't touch matches ever again if he came back, Cindy, I promise I wouldn't.'

She fiercely hugged the limbless doll and rocked to and fro on her knees. 'You know I wouldn't don't you, Cindy? You know I wouldn't.' There was no reply from the doll and Susie thrust it away from her in disgust. 'You never answer me, you naughty girl! You never show you love me!'

She pulled at the pretty plastic head, her arms quivering with the effort, a scream building up in her throat. She suppressed her cry as the head popped free and laughed when she threw it at the stars outside the window. Her body went rigid as the doll's head rebounded off the pane and rolled to the floor. She dared not breathe for a few moments as she listened for footsteps to come thumping along the corridor. She sighed with relief when no such sounds came. They were both asleep. Him, with her, in Daddy's bed. The thought made her angry again. It wasn't just cuddles he wanted. He did other things. She knew, she'd heard, she'd watched.

343

Susie sprang from the bed and padded towards the window, careful not to disturb the toys lying scattered in the dark on the bedroom floor. She examined the pane of glass which had been struck by the doll's head, looking for a crack to show up against the stars outside. It would mean more misery for her if the glass had been broken. She grinned when she saw there was no damage.

Pressing her face to the window she tried to pierce the gloom of the garden below. She spent most of the summer days there when she wasn't at the special school; a prisoner, not allowed to go out on her own. Susie could just make out the shape of the rabbit hutch, weather-beaten and empty, not understanding why they had taken the rabbits away. The baby ones had been gorgeous, lovely to hold, to squeeze. Perhaps if she hadn't squeezed so hard they would have let her keep them.

She returned to the bed and squatted on it, ankles crossed, her arms hugged around her raised knees. The blankets lay rumpled around her. If Uncle Jeremy went away, perhaps Daddy would come back. They could all live together again and be happy, like before. Like before the time she'd been *really* naughty. Before the trouble.

Susie lay back in the bed, pulling the clothes up around her. She gripped the silky edge of the blanket and brushed it rhythmically against her cheek, staring out into the deep blue night framed by the window's edges. One by one she began to count the stars, determined this time to number every one in the rectangle before falling asleep. And one by one, as she silently counted, the stars went out, until only blackness filled the window-frame.

Chapter Two

Bishop glanced discreetly at his watch and was relieved that the two-hour lecture was nearly up. Usual mixed bunch, he thought wryly. Most of them deadly serious, several just curious, one – maybe two – sceptics. And, of course, the token headcase. He smiled generally at the gathering in the small lecture hall.

'So you can see by my list of equipment on the blackboard, parapsychology – the study of paraphysical phenomena – uses technology rather than the more unreliable and, if I may say so, the dubious spiritualistic methods. Graph paper will usually tell you more about strange disturbances in a house than self-imposed mental trances.'

A nervous hand fluttered in the air from the second row. Bishop noticed the man wore a clerical collar. 'May I, er, ask a question?' the equally nervous voice said. All eyes turned to look at the cleric who steadfastly kept his eyes riveted on Bishop's as if embarrassed by his own presence.

'Please do,' Bishop encouraged. 'In fact, we'll spend the last ten minutes discussing any points you might want to raise.'

'Well, it was just that for someone whose profession is the investigation of the paranormal or paraphysical . . .'

'Call it ghost-hunting – it's simpler,' said Bishop.

'Yes, ghost-hunting. Well, it hasn't really been made clear by you whether or not you actually believe in ghosts.'

Bishop smiled. 'The truth of the matter is, having been involved in the study of parapsychology for some years, I'm still unsure. Certainly I've come up against the inexplicable time and time again, but every day science is uncovering new facts about our own powers. Somebody once said that mysticism is just tomorrow's science dreamed today. I think I'd go along with that. For instance, we know concentrated thought, or often

345

unconscious thought, can physically move objects. Scientists throughout the world, particularly in Russia, are now studying the psychokinetic power. Years ago it would have been called witchcraft.'

'But how does that explain spirit sightings?' A middle-aged woman, plump and pleasant looking, had asked the question. 'There are so many cases of hauntings you hear about practically every day.'

'Perhaps not every day, but there are between two and three hundred sightings each year, and probably just as many not publicised. One of the many theories is that ghosts are caused by someone under stress, their minds giving out electrical impulses in the way the heart does, and these impulses are picked up later in particular circumstances.'

The puzzled frown on the woman's face and on the faces of several others in his audience told Bishop he wasn't making himself clear. 'It's rather like a mental picture being transmitted by one individual to be picked up later by someone else who acts as a kind of receiver. Like a television set. This could explain why apparitions are often misty, faded or why sometimes only faces or hands appear: the pictures, or transmissions, if you like, are wearing out, fading until there's nothing left.'

'What about places that have been haunted for centuries, then?' said a young, bearded man in the front row, who was leaning forward antagonistically. 'Why haven't they just faded away?'

'It could be explained by regeneration: the transmission, or apparition, draws on energy from electrical impulses that surround us all. This could account for the appearance of a ghost. A spirit can "live" on indefinitely as long as its image can be seen by others: the ghost is actually telepathic waves, the image created in the mind of a living person years, days, perhaps centuries before and transmitted into the mind or minds of others living today.'

Bishop sighed inwardly: he could see he was losing them. They hadn't expected him to explain ghosts as a scientific phenomenon. They wanted the subject romanticised, the mystic aspect heightened. Even the sceptics among them looked disappointed.

'You're putting it down to electricity, then?' The bearded man in the front row sat back and folded his arms, the slightest indication of smugness in his smile.

'No, not exactly. But an electrical charge given to the nerve tissues of the brain can make a subject see flashes or hear noises. It would seem that a charge given to the appropriate receptive area of the brain can create a phantom image. Remember, the brain functions through electrical impulses and we're also surrounded by them. Impulses picked out of the air by our senses – that's us acting as receivers – isn't a difficult concept to understand. You may have heard of crisis apparitions, where someone sees an image of a friend or relative who is going through some traumatic experience, perhaps dying, many miles away. A voice may even be heard at the same time.'

A few heads nodded appreciatively.

'This can be explained by the person who is undergoing that extreme moment of stress thinking of the person closest to him, perhaps calling out to them. At such times, brain-waves are extremely active – this has been proved by the use of electro-encephalograph machines. When they reach a certain pitch a telepathic image can often be transmitted either to a recipient or into the atmosphere. New factors concerning our own brain power are being brought to light by science at an ever-increasing rate. My guess is that by the end of the century, mysticism and technology will be one. There really will be no such thing as "ghosts".'

A low murmur ran through the gathering as they looked around at each other with various expressions of bemusement, disappointment, or satisfaction.

'Mr Bishop?' The woman's voice came from the back row and Bishop squinted his eyes to see her more clearly. 'Mr Bishop, you term yourself as a ghost-hunter. Can you tell us, then, why you've spent so many years hunting electrical impulses?'

A small ripple of laughter ran through the audience and Bishop smiled with them. He decided to use his reply as a closing statement for the lecture.

'I'm involved in the investigation of hauntings because I believe they have special scientific significance. All phenomena have some rational explanation – it's just that we are not yet advanced enough to perceive that explanation. Any useful information we can gain towards those ends must have value. Mankind is at an exciting stage of development where science and the paranormal are heading towards a meeting point. We have reached the time where parapsychology has to be taken seriously and studied logically with all the advanced technology we have at hand. We can no longer afford to tolerate the fools, the romantics, the misguided; even less can we tolerate the charlatans, the professional ghost-seers, or the mediums who live off the ignorance and distress of others. The breakthrough is nearly here and cannot be allowed hindrance by these people.'

His last words induced a smattering of polite applause from the audience. He held up a hand to let them know he had not quite finished.

'There's one other point. Many people have been emotionally disturbed or frightened by evidence of the paranormal, by "ghostly" appearances: if I can help them understand such occurrences and not to fear them, then that alone justifies my work. Now, I have a list of organisations dealing in physical research, paraphysical studies, metaphysical and ESP research groups and plain old ghost-hunting organisations. There's also a couple of addresses where you can find your own ghost-hunting equipment. Please help yourself to a copy before you leave.'

He turned his back on them, shuffled his lecture notes together and placed them in his briefcase. As usual, his throat was dry after the two-hour talk, and his thoughts now were only of the tall glass of beer that would soothe it. He hardly knew this town, but he hoped the pubs were decent. First, though, he had the gauntlet to run, for there were always those eager to continue the debate on a more personal level long after the allotted time was up. The chief librarian, who had arranged the series of talks in the town library's lecture hall, was the first to come forward.

'Most interesting, Mr Bishop. I'm sure next week's attendance figure will be even higher once word gets around.'

Bishop smiled cynically. He wondered if there would be half as many judging by the disappointment on some of the faces.

'I'm afraid they didn't hear quite what they expected to,' he said without apology.

'Oh no, on the contrary, I think many now realise just what a serious subject the whole matter is.' The librarian rubbed his hands together as if in glee. 'I must say, you've certainly whet my appetite. Let me tell you of the strange experience I had just a few years ago . . .'

Bishop listened politely, knowing he would have to hear several 'strange experiences' from the others in the hall before he could take his leave. As an authority on the subject, he was constantly used as a kind of father confessor by the many who had witnessed real or imaginary phenomena. A small group had soon gathered round and he answered their questions, encouraging them to make a serious study of the paranormal themselves. He also reminded them to keep an open mind and to maintain a careful balance between belief and scepticism. One or two expressed their surprise at his own reservations and he informed them his researches had always been more clinical than biased. The fact that a few years ago an American university had offered £80,000 to anyone who could prove conclusively that there was life after death and as yet the amount was still unclaimed had to have some significance. There was much evidence but still no substantial proof and, although he believed in the continuance of life after death *in some form*, he was still unsure there was a spirit world in the sense of latter- and present-day concepts. While he spoke, he saw the woman who had asked the final question of the lecture period sitting alone at the back of the hall. He wondered why she hadn't joined the group. Eventually, Bishop was able to disengage himself from his inquisitors, mumbling that he had some distance to travel that night and further questions could be asked during the course of the following lectures. Briefcase in hand, he strode briskly down the centre aisle towards the exit. The woman's eyes gazed at him fixedly and when he drew near, she rose from her seat. 'Could I talk to you for just a moment, Mr Bishop?'

He glanced down at his watch as though worried about a pending appointment. 'I really haven't the time now. Perhaps next week . . .?'

'My name is Jessica Kulek. My father, Jacob Kulek, is . . .'

'Is founder and president of the Research Institute of Parapsychological Study.' Bishop had stopped and was looking at the woman curiously as she made her way from her seat towards him.

'You've heard of him?' she said.

'Who in the field of psychical research hasn't? He was one of the men who helped Professor Dean to persuade the American Association for the Advancement of Science to finally accept parapsychologists as members. It was a giant step in forcing scientists throughout the world to take the paranormal seriously. It gave the whole business credibility.'

She gave him the briefest of smiles and he realised she was

349

younger and more attractive than he had at first thought from a distance. Her hair, neither dark nor fair, was short and tucked in closely to the nape of her neck, her fringe cropped high and neatly across her forehead. The tweed suit she wore was stylishly cut and emphasised her slim figure, perhaps too much so – she seemed too slender, frail even. Her eyes were made to look larger by the thinness of her face and her lips were small but finely drawn, like a child's. She seemed hesitant, almost nervous now, yet he felt there was a determination about her that was belied by her appearance.

'I hope my comment didn't offend you,' she said, an earnestness in her expression.

'Hunting electrical impulses? No, I'm not offended. In a way you're right: I am hunting electrical impulses half the time. The other half is spent searching for draughts, land subsidence and water seepages.'

'Could we talk privately for a few moments? Are you staying here tonight? Perhaps your hotel?'

He grinned. 'I'm afraid my talks don't pay well enough for me to stay overnight in hotels. I'd have nothing left over from the evening's work if I did. No, I'll have to drive back home tonight.'

'It's really very important. My father asked me to see you.'

Bishop paused before answering. Finally, he said, 'Can you tell me what it's about?'

'Not here.'

He made up his mind. 'Okay. I'd intended to have a drink before I hit the road, so why not join me? We'd better make our exit fast, though, before the throng back there catches us up.' He pointed over his shoulder at the remaining group of chattering people who were gradually edging their way down the aisle. Bishop took her arm and guided her towards the door.

'You're a little cynical about your profession, aren't you?' she said as they descended the library steps, the cold night drizzle dampening their faces.

'Yes,' he answered brusquely.

'Can you tell me why?'

'Look, let's find a pub and get out of the rain. Then I'll answer your question.'

They walked for five minutes in silence before finding a welcoming pub sign. He led her inside and found a quiet corner table.

'What would you like?' he asked.

'Just orange juice, please.' There was a slight hostility in her tone.

He returned with the drinks, placing the orange juice on the table before her, sinking into the chair opposite with a grateful sigh. He took a long, satisfying swallow of beer before looking across at her.

'Are you involved in your father's research?' he asked.

'Yes, I work with him. You were going to answer my question.'

He was irritated by her persistence. 'Is it important? Has it anything to do with your father asking you to see me?'

'No, I'm just curious, that's all.'

'I'm not cynical about my job – I'm just cynical about the people I come in contact with. Most of them are either fools or publicity seekers. I don't know who are the worse.'

'But you have a good reputation as a psychic investigator. Your two books on the subject are standard reading for any student of the paranormal. How can you deride others who follow the same pursuits as yourself?'

'I don't. It's the fanatics, the idiots steeped in mumbo-jumbo mysticism, and the fools who turn the whole thing into a religion that I despise. The people they prey on, I just feel sorry for. If you've read my books you'll know they're directed towards realism and away from mysticism. For Christ's sake, I've just spent two hours talking about that very thing!'

She flinched at his raised voice and he immediately regretted his impatience. But she came back at him, her lips tight with her own suppressed anger.

'Then why don't you do something more constructive about it? The Society for Psychical Research and other organisations wanted you as a member. Your work could have been invaluable to them. As a ghost-hunter, as you like to call yourself, you're one of the foremost in your field, your services are in great demand. So why do you disassociate yourself from others in your profession, others who could help you?'

Bishop leaned back in his seat. 'You've been checking up on me,' he said simply.

'Yes, my father asked me to. I'm sorry, Mr Bishop, we didn't mean to pry. We just wanted to find out more about your background.'

'Isn't it time you told me why you came here tonight? What does Jacob Kulek want with me?'

351

'Your help.'

'My help? Jacob Kulek wants *my* help?'

The girl nodded and Bishop laughed aloud.

'I'm truly flattered, Miss Kulek, but I don't think there's much about psychic phenomena that I could tell your father.'

'He doesn't expect you to. It's a different kind of information he wants. I promise you, it's important.'

'Not important enough for him to come himself.'

She looked down into her glass. 'It's not easy for him nowadays. He would have come, but I convinced him I could persuade you to see him.'

'It's all right,' Bishop conceded. 'I realise he must be a busy man . . .'

'Oh no, it isn't that. He's blind, you see. I don't like him to travel unless it's absolutely necessary.'

'I didn't know. I'm sorry, Miss Kulek. I didn't mean to be so blunt. How long . . .?'

'Six years. Chronic glaucoma. The nerve structure was already severely damaged before they diagnosed the disease. He'd left it too late before consulting a specialist – he put his blurred vision down to old age and hard work. By the time they realised the real cause, the optic nerves were too far gone.' She sipped her orange juice, then looked at him defiantly. 'He still goes on lecture tours both here and in America and, as head of the Institute, with its growing membership, his days are even more active than before.'

'But if he knows I want nothing to do with organisations such as yours, what makes him think I'd want to help?'

'Because your thinking is not that much different from his. He was once an important member of the Society for Psychical Research until he felt their ideas were at variance with his own. He rejected them too, Mr Bishop, to form his own organisation, the Research Institute of Parapsychological Study. He wanted to research phenomena such as telepathy and clairvoyance to find out if the mind can gain knowledge by means other than the normal perceptual processes. It has nothing to do with ghosts and goblins.'

'All right, so what information does he want from me?'

'He wants you to tell him exactly what you found in Beechwood.'

Bishop's face paled and he quickly reached for his beer. The girl watched him as he drained the glass.

'That was nearly a year ago,' he said, carefully placing the empty glass back on the table. 'I thought it had been forgotten by now.'

'The memory has been revived, Mr Bishop. Have you seen today's papers?'

'No, I've been travelling most of the day. I haven't had a chance to.'

She reached for her shoulder-bag which was propped up against a table leg and drew out a folded newspaper. Opening it, she pointed to the main news item on an inside page. He quickly scanned the bold headline: 'TRIPLE TRAGEDY IN HORROR ROAD'.

He looked enquiringly at the girl.

'Willow Road, Mr Bishop. Where the Beechwood house is.' His eyes returned to the open newspaper, but she told him the details of the story herself.

'Two teenage brothers were blasted by a shotgun last night while they slept. One died instantly, the other is now in hospital in a critical condition. His father is there with him, half his face blown away when he attacked the assailant. He is not expected to live. The madman who did it is in police custody but as yet no statement has been released.

'A fire, which started in the kitchen of a house nearby, burnt through the floor of the bedroom above. The two sleeping people, presumably husband and wife, fell through when the floor collapsed and were burnt to death. Firemen found a little girl in the garden outside watching the flames, petrified with shock. It's not yet known how the fire started.

'In another house, near the end of Willow Road, a woman knifed her common-law husband to death. She then cut her own throat. Their milkman apparently saw the bodies lying on the hall stairs through the glass front door. The report says the woman was in her nightclothes and the man was fully dressed as though he had just come home when she attacked him.'

She paused as if to let the related events sink in. 'All this in one night, Mr Bishop, and all in Willow Road.'

'But it can't have anything to do with the other business. Christ, that was a year ago!'

'Nine months to be exact.'

'So how can there be any connection?'

'My father believes there is. That's why he wants you to tell

353

him everything about the day you went to Beechwood.'

Just the name made him feel uncomfortable. The memory was still too fresh in his mind, the terrible sight he'd witnessed inside the old house still filling his vision like a suddenly projected film slide. 'I told the police everything that happened that day, why I was there, who had hired me. Everything I saw. There's nothing new I can tell your father.'

'He thinks there might be. There has to be something, some explanation. There has to be a reason for thirty-seven people committing mass suicide in one house. And *why* that house, Mr Bishop.'

He could only look down at his empty glass, suddenly feeling the need for something much stronger than beer.

Chapter Three

Jacob Kulek was tall even though stooped, his head thrust forward as if in a constantly enquiring gesture. The ill-fitting suit he wore seemed to hang from his thin frame in draped folds, his shirt collar and tie joining loosely at the very base of his neck. He rose when his daughter showed Bishop into the small room he used as a private study at the Research Institute, the building itself almost anonymous in the medical and financial ghetto of Wimpole Street.

'Thank you for coming to see me, Mr Bishop,' he said, extending his hand.

Bishop was surprised at the firmness of his grip. A muted voice – he realised it was Jessica Kulek's – came from a pocket-size cassette-recorder lying on a low coffee table beside Kulek's easychair. The tall man reached down and switched off the machine, his fingers finding the stop button withoug fumbling.

'Jessica spends an hour each evening recording for me,' he explained, looking directly into Bishop's eyes as if scrutinising him. It was hard to believe he could not see. 'New research information, business correspondence – general matters that fail to receive my attention during the day. Jessica unselfishly shares her vision with me.' He smiled at his daughter, instinctively knowing where she stood.

'Please seat yourself, Mr Bishop,' Jessica said, motioning towards another easychair facing her father's across the coffee table. 'Would you like some coffee – tea?'

He shook his head. 'No, I'm fine, thanks.' As he sat, Bishop glanced around the room; nearly every inch of space on the walls was taken up by volumes of books. It seemed ironic that a man with a mind like Kulek's should surround himself with what must have been the greatest source of frustration imposed by his infirmity.

As if reading his thoughts, Kulek waved a hand generally towards the book-covered walls. 'I know every work in this room, Mr Bishop. Even its position on the shelves. *Masonic, Hermetic, Quabbalistic and Rosicrucian Symbolic Philosophy* – middle bookcase of right-hand wall, third shelf up, seventh or eighth book along. *The Golden Bough* – end bookcase by the door, top shelf, somewhere in the centre. Every book here is important to me, every one taken from those shelves many times before my blindness. It seems that without vision, the mind is more free to turn inwards, to examine more closely one's memory. There are compensations for everything.'

'Your blindness doesn't seem to have affected your work,' Bishop said.

Kulek gave a short laugh. 'I'm afraid it is a hindrance. There are so many new concepts, so many old theories abandoned – Jessica and our little machine have to keep me aware of the changes in thought. My legs are not as strong as they used to be, either. My trusty cane serves both as a guide and a crutch.' He patted the stout walking-stick leaning against the chair almost as though it were a pet animal. 'I have reluctantly cut down on my lecture tours at my daughter's insistence. She likes to have me where she can keep an eye on me.' He smiled reprovingly at his daughter and Bishop felt the closeness between them. The girl had seated herself in a high-backed chair near one of the two windows in the small study as if she were to be an observer only of the conversation about to take place.

'My father would work twenty-two hours a day if I allowed him,' she said. 'The other two he would spend talking about the next day's work.'

Kulek chuckled. 'She is probably right. However, Mr Bishop, to the matter at hand.' His forehead creased into deep lines of concern and his shoulders became even more stooped as he leaned forward. Again, Bishop had to remind himself of Kulek's blindness as his eyes bore into him.

'I believe Jessica showed you the news item on Willow Road last night.'

Bishop nodded, then remembered to voice his affirmation.

'And have you seen this morning's papers?'

'Yes. The man who shot the boys and their father apparently refuses to speak to anyone. The little girl whose parents – no, it turned out to be the mother and her boyfriend – died in the fire is

356

still in a state of shock. The woman who knifed her lover committed suicide, of course, so it can only be assumed that the motive was jealousy or a dispute between them.'

'Ah yes, motive,' said Kulek. 'So it would seem the police have not established a clear motive for each case.'

'There wouldn't be one for all of them. Don't forget, the mother and her boyfriend were killed in the fire. The girl was lucky to get out alive. There's no mention of arson.'

Kulek was silent for a few moments, then he said, 'Don't you think it's rather strange for these three bizarre events to happen on the same night and in the same road?'

'Of course it is. It would be strange if two murders happened over the course of several years in the same road, let alone on the same night. But how could there possibly be a connection between them?'

'On the surface, I agree, there seems to be none other than the time and location. And, of course, the fact that mass self-destruction took place in that same place only months ago. Why were you asked to investigate Beechwood?'

The abruptness of the question startled Bishop. 'Mr Kulek, don't you think you should tell me why you're so interested in the events of Willow Road?'

Kulek smiled disarmingly. 'You're quite right, I have no right to question you without giving you some explanation. Let me just say I have reason to believe the incidents in Willow Road and the suicides of nine months ago have some connection. Have you heard of the name Boris Pryszlak?'

'Pryszlak? Yes, he was one of the men who killed himself in Beechwood. Wasn't he a scientist?'

'Scientist, industrialist – he was an unusual combination of both. He had two main interests in life: making money and the study of energy. A dedicated man in both pursuits. He was an innovator, Mr Bishop, and a man who could turn his scientific achievements into hard cash. A rare man indeed.'

Kulek paused, a curious, hard smile on his lips as if he had a mental picture of the man he spoke of and the memory was unpleasant. 'We met in England in 1946, just before the Communist regime was established in Poland, our homeland. We were refugees: we had realised what was about to happen to our ravaged country. Even then, I could not say he was the kind of man I would choose as a friend, but . . .' he shrugged his

357

shoulders, '. . . we were fellow countrymen and homeless. The situation itself formed our relationship.'

Bishop found it difficult to return Kulek's stare, for the sightless eyes were unwavering. He felt a little unnerved by them. He glanced across at the girl, and she smiled encouragingly, understanding his discomfort.

'One of the other factors that drew us together was our shared interest in the occult.'

Bishop's eyes quickly went back to Kulek. 'Pryszlak, a scientist, believed in the occult?'

'As I said, Mr Bishop, he was a most unusual man. We were friends for a few years – no, perhaps acquaintances would be a better word – then, because our ideas on so many matters differed, we went our separate ways. I settled in this country for a while, married Jessica's late mother, and eventually went to the United States where I joined the Philosophical Research Society under the leadership of Manly Palmer Hall. I heard nothing from or of Pryszlak during those years. Nothing, in fact, until after I returned to England ten years ago. He came to me with a man called Kirkhope and invited me to join their very private organisation. I'm afraid I neither agreed with the direction in which their research was taking them, nor had any sympathy for it.'

'You said the other man's name was Kirkhope. Would that be Dominic Kirkhope?'

Kulek nodded. 'Yes, Mr Bishop. The man who used Beechwood for his occult activities.'

'You know Kirkhope was indirectly one of the reasons I went to the house?'

'I suspected it. His family hired you?'

'No, it was done entirely through the estate agents. Apparently Beechwood has been in the Kirkhope family for years, but never used by them. It was always rented out along with other properties they owned. It seems in the 1930s some strange practices went on there – the estate agents were not allowed to disclose exactly what kind of practices to me – and Dominic Kirkhope became involved. The goings-on were so bad that the Kirkhopes – Dominic's parents, that is – had the tenants forcibly removed. New familes moved in but they never stayed long – they complained the house "wasn't right". Naturally, over the years the house gained a reputation for being haunted and eventually it just remained unoccupied. Because of Dominic

Kirkhope's past association with Beechwood, it became a kind of bugbear to the family, a blemish on their good name. It was neglected for a long time, until just over a year ago they decided to try and rid themselves of the place once and for all. It was modernised, cleaned up, made presentable. But still it didn't sell. There were continuous reports of an "atmosphere". I think sheer desperation made them decide to hire a psychic investigator to try and root out the problem. That's where I came in.'

Kulek and his daughter were silent, waiting for Bishop to continue. They suddenly realised his reluctance to do so.

'Im sorry,' Kulek said, 'I know the memory is unpleasant for you . . .'

'Unpleasant? My God, if you'd seen what they had done to each other in that house. The mutilation . . .'

'Perhaps we shouldn't have asked Mr Bishop to relive his terrible experience, Father,' Jessica said quietly from her position near the window.

'We must. It's important.'

Bishop was surprised at the sharpness in the old man's voice.

'I'm sorry, Mr Bishop, but it's vital that I know exactly what you found.'

'Dead bodies, that's *all* I found! Torn, cut, dismembered. They'd done things to each other that were sickening!'

'Yes, yes, but what else was there? What did you *feel?*'

'I felt bloody sick. What the hell do you think?'

'No, not within yourself. I meant what did you feel in the house? *Was there anything else there,* Mr Bishop?'

Bishop's mouth opened as if he were about to say something more, then it closed and he slumped back in his chair. Jessica rose and went to him; the old man leaned further forward in his seat, puzzlement on his face, not sure what had happened.

'Are you all right?' There was concern in Jessica's eyes as she touched Bishop's shoulder.

He looked at her, his face blank for a few moments, then recognition came filtering through. 'I'm sorry. I was trying to think back to that day, but my mind just seemed to close down. I don't remember what happened, how I got out.'

'You were found in the road outside the house,' Kulek said gently. 'You were lying half-collapsed against your car. Residents reported you to the police and when they arrived, you couldn't speak, you could only stare at Beechwood. That much I

359

found in the official police report. At first they thought you were involved in some way, then your story checked out with the estate agent's. Have you no memory at all of what else happened in that house?'

'I got out, that's all I know.' Bishop pressed his fingers against his eyes as if to squeeze the memory from them. 'I've tried to think back over these past few months, but nothing happens; I see those grotesque corpses, nothing more. I don't even remember leaving the house.' He let out a deep breath, his face becoming more composed. Kulek seemed disappointed.

'Can you tell me now why this is of so much interest to you?' Bishop asked. 'Apart from Pryszlak being involved, I can't see why this business should involve you.'

'I'm not sure that I can be specific.' Kulek rose from his seat and surprised Bishop by walking to the window and gazing out as if he could see into the street beyond. He inclined his head towards the investigator and smiled. 'I'm sorry, my behaviour as a blind man must seem idiosyncratic to you. It's the rectangle of light from the window, you see. It's all my eyes can perceive. I'm afraid it attracts me rather like a moth to a flame.'

'Father, we do owe him an explanation of some kind,' the girl prompted.

'Yes, we do. But what can I really tell our friend? Would he understand my fears? Would he understand, or would he sneer?'

'I'd like the chance to do either,' Bishop said firmly.

'Very well.' Kulek's thin frame swung round to face Bishop. 'I mentioned earlier that Pryszlak wanted me to join his own organisation, but that I did not approve of the direction in which his research was leading. I even tried to dissuade him and this man, Kirkhope, from continuing their dubious pursuits. They knew of my own beliefs relating to the psychic linkage between man and the collective unconsciousness; they thought I would ally myself with their particular cause.'

'But what were they looking for? What were their beliefs?'

'Evil, Mr Bishop. They believed in evil as a power in itself, a power derived from man alone.'

360

Chapter Four

The two policemen began to wonder why they both felt so tense. Their night shift should have been an easy number for them; boring, but easy. The main duty that night was to keep an eye on the road, to report anything suspicious and let their presence be known to the residents by occasionally cruising the road's length in the Panda. Two hours so far, two hours of tedium. Yet their nervousness had grown by the minute.

'This is fucking ridiculous,' the slightly heavier of the two men finally said.

His companion looked across at him. 'What's that?' he asked.

'Sitting here all night just to keep the bleedin neighbours happy.'

'S'pect they're a bit worried, Les.'

'Worried? Murder, manslaughter, bloody house burning down – all in one night? It'll be another hundred years before anything else happens down this road, mate. They've had their lot all in one night.'

'You can't blame them, though, I mean, it's not Coronation Street, is it?'

Les looked out of his side window in disgust. 'Bleedin right it isn't.'

'We'll have another ride down there in a minute. Let's have a smoke first.'

They lit their cigarettes, hands curled round the match flame to cover the sudden flare. Les wound down his window a little to toss the match out, leaving the gap open so the smoke could escape. 'I dunno, Bob. What do you put it down to, then?' He drew in deeply on the cigarette.

'One of them things. Normal road, normal people – on the surface, anyway. Just happens sometimes. Something snaps.'

'Yeah, well it fuckin snapped last year, didn't it? Thirty-seven

361

people bumpin themselves off? Nah, there's something wrong with this road, mate.'

Bob grinned at him in the dark. 'What, touch of the old supernatural? Leave it out, Les.'

'You can laugh,' Les said indignantly. 'Stands to reason something's not right down here, though. I mean, did you see the nutter who blasted those two kids and their old man? Right round the twist, he is. I had a look at him down the cells. Sittin there like a fuckin zombie. Won't do nothin unless somebody makes him. He's an old pouf, you know.'

'Eh?'

'Yeah, got a record. Been done a couple of times.'

'Well how come he had a gun, then? There's no way he'd have a licence, so where would he get a gun from?'

'Wasn't his gun, was it? It was the old man's, the bleedin kids' father. That's the joke of it. This nutter, Burton, broke into the house and found the gun. I reckon he knew they had it. He found the cartridges, the lot. Even reloaded it to do the old man in after he'd got the boys. Then, so the Sarge was sayin, he tried to turn it on himself. Barrel's too fuckin long on a shotgun, though. Couldn't even part his hair with it. Bloody funny, tryin to get it up his nose and he can't even get it past his forehead.'

'Yeah, bloody hilarious.' Bob sometimes wondered if his partner would have been happier as a villain.

There was a silence between them for a few moments and once again the feeling of unease began to build up.

'Come on,' said Bob abruptly, reaching forward to switch on the ignition, 'let's take a ride.'

'Hold it a minute.' Les had raised a hand and was peering intently through the windscreen.

'What's up?' Bob tried to see what his companion was looking at.

'Over there.' The bigger policeman pointed and Bob frowned in irritation.

'Where, Les? You're pointing at the whole bloody road.'

'No, it's nothing. I thought I saw something moving along the pavement, but it's only the street lights flickering.'

'Must be, I can't see anyone. They should all be tucked up in bed, anyway, this time of night. Come on, we'll have a closer look just to be sure.'

The police car slowly crept away from the kerb and crawled

quietly down the road. Bob flicked on his headlights. 'Might as well let anyone who's interested know we're here,' he said. 'They'll sleep more easily.'

They had travelled the length of the road three times before Les pointed again. 'Over there, Bob. There's somethin movin around in there.'

Bob brought the Panda to a smooth halt. 'But that's the house that had the fire the other night,' he said.

'Yeah, so why should anyone be in there now? I'm goin to have a look.'

The burly policeman clambered from the car while his companion radioed in a brief message to their station. He reached back inside and grabbed the torch in the glove compartment. 'Bloody dark in there,' he muttered.

The gate was already open, but Les gave it a brisk kick as he went by; he sometimes liked to warn anyone who might be lurking in the shadows of his approach and give them the chance to get away – confrontations with villains wasn't one of his bigger joys in life. He stopped for a moment, giving Bob a chance to catch up, and shone the powerful torch towards the house. Although the damage to the front, apart from the empty, hollow-eyed windows, was not too bad, the building had a shattered, humbled look, no longer a home. He knew the worst of the damage was at the back, for the fire had started in the kitchen. He swung the light to the attached next-door house. They were bloody lucky, he thought. They could have gone up with this one.

'See anything, Les?' He glanced angrily towards Bob who had crept stealthily up the front path.

'Don't creep about like that, will you?' he whispered. 'Frightened the fuckin life out of me.'

Bob grinned. 'Sorry,' he said in a pleased way.

'I thought I saw someone climbin through a window when we were in the car. Might just have been a shadow from the headlights.'

'Let's have a look while we're here. Bloody stinks still, don't it? Is there anyone still next door?' Bob was moving towards the house and Les hurried to keep up with him.

'Yeah, I think so. Their place wasn't touched.'

Bob left the path and crossed the tiny front garden to reach the glassless downstairs window. 'Bring the torch over, Les. Shine it in.'

Les complied and they both peered into the shattered room beyond the window-frame. 'Bit of a mess,' Les observed.

Bob did not bother to agree. 'Come on, let's have a look inside.'

They walked back to the open front door and the bigger policeman shone the torch along the length of the hall.

'After you, Les.'

'It might not be safe. Those floorboards might have been burned through.'

'No, the carpet's only been scorched. The firemen got here before there was too much damage done to this part of the house. Go on, get in there.'

Les entered the house, gingerly testing each footstep as though expecting to go crashing through the floorboards at any moment. He was halfway down the corridor when a strange thing happened.

The broad, undefined circle of light at the end of the torch beam began to dim as though it had run into a thick blanket of smoke. Except there were no swirling eddies, no grey reflected light. It was as if the beam had met something solid, something that was devouring its brightness. Something dark.

Bob blinked rapidly. It had to be his imagination. There was a movement coming towards them, but there was no shape, no substance. The end wall seemed to be closing in on them. No, it had to be the torch batteries; they were dying, the light becoming dim. But there was still a bright beam along its length, only fading towards the very end.

Les was backing away into him, forcing him to go backwards too. Almost as one, they retreated down the narrow corridor towards the open front door, the torch beam growing shorter as they went until it reached no more than twelve feet ahead of them. Inexplicably, they were afraid to turn their backs on the approaching darkness, fearing that to do so would leave them vulnerable, unprotected.

They had reached the doorway when the torch beam grew strong again and began to force back the gloom. They felt as if an oppression had left them, a fear had been abruptly removed.

'What was it?' Bob said, his voice as well as his legs trembling.

'I don't know.' Les was leaning against the door-frame holding the torch in both hands to control the shaky beam. 'I couldn't make anything out. It was just like a bloody great black wall coming at us. I'll tell you something – I'm not going back in. Let's get some back-up down here.'

'Oh yeah. And tell them what? We got chased out by a shadow?'

The sudden scream made both men jump. Les dropped the torch and it clattered on to the doorstep, its beam dying instantly.

'Oh my Gawd, what was that?' the big policeman said, his legs growing even weaker.

The scream came again and this time both men realised it wasn't human.

'It's coming from next door,' Bob said, a brittleness in his voice. 'Come on!' He ran across the small garden and leapt over the low fence dividing the two properties. Les trundled after him. Bob was pounding on the door by the time the bigger policeman reached him. Inside they could hear a terrible, agonised howling, then another sharp scream sent a coldness running through them.

'Kick it in, Bob! Kick the door in.' Les was already standing back, bringing his foot up high and crashing it against the door lock. The small frosted-glass panel above the letter-box became illuminated and both men stood back in surprise. A faint buzzing noise came to their ears.

Bob thrust his face up to the letter-box and pushed open the flap. His body went rigid and Les could see his eyes widening in shock in the light shining through the letter-box.

'What is it, Bob? What's going on in there?' He had to push his partner aside when he got no reply. He bent down and stared through the rectangular opening. His thumb released the flap as if his own body were rebelling against the sight and refusing to let his eyes see any more. But the sight was already ingrained in his mind. The howling dog pushing its way along the corridor towards him, its back legs slithering frantically in the trail of blood it left behind. Its progress was slow, no more than a panic-stricken shuffle, for it had no front legs, just stumps oozing blood. Behind it, staring down and smiling, stood a man, in his hands a machine of some kind. A machine that whirred, its blades moving faster than the eye could see. He was walking towards the front door as the policeman's thumb had let the letter-box flap drop.

Chapter Five

He was beneath the ocean, swimming downwards, deeper and deeper, away from the silvery light of the sea's calm surface, into the depths where it was dark, the blackness waiting for him, welcoming him. His lungs were bursting, the last bubble of air having escaped an eternity before, yet his body glowed in some strange ecstasy, the pain having no meaning as he reached for the sublimity waiting within that dark, cavernous womb. He entered and swiftly it closed around him, clawing at his limbs, clogging his orifices, choking him as he realised the deception. He gasped for air and the darkness filled him. He floated downwards, arms and legs no longer flailing, his body spinning in a tight circle, faster, faster. Deeper. Then the faint glow, the small shape growing larger, rising to meet him, black waters giving way to its progress. He recognised her face and tried to call her name, but the ocean smothered his cry. She smiled, eyes sparkling in her small, child's face, and reached for him, a plump little hand appearing from the gloom. She still smiled when the other face appeared by her side, her mother's face, the eyes wild, angry, the venom in them meant for him. They began to recede, to grow dim, and he called out for them not to leave him, to help him escape the terrible crushing darkness. They grew smaller, the girl still smiling, the woman's face becoming blank, her eyes lifeless; they disappeared, two tiny wavering flames extinguished, only the total blackness remaining. He screamed and the gurgling became a ringing sound which forced its way into the nightmare, drawing him out, dragging his bedraggled senses back to the surface and reality.

Bishop lay staring at the white ceiling, his body damp with perspiration. The telephone in the hall downstairs refused him time to think of the dream, its shrill cry insistent, demanding to be answered. He threw back the bedclothes and scooped up the

366

dressing-gown lying on the floor by the bed. Slipping it on, he padded down the stairs to the hall, his mind still reeling from the nightmare. He had learned to control the memory, its harshness softened by constancy, but every so often it tore into him mercilessly, shattering the protective wall he had built around his emotions.

'Bishop,' he said into the receiver, his voice dull with fatigue.

'It's Jessica Kulek.'

'Hello, Jessica. Sorry I took so long . . .'

'There was another incident last night,' she interrupted.

His fingers curled tightly around the phone. 'Willow Road?'

'Yes. It's in the morning editions. Haven't you seen them yet?'

'What? Oh, no. I've only just woken up. I had to drive back from Nottingham last night.'

'Can I come over and see you?'

'Look, I told you last week . . .'

'Please, Mr Bishop, we have to put a stop to this.'

'I don't see what we can do.'

'Just let me talk to you. Ten minutes of your time.'

'With your father?'

'He's at a conference this morning. I can come over right away.'

Bishop leaned against the wall and sighed. 'Okay. But I don't think I'll change my mind. Have you got my address?'

'Yes, I have. I'll be there in twenty minutes.'

He replaced the receiver and stared down at it, his hand still resting on the black surface. Snapping himself out of his brooding thoughts, he walked to the front door and pulled the newspaper from the letter-box. The headline sent the remaining nightmare fragments scurrying away.

He was washed, shaved, dressed and drinking coffee by the time he heard her car pull up outside.

'I'm sorry, it took a little longer than I thought,' she apologised when he opened the door. 'The traffic across the bridge was terrible.'

'That's the trouble with being south of the river. You wait till you try to get back.'

He showed her into the small sitting-room. 'Join me in breakfast – coffee?' he said.

'Black, one sugar.' She took off her fawn-coloured topcoat and draped it over the back of an armchair. The slim legged jeans and loose crew-neck sweater she wore combined with her short hair and small breasts to make her look boyish.

'Take a seat. Be with you in a minute,' Bishop told her.

He went back into the kitchen and poured her a coffee, topping up his own. Her voice made him jump, for she had followed him out.

'You live here alone?'

He turned to see her in the doorway. 'Yes,' he answered.

'You're not married?' She seemed surprised.

'Yes, I'm married.'

'I'm sorry, I didn't mean to pry.'

'Lynn is . . . away. Hospital.'

She seemed genuinely concerned. 'I hope she isn't . . .'

'She's in a mental institution. Has been for three years. Shall we go through into the sitting-room?' He picked up the two cups of coffee and waited for her to move from the door. She turned and led the way.

'I didn't know, Mr Bishop,' she said, seating herself and taking the coffee from him.

'It's all right, no reason why you should. And my name is Chris, by the way.'

She sipped her coffee and once again he was bemused by her. One minute she seemed tough, almost brittle, the next, young and timid. An unsettling mixture.

'Did you get a chance to see today's newspaper?' she asked.

'I read the headline, glanced at the story. "More Madness in Horror Road". I'm surprised the Residents Association doesn't take it up.'

'Please, Mr Bishop . . .'

'Chris.'

'Please, the situation is more serious than you think.'

'Okay, I shouldn't be flippant. I agree, a man cutting his sleeping wife's throat with an electric hedge-trimmer, then cutting the legs off his dog isn't a joke. Running out of cable before he could attack two policemen outside is mildly funny, though.'

'I'm glad you think so. You read he turned the machine on himself, didn't you? He severed the main artery in his thigh and died from loss of blood before they could get him to a hospital.'

Bishop nodded. 'Maybe that was his intention from the start, kill his wife, pet dog, then kill himself. He wanted to share his death wish with them.' Bishop held a hand up to ward off her

368

protests. 'I'm not joking now. It's common enough for a suicide to take his loved ones with him.'

'Suicide or not, it was still an act of madness. And why did the other two kill themselves?'

'The other two?'

'The woman who killed her lover and the man who shot the two boys and their father.'

'But he didn't die.'

'He did, last night. My father and I went to the police station where he was being held – we hoped to be allowed to question him. He was dead when we arrived. He was left alone in a cell and he cracked his skull open against the wall. He ran at it, Mr Bishop. From one end to the other, a matter of only eight feet, but enough to split open his head. They said he must have run at the wall twice to cause such damage.'

Bishop winced at the thought. 'The girl. The little girl. . .?'

'They're keeping a very close watch on her. The police are now wondering about the cause of the fire; they seemed to think it may have been deliberately started.'

'Surely they don't imagine the kid set fire to her own home?'

'She has been under psychiatric care for some time.'

'You think that's the link. Everyone in Willow Road is going mad?'

'No, not at all. We've done some checking since we saw you last and discovered that the three people involved in last week's slayings . . .'

'There's no evidence against the child,' Bishop was quick to point out.

'I said the police think the fire may have been deliberately started. There were no electrical appliances switched on, no gas leaks, no fireplace in the kitchen, and they haven't as yet discovered any faulty wiring. What they are reasonably sure of is that the kitchen curtains went up first. A burned-out box of matches was found on the sill. They're now wondering just how the girl got out when the couple in the room next to hers couldn't. Maybe they're wrong in their suspicions, Mr Bishop . . . Chris . . . but the fact that she has needed psychiatric help in the past, that the fire was no accident, and that she got out completely unscathed – and unmarked by smoke – well, it all seems to point in her direction.'

Bishop sighed. 'Okay, so maybe she did cause the fire. What was your point?'

'The woman and the girl were mentally unstable. The woman tried to commit suicide six months ago. The man with the shotgun had been convicted for child molesting. He'd lost his job, had become a social outcast, and the neighbours say the two boys he shot had derided him. It could have been enough to tip him over the edge.'

'You're saying all three were mad?'

'Most people who kill have reached a point of madness. I'm saying something in Willow Road acted as a catalyst.'

'To make them insane?'

She shook her head. 'To direct their instability.'

'Towards murder.'

'Towards an evil act. I don't think it necessarily has to be murder.'

'And you think this is all tied up with the mass-suicide last year?'

Jessica nodded. 'We believe there was a reason for the suicides. Pryszlak, Kirkhope and all those others had a motive.'

Bishop placed the coffee at his feet and stood up. Thrusting his hands deep into his pockets, he walked thoughtfully towards the fireplace. He gazed down at the empty grate for a few moments before turning to her again.

'It's all a bit fantastic, isn't it?' he said mildly. 'I mean, there can only ever be one basic reason for suicide. Escape. That's what it finally comes down to.'

'Release might be another word.'

'Well, yes, release. It's the same thing.'

'No, not quite. Escape means running away. Release is a freedom, something you can embrace. The thirty-seven people who killed themselves in Beechwood were not being persecuted in any way. Not one note was left from any of them to say why they were committing such an act and no individual reasons could be found. There had to be some point in their self-destruction.'

'And you and your father think the events of last week have something to do with it?'

'We're not certain. But we know of the ideals of Pryszlak and his sect. My father told you they wanted his help.'

'He told me they believed in the power of evil. I wasn't quite sure what he meant by "power".'

'He meant evil as a physical entity, a solid force. Something to be used as a weapon could be used. Pryszlak believed this not

370

only as an occultist, but as a scientist, too. He endeavoured to use his knowledge of both to harness that power.'

'But he killed himself before he met with success.'

'I wish we could be sure of that.'

'Oh, come on. At least the man and his lunatic cronies are out of the way. If there is such a power – which I seriously doubt – none of them seems to be around to use it.'

'Unless their very deaths played some part in their search.'

Bishop looked at her in dismay. 'You're not being logical. What good would the knowledge be if they weren't around to use it?'

Jessica's face took on the determined look he had come to recognise. She reached down for her bag and drew out cigarettes. Her hand was trembling slightly when she lit one. She blew out a puff of smoke and regarded him coldly through the sudden haze. 'Then why these sudden acts of violence? Why this sudden madness, Mr Bishop?'

'Chris.'

'Why then?'

He shrugged. 'Who the hell knows? I'm not sure I even care.'

'You're a psychic researcher. You're supposed to have an interest in the paranormal.'

'Sure, but I like to keep my feet planted firmly on the ground. You're flying high.'

'When I first came to you, you seemed to express some respect for my father.'

'I respect his work and his opinion in many things.'

'Then why not in this?'

He turned away from her, resting an elbow on the mantelpiece, his other hand still tucked into a pocket. A small, framed face smiled up at him, the photograph taken when she was only four. A year before she died. Christ, he thought, the bitterness still strong enough to tighten the muscles in his chest, she would have been nearly thirteen now. Even then they could tell she would be the image of her mother.

'Chris?'

He shut the thoughts from his mind. 'It's too implausible, Jessica. And it's all speculation.'

'Isn't all investigation into the paranormal speculation to begin with? You said in your lecture the other night it was your belief

371

that man's natural evolution was reaching the point of break-through, that science and parapsychology were converging to become one and the same thing. Is it beyond you to accept that a man like Pryszlak had already reached that point, had made the breakthrough? At least keep an open mind to it. Isn't that what you tell your students? Isn't that the whole point of your books – openmindedness, with a little realistic scepticism?'

Jessica was on her feet now, her head jutting forward like her father's. 'Or are you too wrapped up in your own personal cynicism? Psychic research needs clear-minded people, Mr Bishop, not cynics, nor fanatics. People who are willing to accept facts and people who are willing to uncover those facts.'

She stabbed her cigarette towards him. 'You're a paid ghost-hunter. All right, we'll hire you. We'll pay for your services. We'll pay you to finish the job you started nine months ago. We want you to investigate that house in Willow Road. Maybe *you* can come up with an answer.'

Chapter Six

Bishop brought the car to a halt, relishing the satisfying sound of crunching gravel. He looked out at the tall, red-bricked, Queen Anne building and said, 'Looks like she's worth a few bob.'

Jessica followed his gaze. 'The Kirkhopes are a great tradition in the shipping industry. At least, they were in the thirties and forties when Dominic Kirkhope's father was alive, but his offspring have had problems now that the shipping boom is over.'

'And she's all that's left?' He tucked his glasses into his breast pocket.

'Agnes Kirkhope is the last of the direct descendants. She and her brother took over when their father died, but, from what I can gather, Dominic played little part in the running of the business.'

'Do you think she'll talk about him? Families are generally reticent about their black sheep.'

'I suppose it depends on our questions. She may not like us digging too deep.'

'When the estate agents hired me to investigate Beechwood I asked to see the owners of the property, but they wouldn't let me. They felt it was unnecessary. In a strict sense they were right – but I usually like to know a house's history. I let it go then because it was just another routine job to me. This time I want to know as much as possible before I set foot in there again.'

'First we have to get her permission to carry out another investigation.'

'Correction: an investigation. The last one wasn't even started.' He switched off the engine and reached for the door-handle on his side. Jessica placed a hand on his other arm.

'Chris,' she said. 'You really think this is for the best?'

He paused before opening the door wide. 'If we tell her the whole story she'll run a mile. Do you really think she'd want her

373

brother's bizarre suicide dredged up again and, even worse, linked with these recent deaths. Let's stick to the story I told her over the phone. She was reluctant enough to see me anyway without giving her further cause for alarm.'

They walked across the drive towards the large main door which opened at their approach.

'Mr Bishop?' a plump, dark-skinned woman enquired.

'And Miss Kulek,' he replied. 'Miss Kirkhope is expecting us.'

The maid nodded, grinning in agreement. 'You come in, Miss Kirkhope is expecting you.'

She busily ushered them into a large, high-ceilinged room off the wide hallway. Pictures of sea-going vessels, from ancient clippers to modern liners, adorned the walls and several detailed models of ships were encased in glass cabinets at various points.

'You wait, please. Miss Kirkhope will be down. She is expecting you.'

The maid left the room, still grinning enthusiastically as though their presence had made her day worthwhile. Bishop ran his eyes around the room while Jessica took a seat on an old Chesterfield, its dark brown bulkiness enhancing the maritime surroundings.

'Business can't be that bad,' he mused.

'It isn't that bad, Mr Bishop, but it lacks the impetus of a few decades ago.'

Agnes Kirkhope's sudden appearance in the doorway startled them both.

'I'm sorry, I didn't mean to be rude,' Bishop apologised.

'That's quite all right, quite all right,' she said striding briskly into the room, her eyes alive with some private amusement. 'I must say this is my most impressive room, though. That's why I receive visitors here.'

She was a small woman, her body thin but ramrod straight, an alertness about her that defied the passage of years. Her hair was pure white but still had a wavy softness to it. She sat at the opposite end of the Chesterfield, her body at an angle so she could still face Jessica, and peered at them through tiny, gold-rimmed spectacles. There was still amusement in her eyes for the embarrassment she had caused Bishop when she spoke.

'I didn't expect two visitors.'

'No, I'm sorry, I should have said on the phone. This is Miss Kulek.'

374

The old lady smiled at Jessica. 'And *who* is Miss Kulek?'

'Jessica works for the Research Institute of Parapsychological Study.'

'Really.' Miss Kirkhope frowned. 'And what exactly is that?'

'We study the paranormal,' Jessica answered.

The old lady's frown increased. 'For any particular reason?'

Bishop grinned.

'To find out more about ourselves, Miss Kirkhope,' Jessica answered.

Miss Kirkhope sniffed as if to dismiss the subject. 'Can I offer you both a sherry? I like to indulge myself at least once a day. Anna! The sherry please!' The maid appeared as though she had been hovering outside the door waiting for the command. She beamed at them all.

'And I think the Cyprus,' Miss Kirkhope added, 'not the Spanish.'

Bishop and Jessica glanced at each other, sharing their own amusement at the slight. They restrained their smiles when the old lady turned her attention back to them.

'Now, Mr Bishop, you said on the telephone you would like to resume your investigation of Beechwood. Hasn't your dreadful experience last time put you off?'

'On the contrary,' Bishop lied, 'it's given me even more reason to investigate the property.'

'Why, exactly? And please do be seated.' She flapped a hand towards an armchair.

He sat on the edge of the seat, resting his forearms on his knees. 'There has to be some explanation as to why all those people killed themselves. There may well be some psychic forces at work in the house.'

'Really, Mr Bishop. The agents told me you were a most practical man despite your profession. You were hired originally to find more material reasons for Beechwood's disturbing atmosphere.'

'Yes, and I still hope to. But we can't just ignore what happened, we have to look for other . . . elements. That's why I'd like to take along Miss Kulek and her father, who is President of the Research Institute. They may discover more than I can on my own.'

The sherry arrived and was distributed by Anna who treated the amber liquid as if it was holy wine and left the room in a fluster of smiles.

'She's new,' Miss Kirkhope explained crisply. She raised her glass. 'Your very good health, my dears.'

They sipped their drinks, Bishop wincing at the sweetness.

'And what has suddenly encouraged you to resume your investigation, Mr Bishop? I wonder if the other recent happenings in Willow Road have rekindled your interest?'

He almost choked on his sherry.

'I ran my father's shipping business practically single-handed for years after his death, with precious little help from dear brother Dominic.' She nodded towards a framed photograph standing on a nearby sideboard; the picture showed a pudgy-faced young man with curly black hair. The resemblance to Miss Kirkhope was minimal. 'True, we eventually went into decline, but that was the case of shipping in general, so please don't take me for a fool just because I'm an old woman. I follow the news and Willow Road is a name I'm hardly likely to forget.'

Jessica spoke up. 'We're very sorry, Miss Kirkhope, I hope we haven't offended you. Chris had no intention of going back to that house until I persuaded him.'

'If we're going to be frank, let's go all the way,' said Bishop. 'Jacob Kulek is hiring me to investigate Beechwood – that is, if I get your permission. We don't want to drag up old memories for you, but Jessica and her father feel there is a link between Beechwood and the recent deaths in Willow Road.'

'Do you feel there is?'

Bishop hesitated before he answered. 'No, I don't. But . . .' he looked across at Jessica '. . . I think it's worth looking into. Jacob Kulek is a renowned figure in his field of work, so any opinion he has on this subject has to be respected. He knew your brother, by the way, and a man named Pryszlak, who was a colleague of your brother's.' He saw the old woman flinch at the mention of Pryszlak's name.

'I warned Dominic about that man.' Her lips were a thin line. 'My brother was a fool, little more than a buffoon, but Pryszlak was evil. I knew it as soon as I set eyes on him. A son of the Devil.'

Both Jessica and Bishop were astonished at the outburst. Just as suddenly, the tension left the old woman's body. She smiled at them, almost mischievously.

'I try not to let things bother me nowadays, my dears, but sometimes memories intrude. Now, assuming I gave you

376

permission to enter Beechwood, what would your plan of action be?'

'You'd have no objections?' Bishop asked, surprised.

'I haven't said that yet,' came the curt reply.

'Well, first I'd like some background history on the house. I'd like to know about the activities that took place there in the 1930s. I'd like to know what your brother was involved in, Miss Kirkhope.'

'And if I decide not to give you any information?'

'Then as far as I'm concerned, the matter is ended. I won't investigate the house.'

Silence descended on the room. Bishop and Jessica studied Miss Kirkhope as she sipped her sherry thoughtfully. She stared down at the floor for a long time and there was a sadness in her voice when she finally spoke. 'Beechwood has been part of my family's history for many, many years. Dominic was born there, you know. An accident really. It was a country house for my parents, you see, built at a time when it really was open country in those parts, long, long before it became a residential area. My father sent my mother and me there for the weekend; he wanted her to rest. He was busy, so very busy, and mother was seven months pregnant. He thought the change would be good for her.' She gave a bitter laugh. 'She had no rest that weekend. Dominic was premature; it was just like him to rush foolishly into the world before his time.'

Her eyes took on a faraway look as though she were studying an image in her mind. 'I was only seven at the time, and I was the one who found her at the foot of the cellar stairs. Why she went down there in the first place nobody ever found out. Mother certainly couldn't remember after the pain she suffered giving birth to Dominic. My God, how she screamed that night. I remember lying in bed listening, praying to God to let the baby die so it couldn't hurt Mother any more. She hadn't wanted to be moved, she would have had Dominic right there in the cellar if the servants hadn't ignored her pleas. I can still hear her screams of agony to this day as they dragged her up those steps. He came in the early hours of the following morning and I heard one of the servants say she wondered what all the earlier fuss was about because of the way he finally just plopped out on to the sheets.

'I don't think Mother ever really recovered from that dreadful night. She always seemed to be frail after that, always sickening for something or other. She loved Dominic, though. Oh, how she

377

doted on that boy! She would never go back to Beechwood after his birth, so father began renting it out rather than let it go empty. It had become too modest for folk as grand as us, anyway! Our fortunes were rising rapidly, you see. I haven't seen the place myself since, had no wish to. But Dominic went back – he must have been twenty-five, twenty-six, I can't remember how old exactly. He was inspecting several properties we owned at that time, doing his duty as father's son, you see. But Beechwood held some strange fascination for him; I suppose it was because he was born there.'

Miss Kirkhope paused to sip her sherry, then suddenly looked up at the other two occupants of the room as if remembering they were still present and that her reminiscences were for their benefit. 'That was the real turning-point for Dominic, I think. Up until then he had certainly been wayward, but that was only the robustness of youth. He returned many times to Beechwood and we naturally assumed he enjoyed the company of the people who occupied the house. There seemed to be no harm in it although my father did warn him it wasn't wise for landlords to become too friendly with their tenants. The area was becoming more populated then and Beechwood was soon surrounded by other properties; it was still an impressive house, perhaps not the most elegant, but firm, solid, a house that would last forever. Dominic became rather an elusive character – we never seemed to see much of him. It was only years later when the police informed my father that they had received complaints about the activities of Beechwood's occupants that we became alarmed. I think my father had already lost hope of Dominic following in his footsteps by that time and, in fact, I myself was fulfilling that role. I was, as they say, on the shelf – I don't know why, I don't think I was unattractive in those days; possibly the shipping business interested me more than men. I think it was a relief to my father that he had at least someone to rely on, someone he could trust to help him in his business ventures. I'm afraid mother had become progressively more fragile over the years and, God bless her, she wasn't much use to anybody. She only seemed to come alive in Dominic's presence which, of course, wasn't very often. Mr Bishop, you've hardly touched your drink. Perhaps you'd like something stronger?'

'Uh, no, it's fine. Thanks.'

'Then perhaps you'd be kind enough to refill my glass. Miss Kulek, another for you?'

Jessica declined and Bishop took the thin glass from the old lady to the silver tray resting on a small, ornately carved table. As he poured he prompted Miss Kirkhope. 'What exactly was going on in Beechwood?'

Anxiety deepened the many lines already ingrained on the old woman's face. 'Some new kind of religious sect was using the house as their church – The Temple of the Golden Consciousness, I believe they called it. Something silly like that. There seemed to be so many ridiculous societies around in those days.' Her anxiety had given way to disdain.

'Unfortunately there still are,' Jessica said.

'Had your brother joined this religious sect, Miss Kirkhope?' Bishop asked as he handed her the sherry.

'Oh, yes, he belonged to it. A full, practising member by that time. My father kept the more sordid details from my mother and me, but I gather sexual orgies played a large part in their worship. I suppose they could have got away with that but for the terrible row they made. The neighbours objected. Father cancelled the lease on Beechwood right away, of course, and ordered the tenants and their strange friends out. Dominic wouldn't come anywhere near us; he hid himself away somewhere. Suffering from shame, no doubt.'

'Who were these tenants?' Jessica asked gently.

'Oh, I can't remember their names, it was too long ago. A man and his wife or mistress – I can't be sure now. They must have been insane, anyway.'

'What makes you say that?' said Bishop.

'They refused to leave. Nothing odd in that, I know, but when they were informed they would be forcibly evicted, they took a rather extreme stand.'

'What did they do? Barricade themselves in?'

'No,' Miss Kirkhope replied mildly, 'they killed themselves.'

Bishop felt his muscles tense and he knew by the expression on Jessica's face she had been startled too.

'For some reason,' the old lady continued, 'nobody seemed to settle in Beechwood after that. Stories, silly rumours spread by neighbours, saw to it. People would move in, stay perhaps a few months, then leave. I think a year was the longest anyone ever stayed in that house. My mother died, my father's health became poor, and I became even more involved in his business activities, so Beechwood was rather lost in the background of things. We

379

had agents who looked after our various properties and they rarely bothered us unless a specific problem arose. I must admit I didn't give much thought to Beechwood over the years.'

'What of your brother?' Jessica enquired. 'Did he ever return to the house? Apart from the . . . last time, that is.'

'I don't know. Possibly. Probably. As I said, Beechwood held a special fascination for him. The only time I had any real contact with Dominic after the earlier scandal was when father died. Le me see, that would be . . . 1948. He came for his share of the inheritance. He gladly relinquished any rights in the family business, but was rather chagrined at being left out on the property. Father, rather wisely, left it all to me, you see. I remember my brother wanted to buy Beechwood from me, but I refused, having recalled what went on there in the past. Quite enraged, he was, like a naughty little boy who couldn't have his way.' She smiled but it was only a sad memory.

'I didn't see much of him after that, nor did I want to. I didn't like what he'd become.'

'What was that, Miss Kirkhope?'

She looked steadily at Bishop, the smile still on her face. 'That is my secret, Mr Bishop. I only heard stories from other people and I had no proof that they were true; but whether they were or not, I've no wish to discuss it.' Her thin, white hands curled around her glass, the fingers locking together. 'The house remained empty for many years, until I decided to put it on the market along with the other properties I owned. I was no longer able to carry on with the business in an efficient manner and I placed responsibility in more capable hands. I still have a nominal place on the board, but hardly any influence in how the company is run. I sold the properties at a time when the company needed a swift injection of ready cash, but the respite, I'm afraid, was only brief. Still, I'm comfortable enough. There's not much financially that can touch me in my last years. That's one of the nice things about old age – you have less of a future to worry about.'

'But you didn't sell Beechwood.'

'Couldn't, Mr Bishop, *couldn't*. That was the irony of it – the one property I wanted to be rid of, no one would buy!' She shook her head in amusement. 'The Kirkhope Folly you might call it. Or the Kirkhope Curse. I even went to the lengths of having it completely renovated, but still nobody wanted it. The agents

380

blamed it on "bad atmosphere'. Apparently it happens occasionally in the property market. That's why your services were called upon, Mr Bishop, to officially "cleanse" the house, if you like.'

'I told the agent at the time I was no exorcist.'

'Nor did you have any belief in ghosts as such. That was why they chose you in particular. The estate agents informed me that unexplained disturbances in a place could often be due to nothing more than an underground stream running beneath the house, land subsidence or even shrinkage.'

'A great many strange happenings can be explained by a detailed site examination, Miss Kirkhope. Rappings, doors opening for no reason, creaks, groans, sudden pools of water, cold spots – there's usually a logical explanation for them all.'

'Well, the agents felt sure you would uncover the cause.'

'Unfortunately, I didn't get the chance to.'

'No. But now you want another crack at it.'

He nodded. 'With your permission.'

'But your motives are not quite the same as Miss Kulek's and her father's.'

'No. Jacob Kulek and Jessica believe there is something sinister in Beechwood. I'd like to prove them wrong.'

'And I thought you were doing it for money,' Jessica said, the sarcasm heavy in her voice.

'There's that too.'

Agnes Kirkhope ignored the sudden antagonism between her visitors. 'Don't you think there has been enough publicity concerning Willow Road? Do you really think it's necessary to drag up the whole terrible affair of Beechwood again?'

'I told you earlier that Jacob Kulek's opinion is highly regarded in the field of psychical research. From what I know of him he's not a man to make rash judgements or speculate wildly. He thinks I may remember something more about the day I went to Beechwood. For my part, I'd just like to finish the job I started and, for reasons of my own, I'd like to prove him wrong about the house.'

'I promise you the investigation would be discreet,' Jessica said earnestly. 'We would report our findings to you before taking any other action.'

'And if you did, and I asked you not to take the matter any further, would you comply?'

'I can't say, Miss Kirkhope. That would depend.'

'On what you discovered?'

'Yes.'

With a loud sigh and a shrug of her shoulders, Agnes Kirkhope surprised them both again by saying, 'Very well. There's very little to interest an old woman like me nowadays. Perhaps this will throw some light into my rather dull life. I take it, then, that you will pay Mr Bishop's fee?'

'Yes, of course,' said Jessica.

'I think I would like to know why Dominic killed himself.'

'There's no way we'll find that out,' Bishop said quickly.

'Probably not. But perhaps I believe more in the mysteries of life than you do, Mr Bishop, despite your profession. We shall see.'

'Then we can go ahead?' asked Jessica.

'Yes, my dear, you can go ahead. There is just one thing.'

Bishop and Jessica leaned forward as one.

'You have a very short time in which to complete your investigation. In four days from now, Beechwood will be demolished.'

Chapter Seven

Night fell with little preamble and the residents of Willow Road nervously drew their curtains against it as if the darkness was a seeing thing. It was quiet out there now, the journalists and TV men having long since departed, their notebooks and cameras crammed with the opinions and fears of the road's inhabitants. Even the sightseers had left, finding nothing in the ordinary, rather drab, road to fuel their curiosity. Two constables strolled the pavements, up the left hand side, down the right, conversing in low tones, their roving eyes studying each house they walked by. At the passing of every twenty minutes, one would speak into his small hand-radio, reporting back to their station that all was quiet. The street-lights were inadequate, the gloom between them somehow threatening, each entry the policemen made into the shadowed areas briefly and secretly considered first.

At No 9, Dennis Brewer switched on the television set, telling his wife to come away from the window where she stood peeking through the curtains. Their three children, a boy of six and a girl of seven sitting on the carpet in front of the television screen, an eleven-year-old boy struggling with his homework on the living-room table, stared curiously at their mother.

'Just checking to see if those policemen are still there,' she said, letting the curtains drop into their closed position.

'Nothing else is going to happen, Ellen,' her irritated husband said. 'Bloody hell, there's not much more that *can* happen.'

Ellen sat on the sofa beside him, her eyes on the over-colourful shapes on the screen. 'I don't know, it's not natural. I don't like this road any more, Dennis.'

'We've been through all that. There's nothing for us to worry about – all those other silly sods were round the twist. Thank God they've all been sorted out in one go, is what I say. Now we can have a bit of peace and quiet.'

'They can't all have been lunatics, Dennis. It doesn't make sense.'

'What does nowadays?' For a second his eyes flickered away from the screen to find the children watching them with rapt attention. 'Look what you've done,' he complained. 'You've frightened the kids.' Disguising his annoyance, he smiled reassuringly at them, then allowed his thoughts to return to the programme.

At No 18, Harry Skeates was just closing the front door behind him.

'Jill, I'm home!' he called out.

His wife came hurriedly from the kitchen. 'You're late,' she said and he was alarmed by her anxious tone.

'Yeah, had a drink with Geoff at the station. You all right?'

'Oh, I'm a bit nervous, I suppose.'

He kissed her on the cheek. 'There's nothing to be nervous about, silly. You've got the law walking up and down outside.'

She took his overcoat from him and hung it in a cupboard under the stairs. 'I'm okay when you're around. It's just when I'm on my own. This road's become a bit frightening.'

Harry laughed. 'Old Geoff was full of it. Wants to know who's going to be bumped off next.'

'It's not funny, Harry. I didn't know the others very well, but Mrs Rowlands was very nice the times I spoke to her.'

Harry shoved his dropped briefcase to the side of the hall with his foot and made his way into the kitchen. 'Yeah, what a way to go. Throat cut by a hedge-trimmer. He had to be potty, that bloke.'

Jill switched on the electric kettle. 'I didn't like him very much. I don't think she did either, the way she spoke about him. She said he hated her dog.'

'Well I don't like poodles much.'

'Yes, but to do that to the poor creature.'

'Forget about it now, love. It's all over and done with.'

'You said that last week.'

He shook his head. 'I know, but who'd have thought anything else would have happened after that. It's beyond all reason. Anyway, I'm sure that's the last of it. Let's have that cup of tea, eh?'

She turned away, reaching into the kitchen cabinet and wishing she felt as confident.

At No 27, the elderly man lay in his bed and spoke to the nurse in a quavery voice.

'Are they still there, Julie?'

The nurse re-drew the curtains and turned to look down at the old man. 'Yes, Benjamin, they've just passed by.'

'All the years I've lived here, we've never had to have police patrols before.'

She walked over to the bed, the table-lamp by its side casting her giant shadow against a corner of the room, creating a deep black void. 'Would you like some milk now?' she asked quietly.

He smiled up at her, his wizened old face parchment yellow in the poor light. 'Yes, I think so, just a little. You will sit with me tonight, won't you, Julie?'

She leaned over him, her full breasts pressing against the high-necked, starched dress she wore in place of a uniform, and straightened the bedclothes around his shoulders. 'Yes, of course I will. I promised, didn't I?'

'Yes, you promised.'

He reached for her plump, but firm hand. 'You're good to me, Julie,' he said.

She patted his hand, then tucked it back inside the blankets, rearranging them again around his frail old body.

'You will sit with me, won't you?' he said.

'I just told you I would,' she answered patiently.

He settled back into the bed, shuffling his shoulders more comfortably into the sheets. 'I think I'll have that hot milk now,' he sighed.

The nurse rose from the bed, tiny beads of perspiration glinting in the fine hairs above her upper lip. She crossed the room and quietly closed the door behind her.

At No 33, Felicity Kimble glared angrily at her father.

'But why can't I go out, Dad? It's not fair!'

'I told you, I don't want you out of the house tonight,' Jack Kimble said wearily. 'I don't want you stopping out late while all this business is going on.'

'But I'm fifteen, Dad. I'm old enough to look after myself.'

'Nobody's old enough to look after themselves these days. I'm not telling you again – you're not going out.'

'Mum!' she whined.

'Your Dad's right, Felice,' her mother said in a softer voice than her husband's. 'You don't know what sort of people all

385

these goings-on have attracted to the neighbourhood.'

'But what could possibly happen? We've got the Fuzz on the doorstep.'

'The police, Felice,' her mother corrected.

'Anyway, Jimmy can bring me home.'

'Yes,' her father said, rumpling his newspaper, 'and that's another reason for not going out.'

Felicity looked at them both, her mouth a tight line across her face. Without a further word, she marched from the room, 'accidentally' kicking over her younger brother's Lego tower as she went.

'Perhaps we should have let her go, Jack,' her mother said as she helped her wailing son reassemble the plastic bricks.

'Oh don't you start,' Jack said, dropping his newspaper on to his lap. 'She can go out as much as she likes when things quieten down a bit. Providing she comes home at a reasonable hour, that is.'

'It's not the same for kids today, Jack. They're more independent.'

'Too bloody independent, if you ask me.'

Upstairs in her room, Felicity flicked on the light and flounced on to her narrow bed. 'Silly old twits,' she said aloud. They treated her like a ten-year-old. She only wanted to go down the club for a couple of hours. Jimmy would be waiting. She'd had enough of it, treated like a kid at school, treated like a kid at home. She was a woman now! She looked down at her ample swellings to reassure herself she was. Satisfied, she turned over on the bed and thumped the pillow with a clenched fist. Bloody silly street, people bumping each other off all the time! She thought a little wistfully of the two brothers who had lived further down the road, both blasted by a shotgun; the younger of the two had been nice looking, she quite fancied him. Not that Dad had a good word to say about either of them. Still, they were both dead now, the younger one having died of his injuries only the day before. He and his father had died within minutes of each other. What a waste! Felicity jumped up from the bed and went to her portable cassette player. She rewound the tape already settled in its deck, then pressed the 'play' button. A soft, slow number began, the kind she preferred, the rhythm emphasised rather than exaggerated. She moved in time with it, lost in the meaning of the words, her resentment towards her parents

386

forgotten for the moment. Her movements led her unconsciously towards the window where her own reflection against the black backdrop made her stop. She pressed her face against the glass, cupping her hands between its surface and her eyes, providing a dark tunnel for her to see through. The two policemen passing below glanced up and continued walking. Felicity watched their progress for a few moments until they disappeared into shadow beyond the street-light. She drew the curtains, her expression thoughtful.

Across the road at No 32, Eric Channing grunted in disappointment. A rectangle of muted light was all he could see of the window opposite. The girl usually left her curtains half-drawn, seemingly unaware that she could be seen from the bedroom across the road. Eric had spent many lonely vigils in his bedroom over the past year, his wife downstairs imagining he was in the small room next door tinkering with his hand-built railway set. He knew Veronica felt his trains were a childish pastime for a man of thirty-eight but, as she often said in company, it kept him out of mischief. It had often been a tricky business, his eyes glued to the window, ears pinned to the stairs, listening for her footfalls. He would rush silently on to the landing as though he had just emerged from the loo when he heard the living-room door open. She would give him hell if she ever found out. He had often sat there for hours in the cold while the miniature train next door whirred round and round on its tireless journey, scrutinising the ten to eighteen inches – depending on how wide she had left the curtains drawn – of bright light across the road, tensing at the flicker of movement, heart almost stopping when she came into view. On a bonus night, she would suddenly appear wearing only a bra and panties. Once, and only once, on a super-bonus night, she had taken off her bra in front of the window! Occasionally he wondered if she really was unconscious of the interest her lush young body caused, or whether she secretly knew he was crouching in the dark as she flaunted herself.

Eric sat there for another ten minutes, his face only inches away from the parted curtains, where the light from the street could not shine directly on to him. He knew from experience that tonight was a minus night: there would be nothing more to see. He would pop up now and again to make sure a gap hadn't appeared in his absence, but he felt certain the evening's performance was over. He had jumped back further into the shadows

387

when she had suddenly appeared at the window. His heart pounding wildly, he realised she was only watching the two policemen below. They must have been the reason for her closing the curtains. Interfering bastards! He reluctantly tore his eyes from the window and slunk dolefully from the room. Sometimes he wished he was Clark Kent and had X-ray vision. Or the Invisible Man and then he could actually be in the room with her.

His wife looked away from the television screen and her knitting stopped momentarily when he opened the door. 'Not playing with your trains tonight, darling?' she said.

'No,' he replied mournfully, 'I'm not very interested tonight, dearest.'

In the street outside, the two policemen strolled in step with each other.

'Bleedin cold tonight, Del,' one said, blowing into his gloved hands.

'Yeah, don't know why they didn't put another Panda on.'

'Can't waste a car on one street every night, can they? We haven't got enough to cover the whole patch anyway.'

'Plenny of helmets, though.'

'Eh?'

'Not enough patrol cars but plenny of helmets. I've had three new ones this year. Keep getting them dented at the matches.'

'Go on.'

'Every time I'm on duty. It's about time they slung those little bastards inside for a couple of weeks instead of lettin them off with piddlin fines.'

'Yeah, I used to enjoy the old football duty. So you've had three helmets then?'

'And a new radio. One of the bastards ran off with the last one. Crowd opened up in front of him like the partin of the Red Sea. Soon came tumblin down on top of me when I went after him, though.'

They walked on in silence for a few moments, their own unisoned footsteps a comfort to them in the quietness of the road.

'Yeah, plenny of em,' Del observed.

'What, helmets?'

'Yeah. Not enough recruits coming into the force, you see. Lots of helmets to go round. And radios.'

'Not enough patrol cars.'

'No. Not enough of them. Beats the old whistles.'

'What does?'

'Radios.'

'Oh yeah. Bit before my time, whistles, Del.'

'Yeah, s'pose it would be. Still handy to have them on us though. You never know when your radio's going to pack in.' They walked in silence for a few steps. 'Too many, you know.'

'What, helmets?'

'No, you silly bastard. Soccer hooligans. Too many of them, not enough of us. We can't control em any more. There used to be just a few troublemakers at a match, now it's most of em. Too many for us to handle.'

'Yeah, nutters, the lot of em.'

'No, most just go along with the ringleaders. They get carried away with the atmosphere.'

'I know what I'd like to do with em.'

Del tutted. 'You're not allowed to, son. They're only victims of their environment.'

'Environment? I've never seen one of em with rickets yet. A bloody good hidin would do em a lot of good.'

'Now, now, that's not the attitude. Mustn't upset our friendly neighbourhood social worker.'

The younger policeman's sneer of derision was hidden in the shadows as they passed beyond the feeble circle of light. He glanced to his left, squinting at the huge, detached building looming up from the general gloom.

'Give me the creeps, that place,' he remarked.

'Yeah, I don't care for it much, either.'

'Another bunch of lunatics.'

Del nodded in agreement. 'This road seems to have its share.'

The younger policeman looked back down the road. 'I wonder whose turn it is tonight?'

Del grinned. 'No, it's due for a bit of peace and quiet, this road. It's had its share of troubles. I don't think there's any more murderers left in those houses.'

'Let's hope you're right,' the younger one said as they continued their watchful journey, the sound of their footsteps fading as they strolled beyond the house called Beechwood.

Julie poured the lukewarm milk into the cup, then drank a little to test it. She wouldn't mind if it burnt the old bastard's throat

389

except it would mean a night of whining. And she wasn't sure she could stand much more of that.

Six years she had been with him: six years of fetching and carrying, nursing, placating, cleaning up his filth, and . . . the other thing. How much longer could he last? When she had first arrived from the private nursing agency, she had expected him to survive for two or three more years at the most. But he had fooled her. Six years! The temptation to slip something into his soup or milk was almost irresistible, but she knew she had to be careful. The circumstances would be too suspicious. His Will would immediately point the finger of suspicion directly at her; there was no one else it could be pointed at. And no one else he could leave his money to. He wasn't wealthy, she knew, but he had enough to pay her salary all these years without any visible means of income, and he owned the property they lived in. Christ, when he went, she would turn it into a glorious house. Perhaps a small residential nursing-home for the elderly. It was certainly big enough. There were a few other similar properties in Willow Road – old Victorian houses that had seen better, grander days, but they, too, had become immersed in the general drabness around them. Yes, it would make a fine nursing-home. Just five or six old people, none with complicated illnesses – that would be too much trouble. And a small staff to do the work. No more skivvying for her! She would merely supervise the running of the place. How much money did the old man have? Her eyes glinted greedily in the dim kitchen light. He'd hinted often enough about his 'little nest egg' that he was saving just for her. She had tried to find out – surreptitiously, of course – just how much that 'little nest egg' amounted to, but the old fool would only grin slyly at her and touch a withered finger to his nose. Cunning old bastard.

She placed the mug of milk on a tray that already held his medicine bottle, spoon, and an assortment of pills. God, he would rattle if she ever picked him up and shook him – and that wouldn't be difficult to do with her size and him being nothing more than skin and bones. Half the pills he didn't really need, but they gave him the impression he was being looked after. They were harmless enough. How much longer, though? How much longer would the stubborn old fool live, and how much longer could she stand being around him? Patience, Julie, she told herself. It will be worth waiting for. Christ, she'd dance on his fucking grave, all right. Maybe the winter would finish him off. The mean old skinflint didn't believe in central heating and the single-bar electric fire he had in his room just about heated the piece of carpet in front of it. She had left his bedroom window open often enough when she went out shopping as well as creeping in to open it in the middle of the night when he was asleep, always closing it first thing the following morning before he woke. If he didn't catch pneumonia before this winter was out, then he was never going to die, he would go on forever. But she had to be careful: sometimes she thought he wasn't as senile as he pretended.

She carried the tray from the kitchen and began to climb the stairs to the bedroom. She almost missed her footing on the gloomy stairway, the milk slurping over on to the tray, and she silently cursed his meanness. The whole house was dismally lit because of his insistence on low wattage light bulbs. Even when one expired it was difficult to get his permission to buy a new one. He scrutinised every bill she presented him with, his whole body suddenly becoming alert, helplessness mysteriously disappearing; it was as though he suspected her of swindling him, that the weekly shopping bill was a concoction of her own making. Crafty old bugger! The only thing he didn't mind paying for was the medicines and pills she fed into him. He regarded this as the mortgage on his life.

Benjamin's rheumy old eyes watched her from over the top of the bedclothes as she entered the room. He pulled the blankets down under his chin and smiled toothlessly at her.

'Bless you, Julie,' he said as she used her broad rump to close the door behind her. 'You're a good girl.'

She brought the tray over to the bed and moved the lamp on the small bedside table back against the wall to make room for it. The shadows in the room adjusted themselves to the change.

'There now,' she said, sitting heavily on the side of the bed. 'Medicine first, then your pills. You can take them with your milk.'

'Help me sit up, Julie,' he said, putting on his weak voice.

Julie groaned inwardly, knowing full well he was capable of propping himself up. She stood and reached under his armpits, heaving his light frame into a sitting position, fluffing up the pillows behind him. He sat grinning at her, yellow, wrinkled and gummy. She turned her head away.

'Medicine,' he said.

She shook the bottle then poured some of its contents on to the spoon. Benjamin opened his mouth wide and she was reminded of a baby gannet waiting to have a worm dropped into its beak. Julie pushed the spoon in, resisting the urge to shove the whole thing down his scrawny throat, and he sucked noisily at the sticky liquid.

'One more, there's a good boy,' she forced herself to say.

He put on a childish mock grimace, then dropped open his lower jaw.

When he had swallowed the second dose, she scraped the spoon up his grizzled chin, shovelling the dribbles back into his mouth. The pills came next, delivered on to his glistening, wavering tongue like communion wafers, and washed down with the warm milk. She patted his mouth with a Kleenex tissue and he sank back down into the bed, his head still propped up by the pillows, a smile of contentment on his face.

'You promised to sit with me,' he said slyly.

She nodded, knowing what he meant. It was a small price to pay for the old bastard's money, she supposed wearily.

'You're good to me, Julie. All these years, you're the only one who's cared for me. You're all I've got in my last years, dear. But you won't be sorry, I promise you that, you won't be sorry. You'll be well taken care of when I pass on.'

She patted his hand. 'Now you mustn't talk like that. You've years ahead of you. You'll probably last me out.' She was only thirty-nine, so there was no bloody chance of that, she thought.

'You'll be well taken care of, Julie,' he repeated. 'Untie your hair, dear. You know how I love to see it.'

Julie reached up behind her head and with a few swift tugs, her lush, dark brown hair cascaded down on to her broad shoulders. It was long and when she tossed her head it fell beyond her shoulders to settle almost to the bottom of her back.

He reached up a trembling hand. 'Let me feel it, dear, I love to touch it.'

She leaned forward so her glistening mane was within reach. He ran a gnarled hand through it, relishing its rich texture. 'Beautiful,' he murmured. 'So thick, so strong. You really have been blessed, Julie.'

She smiled despite herself. Yes, her hair was her greatest attribute. She knew her body was heavy, although her well-rounded curves were not unattractive – Rubenesque would be a way to

392

describe them; and her face too, was a little plump, but then again, not unattractive. Her hair, though – as her drunken old father in Ireland used to tell her – was a 'gift from the gods'. She became coy, playing the game the way he liked it.

'Come on, Julie dear,' he said in mock pleading, 'let me see you.'

'You know I shouldn't, Benjamin.'

'There's no harm in it. Come on now,' he coaxed.

'It might over-excite your heart, Benjamin.' She hoped one day it would.

'My heart is already excited, dear. Won't you give me some reward for the reward I'll be leaving you.'

'I told you not to talk like that. Besides, my reward is taking care of you.'

'Then take care of me now, Julie dear.'

She stood, knowing he would become impatient if the game went on too long. Reaching behind her back, Julie unhooked the clasp at her neck, popping the descending buttons open so the stiff dress hung loose around her shoulders. She shrugged herself free of the top and stood there before him in a fake poise of modesty, her breasts hanging heavily inside her bra.

His mouth opened as he gazed up at her, the corners wet with saliva. He nodded his head in quick jerky movements, encouragement for her to go on. Julie undid the bow that secured her white nurse's apron to her waist, letting it fall to the floor. The rest of the dress was pushed, not without effort, over her hips, and the starched material crackled as she slid it down her legs. The elastic in her dark tights was tucked inside a deep crease around her middle and she dug her thumbs into her flesh to find it. Benjamin groaned when these were pulled from her firm legs and she stood over him; a mountain of white flesh contained only by bra and panties.

'Lovely,' he said, 'so very lovely.' His hands disappeared beneath the covers to scurry around in search of his shrunken member. 'The rest, Julie dear. Now the rest.'

She unhooked the bra, her great mounds spilling free and resting sullenly on the rise of her belly. The bra was dropped on to the pile of clothes at her feet and she ran her big hands over her breasts, squashing them flat and teasing the two pink buttons at their centres until they rose like blunted antennae. She allowed her fingers to run down her large expanse of tummy, hooking her

393

thumbs into the top of her panties and slowly drawing them down over her thighs. He moaned aloud and craned his neck forward off the pillow to see her dark, bushy triangle more clearly.

Completely naked, she placed her hands on her hips and stood before him.

'Yes, yes, Julie. You know what to do now.'

She did. She danced.

Her gross shadow matched her movements around the room, sometimes stretching over the ceiling as she drew near to the lamp, hovering darkly over them both. She weaved and turned, crouched and leapt, flinging her arms high in the air, giving him the chance to see every inch of her fleshy body. She finished with a pirouette, crudely performed and grotesque to see, but he cried, 'Encore!' his eyes alight with the thrill.

Julie slumped breathlessly into a wicker chair standing in one shadowy corner of the room, the wooden struts uncomfortable under her bare skin. But this was where he liked her to sit for stage two of the game.

He watched her expectantly, waiting for her to catch her breath, his own breathing sharp and fast with excitement. If only she knew the money was nearly all gone. Paying her for her services all these years had drained it; there was just enough to last another year, a year-and-a-half at the most, then there would be nothing left. But she had been worth it! By God, she had! He knew as soon as Julie had walked in the door that she would be the one. Everything about her had been sensual: her robust figure, the way she moved, those starchy, high-buttoned nursing frocks she wore. Even her voice with its bare traces of an Irish lilt. And when he had first seen the fully glory of her wonderful hair flowing over her shoulders like a soft, umber waterfall! Bliss! She was the one! The others had done their job well enough, but they cared little for him and his needs. It hadn't taken long to convince Julie her future was with him and not with the nursing agency. Of course, a little deception had been necessary. But after all he had provided for her all these years. It was a shame it had to end, but the money he would get for the house would pay for his last years in a comfortable nursing-home. He would give her a couple of hundred pounds from the proceeds, maybe even three hundred; she had been very obliging. That should keep her happy! Oh yes, Julie, now, do it now!

Julie's legs were stretched wide and her hand was travelling down between her thighs. Her fingers cut a path through her triangle of hair and found the fleshy lips lurking beneath. She moaned, not just for his pleasure, but because her own passion was beginning to awaken. Self-abuse was her greatest pleasure nowadays. Men, on the rare occasions she had found one to smuggle in, were seldom strong enough for her demands. Her teeth bit down on to her lower lip and her face became moist with perspiration as her middle finger forced entry. Her hand moved in a soft, languid motion, but gradually the strokes increased in both speed and firmness as the muscles in her stomach tautened.

Benjamin's hand movements, beneath the bedclothes had increased also, but to no avail. 'Julie,' he called out, 'over here now, please, over here.'

He blinked his eyes as her white, mountainous shape seemed to dim in the poor light. The bulb in the lamp must be dying, he thought, unless his vision was failing along with certain other parts of his tired old body. The shadows in the room became darker and he could hardly see her now, just the ends of her legs from the knees down sticking out of the black patch in the corner, her large feet jerking spasmodically.

'Julie! Please come into bed now,' he pleaded. 'I need you, my dear.'

Her great flabby shape emerged from the shadows and she padded over to the bed. He grinned in welcome as she threw the covers back, and held his limp member upright for her to see. She climbed in next to him and he shivered as her cold feet touched his legs.

'Good girl, Julie. That's my girl,' he murmured as she smothered his thin body with her own oozing flesh.

'Careful now,' he gasped as her weight bore down on him, forcing the air from his lungs. She rolled off and her hand grabbed down at him, brushing his own hands away. He winced at the rough treatment she gave his half-erect penis, pulling and kneading it as though to mould it into a firmer shape.

'Do be careful, Julie,' he complained, 'you're being rather rough.' He could feel her hot breath panting in his ear and his skinny old hands grabbed her wobbling breasts, squashing the two points together, holding them out for his gummy lips to close in on. He sucked at the nipples making baby-like gurgling sounds, then yelped as her arm went beneath him and pulled his body on top of hers with a great heave.

'Come on, you old bastard, give it to me,' she whispered.

'Julie, what . . .'

His words were cut off as she spread her legs and tried to pull him into her. She had to stuff his flaccid organ in with her fingers and it was like dough being forced into an open purse. Her great hands clasped around his fleshless buttocks and she heaved him in, her own hips rising up from the bed to meet him.

'Julie!' he screamed. 'Stop this at once!' He felt as if his lower body was being crushed, his bones ground to powder.

'Come on, you old bastard! Fuck me!' Tears of frustration ran from the corners of Julie's eyes, running into her ears, filling the wells. She rose and pulled, writhed and jerked, but there was nothing of substance inside her. 'Fuck me!' she screamed, and the shadows closed in around them until there was a barely audible fizzing sound as the light bulb splattered into lifelessness and the darkness engulfed them like a black tide.

He was wailing now, hurt in the struggle, desperate to be free. But she would not release him. She held him against her with one hand, her knees rising up on either side of him, her ankles hooked over his reedlike legs. Locking him there. Her hand reached behind her lifted head, gathering up the hair that billowed out on to the pillow. She worked it into one long, thick length and wound it round his scrawny neck.

'Julie, what are you doing? Please stop this! I don't want to play any . . .'

His words were choked off as she began to pull on the hair, tightening it, using her other hand to hold the roots firmly against her head. She pulled harder, tighter, his face twisted to one side, his eyes wide in terror, his mouth spitting small white specks.

'All these years,' she hissed between clenched teeth. 'All these years . . .' Her tears were now because of her own pain, the roots screaming against her scalp. But still she pulled, his gurgling sounds music in her ears. 'All these years . . .'

The darkness in the room became even denser until there was not even light shining through the cracks of the curtains. She could not see anything at all in the blackness. She could only hear his gurgling chokes. And that was enough.

Chapter Eight

He sat in the car, watching the house, afraid. Although the engine was switched off, his hands were gripped tightly around the steering-wheel as though whether to stay or drive off was still unresolved in his mind. The sun was hidden behind troubled clouds this time and the windows were black and secretive. Beechwood was no longer an ordinary house.

Bishop drew in a deep breath and released the wheel, one hand whipping off his glasses and tossing them on to the passenger seat, then reaching back for his case. He strode briskly across the paved area, knowing if he hesitated any longer he would never enter the house. He knew his fear was irrational, but that did not make it any less real. The door opened as he mounted the steps and Jessica smiled down at him. As he drew nearer, he saw the smile was restrained; a nervousness was in her eyes. He understood that nervousness.

'We thought you might not come,' she said.

'You're paying me, remember?' he replied and instantly regretted his harshness.

Jessica looked away and closed the door behind him. 'They're waiting for you.' She pointed to the first door on his left, the one opposite the stairs. For a moment he couldn't move, almost expecting to see the legs still dangling over the stairway, the fallen shoe lying on its side beneath them. They were gone, of course, but the scuff marks on the wall remained.

He felt the gentle pressure of Jessica's hand on his arm and shook the thoughts from his mind. Almost. He walked down the gloomy corridor and entered the room she had indicated. A woman was waiting with Kulek and she rose as Bishop walked in.

'I'm glad you came, Chris,' Kulek said from the armchair he occupied, one hand curled around the top of his walking-stick. 'This is Mrs Edith Metlock. She is here to help.'

Bishop shook her hand and tried to remember where he had heard the name before. She was short and stout, almost matronly in appearance. Grey streaks broke up the blackness of her tightly curled hair and her cheeks bulged ruddily when she smiled. He realised she must have been rather beautiful in her younger days, but plumpness and time had concealed most of that beauty now. Like Jessica, her pale eyes held a nervousness in them. Her grip was firm but, despite the coldness of the room, the palm of her hand was moist.

'Please call me Edith,' she told Bishop, curiosity now mingled with her unease.

'In what way are you going to help . . .?' He stopped in mid-sentence. 'Edith Metlock. Yes, I thought I knew the name. You're a medium, aren't you?' He felt his anger rising.

'I'm a sensitive, yes.' She let go of his hand, recognising the aggression, knowing the scepticism that would follow.

Bishop turned to Kulek. 'You didn't tell me. There's no need for this.'

'It was only decided at the last moment, Chris,' Kulek said placatingly. 'If the house is soon to be demolished, then we do not have too much time. Edith is here to observe. She will assist only if necessary.'

'How? By calling up the ghosts of the people who died here?'

'No, nothing like that. Edith will tell us of the atmosphere of the house, the feelings she receives. She will help you remember.'

'I thought we were going to investigate this house by more scientific means.'

'And so we shall. Edith will be an extra method of investigation if we fail with your, shall we say, more material approach.'

'But you still think there's something I've forgotten from my last visit here. What the hell makes you so sure?'

'I am not sure. But several moments have been lost to you. You found yourself outside the house without knowing how you got there.'

'It's not unusual when someone panics.'

'No, but we *are* talking of an unusual event.'

'May I interrupt?' Edith Metlock said, looking from one to the other. Without waiting for a reply, she asked Bishop: 'Why are you so afraid?'

'Afraid? What makes you say that?'

'Your whole manner, Mr Bishop. The uneasy way you entered this room . . .'

'My God, if you'd seen . . .'

'Your resistance to Jacob Kulek's efforts to discover the secret of this house . . .'

'That's nonsense . . .'

Bishop's protest faded and he stared down at the medium, his face grim. 'Yes, I object to your presence. I've heard you have an excellent reputation as a medium; unfortunately I don't have the same high regard for your kind.'

'My kind?' She smiled at him. 'I have heard of you also, Mr Bishop. You have a reputation for taking great delight in exposing the mistakes of my "kind".'

'Not the mistakes, Mrs Metlock. I'd rather call them the deceptions.'

There was concern on Jacob Kulek's face. 'Chris, please. Edith is here at my invitation.'

She walked over to Kulek and patted his hand. 'That's all right, Jacob. Mr Bishop is entitled to his views. I'm sure he has his own reasons for his attitude. Perhaps he will tell us?'

'I think we've wasted enough time,' Bishop said angrily. 'By all means stay. But please don't try to interfere with my work here.'

Jessica came forward and stood beside the investigator. 'Chris is right. We *are* wasting time. Let's get on with this business, Father.'

'I'll stay out of your way, Mr Bishop,' Edith Metlock said. 'I'll keep to this room while you go about your investigation. If you should need me . . .'

'I won't. But maybe you can help me, Jessica?'

'Of course.'

'What do you intend to do, Chris?' enquired Kulek.

'First I want to take the temperature of each room. I don't know if any of you have noticed, but it's freezing in here, much colder than it is outside.'

'Yes,' said Jessica, 'it was the first thing I noticed when I came in. I thought it was just the fact that the house had been unoccupied for so long.'

'It probably is the reason. It'll be interesting to see if every room is the same, though.' He ignored the faint smile on the face of the medium. 'Miss Kirkhope's agent has managed to supply me with a geological map of the area as well as a two-and-a-half inch scale survey map. One will tell us the type of soil the house is standing on and the general structure of the land around it; the other will show if there are any streams or wells near the property. Tunnels or underground streams beneath the house could cause the chill – or perhaps you would call it "atmosphere", Mrs Metlock.'

'I most certainly would,' the medium said, still smiling. 'I felt it immediately I entered. But I hope you do find some physical reason for it, Mr Bishop.'

'Then I want to test the structure of the house itself. No plans of the building are in existence, unfortunately, but I'll do my own survey. I want to know the materials used in its construction, test the walls for damp, look for shrinkage of any kind.'

'It seems you need a more practical knowledge for your work than just experience of the paranormal,' Kulek remarked.

'Practical knowledge outweighs any other as far as I'm concerned. I used to be a planning surveyor before I took up chasing ghosts, and I needed to know just how houses got themselves built for that.'

'And when you have done all this?' Kulek asked.

'Then I want to set up some equipment to be left here overnight.'

'Equipment?'

'I want to know if there's any activity in this place when it's supposedly empty. I intend to set up a camera connected to a tape-recorder, linked up to photo-electric cells and a sound and vibration detector. If anything moves or makes a noise in this house tonight, we'll know.'

'But you can only set this up in one room,' said Jessica.

Bishop nodded. 'This will be the room. For the others I'll have to rely on powder and black cotton. If we find traces of disturbance in any other room, we'll move the electrical equipment into there for the following night.'

'Have you considered staying overnight in Beechwood yourself?' It was the medium who posed the question.

'Sure. And my considered reply to myself was "no".'

'But I thought you didn't believe in ghosts.'

'I don't believe in being uncomfortable.' He turned to the girl. 'Jessica, I've brought along two thermometers, the greenhouse

400

kind. It would save time if you tested one room while I did the same in another.'

'All right, shall we start down here?'

'No, upstairs. I want to get an idea of the general layout first. Jacob, do you want to come with us?'

'I'll stay and keep Edith company. I'm afraid I wouldn't be much help to you.' He smiled encouragingly at his daughter and Bishop.

Bishop picked up his case and told Jessica to follow him. He paused at the foot of the stairway, looking up into the sombre greyness of the landing above.

'I suppose there's no electricity?'

'No, we tested the lights when we came in,' Jessica said.

Bishop shrugged. 'I didn't really think there would be.'

He climbed the stairs, taking two at a time, his strides swift, leaving the girl hurrying to keep up. He stopped at the top and waited for her.

'That's where I found the first body,' he said, nodding towards the balustrade. 'It was hanging from there.' He saw her shiver.

'Did you come up here, to any of these rooms?'

'No. Just into the main room downstairs. That was enough.' He walked to the end of the landing and drew back the curtains. Light sprang in but made little progress along the hallway.

'Come on,' he called to her and she joined him at the foot of another staircase.

'Two upper floors,' he commented, reaching into his case and producing a torch. 'The principal bedrooms will be on this floor and upstairs will probably be what was once the servants' quarters. There's enough light to see by, but we'll need the torch for looking into cupboards and suchlike.'

His progress up the second staircase was slower and Jessica was able to keep close behind him. There were four doors on the landing above, all closed. Once again he walked to the window and drew back the curtains, a strong musty smell from the material irritating his nasal passages. The daylight revealed the hatchway in the ceiling and he flicked on the torch, shining its beam upwards.

'I'll have a look in the loft later,' he said.

Jessica tried the handle of the door nearest to her. It turned easily and she gave the door a gentle push. The small room was

401

devoid of any furniture, the floorboards bare, dark with age. A tiny, iron-framed fireplace faced her. Bishop pushed past her and walked over to it, crouching and shining the torch up the chimney. He withdrew his head and said, 'Can't see too much, I can't tell if it's blocked or not.'

'Is it important?'

'I need to know where any draughts come from. Or if there are any birds nesting in the chimneys. Our feathered friends are often the cause of "ghostly flutterings".' He took a thermometer mounted on a thin block of wood from his case and looked around for a suitable peg to hang it on. He settled for resting it on top of the small mantelshelf above the fireplace, placing it in an upright position, top resting against the wall. Then he produced a ten-by-eight sketchbook and a felt-tipped pen. There were no curtains at the window, so the light was adequate for his purposes.

'I'm going to make a plan of each room,' he explained, 'then an overall plan of the house. I'll mark on it any draught points, holes that shouldn't be there, rotted floorboards and any structural alterations from the original building. You can help by looking for any signs of dampness.'

'Shall I start in here?'

'No, take this other thermometer into the next room. It'll save time if we move them on when we get a stable reading.'

Jessica took the instrument from him and left the room, stopping for a moment outside. Somehow there seemed to be less light in the hall than before. It was almost as if dusk were falling. That was silly, she told herself. It was still mid-morning. The clouds outside had become heavier, that was all. She moved along to the next door and twisted the handle.

It turned easily enough, but when she pushed against it, the door barely moved before meeting resistance. Jessica pushed harder and the door seemed to sink into something soft yet resilient. This time she put her shoulder to the door and gave it a short, sharp shove. It moved inwards about an inch. She put her eye to the gap, but it was too dark in the room to see anything clearly. Her gaze travelled down the crack and she could just make out the shape of something bulky lying across the bottom of the door. She dared not admit to herself what it might be.

'Chris,' she called out, keeping her voice steady. 'Could you come here for a minute, please?'

He came from the room and frowned when he saw the anxiety on her face. She pointed to the door.

'There's something blocking it.'

He tested the door, pulling it back then pushing against the unseen object. He felt the wood sink into something before meeting firm resistance. Jessica's features were not clear in the poor light, but he could see her eyes were wide.

'It feels like . . .' she said.

'A body? Don't let your imagination run away with you. It could be anything.' Nevertheless, there was a prickling sensation around his scalp.

He gave the door a hard push using the weight of his whole body and it swung inwards six inches. 'Get the torch,' he told her and she quickly disappeared into the other room. He pushed again, keeping up the momentum of the swing, and the door opened wide, one foot, two, a slithering noise accompanying its movement. He took the torch from the girl and stepped halfway into the room, keeping the beam low. Jessica watched his back as he leaned forward and peered around the door. It seemed so dark beyond him.

He looked back at her, a broad grin on his face. A curled finger beckoned her, then he disappeared from view. As she slowly crept forward she could hear his footsteps crossing the floor, then the sound of material being swished back. Dull grey light filled the room.

Jessica stepped sideways through the gap and breathed out when she saw the rolled carpet lying at an angle across the floor, one end resting against the open door.

'This kind of house can make you imagine all sorts of things, Jessica,' Bishop said, one hand still on the heavy drapes he had just pulled back from the window. There was a softness in his voice that she didn't expect from him.

'I'm sorry, Chris. You're right about the house, though: it does stir the imagination. It's so gloomy in here.'

He drew nearer to her . 'The carpet must have been standing in the corner over there. Some disturbance – perhaps when the police were here last – made it topple and block the doorway.'

She managed a weak smile. 'I'll try not to be so shaky from now on.'

'Don't worry about it. It's happened to me in the past. I've come to learn there's generally a rational explanation.'

'And the times when there isn't?'

'That means I haven't been clever enough to discover it.'

Before he could snap up the barrier between them again, she reached for his arm. 'Tell me, Chris, why were you so angry when you found Edith Metlock here?' She saw the coldness flicker behind his eyes.

'It was a surprise to me. I think you're well aware of my feelings towards such people, yet you asked her here.'

'But she's a genuine sensitive. Her reputation is beyond reproach.'

'Is there such a thing as a genuine sensitive? I've no doubt she thinks she is and her belief in the spiritual world is quite sincere. But how much of it is real and how much comes from her own subconscious? I'm sure she is clairvoyant, but then again, couldn't that just be the power of her own mind?'

'It could be, I'll admit that. Whatever it is, it seems to work.'

He smiled at her and some of the antagonism between them melted.

'Look,' he said, 'I've been pretty rude to you and your father – not to mention Mrs Metlock. I'll try to keep my opinions to myself while this investigation is going on and I promise to keep an open mind to whatever we find providing you and your father do the same.'

'But we have.'

'No. Your father seems to be obsessed with this Pryszlak and his view could be clouded by what he knows of the man and his work.'

'My father is totally objective.'

'If he was, he would have brought in a headshrinker to help me remember those forgotten minutes, not a spiritualist.'

She realised he had a point and kept quiet.

His voice was gentle when he spoke. 'I'm sorry, I didn't mean to bark at you again. I'm only trying to make it clear that there are two sides to this and I happen to be in a minority of one. If there is a connection between this house and all the recent killings in the road, then I'd like to find out what it is, too.'

'Let's work together, not against each other.'

'Agreed.'

She looked away from him and, for a moment, he felt she was flustered.

'Okay,' he said, 'set the thermometer up over there then let me know the reading on the other one before you move it on to the next room.'

They worked their way systematically through the upper floor of the house, recording the temperature of each room, checking for draughts and damp, Bishop making detailed drawings. They descended the stairs to the main bedrooms and followed the same routine. The rooms on that floor were much larger than those at the top of the house, but the low temperature seemed constant throughout: five degrees centigrade. The rooms themselves, although in good repair, had the musty smell of emptiness, the creeping decay of walls without the echoes of life.

Jessica stood alone in one room waiting to take an accurate reading from the thermometer she had placed in there moments before. She looked at the solitary bed, its bare springs somehow heightening the loneliness of the room. She wondered why they hadn't taken away the few remaining pieces of furniture and decided they probably meant nothing to Miss Kirkhope neither financially nor for sentimental reasons. When the house came down, then the contents would undoubtedly be crushed along with it. She moved to the window and watched the road below. An old woman shuffled by, not even giving Beechwood a passing glance. A cyclist came into view, his head down, scarf tight around his neck, pedalling steadily, vapour breaths dissolving fast in the cold air. An ordinary suburban street. Like millions of others. But behind certain walls, a difference.

Jessica turned from the window and crossed the room. She stooped to pick up the thermometer propped against a wall and her face creased into a look of consternation. The temperature had dropped from five degrees centigrade to below zero. Even as she watched, the red mercury crept down, the movement slow but visible. When it had reached ten degrees below and was still sinking she placed it back in position and hastily went to the door.

'Chris!' she called out.

'In here.'

Jessica ran to the next room. He had his back to her, scribbling notes on to the sketch he had just made.

'Chris, the temperature next door is dropping rapidly. It's unbelievable. I can actually see it going down.' She was suddenly aware how cold she felt physically.

He turned in surprise, then strode towards the thermometer in that room. 'Christ, you're right,' she heard him say. 'It's below twelve in here.'

The scream made them both jump. It came from the rooms below, screeching its way up the staircase and echoing around the landing walls.

For a frozen instant, Jessica and Bishop stared at each other, then, as one, they raced towards the stairs. Bishop reached them first and as he descended he sensed a blurring before his eyes, shadows hanging like cobwebs in front of him. Jessica saw him sweep a hand before his face as though brushing aside invisible curtains. She followed close behind, but could see no obstruction.

Bishop almost stumbled halfway down, missing a step as though avoiding something lying there. Jessica could see nothing.

He swung round the banister at the bottom of the stairs, then staggered against the opposite wall, a look of bewilderment on his face. Jessica reached him and held him steady. They ran onwards as another scream pierced through the suddenly cloying air and reached the room in which they had left Jacob and the woman. Bishop stopped in the doorway and collapsed on to his knees, his face draining of blood.

The room was filled with people. Their bodies, many naked, writhed and twisted in agony, features contorted as if they were screaming their pain, but no sounds coming from their lips. A woman, near enough to Bishop for him to reach out and touch, swayed unsteadily, her head swung back, beseeching the ceiling. Her blouse was open, the buttons torn away, heavy breasts thrusting the material apart. She wore no clothes from the waist down and her fleshy thighs trembled in some strange paroxysm. Her fingers were curled around a small glass and he could see the whiteness of her knuckles as she strained against it. The glass shattered and its few drops of liquid mingled with the sudden gush of blood from her cut hand. Bishop flinched as spots of blood spurted against his face and he pulled back when the woman fell. She landed in front of him, her back still heaving.

His eyes darted around the room, widening with each individual scene of horror. On the floor, not five feet away from him, three figures were locked in tight embrace, one on top of the other. Their naked bodies shook, but he could not tell whether it was from pain or ecstasy. He realised it was a woman underneath, her legs spread wide, arms scratching at the arms and backs of the two men above her. One had entered her and was

406

moving his hips in unison with the man who clung to his back and who had entered him. The woman's face was pointed towards Bishop, but he could see her eyes were glazed as though heavily drugged. A heavy-set man lumbered towards them, his clothes open to display his genitals. Wild hair and beard almost obscured his face, but Bishop could see this one's eyes were sharp, obsessed. In his hand he held a long, pike-like object, its length black and tapering gradually to a fine point. He held the point against the back of the man uppermost in the tangled heap, pressing it slowly down until it punctured the skin and a tiny drop of blood oozed out. The naked man paid no heed to his injury, continuing to press into the man beneath him. The man with the pike reached upwards and closed both hands against the flat base of the weapon. Bishop opened his mouth to scream as he realised what was about to happen, but the cry stayed locked deep inside his chest. The bearded man plunged downwards and the long, black point sank from view, the pike descending into a fountain of red liquid, its length smoothly disappearing until the man's blood-stained hands were only inches away from his victim's flesh. All three bodies went rigid with shock, then continued trembling, this time the movements jerky, spasmodic, reaching separate crescendoes before falling limp, unmoving. Bishop could see the bearded man laughing, but still no sound came to him.

A young girl, probably in her early twenties, struggled with two men on the room's worn settee which stood beneath the high, bow window. They held her wrists and legs. Her skirt was pulled up around her waist and a woman knelt before her, pushing something bulky between the girl's thighs. The girl looked down at the object, her eyes wide with pleading and Bishop saw the tape sealing her lips. She arched her body and the trapped end of the object rose with her. Bishop raised a hand towards them, but it was as though he was engulfed in a sticky fluid that hindered his movements, bearing down on him with a debilitating force. He saw the woman squeeze the twin triggers of the shotgun and closed his eyes when parts of the girl's body ruptured through her clothes. Even the shotgun blast was silent.

A hand touched his shoulder and he opened his eyes again. Jessica was standing over him, her lips moving.

A man stood behind the door, an insane grin on his face. Liquid drooled from the corner of his mouth and the glass he held slipped from his fingers, landing on the floor without breaking, rolling away from him, then back in a semi-circle. The man slid down the wall, still grinning, his lips only curling down in an expression of painful horror when he reached the floor. His back was stiff against the wall when he slowly toppled sideways, the action like the movement of a second hand against a clockface. His legs kicked out, once, twice, and his chin receded into his neck as his jaw opened to its fullest extent, not even relaxing when he was dead.

A group of men and women sat around the table at the far end of the room, their hands joined across its surface. They waited patiently while one man walked around behind them carefully slitting their throats with a butcher's knife as he went, each member holding on tightly to the hand of the dying man or woman next to them until forced to let go because of their own dying. Soon none of the hands was joined as the bodies lay slumped across the table or had slipped from their chairs. The man who had done the slaying calmly ran the knife across his own up-stretched throat, his chest becoming sodden and red as he sank back to his knees; he fell forward on to his face.

Bishop tried to rise, the girl, Jessica, tugging at his arm to help. A man was watching him from the armchair in which Jacob Kulek had been sitting. His face was thin, cheeks hollow, shadowy, and his eyes seemed to protrude unnaturally from his skull as though he suffered from meningitis. The lips were thin, unformed, the line of the mouth curled at one end in an expression that could have been a smile or a sneer. His hair was black but sparse, swept back from his forehead, making the distance between his scant eyebrows and hairline seem extraordinarily long. His elbows rested on either arm of the chair, his hands raised steeple-shaped before him, a small glass of clear liquid held at their apex. His lips parted as though speaking, then he looked away from Bishop towards a man and woman nearby. They were coupled together, the woman holding the man's head down between her thighs while he thrust himself into her throat. They were frail with age, the skin hanging loosely over prominent bones; their hair was white and brittle.

The mallet was wielded by the bearded man, who laughed when the old man's skull cracked under the blow, his head becoming wedged between his partner's skinny legs. The bearded man knelt beside the aged couple and brought the mallet down hard on the man's buttocks, the woman beneath him suddenly struggling to free herself from his choking member. She twisted her head to one side, but the force of the blows pushed the man's pelvis against her, smothering her, pinning her neck at an awkward angle. It was impossible to know if she died from suffocation, a broken neck, or just shock.

The bearded man was laughing gleefully as he rained blows on the now still bodies. He stopped abruptly and looked towards the man sitting in the armchair. The man was speaking to him, but Bishop could not hear the words. The bearded man shuffled on his knees towards the seated figure, the mallet still grasped tightly in his hand. The glass of clear liquid was offered to him and he took it, hesitated, looked deep into the contents. Then he drank.

The sneer – or was it a grin? – on the seated man's face deepened and he looked towards Bishop once more. He picked up something that had been lying in his lap unnoticed by Bishop. It was heavy, black. A gun. The man took a long, sweeping look around the room, his bulging eyes finally coming back to rest on Bishop. His lips moved, then his mouth opened wide; the muzzle of the gun was pushed in, pointing high into the roof of his mouth. Everything around Bishop seemed to slow down, all movements losing speed, the struggles becoming graceful, a ballet of death. It took a lifetime for the man's finger to slide around the trigger and pull it back tight against the guard, the recoil blurred but still slow, the flame lighting up the inside of his mouth so that Bishop saw the hole appear, could almost follow the bullet's path as it travelled through the man's head, erupting on the other side, carrying bits of brain, mucous, blood, into the air to shatter high against the wall behind leaving a red smear of dripping substance.

Bishop stared at the running pattern and traced a trail of slow-moving blood back to the man below. But it was not the same man. The eyes still bulged, still stood out from their sockets, but it was fear that made them so. Fear of the unseen, sensed only, for the eyes were sightless. It was Kulek who now sat in the chair.

He was calling out and the sounds came creeping through to Bishop. It was as though Kulek was at the end of a long, winding tunnel, and was drawing near, his voice becoming louder and louder at his approach. The figures around Bishop became

409

misty, ethereal, their twisting and writhing becoming even slower until they were still; and as they faded, so another body became clearer, more defined. Edith Metlock lay slumped against the wall, eyes closed, head hanging limply sideways. Kulek's cries came fully to Bishop's ears and with them he found the strength to raise himself, staggering back against Jessica who tried to support him.

He whirled around and she fell to one side, gasping sharply as she went down on one knee. Bishop had to get out, had to get away from the house and the terrible thing that had happened there. That was still happening.

He fell against the door-frame, his body swinging round at the impact so his eyes were looking down into the far end of the hall. There were more moving shapes, fading, slowly dissolving, their bodies grey in the dim light. He pulled himself upright and cried out, 'No!' when he saw the legs hanging above the stairway. They kicked out wildly, scuffing the wall, a shoe falling loose and rolling down several stairs before coming to rest. Dismembered hands clutched at the fading legs, tugging at them, pulling them downwards till they no longer kicked. The hands faded away and only a dim twitching outline of the limbs remained.

Bishop had to get away from the house. He knew the slaughter was going on all over; in the bedrooms upstairs; in the rooms on the second floor. He had to get out. He began to run towards the front door, his legs leaden, his breath drawn in short, sharp gasps. The door beneath the stairway was ajar, a long, narrow gap beckoning to him.

He stopped running and pushed his back against the opposite wall as he had once before. And, like before, the door seemed to be moving outwards as if someone were pushing it from the other side. He found he was reaching forward in repeat motion, his finger clutching the door's edge, afraid to look, but compelled to, something down in that cellar commanding him to. He pulled the small door back and it swung wide, the blackness lurking behind it shuddering and falling away at the sudden light, dim though it was. He heard a movement. A shifting sound. Something on the stairs below. He had to see. Had to.

He approached the open doorway and looked down into the bowels of the house. The darkness at the bottom of the stairs seemed solid, a brooding night that invited him below, a living blackness that waited to devour. And from the blackness a shape began to emerge.

Bishop could not move. Even when the shape grew larger as it mounted the steps and the strange murmurings came to his ears he stood mesmerised. Even when he could see the wild-staring eyes, the long, dark hair hanging forward almost to her waist, the flow broken by huge bare breasts like boulders in a fast-flowing stream. Even when she was near the top step and curling her hair in big hands, stretching it taut across her chest like a thick rope, the words becoming clearer now as she repeated over and over again, 'All these years . . . all these years . . .'

The woman was real, not a spectral shape like the others. As she emerged from the shadows he saw her body had substance and seemed to grow in its firmness rather than fade. And her murmuring, almost an incantation, told him she was not one of those already dead. He backed away, the deranged look on her face as frightening as the visions he had just witnessed. She stopped before him, her hands constantly twisting and turning the thick cord of hair stretched between them. Her big body was shivering, her plumpness no protection against the seeping coldness of the house. Her eyes rolled away from him, searching for something, and she suddenly wheeled away, shuffling down the corridor towards the room he had just left. Bishop slumped against the wall, his forehead beaded with perspiration that turned icy as soon as it escaped from his pores.

Jessica stood in the doorway of the room and held up her arms to ward off the lumbering woman, but she was grabbed roughly and pushed aside, the woman screaming in rage at the feeble obstruction. Jessica fell heavily and for a moment appeared dazed. Bishop could only watch helplessly as the big woman disappeared into the room and he felt a new dread when Jessica uttered a cry of alarm.

She turned her face towards him, pleading in her eyes. 'Help him, please help him!'

He wanted to run in the opposite direction, wanted to be free of the terrible house, away from the horrors that dwelt inside; but her pleas held him there and would not release him from the madness. He stumbled towards her.

Bishop tried to pull the girl to her feet, but she pushed his hands away and pointed into the room. 'Stop her! Help him, Chris!'

The woman was standing behind Jessica's father, leaning over

411

him, her long dark hair curled around his neck. Her knuckles were white as she pulled in opposite directions.

Kulek's face was flushed red, his sightless eyes straining at their sockets, his tongue unwillingly beginning to protrude from his gaping mouth. A rasping, hissing sound came from his throat as the walls of his trachea were squeezed together. His thin hands were wrapped around the woman's wrists in an effort to pull them apart. Bishop ran forward and grabbed her arms.

It was hopeless; she was too strong, her grip too secure.

The old man's body was arched in the seat and he began to slide forward on to the floor, but the woman maintained her hold on him, keeping him from collapsing completely. Bishop knew he was failing, that Kulek would not survive much longer. His grip on the woman's arm was only relieving the pressure slightly, only prolonging the blind man's agony. Jessica had joined in the struggle now and was tugging at the naked woman, trying to pull her away from her father. But the woman had the strength of the obsessed.

In desperation, Bishop released his hold on the woman, stepped swiftly around to the back of the armchair and kicked her sturdy legs away from under her. She fell almost to her knees, supported by the grip she had on Kulek's throat. Bishop kicked out again, the tip of his shoe sinking into the fleshy side of the woman's stomach. She screamed with the sudden pain, her head swivelling towards Bishop, still keeping the pressure on the blind man's neck. Bishop drew a clenched fist back, then swung it with as much force as possible at the round, upturned face. He felt the small bones of her nose shatter under the impact and her lower face was instantly covered in running blood. Still she would not let go.

He hit her again, again, again. And finally her fingers uncurled, releasing the thick rope of hair. She sank to the floor, swaying there on hands and knees, groaning, shaking her gross body as if to shrug off the pain. Jessica ran to her father who was now lying on the floor on the other side of the chair, gasping for air. The injured woman began crawling forward around the armchair and, for a moment, Bishop thought she was trying to reach Kulek again. But she went by, heading for the open doorway, her movements slow, yet determined. He tried to stop her, grabbing her flowing hair and yanking backwards. She half-turned, sweeping a sturdy arm back and knocking him sideways.

412

Her strength frightened him: from her build, he guessed she was a powerful woman, and now her insanity was increasing that strength. She was halfway out the door when he lunged for her ankle, grabbing it and pulling her back. He was in an awkward position, his body stretched out on the floor, elbows supporting him, face exposed to the sudden kick she dealt him with her free foot.

The blow stunned him and he rolled on to his side, his hand releasing her and going to his head. She began crawling forward again and was soon completely through the doorway and disappearing down the hall. Suddenly he knew where she was making for. And he knew he had to stop her.

But before he could move, a figure had dashed past him into the hall. He pushed himself up and staggered through just in time to see Jessica raise Jacob Kulek's stout walking-stick above her head and bring it crashing down against the crawling woman's head. The sharp crack made Bishop wince, but he was relieved to see the woman collapse into a motionless heap, one arm stretched out towards the open cellar doorway. The darkness there was suddenly obliterated as the door was kicked shut. Jessica leaned against the stairway, the weapon she had used against the woman falling from limp fingers and clattering to the floor. Her eyes met Bishop's and for several moments they could only stare at each other.

Chapter Nine

All three looked up expectantly when Bishop entered Kulek's private study at the Research Institute.

'Is it Chris?' the old man asked, his head craning forward.

'Yes, father,' Jessica answered, smiling hesitantly at Bishop, unsure of his grim expression.

'What happened? Are the police still at the house?' Kulek asked.

'They've left a guard outside, that's all.' Bishop sank wearily into a hard-backed chair and rubbed his face with both hands as if to relieve the tension there. He looked across at Edith Metlock. 'Are you all right?'

'Yes, Mr Bishop,' she replied. 'Exhausted but not harmed in any way.'

'You, Jacob?'

'Yes, yes, Chris,' the blind man said a little impatiently. 'My neck feels somewhat tender, but my doctor says nothing was damaged. Some bruising, that's all. Do they know who the woman was?'

The memory of her being carried from the house on a stretcher, her body covered by a thick red blanket, only her face showing, the wide, blank eyes, the constantly moving lips, made Bishop shudder inwardly. Her hair had cascaded over the side of the stretcher, enchancing the madness in her features. Beneath the blanket, heavy straps kept her pinned down.

'A neighbour recognised her when she was taken to the ambulance,' he said. 'She was a nurse or housekeeper to an old man who lived further down the road.'

'But how did she get into Beechwood?'

'The police found a broken window at the back. She must have got in that way. A couple of them went off to see the old man while I was being questioned. Apparently the front door was

414

wide open – it didn't take them long to find the old man's body.'

'He was dead?'

'Strangled.'

'With her hair?'

Bishop shook his head. 'They don't know yet. And from the look of her, it'll be a long time before she answers any questions.'

'If she killed the old man in the same manner she tried to kill me, they'll find strands of hair embedded in his throat.'

'Lilith,' Edith Metlock said quietly.

Kulek turned towards her and smiled kindly. 'I don't think so, Edith, not in this case. Just a demented woman.'

Bishop looked at Kulek in puzzlement. 'Who the hell is Lilith?'

'Lilith was an ancient demon,' Kulek said, the smile on his face implying that his words should not be taken too seriously. 'Some say she was the first woman, before Eve, joined back to back with Adam. They quarrelled constantly and, using a cabbalistic charm, she acquired wings and separation from Adam. She flew away.'

Bishop's voice was cold. 'And what has that got to do with this madwoman?'

'Nothing. Nothing at all. Edith was merely comparing their method of slaying. Lilith also used her long hair to strangle her victims, you see.'

Bishop shook his head in exasperation. 'I think this whole business is bizarre enough without dragging mythical demons into it.'

'I quite agree,' Kulek said. 'It was only an observation on Edith's part. Now please tell us what happened back at the house.'

'They ran me through the mill after they let you go. They were very curious to know exactly what we were doing there.'

'No, all that is not important. I had already informed the local police station that we would be there today with Miss Kirkhope's permission. All they needed to do was check.'

'They did that, all right. But they still wanted to know what a naked madwoman was doing in Beechwood. Finding the dead man in the other house didn't improve their disposition towards me.'

'I'm sure you explained everything adequately . . .'

'I tried to, but they'll be calling on you later. It was only because you – and Mrs Metlock – obviously needed medical

415

attention that they let Jessica take you both away.'

'Chris, the house . . . what did you see?' Kulek's impatience was growing.

Bishop looked around in wonder at the other occupants of the study. 'I saw the same as Jessica and Mrs Metlock,' he said to Kulek.

'I saw nothing, Chris,' Jessica said. She was standing by the window behind her father's desk.

'Nor I, Mr Bishop,' said the medium. 'I . . . blacked out.'

'But that's crazy! You were both there in the room.'

Jessica spoke. 'I heard Edith scream, and I followed you downstairs. I tried to help you when you collapsed in the room. I knew you were seeing something – you were terrified – but, believe me, I couldn't see anything. I wish to God I had. All I know is that you seemed to be having some kind of fit, then you rushed from the room and made for the cellar. I saw the woman come from there – she was real enough.'

Bishop's head swung towards the medium. 'As a sensitive you must have had the same vision.'

'I think I may have caused the vision,' Edith Metlock said calmly. 'You see, I believe I was used by them.'

'You called up the dead?'

'No, I was receptive to them, that's all. They manifested themselves through me.'

Bishop shook his head. 'That's fine if you believe in ghosts.'

'What would you call them?'

'Vibrations. Electro-magnetic images. Jacob knows my theory on such phenomena. An electro-cardiograph shows the heart giving off electrical impulses; I believe someone under stress does the same. And those impulses are picked up later by someone like you, someone sensitive to such impulses.'

'But you saw them, not me.'

'Telepathy. You were the receiver; you transmitted those visions to me.'

Jessica cut in. 'Then why weren't Edith's thoughts transmitted to me? Why didn't I see them?'

'And why not me?' Kulek said. 'If they were only telepathic thoughts from Edith, then why didn't I see them in my mind's eye?'

'And why were you so afraid?' Jessica put in.

'Maybe I didn't actually see anything at all.' They all looked

416

quizzically at Bishop. It could be that I just remembered what I'd seen before in that house. Mrs Metlock may have triggered off something in my subconscious, something so horrible I'd been trying to keep it from myself. And if any of you had experienced it, you'd have been afraid.'

'And the woman?' said Jessica. 'Why was she in the house?'

'She was hiding, for God's sake! She'd killed the old man. She knew Beechwood was empty, so she hid there.'

'But why did she try to kill my father? Why not you? Me?'

'Perhaps she just hates men of your father's age,' Bishop said in frustration. 'Men like her own employer.'

'She went straight to him. She hadn't even seen Jacob, but she went past us both to get to him.'

'She could have heard his voice from the cellar.'

'Yes, the cellar, Chris. You felt it too, didn't you?'

'Felt what?'

'Felt there was something evil in that cellar.'

Bishop rubbed a hand across his eyes. 'I just don't know. It all seems so insane now.'

'Chris, you still haven't told us what you saw or, what, as you would have it, you remembered,' Kulek said quietly.

Angry though she was over the investigator's refusal to accept the reality of what had happened inside Beechwood, Jessica wanted to comfort him when his face became pale.

It was seconds before he spoke, and the words came out dull and flat as if he were deliberately holding back his emotions, afraid he would lose control of them. He described the scene at Beechwood, the mad, perverted suicides, the cruel slayings. Jessica felt the muscles inside her stomach knot into a tight ball. When he had finished, there was a heavy silence in the room. Jacob Kulek's sightless eyes were closed, Edith Metlock's could not look away from Bishop's face. At last, the blind man opened his eyes and said, 'They tried to die in the foulest way possible. They had to.'

Bishop frowned. 'You think there was a motive behind all this?'

Kulek nodded. 'There is always a motive for suicide and murder. Even the insane have their reasons.'

'Suicides usually want to free themselves from the troubles of life.'

'Or the restrictions.'

417

Bishop was puzzled by Kulek's last remark – Jessica had talked of death as some kind of release before – but he felt too drained to pursue it. 'Whatever the motives were, it won't matter after tomorrow. The house will no longer be there.'

They were startled. 'What do you mean?' Kulek asked apprehensively.

'I rang Miss Kirkhope before coming here,' Bishop replied. 'I told her there was nothing in the house except a cold atmosphere and recommended she carry out her plan for demolition as soon as possible. She said, that being the case, she would bring the date forward to tomorrow.'

'How could you . . .?' Jessica said, furious.

'Chris, you don't know what you have done!' Kulek was on his feet.

'Perhaps he is right.' Jessica and her father turned to Edith Metlock in surprise. 'Perhaps the demolition of Beechwood will free their poor souls. I believe the house and everything that has happened there is holding them to this world. Now they may be free to go on.'

Jacob Kulek sank back into his chair and slowly shook his head. 'If only that were so,' was all he could say.

Chapter Ten

'Lucy died three days after her fifth birthday.'

The words were spoken without emotion, as though Bishop had cut himself off from the sadness that went with them. But below, somewhere inside where only he could touch, the pain fed upon itself, weaker now, yet still a living thing, a slow-dying disease of grief. Jessica, walking by his side through the cold London park, remained silent. The physical gap between them somehow symbolised their mutual antagonism, an antagonism that had frequently abated then reared into bitter life again in the few days she had known him. Now, hearing him speak of his daughter, she wanted that gap closed, yet she could not find it in herself to move closer.

Bishop paused to stare into the grey lake, the ducks tucked in close to its edges as if even they found its sombre expanse unwelcoming. 'Laryngotracheo-bronchitis was the indirect cause,' he said, still not looking at Jessica. 'When I was a kid, we called it croup. Her throat closed up, she couldn't breathe. It took us a long time to convince the doctor to leave his warm bed to come and see her that night – even in those days there were many who were unwilling to make house calls. It took three phone calls, the second threatening, the third begging, for him to come. Maybe it would have been better if he hadn't.'

Jessica stood beside him, watching his profile. The heavy cloth of her overcoat brushed against his arm.

'It was a bitterly cold night. The panic rush to hospital may have made it worse for her. Two hours we waited: an hour waiting for the hospital doctor to look at her, another hour waiting for them to decide what to do. They gave Lucy a tracheostomy, but by then she had pneumonia. Whether it was the shock of the operation in her weakened state, or the illness itself that killed her, we never found out. We blamed ourselves, the doctor who refused at first to come, the hospital – but most of all, we blamed God.' He gave a short, bitter laugh. 'Of course, Lynn and I believed in God then.'

'You don't any more?' She seemed surprised and Bishop turned his head towards her.

'Can you believe any Supreme Being would allow all this misery?' He nodded towards the tall buildings as though the city were the container for mankind's torments. 'Lynn was a Catholic, but I think her rejection of God was even stronger than mine. Maybe that's the way it works: the more you believe in something, the more you go against it when that belief is shattered. In that first year, I had to watch Lynn day and night. I thought she'd kill herself. My caring for her may have been the thing that pulled me through – I don't know. Then she seemed to accept it. She became calm, but it was a brooding kind of calmness, almost as if she'd given up, lost interest. In a way, it was unnerving, but at least it gave me something to work on. I could plan our lives again without the hysterics. I planned, she listened. It was something. A few weeks later she perked up, seemed to come alive again. I discovered she had been going to a spiritualist.'

Bishop looked around and indicated a bench on the opposite side of the path behind them. 'Shall we sit for a while? Is it too cold?'

Jessica shook her head. 'No, it's not too cold.'

They sat, and she pressed closer to him. He seemed distracted, almost unaware of her presence.

'Did you believe in spiritualism then?' she prompted.

'What? On, no, not really. I'd never thought about it before. But it was like a new religion to Lynn; it replaced her God.'

'How did she find this spiritualist?'

'A friend, probably well-meaning, told her of him. The friend had lost her husband years before and had supposedly made contact with him again through this man. Lynn swore to me he had found Lucy for her. She told me she had spoken to her. I was angry at first, but I could see the change it had made in Lynn. Suddenly she had a reason for living again. It went on for a long time and I admit my arguments against her seeing the spiritualist were only half-hearted. She was paying him for each session, of course, but not enough for me to suspect he was making a lot of money out of her.' Bishop smiled cynically. 'But isn't that how they operate? Build up a large clientele, accept small, individual "gifts"? It soon mounts up.'

420

'They're not all like that, Chris. There are very few that practise spiritualism just for money.' Jessica stemmed her irritation, not wanting to become involved in another argument with him.

'I'm sure they have all sorts of reasons, Jessica.' The implication was that any other reason was just as bad as that of financial gain, but she refused to rise to the bait.

'Anyway,' Bishop continued, 'Lynn finally persuaded me to go along to one of her meetings. Maybe I wanted to see or hear Lucy again. I missed her so much I was ready to grasp at anything. And for the first five minutes, the man almost had me fooled.

'He was middle-aged, spoke with a soft, Irish accent. His whole manner was soft, in fact; soft but persuasive. Like Edith Metlock, he looked like any other ordinary member of the public. He made no exaggerated claims to me, didn't even try to convince me he was genuine. It was all up to me, he said. The choice whether to believe or not was mine. It was his very casualness that almost convinced me of his sincerity.

'With few preliminaries, the seance began. It was in a darkened room, holding hands around a table – the sort of thing I expected. He asked us to join him in a short prayer to start the proceedings and, surprisingly, Lynn readily did so. There were others at the seance, Lynn's friend who had introduced her to the medium among them, and one by one, their dead friends or relatives were contacted. Frankly, I was a little scared. The atmosphere of the room seemed to be – I don't know – heavy, charged? I had to keep telling myself it was only created by the living people in the room itself.

'When Lucy's voice came through I was shocked rigid. Lynn was grasping my hand tightly, and without looking at her I knew she was crying. I also knew those tears were because she was happy. The voice was small, distant; it seemed to come from the air itself. A child's but it could have been any child's. It was the things she said that made me believe. She was glad I'd finally come. She had missed me, but she was happy now. She'd felt no pain when she died, only a sadness, then a great joy. She had many new friends in the world she was now in and her only concern was that we, her mother and father, were unhappy. I felt my own tears coming, but suddenly, things didn't quite ring true. Lucy was only five when she died and here she was speaking in the manner of someone much older. If you really wanted to

421

believe, you could convince yourself that that was how things were on the other side: you gained a wisdom beyond your mortal years. I wasn't quite that ready to accept, though. I was perplexed when she spoke of things that only we three, myself, Lucy and her mother, knew of. But then they made their first mistake. The voice was reminding me of how once, when Lynn was out shopping, Lucy and I were having a rough-and-tumble in the sitting-room. In the scramble, a favourite ornament of Lynn's got broken. It was a figurine – an 18th Century courtesan, I think – but only reproduction, not valuable. Lynn loved it though, so we knew we were in trouble. Only the head had come off and I spent the next half-hour gluing it back on. It fooled Lynn until she tried to dust it. The head just toppled off again. Unfortunately, Lucy and I were both in the room at the time and we couldn't help going into hysterics at the look on Lynn's face. Anyway, I owned up to it, and that was the last of the matter. Until the giggling voice in the room reminded me of it.

'Okay, seances are full of these trivial incidents related by departed loved ones. It's what makes them seem so genuine, isn't it? Little moments that no one else could possibly know of. That was fine, except they'd got it wrong. It was Lucy who had broken the statuette, not me. I had accepted the blame because Lucy thought she might have been spanked. She wouldn't have, of course, it was an accident. But that's how kids are.

'So now I was even more suspicious. The medium had heard the story second-hand from someone. Who? Lynn? Maybe she had told the story in one of her visits. Or her friend, the woman who had brought her along in the first place. If it was her, there was probably no bad intent. As I said, the Irishman was a soft, persuasive talker. He could have learned many things about us.

'I played along with them for a while, pretending to be convinced, waiting for another mistake. And they made it, all right. A stupid, almost farcical mistake. I suppose they had been lulled into a false sense of security by my act, imagining that here was another punter to be bled. A smoky substance came from somewhere behind the medium. It was near the back of the room, over his left shoulder, where Lynn and I had a clear view of it. An image began to appear in the smoke, hazy, not clearly defined. It was a face, fluctuating between sharpness and a blur. After a few seconds we recognised it as Lucy. The features were hers, the expression was hers; but there was something not quite right. I

422

realised what it was and it was so silly I could have laughed out loud had I not been so angry. Her hair was parted on the wrong side, you see. They were projecting a photograph of Lucy on to a small screen from behind. The screen's edges were well camouflaged, and the smoke helped conceal it even more.

'I lost control when I realised how it was being done and rushed towards the smoke which was coming from a small tube in the wall. I pounded my fist against the screen. It was inside a small alcove that was covered by a panel when the lights were on and made of some kind of black Perspex. I managed to crack it with my fist.'

Bishop leaned forward, resting his elbows on his knees, studying the gravel path. 'Sometimes I wonder what would have happened if I had let it ride. Maybe Lynn wouldn't have had her breakdown.' His bitter smile returned as he remembered the immediate consequences of his action. 'As you can imagine, the seance ended in uproar. The medium was screaming at me, his brogue a little sharp by then. Lynn's friend was in hysterics, while Lynn herself was white-faced and quiet. The others were in various stages of shock and anger. I'm still not sure who their anger was directed at – me or the Irishman.

'I didn't even bother to look for the hidden microphone the child's voice had come from; I'd seen enough. The medium was coming at me looking as if his red face was about to burst open. A good hard shove took care of him, then I grabbed Lynn and got out of there. She didn't say a word for three days after. Then she cracked.

'Her last hope had been shattered, you see. It was as though Lucy had died twice.'

'Oh, God, it must have been terrible for her, Chris. For you both.' Jessica, too, was leaning forward.

'Lynn just seemed to sink further and further into herself over the next few months. I just couldn't reach her. She seemed to be blaming me. I finally got her to a psychiatrist and he explained that to Lynn, I had almost become Lucy's murderer. In her confused mind, I had taken Lucy away from her again. I didn't believe him, I couldn't. Lynn and I had always been so close. When she suffered, I suffered; when I was happy, she was happy. To us, Lucy had somehow represented that closeness, had been a product of it. It was as if with her gone, our ties had been snapped. Lynn tried to kill herself twice before I was forced to have her committed. Once, she tried to kill me.'

423

Jessica shivered, not from the cold, and impulsively placed a hand on his arm. He sat back against the bench as if to shrug her hand off and she quickly withdrew it.

'She took sleeping pills the first time, tried to slash her wrists the second. I managed to get her to hospital before it was too late on both occasions; but I knew there would come a time when we wouldn't make it. After the second attempt, she really hated me. She wanted to be with Lucy and I was preventing her. I woke up one night and she was standing over me with a knife. Why she hadn't struck while I was still asleep, I don't know. Perhaps deep inside the old Lynn didn't want to kill me. When I woke, it must have acted as a trigger. I just managed to move out of the way in time. The knife went into the pillow and I had to hit her hard to make her let it go. After that, I had no choice: I had to have her taken into care. There was no way I could watch her all the time.'

He was silent for a few moments and from the way he avoided looking directly at her, Jessica wondered if he now regretted telling her all this. She wondered if he had ever told anyone else before.

'That happened six, seven years ago,' he finally said.

'And Lynn is still . . .?' she hesitated, unwilling to use a title, afraid it might give offence.

'In the mental institution? She's in a private one – not the best, but one I can afford. The people who run it like to call it a rest home for the mentally disorientated. Kind of takes the sting out of it. Yes, she's still there, and as far as I can see, there's been little progress. The reverse, in fact. I visit her as much as I can, but now she doesn't even recognise me. She's built a protective barrier around herself, I'm told. I'm her biggest threat, so she's cutting me out.'

'It seems such an inadequate thing to say, Chris, but I'm sorry. These past years must have seemed like hell to you. Now I can understand why you hate spiritualists so much.'

Bishop surprised her by taking her hand. 'I don't hate them, Jessica. The real phoneys I detest, but I've learned that many are completely sincere, if misguided.' He shrugged and let go of her hand. 'That first one, the Irishman, was a complete amateur compared to some I've investigated. They've got it down to a fine art. Did you know there's a shop in America where you can buy spiritualistic miracles? A couple of dollars for the Mystery of the Gyrating Tables, a few more for the Joe Spook Spirit Rapper. It

424

even has an Ectoplasm Kit. Spiritualism has become big business with the wave of interest in the occult. People are looking beyond the materialistic side of life and there are plenty of shysters around to cater for their needs. Don't get me wrong – I'm not on any crusade against them. At first I was ready to expose any group or individual I believed was operating fraudulently and I was pretty lucky most times. Their tricks were so obvious when you went along as a complete unbeliever. But other times I was stumped, impressed even. I began to develop a deeper interest in the whole topic of mysticism, keeping my acceptance at a realistic level. I found there was so much that could be explained by down-to-earth investigation. By practical, scientific reasoning, if you like. Of course, there's an awful lot that can't be explained, but we're slowly finding the answers, gradually moving towards the truth.'

'That's what my father's Institute is all about.'

'I know, Jessica. That's why I wanted to speak to you. I've been pretty rough on you, Jacob and Edith Metlock. It seemed to me that events were being exaggerated, moulded into a shape that complied with your way of thinking. It was a kind of hysteria. I've seen it so many times in my investigations.'

He put a finger to her lips to still her protests. 'I believe what you said about this man Pryszlak. Perhaps he *was* on to something. Perhaps he *had* discovered that evil was a physical force in itself and was searching for a way of harnessing that force. But it all ended with his death and the deaths of his crazy henchmen. Don't you see that?'

Jessica gave a deep sigh. 'I just don't know any more. It could be that my father's conviction is swaying my own judgement. He knew the man so well. Their mental capabilities were so alike, so extraordinary. If anything, my father's blindness has enhanced his extrasensory faculties, although it's become a very private thing for him, not one he shares with others.'

'Not even with you?'

She shook her head. 'He will one day, when the time is right.' She smiled, almost whimsically. 'He likens himself to an explorer who cannot lead others until he has found the right path himself. His concern is that Pryszlak was way ahead of him on that path.'

'I've met many like Pryszlak in my investigations. Obviously not as extreme, but all with that same fanaticism that you tell me the man had. It's like a disease, Jessica, it spreads. I've almost

425

caught small doses of it myself when I've been baffled by certain cases.'

'But you've always been content to label them as "unexplained phenomena" and put them aside.' There was no sarcasm in her voice, just a hopelessness.

'For the moment, yes. It's like UFOs: it's just a matter of time before we find the explanation for them.'

She nodded her understanding. 'All right, Chris. Perhaps it's good to have a cynic like you nosing around in this field; we may all be too dedicated to our own causes. I think your experience in that house has shaken you more than you're letting on, though. Your recommendation that it be destroyed immediately could be your way of chasing away your own ghosts.'

He had no answer for her: the truth wasn't clear even to himself. Instead, he tried to make light of it. 'It might destroy a reasonable living if I became a believer.'

She smiled and said, 'Thanks for telling me all this, Chris. I know it wasn't easy.'

Bishop grinned. 'It wasn't, but it helped. It's been good to talk to someone after all this time.' He rose from the bench and looked down at her. 'Tell your father I'm sorry, will you? I didn't enjoy bringing everything to such a sudden halt. I thought it was for the best, though. Really.'

'We owe you your fee.'

'For half a day's work? Forget it.'

He turned to go, but she stopped him by saying, 'Will I see you again?'

His confusion showed before he replied, 'I hope so.'

Jessica watched as he made his way towards the park exit that would take him in the direction of Baker Street. She reached into her shoulder-bag and took out a cigarette. She lit it and inhaled deeply. He was a strange man; intense. But now that she understood his cynicism, all her resentment towards him had evaporated. She wished she could help him in some way. She wished she could help rid her father of his obsession with Pryszlak. She wished it really was all over but, like Jacob, she somehow knew it wasn't.

A screech from one of the ducks startled her and she saw two of them were fighting greedily over a lake-sodden piece of bread thrown by an elderly woman. Jessica rose from the bench, drawing her coat tight around her to keep out the dampness of the air.

She stopped to stub out the scarcely-smoked cigarette on the gravel path, then tossed the broken remains into a nearby bin. Hands tucked deep into her coat pockets, she walked slowly from the park.

The demolition company moved in, their machines battering the walls of Beechwood, the men swinging their sledgehammers with relish. The neighbours gawped, surprised at the sudden attack on the property and some, those who knew the history of the house, were pleased at the destruction. Within two days the building was reduced to rubble, an unsightly scar between the houses of Willow Road, an emptiness that was only filled when nightfall came. A rough wooden barrier was erected to prevent the curious, especially children, from entering the site, for the debris was dangerous, the ground floor not having collapsed completely into the basement area. There were small openings through which someone could fall.

The shadows beneath the rubble welcomed the night, merging with it, becoming more substantial, and the darkness in the cellar seemed to creep from the openings like a living, breathing thing.

PART TWO

Have regard for thy covenant;
for the dark places of the land are
full of the habitations of violence.
Psalms 74:20
(R.S.V.)

Chapter Eleven

Detective Chief Inspector Peck groaned inwardly as the Granada slid to a smooth halt.

'Looks like Armageddon,' he remarked to his driver, who chuckled in response. Peck climbed from the car and surveyed the scene. The smell of smoke still clung to the air and large puddles filled the hollows of Willow Road, forming small, shiny ponds. Water tenders were dampening the ashes of the three fire-ravaged houses, their bright red bodywork a bulky intrusion on the drab greyness of the street. An ambulance stood by, its back door open wide as though expecting a fresh delivery at any moment. A blue-clad figure disengaged itself from an agitated throng and strode briskly towards Peck.

'Chief Inspector Peck? I was informed you were on your way.'

Peck acknowledged the uniformed man's curt salute with a casual nod of his head. 'You'd be Inspector Ross from the local shop.'

'Yes, sir. We've got a right bloody mess here.' He indicated the general background scene with a flick of his head.

'Well, I think the first thing you'd better do is clear the street of anyone not directly involved in last night's business.'

'Just about to do that. Trouble is, half of them *were* involved.'

Peck's eyebrows rose in an arch, but he said nothing.

Ross called his sergeant over. 'Get them all inside their houses, Tom. We'll take door-to-door statements from everyone. And get the Press back to the end of the road; we'll issue a statement later. I thought you posted men at each end to stop anyone getting through.'

'We did. It didn't work.'

'Okay, get on to HQ and have some barriers sent down. Tell them we need more men, too. Right, all civilians off the street. Now.'

431

The sergeant wheeled away and began barking orders at his men and bystanders alike. Ross turned back to Peck, who said, 'Okay, Inspector, let's get in the car and talk quietly for a few moments.'

Once inside, Peck lit a cigarette and opened a side window just enough for the smoke to escape. 'So tell me,' he said, looking distractedly at the activity outside.

The inspector placed his cap on one knee. 'The first sign of trouble was a radio message from one of our constables patrolling this road. Constable Posgate, it was, on surveillance duty with Constable Hicks.'

'Surveillance?'

'Well, not exactly. But it was more than the normal patrol. You've heard about the funny goings-on here recently?'

Peck grunted and Ross took it as affirmation.

'The residents demanded some protection. We gave them the patrol to let them know we were keeping an eye on things, but frankly, we didn't really expect anything else to happen.'

'Seems you were wrong. Go on.'

The inspector shifted uncomfortably in his seat. 'Our man reported what he thought was a scuffle or a mugging going on at the end of the road.'

'What time was this?'

'About half-eleven. They went down to sort things out and got pretty well sorted out themselves.'

'How many involved?'

'Three. Youths. Two white, one black.'

'And they gave your coppers a seeing-to?'

'They were vicious bastards, sir.'

Peck hid his smile by cupping the cigarette against his mouth.

'And it wasn't a mugging,' Ross said seriously.

'No?'

'No. It was a rape.'

'In the street?'

'Yes, sir, in the street. No attempt to drag the victim off into cover. But that's not the worst of it.'

'Surprise me.'

'The victim was a man.'

Peck looked incredulously at the inspector. 'I'm surprised,' he said.

Ross felt a grim satisfaction at shocking his superior. By the

432

end of his report, Peck would be even more shocked.

'Skeates was the name of the man. He lives in the road – a young exec type. Apparently he was just returning home late from the pub.'

'He'll get a cab next time. What about your officers? How badly were they hurt?'

'Hicks has a broken jaw. Not too many teeth left, either. By the time the backup got there, those three bastards had broken both Posgate's arms and were trying to do the same with his legs.'

Smoke escaped between Peck's clenched teeth in a thin, forceful stream. 'Spiteful bitches,' he commented.

Ross failed to appreciate the senior officer's sarcasm. 'There was nothing effeminate about those three. I know, I interviewed them when they were brought in.'

'Was there anything left of them?'

'They'd had a going over. They resisted arrest.'

'I'll bet.' Peck grinned at the inspector's rising indignation. 'All right, Ross, I'm not having a go. I don't blame your lads dealing out some punishment of their own. Did you get anything out of the bastards?'

'No. Like zombies, all three. Haven't spoken a word all night.'

'The victim?'

'My men found him crawling down the street trying to get home. He claims the three youths were just sitting on the pavement as if they were waiting for someone to come along. They don't live in this road, apparently. At least, he's never seen them before.'

'All right, Inspector, I'm already impressed. What else happened here last night?' Peck nodded towards the still smouldering house. 'Apart from the obvious, that is.'

'About half-past one this morning we received a report of an intruder on the premises of number . . .' Ross produced a notebook from his breast pocket and flicked it open '. . . thirty-three. The call came from a Mrs Jack Kimble. By the time my lads got there, her husband had dealt with the trouble himself.'

'Don't keep me guessing.'

'The Kimbles have a fifteen-year-old daughter. She sleeps in a room that looks on to the road itself. A man had forced himself into her bedroom.'

'Not another rape,' Peck said in disgust.

433

'Yes, sir. The intruder lived opposite the Kimbles. Eric Channing was his name.'

'Was?'

'Was. He no longer is.'

'This . . . what's his name – Kimble? . . . took the law into his own hands?'

'Channing had used a ladder to reach the girl's bedroom window. He didn't even bother to open it, just jumped head first through the glass and attacked the girl. While Mrs Kimble was phoning us, Mr Kimble was busy throwing the would-be rapist back out the way he had come. The fall broke Channing's neck.'

'Love thy neighbour, eh? Is there anything dodgy about this Kimble? Is he known?'

'No record. He just over-reacted, that's all.'

'Let's hope the judge doesn't. What else have you got?'

'Well, as if these two incidents weren't enough, all hell broke loose around three o'clock. That's when the fires started.'

'Cause?'

'It started in one semi and took the adjoining house with it. We think flying sparks probably started the fire in the nearest house to them.'

'Yes, but *how* did it start?'

Ross took a deep breath and consulted his notebook again to check on the correct name. 'A Mr Ronald Clarkson, a retired businessman, raised the alarm. He'd been woken up by the smell of burning. It was his wife sitting in the middle of the bedroom floor. She'd used paraffin from one of those oil burners and doused herself with it. He was lucky: she'd doused the bed too. He only just got out in time.'

Peck's eyes were wide now, all complacency gone.

Ross continued, taking some enjoyment from the sight. 'By the time the fire engines got here, the whole house had gone up and there was no saving the one next door. The house opposite was well under way, but they managed to bring it under control before it destroyed the place completely. Eight engines they had here last night; it was like the blitz all over again.'

'Anyone else killed – apart from Clarkson's wife?'

'No. Fortunately, they got out in time thanks to Clarkson giving the warning.'

'Did he give any indication why she'd done it? Burnt herself?'

'He said she'd been depressed lately.'

Peck snorted his disgust. 'Depressed! Jesus Christ!'

'One other thing.'

'Oh, you're kidding.'

'No. This one's not so bad, though. Just as daybreak came, when the firemen were still fighting the blaze and I was running around like a lunatic trying to find out what the hell was going on, a man approached one of my officers and asked to be arrested.'

'It must have made a nice change. Who was it – another nutter?'

'He doesn't seem to be. His name is Brewer. He lives at number nine.'

'And?'

'He was afraid of what he might do to his family. The officer went back to the house with him and found Brewer's wife and three kids all tied up and locked inside a wardrobe.'

'And you say he's not a crackpot?'

'I've spoken with him. He appears to be a nice, ordinary bloke, thoroughly scared of what he did. He can't explain, doesn't know why he did it. But he wanted to be put away so he can't harm them. That's what he's afraid of.'

'I hope you obliged him.'

'Of course we did. He's in a cell now, but later on, when all this is straightened out, we'll get him to a hospital.'

'Do that, but after I've spoken with him. Is that the lot?'

'As far as we know. As I said, we're checking all the houses.'

'Just what kind of crazy road is this, Inspector? Suburbia's crackpot ghetto?'

'Until recently it was just another quiet residential area. We had all that business a year ago, of course.'

'The mass suicide you mean?'

'Yes, sir. The house – Beechwood it was called – was demolished only yesterday.'

'Why was that?'

'From what I can gather, the owner was fed up with the place. It hadn't been lived in for ages and apparently the agents couldn't sell it.'

'Maybe its ghosts have been taking their revenge for the destruction.'

Ross glanced sharply at Peck. 'Strangely enough, some funny business went on in there the other day. Someone called Kulek

435

informed us he was holding a seance or something in the house. We checked that he'd got permission from the owner.'

'So it really was supposed to be haunted?' Peck shook his head, bemused.

'I don't know about that. But they found a naked woman hiding in the cellar. She was a private nurse who, it turned out, had done in her employer, an old man she'd been nursing for years in his house further down the street.'

'Yes, I heard about that. I didn't know about this seance going on, though.'

'I'm not sure it was a seance exactly. I know there was some kind of ghost expert present.'

'All right, I want to speak to this Kulek and anyone else who was with him at the house.'

'You don't think it's got anything to do with ghosts, do you?' There was a curious expression on Ross's face.

'Do me a favour, Inspector. On the other hand, I don't think it's got anything to do with the drinking water. I just think it's about time we collected all the pieces and started putting them together, don't you? Otherwise, before long there'll be nobody left to talk to; they'll either be dead or in the nuthouse.'

A sharp rap on the window at Peck's side made both men look in that direction. A gnarled old face squinted in at them. The woman knocked again, even though she had the attention of both men.

'Are you in charge here?' she rasped, looking directly at Peck.

'What can I do for you, madam?' Peck asked, winding down the window a little more.

'Where's me bleedin dog?' the old woman asked, and Peck was relieved to see the sergeant whom Ross had spoken to earlier hastily making his way towards her.

'Sorry, madam, but if . . .' Peck began to say.

'He's bleedin gone. Been away all night. Why don't you find im instead of sittin there on your arse?'

'Give the details to the sergeant; I'm sure he'll help you find your dog,' Peck said patiently. He gave a sigh of relief when the officer led the grumbling woman away by the arm. 'All this mayhem and she's worried about a bloody dog!'

Inspector Ross shook his head in wonder.

'Excuse me, sir.' The sergeant had returned to the car window.

'What is it, Tom?' Ross asked.

436

'Just thought you'd like to know. About the dog.'

Peck's eyes looked heavenwards.

'Er, it's probably nothing, but that old lady's complaint was the fifth one we've had this morning. It's the fifth family pet that's been reported missing. Seems like they've all run away.'

Ross could only shrug his shoulders when Peck looked blankly at him.

Chapter Twelve

The drive through the peaceful Weald of Kent helped settle Bishop's troubled mind. A sudden, welcoming spring-like change in the weather had taken the dullness from the country-side and, although there was still a definite bite in the air, it could easily be imagined that the seasons had changed order. He had chosen to keep to the minor roads, avoiding the busy main routes that led more directly to his destination, but which would be crammed with other vehicles. He needed time to think.

The madness in Willow Road had persisted; had increased, in fact. The day before, two CID men had paid him a visit at his house in Barnes and had questioned him for almost two hours on his knowledge of Beechwood and the reasons for his investigation of the property. He had told them all he knew: of Jacob Kulek's concerns, of his own determination to prove the house was not haunted, of discovering the naked woman hiding in the cellar. He did not tell them of the hallucination he had had there. When they left they hardly seemed satisfied and gruffly informed him that he would probably be asked for a formal statement within the next day or so; a Detective Chief Inspector Peck would be most interested in his story.

Bishop had later considered contacting Jacob Kulek and Jessica, but something stopped him. He realised he was sick of the whole business, that he wanted to keep away from it. Yet he felt the need to speak to Jessica again and he was confused by that need. The animosity that existed between them had faded with the conclusion of the investigation. The day before, in the park, all his resentment towards her beliefs had dissipated and he was able to look upon her as she really was: an attractive woman. But he resisted the attraction; he had to.

As Bishop kept a watchful eye out for the road signs, he felt the pricking of tiny needles in his stomach. Time for something to eat. He glanced at his watch, knowing he wasn't far from his destination. Good, plenty of time to grab a bite. He wasn't due at the house until three-ish. The phone call had come after the two detectives had left, and the man at the other end had identified himself as Richard Braverman. Bishop had been recommended to him by a friend and he wished to engage his services as a psychic investigator to examine his home in Robertsbridge, Sussex. The new client seemed pleased that he was able to proceed with the investigation the following day. Apart from directions to the property itself, Bishop asked for no information concerning the alleged haunting; he preferred to be on the spot when he asked such questions. He was pleased with the job, wanting to be busy again. That night he had visited Lynn in the mental home and, as usual, had come away disappointed, depressed. If anything, she was becoming even more withdrawn. This time she had refused to even look at him. Her hands were still covering her eyes when he left.

The brightness of the following day had eased the pressure a little and anticipation of the work ahead had kept his mind occupied. He pulled in at the welcoming pub that had suddenly appeared on his left.

An hour later he was back on the road, his mood considerably brightened by a full stomach. When he reached the village of Robertsbridge he had to ask directions for the Braverman house and was guided to a small side road that crossed a railway line and led up a steep hill. At the top a discreet weathered sign, almost hidden in a hedge, reluctantly admitted that 'Two Circles' could be found down the small lane leading off from the main road. 'Two Circles' was the name Braverman had given him. He swung the car into the lane, no more than a rutted track, and almost enjoyed the bumpy ride down to the house; it made driving something to be worked at.

The house came into view and he suddenly understood its unusual title, for it was a converted oast-house, or oast-houses to be more accurate. There were two circular buildings joined together by a more conventional shaped structure which must have been at one time an enormous barn. The conversion was modern and solid, its unique shape pleasing to the eye. Beyond it stretched green fields, their lustre muted by winter, their boundaries marked by fringes of darker green. Bishop drove the car into a wide courtyard that ran the length of the square-shaped building, the adjoining oasts themselves seated in an area of lawn that ran downhill from the house towards the open fields, becoming coarse grass about halfway. Bishop already felt confident about exorcising any alleged ghosts as he strode towards the main door, for large-scale structural alterations like this were often prone to strange creaks and rappings, the owners more concerned that they had aroused a resentful spirit that with the effects of joining new materials to old. He rang the large brass doorbell and waited.

No one came. He rang again.

A movement inside? But still no answer. He rang once more.

Bishop rapped on the door with his knuckles, and called out, 'Hello, anybody there?'

Only us spooks, he told himself.

He tried the handle and pushed the door inwards. It swung smoothly open.

'Hello! Mr Braverman? Anyone about?' Bishop stepped into a long balconied hallway and nodded appreciatively at his surroundings. The wood flooring was stained a rich walnut, light from the many windows bouncing off its highly polished surface and reflecting on to the dark, hessian walls. The odd pieces of furniture scattered around the spacious hallways were interesting enough to be of antique value, and a few carefully scattered rugs managed to diffuse any bareness the flooring may have presented. To his right were two double-doors leading to the circular sections of the house. He walked over to the nearest, his footsteps ringing hollowly around the walls, avoiding a rug in case he dirtied its delicate pattern, and knocked once, then pushed the door open. A huge table imitated the round shape of the room, its surface of the darkest oak. A broad beam, recessed into the curved wall, acted as a mantel to the open, log-filled and unlit fireplace. A small portrait hung just above the mantelpiece and the image it represented seemed vaguely familiar. The floor was covered with a dark brown carpet, its pile deep and springy.

'Mr Braverman? Are you home?'

A noise from behind made Bishop turn. He glanced up towards the balcony. 'Mr Braverman?'

No sound, then a bump. *Someone* was up there.

'Mr Braverman, it's Chris Bishop. You rang me yesterday.'

440

No reply. He approached the stairs. Movement up there. He placed a foot on the first step.

Jessica descended the stairs leading to the Institute's reception area.

'Mr Ferrier?' she said to the small, bespectacled man waiting there. 'I'm Jessica Kulek.'

The man sprang to his feet and nervously turned the brim of the hat he was holding round in his hands like a steering-wheel. A smile briefly quivered on his face, then was gone. His raincoat was dotted with dark specks as if it had just started to rain before he'd entered the building.

'I'm afraid my father hasn't much time to spare today,' Jessica told him, not unused to nervousness in those visiting the Institute for the first time. 'We've been rather . . . busy, lately, and have a backlog of work to catch up on. You said you were from the Metaphysical Research Group?'

Ferrier nodded. 'Yes, it's rather important that I see Jacob Kulek.' His voice was thin and reedy, like the man himself. 'If I could just have ten minutes of his time? No longer.'

'Can you tell me the nature of your business?'

'I'm afraid not,' the little man snapped. Then, realising his brusqueness, he added apologetically, 'It's confidential.'

He saw a firmness stiffen her features and stepped quickly towards her, casting a nervous glance at the receptionist as he did so. The girl was speaking to someone on the phone, but still he kept his voice low.

'It concerns Boris Pryszlak,' he whispered.

Jessica was startled. 'What do you know of Pryszlak?'

'It's confidential,' Ferrier repeated. 'I can only speak to your father, Miss Kulek.'

She hesitated, uneasy. But it might be important.

'Very well. Ten minutes then, Mr Ferrier.'

Jessica led the little man up the staircase and along to her father's private study. They heard the muffled tones of Jacob Kulek's voice before they entered the room. The blind man switched off the dictating machine and looked up at them.

'Yes, Jessica?' Kulek said, knowing her knock, knowing her footsteps, knowing her presence.

'Mr Ferrier to see you. I mentioned his visit earlier.'

'Ah yes, from the Metaphysical Research Group, wasn't it?'

The little man was strangely silent and Jessica had to answer for him. 'Yes, Father. I've explained you're very busy, but Mr Ferrier says it's a matter concerning Boris Pryszlak. I thought it might be important.'

'Pryszlak? You have some information?'

Ferrier cleared his throat. 'Yes, but as I explained to Miss Kulek, it's confidential.'

'My daughter is also my personal assistant, Mr Ferrier. As well as being my eyes.'

'All the same, I'd rather . . .'

'Jessica, perhaps Mr Ferrier would like some coffee. Would you mind?'

'Father, I think . . .'

'Black coffee would be fine, Miss Kulek.' Ferrier smiled anxiously at Jessica, his eyes suddenly hidden by the light reflecting off his spectacles. Her unease persisted.

'I'll take coffee, too, Jessica.' Her father's voice was quietly firm and she knew it would be pointless to argue. She left the study and hurried along the corridor, not wanting to leave Jacob alone with the nervous little man for a minute longer than necessary. She paused when she drew level with her own office, then changed direction and went in. She picked up the telephone.

Anna opened the door and beamed at the two women standing there, her smile as warm for strangers as it was for those she knew.

'Yes, please?' she asked, giving a little bow of her head.

'We'd like to see Miss Kirkhope,' the taller of the two said, returning Anna's smile.

A regretful frown creased the housekeeper's broad face. 'Oh, I don't tink . . .'

'Please tell her it's about her brother Dominic,' the other woman said, face unsmiling, her tone abrupt.

Anna was too polite to close the door fully on the two women and when she returned moments later she found them waiting in the hallway itself. If she was surprised, she did not show it.

'Miss Kirkhope will see you much soon. You will wait in here, please.' She beckoned them to follow and showed them into the 'visitors' room. They seated themselves on the Chesterfield, the taller one smiling sweetly at Anna, the shorter one studying her surroundings, her face impassive.

442

'One moment please. Miss Kirkhope will arrive shortly.' Anna bowed her way from the room.

It was a full five minutes before Agnes Kirkhope entered, insisting that she and Anna finish that particular round of rummy in the kitchen before she received her unexpected guests. The Filipino housekeeper had an uncanny knack of finding black deuces to bolster otherwise unpromising hands and Miss Kirkhope was determined to win back the five pounds she had already lost that afternoon. One card away from victory, she had groaned aloud when Anna had rapped the table and splayed her hand before her mistress, the inevitable black deuce substituting for the Queen of Hearts that Miss Kirkhope held. Why hadn't she plucked a couple of useful cards from the deck when Anna had been answering the door?

Miss Kirkhope looked down at the two women, her irritation plain on her face and in her voice.

'You had something to say about Dominic,' she said without preamble.

'Did you know he was a paraphiliac?' the shorter of the two replied with even less preamble.

'A what?' Miss Kirkhope was taken aback by the coldness in the woman's tone.

'A paraphiliac,' the taller one said, smiling sweetly. 'It's someone who indulges in abnormal sexual practices.'

Miss Kirkhope's hand went involuntarily to her throat. Recovering quickly, she strode stiffly to the centre of the room and glared down at them. 'I suppose this has something to do with blackmail.' She spat the words out.

The taller woman reached into her handbag and said pleasantly, 'Oh no, Miss Kirkhope. Much worse than that.'

443

Chapter Thirteen

Bishop paused on the top step and looked around. To his right were doors leading off to rooms in the square-shaped section of the house; to his left was the balcony rail overlooking the hall below and another staircase leading upwards.

'Mr Braverman?' Bishop called again. He swore under his breath. Was the house empty? Had the noises he had heard just been the house settling? Or the wandering ghosts the owner alleged inhabited the house? One more try, then forget it. Braverman should have been here to meet him.

Light rain began to patter against the windows.

'Is there anybody home?'

Bump. Bump. Bump, bump, bump. The red rubber ball bounced down the stairs, gathering speed, then struck the facing wall. It bounced back against the stairway and lost its impetus, skipping low then rolling towards the wall again where it trickled to a stop.

Bishop craned his neck to see the floor above. It had to be kids playing a prank. 'I've come to see Mr Braverman. Can you tell me where he is?'

Nothing, except a movement. A scuffle of feet?

Bishop had had enough. He mounted the stairs two at a time, annoyance reflected in his forceful stride.

Had they attempted to kill him right away they would have succeeded; but they wanted to enjoy his dying, to relish it. So the blow to his head was too light.

The man appeared in the doorway, the double-barrel held shoulder high and pointed at Bishop's face. The man had enjoyed the game so far and grinned in anticipation at what was to follow. Bishop had stopped dead on the landing, his mouth open and alarm in his eyes; the woman stepped from another doorway, her raised arm which held the hammer already

444

beginning its descent. Stun him, her husband had told her. Hit him just behind the ear, just hard enough to stun him. Then we can have some fun with him before he dies.

The blow knocked Bishop sideways, but he had turned to see the woman coming at him and had instinctively ducked when he saw the falling hammer, so the weapon had glanced across his scalp rather than striking solidly. He fell against the wall and felt himself spinning backwards down the stairs. The woman was too close: her legs became entangled with his and she went with him, the hammer clattering down the wooden steps ahead of them. She screamed as they tumbled and finally slid on to the landing below.

Stupid bitch! the man with the shotgun cursed silently. Trust her to do it wrong! He raised the gun again and aimed it at the struggling figures below. 'Get away from him, you silly cow! Let me get a clear shot!' he bellowed. Bishop would have to be killed outright.

The woman tried to free herself from the tangle of arms and legs and, though he was dazed, Bishop saw the twin-barrels pointing down at him. He pulled at the squirming woman just as one of the black holes exploded with light. Her chest took the full blast, tiny fragments of scattered lead tearing past her body and tugging at Bishop's clothes. She would not stop screaming as he tried to roll clear of her.

The man at the top of the stairs seemed hardly shocked, merely angry, as he lowered the shotgun then raised it again. His aim was more careful this time. Bishop saw the hammer lying propped against the bottom stair and, now on his knees, scooped it up and hurled it towards the man above. It was a wild throw and missed completely, but the man automatically ducked, giving Bishop the chance to gain his feet and run. The second blast powdered the floor behind him. He ran through a doorway leading off from the balcony, sure he could not make it to the front door below before the man had reloaded, praying there would be another staircase leading down at the back of the house. At least this way there would be some cover. He found himself in a room that contained a small bed and ran across to a facing door. The next room also had a bed and little else. Another door, then he was in a dark, narrow corridor. Stairs led down to a closed door.

He could hear footsteps close behind, the man screaming abuse at him. He ran down the stairs, slipping near the bottom, crashing into the door. He scrabbled around in the gloom searching for the handle, found it, jerked downwards. It was locked. A shadow above blocked out what little light there was.

Bishop sat on the second step and kicked out with both feet. The door sprang open, slivers of wood bursting away from the frame. He staggered through, slamming it behind him to stop any gunshot blasted from above. He was in a kitchen and there was a back door.

Footsteps were pounding down the stairs. He ran across to the back door, almost crying out in frustration when he found this, too, was locked. He hurled himself back across the room just as the door leading from the stairs into the kitchen opened. The man was halfway in when the door slammed back on him, trapping the shotgun across his chest, his head jolted back against the door frame. Bishop grabbed the exposed section of gun barrel, pushing against the door with all his strength. The man tried to free himself, but he was in an awkward position, his head turned sideways, his chest crushed by the pressure of the door against the weapon.

The dizziness was beginning to clear from Bishop's head and he concentrated on exerting as much pressure on the door as possible, maintaining his advantage, but not knowing where it would get him. They could hardly stay like that all day. The man's face was beginning to go red as he pushed back against the door; his eyes were wide, turned towards Bishop, glaring their hate. His mouth was open and curved downwards in a snarl, the snarl itself a choking sound. Bishop felt the door moving towards him, slowly pushing him back. He redoubled his efforts, digging his feet into the tiled kitchen floor, his shoulder pressed flat against the woodwork.

The quivering hand that grabbed at his hair from behind made him shriek with fright. He whirled around and saw the woman, her face and chest oozing fresh blood, swaying before him. She had come into the kitchen through another door that must open out into the hallway. The door at his back burst open and he was propelled forward into the mutilated woman. She fell to her hands and knees, the blood flowing freely and forming a deep red puddle beneath her.

Bishop swept his arm round without taking time to look at the man rushing through the door. His elbow caught the man square against the bridge of his nose, abruptly stopping his advance.

446

The decision whether to run or stay was made for Bishop as the gun barrels were raised towards him once more. He had no choice: he had to fight, to run would be suicidal.

He pushed the gun upwards and lunged into the man. They fell back through the doorway on the stairs beyond, their hands locked around the weapon between them. Bishop heaved himself up and the man came with him using the momentum to push Bishop backwards. They staggered into the kitchen once more and Bishop's foot slipped in the spreading pool of blood. He fell to his knees and suddenly his assailant was standing over him, his contorted face only inches away. Bishop's body was arched backwards, his hold on the shotgun now being used against him. He went back on to the floor, his legs forced sideways and out, his shoulders sinking into the sticky redness beneath him. Still he refused to let go of the gun, but he could not prevent the weapon from being turned inwards towards him.

A hand flailed weakly at his face, trying to gouge out his eyes. The woman was still alive, trying to help the man destroy him. He suddenly allowed the gun to turn, bringing it towards him but twisting his body so the twin-barrels struck the floor. The man staggered forward, falling with the gun, and Bishop let go of the warm metal with one hand and struck out, hitting him below the left ear. The man fell sideways and Bishop grabbed at the gun again, but the woman dug painfully into his eyes, forcing him to wrench himself free, to roll his body away from the sharp claws. He realised his mistake when he was halfway across the kitchen floor. The man was free to raise the gun and take a shot at him.

He could only stare as the man grinned in triumph and began to rise to his feet, knowing his quarry was trapped. His fingers had already curled around the two triggers and he was stepping forward when his foot slid in the viscous mess on the kitchen floor. His leg shot out and he staggered to keep erect, but then both feet were in the blood and he fell, going forward, slightly sideways. The gun roared, taking off the top of his head with the double blast. The kitchen ceiling became a shocking canvas of red fluid.

The woman's moan was long and agonised as she stared at the twitching form of her husband and she did not look away nor did the moan die in her throat until his body was still. Then she turned to look at Bishop and held him there sprawled on the floor with her wild-eyed, mesmerising gaze. It was only after the thick

447

gob of blood oozed from her lips that he realised she was dead and her eyes saw nothing. Released, he rose weakly to his feet and stumbled towards the kitchen sink, his stomach heaving in juddering movements. He was still crouched over the metal sink ten minutes later when the pattering on the window panes increased its intensity as the rain became more fierce and the skies overhead darkened.

Jessica hurried along the corridor, her heart thudding. She had just called the Metaphysical Research Group at their head-quarters in Sussex; they had never heard of Ferrier. She reached her father's study and pushed against the door, twisting the handle, prepared to feel foolish if the man and her father were merely engaged in conversation, but somehow knowing that would not be the case. She cried out in alarm when she saw the thin, leather belt around Jacob Kulek's throat, the little man behind him, his hands pulling the belt tight, his body shaking with the effort. Jacob had one hand against his own throat, fingers curled around the improvised garotte as though he had become aware of his assailant's intention just before the little man had struck. His face was a deep red, turning purplish, his tongue emerging from his open mouth, his sightless eyes bulging from their sockets as though a parasite growing inside his head was pushing everything else out. A tight asthmatic wheezing sound came from his throat as he tried to suck in air through his strangulated windpipe.

Jessica ran forward, afraid that she was already too late. The little man seemed almost oblivious of her as she grabbed at his wrists and tried to force them together again to relieve the pressure on the belt. But it was no use; his strength belied his frame. She struck out at his face when she realised that her father's gasps for breath had stopped. Ferrier turned his head away to avoid the worst of her wild blows, but still he maintained the pressure, still he pulled at the leather belt, still his whole body quivered with the effort.

Jessica screamed, knowing she was losing. She pulled at the man's hair, scratched at his eyes, but it had no effect: he was like a robot, unfeeling, governed by something outside his own body. She looked around desperately for something to use against him. The silver paperknife lay gleaming on the desktop.

Frantically, Jessica grabbed it, turning on the man, the

weapon raised high. She hesitated before sweeping her arm down, the intent abhorrent to her, but knowing she had no choice. The narrow blade sank into the side of Ferrier's neck, just above the shoulder bone.

His body suddenly went rigid and, for a moment, his eyes stared unbelievingly at her. Then they seemed to cloud over and with horror she saw his hands resume their pressure. The knife protruded from his neck, only half of its length sunk into his flesh, and Jessica threw herself at him, screaming with frustrated fury, beating at his exposed face, thrusting down on the knife again to sink it in further, praying the blade would find a vital artery.

The little man's body shuddered, and his knees sagged. Then he straightened as if he had regathered his strength. He let go of one end of the belt to sweep his arm around and knock the girl to one side. Jessica staggered against the bookshelves, her eyes blurring at the pain and tears of helplessness that had formed.

'Stop!' she cried out. And then a moan: 'Please stop.'

But both hands pulled at the belt once more.

She heard the footsteps running along the hall and then suddenly, mercifully, there were figures in the doorway. The two men and the woman who peered over their shoulders were members of the Institute.

'Stop him!' she implored.

They were stunned by what was happening, but one, a tall grey-bearded man, generally timid, and usually slow in action, rushed forward, lifting a chair as he went. Without losing stride, he raised it over the desktop and half-threw, half-pushed it into Ferrier's face. The rungs of the chair caught the little man across the forehead, knocking him back, sending him against the window behind, the glass shattering outwards, his body hanging there, hands outstretched to grasp at the window-frame. He seemed to study them for a moment, their actions temporarily frozen, before his fingers uncurled and he let himself fall backwards, his legs rising upwards then slithering down out of sight over the sill.

Jessica wasn't sure whether or not she really heard the sickening squelch of his head bursting open on the pavement below, for the woman was screaming hysterically and she, herself, was stumbling towards her father, who had now collapsed on to the floor. But her mind had recorded the sound, imaginary or not.

* * *

Anna had packed away the playing cards and was on her way back to the 'visitors' room to see if her mistress would require tea for herself and the guests, when the smile disappeared from her face leaving an expression of total incomprehension. Miss Kirkhope had appeared in the hallway, crawling on hands and knees, something wrong with her face, something distorting her features. Her eyes looked beseechingly at Anna, a thin, heavily veined hand reaching towards her, a weak croaking noise coming from a face that was sizzling, the skin popping and tearing.

For Anna, confusion did not turn to terror until she saw Miss Kirkhope's two women guests stroll from the room behind her crawling mistress, each holding what seemed to be nothing more than small bottles of clear liquid. They could have contained water – the fluid looked harmless enough – but the old lady's head shook in horror when the taller woman smiled and raised her bottle. Miss Kirkhope tried to scramble away, but the woman jerked the bottle in her direction, the liquid splashing out and landing in heavy splats on the old woman's back and head. Anna's hands went to her mouth as she heard the faint sizzling sound and saw what looked like small trails of curling steam rise from the wetness.

Miss Kirkhope arched her back inwards, her agonised groans spurring the housekeeper onwards a few paces. But Anna's courage failed her when she saw the shorter of the two women step forward and kick the old lady over on to her back. Anna sank to her knees and joined her hands in supplication when she saw the woman stand astride Miss Kirkhope's slumped body and slowly pour the contents of her bottle in a steady stream into the open, upturned mouth.

The gargled screams filled Anna's head before they became a low rasping sound as vocal cords were burnt away. Anna found she could not rise, not even when she felt the trickle run down between her legs and the floor around her became wet with urine. Not even when the taller woman strode towards her, still smiling, sprinkling the contents of the bottle before her like holy water. Not even when the first splattering of acid touched her skin and began to burn.

Chapter Fourteen

Peck looked disbelievingly across his desk at Bishop. 'Do you know how incredible all this sounds?'

Bishop nodded without apology. 'I find it hard to believe myself.'

'But why should a total stranger try to murder you?'

'Braverman had to be a part of Pryszlak's sect. They didn't all commit suicide. Some were left to carry on his work.'

'Which was killing people?'

'I don't know, Inspector. Maybe we were getting too close.'

'Too close to what?'

Jessica spoke up, and there was repressed anger in her voice. 'The reason for the mass suicide. My father knew there had to be a reason for Pryszlak and his sect to kill themselves.'

Peck sat back in his chair and regarded the girl silently for a few moments, his thumb scratching an itch at the end of his nose. She looked pale and worried, on the surface the type who would crack when things got too rough. But Peck knew better; he had dealt with too many people for too many years to be deceived by appearances. The girl was stronger than she seemed.

'But you still have no idea what this is all about,' he said.

Jessica shook her head. 'I told you Pryszlak came to my father to enlist his help a long time ago, and that my father refused.'

'You think this could be some kind of perverted revenge, then? Instructions carried out by Pryszlak's followers after his death?'

'No, it's not revenge. Why should they try to kill Chris? Why did they kill Miss Kirkhope?'

'And her housekeeper.'

'The housekeeper probably got in their way. Pryszlak's sect has no regard for human life, not even their own. This man, Ferrier, killed himself without hesitation when he saw he was trapped. The motive wasn't revenge. I think the idea was to kill

451

anyone who had any knowledge at all of their organisation.'

'There's been no attempt on your life.'

'Not yet, Inspector,' Bishop said. 'Maybe Ferrier would have turned on Jessica once he'd disposed of Jacob Kulek.'

Peck frowned and turned to Bishop. 'I still don't understand why I haven't booked you for the murder of Braverman and his wife.'

'I came to you, remember? I could easily have left that house without anyone ever knowing I'd been there. I could have wiped away any fingerprints. It would have been easy for the police to have believed that Braverman fought with his wife, shot her, then shot himself. It makes no sense for me to have murdered them and reported the crime myself.'

Peck still looked sceptical.

'And the others,' Bishop went on. 'The attempt on Jacob Kulek's life. The murder of Agnes Kirkhope and her maid. All connected with the Pryszlak business. Kulek, because he was investigating Pryszlak's activities. Agnes Kirkhope, because we had been to see her and told her of our suspicions. And, of course, her brother, Dominic, had been a sect member. It's logical, Inspector, that I should have been a victim too.'

'Nothing's logical about this business, Mr Bishop.'

'I agree. Even more illogical are the events in Willow Road. How do you explain them?'

'At the moment, I wouldn't even try. We've got people locked up and they're like zombies. Even the one man who didn't seem to be as bad as the others has deteriorated – he's now like the rest of them. A man named Brewer – he'd tied his family up and locked them in a wardrobe. But he gave himself up before he could do any harm.'

Bishop noticed the puzzled look on Jessica's face. He was concerned for her: the near-death of her father had left her in a brittle state. He had rung the Research Institute from the house in Robertsbridge, resisting the urge to flee from the blood-stained corpses lying there on the kitchen floor, worried that if an attempt had been made on his life, then the same could happen to Jacob Kulek. He had seen for himself how the mad-woman in Beechwood had tried to get at Kulek. And he knew there was a connection: the portrait he had seen in the round room at Robertsbridge was of Dominic Kirkhope; he had remembered Agnes Kirkhope's photograph of her brother and although there

452

was an age difference between the portrait and photograph, the resemblance was distinct. He had been surprised to find that Detective Chief Inspector Peck, the man who was apparently in charge of the investigation into Willow Road and its mishappenings, was at the Institute. It came as no surprise that an attempt on Jacob Kulek's life had already been made.

'Now all I've got,' Peck was saying, 'are murders, suicides, attempted rape – homosexual and otherwise – mutilation, arson and cells full of people who don't know what time of day it is. To help me with my report to the Commissioner – and which you seem to think explains everything – I've got your information on a nutcase named Boris Prvszlak and his crackpot organisation who believed in evil as a powerful, physical force. How do you think he's going to take it, Miss Kulek? He'd order me to be locked up with the other nutters.'

'I've given you no explanations, just what I know. Your job is to do something about it.'

'Any ideas exactly what?'

'I'd start by trying to find the names of all Pryszlak's associates.'

'You mean the members of his sect.'

'Yes.'

'And then?'

Jessica shrugged. 'I don't know. Keep a watch on them?'

Peck snorted.

'At least you'd find out if Braverman and Ferrier were members,' Bishop said. 'It might even lead you to the murderers of Miss Kirkhope and her housekeeper.'

Peck wished he could make up his mind about Bishop, one way or the other. He had ordered him to stay at the house in Robertsbridge until the local police arrived, and then arranged to have him escorted back to London, to Peck's office in New Scotland Yard. He had questioned the ghost-hunter – what kind of profession was that? – for a solid hour before Kulek's daughter, again under escort, had arrived from her father's hospital bedside. It was getting on for ten now and still he wasn't any nearer to the truth. It would have been easier if he could believe Bishop was either lying or totally innocent.

Peck leaned forward on his desk. 'Okay, we're not going to find out much more tonight. I'm letting you go, Bishop. I'm not convinced, but your story might just be feasible. This Pryszlak may have had friends who didn't like you and Jacob Kulek snooping around Beechwood. It could be that they regarded it as some kind of holy shrine after the mass suicide. The fact that poor old Miss Kirkhope ordered it to be demolished may have been her undoing. We'll put it down to a lunatic fringe for the moment. It still doesn't explain all the disasters in Willow Road, of course, but I can hardly blame you for that. Anyway, we'll be keeping a close eye on you.'

'Don't worry,' Bishop said wryly. 'I won't be running away.'

Peck stabbed a finger against the desktop. 'We'll be keeping an eye on you not just because I'm suspicious – and I bloody am – but for your own protection. That goes for your father, too, Miss Kulek. For protection, I mean. If his assailant was part of Pryszlak's mob, they might have another try.'

Alarm showed in Jessica's eyes.

'Sorry. Didn't mean to frighten you,' Peck said soothingly. 'It's better to be safe than sorry, that's all.' He turned to one of his officers, who had been leaning against the wall, arms folded, bemused by the whole exchange. 'Frank, get someone to show them down, will you?'

As Bishop and Jessica rose to leave, Peck looked up at them, his scowl still in evidence. 'Keep us informed of any more little trips, Mr Bishop. I'll probably want to speak to you again tomorrow. I hope your father recovers, Miss Kulek.'

Jessica nodded her thanks and they left the detective's office.

The officer returned a few seconds later, amusement on his face.

'What are you bloody grinning at?' Peck growled.

'You don't believe in all this bollocks about the power of evil, do you, guv?'

'That's not the point, Frank. *They* believe it, that's what matters. At least, the girl does. I think Bishop hasn't made his mind up yet. To tell you the truth, I don't think *I've* made my mind up, either.'

They drove away from the tall building, silent for a few moments as if Peck could still hear their conversation from his office high above them. The rain had finally stopped, leaving a dampness in the night air. Jessica pulled her coat collar tight around her neck.

'Will you take me back to the hospital, Chris?'

'I'm already headed in that direction,' he told her. 'How was he when you left?'

'Shocked, weak. He was still finding it difficult to breathe.'

'How much damage?'

'Physically, just bruising, as before. The doctor said his difficulty in breathing was more to do with the emotional shock than constriction of his windpipe. Oh God, if I'd have gone back to his study a few seconds later . . .' She left the sentence unfinished.

He wanted to reach out to her, to pat her hand, to touch her; but he felt awkward, a stranger.

'He'll be all right, Jessica. He's a strong-minded man.'

She tried to smile at him, but failed. His attention was on the road ahead, anyway. She studied his profile, noticing the lines of tension around his eyes. 'And you've been through so much, too,' she said eventually. 'It must have been a nightmare.'

'It was even more of a nightmare for Agnes Kirkhope and her housekeeper; one they didn't come out of. What manner of creature could do such a thing?' He shook his head in regret, disgust. 'I think Peck still believes I murdered Braverman and his wife.'

'He can't, Chris. It doesn't make any sense.'

'None of this does. You and I, in our different ways, deal with matters that defy logic all the time. Peck's a policeman: they like some kind of order to things. We can't blame him for his suspicion.'

'Nor his aggression.'

'Nor that.'

He pulled up at traffic lights, floodlights turning the square before them into a daylight scene. Tourists, thousands it seemed, watched the silvery fountains and craned their necks to see the sculptured naval man standing aloft on the huge rising column as though it were the crow's nest on one of his ships. As a brilliantly lit backdrop, the impressive structure of the National Gallery dominated the thriving square, while a constantly surging stream of traffic flowed round and out.

'It's so bright,' Jessica remarked distractedly. 'So alive. It could be daytime.'

The red light blinked off and the green appeared. Bishop edged the car forward into the metal throng, finding a niche and flowing with the tide. 'I wonder how many of Pryszlak's people stayed alive? And why?'

'Perhaps for a time like this.'

He had to concentrate on avoiding a taxi which was making a

455

claim to a three-foot space just ahead of Bishop's car.

Jessica went on. 'If the police can locate them all, perhaps this can end now, before it's too late.'

He snatched a quick glimpse of her. 'What can end, Jessica? Do you and your father know what's happening?'

She hesitated before she spoke. 'We're not sure. We discussed it with Edith Metlock only yesterday – '

They both looked at each other at the same time.

'Christ!' Bishop said quietly.

Bishop turned the car into the wide tree-lined avenue, keeping in second gear and peering from left to right at the houses on either side.

'What number is it?' he asked Jessica.

'I'm sure it's sixty-four. I've never been to her home, but I've often contacted her there.'

'Even numbers on the right. Keep your eyes peeled.'

Once they had passed through London's West End they were able to make rapid progress to Edith Metlock's address in Woodford. Both were angry at themselves for having forgotten the medium, for they realised that she, as a part of the group investigating Beechwood, might also be in danger.

'Fifty-eight . . . sixty . . . sixty-two . . . There! Just ahead.' Bishop pointed towards a small bungalow, twenty feet of garden on either side separating it from its neighbours. He waited for an approaching car to pass, then drew over to that side of the road, stopping just in front of the bungalow.

'She's there,' Jessica said. 'All the lights are on.' Suddenly she felt afraid to leave the car.

Bishop slid his glasses into his top pocket and switched off the engine. 'We're probably over-reacting,' he said unconvincingly, then sensed Jessica's fear. 'Do you want to stay in the car?'

She shook her head and reached for the door-handle.

The garden gate squealed noisily as Bishop pushed it open. Light from the windows spilled on to the lawn on either side of the narrow path leading to the bungalow's porch, the clipped grass a flat green vignetting into total blackness. The porch itself was lit by an external light.

Bishop rang the doorbell and they waited for movement inside. Jessica bit down on her lower lip; her eyes were wide, almost vacant. He touched her arm, at the elbow, giving it a little

456

shake as if to dispel her anxieties. He tried the doorbell again.

'Maybe she's asleep,' he said.

'With all the lights on?'

'She may have dozed off.'

He rattled the letter-box for added noise, then ducked to look through it.

'All the doors in the hallway are open. She must have heard us. Looks like every light is on, too.' He put his mouth to the opening and called out Edith Metlock's name. There was no reply.

'Chris, let's get the police,' Jessica said, slowly backing away from the front door.

'Not yet.' He caught her arm again and this time held it firmly. 'Let's be a little more sure there's something wrong first.'

'Can't you feel it?' Jessica looked around at the shadows surrounding the house. 'It's. . . I don't know. . . unearthly. As if. . . as if something is waiting.'

'Jessica.' His voice was soft. 'You've been through a bad time today – we both have. It's getting to you, eating away at your imagination.' And it was eating away at his, too. 'I'm going to take a look round the back. Why don't you go and sit in the car?'

Her alarm flared to a new level for a brief moment. 'I think I'll stick with you,' she said firmly.

Bishop smiled and moved off, stepping on to the lawn and glancing into a window as he passed. The curtains were drawn wide and lace netting diffused the image inside. He saw it was a small dining-room, the table bare except for a pot containing a leafy plant. There was no one in the room. They moved around the corner of the one-floor building and Bishop felt Jessica draw closer to his back as they found themselves in an area of darkness. The ground became softer beneath their feet as if they were walking through a dormant flower-bed. More light shone ahead and they passed a reeded glass window which Bishop assumed would be the bungalow's bathroom. Beyond, the light was more brilliant, throwing back the night with unimpeded force. The blinds to the kitchen were drawn upwards and Bishop blinked against the harsh neon light.

'Empty,' he told Jessica. 'There's a door over there leading out to the back garden. Let's try it.'

More light flooded outwards from the back of the house and he wondered if it was only because of the natural nervousness of a woman living alone. But Edith Metlock had not struck him as the nervous type.

He tried the kitchen door and was not surprised to find it locked. He jiggled with the handle for a few moments, then rapped on the glass. Maybe she was out and had left the lights on to discourage any would-be burglars. But every light? And the curtains open?

'Chris!'

Bishop turned to see Jessica gazing into a window nearby. He hurried over to her.

'Look,' she said. 'Over there, in the armchair.'

He found himself looking into a bedroom, again the curtains drawn wide. Through the lace netting he could see an unoccupied bed, a bedside table, the lamp on it adding more brightness to the already well-lit room, a wardrobe, a chest of drawers. And in an armchair in the far corner sat the figure of a woman. His vision was hazy through the lace, but he was sure it was Edith Metlock.

'Mrs Metlock.' He tapped at the window. 'It's Chris Bishop and Jessica Kulek.' He used his knuckles against the glass.

He thought he saw a movement, a slight turning of the head, but couldn't be sure.

'Why doesn't she answer?' Jessica said. 'Why is she just sitting there, Chris?'

The thought flashed through his mind that Edith Metlock may have had a stroke; but her body sat erect, not slumped. Was she too afraid to answer?

'I'm going to break in,' he told Jessica. He walked back to the kitchen and angled his body to see through the small glass panels that ran the length of the door. He could just see the end of the key poking from the lock on that side. He half-turned away from the door, then brought his elbow swinging back at a pane alongside the lock. The glass fell inwards and clinked to the floor. He pushed his hand through the opening, carefully avoiding any remaining shards, and twisted the key, grunting with satisfaction as the lock clicked. Turning the handle, he pushed inwards. It wouldn't open. There was less resistance when he put pressure on the top, and solid defiance when he tried the bottom. Without hesitation he kicked in one of the bottom panes, then stooped and drew back the bolt inside. The door swung open.

Jessica followed him in, keeping close, trying to see over his shoulder. Edith Metlock's eyes were closed when they entered her bedroom and they remained so even when they called her name. Her back was stiff, her face pointed towards the ceiling light. Her hands clutched at the arms of the chair.

'She's breathing,' Bishop said and, as if his voice had triggered off something in the medium, her breathing became deeper, her breasts beginning to heave with the effort. Her lips parted and air was exhaled, then noisily sucked in. Her breathing became sharper, gasping, and Jessica knelt before her, touching the medium's shoulders, gently calling her name. The panting became frantic and Jessica looked anxiously at Bishop. He felt useless, tempted to slap the medium and bring her out of her trance-like state, but afraid of what the sudden shock might do to her. Then Edith Metlock jerked forward in the seat, her gasps brought to an abrupt halt. She sat that way for long seconds, then slowly sank back into the armchair, her breath released in a long, drawn-out sigh. The medium's eyelids flickered, opened; her pupils were tiny pinpoints. Her jaw was slack, lips moving, tongue lolling within its cavity as though its muscles were limp. A low murmuring came from somewhere at the back of her throat.

'She's trying to say something, Chris. Can you understand her?'

Bishop leaned his head closer to the medium's and listened. Slowly, the words began to take form, began to shape themselves into a meaning.

'Keep . . . it away,' Edith Metlock said, her voice slurred but just coherent. 'Keep . . . it . . . away . . . The dark . . . keep it away . . .'

Chapter Fifteen

The home crowd was angry, its wrath rolling around the stadium in a mighty roar. The ref was a wanker: even the minority away-fans, delighted though they were at his dubious decisions in their team's favour throughout the match, had to admit it. Now even the goalkeeper was going into his book for dissent and *he* had never received a booking in fifteen years of soccer. The over-whelming anger reached fever pitch when the tiny yellow card was raised into the air and the away-fans – except for the lunatic few whose brains were in the tips of their tongues – refrained from jeering. The hostility around them had made them nervous.

The home team had been playing well all season, and the smell of the First Division was in their fans' nostrils. They had com-pletely dominated their rival clubs in the Second Division. Their new striker, imported from Italy for an incredible sum of money (to make up the loss, the club had had to sell two players, one mid-field, the other a popular left-back, and admission prices had been raised) had contributed remarkably to their success. But after only ten minutes, the Italian had been stretcher carried off with a leg injury. The word spread around at half-time like an uncontrolled brush fire that his leg had been broken. In two places.

The away-team had played like non-league factory workers throughout the match, their studded boots scything opponents rather than playing the ball. It had been the same on Saturday when ugly brute force at their own ground had earned them the draw. Their fear of relegation next season had turned them into eleven crude defenders, only occasional bouts of real skill reminding the crowd they were playing football and not rugby. Tonight the match was a gruelling affair and already several fights had broken out among the crowd. The policemen seated on benches placed strategically around the pitch, helmets at their feet, glanced nervously over their shoulders at the ranting mob, the surge of faces merged into a dark swaying mass behind the brilliant glare of the floodlights. The mood was ugly.

Eddie Cossins pulled his girlfriend, Vicky, closer to him. He was beginning to wonder if it had been wise to bring her tonight. She didn't even like football as a rule and he suspected her insistence on coming with him was more to do with ingratiating herself with him than interest in football itself. Five weeks was a long time to be going out with a bird. Too long, really. They started getting ideas.

'What's he booked him for, Eddie?'

He barely heard her shrill voice above the uproar even though she had stood on tiptoe and bellowed into his ear.

'Ref don't like bleedin arguments!' he yelled back.

'What's he arguing about?'

Eddie groaned. 'The ref's given the other side a penalty. Any-one could see the player took a dive. All the bleedin fouls they've done and they get a penalty. What a tosser!'

Vicky sank back inside her heavy overcoat, pulling Eddie's club scarf tighter around her neck. Stupid game, she told herself. Grown-up men kicking a bag of wind around a field. And the crowd getting upset just because their team wasn't winning. Like a load of kids. Eddie too. Look at him shouting at the referee as if he could hear him. Poor little man was only doing his job. So this was what she had to compete against. Another girl might have been easier. Oh no. Now it's raining. Jostled, pushed, crushed, touched-up by invisible hands – and now a soaking! It wasn't worth it. He could have his bloody football! He was spotty, anyway.

The crowd hushed as the away-team's skipper placed the mud-smeared ball on the penalty spot. His left foot was renowned.

On the terraces, Jack Bettney held his breath, almost afraid to watch. Twenty-five years he'd supported the club, through the good years and the lean. After a long stretch in the Second Division they were on the way up again, back to their rightful place among the leaders of the game. They had won back their old days' glory last season and this one. Nothing would stop them now. Nothing except a team full of cowboys and a bent referee. He kept the anger tight within himself.

He blinked away rainspots from his eyes and watched the enemy pace himself away from the ball. The goalkeeper danced

461

nervously from foot to foot and finally settled down on his line, heels raised from the muddy earth. To the right, son, he'll aim it at the bottom right-hand corner, Jack Bettney told him silently. He knew the opposing captain's favourite spot. Jack could feel the tenseness around him; the apprehension passed through the mass of tightly packed bodies like an electric current. The enemy began his run, pounding up to the glistening ball like an express train. To the right, son, to the right.

Animal, sometimes known as The Beast to his friends, whooped with glee when the ball shot into the bottom left-hand corner of the net, the goalkeeper left sprawled in the mud on the other side of his goal-mouth. Animal leapt in the air using the shoulders of a fellow supporter in front to hold himself aloft. His friend's knees buckled under the seventeen stone weight, but others grabbed his arms to keep him upright. It would have been difficult to get up again in that crowd.

'Fuckin magic, fuckin magic!' Animal screeched. Hostile eyes turned to look in his direction.

He chortled as the goalkeeper dejectedly retrieved the ball from the back of the net. 'What a load of wankers!' he chanted.

'Leave it out, Animal,' one of his companions said nervously, feeling the resentment around them. 'We're not bloody at home now.'

Animal didn't give a shit and he let the home supporters around him know it. Personally, he didn't care much about the game either. It was the excitement he liked, not the excitement of the competition but, although he couldn't have expressed it himself, the raw emotion the game produced, feelings that could be demonstrated without embarrassment.

He turned to face the crowd behind him, his thick, porky arms raised, middle and index fingers stiff and parted in his favourite up-yours gesture. The rain suddenly fell as though someone had pulled the plug from the clouds above and it spilled on to his fat cheeks and open-necked shirt. He laughed, catching the torrent in his mouth. Their faces were just a watery blur, but he could feel their hate and it cheered him.

He found another pair of shoulders to leap on and this time his companion went down, Animal collapsing with him. He giggled in the darkness, thrashing out at the jostling legs around him. It was like being underground, subdued light sinking down through cracks in the earth, the surrounding legs like moving tree roots.

He giggled louder at his friend's muffled cursing, maliciously pushing his gross body on hands and knees further into the throng, causing those above him to lose their balance and spill over. He liked the darkness as much as he liked being in a crowd. It was almost the same thing: you couldn't be seen. For a moment it had become too black down there, as though the crowd had joined together to form a solid crust above him, and he felt a little afraid. The darkness somehow had a gooey thickness to it.

Animal burst to the surface like a whale from the sea, throwing those nearest to him backwards, laughing at their shouts of anger. The fact that their club scarves differed from the one he wore tied around his wrist didn't bother him at all: Animal was afraid of nothing and no one.

Fans at the back resented the crowd ripple that had thrust against them and several saw the cause of it, the fat grinning face turned away from the pitch in their direction, thick bare arms, despite the weather, raised in defiance against them, the opposition scarf tied to one wrist. The rain had drenched them, their team was losing – and this fucker was taking the piss. They surged forward as one, a ripple that grew into an onrushing wave, gathering momentum, gaining force, breaking over the fat man and pounding him like a rock on the sea-shore.

Eddie and Vicky had been standing halfway between the grinning monster and the fans at the back who had started the push. The girl screamed as they were carried forward, her feet swept off the ground, her body held tightly aloft, desperately clinging to Eddie who was powerless to resist the torrent. Eddie had been used to crushes like this before, but he had never had a girl to look after. He knew these sudden rushes could be dangerous, fights inevitably breaking out in the aftermath. The thing was not to go down – you'd be kicked to death beneath all those feet. It was the poor sods at the front who took the full weight of it: they'd be crushed against the barriers. He managed to get an arm around Vicky's waist, his other arm locked tight against his body. He shouted a warning to the girl when he saw what was happening ahead of him. Bodies were going over, *going down!*

Jack Bettney felt the swell reach him. Fortunately, he was away from the path of the main stream, but even so he and the other fans around him were pushed back then sucked in with the flow. He kept his balance, well experienced nowadays in the art of surviving a football match. Silly bastards! he thought. No wonder the armchair was the best place to watch a game these days. Those nearest to him managed to steady themselves and they jigged on tiptoe to see what was happening in the other part of the crowd. A great hole had appeared and they realised many of the people had gone down, more bodies toppling over them as the surge continued.

Jack winced. There'd be a few broken bones among that lot. His woolly cap was sodden now, and rain ran off the end of his nose. He blinked and saw the ball was in the centre of the pitch again, the players deliberately oblivious of the reaction in the crowd. They probably couldn't see too much against the glare of the floodlights anyway. Jack turned his attention away from his team's centre forward who was preparing to tap the ball towards a mid-field player, and tried to see what was happening to the fallen spectators. The atmosphere in the stadium was bad tonight and he was glad he was a home supporter. The hostility towards the away-fans had been growing since the beginning of the match and the commotion over there was just the start of the trouble to come. Needle matches always infected the fans and tonight the infection was going to run wild. He could feel it.

A flickering behind and high above distracted him. He looked up at the tall metal tower set into the concrete terraces towards the back of the stadium, sixteen blinding lights at the top helping three other similarly situated towers around the ground to turn night into day on the pitch. Fifteen lights. One was spluttering, going dim, reviving briefly, sparks flying into short-lived arcs, then fading completely. Bloody rain. That shouldn't be happening, though. When was the last time they were checked? A cheer rang out from the other side of the pitch as another light abruptly popped off, then another. More sparks began to fly and soon the whole array of lights was fizzing and smoking. The section of the crowd beneath the tower began to grow anxious and started backing away from the area beneath it, pushing at those around them for room. All the lights suddenly exploded at once, glass and sparks falling with the rain on to the people below and a sharp, tangy smell was carried into the air. The gloom on that side of the stadium suddenly became denser and Jack felt the panic as a crowd wave started again, this time rippling outwards, the movement resembling a pond's surface disturbed by a stone.

Animal was on the ground kicking out with heavy boots,

464

trying to clear a space for himself. It had become darker now, almost black and, strangely, rather than fearing the blackness, he welcomed it. Someone was on top of him and he managed to get one beefy hand beneath the man's chin. He pushed up sharply and was delighted to hear above the clamour of the spectators – or had he only felt it? – something snap. The body fell limply against him and Animal felt good. He had enjoyed that. Something chuckled in the blackness of his mind and it wasn't him.

A foot came down on his cheek and he twisted his head to dislodge it. He heaved the body on top of him away, but there were others, alive and thrashing, to take the man's place. Animal managed to get an elbow beneath himself and raised his shoulders from the ground. A figure crashed down beside him – man or youth, he couldn't tell – and this time he definitely heard the crack of skull on concrete. He lifted the fan's head by the hair and shoved it down to hear the sound again. Nice one.

Eddie tried to pull Vicky closer to him, but he was pinned to someone else's back. The body beneath him squirmed to free itself, but there were others on top of Eddie. Vicky's screams could be heard clearly over the predominantly male cries of alarm and anger and he tightened his grip around her waist, determined not to let her go. He felt a blow behind his ear, then another. For fuck's sake, someone was hitting him! Twisting himself around, he spilled the two on top of him over, using his elbow to help them on their way. He rolled on to someone else and he realised it was Vicky.

Pushing himself up, not caring if he was treading on anybody, he pulled at the girl, drawing her halfway out of the scrambling heap.

Hysteria was in her eyes as she grabbed wildly at him.

'Take it easy, Vicky!' he shouted. 'You'll have me over!'

Something thudded into him from behind, causing him to lose his precarious balance. Then someone had him by the throat and was pounding a fist into his face to the accompaniment of Vicky's screams. Rage replaced the fear inside him as he struck back at his aggressor. No one was going to belt him and get away with it! And as he fought, a blackness seemed to fill him.

The girl felt the mob violence. It wasn't just the physical aggression of the crowd; it was something else, something that slowly, stealthily, smothered them all. Her head snapped upwards when she felt icy, black fingers tapping on the surface of her mind, fingers that wanted to scratch their way through and explore inside. She screamed again, fearing the dark hand more than the madness around her. Someone was pulling her up and she opened her eyes, grateful for the firm grip beneath her arms. The face was smiling, she could just make that out in the gloom. But she sensed there was no humour in the smile. It was a huge bloated face, the hair closely cropped and plastered to his scalp by the rain. His body was big, his arms bare, and he held her upright against the frenzied tide surrounding them. She knew the evil that was in the air was also in him. The cold black fingers had found easy access into this man.

Animal's smile became a grin as the voices inside told him what to do.

Something was tugging at Jack Bettney and it had nothing to do with the spectators who were clawing at each other to get clear of the crush. It was something nipping away at his thoughts. No – it was something nipping away at his will, he was sure of it. He had read somewhere about mass-hysteria, how panic or even adulation could pass through a crowd, hopping from mind to mind, touching every person present until they were enveloped in a binding cocoon of emotion. That was what was happening here! But it was something more than panic. There was a savagery about these struggling, heaving people. Not all of them, for many were under attack from others; but the earlier hostility had somehow manifested itself into an overwhelming madness. It was the madness that was tugging at him!

He began to hit out, not caring who he struck, knowing he had to get away from them, sensing he was different – *he was not with them*. They would sense it too!

Hands reached out to him, grabbing at his clothes, pulling the woolly cap from his head, reaching for his eyes. He went down and as he lay underneath the trampling feet, the darkness all around, he began to give in to the silent, pounding voices, wanting to join them if it would give him peace, agreeing to be part of them, whatever their intent. Realising too late they were not offering him peace.

Animal was finished with the girl. Others wanted her even though her body was limp, no life left in it. He let her fall and pushed a way through the mob, making slow but firm progress, eyes fixed on the metal structure protruding from the mass of human flesh and towering over them like a soulless sentinel.

All activity on the field below had stopped, the players, linesmen and referee staring in bewilderment at the crowd on that side of the pitch. Policemen had left their benches and were hurrying around to gather just below the section where the trouble had started. But there was no longer one place of activity, for the skirmishes had spread, joined, merged into one massive battle, everyone on that side of the stadium involved. None of the constables felt inclined to wade into the thick of it, nor did the officer in charge encourage them to do so. Suicide was not part of their duty.

Animal finally reached the base of the floodlight tower, the short journey through the press of bodies taxing even his great strength. But adrenalin was coursing through him, for he knew what he had to do and it excited him. He was pushed up against the metal, its surface slimy wet with rain; he reached inside for the junction box from which heavily protected cables emerged, soaring their way up towards the rows of burst lights above. The cover to the box would not budge, for it had been built to resist the attention of destructive fans. Animal climbed the first two cross-struts of the tower and poked his foot inside. He kicked at the box, his heavy boot scarring and denting its surface. It took long minutes for the cover to work itself loose but, for perhaps the first time in his life, Animal had patience. He kept doggedly at his task and whooped with glee when the cover finally fell away. Then he reached inside and curled his huge hand around two of the heavy cables. He began to tug, the crowd pressed tight around him, the rain drenching everyone and everything.

The cables finally came away, for Animal was strong, and the power passed through him into the wet, tightly-packed crowd, sweeping outwards with paralysing swiftness, spreading like a deadly germ. Hundreds had been touched before the current finally blew itself out and plunged the entire stadium into total, screaming darkness.

Chapter Sixteen

Bishop studied Lucy's tiny face, holding the framed photograph in one hand, his other hand resting on top of the mantelpiece. His thoughts of her had become frozen moments, still-life images like the photograph he held, single frames his memory had captured. He could still hear her squeaky giggles, her panting sobs, but they were echoes, not attached to Lucy herself. He missed her and, with a slight feeling of guilt, realised he missed her more than Lynn. Perhaps it was because in reality his wife was still there: only her mind was dead. Did it amount to the same thing? Could you still love a person when they had become someone else? Something else? You could, but it wasn't easy; and he wasn't sure he was capable anymore.

He replaced the photograph and sat in an armchair facing the empty grate. A new guilt was rising in him, compounding the old, and it was to do with Jessica. Perhaps it was because she was the only woman he'd had any real association with for a long, long time. Since Lynn's illness he hadn't sought female company, nor missed it. So much had been drained from him after Lucy's death and Lynn's breakdown; only resentment had been left, the remnants of his own sorrow. The resentment had become a fierce anger which had been channelled into the new work he had found for himself. But even that had begun to die, leaving only the bitterness that clung like a withered vine to a crumbling wall. Now something inside that had lain dormant for many years had begun to breathe again, lightly at first, stirring gently, unfurling, becoming steady. The old feeling had moved aside a little, making room for the new. Was it because of Jessica or because of the passage of pain-healing time? Could any attractive woman coming into his life at that point have had the same effect? He didn't have the answer, nor did he want to ponder the question. One day, Lynn might become whole again. And if she didn't . . . she was still his wife.

Restless, he heaved himself from the chair and went into the kitchen, taking a can of beer from the fridge. he pulled the tab and drank straight from the can, half its contents gone before he took it from his lips again. He returned to the armchair, his thoughts dark and brooding.

It was crazy. Everything that was happening was crazy. The madness was growing, a virulence that was spreading like an ancient, uncontrolled plague. An exaggeration? The suicides at Beechwood had been the beginning. Then the insanity that developed a year later, a madness that had soon enveloped most of those living in Willow Road. An attempted murder on himself and Jacob Kulek. The slaying of Agnes Kirkhope and her housekeeper. And then the riot at the football stadium last night. *Nearly six hundred people dead!* Hundreds electrocuted, floodlight wiring torn loose and the current directed into the rain-soaked crowd. Hundreds of others beaten, kicked to death by the mob. The rest – mass suicide. Any way they could find. Climbing then leaping from the floodlight towers or the girders supporting the covered stand area. Or hanging themselves with their club scarves. Belt buckles, metal combs – other concealed weapons that troublemakers always managed to smuggle in – anything that was sharp used to sever arteries. There had been a record gate for a midweek match in the small Second Divison ground: twenty-eight thousand. Nearly *six hundred dead!* What kind of nightmare must it have been inside that darkened stadium? Bishop was unable to control the shudder that ran through him. The beer spilled on to his chin when he raised the can again and he realised his hand was shaking.

Others had run into the streets, most to escape the bedlam, many seeking alternative means of destroying themselves. Hands had been smashed through shop-front windows, the jagged shards used to slash wrists. Twenty youths had run into the nearby railway station and jumped as one from the platform when an express hurtled through. The nearby canal was still being dredged for the bodies of those who had chosen drowning. Tall buildings had been used to leap from, lorries or buses to leap under. Cars as weapons. The destruction had gone on through the night. *Six hundred!*

When daylight finally came, scores of them had been found wandering the streets, their faces blank, their minds seemingly empty. The word *zombie* flashed through Bishop's head, a word

469

that had always held humorous connotations for him in the past; but now the description had a true, sinister meaning. That was what these people had become. Zombies. The walking dead.

Just how many had been found in this state was not yet known; but according to the news media, there were more still not accounted for. Still wandering mindlessly? Dead but not discovered? Or had they found a place to hide? The horror of it had been with Bishop throughout the day, for he had made the connection, the obvious connection. And so had Jacob Kulek, who was now out of hospital, and Jessica – Bishop had spoken to her earlier that day. The insanity was not confined to Willow Road: it had travelled a distance of nearly a mile to the football ground.

He wondered if Edith Metlock had been touched by the same madness. When he and Jessica had found her in her home two nights before, she had mumbled something about the dark over and over again as though she were afraid that the night outside might enter the house and somehow consume her. Bishop had wanted to get her to a hospital, but Jessica had told him she had often seen mediums in this state, that Edith had become lost within herself and could only find her way back on her own. The trance would tear off; all she needed was protection until it did. They had put the medium on to her bed, Jessica covering her with a quilt, propping her head up with a pillow. While Bishop had checked every room in the house and relocked the kitchen door, Jessica had rung the hospital where her father was being kept for observation. He was fine, sleeping under mild sedation and there was no point in her coming over that late; unless there were any unforeseen developments overnight, she could come and collect him in the morning.

They had sat with Edith Metlock all night, and they had talked, occasionally breaking off to listen to the medium's sudden disturbed murmurings. It was well past three before the tension drained from Edith's face and she seemed to drift off into a deeper, peaceful sleep. By that time, Jessica's eyes were closing and he finally persuaded her to lie down on the end of Edith's bed. He found a blanket to cover her with and, half-asleep, she had smiled when he touched a hand to her cheek; then she was gone, her breathing becoming deep and regular to match Edith Metlock's.

Bishop had sat in the chair previously occupied by the medium, uneasy at being left alone with the oppression that seemed to surround the house. It was just his imagination, he told himself. There was nothing out there. It was just the result of everything that had happened catching up. Eventually the oppression seemed to lift. His eyelids grew too heavy and he slept.

Gentle prodding had woken him the following morning and he had found Jessica kneeling before him, her smile a welcome sight. Edith Metlock was propped up on the bed and, although she appeared to be exhausted, she thanked them both for staying with her through the night. She seemed nervous and constantly glanced around the room as though expecting someone else to be there hiding in the shadows. She was too confused to tell them what had happened the night before – Bishop suspected she wasn't sure herself. Fortunately, because of her unsettled state, it had not occurred to Edith to ask them what had brought them to her house, and they deemed it wise not to tell her.

After a light breakfast cooked by Jessica, they had persuaded the medium to stay at Jacob Kulek's house for a few days. Edith had declined at first, but when Jessica mentioned that her father had had a slight 'accident' – she would explain later – and that it would be enormously helpful if Edith could take care of him for a few days until he was better while Jessica organised the day-to-day running of the Institute, she readily agreed. There was much she and Jacob could discuss over the next few days, Edith told them, a distant look in her eyes.

By the time they were ready to leave the house, some of the colour had returned to the medium's cheeks, although they still found her occasionally glancing around the room in a perplexed manner.

Bishop was surprised when he saw the home in which Jacob Kulek and his daughter lived. It was in a small, secluded lane just off Highgate Village and, as they turned into the narrow driveway almost hidden by trees, it was as if they were approaching a building constructed entirely of broad sheets of shining bronze, the sun reflecting from their surfaces, a dazzling contrast to the surrounding sombre winter greens.

'It's iodised glass,' Jessica had explained, amused by his reaction. 'You can see out, but you can't see in. At night, when it's lit inside, vertical blinds give us our privacy. My father can see shadows, you see. With daylight all around he can see any movement inside the house. It's the only vision he can enjoy.'

Jessica had rung the hospital again from the house and was

471

relieved to hear Jacob was well and would be allowed home later that morning after one or two tests had been carried out. Bishop left and before he turned from the driveway into the small lane, he glanced in his rearview mirror and saw Jessica standing at the door of the house, watching him. He almost raised a hand to wave back, but stopped himself.

Once home, the drive through the rush-hour filled city having wearied him even further, he had undressed and thrown himself into bed, not waking until five that evening. A phone call to Jessica's had disappointed him, for Edith Metlock had answered. Jacob Kulek was resting, she herself was fine although still not quite clear on what had happened the previous night, and Jessica was at the Institute. He put down the receiver and stood by it for a few moments, debating whether or not to ring Jessica's office. He decided not to.

He cooked and ate a lonely dinner, then settled down to work for the rest of the evening. A publisher was interested in a new book he had planned and had already agreed on a small advance on production of a synopsis. Bishop's idea was to write a detailed study on the many occult associations that were now thriving in different parts of the world, organisations as varied as the Institute of Parapsychology and Cybernetics Inc., in Texas, to the Foundation for Research on the Nature of Man, in North Carolina. A list of all these associations and societies had been drawn up by him, but he would have to sift through and choose those he would major on, for there was no possibility of visiting every place in person and, indeed, some were behind the Iron Curtain and access to them might prove difficult. Several of these, however, sounded intriguing: the Czechoslovak Coordination Committee for Research in Telepathy, Telgnosis and Psychokinesis, and the Bioelectronics Section of the Polish Copernicus Society of Naturalists were just two he was determined to see for himself. His publisher had agreed to pay his travelling expenses as part of the advance, this later to go against royalties, and Bishop hoped that many of the associations would receive and accommodate him as a guest; most were eager to have their work recognised. He planned an objective study on these foundations, societies, associations, institutes – whatever they termed themselves – keeping his own attitudes carefully in check until the conclusion of the book. It was only then that he would know himself what those attitudes would be. In a way, the exercise

472

was almost self-indulgent: he wanted to discover more about the paranormal. When he had begun his strange career as a psychic investigator, he had had an intransigent prejudice against mysticism in any form and had quickly come to learn that there was a great difference in what was commonly termed the supernatural and the paranormal: one had mystical connotations while the other was an unknown science, perhaps – and, as yet, no one was *really* certain – the science of the mind. He felt sure that by studying the activities of these various groups he would have a clearer picture of the overall progress this relatively new field of science had made. The growth in public interest was incredible. The young were shying away from materialism and seeking their own higher levels, their elders seeking a refuge from the chaos around them. It seemed that for many, conventional religion had failed to provide that comfort, for prayers and paying homage did not always work. In fact, for most, it rarely worked. Where was justice, where was right? The more communications improved throughout the world, the more the injustice could be seen. When the new generations looked at religion they could only see manmade ritual, manmade hypocrisy. Even history told them the pursuit of God had meant the slaughter and suffering of millions. Many turned to new cults, fringe religions such as the Scientologists, the Moonies, the People's Temple (what was the real reason for *their* mass suicide?). Gurus had replaced messiahs. Psychiatrists had replaced priests. Para-psychologists might eventually replace both.

There was a growing belief that man's soul was hidden deep in some dark recess of his mind, not an invisible entity filling his whole being. If it was there, it could be found; the scientists needed only to know where to look and produce the instrument to trace it. And science in its study of the paranormal, was slowly, very slowly, homing in. Bishop had to smile at his own uncomplicated logic; Jacob Kulek could probably improve on the substance of his reasoning, but he felt their separate conclusions would not be that far apart. He made a mental note: Kulek's Research Institute would be a good place to start with for his book.

Bishop worked late into the night, outlining the structure of his thesis, drawing up a shortlist of associations he would include, making a note of their locations and any specific field of the paranormal they were involved in. It was well past one when he

473

went to bed and sleep quickly claimed him. The nightmare returned and he was once again sinking into the black, brooding depths of the ocean, his lungs crushed by the pressure, his limbs stiff and useless, his body's leaden weight dragging him below. A face was waiting for him down there, a greyish blur that grew clearer as he plunged. This time it was not Lucy's. It was a man he recognised, yet did not know. The man was grinning, and withered lips called Bishop's name. His eyes seemed to bulge unnaturally from their sockets and Bishop saw there was nothing but evil in them, a cold, mesmerising darkness that sucked him in, that drew him into a blackness that was even deeper than the ocean. The grin was a sneer and Bishop suddenly knew it was the same man he had seen in Beechwood, the man who had watched his followers kill each other and themselves before putting a gun into his own mouth. the lips parted, yellow, ill-formed teeth guarding the glistening cavern inside, the fleshy, quivering tongue resting on the entrance floor like a huge slug waiting to curl around and engulf any intruder. Bishop floated through, the jaws closing behind him with a thunderous steely clang, and he was totally blind and screaming, the soft enveloping surface of the tongue reaching up for him and moulding itself around his feet. He tried to tug himself free but only sank further into the gripping slime and in the darkness he sensed the tongue curling round, rearing over him to descend upon his shoulders. His own panic-stricken screams deafened him as white, floating shapes came into view, rising from the tunnel that was the man's throat, their faces familiar, the images of those who had died in Beechwood. Dominic Kirkhope was with them. And so was Lynn.

Her eyes were wild, both terror and beseeching in them. Her lips formed words that were cries for help. She begged him. She pleaded. Help me.

And he couldn't; the tongue was pressing down on him, smothering his head and shoulders, choking him with its sticky juices, forcing him to fall, crushing him in a cushion of softness. Until everything exploded. And he was the bullet smashing its way through the man's brain. The man he suddenly knew was Boris Pryszlak.

He awoke still screaming, but no sounds came from his lips. It was light outside and he almost wept with relief.

The beer can was empty and Bishop placed it on the floor at his feet, then slumped back into the armchair, one elbow resting on the arm of the chair, hand across his brow as though shielding his eyes from the lamp-light. His head ached and every muscle in his body felt lifeless. He had spoken with Jessica that morning, ringing her as soon as he'd heard the news on the radio. She had been at home and told him she would stay there today to look after her father. Jacob had also heard the news of the bizarre tragedy at the football stadium and he, too, felt sure it was related to the incidents in Willow Road. He was still weak from the attack, but had made her promise to arrange a meeting for all of them later that evening, a meeting that would include Detective Chief Inspector Peck. Even if the policeman thought they were all insane, they had to try to convince him there was a connection between the Pryszlak sect and the recent events. Bishop had agreed to keep himself available that evening; she would ring him when she had fixed a suitable time.

He still hadn't heard from her and he was becoming concerned. That concern finally drove him out of the armchair into the hall. He was just reaching for the phone when it rang.

'Jessica?'

'Uh, no. Mr Bishop? Crouchley here. From Fairfields.'

Fairfields. The mental home.

'Has something happened to my wife?' Dread hit Bishop's stomach like a lead weight.

'It's important that you come over right away, Mr Bishop.' said the metallic voice.

'Is Lynn all right?'

There was a slight pause at the other end. 'We've had what you might call a slight breakthrough. I think we rather need you here. I'll explain when you arrive.'

'It'll take me twenty minutes. Can't you tell me a little more now?'

'It's better that you see for yourself.'

'Okay. On my way.'

Bishop's heart was thumping as he raced upstairs to grab his jacket. What did a 'slight breakthrough' mean? Was Lynn at last beginning to emerge from the shell she had retreated into? Would there be some warmth, no matter how faint, in her eyes when she saw him? He tugged on his jacket and raced back down the stairs, a new hope urging him on.

When the phone rang again only moments later, the house was already empty.

Chapter Seventeen

Bishop had to force himself to concentrate on driving as he sped towards Twickenham, the rain splatting off the road like tiny cannon shots. Fortunately, the traffic was light and he was able to make good progress. He was filled with apprehension; there had to be good reason for Crouchley to call him out at that time of evening. If Lynn had finally . . . he refused himself the thought. Better not to expect too much.

It was not long before he reached the quiet cul-de-sac at the end of which stood the Fairfield Rest Home. He drove straight through the tall entrance gates into the wide drive. Slamming the car door, he hurried up the steps leading to the building's main door, rain speckling the driving glasses he had forgotten to remove. He whisked them off into his top pocket, ringing the doorbell with his other hand as he did so. The home was a large redbrick building which in appearance could have been anything from a small, private school to a residence for geriatrics. Only when the discreetly lettered sign mounted on the front railings had been read did the building take on a faintly daunting atmosphere. The fact that most of the interior lights seemed to be off, made it look even more grim.

Bishop heard the lock click, then the door opened slightly.

'I'm Chris Bishop. Dr Crouchley asked me to come over.'

The door opened wider and he saw the silhouette of a short, plumpish woman standing there. 'Oh, yes, we were expecting you, Mr Bishop. Won't you come in?'

He stepped into the home's reception area and turned anxiously towards the small woman as she carefully locked the door again.

'Is my wife . . .?'

'We'll take you straight up to see her, Mr Bishop,' a voice said from behind and he turned to see another woman sitting at the reception desk to one side of the hall. Her face was turned away from the small desk-lamp that did its feeble best to light up the gloomy surroundings. The figure rose and came around the desk towards him.

'I'm sorry about the poor light,' she said as if reading his mind. 'We always keep the lighting subdued after eight o'clock. We find it's restful for our patients.'

She was taller than the woman who had let him in and Bishop realised he had seen neither of them before. Perhaps they were new, the tall one certainly, for patients were never referred to as such in Fairfield – they were always 'residents'.

'What's happened to Lynn?' he asked. 'Dr Crouchley wouldn't tell me over the phone.'

The two women eyed each other and a pleased look passed between them. 'I think you'll find a marked improvement, Mr Bishop,' the taller one said. 'Would you like to follow me?'

They walked towards the broad staircase that led to the first floor of the home, the smaller woman falling in behind Bishop, hands thrust into her white medical coat. The taller woman kept up a flow of conversation as they climbed the stairs, but he hardly listened; his mind was on Lynn. The corridor on the first floor was also lit only by a small lamp on a table at the far end and he found the dimness disconcerting. He hadn't realised they kept the lights to a minimum after visiting hours; it was more depressing than subduing. A door opened as they passed, the room beyond in total darkness; the smaller woman hurried over and stretched out an arm as if to gently push someone back towards their bed. The taller woman smiled sweetly at him as though nothing had happened.

Bishop had always found the mental home slightly unnerving, which was natural enough; but at this time of night, without the usual bustle of visitors and staff, it was more than that. His mouth felt dry and he wondered if the tension was because of Lynn or because he had become a little afraid of the place. They passed more doors and he wondered what lay behind them, what was going on inside those damaged minds.

'Here we are.' The tall woman had stopped outside a room he knew Lynn shared with three other residents. The wards were kept small at Fairfield, the doctors reluctant to separate their charges from each other, although they believed in keeping the numbers to a minimum.

477

'Won't we disturb the others?' Bishop asked.

'They're sleeping soundly – I checked just before you arrived. Please go in, your wife is waiting for you.'

'Is Dr Crouchley with her?'

'He'll be along shortly. He wants you two to be alone for a few moments.'

Bishop's face lit up, the tension beginning to leave him. 'She's . . .?'

The white-coated woman put a finger to her lips, then smiled pleasantly, her eyes sparkling at his anticipation. She pushed open the door and motioned him to enter. He said a quiet 'Thank you' and went into the room. The door closed behind him.

Lynn's bed was in a corner by the window and a small nightlight had been placed on her bedside cabinet. She was propped up on pillows, her head turned to one side as if she had dozed off while waiting for him. He tiptoed towards her, conscious of the grey, sleeping forms in the shadows around him, his eyes moist, throat still dry.

'Lynn?' he said gently when he reached her side. 'Lynn, are you awake?'

He touched her hand lying on top of the bedsheets and softly shook it. Her head slowly came round towards him and in the poor light he saw the grin on her face. His body went rigid and all the openings in his body seemed to curl inwards.

'Lynn?'

Her eyes still bore the look of insanity. Her grin reflected the madness. She began to sit up and he was aware that the others in the shadowy beds around the ward were rising also. Someone snickered.

Lynn's lips were glistening wet as she pushed back the bedclothes and began to reach for him. He had to stop himself from backing away.

'Don't get out of bed, Lynn.'

Her grin widened.

One leg slipped from the covers.

Her hand touched his shoulder.

'Lynn!' he screeched as her other hand whipped up and clawed at his face.

She was laughing and it wasn't Lynn at all: the features were the same – same mouth, same nose, same eyes – but they were distorted, twisted into an ugly grimace, someone else, something else, behind those wild eyes.

478

He grabbed her wrists and held her away from him, her body exploding into violent motion. Screams were mixed with her laughter as she kicked out at him, snapping her teeth like a rabid dog. He pushed her back towards the bed, unnerved by her strength, frightened by her condition. The bloody fools! Why had they dragged him here to see this? Had she fooled them, made them believe she was changing for the better? Or had just the sight of him broken down what good had been done?

She was on the bed now, her head thrashing around on the pillows, her flimsy nightdress kicked high over her thighs. She hissed and spat at him, the bubbled saliva smearing his face. He was dimly aware that other shapes were moving towards him from out of the darkness, but he was afraid to let go of his wife's wrists, afraid of those claw-like nails.

His head was jerked back as a hand grabbed his hair from behind; he twisted his neck, trying to pull himself free. But the hand grasped him tightly and another reached around and across his throat. Bishop was forced to let go of Lynn and clutch at the arm that was squeezing his neck. She was off the bed immediately, coming at him, hands flailing, her mouth snapping at him once more. They went down in a heap, the woman behind losing her grip on his throat, but still gripping his hair at the roots. He blinked away the blur in his eyes and rolled over, taking Lynn with him, the other woman scrabbling at him with her free arm.

He managed to get a foot up and kicked out at Lynn, her cry of pain a terrible sound, but knowing he had no choice. She scudded away from him and he turned on the woman still clinging. A fierce backslap of his hand stunned her and she shrieked with the shock. Even in the darkness he could see she was an old woman, her hair white and frizzed out as though filled with static.

A bare foot kicked him, striking his cheek and knocking him sideways. Two other nightgowned women were standing over him, their faces masks of grinning hate. They ran forward, kicking out, crying their triumph. A body landed on him and teeth sank into his neck. In the nightmarish confusion he knew it was Lynn. He broke her grip, but felt skin tear away and a spurt of blood run into his collar. He grabbed a foot that was pushing at his chest and twisted it forcefully, the woman above him falling back with a scream. He got a knee beneath him and pushed himself upwards, taking Lynn with him, a figure in front pounding his face with clenched fists. He struck out, hitting the woman on the forehead, sending her hurtling backwards into the shadows. He held Lynn to him, pinning her close to his body, trapping her arms. The white-haired woman was slowly creeping towards him like a ghost from the mists, arms stretched out before her holding what looked like a rolled-up bedsheet, a twisted shroud he knew was to go around his neck. He almost collapsed with relief when he saw the door behind her begin to open, the dim light from the hallway casting dark shadows into the room.

The silhouettes of the two women who had shown him in, the tall one and the short one, stood there.

'Thank God,' Bishop said, the moans, the giggles, the screams – Lynn's squirming – suddenly coming to a stop. Even the old woman bearing the twisted bedsheet paused and looked back over her shoulder.

The tall woman stepped into the room and the other one followed. The two women moved to the side, opening the door wide, and he heard the tall one say: 'Bring him along.'

They poured into the room, demented, arm-waving creatures from hell, the women dressed in plain, shapeless smocks that served as nightgowns, the men in similar garments. Bishop backed away, almost believing he had walked into a terrible dream.

Lynn broke free and suddenly the twisted bedsheet was thrown around his shoulders, then jerked tight. He was pulled forward and a screaming mass of bodies enveloped him, hands tearing at his clothes, darkened manic faces appearing before him, disappearing as others brushed them aside to see their victim. Bishop blindly hit out, their screams deafening him, his fists sinking into fleshy parts of bodies and sometimes striking hard bone. Those that fell back were immediately replaced by others and he began to go down, clutching at their robes to stop himself. A knee came up into his face and for a second he felt only white-hot shock, the numbing pain reaching him split seconds later. He went down on to his knees and a hard slap rocked his head backwards. His hands spread themselves on the floor before him and he felt the sheet around his neck tightening. Bruising feet toppled him over.

They used the sheet to drag him towards the door.

The tall woman looked down at him, the gloomy light from the hallway throwing her face into half-shadow; the pleasant smile was still there. He lay on his back staring up at her and she and her short companion took delight in his horror. She held up a hand and for a moment the clamour died, just a sigh, a moan, a giggle, coming occasionally from the shadows.

All she said was: 'It's too late, Mr Bishop. It's already begun.'

Then they were on him again and he was half-carried, half-dragged into the hall. He thought he heard Lynn laughing with them.

He managed to get his feet beneath him and forced himself erect, digging his heels into the tough cord carpet, pressing himself back against the mob, unwilling to go wherever it was they wanted to take him. He groaned aloud when he saw what lay ahead of him in the corridor.

The bodies of the mental home's staff had been tumbled out from the rooms on either side of the long corridor. Very little white showed through their bloodstained uniforms. With revulsion, he saw they had not just been murdered; mutilation had taken place. Whether or not they had been dead before . . . He shook the thoughts from his mind.

He was shoved forward and the fury inside him broke. He did not know what had happened to them all, why or how their unbalanced minds had turned to such appalling violence, but he hated them for it. Events of the past weeks told him they were not responsible – their enfeebled minds had been taken over by a greater madness. It was *that* madness he felt hate for, but they were its hosts, they were its perpetrators. They had allowed themselves to be used. They were no longer human.

The short woman stepped in front of him, her face pinched and malicious, ready to taunt. His foot came up and caught her just below her plump belly, and her ducking face met his swiftly lifted knee, choking off her piercing shriek.

Those holding him were momentarily stunned and a dagger of fear found its way through their insanity. Bishop tore an arm free and twisted himself to strike the madman holding his other arm. He felt a fleeting satisfaction as the man's nose squelched beneath his knuckles. The sheet around his neck loosened and he quickly pulled it over his head, already jumping away from the mob crowding into the corridor. The cries reached a new pitch as he shoved the man who had been holding on to his other arm back into the mob. Hands were clutching at him, trying to drag him back into their midst.

481

He was backing away, slapping at their hands as though they were naughty children grabbing for sweets. He almost stumbled over the outstretched legs of a male nurse and then he had turned and was running for the stairs, the sight of the dead man looking up at him, deep red holes where his eyes should have been, completely unnerving him. The residents chased after him, stumbling and giggling over the bodies of those they had already slain.

Bishop reached the top of the stairs and fell against the banister. Two figures, clad in the white starched trousers and jackets that were the Fairfield uniform, were mounting the steps, their faces hidden in the shadows. One held a long iron bar that he was rattling along the uprights of the banister and, when their heads and shoulders came into view, Bishop saw the same wild-eyed glee in their eyes that belonged to the mad men and women behind him. He staggered up the staircase leading to the second floor.

A hand curled round his ankle, bringing him down, and he grasped at the banister to stop himself from sliding to the bottom. He twisted and found it was Lynn holding on to him, a chuckling, drooling Lynn, a Lynn he no longer knew, who was enjoying the game, who wanted him dead. He had to close his eyes when he brought his foot down into the upturned face.

The metal bar crashed against the rails his fingers clung to, only inches away, and the grinning face of the male nurse peered up at him from the other side. The mob at the foot of the stairs were tripping over the fallen body of Lynn as Bishop lumbered onwards, taking the stairs three at a time, the terrible fear that his legs would turn to lead fuelling his panic. He used the rail to pivot himself around the bend in the stairs, the mob now trampling over Lynn to reach him. He reached the second floor corridor and it was dark. But not so dark that he couldn't see the white clad figures drifting down the corridor towards him, doors opening on either side and others stepping out, dim spectres in a world of blackness and screams.

He was trapped.

Except for a door on his left that had not yet opened.

He burst through and slammed it behind him, leaning back against it to prevent them from following, sucking in huge swallows of air. Keeping a shoulder against the door, he scrabbled around for a key in the lock. There was no key. Not even a bolt.

He could hear them gathering outside.

And his feet were wet.

482

He reached for a light switch, found nothing, but felt something brush against the back of his hand. A cord. A light. He pulled. He was in a bathroom, the white tiles stark and blinding. That was why there was no lock on the door: mad people were not allowed to lock themselves in rooms. The floor was covered in puddles and the deep, claw-footed bathtub was filled to overflowing, the water smooth and placid, its highest level reached.

A chair with two carelessly dropped towels draped over its back stood in a corner next to him. He reached for it gratefully and jammed it against the door at an angle, its back beneath the handle. It might hold them for a precious few moments, time enough to reach the high window opposite. He saw the frosted glass was reinforced with metal wire and prayed he would be able to break through, already sure the frame was set in its surround, unable to be opened naturally. He splashed across the bathroom floor, ignoring the shrill laughter from outside. And as he passed by the huge bath, he realised it had all been an evil game for them, that they meant to let him escape to the second floor, that they had directed him to this particular room. They had wanted him to see what lay beneath the unstirring water in the bath.

Chapter Eighteen

The house surprised Peck. Not the kind of place he expected Jacob Kulek to live in; somehow he thought the old man would have preferred oak beams, roses running up the outside walls, or maybe something Georgian, tall and elegant. Still, his kind was unpredictable; something a little cranky about most of them. Seemed well-balanced enough until you started listening to what he was saying.

'Some shack, eh, guv?' Frank Roper, his DI said as Peck pressed the doorbell. 'All glass and chrome. I'd hate to be their window cleaner.'

Peck grunted, his thoughts now distracted. He was wondering why Kulek had insisted on seeing him, especially at this time of night. The insanity of the night before had meant an overload – and that was an understatement – for everybody: how the hell do you deal with mass murders by a mass of murderers? And what was the connection between the incidents at the football ground and Willow Road? Or, to be more specific, the house that had once been there: Beechwood. Because there was a definite link now. If Kulek hadn't asked for the meeting, then Peck, himself, would have wasted no time in interviewing the old man. It seemed he was the only person who could give some clue as to what was going on.

The door opened and Jessica Kulek's white nervous face peered out at him.

'Come in,' she said, opening the door wide.

'Sorry we're a little late,' Peck apologised. 'As you can imagine, we've been pretty busy today.'

'That's why my father wanted to see you, Inspector. It's about what happened last night.'

'You're going to tell me there's a link. And you'd be right.'

Jessica's eyebrows arched in surprise. 'You think there is, too?'

'Let's say it's a strong possibility.'

Kulek was waiting for them in a large L-shaped lounge, the room itself, like the house, of modern design, although the furniture seemed old, possibly antique; surprisingly, the combination worked. Peck noticed everything was set out in straight lines or at right-angles to each other and he realised a blind man wouldn't want odd bits of furniture scattered at random around the room. The vertical blinds were drawn against the night.

'Good of you to come, Inspector,' Kulek said. He was standing by an armchair, one hand resting on its back, whether for support or merely guidance, Peck wasn't sure. He looked older than when the policeman had first met him, but infinitely better than when he had seen him in the hospital two days ago. His skin had taken on a dry, pale yellow cast and his stoop had become more pronounced. A silk scarf peeping over the top of his shirt-collar hid his bruised neck.

'You've met Detective Inspector Roper,' Peck said without looking at his colleague.

'Yes, indeed. And this is Edith Metlock.'

The medium smiled briefly at the two policemen.

'Won't you sit down? Can we offer you something to drink? Something stronger than tea or coffee?'

Peck relaxed his body into a sofa while Roper chose an uncomfortable hardbacked chair. 'Whisky, a little water, for me,' Peck said. 'I believe Inspector Roper will have the same.'

Roper nodded and Jessica made herself busy at the drinks cabinet.

'I thought you said Chris Bishop would be here tonight?' Peck said.

Kulek seated himself in the armchair he had been standing behind. 'My daughter has been trying to contact him for the past half-hour. He must have left his house.'

Jessica came over with the drinks. 'Chris may have decided to come over anyway. I said I would ring him as soon as I fixed the time for the meeting with you. I'm afraid you weren't easy to reach today.'

'Well, we can soon find out where he is. I've had two men watching him all day. Frank, tell Dave to radio through, will you?'

Roper placed his glass on the deep red carpet and left the room.

Kulek spoke. 'Jessica tells me there has been a man in a car parked near this house for the last two days.'

'For your protection, sir. There's been one attempt, no sense in risking another.'

An awkward silence followed Peck's statement before the detective cleared his throat and said: 'I had planned to see you first thing in the morning, Mr Kulek. I think there's a lot we have to discuss.'

'Yes, Inspector, indeed there is. But I gave you all the facts concerning Beechwood and Boris Pryszlak at our first meeting. Tonight I wanted to talk theory with you.'

'I'm always interested in theories. Provided they're sound, that is.'

'I can't promise you that. What may be sound to me might be completely irrational to you.'

'I'm prepared to listen.' Peck turned to Edith Metlock. 'Mrs Metlock, one of my detectives spoke to you the other day, after the madwoman was found in Beechwood. You were there at the seance.'

'It wasn't a seance, Inspector,' the medium said. 'At least, it wasn't planned as such.'

'You said you saw nothing yourself of this, uh, vision or hallucination – whatever you might call it – that Bishop claims to have seen.'

'No. As a medium, I seldom see or remember such things. My body is used as a receiver by the spirit world. They speak to others through me.'

'And you think this is what happened at Beechwood? The spirits of Pryszlak and his people used to speak to Chris Bishop? He was the only one who saw them, wasn't he?' Peck shifted uncomfortably in his seat, glad that Roper wasn't in the room to hear his line of questioning.

'They didn't speak to him,' Edith replied. 'He was shown what had happened there.'

'Why not you, Mr Kulek? Or your daughter, Jessica?'

'We don't know,' the old man answered. 'Perhaps it was because Chris Bishop discovered the bodies originally. Perhaps Pryszlak was mocking him with the truth of what had happened.'

'Pryszlak's dead.'

This time there was no reply.

486

'There could be another, more reasonable, explanation,' Peck said finally. 'Bishop had a mental block on what he stumbled across in Beechwood for nearly a year. It could be that going back into the house shocked him into seeing it all over again.'

'But he only discovered them when they were all dead,' said Jessica. 'The other day he actually saw them killing themselves and each other.'

'We only have his word that they were already dead.'

Jessica looked at her father, who said: 'Wasn't there a witness who saw him go into the house? A woman with a child who was passing by at the time?'

'Yes, I've read the report. But how do we know he hadn't already been to the house, hadn't actually been present when the suicides and executions took place. From what I've learned of this Bishop, he believes in a more scientific approach to the supernatural. Didn't you tell me Boris Pryszlak also had a scientific interest in these matters?'

'Yes, but . . .'

Peck went on. 'You see, it could be that our Mr Bishop is part of Pryszlak's secret sect himself. It could be that he was a member chosen to stay behind to carry on whatever fanatical cause they were all involved in.'

'That's nonsense!' Jessica's face was flushed red, 'Chris was also attacked two days ago!'

'He says.'

Kulek's voice was calm. 'I think you're wrong, Inspector.' His sightless eyes looked towards his daughter and Edith Metlock. 'We all think you're wrong.'

'I also got the impression that he wasn't entirely in favour of your investigations into Beechwood.'

'That's true,' said Jessica, 'but only in the beginning. His opinion is different now. He's trying to help us.'

'Is he?' Peck's tone was flat.

Roper came back into the room and sat in his chair again, retrieving the whisky glass from the floor with an undisguised look of relish. He glanced over at Peck before he drank.

'Bishop went out just after eight. Our obo followed him to a place near Twickenham, Er, Fairview . . . no, Fairfield Rest Home.'

Jessica said, 'It must be the home where his wife is a patient.'

'A mental home?'

She nodded and couldn't read the expression on Peck's face.

'Get back on the radio, Frank. Tell them to bring Bishop here. I think he could be useful to this little gathering.'

'Now?' Roper's lips were poised over the edge of his glass.

'Right away.'

The policeman replaced his glass and left the room once more.

Peck slipped at his own whisky and water and regarded Jacob Kulek over the rim of his glass. 'Okay, sir, you said you wanted to talk theory.'

The blind man's mind was still on Bishop. No, it wasn't possible. Chris Bishop was a good man, he was sure. Confused. Angry. But not of Pryszlak's kind. Jessica had finally come to like the man and she was the best judge of character he knew. Sometimes he felt her judgement was a little too good, a little too critical . . . The few men in her life had never come up to her expectations.

'Mr Kulek?' There was a note of impatience in Peck's voice.

'Sorry, Inspector. My mind was wandering.'

'You have a theory?' Peck prompted. Kulek's eyes seemed to be boring into him and he could have sworn he felt the back of his mind being searched.

'It's difficult, Inspector. You are a practical man, a down-to-earth person who does not believe in ghosts. But, I think you are probably very good at your job and therefore, you may have some imagination.'

'Thank you,' Peck said drily.

'Let me start by telling you of the strange experience Edith had two nights ago. Or perhaps she will tell you herself?' he turned to the medium.

'As a sensitive – medium, spiritualist, are words you are probably more familiar with, Inspector – as a sensitive I am more susceptible to forces, influences, that are outside our daily lives. Forces from a world that is not of our own.'

'The spirit world.'

'If it can be called that. I'm not sure any more. It may be that we have a misconception about what we term "the spirit world". There are others in my profession who are beginning to have the same doubts.'

'Are you saying there are no such things as, er, ghosts?'

Roper had re-entered the room and he gave Peck a bemused look. He nodded at his superior to indicate that his instructions were being carried out, then took his place in the chair and reached for the glass at his feet.

'Perhaps not as we have always considered them,' the medium replied. 'We have always thought of them as individual spirits, existing in another world not unlike our own, but on a higher level. Closer to God, if you like.'

'And that's all wrong?'

'I'm not saying that.' There was a trace of irritation in her voice. 'We just don't know. We have doubts. It may be that this spirit world is not as far removed from our own as we thought. And it may be that they do not exist as individuals but as a whole. As a force.'

Peck frowned and Roper gulped his drink noisily.

'Inspector, I will try and explain later,' Kulek interrupted. 'I think Edith should just tell you what happened two nights ago.'

Peck nodded his agreement.

'I live alone in a small house in Woodford,' Edith told him. 'On Tuesday evening – it was late, some time between ten and eleven, I think – I was listening to the radio. I like those phone-in programmes, you know. It's good to hear what ordinary people think of the state of the world occasionally. But the set kept crackling as if someone nearby was operating a machine without a suppressor. I tried twiddling the knobs, but the interference kept coming back. Short bursts of it, then longer. In the end it was one continuous buzz so I turned the radio off. It was then, sitting there in the silence, that I noticed the change in the atmosphere. I suppose my attention had been too fixed on that blessed radio interference for me to have noticed it before. There was nothing alarming about it – presences have often made themselves known to me in the past without invitation – so I settled back in my armchair to allow it through. It took me only a few seconds to realise it was unwelcome.'

'Hang on,' Peck interrupted. 'You've just been telling me you aren't sure there are such things as ghosts.'

'Not as we think of them, Inspector. That doesn't mean something other than what we see or feel does not exist. You can't ignore the incredible number of psychic experiences that have been recorded. I must stress that at the moment I'm confused as to just what it is that communicates through me.'

'Please go on.'

'I felt my house was being surrounded by a . . . a . . .' she

489

searched for the word '. . . a dark shroud. Yes, as though a blackness were creeping around my home, pressing itself up against the windows. And part of it had already reached me. Part of it was already in my mind, waiting to spread itself, waiting to absorb me. But it needed to smother me physically and something was holding it at bay.'

'Your will power?' Peck said, ignoring Roper's grin.

'Partly that, yes. But something else. I felt darkness was its ally, its travelling companion, if you like. I don't know what made me do it, but I switched on every light in the house.'

Nothing unusual in that, thought Peck. He didn't personally know of any woman living alone who wasn't afraid of the dark. Plenty of men, too, although they wouldn't admit it.

'I felt as though a pressure had been taken off me,' the medium said, and Peck could see by her expression she was reliving the experience. 'But it was still outside . . . waiting. I had to block my mind, resist the urge to let it flow through me. It was as though something were trying to devour me.' She shivered and Peck himself felt a certain coldness at the base of his neck.

'I must have gone into a trance – I can't remember any more. Except for the voices. They were calling me. Mocking me. But enticing me, also.'

'What were these voices saying? Can you remember that?'

'No. No, not the words. But I felt they wanted me to turn off all the lights. Somehow, a part of me knew if I did I would be lost to them. I think in the end I just retreated into myself, fled to a corner of my mind where they couldn't reach me.'

That would be a nice trick for me to use when the Commissioner asks me what I've uncovered so far, thought Peck, holding back a weary smile.

They sensed his cynicism, but understood it. 'Edith was in that state when Chris and I found her,' Jessica said. 'When we left you that evening, Inspector, we were suddenly afraid that something might happen to her. Chris, my father, and Mrs Kirkhope had been attacked; we'd forgotten about Edith.'

'And what did you find at Mrs Metlock's house? Apart from the good lady herself.'

'We didn't *find* anything. We sensed an atmosphere. A cold, oppressive atmosphere. I was afraid.'

Peck sighed heavily. 'Is this really getting us anywhere, Mr Kulek?'

490

'It might help you to understand my . . . theory.'

'Perhaps we can get on to that now?'

The blind man smiled patiently. 'Believe me, we understand how difficult this is for you. We cannot give you solid evidence, no hard facts. However, you must *not* dismiss us as cranks. It's vital that you seriously consider whatever we tell you.'

'I'm trying, Mr Kulek. You've told me very little so far.'

Kulek bowed his head in acknowledgement. 'My daughter and Chris Bishop brought Edith here – they thought she would be safer. As you know, I was in hospital but returned home later that day. It wasn't until yesterday evening that Edith began to talk of what had happened. When she had been found she was in an extreme state of shock, you see, and it took some time for her to emerge from that state. The only words she had said before then were, "Keep the dark away." It seems the darkness was somehow symbolising whatever it was she feared. Now I'm sure it hasn't escaped your notice that everything that happened in Willow Road recently has taken place at night.'

'The woman who attacked you in Beechwood. That was in the daytime.'

'She had killed her employer the night before. I believe that was when the madness hit her. Remember she was hiding in the cellar of Beechwood; in the dark.'

'The murder of Agnes Kirkhope and her housekeeper? The further attack on you? Bishop's alleged attack? These were all during the day.'

'It's my belief that the perpetrators were disciples of Boris Pryszlak. Their's was a different kind of madness. I think they were a physical guard left behind by Pryszlak to carry out certain duties. Protectors, if you like.'

'Why should he need protection if he's dead?'

'Not for *his* protection. They were left as a safeguard to his plan. Perhaps a tangible force to support his ethereal force.'

Peck and Roper exchanged uncomfortable glances. 'Could you explain exactly what you mean by "ethereal force"?'

'A force not of this world, Inspector.'

'I see.'

Kulek smiled. 'Bear with me; you might see some sense to it by the time I've finished.'

Peck hoped so, but he wouldn't have laid odds on it.

'When Boris Pryszlak came to enlist my assistance some years

491

ago, he told me he was a man who did not believe in the existence of God. For him, science was the key to mankind's salvation, not religion. Disease and deprivation were being overcome by technology, not by prayer. Our economic and social advances were achieved by science. The decision to create new life was now our own; even the gender of the newborn would one day be decided by ourselves. Death itself, if not entirely thwarted, could at least be delayed. Our superstitions, our prejudices and our fears were steadily becoming obsolescent in the face of new scientific discoveries. World wars had been virtually eradicated not because of Divine Intervention, but because we, ourselves, had created weapons too fearsome to use. Old barriers had been broken down, new barriers smashed through – by mankind's own ingenuity, not by some superior being in the heavens.

'Pryszlak claimed that one day we would even discover scientifically how we gained that ingenuity; how, in fact, we were not created by a mystical Someone, but created ourselves. We would prove by science that there was no God.'

Kulek's words were said calmly, his voice soft and even, but Peck could feel Pryszlak's madness in them. It was the cold logic of a fanatic and Peck knew these were the most dangerous kind.

The blind man went on: 'So, if there was no God, there could be no Devil. Yet, as a pragmatist, Pryszlak could not deny the existence of evil.

'Through the centuries, religious and mystical leaders had always played on the superstitions and the ignorance of their fellow men. The Church had always insisted that Satan was a reality: for them it helped to prove the existence of God. Freud had confounded the Church and demonologists alike by explaining that each of us has been through a phase of individual development corresponding to that animistic stage in primitive man, that none of us has traversed it without preserving certain traces of it which can be re-activated. Everything which now strikes us as "uncanny" fulfils those vestiges of animistic mental activity within us.'

'You're saying that somewhere in here –' Peck tapped his temple' – is a part of us that still wants to believe in all this "evil spirits" nonsense.'

'Freud said this and, in many respects, I believe he was right. In thousands of cases where ecclesiastical exorcists have tried to rid disturbed men and women of so-called diabolic possessions, rational examination has revealed a varied range of psychoses in those same people. Philosophers such as Schopenhauer advocated that evil sprang from man's fear of death, his fear of the unknown. It was man's will to survive that brought conflict to the world, and within himself. But his own iniquity had to be blamed on something – *someone* – else: Satan provided the ideal psychological scapegoat. In the same way, because of the adversities inflicted on man throughout life, and because he knew his own inadequacies, man needed a god, a superior, someone who would help him, someone who, in the end, would provide the answers. Someone who would pull him through.

'Unfortuntely for the Church, the age of rationality is here; perhaps one could say that education has been the greatest enemy of religion. The edges have become blurred, questions are being asked: How could atrocities be committed to achieve right? Wars, killing, executions – how could "bad" acts achieve "good"? How could men the world knew to be evil claim God was on their side? Would a civilised country ever fight a religious war again? In the late seventies, who had been the more evil, the dictatorial Shah of Persia or the religious fanatic, Ayatollah Khomeini who overthrew him? Idi Amin claimed to have conversed with God several times. Hitler claimed God was on his side. The persecution of so-called heretics throughout the centuries by the Church itself has still not been answered. This dichotomy has been challenged and Pryszlak saw it as man's recognition of his own powers, a predetermination over his own destiny. He had discovered his own Original Sin and decided it wasn't as evil as the Church had always taught him. Satan has now become a source of ridicule, of entertainment, even. A comical myth. A bogeyman. And evil came from man alone.

'Pryszlak believed it was a physical energy field within our mind and, just as we were learning to use our psi faculties – energies such as telekinesis, extrasensory perception, telepathy, telergy – so we could learn to use physically this other power.'

Kulek paused as if to allow the two policemen's thoughts to catch up on all he had said. 'I think Pryszlak developed his concept into a proven fact: he located this source of energy and used it. I believe he is using it now.'

'That's impossible,' said Peck.

'Many things in your own lifetime that you once thought

493

impossible have been achieved by science, and knowledge in every field of technology is in escalation. Man has accomplished more in the last hundred years than in the previous thousand.'

'But for Christ's sake, Pryszlak is dead!'

'I think he had to die, Inspector. It's my belief that Boris Pryszlak and his followers have become that energy.'

Peck shook his head. 'I'm sorry, you know I can't buy all this.'

Kulek nodded. 'I didn't expect you to. I just wanted you to hear a theory I'm convinced is true. You may have cause to reflect upon it over the next few weeks.'

'What do you mean by that?'

'The madness will get worse, Inspector. It will spread like a disease. Every night there will be more who will succumb to its influence, and the more minds it takes the stronger it will grow. It will be like the raindrops on a windowpane: one small drop will run into the one below, then both into the one below that, growing in size and weight until it is a fast-flowing rivulet.'

'Why night-time? Why do you say these things only happen when it's dark?'

'I'm not sure why it should be so. If you read your Bible you'll see evil is constantly referred to as darkness. Perhaps that terminology has more significance than we thought. Death is darkness, Hell is in the dark, fearful underworld. The Devil has always been known as the Prince of Darkness. And isn't evil expressed as the darkness in one's soul?

'It could be that darkness is the physical ally to the manifestation of this energy. Perhaps the biblical concept of the constant battle between Light and Darkness is a true, scientific concept. Whatever energy light rays contain, be they from the sun or artificial, it may be that they counteract or negate the catalystic qualities of darkness.

'Pryszlak inferred much of this at our last meeting and I must admit that although I often found his ideas fascinating, this time I thought there was some madness in his thinking. Now I'm not so sure.'

Kulek's frame seemed to relax imperceptibly in his chair and Peck realised the blind man's disquieting statement was over. He looked at each individual in the room and noticed even Roper's secretive smirk had disappeared.

'You realise everything you've just told me is totally useless to my investigations, don't you?' he said bluntly to Kulek.

'Yes. It is at this moment. Soon I think you will change your mind.'

'Because more is going to happen?'

'Yes.'

'But even if what you say is true, what would be the point for Pryszlak?'

Kulek shrugged, then said, 'Power. More power than he had when he was alive. A larger following, one that will grow.'

'You mean he can still go on recruiting?'

Kulek was puzzled to find no trace of sarcasm in Peck's question. In fact, he was surprised the policeman had listened so patiently. 'Yes, others will join him. Many others.'

Peck and Roper exchanged sharp glances which were not lost on Jessica.

'Is there something you haven't told us, Inspector?' she asked.

Peck looked uncomfortable again. 'The crowd that ran amok last night – those that got away, that is – dispersed into the surrounding area. We've been picking them up throughout the day. Many have been dead when we've found them, mostly killed by their own hand. Others have been . . . mindless, wandering around lost.'

His face was grim, as though he did not like what he had to say next. 'Quite a few made straight for Willow Road. They smashed the barrier surrounding the Beechwood property. We found them standing there in the debris, just waiting like bloody vultures.'

495

Chapter Nineteen

Bishop stared at the still body lying in the bath. The white, contorted features stared back.

He had spoken to Crouchley many times over the past few years, their conversations confined to Lynn's mental progress – or regress, as it turned out – and always on a professional basis. He couldn't say he ever got to like the man, his approach was a little too impersonal for Bishop; but he had respected him as a doctor and he had soon realised the man's dedication to his patients' welfare went beyond professional bounds. In the end they had turned on him.

The two women who had let Bishop in: had they been patients? He thought not; there seemed to be no insanity in them. Were they tools of Pryszlak as Braverman and his wife had been? Probably. They had taken over the home, the patients becoming their allies, and murdered those of the staff who had not succumbed to this new, deadly madness. Then they had forced Crouchley to ring him. After that, they had dragged him up here and drowned him.

Crouchley's mouth was open, the last bubbles of life-giving air having long exploded from his lungs to fight their way to the surface. His fair hair had turned dark beneath the water and now floated softly around his head like pondweed. Even though he was dead, fear still showed on his face.

They were banging on the door now, laughing and screaming Bishop's name, taunting him with the terror to come. The small wire-toughened window was on a level with his face and he saw, as he had expected, the frame was fixed into its surround. He looked around desperately for something to smash it with, but the bathroom was bare of implements. The chair may have helped, but that was the only thing keeping his pursuers out. The blows on the door had become harder, their rhythm more

496

definite, as though the crowd had stood back to allow someone to use his boot against it. The angled chair shuddered.

A faint hope fluttered inside him when he saw the towel rail hooked over the bathroom's radiator. It was made of chrome and felt heavy enough to have some effect when he lifted it clear. The large towel that had been draped over it slid to the floor when he raised the rail to shoulder level. With one hand behind the triangular shaped hook and the other around the long metal rail iself, Bishop ran at the window and thrust it at the frosted glass, his feet almost slipping in the puddles beneath him.

The glass fractured, a jagged hole appeared; the wire reinforcing the glass held it together. Bishop drew the rail back and thrust again. Still the wire held.

The chair shook.

He thrust again.

The chair legs moved a fraction.

Again.

Another fraction.

This time the hook at the other end of the towel rail became entangled with the wire mesh and Bishop pulled inwards, twisting the hook to entangle it more, drawing the wire with its clinging fragments into the room, stretching it until it snapped, dropping the rail and pushing his fingers through the tiny holes, ignoring the sharp pain as the wire bit into his flesh, tugging frantically, hearing the sound of the chair scraping on the damp bathroom floor, feeling the cool night air breathing on his face through the opening that was growing wider, the wire and glass coming loose from its frame, feeling the draught grow stronger, sucked through as the door behind him burst open, tearing and twisting the wire and glass free, seeing there was enough room for him to squeeze through . . .

. . . feeling the hands on his shoulders . . .

They clawed at his body, dragging him to the floor, their screams shrilling in his head as they bounced from the tiled walls. He kicked out, his own cries joining theirs. They bore down on him, smothering his thrashing limbs with their own. A hand reached into his open mouth in an effort to pull his tongue from its roots and he bit hard, tasting blood before the scrabbling fingers jerked themselves free. He screamed when excruciating pain stabbed up from his groin area, manic hands squeezing him in a merciless grip. His shirt was ripped open and sharp

497

fingernails dug into his chest, sinking into his skin and drawing short jagged lines of blood.

His wrists were being held and even through the confusion he could feel someone bending the fingers of one hand back, trying to snap them. Before they could succeed, he was lifted, his squirming body held in eager grips. Wild deranged faces were around him and, as he twisted his head to and fro, he caught a glimpse of the two women, the tall one and the short one, standing in the doorway. Their smiles were not sinister, merely pleasant.

He arched his body upwards, the circular light set in the ceiling a huge sun filling his vision, almost blinding him. Shock hit him as he was plunged downwards and water engulfed his body. He choked as it rushed into the canals of his nose and throat, forcing out air in huge explosive bubbles. The light above was broken into frantic patterns as the water's surface scattered into stormy motion and he could see the blurred silhouettes of those who leaned over the bath and held him down. The body of the dead man stirred beneath him.

The illogical thought that Crouchley was suddenly waking from the dead threw yet more panic into him even though whatever reason was left inside told him it was only the water's disturbance that made the body move. He pushed himself upwards, resisting the hands that held him back, forcing his head above the surface. He coughed water from his lungs, retching and gasping in air at the same time. His head was gripped and he was forced down again, hands tugging at his legs to jerk him back. The water splashed at his face, covering his chin, nose, eyes. Then he was below the surface again, the world suddenly going quiet, the screaming an imaginary sound in his head. His hands reached upwards for the side of the bath and fierce pain told him they were being battered, prised away from the slippery, enamel surface. A shadow loomed over him and he felt a crushing weight on his chest. Another sudden weight on his hips pinned him helplessly to the body beneath him. They were standing on him.

His breath was beginning to go, the weight on his chest forcing it out. He closed his eyes and the darkness was tinged red. His lips were closed tight but the air bubbles steadily forced their way from them. Like his body, his mind began to drown and he felt it plummet downwards. There was no redness anymore, only the deep sucking blackness and now he was living his constant nightmare, his body sinking down into the depths, small white blobs that he knew were faces waiting for him below. Pryszlak wanted him. But Pryszlak was dead. Yet Pryszlak wanted him.

He was fathoms beneath the ocean now and his body was still, struggling no more, resigned to its death. The last silvery pearl of air fled his lips and began its hasty mile-long journey to the ocean's surface above. There were many, many faces waiting below for him and they grinned and called his name. Pryszlak was among them, silent, watching. Dominic Kirkhope, gloating. The man who had tried to shoot him, Braverman, and his wife, were laughing. Others, some of whom he recognised from his vision in Beechwood, were reaching up with shrivelled, water-crinkled hands.

Then there was anger in Pryszlak's face and the others were no longer grinning. Now they were howling.

Bishop felt himself rising, rushing to the surface. He was suddenly worried about the rapid change of pressure, that nitrogen bubbles would be trapped in the tissues of his body and he would suffer what every deep-sea diver dreads: decompression sickness – 'the bends'.

Then he was above the surface, spilling bath water from his mouth, wheezing in air when he could, choking as uncleared water rushed back down his throat. Strong hands held the lapels of his jacket collar and above the roaring in his ears he heard a distant voice shout, 'There's another one underneath him!'

He was dragged from the bath and allowed to fall on to the wet, tiled floor. He sucked in air, his senses spinning. Crouchley's staring face appeared before him, his limp body hanging over the side of the bath, water flowing from his mouth as though it were the end of a drainpipe.

'This one's dead,' the distant voice said.

Bishop was pounded on the back and he retched up the rest of the water inside him. He was pulled to his feet.

'Lean against me, but try and stand, mate. We'll get you out!'

Bishop tried to see who was helping him, but the room spun dizzily. He wanted to be sick.

'Get back!' A cannon roared and he saw splinters of wood fly from the wooden frame around the open doorway. White shapes scurried back into the shadows.

'Come on, Bishop, you'll have to help me. I can't carry you on my own.'

The voice was coming nearer, the words becoming more clear. The man had slid a shoulder beneath Bishop's arm and was holding him up. Bishop tried to push himself away, thinking the man was one of the maniacs, but the grip tightened.

'Hold up, pal, we're on your side. Try to walk will you? Move your legs.'

'They staggered forward and Bishop felt the strength willingly flow back into his body.

'Good man,' the voice said. 'Okay, Mike, I think he's going to be all right. Keep that bloody mob back.'

They lurched into the dark hallway and began a slow, stumbling march towards the stairs. Something moved in the shadows ahead and the man in front of Bishop and his helper fired a shot into the air. The hallway was lit up for a split-second by the gunflash and he saw the mad creatures crouching there, afraid but ready to pounce.

Bishop and his two men had reached the bend in the stairs when the mob decided to attack.

They came tumbling out of the darkness like screaming banshees, pouring down the stairs in an unbroken, human stream.

Bishop fell back into the corner as his support was taken away and he saw both his helper and the other man raise their guns and fire into the crowd.

Cries of pain and fear rang through the corridors of the large house and he heard bodies falling, those behind toppling over the injured in front. Something slumped across his outstretched leg and began to writhe there. Bishop kicked the body away.

A hand tugged at his arm and he pushed himself upright, ready to fight.

'Come on, Bishop, let's keep moving.' With relief he realised the hand belonged to his helper.

'Who the hell are you?' he managed to say as they descended the next flight of stairs. It was lighter down there, but the man leading them improved matters by flicking on a switch. The hall and stairs were flooded with light.

'Never mind that now,' the man helping him said. 'Let's just get away from here first.'

A sudden thump on the stairs behind made them whirl. The male nurse who had tried earlier to attack Bishop with an iron bar stood above them. He still held the iron bar.

A blast from the gun and his white uniform became a shredded

500

mass of red just above the knee. His leg buckled and he fell back on to the stairs, the bar clattering down noisily. He clutched his leg and burbled his pain. Others were creeping round the bend in the stairs behind him, their eyes wide and fearful.

Bishop and the two men backed away to the next flight of stairs which would lead them to the ground floor. His clothes felt heavy with water, but noradrenaline was coursing through him once more, giving him the strength he needed.

The two women were waiting below. The short one was splashing liquid from a can on to the wide stairway. She stood back, placing the can at her feet, and smiled up at her companion. The taller woman struck a match and flicked it at the stairway.

The petrol ignited in a brilliant *whoosh* and the three men at the top of the stairs raised their arms against the fierce heat. The flames hungrily climbed the wooden staircase towards them and beyond they could see the two women backing away, grinning delightedly.

'We can't get down,' one of the men shouted. 'There must be another way out. They've got to have a fire escape.'

Bishop's head was still reeling, but through the confusion he heard the other man say, 'Can you make it, Bishop? We're going to try the back way.'

He nodded and all three men turned as one, ready to run towards the back of the building. A ring of white-robed people blocked their way.

The patients shuffled forward, their nightclothes tinged red from the rising flames, and Bishop saw Lynn was among them.

'Lynn! It's me, Chris!' he cried, moving ahead of the two men to plead with her. 'Come with us, Lynn, before the whole building goes up.'

For a brief moment, Bishop thought he saw a tiny flicker of recognition in Lynn's eyes, but if she had realised who he was, the memory only renewed her hatred. She tore herself away from the crowd and ran at him, arms flailing, hands outstretched, claw-like. In his weakened state he could not hold her; he fell and she toppled over him. Her hands clutched at the stairs as she slivered down towards the flames and Bishop desperately tried to grab her ankle. He touched her heel but the limb was gone before he could gain a hold. Her screams pierced all other sounds as she slid into the fire and her nightdress and hair became a blaze. Her tumbling body was lost in the inferno and her screams stopped abruptly. Something fell half out of the flames into the hallway below, a blackened, charred shape that bore no resemblance to a human body. It was quickly covered as the flames spread.

'No! No!' Bishop's cry descended into a low moan.

He was pulled away from the raging heat by the two men, his body totally limp now, his senses numbed with shock.

The patients had cowered back, the full horror of their companion's death striking fear into their disordered minds. The men with Bishop saw that whatever extreme madness had driven them to this, it had been overcome by their own natural terror of the fire. The patients began to whimper as the heat grew in strength, and smoke filled the hallway.

'Let's get going while we can, Mike,' one of the men holding Bishop said just loud enough to be heard.

'Right,' his colleague agreed, his back beginning to feel singed by the heat.

With Bishop between them, their Webley .38s pointed at the figures in the crowded hallway, they cautiously moved forward.

'This way, Ted,' the man called Mike said, indicating to the right with the muzzle of his gun. 'There's a window down at the end of the corridor. Oh shit!'

The lights in the hallway had suddenly gone off. Had the fire burned through the wiring or had someone pulled the master switch? Both men thought of the two women who had started the fire.

'Let's move,' Mike said grimly.

The hallway was bathed in a red, weaving glow, dark shadows rising and dancing against the walls. The whimpering patients glared at the men who were retreating down the hall and carefully stepping over the sprawled bodies lying there. The white-gowned figures edged forward and doors on either side of the three men began to open.

The man called Ted glanced nervously from left to right. The only sound that could be heard now was the crackle and roar of the spreading fire. 'They're going to rush us again,' he said.

Figures were stepping into the hallway, hemming them in, watching silently, not yet raising their hands against them.

But the tension was rising, a huge bubble of hysteria that was swelling to breaking-point, and when it broke the retreating men knew they would be easily overwhelmed. As they backed further down into the blackness at the end of the hall, each of the three

502

men felt something else nudging against the walls of their mind, something that seemed to be seeking access.

The fresh attack was started by one old woman who stood in the centre of the hall near the burning staircase. Her brittle legs were wide apart, her hands clenched and arms held rigidly to her sides; flames licked up at the ceiling above her. The cry started somewhere low in her abdomen and began to build, rising to her chest then up through her throat until it came out as a shrilling scream. The others had joined in with her mounting cry and when it broke, so they broke and came running towards the men.

The ceiling above the staircase and the next flight of stairs had become potent with heat; the flames below billowed upwards, old timbers eagerly giving themselves to the fire. A huge ball of flame spilled into the hallway, enveloping the white-robed figures who stood in its way, searing others who were too near.

Black smoke swirled towards the three men and they began to choke, their eyes already stung by the heat of the fireflash.

Bishop was dragged to the window, his body heaving as his lungs tried to eject swallowed smoke. He was pushed into a corner while the two men struggled to open their only means of escape. The fire spread rapidly and patients were running into open doors on either side of the hallway, many of them with nightclothes on fire.

'It's fucking locked!' Bishop heard one of the men shout.

'Shoot the bloody glass out!' his companion told him.

Both men stood back from the large single-framed window, raised one arm each to shield their eyes, and pumped bullets through the glass. The window shattered and a cold blast of air sucked in towards the flames.

Bishop was yanked away from the corner and steered towards the window. He drew in a deep breath of air and felt some reason returning as he leaned out into the night.

'There's – there's no fire escape,' he managed to gasp.

'Jump! It's only one floor up!'

He climbed on to the sill and let himself go. It seemed a long time before he hit the soft earth below.

Chapter Twenty

Peck gazed down at the slow-moving traffic and filled his lungs with cigarette smoke. He wondered if the people scuttling around below in their tiny Dinky-toy cars had any real idea of what was going on in their city. It was impossible to keep an absolute clampdown on the bizzare events of the past few weeks; the media had made the connection between the events at the stadium and Willow Road days ago, but had reluctantly agreed to contain the full story until the authorities had come up with some rational answer to quell the mounting anxiety of the general public. It was an uncomfortable collaboration between the authorities and the media and one that would undoubtedly fail when the next major incident occurred. The newsmen could only be suppressed for so long.

He took the half-smoked cigarette from his mouth using his index finger and thumb, the palm of his hand curved around the butt. Janice was always telling him he'd never make Commissioner if he continued to smoke cigarettes with such mannerisms. Sometimes he thought his wife was serious.

Peck turned away from the window and slumped into the chair at the desk, stubbing the cigarette out against the side of his waste-paper bin and dropping the butt inside. Mannerisms? It had taken her ten years to stop him rolling his own. The knot of his tie was hanging loose over his chest, shirtsleeves rolled up to the elbows. He rubbed a hand across his face, conscious of the scratching sound his chin made, and studied the last page of the report he had just completed. Better grab a quick shave before I show this to the Deputy, he told himself. It wouldn't matter to that pompous bastard if you'd just arrested Jack the Ripper if you hadn't shaved beforehand.

As he re-read the last lines in his report his hand unconsciously travelled towards the back of his head, cold fingers breaking

504

through his concentration to tell him no new hair had miraculously grown overnight. In fact, he thought, his attention now fully with his probing fingers, a few more had said their last farewells. He quickly dropped his hand lest any of his new men saw him through the glass panelling of his office. He'd rather be caught playing with himself than caught checking to see how his baldness was coming along. Getting old and feeling it, he silently grumbled. Still, they said baldness meant virility. He couldn't say he'd noticed lately.

He closed the report and sat back in his chair, taking another cigarette from the pack on the desk as he did so. He flicked the Zippo and stared through the billow of smoke as it escaped his lips.

What the fuck is going on? he asked himself.

The football incident had been the biggest so far, but there had been others just as alarming. The burning down of the Fairfield Rest Home, for one. The riot in the boys' Remand Home, for another – the little bastards had turned on their wardens and then on themselves. Sixteen dead, twenty-four terribly injured. The rest? Where were the rest? The inmates of another mental home, this one run by the National Health, therefore known more accurately as a hospital for the insane, had turned on the staff first and then, as with the boys' home, themselves. Fortunately, the alarm had been raised before too much damage was done, but five were dead – two nurses, three patients – before the police had arrived in force. The mystery was why several of the staff had joined in the riot.

There had been many smaller incidents and if anything some of these were even more disquieting than the major events. Perhaps it was because they had involved perfectly normal people – at least considered to be normal before they had committed their individual acts of madness. A man had slaughtered every animal in the pet shop he owned, afterwards taking to his bed with the one fortunate creature he had spared, the show-piece of his collection: a ten-foot long South American boa constrictor. He had been found dead with the snake wrapped around his throat like a muffler. Three nuns had gone berserk in their convent, creeping through the corridors one night and attempting to smother several sleeping sisters with pillows: they had succeeded twice before they were discovered. A doctor on night duty – the enquiry discovered he had worked non-stop for two days and

505

nights – had toured the wards of his hospital injecting patients with a lethal dose of insulin. Only the intervention of a duty-nurse had prevented more than a dozen deaths – she herself had been injected and killed when she had struggled with the doctor. A labourer, working late to finish an urgent job on a block of offices that was undergoing modernisation, had knocked his foreman semi-conscious, then pinned him to the wall with a nail-gun. The gun individually shot six-inch nails with a force strong enough to pierce concrete and by the time the other work-men got to the unfortunate foreman, his arms and legs were firmly pinned. The crazed workman managed to fire a nail through his own head before they could get to him and another labourer had narrowly missed being punctured when the nail had emerged from the other side without losing any impetus. Perhaps the most bizarre of all was the butcher who had served his chopped-up wife to his customers – Today's Special, regular customers only. A section of thigh was still missing and the police were desperately trying to trace the unlucky housewife who had made the 'bargain' purchase.

There had been other crimes, other suicides, but it was not yet known if these were connected with the more bizarre incidents. And what exactly could the connection be other than the fact that each horrendous act had seemingly been carried out at night? Could the dark really have something to do with this madness as Jacob Kulek had suggested?

Peck had included the blind man's theory in the report, but had left it as a separate section, adding no personal comment himself. He had been tempted to leave it out completely and if he could have offered any reasonable theories himself, then perhaps he would have done so. What the Commissioner would make of it all he dreaded to think but he, Peck, was only a small cog in the operation now; the big boys had taken over. All he could do was provide them with every scrap of information he had. A couple of weeks ago Peck had considered Kulek to be a little crazy; now too much had happened for him to dismiss the man as such. If only they could find out more about Boris Pryszlak. His home had been a flat in a huge apartment block near Marylebone although, according to his neighbours, he was hardly ever there. The flat itself offered no information whatsoever; it was a spa-cious accomodation which held little comfort in the way of furni-ture. There were no pictures on the walls, no bookshelves, few

506

ornaments of any kind. What items of furniture there were were expensive but functional and bore little sign of wear. It was obvious the man used the apartment only as a base, his activites – whatever they may have been – keeping him away most of the time. Even the information gathered at the time of the mass suicides in Beechwood had revealed little. If Pryszlak was head of some kind of crazy religious sect, then his organisation kept an extremely low profile. They seemed to have had no specific meeting place, and there was no indication of how they gained recruits. Also there was no record of the work – scientific or otherwise – Pryszlak had become involved in. Several of the people in the house had been wealthy, Dominic Kirkhope being a prime example, and Peck felt it reasonable to assume they were sponsoring Pryszlak with his project in some way. Did they have genuine aspirations or were they just a bunch of deviates who enjoyed getting together on odd occasions for orgies? The information gathered so far on Kirkhope and some of the others indicated that their sexual preferences were somewhat bizarre. Dominic Kirkhope had once owned a farm in Hampshire which, acting on complaints from neighbouring properties, the police had investigated. It seemed the animals kept there were not being used for natural purposes. The scandal had been hushed up, for the indignant landowners in the surrounding properties did not want their tranquil existence shattered by such adverse publicity. No charges had been brought against Kirkhope and his guests, but the farm itself had changed hands soon after the police raid. Kirkhope had been watched for a while after that, but if he indulged further in such sexual malpractices, then he did so very discreetly.

The backgrounds of Braverman, his wife and Ferrier, the man who had fallen from the window at Kulek's Institute, were being checked: so far, nothing unusual had been unearthed about any of them. Braverman had been a creative director of an advertising agency, a leading figure in his field. Ferrier had been a librarian. There seemed to be no obvious social connection between either party. Could they have been followers of Pryszlak?

There was only one lead on the murders of Agnes Kirkhope and her housekeeper. Two women had been spotted strolling past the Kirkhope property by neighbours on the day of the murders. Had it not been a quiet residential area, then they probably would not have been noticed; as it was, they had been observed walking by Miss Kirkhope's house two or three times by different people. It could be that they were waiting for the right moment to strike. One woman had been tall, the other short.

Chris Bishop had said that two women, one tall, the other short, had let him into the Fairfield Rest Home. Were they the same two? It was possible. Probable in fact. Peck had almost lost all suspicions regarding the psychic investigator now. He was involved all right, but only as a potential victim, of that the detective was sure. Whoever – whatever – was behind all this was trying to get at Bishop. Why? Who the hell knew? None of it made any sense.

It had been fortunate for Bishop that Peck had ordered an obo on him. The two officers on observation duty that night had followed him to the mental home, then gone in to bring him to Kulek's house as instructed over the car radio. They had found the patients trying to drown Bishop in a bathtub. It was a good thing that the two detectives had been armed – Peck had suspected Bishop of murder at that time and was taking no chances with the lives of his own men. Without firearms, they would never have fought off the berserk residents. His men had also seen the two women at the mental home who had set light to the staircase. The home had been razed to the ground, burning almost half the patients to death, and Bishop – poor bastard – had lost his wife in the fire.

All the nursing staff had been killed, whether in the fire or before it, no one would ever know – Bishop and the two detectives had seen several staff members already dead before the fire had struck. Some of the patients had leapt from the same window Bishop and Peck's men had escaped through, and had run off into the night to be picked up later by patrol cars; others had managed to use the fire escape on the other side of the building and these, too, had been found wandering the streets later that night. But a few had disappeared completely, the body count of those living and dead carried out the following day failing to tally with the known number of residents and staff.

Peck scratched the bottom of his nose with his thumb. He briefly wondered if he should recommend that a general alert be put out, to warn the public of the menace that was roaming the streets, then discarded the thought. Why be accused of over-reacting when it was up to the boys upstairs to make such drastic

508

decisions? Besides, the trouble was still confined to an area south of the river. No point in causing panic in the rest of the city. No, he would just hand in his report and let his superiors get on with it. The only thing was, he thought, studying green pins on the large map of London he had stuck to his office wall board, the trouble was growing outwards, the pins spreading from the centre like a green starburst. Each pin indicated a fresh incident, the common denominator being that they had happened at night and that there was some kind of evil lunacy involved. What was it Kulek had said about rainspots on a window? It did seem to be gathering momentum.

The police cells and hospital wards were full of people who had had to be taken into custody for their own protection. Not all had committed acts of violence, but every one of them had that same brainless appearance. There had to be several hundred people being held at that moment, most of them part of the football crowd. The football match incident had been put down to crowd hysteria. Crowd hysteria! Jesus, the understatement of all time. Fortunately, it had been regarded as a single major phenomenon by the public and the authorities had played down the other comparatively 'minor' incidents, never once suggesting and always refuting any connection between them. The condition of those held seemed to be deteriorating rapidly, the first ones taken into custody having become nothing more than empty shells. Dozens, particularly those from Willow Road, had somehow managed to take their own lives, for there was no way such vast numbers could be watched all the time. Many were being fed intravenously, all will to live seemingly gone. Zombies, that was the word Bishop had used when he had spoken with him earlier that week. It was a good word. Apt. That's just what they were. Many shuffled around all day, some murmuring, others silent and immobile, lost within themselves. The medics were baffled. They said it was as if part of their brains had decided to close down, the part that controlled motivation. They had a fancy name for it, but however it was termed it amounted to the same thing: they were zombies. Only one thing seemed to stir them, one thing that had them all staring at the windows of their wards, rooms or cells: the coming of night. They all welcomed the darkness. And that worried Peck more than anything, because it gave substance to Kulek's theory.

The other matter that concerned Peck almost as much was the

fact that over seven hundred people had been reported missing, most of them part of the crowd that had run amok at the football match. His chair scraped noisily against the floor as he pushed it back. He straightened his tie and began to roll down his sleeves as he walked to the window once more. He dragged on the cigarette, deep, sharp breaths, wanting to finish it before he went to see the Deputy Commissioner. *Seven hundred*! He gazed down at the slow-moving traffic once more. Where the hell could seven hundred people disappear to?

'Gorn, out of it!' Duff aimed part of a crumbled brick at the creature caught in the beam from the lamp fastened to his safety helmet. The rat scuttled from the narrow ledge running alongside the sewer channel and plopped into the foul-smelling water. It vanished into the darkness ahead.

Duff turned to his companions and said, 'Watch yourselves along here. It's part of the old network – bit dodgy.'

The man immediately behind him wrinkled his nose against the heavy nitrous smell in the sewer, cursing the bright spark at the GLC who had thought up this unpleasant little assignment for him. There was a growing concern over the decaying state of the major cities' sewer networks and inspections were being hurriedly carried out to see if what was happening in Manchester could happen elsewhere. Huge holes had appeared in the busy roads in the northern town, holes big enough for a bus to drop through, caused by the collapse of the underground walls. The danger had been coming for years, but it was something out of the public eye and therefore something that could be put off to a later date. Now the worry was that it would soon be very much in the eyes of the public as cracks and holes appeared in the streets; in their noses too, as the stench wafted upwards. Berkeley, the lucky man in his department chosen to study this section of London's sewer network, shivered in the damp air and had visions of the whole city collapsing inwards into the slimy catacombs beneath. So long as he wasn't down here when it happened he didn't give a damn.

'All right, Mr Berkeley?'

He shielded his eyes against the glare of Duff's headlamp. 'Yes, let's get on with it. You say there's a section ahead that's particularly bad?'

'Last time I had a look at it. That was about two years ago.'

510

Wonderful, Berkeley thought. 'Lead on,' he said.

There were three men in the inspection team: Charlie Duff, senior repairs foreman for the water authority, Geoffrey Berkeley from the ministry, Terry Colt, assistant to the foreman. They were forced to stoop as they moved along the old tunnel and Berkeley tried to touch the fungus-covered walls as little as possible. His foot slipped at one stage and his leg disappeared up to the knee into the murky waters flowing beside them.

Terry Colt grinned and reached down to grasp the man's elbow, saying jovially, 'Slippery, innit?'

'Be all right in a minute, Mr Berkeley,' Duff said, also grinning. 'Tunnel widens out up ahead. Just have a look at this brickwork.'

He reached up and prodded the ceiling with a spiked metal bar he always carried when inspecting the sewers. Loose cement and brickwork crumbled away and plopped down into the centre channel.

'I see what you mean,' said Berkeley, shining his torch upwards. 'Doesn't look too good, does it?'

Duff grunted his reply and moved further along, poking the ceiling as he went. Suddenly a small section of brickwork came away completely causing Berkeley to cry out in alarm.

Duff merely stared up at the damage, shaking his head and mumbling to himself at the same time.

'I suggest you are less forceful with your probing, Duff,' Berkeley said, his heart pounding wildly. This job was unpleasant enough without adding danger to it. 'We don't want the whole roof down on top of us, do we?'

Duff was still grumbling to himself, his torch beam weaving from side to side as he shook his head. 'All these old tunnels are the same, you know,' he finally said to Berkeley. 'It's gonna cost millions to put them right. Solid enough when they were built, but all that traffic up there over the years, all those bleedin juggernauts, all those buildings goin up . . . People who built these never dreamed they'd have to bear such a load. Never thought they'd have to carry so much shit, either.'

Berkeley wiped his slime covered hands on his overalls. 'Fortunately, that's not my problem. I only have to submit a report.'

'Oh yeah?' said Terry from behind. 'An who d'you think pays for it, then? Only comes out of our pockets, dunnit?'

'Shall we move on? It's rather uncomfortable crouching like

511

this.' Berkeley was anxious to get the inspection over with.

Duff turned and made his way further down the tunnel, keeping his experienced eye on the ceiling, looking for breaks and signs of sagging. He saw plenty.

His assistant's voice came from the rear. 'D'you know what? If you got lost down here on your own, Mr Berkeley, you could wander around for years and never find your way out.'

Silly sod, Duff thought, but grinned to himself all the same.

'There's miles and miles of tunnels,' Terry went on. 'You could get from one end of London to the other.'

'Surely you would have to stop at the Thames?' came Berkeley's acid-toned comment.

'Oh yeah, if you could find it,' Terry answered, unabashed. 'You could drown before you did, though. You should see some of these tunnels after heavy rainfall. Some of em fill right up. Just think of it, wanderin around down here, your lamp battery runnin down, things scuttlin around in the dark. I think the rats'd get you in the end. Some big bleeders down here.'

'All right, Terry, leave it out,' said Duff, still grinning. 'It's gettin wider up here, Mr Berkeley. we'll be able to stand up soon.'

Berkeley wasn't bothered about Terry's remarks – he knew the idiot was only trying to intimidate him – but he could not help being afraid of the tunnels themselves. He felt a huge pressure bearing down on him, as though the city above were slowly sinking, pressing down on the tunnel roofs, compressing them, squeezing them flat, inch by inch. He would be forced into the slime flowing beneath him, the ceiling pushing him underneath, holding him there until he had to swallow, the filthy waters gushing down his throat, filling him . . .

'There you go!' Terry had spotted the opening ahead where their tunnel joined another.

Berkeley was grateful to step through into it and stand erect. This branch of the sewer network must have measured at least twelve feet across and the domed ceiling was high at its apex. The causeways on each side of the channel were wide enough to walk along comfortably.

'This looks fairly sound,' he commented, his voice ringing out hollowly against the damp curved walls.

'Should be all right along this stretch,' said Duff. 'It's the pipes and small conduits that give us the most problems – you'd

512

never believe just what they get blocked up with.'

'No, I meant the brickwork here. It seems solid enough.'

Duff took the lamp from his helmet and flashed it down the tunnel, searching walls and ceiling for breaks. 'Looks okay. There's a storm weir further down. Let's just have a look at it.'

By now, Berkeley had lost all sense of direction, not knowing whether they were heading north, south, east or west. The foreman's assistant was right: it would be easy to get lost in the maze of tunnels. He heard Duff poking at the walls with his metal pike and briefly wondered what would make a man take up this kind of work for a career. Career? Wrong word. His kind didn't have careers – they had jobs. And the young man behind – surely working in a garage or a factory was better than creeping around in the dark among the city's filth. Still, Berkeley reflected, thank God someone was stupid enough to do it. He peered into smaller openings leading into the main channel as he passed, shuddering at the total blackness they presented, his beam seeming to penetrate very little of their length. He imagined one of the huge rats the foreman's assistant had spoken of lurking there, waiting to pounce on any unfortunate who would unknowingly wander into its lair. Or a giant spider, huge and malformed, glutted on the slivering dark life all around, never before seen by human eyes, its web strung completely across a tunnel, waiting for an unsuspecting victim . . . Or a giant slug, blind and slimy, sucking itself to the lichen-covered walls, living in perpetual darkness, greedy for the next human feast . . .

'Oh my God!'

Duff swung around at the sound of Berkeley's shriek. 'What is it?' he asked, his voice a little higher-pitched than he'd intended.

The ministry man was pointing into a tunnel. 'Something moved in there!' His hand was trembling uncontrollably.

Duff lumbered back to him thinking, *silly sod*, and peered into the opening.

'You probably saw a rat,' he said reassuringly. 'Lots of em down here.'

'No, no, it was much bigger.'

'Trick of the light, probably all it was. It's the imagination that does it, every time. Takes a while to get used to things down here.'

Terry was peering over Berkeley's shoulder into the opening, a big smile on his face. 'They say the sewers are haunted by murder

513

victims whose bodies've been dropped into them to get rid of the evidence,' he brightly informed the ministry man.

'Hold your noise, Terry,' Duff told him, 'You'll be givin me the bleedin creeps next. Look, Mr Berkeley, there's nothing down there.' The combined lights from their lamps forced back the darkness in the tunnel, revealing nothing but green-and-yellow-streaked walls. 'It must have just been your light throwin a shadow as you passed. Nothin to worry about.'

'I'm sorry. I'm sure . . .'

Duff had already turned away and was marching onwards, whistling tunelessly to himself. With a last look into the tunnel, Berkeley followed, feeling foolish, but none-the-less, still nervous. Stinking bloody job to send him on!

As Terry moved away from the opening he thought – just thought – he heard a sound from its depths. 'Frightened me bloody self now,' he muttered under his breath.

Berkeley was hurrying to catch up with Duff, finding a small comfort in the man's no-nonsense, down-to-earth attitude, when the foreman came to an abrupt stop, causing the ministry man to bump into him. Duff was pointing his lamp down into the channel at their feet.

'There's something in the water,' he said.

Berkeley looked towards the centre of the wide torch beam. Something was floating lazily along, drifting with the slow-moving current, its progress hindered as it bumped against the raised side of the causeway. It looked like a large sack in the inadequate light.

'What on earth is it?' Berkeley asked curiously.

'It's a body,' said Terry, who had now joined them.

This time Duff knew his assistant wasn't joking. He knelt down on the edge of the causeway and caught the drifting shape with his metal bar as it came close. He pulled and the body turned languidly over in the water. All three men gasped when they saw the white bloated face and wide, staring eyes.

Berkeley found himself bent double against the moist wall, his stomach heaving up and down like a berserk lift. Through his dizziness, he heard Terry say, 'Christ Almighty, there's another one!'

He forced himself to look when he heard a splash. Terry had dropped into the sewer, his thigh-high boots giving him adequate protection against the foul-smelling stream that reached a point

514

just above his knees. He was wading to another floating form on the other side of the channel.

'This one's a woman, I think!' he called back over his shoulder.

'Okay, Terry. Try and lift it on to the causeway,' Duff told him. 'We'll go back and get a team to come down and collect em. Mr Berkeley, give us a hand to pull this one out, will you?'

Berkeley shrank back against the wall. 'I . . . I don't think . . .'

'Would you believe it?' It was Terry's voice again. 'There's another one comin down.'

Duff and Berkeley followed his gaze and saw the shape floating towards them. As it approached they saw it was the body of another woman, a white shape that could have been a nightdress billowing out around her. She was on her back, glazed eyes staring up at the dripping ceiling. Fortunately for Berkeley's stomach, her features did not have the puffiness of the first person they had found.

'Grab her, Terry,' Duff ordered.

The assistant heaved the body he was holding on to the causeway, then waded towards the new one. They watched him as he caught a leg, Duff with his hand grasped around the lapel of the dead man below him, Berkeley wondering at the assistant's lack of nerves. Perhaps the boy was too thick to be bothered.

Terry leaned over the floating woman, his arms going around her waist and reaching to grip her beneath the armpits. What happened next caused the same reaction in both men watching but with different results.

As Terry's head came close to the woman's, two pale-fleshed arms slid from the water and encircled his neck. He screamed as he was pulled down, the scream broken off by a choking gurgling sound as he plunged beneath the water. The oozing fluid became a white-foamed eruption as he struggled to free himself from the deathly grip, but the creature held on to him, dragging him down in her embrace.

Berkeley's mouth dropped open in a soundless scream and he was only dimly aware of the hot excreta that had been jettisoned down his sagging legs. He staggered back against the wall again, the knuckles of both hands filling his open mouth.

Duff's initial shock was instantly followed by a paralysing pain that began in his chest and swiftly travelled up to his neck and arms. A red, blinding mist closed the vision before him and

515

he toppled forward into the water, his heart already given up before he could be drowned.

Berkeley watched as Terry rose from the water just once and he saw the assistant's eyes were staring into the face before him as if in disbelief. The woman hugged him tight, a lover's embrace, and her cracked and bitten lips were smiling. The boy stumbled backwards and the creature fell with him. Berkeley could see the dim glow of his lamp beneath the churning, green slime, but it grew weaker as he watched, the disturbance becoming no more than ripples, the ripples themselves fading after the last confusion of bubbles shot to the surface. Finally the light shrank to nothing.

The water was still.

Until she slowly emerged.

Green slime running from her body.

Looking at him.

Smiling.

Berkeley's shrieks echoed around the dingy caverns, the sound multiplied into a hundred screaming voices. There was more movement further down the tunnel. Figures were stepping from black openings into the main sewer. Others were in the water, wading towards him from the direction in which he and the two workmen had come. He didn't want to look, but he couldn't help himself, the headlamp swinging in a frantic arc towards the approaching figures. A cold, wet hand closed around his ankle.

The woman was standing close to him and he jerked his foot away from the edge of the causeway. Her long damp hair hung like the tails of rats over her face and the white gown she wore was ripped almost down to her pubic area, revealing sagging breasts and a stomach that was strangely distended as though she had not eaten for a long time. He cowered before her in the darkness and wondered if she was dead.

The woman reached for him again and began to clamber on to the causeway.

'No!' He kicked out at her and scrambled away on all fours. 'Leave me alone!'

He staggered to his feet and pushed himself against the wall, scraping lichen off with his back as he moved away. She began to crawl towards him. The others were moving closer.

He fell into an opening behind him and, as he looked for a

516

means of escape, white, shaking hands reached for him from within. He tumbled back into the main tunnel, gasping, whimpering sounds burbling from his lips. He slipped from the causeway and fell headlong into the slow-moving fluid, emerging spluttering and crying, but still running. The water, thick with soilage, clung to his legs as though mud creatures at the bottom were gripping his feet and holding him back. Lifting his knees high, he splashed down the channel, away from the dark figures that followed, away from the woman who held her arms out to hug him. He was conscious of more and more objects bumping into his legs and was afraid to look down, knowing what they were, knowing arms would reach up to drag him down if he did look. The sewer opened up into a huge chamber, the ceiling some thirty or forty feet above him and supported by sturdy iron pillars. The massive weir controlling the flow of water through the sewers stood opposite. But he did not see it. For this was where they were all waiting.

They stood around the edges of the chamber, others in the water itself. More were crammed into the many openings in the circular wall. The water at the bottom of the chamber was full of bodies, several drifting away into various outlets as he watched. His headlamp swung round from face to face and he had the eerie sensation of being in a dark underground cathedral, the black-smeared people choristers awaiting the arrival of the choirmaster. The lamp beam seemed to be growing weaker, the surrounding darkness closing in around it, slowly stifling its brightness. Hundreds of eyes watched him from the shadows and the gaseous fumes from the chamber assailed his nostrils with added force. The stench here was somehow more acrid.

He began to back away from the crowded chamber. But a damp, white hand on his shoulder told him there was nowhere to run.

Chapter Twenty-One *

The cat kept to the shadows, its progress along the rain-freshened street silent and unseen. The rain had stopped, otherwise the cat would still be skulking somewhere under cover. It was an animal that had no owner, one that needed no permanent home; it lived on its own cunning, its own stealth, its own speed. Humans would never pet its kind, nor welcome it into their homes, for it was a scavenger and had the looks of a scavenger. The black fur on its back was sparse, almost bare in places where the cat had come off worse in fights with others of its breed. One ear was just a mangled shape, a stub protruding from its head; the dog that had inflicted the wound could now see only from one eye. Its claws were stunted from too much running on concrete, but were still lethal when fully extended. Its pads were hard, like tough leather. The cat sniffed the damp night air and its eyes, caught in the dull glow of an overhead streetlight, were glassy yellow.

It turned into an alleyway and padded towards the dustbins hidden there in the dark doorways. The scent of other night creatures was strong in its nose. The cat recognised most of the individual smells, some friendly, others producing a new sharpness to its already acute senses. The furtive, sharp-nosed, long-tailed creatures had been here, a cowardly enemy that would always choose to run rather than fight. They were gone now. Its own kind had been there earlier, but they, too were gone.

The cat sniffed its way through the litter on the ground, then leapt on top of a dustbin, disappointed that its lid was sealed tight. The lid of the next dustbin was at a slight angle and the smell of corrupting food wafted through the narrow, new-moon gap. The cat poked its nose inquisitively into the opening, poking a paw through to tug at the loose paper and rubble at the top. The lid moved a little under the cat's insistent probing, then even more when the creature pushed first its head then its shoulders through the widening gap. The metal lid finally slid gratingly across the rim of the dustbin and landed with a loud clatter on the ground. The cat fled, alarmed by the noise of its own making.

It paused at the entrance to the alley, its one good ear pricked for unfriendly sounds, nose held high and twitching for hostile scents. The animal stiffened when it detected the slight acrid smell in the air and the sparse hairs on its back began to bristle. As its fellow creatures had been only minutes before, the cat became aware of a strange presence that somehow belonged to man, yet wasn't man. It crept over the paralysed cat like a crawling thing, a shadow that mixed with the other shadows. The terrified creature bared its teeth and hissed. Something was moving in the middle of the glistening wet road.

The cat arched its back, every hair on its body stiff and erect, mouth wide in a hissing snarl. It spat its defiance, afraid though it was, and its eyes narrowed, full of venom. The streetlights had dimmed as though a mist had drifted across them and the pavements no longer offered any reflections in their wetness. A heavy, metallic sound came from the road's centre as the manhole cover shuddered, then began to rise. It was pushed higher, one side resting on its base, and something black began to emerge. The cat recognised the shape that came over the edge of the hole. It knew it was a human hand. Yet instinctively, it knew the hand did not belong to a human.

The cat hissed once more, then fled, for some reason heading for the lights rather than the shadows.

The three youths waited in the weather-battered shelter on the common. Two were white, one was black. They puffed on cigarettes and jiggled their knees to keep out the cold.

'I ain't stayin much longer,' the coloured boy said. 'It's too fuckin cold.' His name was Wesley and he was on probation for purse snatching.

'Shut up an wait a minute. Won't be much longer,' said one of his companions. His name was Vincent and he was on probation for half-killing his stepfather.

'I dunno, it's gettin late, Vin,' said the third youth. 'Don't think there'll be no one about.' His name was Ed – his friends thought it was short for Edward but, in fact, it was short for

Edgar – and he had recently finished his villain's apprenticeship in an approved school.

'What you wanna do, then, go ome?' asked Vince of his two friends. 'Got any money for tomorrow night?'

'No, but, I'm fuckin cold,' Wesley told him again.

'You're always fuckin cold. Miss the old Caribbean, eh?'

'Ain't never been there. Born in bloody Brixton, were'n I?'

'Get out of it. In your bloody blood. You all miss your bleedin sunshine. It's what makes your hair curly.'

'Leave im alone, Vin,' said Ed, peering around the edge of the shelter into the gloom. 'He's joinin the Front, inne?'

'Do me a favour! They won't have im! He's a nig-nog imself.'

'Yeah, but I don't want no more of them comin over ere. Specially those Pakis,' Wesley protested. 'Too bloody many.'

The other two youths shrieked with glee. The thought of Wesley marching along with the National Front holding a banner saying 'KEEP BRITAIN WHITE' was too much. Wesley was too puzzled by their laughter to feel aggrieved. Soon he was laughing with them.

'Ang on, ang on,' Ed said suddenly. 'I think there's someone comin.'

'Right. Down to you Ed,' said Vin, springing to his feet. 'Me an Wes'll be over there in the bushes.'

'Why always me?' Ed protested. 'You av a go.'

Vince patted him on the cheek, the last pat a little more forceful than the rest. 'You're so pretty, that's why. They like you more than us. Think you're one of them, don't they?'

Not for the first time, Ed cursed his own blond good looks. He would much rather have had Vince's tough, pock-marked features and short ginger hair than his own almost girlish looks. 'What about Wes, then?'

'Nah, they don't trust coloureds, do they? Think they're all fuckin muggers.' He gave his black friend a playful shove. 'Right, innit, Wes?'

Wes grinned in the dark. 'They's fockin right, man,' he said, mimicking his own father's accent.

Vince and Wesley ran quietly from the shelter, both sniggering and prodding each other as they went. Ed waited silently, taking a last drag from his cigarette and listening for the approaching footsteps. The common was a favourite haunt for clandestine lovers of all varieties, that variety having increased since the surrounding working-class area had been infiltrated by middle-class residents. The cost of travelling every day from the surrounding suburbs to their jobs in London had become too much for the *nouveau-pauvre*. The area that had become multi-racial over the years was now fast-becoming multi-class. Ed threw the half-inch butt on to the ground, then took another loose cigarette from the pocket of his denim jacket. He was about to step from the shelter into view when he realised there were two sets of footfalls. He slunk back into the shadows.

The couple walked past the shelter, arms tight around each other's waists; Ed was worried that they were going to make use of his hideaway for their own purposes, but when they moved on he realised the stink of stale urine in the shelter would put any lovers off, no matter how desperate. He cursed under his breath and dug his hands deep into his pockets. There'll be no gingers about now, not this late, he told himself. Yet he knew from previous experience that the lateness of the hour meant nothing to certain lonely men, nor did the remoteness of the locations they wandered through. Sometimes Ed wondered if they went out of their way to be attacked. Maybe they enjoyed it. Or maybe it was their own subconscious way of punishing themselves for what they were. The last, deeper thought was immediately dismissed by one more obvious to Ed's way of thinking; maybe they just got more horny at night.

He looked out into the darkness towards the spot where Vince and Wes had disappeared. The feeble glow from a nearby lamppost did little to pierce the shadows. He was about to call out to them, imagining them both giggling and playing around in the dark, when he heard more footsteps. Ed listened, making sure they belonged to one person. They did. The man came into view seconds later.

He was slightly built, about Ed's size. A heavy belted overcoat hung loosely on him, emphasising his narrow shoulders rather than compensating for them. Definite pouf, Ed told himself, not sure if he was pleased or displeased with their luck. He knew these men were easy pickings, that there was little danger from them; but something inside always made him scared of them. Perhaps that was why in the end he always used more violence against them than his companions did. The memory of when he had decided to tackle one on his own was still fresh in his mind for, instead of attacking his intended victim and relieving him of

521

his wallet, he had let himself be used, then run off sobbing before he could even be paid. The shame of it still stung his face, and he knew his skin had become bright red in the darkness. If Vince and Wes ever found out . . .

'Got a light, John?' Ed had pushed all further thoughts away and stepped on to the pathway leading across the common.

The man came to an abrupt halt and glanced around nervously. The boy looked all right, but was he really alone? Should he walk on or . . . should he take a chance?

He took out his own cigarettes. 'Would you like one of mine?' he asked. 'They're tipped.'

'Oh, yeah. Thanks.' Ed stuck his battered cigarette back into his pocket and reached towards the proffered pack, hoping the man hadn't noticed his hand was shaking slightly.

'You can have the pack, if you like,' the man said, his face serious.

My Gawd, a right one ere, Ed thought. 'Oh, great, thanks a lot.' He pushed the pack into another pocket.

The man studied the boy's face in the glow from the cigarette-lighter. It became indistinct when he drew back, his cigarette lit. The man snapped out the small flame.

'It's rather cold tonight, isn't it,' he said cautiously. The boy was attractive in a rough sort of way. Was he genuine or just a tart? Either way, he'd want money.

'Yeah, bit nippy. Just out for a walk?'

'Yes, it's nicer when it's quiet, I hate crowds, I feel I can breathe at night.'

'It'll cost you a fiver.'

The man was slightly taken aback by the boy's sudden bluntness. He *was* a tart.

'Back at my place?' he asked, the excitement that had been triggered off at the boy's approach now accelerating.

Ed shook his head. 'No, no, it'll ave to be ere.'

'I'll pay you more.'

'No, I ain't got time. Got to be ome soon.'

The boy seemed a little afraid and the man decided not to push his luck.

'All right. Let's find somewhere nice.'

'Over there'll do.' The boy pointed towards a clump of bushes and trees and this time it was the man's turn to become a little nervous. It was so dark over there: the boy could have friends waiting.

522

'Let's go behind the shelter,' he suggested quickly.

'No, I don't think . . .'

But the man now had a surprisingly firm grip around Ed's shoulders. The boy allowed himself to be propelled towards the back of the wooden shelter, hoping his friends were watching. It would be just like those two bastards to leave it till the last minute.

They squelched through the mud at the side of the hut, the man warding off bushes that threatened to scratch their faces. They turned a corner and Ed found himself pressed against the back of the hut. The man's face was looming larger in front of him, his lips only inches away, and Ed felt the revulsion rising in him. Fumbling fingers pulled at the zip of his jeans.

'No,' he said, turning his head to one side.

'Come on. Don't be coy. You want it as much as me.'

'Fuck off!' Ed screamed and pushed at the man's chest. His face had grown red-hot again and his vision had become blurred with sudden tears of rage.

The man was startled. He staggered back and stared at the youth. He began to say something but the boy rushed at him, lashing out wildly with his fists.

'Stop it, stop it!' the man screamed, falling backwards. Ed began to kick him.

'You dirty fuckin queer!'

The man tried to rise, whimpering with fright now. He had to get away, the boy was going to hurt him. And the police might hear the disturbance.

'Leave me alone! Take my money!' The man managed to reach his inside pocket. He threw his wallet at his attacker. 'Take it, take it, you bastard! Just leave me alone!'

Ed ignored the wallet and continued to rain punches and kicks down at the curled form at his feet until his arms and legs grew heavy and his anger began to subside. He stumbled back against the shelter's wall and stood there leaning on it, chest heaving and legs weak. He could hear the injured man crying out but, for some reason, he could no longer see him lying there on the ground. The night darkness had somehow become more dense.

'Vin! Wes!' he called out when he had recovered enough breath. 'Where are you, for fuck's sake?'

'Ere we are, Ed.'

The youth jumped at the close proximity of their voices. It was almost as if they were inside his head. He could just see their dark outlines as they stood at the corner of the shelter.

'You took your time, you bastards. I ad to deck im on me own. Let's get is money and split.'

'Nah, I don't think so, Ed.' It was Vince's voice. 'Let's av some fun first.' He heard Wesley giggle.

This is stupid, Ed thought. It'd be better to get away . . . but it would be nice to do something to this cunt . . . something nasty . . . he was helpless . . . there was no one around . . . something that would hurt him . . . something . . .

There were other voices inside his head now, not just his own. Something was creeping along corridors in his mind, cold fingers that probed and searched, fingers that spoke to him and laughed with him. And he was leading them on, guiding them. The coldness was all-enveloping as it suddenly lunged and caught him in its icy grip, and he was pleased to receive it, the shock turning into pleasure like the swift effect of an anaesthetising injection. He wasn't alone anymore. The voices were with him and they told him what to do.

Vince and Wes had already begun and the damp earth that was being pushed into the struggling man's mouth stifled any screams.

The filling station stood at the edge of the common, an oasis of light in the surrounding darkness. The yellow Ford Escort pulled into the forecourt and came to a smooth halt before a petrol pump. The driver turned off the engine and settled back to wait for the attendant to emerge from his office. The car's occupants did not know that the man on duty, who was, in fact, the garage manager, had popped round to the back of the building twenty minutes earlier to lock up the toilets there; he didn't want any lingering customers at that time of night. Regretfully, he had had to let his usual attendant leave earlier; the man was obviously coming down with a bad attack of flu and the manager wasn't taking the risk of catching it himself. His profit margin was small enough without his being off sick and leaving the staff to run the garage. He'd go broke within a week with their fiddles. It was normally bad policy to man a garage alone at night, for it made the station an easy mark for villains; but tonight he had no choice. He kept the door of the office overlooking the forecourt permanently locked and scrutinised every customer that came in for petrol before unlocking it. If he didn't like the look of them, he turned the OPEN sign around to CLOSED and ignored their muffled curses. It had been well after twelve when he remembered the toilets were still unlocked.

'You sure it's open, George?' the woman next to the driver said testily. 'There doesn't seem to be anyone around.'

'It says "open" at the entrance,' her husband replied. 'And look, on the cashier's door. There's another "open" sign.'

'I should give him a toot, George,' said the driver's father-in-law from the back seat.

'I'll give him a minute. He might be round the back.' There was nothing pushy about George.

His wife, Olwen, pulled the hem of her flouncy, sequined dress into a tight bunch over her knees, afraid the chiffon and layers of netting would pick up dirt from the car's interior. A large polythene bag was draped over the passenger seat to protect her meticulously made ballroom frock and fur shoulder-cape from any hidden grime. Her high coiffured hair brushed against the car roof as she stared through the windscreen, her mouth set in a firm, straight line.

'We should have won,' she announced grimly.

'Now, Olwen,' George said patiently, 'Nigel and Barbara were very good.'

'That's right, defend them. I suppose it doesn't matter that they bumped us twice on the dance floor. Never even apologised afterwards. You'd have thought there was no one else in the ballroom the way they pranced around. We should have objected. Bloody judges should have spotted it.'

'Well, we were runners-up, dear.'

'Runners-up! That's the story of your life, isn't it, George? That's all you'll ever be.'

'There's no call for that kind of talk,' Olwen's father rebuked.

'Shut up, Huw,' said Olwen's mother who sat cramped in the back with her husband. 'Olwen's quite right. She could have been ballroom champion by now, that girl.' She did not add, 'with a different partner'. There was no need to.

'Take no notice, George,' Huw said. 'Neither of them are ever satisfied.'

'Satisfied? What have I got to be satisfied with? What have you ever given me?'

'I'll give you the back of my hand in a minute.'

'Dad, don't speak to mother like that.'

'I'll speak to her however I . . .'

'You certainly won't. You see what he's like, Olwen? You see what I've had to put up with all these years?'

'Put up with? I've had your nagging . . .'

'Nagging?'

'Mum doesn't nag.'

'She nags all the time. Same way you nag poor old George.'

'Me nag George? I never nag George. Do I ever nag you George?'

'The attendant's a long time,' said George.

'Well bib him.' Exasperated, Olwen reached across George and thumped the car's horn. 'Lazy bleeder's probably sleeping under the counter.'

George ran his finger and thumb along his thin pencil-line moustache, smoothing down the Brylcreemed hairs, and briefly wondered what would happen if he punched Olwen on the nose. She'd punch him back, that's what would happen. And she could punch harder.

'Ah, here he comes,' he said, pointing to the figure that had emerged from the darkness at the rear of the garage.

'It's about bloody time,' said Olwen.

'Don't swear, dear, it's not very nice.'

'I'll swear if I like.'

'George is right, Olwen,' said her father. 'It's not very lady-like.'

'Leave her alone, Huw,' said her mother. 'She's had a lot of stress this evening. George didn't help by letting her fall on her bottom in the *pas redoublé*.'

'Best part of the bloody evening,' her father remarked, smiling at the memory.

'Dad!'

'Take no notice, Olwen. It's just like him to enjoy seeing his own daughter make a fool of herself.'

'Mum!'

'Oh, I didn't mean . . .'

'Five of 3-star, please.' George had wound down his window and was calling out to the approaching figure.

The man came to a halt, smiled at the occupants of the car, and looked over towards the petrol pumps. He made towards them.

'He's slow enough, isn't he?' remarked Olwen's mother. 'And what's he got that silly grin on his face for?'

'Look at the state of him,' said Olwen. 'You'd think he'd been

526

down the mines. I wonder if the manager knows his staff walk around like that?'

'Perhaps he is the manager,' said her father, chuckling in the back, not knowing that the manager lay dead on the floor of the toilets, his skull cracked open like an egg from the repeated blows of a brick.

They watched the man as he lifted the dispensing nozzle from the rack set in the pumping unit. He came towards the car holding the hosecock alongside his head like a duelling pistol. His eyes were half-closed as though they had not yet adjusted to the contrast between the harsh overhead lighting and the darkness from which he had just emerged. He grinned at the four people watching him from the car.

'Silly bugger,' Olwen remarked.

George poked his head out of the window. 'Er, no, old chap. I did say 3-star. You've still got it switched to 4-star.' He drew back quickly when he found himself staring into the black hole of the dispensing nozzle.

In the back of the Escort, Olwen's father had a puzzled frown on his face. He had seen movement in the fringes of darkness around the service area. There were shapes moving closer. They were stepping into the lighted area, then stopping. They were waiting. Watching. Others stood behind them, still in the shadows. What the hell was going on? Why were they staring at the car? He turned to say something but stopped himself when he saw the metal nozzle from the petrol pump stretching into the car window and George, a startled expression on his face, leaning away from it. Olwen's father could only watch in dumbstruck amazement as the index finger on the hand holding the nozzle began to tighten.

The petrol gushed out, covering George's head and shoulders in a filmy fluid. Olwen began to scream when the nozzle was aimed down into her husband's lap. Her father tried to push forward and grab the long barrel of the hosecock, but it was turned in his direction and he fell back, choking on the petrol that had poured into his open mouth. Olwen's mother was screaming now, knowing she and her husband were trapped and helpless in the back of the two-door vehicle.

Olwen's screams became even louder as her dress was suddenly splashed by the foul-smelling liquid. She tried to reach for the door-handle on her side, but her fingers slid from the petrol-soaked metal.

527

Her father, still choking on the fuel he had swallowed, could only watch in horror as the nozzle waved around, the petrol pouring out in a solid stream and filling the car with its noxious fumes and deadly liquid. George was striking out blindly, his eyes stinging and useless. Olwen's hands were covering her face as she cried out and beat her feet against the car's floor. Her mother was trying to burrow her way down into the gap between the back of the driver's seat and her own. The flow of petrol abruptly stopped and the nozzle was withdrawn.

Olwen's father could only observe the middle portion of the man through the windows; it was enough to see him drop the nozzle and reach into his jacket pocket for something. Huw began to moan when he saw the box of matches, the sudden bright flare as one was lit, the small arc of smoke as the match was tossed into the car.

The man stood back as the Escort's interior burst into a blinding cauldron of flame, his face peeling instantly as the fire licked out at him. He did not seem to feel the pain as he reached down for the hose at his feet and drew the dispensing nozzle towards himself. His fingers curled around the trigger and squeezed.

He walked around the forecourt as far as the hose could allow, splashing petrol everywhere, becoming saturated himself, but seeming not to care. Then he turned back towards the little yellow car that had by now become a raging inferno, the sounds of its occupants no longer heard, and he aimed the jet of fuel at it. The flames rushed towards him and he stood there and screamed as he became a black charred shape. His companions turned away from the heat and light, sinking into the darkness that was iself forced back when the filling station exploded into a huge ball of fire that rose hundreds of feet into the air and lit the night sky.

The Dark drifted on, an evil, creeping blackness that had no substance, yet was full of invisible energy, an expanding shadow that existed only in other shadows, an incorporeal thing that sucked at human minds, invading and searching for the hidden repressed impulses that were of itself. There were solid, dark shapes within it and these were the forms of men and women whose will it did not just govern, but who embodied the material part of it, those who physically enacted the evil that it was, its earthly force. It had a smell, a faint acridity that tainted the air it filled, a bitter aroma that men were aware of when lightning struck the ground, or when electric cables discharged sparks into the air. It was a dark stain on the night.

The blaze was left far behind with the wailing sirens and distant shouts, and the Dark relished the blackness it crept into, its edges probing like tentacles at the shadows before it, sensing a fresh force that was somewhere near, a huge source of energy that was as yet untapped, a chained gathering of dark minds that was the very substance it needed.

It seeped across the grassland on to an open road, shying away from the orange-glowing streetlights, surging around them like a stream around rocks projecting from its bed. The shadowy figures drifted with it, several collapsing, their bodies drained, lack of food or water finally bringing them down like machines not fuelled or oiled. Some died – the others would follow later – and as they did, a part of them was released: the darkness within them was welcomed by the mass.

The long wall loomed up high and the darkness flowed over it, leaving the men and women who walked with it below, helpless and suddenly afraid. It rushed towards the sleeping inmates of Wandsworth Prison, creeping into the openings, pouncing and absorbing, the recumbent minds receptive and eager. Not all though. But these did not last long.

Chapter Twenty-Two

The ringing phone woke Bishop from a deep sleep. It was strange, but since Lynn's death two weeks before, his recurrent drowning nightmare had left him. Perhaps it had been purged from him by the experience in the mental home that night, living out the dream, almost taking it to death's conclusion. He pushed back the covers and switched on the bedside lamp. The small alarm clock told him it was just after two o'clock. Alertness spread through him as he heaved himself from the bed and padded down the carpeted stairs to the hall. He grabbed the phone.

'Bishop? Detective Chief Inspector Peck here.'

'What's wrong?' All drowsiness had completely left Bishop now.

Peck's voice was urgent. 'I haven't got long, so just listen and do as I tell you.'

Something knotted inside Bishop's stomach.

'I want you to lock your doors, front and back,' Peck went on. 'Check all your windows, make sure they're locked, too.'

'What's going on, Peck?'

'Have you got a room you can lock yourself into?'

'Yes, but . . .'

'Then do it. Barricade yourself in.'

'What the hell are you talking about?'

'Look, I haven't got time to explain. All I can tell you is that something is going on near your part of London. Our Information Room is being flooded with emergency calls. Our biggest problem is a riot in Wandsworth Prison.'

'Jesus. Can they break out?'

'It looks like they already have.' There was a short pause at the other end of the line. 'It seems some of the prison warders themselves may have been involved. To make matters more confused, a garage on the other side of the Common has been blown up.'

'Peck, has all this got something to do with the Pryszlak business?'

'God only knows. If it has, some of these maniacs may come after you. That's why I want you to lock yourself in. I'm afraid I haven't got enough men available to send you any protection. I could be wrong anyway.'

'Thanks for the warning. Have you told Kulek and Jessica?'

'I still have a man watching their house. I've sent a radio message telling him to inform Kulek of what's happening. I've let the guard stay there, even though we can't really spare him. Unfortunately, the officer keeping an eye on you had to be called in – that's why I'm ringing you. You'll be okay if you do as I say.'

'All right. Just tell me one thing. Do you now believe Jacob Kulek's theory?'

'Do you?'

'I'm beginning to more and more.'

'Well, maybe I am too. I don't *understand* it, but there's nothing else to explain what's going on. The thing is to convince my governors. I've got to get back now. You just sit tight, understand?'

The receiver was replaced before Bishop could answer. He quickly checked the front door to make sure it was bolted as well as locked, then went out to the back. The kitchen door leading to his tiny rear garden was also locked. Next, check the windows, he thought, but instead he decided to first ring Jessica; even with police protection she was probably scared to death. He had seen her only twice since Lynn's death: once when she had come to his house after learning about the tragedy in the mental home, and then a couple of days later, at a meeting held by Peck and several of his superiors, including the deputy commissioner. Since then she had left him alone and he was grateful that she realised he needed time to get over the shock of losing Lynn, this time permanently. It disturbed him that rather than feel remorse, he felt anger at his wife's death. To him, she had begun to die years before, a long, lingering illness of the mind from which he somehow knew she would never recover; it was the manner of her death that angered him. She had been used, controlled by an unknown power along with the others at the home. Her death had been horrible, although mercifully quick, and he wanted it avenged. If Pryszlak was in some bizarre way involved, then he,

Bishop, would find a way to strike back. There had to be a way.

He dialled Jessica's number, hoping she would still be awake after the policeman's message. It was several long moments before the receiver was lifted and Jessica's voice came through.

'Jessica, it's me, Chris.'

Her tone became alert as had his only minutes before when Peck had called him.

'Chris, what is it? Are you all right?'

'Didn't you get Peck's message?'

'No, what message? It's the middle of the night, Chris. We've been asleep.'

'But there's a policeman on guard outside. Hasn't he told you?'

'Nobody's told us anything. What on earth's going on? Tell me what's happened.'

Bishop was puzzled. 'Peck rang me a few moments ago. He said he'd got a message to you. There are more incidents being reported, Jessica. All on this side of the river, it seems.'

'What kind of incidents?' Her voice was calm, but it had an edge to it.

'A riot in Wandsworth Prison. Something else about an explosion in a garage nearby. Others that he didn't have time to tell me about.'

'And he thinks there's a connection . . .?'

'With Pryszlak and his sect? He's not sure, but he felt he ought to warn us, anyway. Jessica, he said they might come after us again if there is a connection.'

'Oh, Chris.'

'Don't worry, you'll be all right. So far, all the trouble is over here. You've got a man outside who will contact his headquarters if anything begins to happen there.'

'But what will you do?'

'I'll barricade myself in, don't worry. We're all probably going to feel embarrassed later when we learn these are entirely separate incidents that have nothing to do with us.'

'I hope . . .' Jessica's voice broke off. 'There's someone at the door now. Our guardian policeman, no doubt. I'd better let him in before he wakes my father – if he isn't already awake, that is.'

'I'm sorry, Jessica. I just wanted to make sure . . .'

'Don't be silly, Chris. I'm glad you rang. Just hold on for a minute while I open the door.'

532

Bishop heard the clunk of the receiver being placed on the small table he remembered the phone rested on in the long hallway. There was silence for a few moments save for the strangely hollow sounding atmospherics in his own earpiece, then he thought he heard the distant noise of the front door being unlocked. For some reason he began to feel uneasy. Why had the detective been so slow in delivering his message? Perhaps he had taken it into his own head not to disturb the sleeping household – what they didn't know couldn't hurt them. After all, the policeman was keeping a watch on the place. The hall light being switched on by Jessica as she answered the phone could have prompted him to change his mind and inform them there and then. Yet Bishop could not imagine any of Peck's men not carrying out his instructions to the letter. He had said he'd told the officer to inform Kulek immediately.

Bishop's hand tightened around the receiver, his knuckles becoming white. 'Jessica, can you hear me?'

He listened and thought he heard approaching footsteps at the other end.

'Jessica?'

A click, then a burring noise as the receiver was dropped on to its cradle at the other end.

Bishop slowed the car as he turned from the main Highgate High Street into the village itself. The drive across London had been swift, for there was little traffic around at that hour, although there had been much activity in the Westminster area as police vehicles and minibus 'pixies' were deployed to deal with the emergencies across the river. Bishop had tried to ring Jessica back, but this time only got an engaged tone. He had also attempted to contact Peck again, but the detective had already left his office. Not sure if he wasn't exaggerating the situation, Bishop left a message and set off for Jacob Kulek's house himself, a little wary as he stepped outside his front door, almost expecting to be attacked. The street was deserted.

He found the narrow lane leading to Kulek's house and headed into it, the car's headlights casting their twin beams far ahead, pushing back the darkness. Small, elegant houses sped by and, because the lane was downhill, he could see the bright glow of the city in the distance. He applied the brakes gently and changed down to a lower gear, sure that Kulek's house lay just ahead in a turn-off to the right. He brought the car to a halt when he saw the vehicle parked opposite the entrance to the house. It was tucked well into the side of the lane, the passenger doors no more than six inches away from a high brick wall that gave privacy to a residence beyond. Bishop pulled in behind and saw that the car appeared to be empty; he wondered if the policeman might be slumped down in the driver's seat – asleep or perhaps dead. He switched off his engine, but left the headlights on. Discarding his driving glasses, he stepped from the car.

The night was cold, but he wondered if the sudden chill he felt was due to something more. He cautiously approached the other vehicle and bent down to peer into a window. It was empty.

Bishop tried the handle and, finding it unlocked, pulled the door open. The radio equipment inside told him he hadn't been mistaken – it *was* a police car. Where was the policeman himself, though? He must have gone into the house. Bishop felt somewhat foolish for having panicked so easily. Yet, with all that had happened recently, he had reason to be a little jumpy. Peck may have told his man to stay inside Kulek's house – it seemed to make sense if Peck's concern for Jessica and her father's safety had suddenly been heightened by that night's events. Why had the phone been put down on him, though? Then he cursed himself, feeling even more foolish. The line had been engaged when he had tried to ring Jessica back – she must have realised she had cut him off, then tried to reach him again! He was behaving like a frightened old woman.

He went back to his own car, switched off the headlights, and strode across the lane towards the driveway leading to Kulek's house. From the entrance he could see a light shining ahead, a long rectangular glow that had to be the glass side-panel that ran the length of the front door. At least, if Jessica and her father were asleep, the policeman would be awake and could let him in. Yet, despite all the rationalisation, his anxiety still persisted. Somewhere inside him he knew things were wrong. If he could have seen the corpse of the policeman, his throat slit from ear to ear, lying in the darkness of the undergrowth only two feet away, Bishop might have turned away from the house.

His feet crunched on the gravel drive as he approached the glass-structured building, its smooth exterior as black as the night around it. The light from the side panel guided him towards the door and he hesitated when he had stepped on to the wide porch area. He was afraid to ring the doorbell.

He did not need to – the door was already opening. The light from behind threw her shape in silhouette, but her voice was strangely familiar to him.

'Welcome again, Mr Bishop. We've been waiting for you,' the tall woman said.

Jacob Kulek and Jessica were in the living-room. Both were seated and dressed in nightclothes. The short woman was holding a knife at the blind man's throat, a long butcher's knife that had dark, reddish stains on its blade. She smiled at Bishop.

'Are you all right, Jessica? Jacob?' asked Bishop, standing in the doorway.

Jessica could barely tear her eyes away from the blade at her father's throat.

'We are all right for the moment, Chris,' the blind man answered. 'Unfortunately, our guard, we are told, has been murdered.'

A gentle push from behind with the small Beretta the tall woman held urged Bishop further into the room.

'Yes, Mr Bishop,' she said. 'You passed the poor policeman on your way in. I must say he was very easy to kill. But then would you suspect Miss Turner there would cut your throat if you didn't know better?'

The smile on the small woman's face broadened. 'The silly man thought I was a helpless old bag who'd had too much to drink.'

'We knew he was there, you see. We, also, have been watching this house all week. Would you please sit down, Mr Bishop? We don't want any more deaths just at the moment, do we? Later, of course, but not just yet.' The tall woman pointed to a place on the settee next to Jessica.

Bishop sat and saw the terror in Jessica's eyes. He took her hand and held it.

'Yes, very touching, Christopher. May I call you Christopher?' It was hard to imagine the tall woman was anything more than a member of the Women's Guild, the type who sold paper flowers on Poppy Day. The small gun in her hand and her next words reminded Bishop just how evil she really was. 'Have you forgotten your wife already, Christopher? Did she mean so little to you?'

535

He began to push himself from the seat, his rage smothering any fear, but Jessica caught his arm.

'No, Chris!' she cried out.

The pleasantness had suddenly left the tall woman's manner. 'Take notice of her. Christopher. She has been told her father will die instantly if there is any trouble from you.'

He sank back, the anger making him tremble.

'That's right,' the tall woman said soothingly, her pleasantness returned. She sat down in a straight-backed chair which stood against the wall, keeping the gun pointed in Bishop's direction. 'You're an interesting man, Christopher. We have been finding out more about you over the past few weeks. I've even read one of your books. In a strange way, your theories are not too distant from Boris Pryszlak's. Nor Jacob Kulek's here, although I gather you care more for explainable science than the unexplainable.'

'May I ask what Pryszlak was to you?' Kulek asked. 'And may I also ask that this knife be taken away. It is rather uncomfortable. Surely the gun that you hold is enough.'

'Yes, Judith, I think you can relax a little now. Why don't you sit on the arm of the chair and keep the knife pressed against Kulek's heart?'

'I don't trust the old man,' the short woman replied. 'I don't trust any of them.'

'No, dear, nor I. But I don't imagine there is much they can do in the short time they have left. I'll keep my gun pointed straight at Mr Bishop's head.'

The short woman grudgingly changed her position and Kulek felt the tip of the knife pressed against his chest a little harder than was necessary to make him aware of its presence.

'Will you now tell us of your relationship with Pryszlak?' he asked, seemingly unaffected.

'Of course. There's no reason why you shouldn't know. Judith and I – my name is Lillian, by the way, Lillian Huscroft – were introduced to Boris many years ago by Dominic Kirkhope. Dominic knew the sort of games Judith and I enjoyed – I could say his knowledge was intimate – and he knew we were reasonably wealthy. Boris needed money at that time for his experiments. He also needed people, people of his own kind. If there was an overall characteristic among the members of his specially chosen group, I suppose you could call it "moral

536

wickedness". We were all evil, you see. But we regarded that as a virtue, not a weakness. A quality held by many, but repressed because of the distorted prejudices so-called civilised society had thrust upon us. We found our freedom with Boris. Every sinful act we committed was a step nearer to our ultimate goal.'

She gave a short laugh and looked mockingly at her three captives. 'The police in this country would be amazed how tidy their files on unsolved crimes would become if we revealed the part many of our members played in them. The hardest crime to solve is the one without apparent motive and I'm afraid our dear law enforcement officers find the concept of evil for the *sake* of evil hard to grasp.'

'I find it somewhat hard to grasp myself,' said Kulek calmly.

'That, if I may say so, is why Boris is a great innovator, while you are merely a mundane theorist. It was a pity you did not accept his offer – you may have become as great as he.'

'You said "is". Are you telling me that Pryszlak is not dead?'

'No one really dies, Jacob.'

'The policeman outside is dead,' Bishop said evenly. 'My wife is dead.'

'Their bodies are discarded shells, that's all. Your wife, I believe, is still very active. As for the policeman – it's up to him how he continues. It will depend on which were the stronger powers within him. I can assure you, the fact that he was a law enforcer does not mean his powers for "goodness" were necessarily the more dominant. Far from it.'

'What the hell are you talking about?'

'She means there are two invisible powers that control the destiny of mankind,' Kulek explained. 'If you were a religious man, you might label them the Powers of Light and the Powers of Darkness. The Bible refers to them often enough. What we've never realised or, if you like, what we've forgotten over the centuries is that they were scientific concepts, not merely religious imagery. It seems Pryszlak did find a way of tapping that power. He used his knowledge of psychism to find the key. Others have achieved it in the past, only we've never recognised the fact. They probably did not fully realise it themselves. Just think of the tyrants, the mass murderers, the *evil* geniuses of the past. How did ordinary men like Adolf Hitler gain such incredible power?'

'Excellent, Jacob,' said the tall woman. 'You really could have been helpful to Boris.'

537

'But what was that key?' Kulek had involuntarily leaned forward and the sharp pain from the knife prick made him move quickly back.

'Don't you know, Jacob? Ah, but of course, you are not a scientist. You know little of the powers of pure energy. Have you any idea of the immense energy in one person's brain? The electrical impulses created by chemical reaction that keeps our bodies functioning throughout our lifetimes? An energy that cannot disappear, cannot dissolve just because our bodies die? An electrical force, Jacob, that can be reached. Its potential is limitless. Have you any concept at all of its collective force?' She laughed again, enjoying the moment, and her companion smiled with her. 'Of course you haven't. None of us has! But we will. Soon!'

'Electrical energy.' Kulek's face had gone deathly white. 'It's not possible. We must be more than that.'

'We are, Jacob. But then energy itself is more than just that. It is a *physical* thing but, you see, we underestimate the term. The paranormal is perfectly normal. We just need to understand it. I believe that is one of your own doctrines.'

'Matters that today we believe are extraordinary will not be so in the future.'

'Yes, scientific progress will see to that. And the momentum of that progression is increasing. Boris was far ahead of us all, and he had the courage to take the final step to give proof of his discovery.'

'By killing himself?'

'By freeing himself.'

'There has to be more to it.'

'Oh there is, and it was very simple. For a man like Boris, that is.'

'Won't you tell us?'

'I think not. You'll find out yourselves soon enough.'

'Why are you holding us here?' said Bishop. 'What are you waiting for?'

'You'll see. It shouldn't be long now.'

'Is it anything to do with the trouble that's going on tonight on the other side of the river?'

'Yes, it is very much to do with it.'

Jessica spoke. 'What is happening there, Chris? You said on the phone there was a prison riot.'

'All I know for sure is that the police are being kept pretty busy – and not just with the riot.'

Kulek sighed heavily and said, 'It's the Dark, isn't it? It's growing more powerful.'

The two women only smiled more meaningfully. 'No more questions,' the tall one said.

Bishop was puzzled. Kulek had just referred to the dark as if it were some special entity, a force on its own. The powers of Darkness, he had said before. Was it possible that the night could harbour such adverse potency? Bishop was confused and he forced himself to push the thoughts away to concentrate on the immediate problem. He felt helpless. If he made a move towards the tall woman Kulek would be stabbed in the heart. If he tried for the short woman, he would himself be shot in the head. Their only chance would be the failure of the policeman to report in – surely he would have to report back to HQ every so often? But then with all the confusion going on over the other side of London it might go unnoticed. Beside him, Jessica trembled and he reached for her hand again.

'Stop,' the tall woman ordered. 'If you move again, I'll kill you.'

Bishop let his hand drop and tried to smile reassuringly at Jessica. 'I think the waiting is making them more nervous than us.'

'Shut your mouth,' the short woman hissed. 'Why don't we kill him now, Lillian? He's not important.'

'We'll wait. But I warn you, Christopher, if you move or speak again, I *will* shoot the girl.'

As the minutes ticked by, the tension in the room began to mount. Bishop noticed the short woman kept glancing over at the dome-covered clock resting on the sideboard and then at her companion, agitation plain on her face.

'There isn't much time,' she finally said.

'Just a little longer. Concentrate, Judith, help me bring it here.'

The tall woman's face became damp with perspiration and occasionally her eyes would half-close, the hand holding the gun wavering slightly. The short woman seemed to be undergoing a similar stress. Bishop tensed his muscles, waiting for the right moment.

Suddenly, the one called Lillian took in a sharp breath and

539

then she was smiling again. 'Can you feel it, Judith? It's coming. It knows.'

'Yes, yes.' The short one had her eyes closed as though in a trance, but the knife was still pressed into Kulek's nightclothes.

The tall woman's expression was almost orgasmic and Bishop shifted his weight forward when her eyelids began to flutter. She knew his intentions, though, for her eyes abruptly became sharply focused on him. 'I'm warning you not to move!' The words were almost spat out.

'No!' Jessica and Bishop looked across at Kulek who had cried out. The blind man's hands were like claws around the sides of the armchair and his neck was stretched upwards, tendons standing out like stiffened rods, eyes gazing sightlessly at the ceiling. 'It's so close.'

The short woman began to laugh, her plump, round shoulders heaving spasmodically. The tall woman rose from her chair and approached Bishop, the gun only inches away from his head.

'Now you'll see,' she said, her breathing jerky, sharp. 'Now you'll see the power.'

He shuddered, the tension in the room reaching a peak, but now a stifling oppression seeming to mingle with it. Short gasps were coming from Jessica and he knew she was terribly afraid. And he, too, felt the same fear.

The figure that appeared in the doorway caused the scream that had been building up inside Jessica to finally break free.

Chapter Twenty-Three

Bishop grabbed the tall woman's wrist and pushed the gun away from his exposed face, at the same time driving his clenched fist hard into her midriff. Her shout became a breathless gasp as she bent double and Bishop wrenched the Beretta from her grasp. He threw her away from him as he rose and turned to face the short woman, who was still staring at the figure in the doorway. She realised Bishop's intentions and drew the knife back to give it added thrust when she plunged it into the blind man's heart. But Kulek was faster: he thrust out and she toppled from the arm of the chair, not falling completely, but unbalanced enough to reach out wildly to save herself from going down. She grasped the back of the armchair and Bishop quickly stepped closer, bringing the pistol butt down on her forehead. She let out a yelp and collapsed on to the floor, helped by Bishop hooking a foot under her knee and jerking it from beneath her. He leaned forward and took the knife away, slapping her with fist and gun as she tried to resist.

Jessica ran to her father and held him. 'I'm all right,' he told her, then turned his face towards the door, knowing someone was there even though he could not see.

Edith Metlock looked pale and frightened. Her eyes went from one figure to the next, confused and unable to take in the situation. She slumped against the doorway, her head shaking from side to side. 'I came to warn you,' she managed to say.

'Edith?' asked Kulek.

'Yes, Father, it's Edith,' Jessica said.

Bishop went to the medium. 'You couldn't have arrived at a better moment.' He took her arm and drew her into the room.

'I came to warn you,' she repeated. 'The door was open.'

'They were expecting someone – or something else.'

From the floor, her mouth still open and desperately sucking in air, the tall woman stared at the medium. Bishop kept a cautious eye on her, ready to use the gun if necessary.

'Edith,' said Kulek, 'what brought you here? How did you know we were being held by those two?'

'I didn't. I came to warn you of the Dark. It's coming for you, Jacob.'

The blind man was on his feet and Jessica led him over to the medium and Bishop. His voice was full of interest rather than fear when he spoke. 'How do you know, Edith?'

Bishop let her down on to the settee and she slumped back as though exhausted. 'Voices, Jacob. There are hundreds of voices. I was at home, asleep. They invaded my dreams.'

'They spoke to you?'

'No, no. They are just there. I can hear them now, Jacob. They are becoming louder, clearer. You must get away from here before it's too late.'

'What are they saying, Edith? Please try to stay calm and tell me exactly what they are saying.'

She leaned forward and clutched at his arm. 'I can't tell you. I hear them, but there are so many. They're so confused. But I hear your name, over and over again. He wants his revenge, Jacob. He wants to show you just what he has achieved. And I think he fears you, too.'

'Ha!' The tall woman was on her knees now, wary of her own gun that was pointed in her direction. 'He fears nothing! He *has* nothing to fear!'

'Pryszlak? Do you mean Pryszlak, Edith?' The blind man spoke more sharply.

'Yes. He's nearly here.'

'I'm going to call the police,' said Bishop.

'They can't help you, fool!' the tall woman's face was twisted into a malicious sneer. 'They can't harm him.'

'She's right,' said the medium. 'Your only chance is to run. That's all anyone can do.'

'I'm calling the police anyway, even if it's only to take these two away.'

'It's too late, don't you see?' The tall woman was rising, her eyes gleaming. 'It's here. It's outside.'

The arm that encircled Bishop's throat from behind was plump and powerful. His body was arched back as the short woman brought her knee up against the base of his spine. One hand was reaching for the knife he held.

Jessica tried to force the little woman away from him, grabbing at her hair and pulling, but it had no other effect than to overbalance the two figures and send them crashing to the floor. Bishop tried to twist himself away from the tenacious woman, unable to break the grip around his throat. He raised his elbow, then swiftly drew it back, feeling it sink into her fatness. He repeated the action, using all his strength, and felt her legs flailing out beneath him. The tightness against his throat began to slacken and he renewed his efforts. He managed to turn his body and, because she would not let go of either his neck or hand, the knife sliced across her plump breasts and blood spurted from them. She screamed.

At last he was able to pull himself free and he turned his head, expecting to see her tall companion bearing down on him. But she was gone.

Hands clawed into his face and his attention was drawn back to the squirming woman beneath him. Her chest was now a mass of red stickiness, yet still she fought on, her lips bared to reveal stained, yellow teeth. The sounds she made were like those of an enraged dog and her eyes were becoming clouded. Her struggles began to weaken as the wound sapped her strength; only her will prevented her from collapsing. He pushed her hands away and staggered to his feet, feeling no pity as he looked down on her, her hands still scrabbling feebly at empty air.

'Chris.' Jessica clung to his arm. 'Let's get away. Let's call the police from somewhere else!'

'It's too late.' Edith Metlock was looking over her shoulder at the glass walls behind. 'It's already here,' she said tonelessly.

Bishop could see their own reflections against the darkness outside. 'What the hell are you talking about?' he found himself shouting. 'There's nothing out there!'

'Chris,' Kulek said quietly. 'Please go and make sure the front door is locked, Jessica, turn on every light in the house, outside lights, too.'

Bishop could only stare wordlessly at him.

'Do as he says, Chris,' Jessica urged.

She ran from the room and he followed. The front door was ajar and before he pushed it closed, Bishop peered out into the night. He could barely see the trees that lined the narrow drive

543

leading to the house. After slamming the door, he pushed home the bolts and turned to see Jessica flicking down all the light switches in the hall. She pushed past him to climb the stairs leading to the rooms on the upper level; Bishop followed.

'In there, Chris!' Jessica pointed at one of the doors leading off the upstairs hall as she disappeared through another. Still puzzled, Bishop obeyed and found himself in a large, L-shaped bedroom. This side of the house overlooked the city and he realised that on any other night, the view would have provided a dazzling display of lights. On this night, though, there was some- thing odd about the shimmering glow. It was as if he were watch- ing it through a moving lacy veil, the lights twinkling and growing faint, then emerging brightly again. It wasn't like fog, for that would have shrouded everything in its rolling grey mist; it was a shifting inky darkness punctured by the brightest of the lights, smothering those more distant, dulling their luminosity.

'Chris?' Jessica had entered the room. 'You haven't turned on the lights.'

He pointed towards the glass wall. 'What is it, Jessica?'

Instead of answering, she flicked down the light switch, then hurried over to a bedside lamp and put that on also. She left the room and he heard other doors opening. Bishop went after her and caught her arm as she emerged from one of the rooms.

'Jessica, you've got to tell me what's going on.'

'Don't you understand? It's the darkness. It's a living entity, Chris. We've got to keep it away.'

'By turning on lights?'

'That's all we can do. Don't you remember how Edith had kept it away that night we found her? She knew by instinct that that was the only way.'

'But how can darkness harm us?'

'It's what it does to people. It seems to prey on weak or evil minds, it somehow makes the badness in them dominant. Can't you see what's been happening? That night at the rest home – don't you see how it used their enfeebled minds.' She saw the pain in his eyes. 'I'm sorry, Chris, but don't you see how it affected Lynn? She wanted to kill you again, and so did all the others. They were being directed, don't you see? Their minds were being used. The same happened at the football match – in Willow Road itself. Pryszlak has found a way to use the evil lying in everybody's subconscious. The stronger that evil, or the

544

weaker the person's mind, the easier it is for . . .'

'Jessica!' Jacob Kulek was calling from the foot of the stairs.

'I'm coming, Father!' She looked earnestly up at Bishop. 'Help us, Chris. We have to try and keep it out.'

He nodded, his mind a jumble of thoughts, everything he'd seen and heard in some crazy way confirming her statement. 'You go down to your father, I'll see to the rest of the lights up here.'

Bishop checked every room, even turning on the bathroom light for, though its two outside walls were part of the rare brick segments of the structure, it had a huge glass skylight in the ceiling. He also twisted a wall spotlight around and directed it towards the skylight. When he finally descended to the ground floor, Jessica had switched on the outside lamps, flooding the grounds with their brightness.

Bishop, Jessica and Kulek stood in the main lounge again, Edith Metlock trying to stem the flow of blood from the injured woman lying on the floor with a white linen towel Jessica had found for her. The wounded woman, Judith, lay still, her eyes staring up at the ceiling and occasionally flicking towards the huge window-wall.

'What now?' Bishop asked.

'We can only wait,' Kulek replied. 'And perhaps pray.' Almost to himself he added, 'Although I'm not sure that will help any more.'

'I'm going to try and reach Peck again,' said Bishop, heading for the hallway. 'We'll need an ambulance too – for her.' He indicated the injured woman lying on the floor.

Jessica clung to her father, both of them feeling the oppression that now hung over the house. 'Is it really possible for this to happen? Could Pryszlak have really found a way of tapping this power, Father?'

'I think he has, Jessica. Those who have studied the subject have always known it existed. The question is: does Pryszlak control the power, or does it control Pryszlak? I think we shall soon find out if what the woman called Lillian said is true. Will you find my cane for me? Then you must help Edith with the injured woman.'

Jessica found Kulek's stout cane lying behind the armchair in which he had been sitting; she gave it to him then went to the medium who was still kneeling beside the recumbent figure.

'How is she?'

'I . . . I don't know. She seems to be in a state of shock. If she's in pain, she doesn't show it.'

545

The linen towel was no longer white. Edith held it against the long slash, her hands, along with the cloth, red from the woman's blood. 'I don't think it's too deep, but she's losing a lot of blood.'

'I'll get another towel. We'll have to open her blouse and try to cover the whole of her chest.' Jessica felt herself shudder as she gazed down. The still woman's pupils had retracted to small pinpoints and for some reason, there was a distant smile on her face. She seemed to be listening.

The medium looked up at the glass wall. She, too, could hear something.

'Edith, what is it?' Jessica shook her.

'They're all around us.'

Jessica looked towards the windows, but could only see the glow of the outside lights. They didn't seem as bright as they should have been.

Bishop returned to the room, a determined look on his face. 'Peck was still unavailable, but one of the men in his department told me the trouble seems to be shifting over to this side of the river. There's been a constant stream of emergency calls and they're pretty thin on the ground for reinforcements. His advice is to sit tight and he'll get someone out to us as soon as possible. Even telling him one of their own officers has been murdered didn't get me too far. It seems he's only one of many dead policemen tonight.' He took out the small gun that he had put into his jacket pocket earlier. 'If anyone tries to break in, I can try and hold them off with this. Have you any other guns in the house, Jacob?'

The blind man shook his head. 'I have no use for them. And I think weapons of that sort will not help us.'

'Jacob, the lights outside are dimming.' There was dread in Edith Metlock's voice.

'There must be a reduction in power somewhere,' Bishop said, walking towards the glass wall.

'No, Chris,' said Jessica. 'The lights inside the house haven't been affected.'

Kulek turned towards the sound of Bishop's voice. 'Chris, are you by the window? Please keep back from there.'

'There's nothing outside. No movement, except . . .'

'What is it? Jessica, tell me what is happening.'

'The shadows, Father. The shadows are drawing closer to the house.'

Bishop spoke. 'The lights are just a dull glow now. There's a . . .

546

sort of . . . blackness creeping forward. It's only a few feet away from the windows. It's moving all the time.' He began to edge away from the glass wall, stopping only when he had reached the back of the settee. Suddenly, all they could see was their own reflections, the outside lamps hardly visible. The feeling of oppression had increased: it seemed to be bearing down on all of them, straining against the very house itself, pressing, crushing.

Edith Metlock slumped against the settee, her eyes closed. Jessica reached for her father but found she was too frightened to move towards him. Kulek stared out at the darkness as though he could see it and, in his mind, he could. Bishop raised the gun towards the glass wall, knowing he could not pull the trigger.

'It can't get in!' Kulek shouted, his voice raised even though there was total silence in the room. 'It has no material form!'

But the bulging inwards of the huge sheets of glass joined by thin metal strips belied his words.

'Jesus Christ, it's not possible.' Bishop couldn't believe what he was seeing. The glass was bending like the distorted mirrors in a funfair's crazy house. He put his other hand up to protect his eyes, sure that the windows would burst inwards at any moment.

The injured woman pushed herself into a sitting position, the stained linen towel falling away from her chest and blood flowing freely into her lap. She watched the windows and laughed. The cackling sound she made died when, without warning, the bulges in the glass subsided and the windows returned to their normal shape. For several moments, no one in the room dared to speak.

'Is it ov . . .?' Jessica began to say when an ear-splitting *crack* made them all jump back in alarm.

The middle section of the wall was split from top to bottom, jagged streaks running from the main crack like forked lightning. Again the sharp sound of splintering glass came to them and they watched in paralysed horror as the section next to it began to split. They saw the thin cracks travelling in different directions, patterning a jigsaw of sharp lines on the treated glass. Soon the lines resembled a spider's web. Another *crack*, and the section on the other side of the centre piece began to break, this time two lines travelling up from the base and joining near the top, etching out a jagged mountain shape.

With explosive force, all the sections shattered inwards, showering the occupants of the room with thousands of lethal glass shards. The sound was that of a hundred pistols being fired at once. Bishop fell back over the settee, his clothes and hair covered in silver fragments. Kulek instinctively turned his body and ducked, his dressing-gown instantly covered in tiny porcupine quills of glass. The shock had sent Jessica reeling back, the long settee between her and the windows protecting most of her body; she screamed when a section of glass the size of a dinner plate scythed along the side of her raised arm as she fell. The settee served to screen Edith Metlock and the short woman completely from flying glass.

Bishop had rolled on to the floor, tumbling over the injured woman. He lay still for a few moments, waiting for the ringing in his ears to clear, then forced himself to stand. He saw Kulek groping his way towards Jessica, calling out her name.

'I'm all right, Father.' She was pushing herself up on to one elbow and Bishop winced when he saw the long, red tear in her arm. He reached her just as Kulek was leaning forward to help her up, pieces of glass falling from their bodies like brushed snow. There were many tiny cuts on Jessica's forehead, neck and hands, but the rent along her arm was the worst damage she had suffered. He held her with Kulek and all three looked across at the broken wall, cold air flowing in unhindered and chilling them.

There was nothing outside now but blackness.

They kept still, scarcely daring to breathe, waiting for something to happen. The first figure appeared, standing just beyond the area of light so his body was ill-defined, shadowy. Bishop realised he had dropped the gun.

The figure stepped over the threshold, out of the darkness, into the light. He stood there, head turned slightly sideways, eyes blinking as though the light was hurting his eyes. The man was filthy, his clothes torn and covered with grime. Even in their dazed state, they could smell his corruption.

'Who is there?' asked Kulek softly, his question directed at Jessica and Bishop. Neither could answer.

The man's head was slowly turning towards them and, even under the dirt that covered him, they could see his face was drawn and emaciated. His eyes were still half-closed, and there were no whites to them, only a dull, greyish-yellow. His movements were sluggish as he walked towards them.

Jessica began to back away, dragging her father with her, but Bishop stood his ground. There was a hollow, vacant expression

548

on the man's face and Bishop felt revulsion when he saw the dried mucous and spittle that covered the lower half of his face. His revulsion heightened when the man grinned at him.

Bishop ran forward, afraid yet repulsed enough to want to crush the thing before him as though it were a loathsome spider. He pushed the man and to his surprise felt no resistance; it was as if he had no strength left at all, that his body had wasted into a debilitated state, a withered frame that was hardly living. The man staggered back and Bishop followed through by lifting him and throwing him back out into the darkness. He stood there, panting from fear rather than exertion, and looked out into the night. There were many more standing in the shadows, watching the house.

He backed away and, as he did so, three figures came running forward from the blackness. They leapt into the room and came to an abrupt halt as the sudden glare blinded them. There were two men and one woman: the men wore grey denims, and one of them was shoeless; the woman was dressed normally. Bishop realised these three were not in the deteriorated state the first man had been in. He quickly looked around for the lost Beretta and gratefully lunged for the pistol when he saw it lying on the floor half-under the settee. He was on one knee retrieving the weapon when Jessica shouted; he turned to see one of the men rushing at him. His intention had been to try and warn them off, but without thinking he swung the gun in the advancing man's direction and squeezed the trigger. His would-be assailant spun arounnd and fell to the floor as the bullet spat into his shoulder. The woman fell over the sprawled figure, but the other man skirted them both and came running towards Bishop, who was still crouched low. The next bullet punctured the second man's neck.

'Chris, there are more of them outside!' warned Jessica.

He saw them hovering just beyond the area of light. 'Quick, upstairs. We haven't got a chance down here!'

Leaping over the back of the settee, he pulled Edith Metlock to her feet. 'Take your father up, Jessica. We'll follow.' He did not allow his eyes to stray from the broad wall of darkness before him, the gun held up, trembling slightly, towards it. His first two shots had been lucky, for he was not at all familiar with guns, nor was he used to maiming or killing people; but he was aware that at such close range it would be virtually impossible to miss and he would not hesitate at firing at anyone entering the room. He

549

pulled the medium along with him and she allowed herself to be led, her hands over her ears as though the sound of the breaking glass was still reverberating in them. She looked dazed and pale. Bishop felt perspiration trickling into his eyes and he hastily wiped the back of his hand over his forehead. He was surprised to see his hand smeared with blood when he brought it away; parts of his face must have been lacerated by flying glass.

'They're at the front door,' he heard Jessica call out. 'They're trying to force it open!'

He could hear the muffled thumps coming from the hallway. 'Up the stairs, quickly,' he ordered. At least they would not be able to rush him up there and he might just be able to hold them off until the police arrived. *If* they arrived.

The hand that hooked itself behind his knee and brought him down belonged to the short woman. He fell heavily, taking the medium with him, and the injured woman threw herself on top of him, oblivious of the pain she suffered. Twisting his head to avoid the sharp-edged fingers, Bishop saw the woman who had leapt into the room with the two men crawling towards him, a long sliver of glass held in her hand like a knife blade. He brought a knee up and it sank viciously into the plump side of the woman above him, causing her to topple sideways. His back still against the floor, he pointed the gun straight into the advancing woman's face. She did not seem to notice; or she did not seem to care. Panic-stricken though he was, Bishop could not pull the trigger. He twisted away as the jagged glass came rushing down at him and heard it break against the floor. The woman stared at her bloody hand, then reached for him again. He swiped away the arm that supported her weight and brought the end of the pistol down on the back of her head as she collapsed. Kicking himself free of the short woman, whose legs were still tangled with his, he pulled himself clear. A well-aimed shove sent her crumpling back against the settee and he thought she would not be able to rise again. Incredibly, he was wrong.

She flew at him with a strength that was frightening for someone in her condition and her blows sent crystals of glass that had already pierced his face deeper into the skin, making him cry out. Others were in the room now, men and women who had stepped from the cover of darkness they seemed to favour, some of them shielding their eyes from the harsh glare, others squinting their eyes against the light. Bishop felt the plump woman's body shudder as the bullet entered her groin, but it took two more to stop her struggles. As she slid away, he saw there was no fear in her eyes, only a strange look of pleasure.

He fired into the crowd that had invaded the room and, for a brief moment, their disorganised rush was halted. It gave him just enough time to gain his feet and stagger towards the door. Roughly pushing Edith Metlock through, he pumped two bullets into the nearest man, this one also dressed in grey denims which Bishop suddenly recognised as prison clothes. The man fell forward just as Bishop pulled the door closed and the wood shook as his body crashed into it on the other side.

Jessica and her father were on the stairs, the girl looking down over the balustrade at him. Her face was streaked with tears that came from absolute terror. Bishop felt the handle twisting beneath his grip and he knew he would not be able to hold the door shut for long.

'Move yourselves!' he shouted. 'Take Edith with you!'

Jessica was galvanised into action by the harsh command. She reached down over the balustrade and guided the medium around to the stairs. Bishop waited until they were out of view before he released the door-handle. It flew open and he kept firing into the room beyond until the gun made only a sharp click. It was empty, empty and useless. He turned and fled.

As he passed the glass panel that ran the length of the heavy, wooden door, it broke and a hand reached in and grabbed his arm. Another hand shot forward and pulled at his hair. It was then that all the lights in the house went out.

Even as he struggled, he realised someone had broken into another part of the house and found the main power switch. He tore himself away from the grasping hands, feeling his jacket rip and some of the hair pulled from his scalp. He collapsed on to the stairs, hearing the rush of footsteps in the darkness, the shrieks of the possessed, their cries of triumph. Hands groped at him through the banister rails as he forced himself upwards. They tore at his face and hands, ripping his clothes, trying to pin him down. A steel-like grip closed around his ankle and he was pulled back down the stairs. He groaned aloud as he held on to the balustrade, desperately trying to halt his descent back into the mob. Wild screams and laughter filled his head, then a voice, a voice that barely pierced the babble, but a voice he knew to be Jessica's. But the words made no sense.

551

'Close your eyes, Chris, close your eyes!'

The brilliant flash that lit up the hallway stung his vision and silver and red images danced beneath his closed eyelids for long seconds after. He felt himself released and heard the howls of anguish.

'Come on, Chris!' It was Kulek's voice this time. 'Up, up! While they are blinded!'

Bishop moved fast, even though dazzled; he knew which way was up. He reached the landing and fell against the facing wall, his vision still swimming with swirling lights. More hands grabbed him and he knew these were friendly.

'This way, into the bedroom,' he heard Kulek say.

Heavy footsteps came from the stairway as the blind man guided him into a nearby room and Jessica's fear-filled voice cried out, 'Close your eyes!' just before the brilliant flash froze everything into an eerie white stillness. Screams and the sound of tumbling bodies came to them. Bishop felt rather than saw Jessica rush into the room and quickly close the door; he rubbed his eyes, trying to clear the dazzle from them.

'Quickly, we must barricade the door!' Kulek shook Bishop's arm.

Jessica locked the door, then hurried over to a heavy-looking dressing-table. 'Help me, Chris, Edith.' She began pulling it away from the wall it rested against.

Bishop blinked several times and gradually began to make out shapes in the room. Just enough light filtered through the long window-wall for him to see the two women struggling with the dressing-table. He joined them and soon the unit was up against the door.

'Let's get the bed!' Bishop shouted. They tipped it up and he was relieved to feel its heavy weight. It crashed against the dressing-table, reinforcing the barricade. Footsteps came running along the hallway and they heard movement in the room next to theirs. More running, then the footsteps stopped outside their door. The handle turned and Bishop leaned against the makeshift barricade, whispering to the others to do the same. The pounding that started made them all jump even though they were expecting it.

The door shook in its frame, but mercifully held.

'Who are they? Where have they come from?' Jessica was next to Bishop and he could just make out the white blur of her face in the gloom.

552

'Some of them are from the prison, I'm sure. They must have escaped in the riot.'

'But there are women among them, and other men. They're in a terrible state.'

'The missing people! It must be them! God knows how they got into that condition.'

'What condition?' asked Kulek, who was also pushing against the upturned bed.

'They're filthy, their clothes in rags. They look starved, too. The first one I tackled was as weak as a kitten.'

The banging against the door became louder as though those outside had found heavy objects to beat at the wood with.

Kulek's voice was grim. 'They were the first victims. Whatever it is that possesses them has no regard for their lives. It uses them and destroys them.'

'And the stronger are the more recent victims? Like the convicts?'

'It would seem so.'

The whole barricade trembled a fraction and Bishop knew the door lock had been broken. He dug his feet more firmly into the carpeted floor and pushed harder against the bed, one hand reaching round to steady the dressing-table behind it. He was vaguely aware that Edith Metlock had sunk to the floor and was swaying on her knees, head in her hands.

A crash from behind made them all turn sharply towards the long windows. Jessica covered her face, expecting the glass to shower inwards again, but as they watched, a black object sailed into view and smacked against the window again.

'They're throwing things at the window,' Bishop said breathlessly and was suddenly aware that the banging against the door had ceased. 'Keep pushing against the bed,' he told Jessica and her father as he crossed the room. In the gloom, he kicked something lying on the floor and he almost smiled when he saw it was a camera, a rectangular attachment fitted. Jessica had used the flashgun against the mob chasing him, blinding and stopping them with its brief but powerful light.

He reached the window just as another object crashed against it and he pulled away in reflex action. Fortunately the treated glass was extremely strong and, although a whitish crack appeared, the glass did not break. Cautiously, Bishop crept forward again and looked down into the grounds below. The bedroom overlooked the rear garden and he could see figures standing in the shadows of the shrubbery and trees. As he watched, a man began pulling at the brickwork of a low garden wall, then stepped out on to the lawn and raised the object of his efforts, his body leaning backwards for the throw. But the brick never came towards the window; it dropped from the man's fingers and thudded to the grass.

The man moved back, his gaze still on the window from where Bishop was watching; he sank into the shrubbery behind him and Bishop noticed that the other figures had now disappeared. The man became part of the shadows and then, like the others, was gone.

A movement by his side made Bishop turn his head; Edith Metlock was staring over the treetops at the city beyond. 'They're leaving,' she said simply. 'The voices have gone.'

Jessica and Kulek joined them at the window.

Bishop shook his head. 'Why should they suddenly go? We had no chance against them.'

There was a tiredness in Jacob Kulek's voice when he spoke and, as Bishop turned to him, he saw the tiredness was in his deeply lined face too. And, even as the blind man said the words, it occurred to Bishop that there *was* enough light to see him.

'The dawn is here,' Kulek said. 'There is a greyness in my eyes where before there was only blackness. They have fled from the morning light.'

'Thank God,' Jessica said softly as she leaned against Bishop and held on to his arm. 'Thank God it's over.'

Kulek's sightless eyes were still directed towards the approaching light, the world outside grey, almost colourless, but no longer black. 'No, it is not over. I'm afraid it has only just begun,' he said.

PART THREE

They will growl over it on that day,
like the roaring of the sea,
And if one look to the land,
behold, darkness and distress;
and the light is darkened by its clouds.
                                    Isaiah 5:30
                                    (R.S.V.)

Chapter Twenty-Four

Many were found wandering aimlessly through the streets of the city, confused, their eyes half-closed, hands acting as shields against the glare of the sun. Others cowered in darkened rooms or hid in the basements of any building they could find access to. The London Underground system was brought to a halt when shocked motormen staggered from their trains, the sight of countless bodies they had ploughed through in the black tunnels a nightmare they would never forget. A search of the sewer network was ordered – three men on inspection duty the day before had been reported missing – and the searchers did not return. Corpses were found in the streets, many with bodies wasted, clothes bedraggled. Some had taken their own lives, others had died through self-neglect. Not all were in a helpless state: a large number were bewildered, remembering the violence they had committed during the night hours, but unable to explain it. Many of these, if they managed to find their way home, were hidden by their families. Once safely inside, they insisted that the curtains be drawn against the daylight; they listened apprehensively to the reports of the previous night's mass-violence, aware they had been a part of it, but afraid to go to the police. Those close to them could only watch, frightened by what had happened, but reluctant to seek outside help, for they knew that anyone involved in the riots was being rounded up and taken away. It was midday before the wailing sirens of fire-engines ceased, but the sounds of ambulances rushing through the streets went on well into the afternoon. It was never truly estimated just how many lives had been lost or how many minds had been taken on that first night of terror, for events after that took on such major proportions and with such rapidity that it became hopeless to keep accurate accounts of human or material damage. The prime objective was to survive, not to record details.

557

It began all over again the following night. And continued the night after that. And the next.

The congregation inside the Temple of the Newly Ordained had gathered earlier that afternoon, for they knew the five o'clock curfew would not allow them to leave their homes and travel to the modern, white-painted building. They had been ordered to keep silent while they waited – Brother Martin did not want their presence inside the church to be known – but their minds were in a turmoil of excitement. They were afraid, but eager, too. Their leader had told them of what was to come and they had faith in his word. Brother Martin had the knowledge, for he had spoken with the Dark.

In a room at the far end of the church which was not really a church but rather an assembly hall with rows of benches, near the altar which was not really an altar but an elaborate lectern, sat a neatly dressed man, his features lit only by a solitary candle that stood on the table before him. The man's eyes were closed and his breathing was deep and rhythmic. He felt the tension emanating from the hall next door and smiled. It would help; the vibrations of the thought-flow would act as a guide. He was ready and they were ready. Nearly a hundred and fifty people. The Dark would make them welcome.

His eyes snapped open as a soft tap on the door roused him from his deep thoughts. One of his followers, a tall coloured man, entered the room. The coloured man was in his early thirties, his hair allowed to grow Afro-style, but his suit conservative. Brother Martin smiled at him.

'Is everything ready?' he asked.

The coloured man was too nervous to return the smile. 'Ready,' he affirmed.

'Are you afraid, Brother John?'

'Brother Martin, I'm shit-scared.'

Brother Martin laughed aloud and his follower managed to join in.

'There's nothing to fear any more, John. This moment has been a long time coming – we mustn't balk at it.'

Brother John seemed uncertain. 'I know that, I know that. But what if you're wrong?'

Brother Martin's hand snaked out and struck the coloured

man across the cheek. No resistance was offered, even though Brother John was at least a foot taller than his aggressor.

'Never doubt me, Brother John! I have spoken with the Dark and I have been told what we must do.' His voice became softer and he reached out and touched the cheek that now bore the marks of his hand. 'We've enjoyed what we've gained from these people, Brother, but it's time for something more, something better. Their faith has given us wealth; now they can help us reach something that transcends material gain. He went to the door and turned towards his companion. 'Is the potion ready?' he asked.

'Yes, Brother Martin.'

'Let your faith rest in me, Brother John.' He opened the door and stepped into the hall beyond.

'Faith, shit,' the coloured man muttered. It had been good for them once, convincing the people they would find their salvation with Brother Martin, accepting their donations, travelling the country looking for more. They had trust in their leader, the man who preached that love was the giving of one's-self, the giving of one's possessions. And Brother Martin was there to receive everything they gave. Especially the women. Brother Martin would never turn away even the ugliest. It could churn a man's insides to think of some of the dogs Brother Martin had bedded. He, Brother John, had been more choosey.

The followers were grateful to be told lust was just as much a part of love as was affection: lust meant procreation and that led to more offspring to follow God's way. They loved to hear that to sin was good, for sin meant repentance, and only by repenting could they know humility, and only by feeling true humility could they reach the Almighty. Sin today, regret tomorrow – what could be better? The only problem was that Brother Martin had come to believe his own preaching.

They had both been surprised eight years ago when what had started out as a small-time confidence trick to gain a little extra cash had turned into an ongoing, lucrative profession. Those early years had been one great merry piss-take, both of them cracking up after meetings, their eyes too filled with laughter tears to count the night's take. They had both soon learned that money was not the only pleasurable benefit from their operation: the weakness of the flesh had quickly been established as a worthy sin for remorse. The more remorse he could help them feel, the more he praised the Lord he had been given to them as an instrument of sin. Privately, he would wink at John and ask: 'Who could resist the concept that to fuck illicitly is good for the soul?' But since Brother Martin, alias Marty Randall, had caught the syph three times in two years, his attitude had changed. Wasn't it only gonorrhoea that was supposed to drive you nuts? Gon today, gone tomorrow? Maybe it was just the idolisation they had thrust upon Brother Martin that had made him begin to believe it all himself. Up until founding the Temple of the Newly Ordained, Randall – Brother Martin – had been small-time: now he had become something to be worshipped. It was enough to turn any mother's head. He, Brother John alias Johnny Parker, had watched with awe as Randall had begun to change over the years: his sermons had become more emotional, each one always reaching a crescendo that would leave the whole congregation on its feet, clapping and yelling, 'Amen, Brother Martin!' There were still the odd occasions when the two of them would snigger at each other and congratulate themselves on their good fortune and their flock's gullibility, but these occasions were becoming less and less frequent. Now, tonight, Brother Martin seemed to have really flipped his lid. Would he go through with it or was it just to test them all, a megalomaniac's way of proving his command over them, an experiment to be halted at the last moment? Brother John, alias Parker, hoped it was the latter.

Brother Martin strode to the lectern, his eyes quickly becoming accustomed to the brightness of the hall after the gloom in the small room next to it. A bustle of excitement greeted his entrance and the people nervously glanced at each other, afraid of what was about to happen, yet eager for this new and far-from-final experience. There were a few in the crowd who still doubted, but these were not too concerned with living anyway. Everything that was happening in the city gave credence to what Brother Martin told them. The time had come and they desired to be among the first.

Brother Martin directed their attention towards the three punch bowls that stood on a table at the head of the centre aisle. 'You see there, my dear brothers and sisters, our elixir,' his voice boomed out. 'With just one sip you will be eternal. You have seen for yourselves the chaos outside, the people who are dead yet still refuse to give up their bodies. Will you allow the torturous

560

degenerations of the shell you inhabit, or will you follow me, cleanly, without stress? With purity!'

He allowed his eyes to glance over the congregation so that each member felt the words were meant for him or her alone. 'There are some among you who are afraid. We will help you overcome that fear. There are some among you who still doubt: we will help you overcome that doubt. There are many among you who hate the world and the terrible hardship it has caused you: and I say that is good! It' good to hate, for the world is a vile, loathsome place! Detest it, brothers, revile it, sisters! Remember the words: "Is not the day of the LORD darkness, and not light, and gloom with no brightness in it?" This is the day of the LORD! The brightness has gone!'

Brother Martin waved a hand and, at the signal, all the lights in the hall were flicked off by Brother John, who stood by the main switches. A moan came from the crowd as the hall was plunged into darkness, except for the poor light cast from the flickering candles strategically placed around the walls.

'Open the doors, Brother Samuel,' their leader commanded and a man standing by the temple's double-doors swung them wide. The darkness outside became part of the darkness inside. 'Concentrate, my brothers and sisters, bring the Dark to us. We must hurry.' He could see the street-lights beyond the temple grounds, the houses with every light in them turned on. The order had been given for every possible light in the capital to be left on overnight: the authorities knew the Dark's strength. Night after night it had returned, the natural darkness its ally, and each time the chaos had become greater. No one could tell who would succumb to its influence – father, mother, brother, sister. Child. Friend. Neighbour. What evil lay tethered in each of these, waiting to be freed, yearning to be cut loose. The light was the only barrier. The Dark feared light. 'The light shines in the darkness, and the darkness has not overcome it.' Gospel according to John. But *man* can overcome the light. Brother Martin chuckled to himself, the sockets of his eyes dark shadows in the candlelight.

'Come forth, drink of the liquid that will make us whole.' Brother Martin held out his arms towards the congregation.

Despite the chill sweeping in through the open doors, beads of sweat broke out on Brother John's forehead. Oh man, oh man, he's really going through with it. He really wants to kill them all.

561

Randall really believed all this shit the people upstairs were putting out about the Dark. Jesus, didn't he know it was just jive? The word was out on the street: it was a chemical gas that couldn't activate under sunlight or any other fucking light. Nobody knew who had released it – a foreign power, terrorists? The fucking British scientists themselves? Nobody on the street knew. But the motherfuckers in power did. Only they weren't saying. Stay inside at night, keep your lights on – that's *all* they were saying. Police and troops patrolled after curfew to make sure the rule was obeyed, using powerful searchlights themselves for their own protection. And this stupid fuck Randall was disobeying the law, turning all the lights out, ordering the doors opened. What the hell would happen when he discovered the mixture in those punch bowls had no cyanide in it? What would he do when the stupid fucking sheep who followed him didn't drop dead after they'd tasted Potion 99? He'd know who to blame: it was sweet Brother John who'd been given the order to get the poison. Where the fuck did Randall expect him to find enough cyanide to kill off a hundred and fifty mothers? Brother John began to edge his way down the side aisle, away from the three containers of harmless Sainsbury's own-brand wine towards the open doorway. Time to split. Should have done it a long time ago.

The congregation were filing forward, each holding a plastic beaker they had been issued with on entering the temple. Brother Martin smiled benignly as they passed him. A woman in her early forties threw herself at him, her face soaked with tears, nose running. Helpers broke her hold on Brother Martin and gently led her away, soothing her with words she hardly heard. A man in his sixties passed before him, eyes downcast.

'I'm afraid, Brother Martin,' he said.

Brother Martin reached out with both hands and touched his follower's shoulders. 'We all are, Brother . . .' what the shit was his name? '. . . dear friend, but our fear will soon be replaced by great joy. Have faith in me. I have spoken with the Dark.' Now move on, you silly bastard, before you frighten the others.

It was important not to allow the mood of euphoria, albeit a tense euphoria, to be broken: if one panicked, then others would follow. He needed them all, wanted their strength, for he really *had* spoken with the Dark. Or at least, he had dreamt he had spoken with it. It amounted to the same thing.

The Dark wanted him, but it also wanted his people. The more life that was given to it, the stronger it would become. Brother Martin, alias Marty Randall, was happy to be the Dark's recruitment officer.

The people moved in an orderly flow to the punch bowls and then back to their seats, disguising Brother John's progress towards the doorway; the general dimness of the interior also offered concealment. However, he expected to hear Brother Martin calling him back at any moment, and the further he moved away from his leader the more nervous he became. He licked his lips, aware his throat had become very dry. Some of the flock looked at him enquiringly and he had to nod and smile at them reassuringly. He was thankful that the light was so poor, for it meant they could not see the perspiration he felt on his face. Brother Samuel was still standing near the open doors and Brother John approached him cautiously. This man was a devout follower, a mother who would lay down his life for their leader, a honky whose brain functioned only under the guidance of someone else. Just the kind of dogshit Randall needed to keep his followers in order. The big man cocked his head to one side like a curious labrador when Brother John drew near. He didn't like black men and he particularly didn't like Brother John. The nigger always seemed to have a smirk on his face, as if he were taking the piss all the time.

Brother John leaned forward and whispered into the big man's ear. 'Brother Martin wants you to go forward, Brother Samuel, and drink with the others. He feels they need your encouragement.'

Brother Samuel cast an anxious glance over the shadowy congregation. A deep moaning noise came from some of them, while several of the women were openly wailing. He tucked his hand into his jacket pocket and closed his fingers around the gun lying there. Brother Martin had warned him it might be necessary to persuade some of the followers to carry out what was required of them. But he had also told him that he was to wait until last, just in case any were not killed by the poison, or had only pretended to drink. A bullet in the head was to be the answer to that. Why had Brother Martin changed his mind?

'He told me to stay by the door.'

'I know, Brother Samuel,' the black man said patiently, aware that his legs were beginning to feel weak. He could hear Randall's

563

voice from the front urging the people to concentrate, to draw the Dark to them. 'He's changed his mind. He needs you up there, Brother.'

'Who'll watch the door? Who'll see no one gets out?'

'No one's leaving. They want to follow Brother Martin.'

A crafty look came into the big man's face. The nigger wasn't wearing his usual smirk. And at this close range, he could see he was sweating. Brother John was afraid. 'Then why does he need me up there if they want to follow Brother Martin?'

Oh shit. 'One or two need help, Brother Samuel. They're not all as strong as you.'

'Are you as strong as me, Brother John? Do you need help?'

The coloured man tried to keep his hands from shaking. 'No, Brother Samuel. It's the others. Now you do what the man says, Brother, and get yourself up there. He's gonna get mad if you don't.'

The big man seemed uncertain. He looked towards Brother Martin, his hand leaving the weapon inside his jacket pocket.

Brother John was cursing himself for not having left sooner. He should have vanished as soon as Randall had begun his crazy suicide talk. It had become a fascination with him after the mass self-destruction of the People's Temple sect in Guyana several years before, and kindled even further by the other group suicide that had taken place in the suburbs of London just about a year ago. During the last few weeks it had become an obsession; it was as though he had discovered the ultimate truth. Oh Jesus, he should have scooted when Randall ordered him to get the cyanide. He couldn't believe the man intended to go through with it. It was no place to be when they all sat around gawking at each other, waiting to drop like flies. They wouldn't be amused and neither would Brother Martin.

'Come on, Brother Samuel, don't keep him waiting.'

Unfortunately for the coloured man, Brother Martin had been scanning the crowd for him. Brother John's faith had seemed a little shaky over the last few days. He needed help, perhaps coercion. Of late he had become a cause of concern, his enthusiasm for Brother Martin's way seemed to be waning. It might be a good idea to let him be the first to taste this nectar of the after-life.

'Brother John, I can't see you? Where are you?'

The coloured man groaned inwardly. 'Right here, Brother Martin,' he said aloud.

'Come to the front, Brother, where we can see you. Yours will be the honour of leading the way.'

'I, uh, I'm not worthy of that honour, Brother Martin. Only you can lead us.' Brother John licked his lips and glanced nervously towards the doorway.

Brother Martin laughed. 'We are all worthy! Come now, drink first.' He walked over to a punch bowl and dipped a white beaker into the dark red liquid, then proffered it towards the black man. Heads began to turn and look towards Brother John. As if guessing his intention, Brother Samuel moved his big frame into the entrance, blocking any escape.

Oooooh shit! Brother John's head screamed and he brought his knee up into the big man's groin area. Brother Samuel fell to his knees, his hands clutching at his genitals. Brother John jumped through the open doorway into the even greater darkness outside. And stopped.

It was around him like cold clammy hands, like icy treacle smearing itself over his skin. He shivered and looked wildly around, but could see only blurred pinpoints of light in the distance. He backed away from it, but it came with him as though it were stuck to his body. He felt an eerie kind of probing going on inside his head and cried out when the cold fingers touched something inside his mind. No, I don't want this! Something inside him screamed, but another voice answered, yes, yes, you do!

Other hands reached around his throat, and these were real hands, the big, strong hands of Brother Samuel. The grip began to tighten as the inky blackness enveloped both men, and Brother John's thoughts tumbled over themselves to run from the unreal dark fingers that touched and ravaged his mind. He sank to the hard paving stones leading up to the temple, the big man standing behind him, never letting go, and slowly he realised Brother Martin was right: this was the eternity they had been seeking. Although his body was trembling with the pain, something inside him was dancing with happiness. Oh, you *mother*, you were right, Brother Martin, Brother Marty Randall, you were *soooo* right. Even as his closed throat strained to suck in air through to his lungs, his lips were parted in a rapturous smile. His red-filled vision began to cloud into a deepening blackness and soon that was all there was – total, welcoming darkness. Amen to that.

Brother Samuel dragged the limp body back into the temple and the Dark followed, flowing in greedily, spreading and seeping, dimming the already faint light from the candles. Brother Martin closed his eyes and spread his arms wide, ignoring the sudden cries of fear around him, welcoming the Dark into his church.

'We will drink the poison and join you,' he said aloud and wondered at the mocking laugh he thought he heard. It had sounded like Brother John. One by one, the candles sputtered and finally went out.

'Tell them to keep the noise down, Alex. If the Law finds out you've got a meeting going on in the back, they'll have your licence.' Sheila Bryan held the glass up to make sure she had wiped away all the smears in the bottom of the pint glass. It wasn't often the pub's glasses received such close scrutiny, but then it wasn't often a curfew was imposed. She briefly wondered if there had been such restrictions during the war. She didn't think so, but couldn't be sure; it was before her time.

'They're all right. They're not disturbin anybody.' Her husband, Alex, regarded Sheila with ill-disguised impatience. He was a hefty man, large of gut, loud of voice, and it needed a woman with similar attributes to handle him. He was just approaching forty, she had just said goodbye to her twenties; their mutual largeness somehow made them appear the same age.

'I don't know why you have anything to do with them, anyway,' Sheila said, placing the glass next to its dry companions on the bar. Ash from the cigarette dangling between her lips fell into the murky washing up water as she leaned forward and reached in for another glass.

'They've got the right idea, that's why,' Alex retorted as he dumped the tray of glasses on the draining-board next to the sink. 'They want another round.'

'Well they'll have to use those. I'm not using fresh glasses.'

'Of course they'll bleedin use these. Who's askin for new ones? I don't know what gets into you at times. We wouldn't be makin a penny if we didn't av that lot tonight. Bloody filth keepin everyone indoors.'

'The Law says it's dangerous to go out at night.'

'That's all bollocks. They've got somethin goin on, that's all, somethin they don't want anybody to see.'

'Don't be bloody daft. You've seen what's going on on the telly. Riots, fires – all those murders.'

'Yeh, because somebody's used a nerve gas on us, that's why.

566

Bastard Lefties, that's who's done it, brought it in for their friends abroad.'

Sheila stood up from the sink and took the cigarette from her mouth with damp fingers. 'What are you talking about now?' she said, looking at her husband with disdain.

'Everyone knows the Commies are behind it. They won't tell you on the news, but just you ask anyone. It'll be New York next, maybe Washington. You wait and see. Then Paris, then Rome. All over. Won't appen in Russia, though.'

'Oh you do talk wet, Alex. That mob next door been filling your head with ideas again?'

Alex ignored the question and began filling the glasses with their appropriate drinks. 'It makes sense when you think about it,' he said undeterred as he poured.

His wife raised her eyes towards the ceiling and resumed polishing the glasses. It *was* worrying, though, the whole town being placed under some kind of martial law. It was the sort of thing you expected to happen in foreign parts, but not England. Not London. Why should they have to keep all lights on as though they were afraid of the dark? The Dark: that was what everyone was calling it because it only happened at night-time. They said people were losing their minds with it, roaming around the streets setting fires, killing. There was no sense to it. She, herself, had seen the army trucks searching the streets in the early hours of the morning, picking up people who seemed to be wandering loose and taking them away somewhere. She'd watched them from the window upstairs one morning when she couldn't sleep. Some poor sod had been just lying in the road, covering his head with his hands. There had been blood on his fingers because he had been trying to pull up the manhole cover in the middle of the road, but it must have been too heavy, or he couldn't get a grip. He didn't say a word when they slung him into the truck, and his face had been deathly white, white as a ghost, and his eyes black and half-shut. She shivered. It was like one of those old horror films, like Quatermass.

'Where's all the fuckin light ales?'

Her attention was abruptly drawn back to her husband. 'Don't swear in the bar, Alex, I've asked you before.'

He looked back at her, then around at the empty saloon bar. 'There's no one ere, you know.'

'That's not the point. You've got to get out of the habit. It's not necessary.'

567

Silly cow, he said to himself. Then aloud, 'We can't av used all the light, we've only ad lunchtime trade the past couple of weeks.'

'Alex, there's plenty in the cellar if you'd like to make the effort and go down and get it.'

Alex's sigh turned into a grunt when he leaned forward and pulled at the ring set into the trapdoor behind the bar. He heaved it open and stared down at the blackness below. 'I thought we were supposed to turn on all the lights,' he said.

'I did,' his wife replied, looking over his shoulder into the square of darkness.

'Well that one's not bleedin on, is it?'

Sheila walked over to the set of light switches that lay near the doorway to a small back room they used mainly as an office, their living quarters being on the floor above. 'They're all on,' she called back to her husband. 'The bulb must have gone.'

'Oh fuck it,' her husband groaned.

'I'll get you another one, Alex. You can put it in.'

'Great,' Alex replied wearily. He wanted to get back to the meeting; he enjoyed listening to the boys and tonight, because there were no other customers, was the ideal opportunity to sit in on their discussions. Fortunately, his was a Free House, so no interfering nosey-parker could inform any brewery of the type of organisations he allowed to hold meetings in his pub. One of his mates, a publican in Shoreditch, had had to vacate when the brewery which owned the pub discovered he was letting his back rooms out for National Front meetings. That was the trouble with being a tenant-landlord – you had to dance to someone's else's tune. 'Come on, Sheila,' he called out, 'let's av it!'

She returned, a cold look on her face, and handed him a torch and a new light bulb.

'Forty watt?' he said disgustedly. 'This ain't gonna be much cop, is it?'

'It's all we've got,' she replied patiently. 'And you can bring up some Babycham while you're down there.'

'Babycham? Who the ell's gonna be drinkin that tonight?'

'It's for tomorrow lunchtime. You know we're packed during the day now.'

'Yeh, they're all makin up for what they can't get in the evening.'

'Just as well they are, otherwise we'd soon go broke. Hurry up, or your mates will be screaming for their beer.'

'They're not me mates.'

'You could have fooled me. You spend enough time with them.'

'I just appen to agree with a lot of what they say. You've seen ow many blacks there is around ere. More of them than us.'

'Oh go on, get down there. You talk like a big kid at times.'

Alex hoisted his frame on to the ladder. 'You mark my words, they'll be comin in ere to drink next.' His big, round head disappeared from view.

'Heil Hitler,' Sheila commented drily and took another puff of her cigarette. With a resigned sigh she returned to polishing the glasses.

Below, Alex flashed the torch around the grimy, beer-smelling cellar. The beam soon found the naked light bulb hanging from the low ceiling. Better have a stock-take tomorrow, he told himself as he crossed the dusty stone floor. Running low on – oh *fuck*! He stepped out of the puddle and shook droplets of stale beer from his shoe. He shone the torch down and dazzled himself with the reflection off the thinly spread liquid. The cellar floor sloped towards its middle so that all spillage would run into a centre channel then into a drain. He followed the direction of the channel with the torchlight and saw rags or sacking were blocking the flow.

'That silly bastard Paddy,' he said under his breath, referring to his daytime barman. It was the little Irishman's job to stock up the bar each morning, using the dumb-waiter to carry the drinks to the floor above. He must have dropped the rags or whatever it was. 'Bloody Irish twit,' he muttered, kicking the damp bundle aside. He's been dipping into the till again, too. Christ, it was difficult to get honest bar staff. Alex watched the strong-smelling mixture of combined beers gurgle into the square, grill-covered drain. At least it wasn't blocked. If there was one job Alex could not abide it was unblocking drains. All that shit and slime. The drains had to be kept clear otherwise the basement would be ankle deep and stinking like a brewery within a week with all the breakages that went on down there. The delivery men didn't give a sod. Slung the crates down any old how. He thought he saw something scuttle away from the circle of light cast by the torch. 'Don't say we've got rats down ere now,' he groaned aloud.

He swung the beam around but found nothing, only retreating blackness.

Alex plodded over to the dangling light bulb, not sure if he had only imagined the dark thing scuttling away. He hadn't heard any movement. The light itself hung over the drain and the publican stretched upwards to reach it, torch held precariously with the fingers of one hand and pointing up at the ceiling. His feet were spread out on either side of the drain.

'Ouch!' Alex cried out when his fingers touched the hot glass. The bulb must have blown just before he opened up the cellar. He jerked his hands away and the torch fell from his grasp. 'Oh *fuck* it!' he shouted when it crashed to the floor and its light was extinguished. The open trapdoor at the far end of the cellar threw down a little light, but its range was not enough to reach where he stood. He dug into his pocket and pulled out a handkerchief, his other pocket bulging with the new light bulb. Alex reached up for the dead one, this time using his handkerchief for protection against the heat.

The gloom did not bother him, for he had never been afraid of the dark, not even as a kid. But the prickling at the back of his neck warned him that something was not quite right in the cellar.

Sheila rested her elbows on the bar top and stared reflectively at the locked door. A fresh cigarette dangled from her lips and her large breasts lay comfortably on the bar's wooden surface like full sacks of graded flour. She didn't know how many more nights like this she could stand. Dolling herself up, slipping into the mental gear necessary to sustain herself through the evening's jollifications or commiserations, whatever the individual customer's mood required, being nice to everybody, firm to those who took liberties. It was like showbiz in a way, only these nights there was no biz. Surely they were going to get rid of this gas, or whatever it was soon. The whole town would go to pot otherwise. Still, she supposed she should have been grateful for the small amount of evening trade she had in the back room, as much as she disliked their views. It was only because they had booked the room a month in advance that she had let Alex persuade her to allow the meeting to be held. He was one of them, even though he wouldn't admit it. They'd have to pay for the use of the room all night, of course; there was no chance of any of them leaving before tomorrow morning. They'd be nicked if they were caught out on the streets at night. Where was Alex? He was taking his time. Who was it who came on telly the other night? A cardinal or bishop, wasn't it? Told them all to pray. Hah, that was a laugh! She could just see old Alex going down on his knees to pray.

Probably would if someone held a gun at his head. What were they supposed to pray for? What good were prayers against a nerve gas, as Alex said it was? It was the scientists who had to do the praying. It was down to them, all this mess. Let them come up with something. And not prayers.

'Sheila.'

She looked around. What was that?

'Sheila.'

She sighed and lumbered towards the open trapdoor. 'What're you up to, Alex. How long does it take you to send up a crate of light and Babycham?'

She peered down into the blackness.

'Haven't you put the bulb in yet?' she said, irritated.

'Sheila, come down.'

'Where are you, Alex? I can't see you.'

'Come down.'

'Do what? Me, come down there? Do me a favour, Alex.'

'Please, Sheila.'

'Are you sodding about, Alex? I'm not in the mood.'

'Come on, Sheila, come down. I've got something to show you.'

The publican's wife chortled. 'You can show me that later, in bed.'

'No, come on, Sheila, now. Come down.'

Alex's voice sounded strangely urgent.

'It's dangerous, Alex. I might fall.'

'You won't, Sheila. I'll help you. Come down.'

Oh my Gawd, Sheila said to herself. The things I do for love. 'All right, Alex,' she called down, a giggle escaping her. 'It had better be worth it!'

She gingerly lowered herself on to the metal-runged ladder, her hands firmly grasping the wooden sides. Sometimes she wondered if Alex was all there, the strokes he pulled. But he was good for a laugh, she had to give him that.

'Alex? Alex! Where are you?' She was halfway down the ladder and looking around, trying to pierce the gloom. 'I'm going up again if you don't stop hiding right this minute.'

'I'm right here, Sheila, waitin for you.'

'Well what do you want?' Sheila had decided she didn't really like this game. The cellar stank – beer dregs and something else. What? Funny smell. It was cold and dark there too. 'I'm going up, Alex. You're acting stupid, true to form.'

571

She waited for a reply, but there was only silence.

Sheila came down two more rungs then stopped. 'Right, that's it. This is as far as I come unless you come over here into the light.'

Alex didn't make a sound. But she heard his breathing. She suddenly felt uneasy.

'Bye, Alex.' She began to climb back up the ladder.

Alex came out of the dark, a lumbering shape that held something high above his head. Sheila just turned her head in time to see the mallet used for opening kegs of beer descending. There was no time for her to scream and no time to wonder what had come over Alex.

She fell to the floor and lay still, but the heavy wooden mallet continued to batter her head and soon it was blood that flowed down the basement's centre into the dark, noxious dark.

Alex climbed through the trapdoor minutes later, a smile of pleasure on his face. He heaved his heavy body through the opening, the bloodied mallet still held in one hand. Reaching up to the bartop with his free hand, he pulled himself to his feet. He walked to the set of switches that controlled all the downstairs lights in the public house and ran his hand over every one until both bars and back rooms were plunged into darkness. He walked back the length of the bar, careful not to fall into the even blacker hole that was the open trapdoor. Confused voices coming from one of the back rooms guided him, although guidance wasn't really necessary, for he knew his pub like the back of his hand. He hurried to rejoin the meeting. They would be pleased to see him. They would be pleased to see what he had brought along with him.

He looked to the right, studying the wide road for several long seconds before directing his gaze to the left. All clear. No police, no patrolling army vehicles. It was now or never. He ran, heading for the road leading to the big park. To where it was empty. And dark.

His gait was awkward, more of a waddle than a run, his short legs treading the hard, smooth road's surface as though it were cobblestones. The thought of the jogging which several of his colleagues in the House had taken up when it had become fashionable a couple of years back made him wonder at their sanity. Moving at any speed faster than a brisk stroll *had* to be damaging

572

to one's health. No wonder some of them had collapsed with heart attacks. He remembered the leaflets all the Members had received encouraging them to use the Parliament gym, telling them that by keeping a healthy body, they would have the stamina to serve their constituents better. Well, his stamina was in the mind, not in the body. As far as he was concerned, each leaflet should have been issued with a GOVERNMENT HEALTH WARNING. You couldn't serve your constituents very well from a wooden box six feet under the earth. And if his heart was going to collapse, he would rather it was due to the demands of a good whore than running through the park in plimsolls. He paused at the entrance, his rotund body heaving and sucking in huge, rasping lungfuls of air. He studied the broad expanse of darkness before him, afraid now, then forced himself on, the night swallowing him up as though he had never existed.

Once he was safely inside the black sanctuary, he slumped to the grass, heedless of its cold wetness, and endeavoured to recover a normal rate of breathing. The lights of the city blazed away in the distance, but they barely penetrated the fringes of the park. He was in the Kensington Gardens section, deeming it wise to keep well away from Hyde Park on the other side of the Serpentine where a police station operated. He would find it difficult to explain his presence. Even being a Labour MP for the past sixteen years would not prevent his immediate arrest. Any Member of Parliament on government business had to have an army escort after nightfall, otherwise they had to stay indoors like other citizens. The uproar over the restrictions still raged every day in the House, but the PM and the Home Secretary were adamant. Anyone who wished to leave the capital while the emergency was on was perfectly entitled to do so, but if they remained, then they came under the government edict. Until the solution was found to this madness, conditions for living in London were severe. Never mind the solutions, backbenchers on either side had cried out, what was the problem? Just what was happening each night? Why was there, as yet, no official statement? The public were entitled to know. *The Members of Parliament themselves were entitled to know*! They had been astonished, then disbelieving, when they were told of the ethereal mass of dark substance that had strange effects on the brain, a mass that had no defined shape nor, as far as anyone could tell, material form. It was neither a gas, nor a chemical. Autopsies on the brains of victims affected by it, and who had taken their own lives, revealed nothing unusual. Why those that could be found wandering the streets by day were docile and in almost trance-like states, no one knew. Paranormal connotations were still being denied, as could be expected.

He rose to his feet, brushing the dampness from his knees. His eyes had become accustomed to the gloom and he realised the patch he was in was considerably lighter than the heavy blackness ahead. He shuffled forward, eager to be completely enveloped by the darkness. The bloody fools didn't understand the significance of it all! This was a new entity – no, not new: it was as old as the world itself. It was a power that had existed even before human life, a dark power that man had allied himself with from the beginning. Now it dwelt in man. It had always been there, the darkness where evil lurked, the darkness that bestial things crept in, the darkness waiting for man to give himself up completely to it. And now was the time.

He froze. Something was moving in the shadows ahead. No sounds. No more movement. His eyes must have been playing tricks on him.

The Dark had called to him, told him what he must do. The power of politics was nothing to the power he had been offered. It was a giant step to take, but the rewards were infinite. No hesitating now, no second thoughts. He had been chosen.

It was difficult to see anything in front of him, for the moon was behind heavy clouds. He could see lights through the trees coming from the hotels that edged the opposite side of Park Lane, but they were far away and had nothing to do with the void of blackness he stood in. Was this *the* Dark around him? Was this the force he had come in search of? Let it happen, then. Absorb me, take me in . . . He stumbled over a figure sitting on the ground.

The politician fell heavily and rolled on to his back.

'Who's there?' he asked querulously when he had recovered from his surprise.

He heard a mumbling sound, but could make no sense of it. He squinted his eyes, hoping to see better. 'Who's there?' he repeated, then became a little bolder. 'Speak up!' His voice was still a whisper, though the words were spoken harshly.

He cautiously crawled forward, afraid yet curious. 'Come on, speak up. What are you doing there?'

'Waiting,' came the murmured reply. It was a man's voice.

The politician was taken aback, somehow not really expecting an answer. 'What do you mean "waiting"? Waiting for what?'

'Waiting like the others.'

'Others?' The politician looked around and suddenly became aware that what he had thought to be dark shapes of bushes and shrubs were, in fact, the figures of people, some squatting on the ground, others standing. All were silent. He grabbed the man by the shoulder.

'Do they – do you – know about the Dark?'

The man shrugged his shoulder away. 'Piss off,' he said quietly. 'Leave me alone.'

The politician stared at the shadowy figure for a while, still unable to make out his features. Finally, he crawled away and found a space of his own. He sat there for a long time, confused, then ultimately, resigned. It made sense that he would not have been the only one; others would have been chosen. At one point, when the quarter moon was able to free itself of clinging black clouds for a few seconds, he was able to look around and see how many others there were waiting with him. At least a hundred, he thought. Perhaps as many as a hundred and fifty. Why didn't they communicate? Why were they not speaking? He realised that, like him, their minds were too full of what was going to happen, opening themselves to receive the probing darkness. Willing it, demanding it. The clouds covered the moon and he was alone once more, waiting for the Dark to come.

When the first haziness of dawn edged its way over the tall buildings on the horizon, he rose wearily and stiffly to his feet. His overcoat was covered in a layer of morning dew and his body ached. He saw the others were rising, their movements slow and awkward as though the night's long wait had rusted their joints. Their white, early morning faces were expressionless, but he knew they felt the same bitter disappointment as he. One by one they drifted away, the low-flying dawn mist swirling around their feet.

He felt like weeping with frustration and shaking a fist at the vanishing shadows. Instead, he went home.

Chapter Twenty-Five

Bishop sipped his scotch, then lit his third cigarette since he had been sitting in the hotel bar. He glanced at his watch. The conference had been running for over three hours already and when he had left just half an hour earlier, it seemed far away from any firm conclusions. With so many now involved he wondered if there would ever be any real agreement between them. The combination of scientists and parapsychologists, with government ministers trying to find a common ground between both factions, was hardly ideal for a conducive atmosphere. An American Research Society had expounded on Jung's collective unconscious theory – 'Just as the human body shows a common anatomy over and above all racial differences, so too the psyche possesses a common substratum transcending all differences in culture and consciousness' – and maintained that this collective unconsciousness consisted of latent dispositions towards identical reaction, patterns of thought and behaviour that were a common heritage of psychological developemnt. Different races and separate generations had common instincts – why else the similarity between various myths and symbols? And perhaps one of man's most shared instincts was that for evil. It was argued that surely good was the more predominant instinct throughout history, despite the terrible atrocities that had taken place, and the speaker had agreed, but had gone on to add that perhaps after centuries of enforced suppression, the evil instinct had broken free of the mind's confines. It had finally evolved into a material form.

Bishop, seated in the back row of the modern auditorium, had almost smiled at the perplexed looks that passed between the Police Commissioner and the Army Chief of Staff. If they hadn't had official reports as well as personal eyewitness evidence of the massive unexplained destruction taking place in the nation's capital each night, they would have dismissed such jargonised theories out of hand. However, when a member of the delegation from the Institute of Human Potential insisted that this new madness was the final breakthrough to sanity, their looks turned to mutual anger. It was the Home Secretary, himself, who delivered a severe rebuke to the man who went on to explain that what society considered to be the norm was not necessarily so, and that the condition of alienation, of being asleep or unconscious, of being out of one's mind, was the natural condition of man. The men and women who had been affected had all been in a trance-like state, an altered state of consciousness, an *enlightened* state. They had a mission that so-called normal people – which included everyone in the conference theatre – did not yet understand, nor appreciate. The Home Secretary warned the man and others of his group that they would be removed from the auditorium if they persisted in putting forward these non-productive and rather absurd arguments. The country was in a state of emergency and, while every opinion was valued at this juncture, frivolous speculation would not be tolerated.

Relief on the faces of the Home Secretary and several of his ministerial and law enforcement colleagues showed visibly when the general discussion took on a more medically scientific aspect, but they were soon disappointed by the statement of a prominent neurosurgeon seated in the front row of the audience. He explained how he and a special team of surgeons had performed craniotomies on several of the London victims, the dead as well as the living, in an attempt to find out if their brains had been affected physically in any way. The results had proved negative: no inflammation of the membranes or nerves, no deterioration of tissue, no blockage of cerebrospinal fluid, no bacterial infection, no blood clots or restriction of blood flow to the brain. The surgeon went on to list further defects such as chemical deficiencies that could have damaged the brain's normal functioning, and assured everyone present that none of these had been present. Other tests had been carried out, more in desperation than in hope, and these, too, had proved negative. There had been no lack of enzyme in the victims' systems – without this there would have been an accumulation of amino-acids such as phenylketonuria in the blood. Nor had there been any sudden imbalance of chromosomes in the body cells. A thorough examination had been made of the central region of the brain, particularly the regions grouped around the fluid-filled cavities called the ventricles. One of these regions, the hypothalamus, controlled hunger, thirst, temperature, sex drive and *aggression*, and a close study of the collection of structures around that area forming the limbic system – the septum, fornix, amygdala and hippocampus – which were believed to be particularly responsible for emotional responses such as fear and aggression – had revealed nothing unusual. That is, as far as they could *tell*; no matter how far science had come, the brain was still very much a mystery.

The participating audience, many of whom had become lost with the eminent doctor's medical terminology, stirred uncomfortably. The Home Secretary, anxious to have as many opinions as possible aired in the time available, asked for the view of the psychiatrist seated next to the neurosurgeon, and the two main psychoses of the emotionally disturbed were quickly and clearly explained in a voice that was loud, yet somehow soothing. In manic depressive psychosis, the patient's mood changed from deep depression to mania, which might possibly explain the victims' trance-like quietness during the day and the uncontrollable urges to commit acts of destruction at night. Yet treatment with drugs such as lithium had had no affect on these people. The other chief psychosis was schizophrenia, which generally occurred in those with a hereditary disorder in their metabolism. The symptoms were irrational thinking, disturbed emotions and a breakdown in communications with others, all of which applied to the recent victims. Phenothiazines, also used as tranquillisers, and other drugs such as fluphenazine, had been used unsuccessfully on the victims. As yet, shock treatment had not been tried, but the psychiatrist had also expressed his doubts as to the effectiveness of this method. An alternative which would undoubtedly succeed would be a lobotomy on each individual, but he did, of course, understand that this would be impractical with so many victims. He looked steadily up at the Home Secretary and his hastily appointed 'emergency' council seated on one side of a long, highly polished table on the small stage, remaining silent until the minister realised the psychiatrist had nothing more to say. It was then that a member of an organisation called the Spiritual Frontiers Fellowship Rescue Group rose to his feet and informed those present that the phenomenon being witnessed in London was no more than a large gathering of

578

discarnate beings who did not know they were dead and were possessing others in their confusion. The destructive acts of violence that the possessed were committing were caused because the lost spirits were frightened. He asked that mediums be allowed to guide the tormented souls onwards, to leave their earthly ties behind. Bishop had decided he needed a drink at that point in the proceedings.

He had crept from the conference theatre as unobtrusively as possible, pushing his way through the throng of journalists cramming the back of the auditorium. The hotel bar was empty and the lone barman seemed relieved to have some company. Bishop, however, was in no mood for conversation. He swallowed the first scotch fast, then nursed the second.

The meeting was being held in an hotel at the Birmingham Conference Centre, a huge complex of exhibition halls and conference rooms. The complex was, in fact, some miles from the town itself, in a position easily accessible from the M1 motorway. The authorities considered it too risky to use a more convenient London venue for, although the danger only presented itself at nightfall, the situation in the capital was unpredictable. It was feared that many of the various organisations invited to take part in the general debate might have declined the offer if it were held in the danger zone. And anyway, as the Army Chief of Staff had said: 'A general doesn't hold his war council on the field of battle!' When Bishop had arrived with Jacob Kulek, Jessica and Edith Metlock earlier that morning, the hotel lobby had been filled with clamorous groups of scientists, medical experts and parapsychologists. Outside had been an even larger gathering of media people, many of these too, from other parts of the world. Bishop was unsure if the conference was being held merely for cosmetic reasons to show that the government was taking some action, or out of sheer desperation because they had no solution to the problem. Probably for both reasons, he decided.

Jacob Kulek had become adviser to the special action committee formed to deal with the crisis, his Institute suddenly becoming almost another branch of the Civil Service. Just as Winston Churchill had introduced an occult bureau into the Secret Service during World War Two, so had the Home Secretary adopted what he considered was a similar, ready-made organisation. The government was not convinced it was dealing with a paranormal

579

phenomenon but, because it had not found any other answers, it was not ruling out the possibility. Hence the conference with its diverse groups of experts. At the moment, the 'trouble' in London was being contained, although the city was too vast to be effectively policed for long. New disturbances broke out every night, more victims were found cowering in the streets each morning. The sewer exits were being watched.

How long the police and troops could maintain control was anybody's guess; the night was already beginning to catch up with the mopping-up exercises of the day. And how many more victims affected or infected – still nobody was sure of the correct term – by the Dark could be kept under lock and key was another problem that was reaching crisis point. The exodus of London residents was relatively small so far, but the sudden influx of outsiders gave cause for alarm. Why would men and women flock to the city when such danger stalked the streets at night? And why were so many flouting the 'lights-on' regulations? It was almost as if some welcomed the phenomenon that had become known as the Dark. Bishop sat in the bar, pondering over the imponderable. Were they faced with a crisis that could be dealt with by scientific means, or a crisis whose cause lay in the paranormal and therefore, could only be answered by psychic means? He, himself, felt they were about to discover there was a definite link between the two.

He drained his glass and waved it at the barman for another.

'I think I need the same,' came a voice from behind him.

Bishop turned to see Jessica had entered the bar. She perched herself on the stool next to him and he ordered her a scotch.

'I saw you leave the conference theatre,' she remarked. 'I wondered if you were okay.'

He nodded. 'Just weary. The discussion doesn't seem to be getting far. Too many fingers in the pie.'

'They feel it's necessary to get as many views as possible.'

'Some of those views are a little eccentric, wouldn't you say?' Bishop passed Jessica's drink over to her. 'Water?' he asked.

She shook her head and sipped the scotch. 'Some are fanatical in their beliefs, I agree, but the others are well respected in their particular fields of psychic research.'

'Will any of it help, though? How the hell can you beat something that apparently has no material form?'

'The idea of germs being living organisms was unknown not

too long ago. The Bubonic Plague itself was at first thought to be the work of the devil.'

'I thought you believed this was.'

'In a way, I do. I think our terms are wrong, though. Many think of the devil as a creature with horns and a long forked tail, or at least, a living creature who pops through the gates of hell every now and again to create havoc. It's a belief the Church has done nothing to discourage!'

'And the devil is behind all this?'

'As I said, our terms are wrong. The devil is within us, Chris, just as God is.'

Bishop sighed wearily. 'We are God, we are the devil?' There was disdain in his words.

'The power for good and the power for evil is in us. God and devil are just symbolic names for an abstraction.'

'That's some abstraction if, as you're implying, it's the root cause of everything good and everything bad that's happened in the world.'

'It's an abstraction that's fast becoming a reality.'

'Because Pryszlak has found a way of using it?'

'He's not the first.'

Bishop stared at her. 'This has never happened before.'

'How do you know? Read your Bible, Chris; it gives us plenty of indications.'

'But then why this evil power? Why hasn't someone used the power for good?'

'Many have. Jesus Christ was one.'

Bishop smiled. 'You mean all those miracles were due to a force He knew how to tap?'

'Miracles are more common than you think. Christ may have been a man who knew the process of using that power.'

'Would that make Pryszlak the anti-Christ? I mean, he went for the other extreme.'

Jessica ignored the mockery in Bishop's question. 'There have also been many anti-Christs.'

The whisky on an empty stomach had begun to make Bishop feel slightly light-headed, but the earnestness in Jessica's eyes made him bite back his cynicism. 'Look, Jessica, if you say miracles are fairly common, why is it that no one else is using this other source in the way Pryszlak apparently is?'

'Because we're still learning. We haven't yet grasped it. When it is used, it's done unconsciously. When we learned to walk, did we think about it first, or did the realisation come after? Once we were aware that we could walk, that it was physically possible, we could learn to do other things. Run, then ride, use implements, make vehicles to carry us. It's a gradual process, Chris, and only our own awareness can speed up that process.'

Bishop wondered why he was resisting the argument, for it explained much of his own thoughts regarding the paranormal. Perhaps it was because it all seemed too simple, too obvious an answer; but then, who said the answer had to be complicated? Everything came from the individual, no outside force was involved; and when each personal source was discovered, then, united with others, that collected power became massive. It did seem that the Dark affected those people who were in some way mentally disturbed, whether they were criminals, insane, or – his grip on the glass tightened – or had evil in their minds. Many of the cases he had heard of over the past few weeks concerned individuals who held some grievance against others – even mere dislike – and it seemed the madness around them had triggered off their own violence. If the Dark could seek out this evil, invade their minds and draw out that force, uniting with it, reinforcing its own strength like some giant, rapacious organism, then where would it end? As it grew stronger, would it be capable of swamping any opposing force for good in the mind, finding the evil that lurked in every living soul and using it? Was the reason for that power not having been developed more fully in the past because of the conflicting oppositions within everybody, only those rare beings who were truly good or truly evil being capable of harnessing it in their own way? And when you died, did that entity die with you or was it released into . . . into what? Bishop realised that Jessica's answer had not been simple at all: it was as complex as man's own evolution.

'Chris, are you all right? You've gone deathly white.'

Jessica's hand was over his own, and he became aware of the crushing grip he had on the glass. He placed the scotch back on the bar, but still she kept her hand on his.

He took in a deep breath. 'Maybe it's all catching up with me.'

Misunderstanding him, she said. 'You've been through so much. We all have, but you more than most.'

He shook his head. 'I don't mean that, Jessica. Lynn's death is something I'll never really get over, but it's something I know I'll learn to accept, just as I've accepted Lucy's. The hurt will always be there, but it'll become controllable. No, what's shaken me is your explanation for the Dark. I take it Jacob shares your view?'

'It *is* his view. I agree with him.'

'Then there's no way we can overcome it.'

She was silent for a moment, then replied. 'There has to be a way.'

Bishop turned his hand over so that the palm joined with Jessica's. His fingers curled around her hand and gently squeezed; but he said nothing.

He was still awake, sitting in the uncomfortable armchair in his hotel room, facing the large picture window and wondering what fresh atrocities were breaking out in London, when the light rapping on the door disturbed his thoughts. He glanced at his watch and saw it was 10.30. The rapping came again. Crushing his half-smoked cigarette into the ashtray resting on the arm of the chair, he rose and walked over to the door. He hesitated before turning the twist-lock handle, apprehension having become a part of his life-pattern now. Jessica's voice dispelled his anxiety.

He opened the door and found himself looking into the sightless eyes of Jacob Kulek, Jessica standing just behind her father.

'May we come in, Chris?' Kulek said.

Bishop stood aside and Jessica guided her father into the room. He closed the door and turned to face them.

'I'm sorry I have not been able to speak with you during the day, Chris,' Kulek apologised. 'I'm afraid my time is governed by others nowadays.'

'It's all right, I understand. These people seem to expect a lot of you, Jacob.'

The blind man gave a small laugh, but Bishop noted there was a tiredness to it. 'The scientists and medical people on the one hand are sceptical, while most of the psychists on the other are cautious – they see this as an opportunity to prove everything they have preached over the last few decades. The irrational ones among them have, thank God, been largely ignored. The authorities are stuck somewhere in the middle of both groups, naturally leaning more towards the logical or, if you like, the scientific, point of view. I believe it is only because the scientists have not as yet provided any clues, let alone answers, that our

583

opinions are being sought. May I sit, Chris? It's been a wearisome day.'

'Please.' Bishop turned round the armchair he had just vacated to face the room and Jessica guided her father into it. She smiled warmly at Bishop as she sat in the chair provided with the room's dressing-table. He settled on the edge of his bed and returned her smile.

'Can I order you both some coffee?' he asked.

'No, thank you. I think a large brandy might help to ease my ageing bones, though.' Kulek inclined his head towards his daughter.

'Coffee will be fine for me, Chris.'

Bishop picked up the phone and ordered two coffees and one large brandy. When he replaced the receiver he said, 'Is Edith okay?'

'Tired, frightened, like all of us. Our smaller, more intimate meeting in which she was included, broke up only twenty minutes ago. The select committee had to discuss all the points raised at the conference today – the valid points, that is.'

'Who decided which were and which were not?'

'I suppose you could say moderation did. Our Home Secretary is not one for extremes, you know.'

'From what I hear, he's not one for actions, either.'

'Then his decision may surprise you.'

'Oh?'

'I'm not sure he's convinced, but he has agreed to – what shall I say? – to an experiment.'

Bishop leaned forward, arms resting across his knees, interested.

Kulek pinched the sides of his nose and squeezed his eyes tightly shut for a few seconds to ease the ache in his head. His face looked drained when he raised his eyes again. 'We are going back to Beechwood. That is, what's left of Beechwood.'

Bishop was stunned. 'Why? What good could that possibly do? As you said, the place is in ruins anyway.'

Kulek patiently nodded and rested his long, thin fingers over the top of his walking cane. 'It was, and still is, a focal point in this whole affair. Every night, more and more unfortunate victims of this thing we call the Dark gather there. Some die, others are found the following morning either standing or lying helpless in the rubble. There has to be a reason for them to go there,

584

something that draws them to it.'

'How could it help for you to go there? We tried it before, remember?'

'And something happened, Chris,' Jessica broke in.

'Jacob nearly got killed.'

'And you had a vision,' the blind man said quietly.

'You saw what went on in that house,' Jessica added. 'You saw how Pryszlak and his followers died.'

'Don't you see, Chris, there are strong vibrations around that area? Even though it is only a ruin, there will be those same energies.' Kulek fixed Bishop with his sightless gaze.

'But the danger. You . . .'

'This time we will have protection. The area will be guarded by troops, we will have powerful lighting . . .'

'You're not thinking of going back there at night?'

'Yes, that would be the only time for what we have in mind.'

'You're crazy. Jessica, you can't let him do this. The Army won't be able to protect him.'

Jessica looked at Bishop steadily. 'Chris,' she said, 'we want you to come with us.'

He shook his head. 'This is wrong, Jessica. There's no point to it. What can we do there, anyway?'

Kulek replied. 'The only thing that is left to us. We are going to make contact with the Dark. We will try to talk with Boris Pryszlak.'

The discreet knock on the door announced the arrival of the coffees and brandy.

Chapter Twenty-Six

It could have been daytime, the lights were so dazzling. Every house in Willow Road had been cleared of its occupants; not that there were many of them left – the road had attracted the attention of too many victims of the Dark for any residents to feel safe. Army vehicles were parked along the kerbside, all pointed in the same direction, and heavily guarded barriers had been placed across both ends of the road. Two powerful, wide-beam searchlights mounted on trucks and powered by their own generators, were directed into the open space that had once been Beechwood. Most of the rubble had been cleared to allow for an array of equipment to be set up, instruments ranging from sound and video recording machinery, to geiger-counters and other sophisticated gadgetry that Bishop had never seen before, let alone put a name to. Arc lamps, hooked into the main electricity system of the area, were placed at strategic points around the grounds. The whole scene had an unreal look and Bishop could not help feeling he had wandered on to a film set, the various cameras operated by army personnel adding to the illusion. Nearby, Jacob Kulek was having angry words with the Principal Private Secretary to the Home Office over the amount of machinery and reinforcements that were in evidence, all of which, Kulek claimed, might interfere with the energy patterns in the atmosphere and impede any mental contact that might be made with the Dark. The Private Secretary, a thin, waspish little man name Sicklemore, testily replied that they were conducting a scientific operation rather than a parlour seance and his instructions had been to gather and record all necessary data from the experiment while providing every protection possible to civilian life. He added that for decades parapsychologists had urged scientists to work hand in hand with them, so Kulek should not complain now that this was happening. The blind man had to concede the point, realising the crisis was too grave for petty bickering. Jessica, standing by her father's side, looked relieved that the minor flare-up between the two men was over.

Bishop eased his way through the throng of technicians, police and army personnel, all of whom seemed to have some specific task to perform, and saw Edith Metlock sitting alone among the confusion in a canvas-backed chair. He went over to her and sat in the empty seat next to her.

'How do you feel?' he asked.

Her smile was faint. 'A little nervous,' she replied. 'I'm not sure this is the right way.'

'Jacob seems to think this might be the only way.'

'He's probably right.' Her mood was one of resignation.

'We've got plenty of armed protection,' he said to reassure her.

'You don't understand, Chris. I have to let this . . . this darkness enter my mind. It will be like allowing an evil spirit to invade my body, only in this case there will be several hundred demons.'

He pointed towards two men a few yards away who were talking in low tones. 'They'll be with you.'

'They're both sensitives of high repute and it's a privilege to be working with them. But our combined strength is nothing compared to the evil influences that have accumulated. I can feel their presence already and it frightens me.'

'Maybe nothing will happen.'

'In some ways, I hope you're right. It has to be stopped, though, before it's too late.'

Bishop was silent for a few moments, his head bowed as if studying the dirt at his feet. 'Edith,' he said finally, 'back in Jacob's house, when we were being held hostage by those two crazy women. Before you arrived, one of them said that Lynn, my wife, was still "active". Can you tell me what she meant?'

The medium patted his arm sympathetically. 'She probably meant that your wife's spirit was tied to those others controlled by the Dark.'

'She's still part of it?'

'I can't say. She may be. Is that why you're here tonight?'

Bishop straightened his body. 'There's a lot I've had to accept recently. I admit I'm still confused by many things, but just the thought of how they murdered Lynn . . .' With effort, he controlled his anger. 'If there's anything I can do to help smash this

587

thing, I will. Jacob said he was unsure of what caused the manifestations in Beechwood before – you, or me, or a combination of both of us. I suppose I'm just an ingredient he wants handy to throw into the pot.'

A shadow fell over them and they looked up to see Jessica. 'Everything's nearly ready, Edith. Jacob would like you and the others to take up your positions.'

Bishop helped the medium to her feet and could not help noticing how the robustness had left her demeanour. They walked towards Jacob Kulek who was talking to a group of people which included the Police Commissioner, a youngish-looking army major, and several men and women whom Bishop knew to be scientists and metaphysicists. It's like a bloody circus, he thought grimly.

Kulek broke off his conversation when Jessica tugged at his sleeve and said something to him. He nodded, then spoke to the group around him. 'Anyone who is not necessary to this operation must leave the site. Will you please see to that, Commissioner? The very minimum of guards, the very minimum of technicians. Conditions for what we are about to attempt are poor enough without making them worse. The searchlights will have to be switched off, Major.'

'Good Lord, you're not serious?' came the immediate response.

'I'm afraid I am. The arc lamps, too, will have to be dimmed considerably. Edith?'

'I'm here, Jacob.'

'I'm sorry about these conditions, my dear, I hope they will not be too much of a distraction for you. Mr Enwright and Mr Schenkel, you are both ready?'

The two mediums whom Jessica had also brought over answered that they were.

'Is Chris there? Chris, I want you seated next to Edith. Could everyone please take their positions?'

Bishop was surprised: he had thought that he would be somewhere on the sidelines. Suddenly, he was even more afraid.

Six chairs forming a rough semi-circle had been placed in a flattened area of the site. To his further discomfort, Bishop realised they were in a spot close to where the main room of Beechwood would have been. Rough boards beneath his feet covered any gaps leading to the cellar below. Glancing at his watch, he saw it was just after ten. The medium called Schenkel sat in the end seat, Enwright next to him. Then came Edith Metlock, himself, Jacob Kulek, with Jessica sitting slightly back from the group just behind her father.

'Please, we must have complete silence.' Kulek's voice was barely raised, but everyone on the site heard. 'The lights, Major. Could we have them down now?'

The searchlights blinked off and the specially fitted dimmer switches of the arc lamps were turned down. The scene that had been brightly lit became gloomy and immediately sinister.

Kulek turned to Bishop. 'Think back to that first day, Chris. That first time you came to Beechwood. Remember what you saw.'

But Bishop already had.

He knew what he had to do. They had told him.

The inside of the power station was like a huge cavern, a giant's lair that roared and throbbed with the sound of the massive furnaces and turbines. He passed between them, monster steel-plated turbines on one side, furnaces and boilers that stretched up from the basement thirty feet below, almost touching the ceiling over a hundred feet above, on the other. The turbines were painted a bright yellow, each one equipped with an instrument console that kept a watchful eye on their activity. The furnaces and boilers were deceptively cool grey in colour, though the effort of burning a ton of oil per minute made them dangerously hot to touch. Heavily insulated pipes ran from them combining with the boiler pipes in the basement to carry the steam at a pressure of fifteen hundred pounds per square inch to drive the turbine blades.

He passed a technician checking the rows of dials which monitored one of the furnaces and he gave no acknowledgement to the waved hand. The technician frowned, puzzled by his colleague's unkempt appearance, but his thoughts quickly returned to the instruments before him; the loads were heavy these nights because of the government edict that every possible light in the city should be turned on.

The man headed for the stairs leading to the administration floors. And the main switching room.

For two days and nights he had hidden in his basement flat, the curtains drawn, the two rooms he occupied kept in a shadowy

589

gloom during the day, a total darkness during the night.

He was a squat man of twenty-eight, his face still riddled with acne that should have disappeared years before, his hair already leaving his scalp in disloyal batches. He lived alone, not by choice, but because no others, male or female, had any inclination to live with him. His contempt for the human race in general was only thinly disguised and it was a feeling he had nurtured ever since he had realised the world was contemptuous of him. He had thought that leaving school would mean the end of being treated like some loathsome object by immature minds, only to find that the minds at the college he had gone on to, although older, were still as immature. By the time he had become a chemical engineer, the damage was entrenched within him. His parents were still alive, but hardly seen by him. They had never offered him real comfort. Their finding him spying on his rapidly-developing sister on several occasions had earned their early disenchantment with him. They had let him know that the thick lenses he had to wear which made his eyes look like black buttons swimming in silvery pools were a punishment from God. So did He also give him the spots because he couldn't stop abusing himself? And did He make his body smell more than others because he hated his sister, even though he spied on her? And now was He making his hair fall out because he never stopped having dirty thoughts? Did He do all that? Well forget Him, there were other gods to worship.

He climbed the stairs to the offices, passing no one else on the way; the generating station needed little more than a complement of thirty staff and technicians to keep it functioning, a small group of people who controlled the power used by millions. Being in charge of the energy used by so many was what had attracted him to the job in the first place. There were three ways of depriving people of their light and power in the area supervised by his particular station: one was to blow the whole plant up; two was to systematically shut down the generators and turbines, and cut the fuel supply; three was to turn off everything, apart from the furnaces, by the remote controls in the main switching room. He had no access to explosives, so blowing up the plant was out of the question. Shutting everything down and cutting the fuel supply manually would take too long and the other technicians would stop him before he'd managed one turbine. So the answer was in the control room. Cut the switches and

590

everything would be black. Black as the night. A look of peasure came into his eyes.

The main switching room was a large glass-fronted box projecting out into the generating hall, crammed with consoles containing dials, and a row of television screens that kept an eye on every part of the power station. The supervisors had been even more alert than usual over the past few weeks, for the danger of allowing a power failure in any area covered by their plant had been carefully explained to them. The danger within their own ranks, however, had been unforeseen.

The duty supervisor looked up in surprise as the man entered the room and was about to ask where he'd been the last couple of days when the bullet from the Beretta punctured his forehead. The other supervisors were too stunned to react quickly and he carefully shot them, each bullet finding its mark with precisioned nonchalance. He was amazed at his own accuracy considering he had never handled a gun before, but not amazed at his own calmness. The stranger, the tall lady, had shown him how to use it when she had come to his basement flat earlier that day, but it was not she who had instilled the calmness in him. The Dark had done that.

He sniggered as the bodies of his colleagues tumbled to the floor and he took time to watch their twitching limbs for a few moments. His lips glistening, made wet by the tongue that constantly flicked across them, he stepped over the bodies towards the control panels. His hand was trembling as he reached for the first switch.

Bishop blinked his eyes rapidly. Was it his imagination or was it becoming even darker? He felt the tightness in his throat as he tried to swallow. It seemed as though there were four walls around him, transparent walls through which he could see the hazy figures of the others on the site. The walls grew more solid. A window to his left, curtains closed. Another window to his right, further down. Shadows moving like wispy smoke.

He resisted.

Edith's eyes were closed, muted sounds coming from her. Her head slowly sagged forward until her chin rested on her chest. The other two mediums were watching and Bishop saw their alarm. The one on the end, Schenkel, began to shiver. His eyelids fluttered and his pupils rose upwards into his head before his eyes

591

closed completely. Enwright had not noticed what was happening to his colleague, for he was still watching Edith Metlock. Strong fingers curled around Bishop's arm and he snapped his head around to find Kulek's sightless eyes peering intently at him.

'Chris, can you see them again?' Kulek whispered. 'I can feel there is something malevolent here. Is it them, can you see those same faces again?'

Bishop was unable to answer. It was too sudden; no sooner had the lights been dimmed than the presence was with them. As though it had been waiting.

The room was solid and figures wafted before him, floating into focus then becoming vague again, blurred images. The room seemed smaller. Sounds buzzed in his ears, voices bursting forward then disappearing abruptly, replaced by others, as though a frequency dial was being aimlessly turned across the airwaves. He looked back at Edith and saw a black substance was seeping from her lips, dribbling down her chin and on to her chest. It could have been blood, yet he knew it wasn't. He reached out a hand to touch and there was nothing there, no black stickiness on his fingers, nothing on her chin. He withdrew his hand and the substance dribbled from her lips once more. Bishop looked up and the room seemed even smaller.

Schenkel fell from his chair and lay still on the rough boards and earth covering the cellar below. No one stepped forward to help him, for they had been warned not to interfere unless something drastic occurred. Enwright glanced at his companion but ignored him. Edith Metlock moaned aloud and something dark was expelled from her mouth like a billow of smoke. The voices inside Bishop's head were laughing now and he saw that the room was shrinking, the walls and ceiling reaching in towards him. He knew he would be crushed and he tried to rise from the chair. His body had become frozen solid and he could feel the frost heavy on his eyelids, sealing them tight. His hair prickled as each one became a brittle icicle. The walls were only feet away.

A cold hand touched his and somehow warmed it. Edith had reached out to him. His other hand was being held by someone else and, although his head was frozen tight, he knew it was Jacob Kulek who gripped him. The warmth returned to his body and he felt something falling away from him, something that had threatened to smother him. The walls and ceiling had vanished, but a swirling darkness filled his vision.

The sound came from Enwright, but it was not his voice, nor the voice of any living thing. It was a high squealing sound, a tortured wailing. The medium stood, his palms pressed against his temples, his head turning from side to side as though he were trying to shake something from it. His eyes looked wildly around until they came to rest on Bishop.

The after-image of those staring eyes stayed in Bishop's vision as the dim lights went out and everything succumbed to the crushing blackness.

Chapter Twenty-Seven

The hands closed around Bishop's throat and began to tighten. He could only see a black shape before him, but he knew it was the medium, Enwright, who was trying to choke the life from him. He gripped the man's wrists and pulled at them, his chin automatically tucking itself downwards, neck muscles taut, to resist the increasing pressure. Even as he struggled, Bishop was aware of the confusion around him, the shouts, the running feet, the sudden small flares as matches or lighters were lit, then the long torch beams cutting out bright sections in the night.

A dizziness made the scene even more chaotic and he knew he would soon begin to lose his senses if he did not break the choking grip, but no matter how hard he pulled at the wrists, the pressure still increased. He did the only thing possible. Releasing his own hold, he grabbed the medium's clothing and pulled the man towards him, pushing his heels hard into the boards beneath them. His chair leaned back at a precarious angle, then both men went toppling over, Bishop increasing the momentum with an added thrust of his heels. They landed heavily, Enwright's head smashing on to the boards with a loud crack, his body immediately becoming limp. Bishop had curved his back and hunched his shoulders so the impact had little effect on him. He pushed the sprawled body away and sat up, looking quickly around, then closing his eyes for a few seconds to help them adjust to the darkness more easily.

'Get those bloody searchlights on!' he heard someone shout and almost immediately a broad expanse of light lit up half the site.

'The other searchlight!' cried the same voice and Bishop could now see it was the army major who was shouting the commands. 'Get it bloodywell on!'

But something was happening at the vehicle on which the

second searchlight was mounted. Bishop could just make out struggling figures and he flinched when a shot rang out. Other soldiers began to run towards the vehicle, their 7.62mm self-loading rifles held across their chests, ready for use.

More movement before him caught his eye and he saw Edith Metlock was tossing her head from side to side, her hands waving in the air as though warding something off. The other medium, Schenkel, was now on his knees, body bent forward and hands covering his face.

'Chris, help me!'

Jessica was trying to pull a man away from her father, a man who wore the dark blue uniform of a policeman. The realisation struck Bishop in a flash of new dread: the Dark had penetrated the minds of some of those meant to protect them. He staggered to his feet and ran towards Jessica, but another figure reached them first. The policeman was behind Kulek and was dragging him backwards, an arm locked around his throat, Jessica in front of both men trying to wrench the arm away. The other man came up behind the policeman and dug rigid thumbs into the flesh points just under the uniformed man's jawline, digging them in deeply with a screwing motion. The policeman screamed and was forced to release Kulek; as he turned, the second man brought the heel of his hand sharply up beneath the policeman's nose, snapping his head backwards. A swift chop at the exposed wind-pipe sent the policeman reeling to the ground where he lay squirming and gasping for breath.

By then, Bishop had reached them and he recognised the man who had saved Kulek as Peck's DI, Roper.

'Bleedin wollies,' Roper said, barely giving the injured police-man a second glance.

Just then, Peck himself emerged from the general confusion. 'Are you okay, sir?' he asked, a hand reaching out to steady Jacob Kulek.

The blind man drew in deep breaths as Jessica held on to him. 'I'm . . . I'm learning how to resist such attacks,' he managed to say and Peck allowed a brief flicker of amusement to cross his face.

'We'd better get you out of here,' he said. 'It looks as if the power supply to half of London has been switched off. Anything can happen now.' He turned to Bishop. 'You all right? I saw that bastard ready to attack you just before the lights blew. Sorry I couldn't get to you in time.'

'I'm okay. How could the power fail?'

Peck shrugged. 'Overload, maybe.'

'Or sabotage.'

'For the moment, it doesn't matter. The main thing is to get you all somewhere safe.'

'Edith. Where is Edith?' Kulek was clutching at Jessica, frustrated by his own blindness.

'She's still in her chair, Father. She's in a trance state. I think she's trying to break free of it.'

'Quickly, take me to her before it's too late.'

'I think we ought to get away from here, sir,' Peck interjected.

'Edith first,' Kulek said firmly. 'We must take her with us.'

Jessica led him over to the agitated medium and Roper looked uneasily towards his superior.

'I don't like this, guv,' he said. 'We don't stand a chance if that searchlight fails.'

'Get over to the cars, Frank. I want all their lights on right away. Where's the bloody Commissioner? And the army major – he should have had things organised by now.'

But more gunfire told him that organisation under those circumstances would prove difficult, and when the shattering of glass preceded the extinction of the remaining light, leaving the site filled only with individual torch beams, they knew it would prove virtually impossible.

'The cars, Frank, quick. Get those lights on.' Someone bumped into Peck and he roughly pushed the figure away. He reached inside his jacket for the Smith and Wesson holstered discreetly at his hip and drew it.

'Bishop! Where are you?'

'Right here.' He had been following Kulek and Jessica before the remaining light had blown and now stood midway between them and Peck.

The detective cursed the lack of moonlight. What a bloody silly night to choose! 'Can you reach Kulek?' He had to shout to make himself heard over the general clamour.

'Yes, they're not far . . . Jesus!'

Peck made his way towards the dark shape a few feet away when he, too, felt the coldness stab inside him. It blanked out his thoughts for a few moments, a numbling iciness that seemed to fill every secret crevice of his mind. He stumbled against someone.

'Bishop? What is it? Can you feel it, too?'

'Don't give in to it, Peck. Force it out!'

'What is it?' Peck was shouting, his free hand against his eyes and forehead, the gun held away from him.

'It's the Dark. It's probing your mind. You can resist, Peck, but you've got to want to.' Bishop's mind was clearing fast after the first paralysing assault on it and he suddenly understood that the Dark could only claim those who allowed themselves to be claimed. The Dark had to be accepted before it could take, like the mythical vampire who could not cross a threshold unless invited.

He grabbed Peck and shook him. 'Fight it!' he yelled. 'It can't touch you if you fight it!'

Bishop lost his grip as Peck slid to the ground. 'Get them . . . get them out of here!' he heard the detective say.

Bishop wasted no more time: only Peck could save himself now. More shots were ringing out and the brief gunflashes lit the scene into frozen actions. The darkness around them was heavy, cloying, but his eyes were slowly adapting to it and he was able to make out shapes more clearly. He moved towards Jessica and her father, finding them crouched beside Edith Metlock, who still writhed in her chair.

'Jessica,' he said, kneeling next to her, 'we've got to leave here. It's too dangerous to stay.'

'They're torturing her, Chris. She can't bring herself out of the trance.'

Kulek was clutching the medium's shoulders. He softly called her name over and over again. Her body heaved as she began to retch, the sound dry and agonised until she slid from the chair and vomit spurted from her mouth in an arched stream. Bishop felt warm, sticky particles spatter his face and a foul stench came to his nostrils. He brushed the speckles away with the sleeve of his jacket, then reached down for the medium and pulled her into a sitting position. Lights began to spring into life from the roadway and two sets swung their beams on to the site as drivers manoeuvred their cars. Edith's eyes were wide and staring and, although she still shook, the wild writhing had stopped.

Bishop stood and dragged her up with him. She offered no resistance and he was relieved she could stand albeit only with his support. 'Jacob, hold on to Jessica. We're getting out now.'

'We made a mistake. We did not realise the madness we were dealing with, the evil that is around us.'

597

'You're telling me. Now come on, let's go!' There was an anger in Bishop that he did not understand, but was glad to have; it somehow threw strength into him.

He half-carried, half-dragged Edith across the site, making for the road where the lights were, urging Jessica and her father to keep close to him. The soldier who stood in his way took his time in raising the rifle and aiming it at Bishop's head.

All Bishop could see was the black silhouette against the glare from the nearest car, but he knew the soldier's intention. He started at the shot that rang out and watched the soldier's body slowly crumble.

'You going to stand there all night?' said Peck, emerging from the shadows to one side of the bright twin beams. Bishop almost cried out with relief; he never thought Peck would have been such a welcome sight. He tightened his hold on the woman, who still stared blankly ahead, and moved forward, Peck joining him and helping to support her weight.

'I thought it had me back there,' Peck said loudly. 'Couldn't move, like being doped up for an operation but not as pleasant. Scared the life out of me. Keep up with us, Miss Kulek, we'll soon be out of this!'

The site was further lit by the first searchlight coming back into action again and, as Bishop swung his head to survey the scene, he saw there were many individual struggles taking place, soldier against soldier, policeman against policeman, and a mixture of both. There were others on the site now, men and women who had not been there before, and these people cowered under the naked glare, shielding their eyes with raised arms. Where they had come from, he could not even guess, but it was evident that they were victims of the Dark. Bodies of policemen or soldiers whom they had attacked lay at their feet. He couldn't be sure, but one of these recumbent figures looked like the Police Commissioner himself.

They stumbled over the rubble around the edges of the site and crossed the small concreted area that had once been Beechwood's car space. To Bishop it seemed like only yesterday that he had crossed that area for the first time, yet so much had happened since, it could well have been years ago.

Willow Road and the Beechwood ruin were a bubble of light in that broad section of the city, the glow tingeing the night sky so that it could be seen for miles around. People were stirring, looking out from their windows at the bright glow, wondering why it was lit when their streets were in total darkness. Others left their homes, or emerged from sewers and other dark places to make their way towards the light, already knowing what they would find there.

Bishop squinted his eyes against the headlights, the shouts, the screams, the crackle of gunfire spurring him on. They reached the first car and almost fell against the bonnet in their haste.

'Over here, guv,' came a familiar voice.

Policemen, uniformed as well as those in plain clothes, were all around, and Peck led the small party through them towards Roper who was standing by another car.

'Bloody murder going on back there,' the Detective Inspector said. 'I didn't think you'd make it.'

'Yes, me too,' Peck replied. 'Have you been on to HQ?'

'Yeah, they're sending all available help. They've got their own problems, though; trouble's breaking out all over again.'

Peck called a uniformed sergeant over. 'I want one more car swung round to point its lights into the site. Back as many of the others as possible up against one another to give us a circle of light around us. Let's keep any marauding maniacs away, or at least see them before they get too close.'

They ducked instinctively when a bottle shattered into the road near them. They tried to see who had thrown the missile, but were dazzled by the other car lights parked further down. Another bottle came sailing through the air and this one broke against the shoulder of a plain-clothes policeman. The man went down on one knee, then rose again, apparently not badly hurt. Shadowy figures flitted momentarily through the beams of light before disappearing into the surrounding darkness once more. Peck knew he would have to get his men organised quickly – their fear was becoming greater because of their confusion.

'Bishop, I want you and these people out of the area. My driver, Simpson, will get you over to the other side of the river.'

Bishop thought Kulek might offer some resistance to Peck's directions, but when he turned to the blind man he saw only a look of utter defeat on his face.

'Jacob?'

'It's become too stong. I did not realise.' The words were spoken to no one in particular; it was as if Kulek had retreated within himself.

599

'We must leave, Father. We can't do any good here,' Jessica urged him.

Peck was already opening the doors of the Granada. 'In you get,' he ordered crisply. 'Kulek and the two women in the back, you in the front, Bishop. Frank, grab a patrol car and go with them. Take a couple of wollies.'

Roper dashed off to commandeer a white Rover nearby, its driver immediately gunning the engine, relieved to be on the move. The car screeched over to the Granada as Peck slammed the door after Kulek and the two women. Other police cars were positioning themselves in the road, tyes screeching as they turned their vehicles so their headlight beams shone outwards. There were several muffled thuds as bodies of people lurking in the darker areas were struck by the fast-moving vehicles. Peck was surprised at just how many people were advancing on them, their forms frozen in the swinging lights reminding him of paralysed foxes caught on country roads at night. Whether or not they were all victims or some had merely come to investigate the lights and commotion, there was no way of knowing; there was no choice but to treat everyone as a potential enemy. He leaned into the Granada's passenger window and spoke across Bishop to his driver.

'Back to HQ, and don't stop for anything. Just follow the patrol car.'

Bishop called after Peck as the detective made his way towards the Rover. 'What will you do?'

Peck turned and said, 'We'll get the Commissioner and the civilians out of here, then head back over the river. The Army can sort themselves out!'

He turned and shouted instructions at the driver of the patrol car before Bishop could tell him he thought he had seen the Police Commissioner either dead or unconscious on the ground. Peck banged his hand down hard on the Rover's roof and the car shot forward. Bishop was thrown back into his seat as the Granada lurched after it. They had only travelled a hundred yards when the red brakelights of the car ahead blinked on and both cars screeched to a halt. Bishop poked his head out the passenger window and a wave of despair swept over him.

The end of the road was completely blocked by crowds of people. They moved forward, some running, others walking slowly as if by automation. He could see that many were in a bad

600

state of deterioration, while others were alert, their actions quicker, the light not seeming to bother them as much. There was no way of knowing just how many were out there, but it seemed like hundreds, an unbroken mass of advancing bodies. As they drew nearer, he saw that many carried weapons ranging from iron bars to knives and milk bottles. One of the running men held what looked like a shotgun.

Jessica, directly behind Bishop, was leaning forward in her seat, unable to see clearly. 'What is it, Chris?'

He had no time to reply, for the driver in the car ahead had decided what to do: the Rover accelerated towards the mob and the Granada followed. If the policeman in the first car expected the crowd to jump aside and leave a path clear for him, he was mistaken: they stood their ground and the Rover plunged into them.

Jessica screamed when she saw the bodies tossed into the air, the headlights of the Granada illuminating the scene in shocking relief. Their car skidded as the driver turned the steering-wheel to avoid crashing into the back of the now stationary Rover; instead, the Granada's side smashed into the lead vehicle, throwing the patrol car's occupants forward and shaking Bishop and the others badly.

Roper's head appeared out of the white car's rear passenger window and he waved his arm in a forward motion at them. His own driver was quickly recovering from the shock of running down so many people and was starting his stalled engine once more when a man appeared near the bonnet of the Rover. He carried a shotgun and he aimed it at the windscreen.

Bishop heard the blast and saw the glass shatter leaving an irregular opaque fringe of glittering silver around the edge of the black hole it had created. Both policemen in the front of the patrol car jerked backwards, then their bodies slipped from view. Roper was already pushing his door open when eager hands grabbed at him. He raised his gun, but the weapon was forced aside as he was mobbed.

'We've got to help him!' Bishop cried as he reached for the door-handle on his side.

The driver grabbed him and pulled him back. 'No way. My orders were to get you lot out of here and that's what I'm going to do.'

'We can't just leave him!'

601

'We'd have no chance out there – there's too many!'

Even as he spoke, their own car was being surrounded, fists and makeshift weapons pounding on the roof. Hands reached in and tore at Bishop's arms and face; the driver had wisely kept his window closed throughout. Bishop pulled himself away from the grasping hands and struck out at them, feeling no pity for these people and what they had become, just a loathing fear. Metal scraped against metal as the Granada lunged forward once more, friction between the two cars sending a shower of sparks into the air.

Jessica watched with horror as one man refused to let go of the door on Bishop's side and was dragged along with the vehicle as it gathered speed. Slowly and deliberately, Bishop prised the man's fingers away from the door-frame until the hands fell away; Jessica felt the slight but sickening bump as the car ran over the man's trapped ankles.

Simpson headed towards the pavement which seemed less congested than the road itself. A woman leapt on to the bonnet and managed to cling there staring with manic eyes through the windscreen before the car mounted the kerb and she was tossed off. Bishop looked back, but could see nothing of Roper, just a mass of black shapes swarming over the Rover. Another blast, then a great roar as the patrol car's tank exploded; someone – probably the same man who had shot the driver and his partner – had deliberately fired into the Rover's bodywork. A great ball of flames rose into the air, killing those too close, burning others. Most of the road was lit up by the explosion, but the shadows quickly regained ground, beaten back only by the red glow from the ensuing fire.

The Granada bounced back on to the road, the main body of the crowd having been skirted, and sped on, heading for the T-junction at the end of Willow Road. The headlights caught the figure of a man as he ran forward and hurled a milk bottle at the windscreen. Both Bishop and the driver raised their arms to protect their faces as their view became a web of fractured glass. Barely slowing, the driver punched a hole through the windscreen and shouted to Bishop. 'Take my gun – smash out the glass.'

He had flipped back his jacket and Bishop could just make out the gun butt protruding from the holster at the driver's waist. The policeman loosened the restraining grip, his attention still firmly directed through the jagged hole he had created. Bishop pulled out the gun and used it to smash a larger hole in the glass. the wind rushed through the gap, but they hardly noticed it. The car tore into the street at the end of Willow Road, the tyres flattening out and desperately biting into the road's surface for grip. Bishop was thrown against the passenger door and he grabbed the frame to hold himself there until the car had regained stability. He had one last look at Willow Road through the windows opposite him before they had turned the corner completely and houses blocked his view. Lights, flames and milling people were all he had seen. Now there was blackness around them, probed only by their own headlights.

Bishop became conscious of the cold steel he held. He proffered the weapon towards the driver. 'Here's your gun.'

The policeman's eyes were screwed into narrow slits against the wind rushing at his face and he did not take them from the road ahead. 'You keep it, I've got to concentrate on driving. Don't hesitate to use it if necessary.'

Bishop was about to protest, but thought better of it. The man was right: he could hardly protect them and drive at the same time. It was fortunate that all senior policemen had been issued with guns – the whole force would have been armed if there had been enough weapons to go round – for the numbers of victims claimed by the Dark was growing day by day. Or, more appropriately, night by night.

He wound up his side window, then turned to the three passengers in the back. 'Are you okay?' he asked above the noise of the engine and the wind rushing through the interior. Their shapes were barely discernible in the darkness. Jessica's face came close to his.

'I think they're both in a state of shock, Chris.'

'No, no, I'm all right.' It was Kulek's voice. 'It was just so . . . so . . . overwhelming. The power has become so great.'

Bishop sensed the blind man's utter weariness and shared in his feeling of defeat. How did you combat something so intangible, something that had no material form, no physical nucleus? How did you destroy energy from the mind? The living people who gave themselves up to the Dark could be controlled, killed, but the killing itself allowed that energy to become stronger.

A wild skid as the driver tried to avoid a group of people in the centre of the road caused Bishop to clutch at the back of his seat.

603

The car swerved into a narrow sidestreet, leaving the group calling after them; they may or may not have been victims, but the driver had no inclination to stop and find out. Dull glows were coming from the windows of many houses they passed as though the occupants were lighting fires or candles to create a natural light. They saw that other people were leaving their homes, leading or carrying children, and jumping into their cars, switching their headlights on.

'Looks like we're not the only ones heading for the bright lights,' the driver remarked as he swerved around a car that was just pulling out ahead of them.

There were more headlights in the distance as people followed the example of neighbours and hurried out to their own cars, not understanding what was happening, but knowing enough to realise the darkness around them was dangerous.

'It's going to be bloody chaos soon!' Simpson shouted. 'They'll all be trying to get to the other side of the river!'

'Who can blame them?' Bishop replied.

Their car was forced to stop when two cars on opposite sides of the road swung out and collided. Their speed had not allowed any serious damage, but the cries of anguish and panic could be plainly heard. Another car screeched to a halt behind the Granada.

'The silly bastards have blocked the road.' The policeman looked behind, hoping to reverse away from the situation. Yet another vehicle had pulled up behind the car blocking their exit and horns began to bellow their annoyance.

The police driver looked swiftly from left to right, searching for a way out. 'Hold on tight!' he yelled, then jammed the gearstick into reverse and struck down hard on the accelerator pedal, braking almost immediately after. The Granada shot back a few feet, crunching into the car behind and pushing it back, allowing the policeman valuable room ahead to manoeuvre. He spun the wheel round and once more mounted the kerb. Bishop sank back into his seat, his heels pressing involuntarily into the flooring as though to brake, sure there was no way the Granada could pass between the lamp-post and the low garden wall on their left. They got through only because the car itself widened the gap considerably by taking much of the garden wall with it. The tearing of metal and crumbling brickwork on the passenger side made Bishop lean towards the driver, expecting his side of the car to rip free at any moment. The policeman found his way back on to the roadway, the two crashed cars successfully passed.

'Always wanted to do that,' he said, grinning despite the tension.

'Sunday drivers,' Bishop commented, relieved to still be in one piece.

'There's a main road ahead. We should be able to make better progress.'

The driver's optimism, however, was misguided, for as they tore into the wide road, they saw that the intersection ahead which was normally controlled by traffic lights was jammed solid with vehicles.

'The sideroad – there!' Bishop pointed at the narrow turning to their left and the driver directed the car into it without hesitation. At the far end they could see a building blazing, figures standing in the road watching.

'Right!' Bishop shouted, but the driver had already seen the turning and was reducing speed. The car struck something that made a dull thud against the metalwork; neither of the two men in the front had seen whether it was a man, woman or stray animal. The driver accelerated once more, saying nothing.

The sidestreet ran into another main road and the Granada came to an abrupt halt halfway across it. To their right was the jammed intersection they had just avoided and now they could see people being dragged from the cars and attacked. Again, there was no way of knowing whether or not the attackers were Dark victims or merely angry motorists frustrated at not being able to escape the lightless area of the city. As they watched, a man, lit by the headlights, leapt on to the roof of his car while hands reached up and clawed at him, trying to drag him down. His resistance came to an abrupt halt when his legs were swept from beneath him by a stick or iron bar of some kind; he fell on to his back, then slid from the roof, fists pummelling him as he went down. Screams directed their attention to another spot in the jumble of machines: a woman was being stretched across a car bonnet, her clothes ripped from her body, arms and legs pinned down by eager hands. The rush of others towards her obscured what followed, but as the screams became more shrill, there was little doubt as to what was happening to her.

Bishop's hand tightened on the Smith and Wesson as Jessica said, 'We've got to help her, Chris, please, stop them!'

He looked towards the policeman who shook his head. 'Sorry,' Simpson said, 'we'd have no chance. There's too many.'

Bishop knew the man was right, but he was unable to sit there and let the atrocity happen. The driver sensed his mood and quickly stabbed down at the accelerator pedal. He swung the car around in a tight quarter-circle, heading away from the inter-section. Anger burst from Bishop and for a brief second he con-sidered levelling the gun at the policeman's head.

Then Edith Metlock began to laugh.

He swivelled around to look at her, the gun poised, barrel angled towards the car's roof. Kulek and Jessica had recoiled away from the medium and were staring at the dark form sitting opposite them.

The laughter did not belong to her. It was deep, nasty, a man's heavy laughter.

The driver kept his foot down, knowing it could be fatal to stop in that blacked-out area, but he experienced the same dread as the others: the coldness seeping through him, the feeling of fluttering pressure just below the back of his neck, the loosening of sphincter muscles. The laughter was unnatural.

'Edith!' Kulek said sharply, the weariness now gone from his voice. 'Edith, can you hear me?'

Oncoming cars flashed by, their lights briefly casting beams into the interior of the Granada, the drives unaware that the way ahead would be blocked by the jam at the intersection. Edith's face was momentarily illuminated as each fleeing vehicle swept by and they could see her eyes were full of a malice that was alien to the woman herself. Her mouth was open, but her lips did not curve upwards into a smile; the laughter rattled from somewhere deep in her throat.

Kulek blindly reached out towards her, his searching hand finding her immobile face. The wind blew in through the broken windscreen and howled around the interior of the car. Still she laughed.

'Force him from you, Edith!' Kulek shouted above the noise of the wind and the car's engine. 'He cannot take you unless you allow him to!'

But the laughter had become that of many now. And the wind had stopped.

It was as though they were in a vacuum; even the noise from the engine could not be heard. Only the hollow laughter of things that were dead filled their heads, mocking them and enjoying their fear.

The driver nervously glanced back over his shoulder, unsure of what was happening, the sounds making him hunch his body over the steering-wheel as if he were warding off something physical. 'For Christ's sake, make her stop! Hit her, do something!'

Kulek began to talk to her again, his voice low and soothing; the others could not hear him, but each time the interior was lit up, Bishop could see the blind man's lips moving, and he knew Kulek was urging the medium to rid herself of the demons using her body.

'Oh, no!' It was the driver again.

Bishop turned and saw the policeman was staring at the road ahead; he was heaved towards the smashed windscreen as the brakes were slammed on. The car skidded to a halt and rocked backwards and forwards on its suspension; the three passengers in the rear were thrown against the backs of the front seats.

Because of the remaining shattered glass in the windscreen, Bishop could not see what had made the driver stop. He quickly leaned over towards the steering-wheel and peered through the gaping hole in the glass. He drew in a sharp breath.

A line of vehicles stretched across the road, those at each end jammed into shop doorways so there was no possible gap for other cars to break through. The blockage had been deliberately set up to prevent the main road being used as a means of escape to the other side of the river. They saw the wrecks of other cars that had reached that point before them, their bonnets buckled and bent because the drivers had not braked in time. Faces peered over the top of cars at the Granada, then fingers leapt over the barrier and appeared from doorways on either side of the road, streaming towards them. Their cries snapped the policeman into action, but not before the first man had leapt on to the car bonnet and was curling his fingers around the jagged windscreen glass for grip. Another joined in, this one a woman, her face black with dirt and her body emaciated.

The door on Bishop's side was pulled open just as the car shot backwards away from the blockade, swinging wide with the added momentum. Bishop felt Jessica's hands on his shoulder as he nearly tumbled out on to the road. A man clung to the door, his legs stretched out behind him as he was dragged along. The woman on the bonnet was thrown off and landed in the road, her piercing scream instantly cut off as her skull cracked against the hard surface. The first man still miraculously clung to the broken window and was hauling himself forward against the gravitational pull, his free hand reaching in and clutching the steering-wheel.

'Shoot him, Bishop!' the policeman cried and, almost in a reflex action, Bishop raised the weapon and pointed it at the gaping hole in the windscreen. Instead of squeezing the trigger, he brought the gun down hard on the man's knuckles. The hand opened and glass snapped from the windscreen as the man flew away from them.

The Granada gathered speed, the driver silently praying that no other vehicle would suddenly appear behind them. Without warning he jumped on the footbrake and spun the wheel into full lock. The car did a hundred and eighty degree turn, its nose ending up pointed in the direction from which they had come. The passenger door swung shut, sending the man clinging to it skidding and bouncing across the road.

Once again the accelerator pedal was pressed and the car leapt forward. Bishop was too breathless to make any comment on the driver's skill; he checked behind to see if the others were still in one piece, but even before he could ascertain whether or not they were, the car was screeching around to their right, the driver knowing it was useless to go back the way they had come. When Bishop had righted himself again he saw they were speeding along a street that had high-rise buildings on one side, a row of shops on the other.

Somehow, he knew there was something ominous about the headlights that swung into view ahead of them.

Simpson raised an arm to shield his eyes from the glare. 'Silly bastard – he's on full beam.' He flashed his own headlights to warn the other driver, but the advancing beams were not dipped in acknowledgement. Their faces were brilliantly lit by the oncoming lights and Bishop realised the vehicle coming towards them had to be a lorry or a truck of some kind – its lights were too high above the ground for it to be a car. The policeman steered over to his right, for the other vehicle was on the wrong side of the road. The other driver matched his direction, pulling to his left.

'Jesus, he's trying to hit us!' the policeman whispered, but the wind was back in the car and no one heard his words. The glare became even more harsh, the dazzle painful. It filled their vision, drawing closer like a fiery comet dashing across a black void. Bishop could hear Jessica screaming, the policeman shouting. The laughter of the dead.

He closed his eyes and pushed himself back against his seat, bracing himself for the impact.

Chapter Twenty-Eight

For Bishop, there was no sense to the next few moments, just the shock of screaming noise and whirling lights. The police driver had spun his steering-wheel to the left in an effort to thwart the oncoming vehicle, but the other driver had altered his direction just enough to clip the Granada's rear wing, sending the car into a screeching spin, the occupants violently jarred by the blow. The policeman was powerless to control the skid and the car turned completely around almost in its own space, before careering across the forecourt of a block of flats to their left. Most of the glass in the windscreen had been shaken loose and Bishop opened his eyes in time to see the entrance to the high-rise building tearing towards them; he jammed his feet hard into the footwell in front of the passenger seat and pushed both hands against the dashboard to prevent himself going through the windscreen when the car hit concrete.

Even though the driver had the brake pedal fully-pressed and was turning the wheel to avoid hitting the building head on, the impact, when it came, was tremendous. The bonnet buckled upwards as it met the corner of the entrance, the radiator cut in half and each segment pushed back into the engine in a shower of scalding steam. Bishop was thrown forward, but was saved from going through the windscreen by the position he had taken up moments before; his chest hit the dashboard and he was thrown back into his seat. The driver clung to the steering-wheel which collapsed against his weight and he found himself out of the windscreen, his face against the risen metal of the bonnet, unaware of the body that slammed past him. Edith Metlock was saved from flying over the front seats because she had been knocked to the floor when the lorry had struck the wing on her side; Jessica had already been clinging to the back of Bishop's seat when they had first been hit and her grip had tightened so that when they plunged into the building she was able to prevent herself from being propelled forward. Jacob Kulek was less fortunate.

The total silence that followed did more to rouse Bishop than any voices or body-shaking hands could have; the screams, the laughter, the screeching tyres, had all culminated in the strident cry of torn and crushed metal, and now the contrasting quietness seemed to prod him physically.

He pushed himself upright, his movements slow and deliberate, waiting for sudden pain to tell him he was injured. None came, but a general numbness gave a hint of the pain to come from the bruising he had received. He heard a whimper from behind.

'Jessica?' He twisted his body to see. Somehow the headlight on the passenger side had remained undamaged, although its twin was completely shattered, and just enough light was reflected back from the cavern of the building's entrance to enable him to make out shapes in the car's interior, 'Jessica, are you hurt?'

He half-knelt on his seat to reach her. Her face came up from the top of his seat where it lay, her eyes still closed, beginning to open. She whimpered again and shook her head slightly as if to clear it. Her eyes opened fully and she stared blankly at him.

Movement on the driver's side caught Bishop's attention; the policeman was cautiously drawing himself back from the glassless windscreen into the car. He groaned aloud as he slumped back into his seat. There was blood on his forehead and Bishop could see tiny sparkles of imbedded glass. The policeman gingerly rubbed his chest then drew in a sharp breath when his probing fingers reached his ribs.

He groaned. 'Cracked one, I think,' he said turning to Bishop. 'Maybe just bruised. You okay?'

Before he could reply, Edith Metlock's head and shoulders came into view. 'Where are we? What's happened?' she asked.

Bishop and the policeman exchanged quick glances. 'It's all right, Edith. We've had an accident,' said Bishop gently, aware of the obviousness of his statement.

'Come on,' Simpson said abruptly. 'We'd better get out of here. We're sitting ducks. Did you lose the gun?'

Bishop felt around the floor of the passenger footwell and his fingers touched cold metal. 'Got it.'

'There's a torch in the glove compartment – get that, too.' He pushed open his door, grunting with the effort.

Bishop took the torch and stepped from his side of the car knowing they were lucky not to have been seriously injured: the damage to the front of the Granada was appalling.

'Father!' Jessica's scream sent Bishop rushing to open her door. She tumbled out and pushed past him, running towards the wrecked part of the car. He realised what must have happened when he saw only Edith Metlock in the back passenger seat: Jacob Kulek had been hurled through the windscreen.

He found Jessica kneeling beside the still body of her father. Slipping the gun into his jacket pocket, he knelt and shone the torch on to Kulek's face. The blind man had the look of death on him, his eyes narrow slits through which only the whites showed, his mouth partially opened, a faint, empty smile on his lips. Bishop frowned, for he could see no outward physical signs of injury. He probed the skin beneath Kulek's jawline with two rigid fingers and was surprised to find the pulse fluttering weakly.

'He's alive,' he told Jessica and her sobs subsided. She slipped her arm beneath her father's head, raising him slightly from the paving. The blood from his skull began to flow freely.

Bishop became aware that the driver and Edith had joined them.

'Dead?' the policeman asked brutally.

He shook his head. 'Unconscious. His skull may have been fractured.' Bishop took a handkerchief from his pocket and helped Jessica place it against the wound; the cloth immediately became a soggy, red mess. But Kulek moved and a murmuring came from his parted lips.

Jessica called his name, touching his cheek with her free hand and, for a moment, his eyelids flickered as though he were going to open them.

The policeman crouched low and said urgently. 'We've got to get going, Bishop, it's too dangerous to stay here.'

Bishop stood, passing the torch over to Edith who had replaced him by Kulek's side. Although still bewildered by her surroundings, she had the presence of mind to loosen the blind man's tie and shirt collar.

'We shouldn't move him,' Bishop said to the policeman in soft tones so Jessica could not hear. 'We don't know how badly he's

612

hurt. Fortunately, most of the glass was out of the windscreen, but he must have gone through the opening with some force. Either the top of the car or the concrete pavement must have . . .'

The policeman cut in. 'We've got no choice – we'll have to carry him. We'll need to find some other transport to get us away from here.'

'There are plenty of parked cars around, but how can you get one started?'

'That's no problem – it's just a matter of jumping the wires. I'm going . . .'

This time it was the policeman who was interrupted as the revving of an engine came to their ears. They turned and looked back in the direction from which they had come. Probing head-lights lit up the street throwing elongated shadows from the many figures making towards the wreck.

'They're coming for us,' Bishop said quietly.

The sound of the lorry's engine grew to a roar as it began to gather speed, several of the walking people silently disappearing beneath its wheels as if they were unaware of the vehicle's presence, even when they were crushed. Bishop and the policeman guessed the driver's intention.

'Get back into the building!' the policeman ordered the two kneeling women. Jessica opened her mouth to protest, but quickly saw what was happening. Bishop and the driver reached down for the injured man, pushing the two women towards the swing doors just beyond the lifts in the entrance hall. They roughly pulled Kulek towards the doors, a hand each beneath his shoulders, allowing the rest of his body to drag along the floor.

The whole of the entrance became bright as the lorry drew nearer, the driver beginning to angle his vehicle towards the block of flats and the wreck in its forecourt. Jesica and Edith pushed at the yellow swingdoors; they were stiff and opened only slightly. The women used their shoulders and swung the doors wide, holding them open for the two men to drag Kulek through.

'Use the gun!' the policeman shouted. 'Try and get the bastard before he reaches us!' Bishop let go of the injured man and ran back to the entrance, drawing the Smith and Wesson from his pocket. The lights were blinding once more and he kept his eyes narrowed against the glare. With both hands curled around the butt of the gun he took careful aim, amazed at his own coolness, knowing he had to somehow divert the lorry – if it hit the entrance square on, the impetus would easily carry much of the bodywork straight through to the rear stairwell. He aimed the gun at a point just above and slightly to the right of one circle of light, to where he hoped the driver would be. The vehicle was no more than seventy yards away, going into a sharp turn that would bring it head on across the forecourt towards the entrance. Fifty yards away. Bishop squeezed the trigger.

Nothing happened. Forty yards.

He resisted the urge to run and fumbled at the safety catch. Thirty yards.

Squeeze. Recoil. Three times.

One of the headlights went out. Glass shattered. The lorry came on. Bishop ran.

He threw himself at the swingdoors that Jessica and the medium held open and heard the explosion of metal against concrete behind, his fully-stretched body sliding on the tiled flooring and tipping over the few steps leading down to the building's rear exit. The two women fell away from the released doors which were slowly closing, covering their faces with their hands, more against the horrendous tearing noise than the flying wreckage. As Bishop rolled on to his back, the building itself seemed to jolt and he saw something bulky shoot from the cabin of the lorry and scrape itself along one wall of the entrance, leaving a large smear of red as it went. It smashed against the swingdoors, an arm becoming trapped between them, preventing them from closing completely. Bishop just had time to see the driver's bloody face peering at them through the reinforced glass, his neck propped up at an impossible angle, before flames billowed out and filled the entrance in a great, leaping ball of fire.

He drew his knees up and covered his head as a blast of hot air swept through the partially open doors; for a moment he thought he was alight, but the searing feeling quickly passed as the air was funnelled up the stairwell. Cautiously raising his head once more, he looked over the top of the three stairs he had fallen down and saw the flames had retreated, but the burning cabin of the lorry completely blocked the entrance. The hallway was filled with chunks of twisted metal, much of it smouldering and black, and the vehicle had struck the entrance at an angle, totally destroying the crashed Granada. Edith Metlock had fallen to one side of the swingdoors and had been protected by the solid wall facing the stairway leading to the upper floors. The police driver was half-sitting against the exit doors, the body of Kulek sprawled beside him.

Bishop put the gun back into his pocket and crouched beside Jessica whose legs were stretched out on the lower two steps. He helped her into a sitting position and when she saw the burning lorry in the entrance, she clung to him. His fingers sank into the soft hair at the back of her neck and he held her to him, her small, trembling body feeling vulnerable to his touch.

She pulled her head away from him and looked quickly around. She found her father and tore herself away. Kulek's eyes were fully open now and confusion was clear on his face, which was bathed in a flickering warm glow from the fire. His mouth opened and closed as if he were trying to speak, but no words came.

Bishop rose to his feet and pushed at the exit doors. They were locked.

The policeman looked up at him. 'Don't worry about them – we might be better off staying inside this building.'

'But the fire.'

'It won't spread. They built these blocks of flats to contain any fires. Let's get upstairs and find a phone – at least they shouldn't be affected by the power cut. We'll get some help sent to us.' He eased himself into a standing position, keeping his grip on the blind man. 'Right, let's get him up.'

Together, they managed to get Kulek on his feet. 'Jacob, can you hear me?' said Bishop.

Kulek slowly nodded, a hand trying to reach behind his head.

'It's all right. You've had a bad knock. We're going to try and get into a flat upstairs and find some help.

The old man nodded, then managed to say his daughter's name.

'I'm here, Father.' She had found another handkerchief or a piece of cloth from somewhere and was holding it against the wound on Kulek's head. Fortunately, the blood was not flowing as badly as before.

Bishop put his shoulder beneath Kulek's arm, grasping the wrist around his neck, his other arm around the blind man's waist. 'Can you walk?'

Kulek took a tentative step forward, Bishop holding him tightly. The policeman held his other arm, supporting him, and between them they managed to get the blind man up the first three steps. Edith came forward from the corner she had been crouching in.

'Lead the way,' Bishop told her. 'Upstairs to the first floor.'

They half-carried, half-dragged the weak form of Kulek up the stairs, going fast, thankful that the lorry was partially blocking the entrance to the flats, the flames preventing anyone from passing through any gaps. Neither Bishop nor the policeman had forgotten the approaching figures.

The fire from below lapped over the balcony of the first floor, so they decided to continue upwards to the second. Edith led the way down the short hallway to the open landing, a four-foot high balcony running in either direction along the length of the building. The block of flats seemed comparatively small against normal high-rise buildings. There were only three apartments to each floor and as yet they did not know how many floors there were, but Bishop guessed there were probably nine or ten. There were two flats on the landing to the left of the short hallway, one to the right. The policeman helped Bishop prop Kulek against the balcony, then hurried along to the single flat on their right. While he banged on the door, Bishop looked down into the forecourt and street below.

Smoke rising from the burning wreck stung his eyes and he quickly drew back, but not before he had seen the people standing just beyond the ring of light thrown by the flames. Their faces were turned upwards as though watching him.

'Police. Come on, open up in there!' the driver was calling through the door's letter-box.

Bishop left Jessica steadying her father with Edith helping her, and hurried over to the irate policeman.

'There's someone in there,' he said, turning to Bishop, 'but they're too scared to open the bloody door.'

'Have they said anything?'

'No, but I can hear them moving around.' He put his face to the letter-box again. 'Look, it's the police – we're not going to hurt you.' He rattled the flap when no reply came.

Bishop looked back over the balcony and did not like what he saw. The flames below seemed to have lost much of their intensity; soon they would be low enough for those waiting to get through to the stairs. And although they were only shadowy blurs, there were many more people down there than he had at first thought.

'Let's try another flat,' he said hastily to the policeman.

'Yeah, I think you're right; wasting our bloody time here.' He stooped for one more try. 'Look, if you won't let us in, at least call Emergency. Ask for the police *and* an ambulance – we've got an injured man here. My name's Simpson, driver to Detective Chief Inspector Peck. Got that? Chief Inspector Peck. Tell them I've got Jacob Kulek with me and to send immediate assistance. Please do it!'

He rose once more, shaking his head. 'Let's hope they listened.'

'Let's hope they've got a phone,' Bishop replied, leaving the policeman staring after him as he returned to the two women and Kulek.

'Shit,' Simpson said to himself, then followed Bishop. 'Let's get up to the next floor,' he said. 'These other buggers won't open their doors now they know their neighbours wouldn't.'

This time Jessica helped Bishop move her father as Edith and the policeman led the way, the medium shining the torch ahead of them in the darkened stairwell. On the next landing, Simpson went to the first door on their left and rattled the letter-box.

'Hello in there. This is the police. Open up, please.'

They leaned the injured man against the wall in the hallway, Bishop reluctant to be seen by the victims below.

'Edith, bring me the torch,' he called out softly, and the medium left the policeman to come round to them. 'Shine it on Jacob; let's see how he is.'

He looked a hundred years old, his face drawn and pale, the lines in his skin somehow more deeply etched than before. His sightless eyes blinked against the light, but there seemed to be little thought behind them. Bishop knew by the way his tall but frail body sagged that he would collapse without their support. Just how badly he was hurt, there was still no way of knowing; he had known men to be conscious even with a fractured skull. Yet, it seemed impossible that Kulek could even be semi-conscious after being tossed through the windscreen with such obvious force.

'Father, can you hear me?' Jessica anxiously bit her lips when she received no reply, and looked across at Bishop pleadingly.

'He's a strong man, Jessica. He'll be okay once we get him to a hospital. Hold him, Edith, while I see how Simpson is getting on.' Bishop really wanted to find out what was happening below

617

without alarming the two women. Allowing the medium to slide into his position without losing grip on Kulek, he turned the corner, then peered warily over the balcony. The area of light below had become smaller, the blaze on the lorry and the Granada having become several separate, weaker fires rather than one large inferno. The ring of waiting people had drawn closer. Bishop shuddered at the thought, but it seemed as though these people knew who had been in the Granada, knew that Jacob Kulek was in the block of flats. Was it possible? Was there some telepathy between them and the Dark? This strange force possessed and directed them; did it really have an intelligence?

Someone stepped into the area of light below and looked directly up at him; it was a woman and there was something vaguely familiar about her. He reached for the spectacles he used for driving, pulling them from his breast pocket and slipping them on. For the first time that night, anger became more dominant than his fear. It was her, the tall woman, the one who had helped kill his wife. His fingers tightened around the balcony rail and for one wild moment he wanted to run back down the stairs and throttle the life from her. How had she known where to find them? Had it been what Pryszlak had wanted all this time – to trap them in an inescapable area of darkness? And why? Was it just revenge on a man who had refused to help him so many years before? Or was Jacob Kulek a threat? The questions flooded his mind, but they remained mere questions, for he had no answers at all.

'Someone's coming!'

The policeman's voice brought Bishop back to the situation behind him.

'Will you open the door please?' Simpson said, this time keeping any harsh authority from his request. 'There's nothing to be afraid of. I just want to use your telephone if you have one. Look, I'll put my identification card through the letter-box, then you can examine it under any light you've got in there.' He lifted the letter-box flap and slid his wallet through. 'Okay. Now please have a look at it, then let me in. We've got an injured man out here and we've got no time to waste.'

Bishop could just see a vague shape through the window next to the flat's hallway, in a room that was probably the kitchen. It moved from view and again there seemed to be movement behind the reeded glass of the hall door.

Simpson looked across at Bishop and said, 'I think we're in luck this time.'

There were noises inside, a bolt being drawn back, a door-chain being loosened. Finally the lock turned and the door opened fractionally. Bishop thought he could see a face peering out at them, but it disappeared when the policeman moved closer.

'Hello?' Simpson said. 'Don't be alarmed, no one's going to hurt you.' He reached towards the door and gave it a gentle shove. It opened a litle wider and he poked his head into the gap. 'Have you got a phone?' Bishop heard him say.

The policeman pushed the door all the way open and stepped into the blackness of the hallway. For a moment, Bishop lost sight of him; then he appeared again, backing out of the doorway. He slowly turned, his eyes looking pleadingly at Bishop, who now saw the hilt of the carving knife protruding from a point just below the policeman's rib-cage. Simpson sank down the door-frame to the floor, one leg buckling awkwardly under him, the other sprawling outwards so he was propped there. His head gently lowered itself to his chest and Bishop knew he had died.

The shock had dulled Bishop's reactions, for he was not even reaching for the gun in his jacket pocket when the figure came lurching out of the blackness. He reached up automatically to ward off the thin clutching hands. The glasses he had just donned were knocked away, the lenses having prevented his eyes from being raked by sharp-nailed fingers. The creature he struggled with hissed and spat at him and he realised that it was an old woman. Her wrists felt brittle in his grasp and although she only had the feeble strength of the aged, she fought with an intensity that was frightening. She pushed him back so that his shoulders were over the balcony, her fingers curling closed then open like talons. It was Jessica who ended the battle by coming up behind the old woman, reaching both arms around the scraggy neck, and pulling her away from Bishop. He felt no remorse when he clenched his fist and struck the ranting woman's jaw as hard as he could; to him, she was no longer a human being, just a shell, a host for an energy that was pure evil. She gave a sharp cry and staggered from Jessica's grip, falling backwards over the sprawled leg of Simpson into her own hallway. Her head cracked against the wall inside and she went down in a heap, her body crumpled like a bundle of old rags.

Bishop had to draw Jessica away from the still form of the

policeman and she moaned softly as she leaned against him.

'How many, Chris? How many more will it take?'

He was afraid to reply for the answer depended on how much evil existed and in how many minds. Who knew what dark thoughts a friend, neighbour or brother kept hidden? And who didn't possess such thoughts? He led her back to Edith and her father.

'Let me have the torch, Edith. I want you to wait for me here while I search the woman's flat for a phone.'

'Can't we lock ourselves in there?' said Jessica. 'We'd be safe, wouldn't we?'

'If I can call the police from there, maybe.' He hesitated before deciding to tell them the truth of the situation. 'There's a crowd down in the forecourt – I think they want us, or at least, Jacob. It wouldn't take them long to break down the door or smash the windows. We'd be trapped.'

'But why should they want my father?'

It was Edith Metlock who answered. 'Because they fear him.'

Both Bishop and Jessica looked at her in surprise, but the sounds of footsteps prevented any further questions. Someone was coming along the landing from the single flat on the other side of the hallway; a faint glow preceded the footsteps. Bishop pulled the revolver from his jacket pocket, and pointed it towards the approaching light, hoping there were still bullets left in the chamber. The man peered cautiously around the corner, holding the candle well before him. He was dazzled by the torchlight.

'What's goin on ere?' He blinked his eyes against the light.

Bishop relaxed slightly; the man seemed normal enough. 'Step out where I can see you,' he said.

'What's that – a gun?' The man raised the long, iron bar he was carrying.

'It's all right,' Bishop assured him. 'No one's going to harm you. We need some help.'

'Oh yeah? Well put the gun down first, mate.'

Bishop lowered the pistol, holding it by his side, ready to be raised if necessary.

'What appened to the old lady? I saw her run out at you from me door.'

'She killed a policeman who was with us.'

'Bloody ell. I'm not surprised though – she was always a bit crazy. What did you do with her?'

620

'She's unconscious.' He decided not to tell the man she was probably dead. 'Can you help us?'

'No, mate. I'm looking after meself and the family, that's all. Any bastard who comes through my front door cops this.' He brandished the iron bar in the air. 'I don't know what's going on lately, but I ain't trustin no one.'

'My father's hurt, can't you see that?' Jessica pleaded. 'You've got to help us.'

There was a short silence, but the man had made up his mind. 'I'm sorry about that, miss, but I don't know who you are or what you are. There's too many nutters around for me to take any chances. I mean, who crashed the bleedin lorry down there, for a start? Thought the buildin was coming down.'

'We were being chased.'

'Oh yeah? Who by?'

Bishop was beginning to grow irritated by the man's doubting attitude. 'Look, we wanted to use that woman's telephone. That's what I'm going to do now.'

'You'll be lucky: she ain't got one.'

'What about you? Have you got one?'

The man was still cautious. 'Yeah, but I ain't lettin you in.'

Bishop raised the gun once more.

'I'll av you with this first, mate,' the man warned, holding the iron bar in front of him.

'Okay,' Bishop said resignedly, knowing it was pointless to argue; any man who thought he could beat a bullet with an iron bar either had to be very dim or very sure of himself. 'Will you ring the police for us? Tell them where we are and that Jacob Kulek is with us. We need help urgently.'

'They're likely to be a bit busy, aren't they?'

'I think they'll make the effort. Just remember to tell them Jacob Kulek is here.'

'Kulek. Right.'

'Tell them to get here fast – there's a mob downstairs after us.'

The man took a quick peep over the balcony. 'Oh my Gawd,' he said.

'Will you do it?' Bishop persisted.

'All right, mate, I'll get on to em. You ain't comin in though.'

'Just keep your door locked and barricade yourself in. You should be okay – it's us they want.'

The man backed away, the iron bar still pointed forward,

his eyes never leaving the group in the hallway. They heard his front door close and the bolt being drawn.

'Nice to see the old blitz spirit coming back,' Bishop remarked wearily.

'You shouldn't blame him,' said Edith. 'There must be millions like him, totally confused by what's going on. He had no reason to trust us.'

'Let's hope he at least rings the police.' Bishop glanced towards the balcony and saw the glow from the fire had dimmed considerably. 'We'd better move on,' he said to the two women.

'Where can we go to?' Jessica asked. 'We can't get out.'

Bishop pointed upwards. 'There's only one place to go. The roof.'

Inside the flat, the man was trying to calm his terrified family. 'It's all right, it was just some people in trouble – nothin for us to worry about.'

'What are they doin ere, Fred? his wide-eyed wife asked, clutching her ten-year-old daughter to her. 'Were they in that crash downstairs?'

'I dunno. They wanted me to get the police.'

'Are you goin to?'

'I'll av a go, won't do no arm.'

He pushed past his wife and entered the sitting-room, walking over to the telephone resting on a sideboard. 'Keith!' he called back to his teenage son, 'get somethin up against the door – somethin solid.' He laid down the iron bar and leaned close to the telephone, using the candle to see the dial.

He let it ring for a full two minutes before replacing the receiver. 'Would you believe it?' he said incredulously to his wife who had followed him into the room. 'It's bloody engaged. Their lines must be jammed solid. Either that or they're out of order.'

He shook his head regretfully. 'Looks like those poor beggars out there are on their own.'

622

Chapter Twenty-Nine

They had only reached the sixth or seventh floor – Bishop had lost count – when they heard footsteps on the stairs below.

He leaned against the rail, gasping for breath, trying to listen. Jacob Kulek was now over his shoulder in a fireman's lift, and with each step Bishop took, the blind man seemed to grow heavier.

'They're in the building.' He looked into the blackness below and could see nothing. The acrid smell of smoke from the burning wreck seemed to fill the stairwell even though it was apparent that the worst of the fire was over.

Edith Metlock shone the torchbeam downwards and they saw what looked like tiny white creatures sliding upwards along the stair rails; they soon recognised the shapes as the hands of ascending people, the rest of their bodies hidden by the overhanging staircases. It was an eerie sight, for the hands seemed to be disembodied, a nightmare army of marching claws.

'We'll never make it!' Jessica cried. 'They'll catch us before we reach the top!'

'No, they're moving slowly – we've still got a chance.' Bishop pushed himself upright again, adjusting the weight of the semiconscious man on his shoulder. 'Take the gun from my pocket, Jessica. If they get close, use it!'

They went onwards, Edith leading the way, shining the torch ahead of them. Bishop felt his legs weakening, his body slumping more and more under the load. His teeth bit into his lower lip with the effort and the muscles in his back protested their agony. They reached another floor and he fell to his knees, unable to stop himself. Kulek slid from his shoulder and Jessica just caught her father's upper body before it touched concrete. Bishop drew in sharp breaths, his chest heaving. He leaned his head against the bars of the stair rail, his face wet with perspiration.

'How far down are they?' he asked between gasps.

Edith shone the torch downwards once more. 'Three floors below us,' she said quietly.

He grabbed the rail and jerked himself to his feet. 'Help me,' he said, reaching down for Kulek.

'No,' Kulek's eyes were open and he was pushing himself into a sitting position. 'I can walk. Just get me to my feet.'

The way in which the blind man was drifting in and out of consciousness was somehow more worrying to Bishop than if he had just remained unconscious. Kulek groaned aloud and clutched at his stomach as they lifted him. His body was stiff as he forced himself upright.

'I'll be all right,' he reassured Jessica as she held on to him. A trembling hand reach for Bishop's shoulder. 'If you will just bear my weight,' he said.

Bishop slipped the blind man's arm around his own neck and they turned the bend to the next flight of stairs. They began to climb and he felt Kulek wince at every step. 'Not far, Jacob,' Bishop said. 'We're nearly at the top.'

Kulek hadn't the strength to reply.

'LEAVE HIM, BISHOP. HE'S NO USE TO YOU NOW!'

They froze on the staircase as the words spiralled upwards. It was a woman's voice, and Bishop knew it was the tall woman, the one called Lillian.

'He's dying, can't you see that?' The words were no longer shouted, echoing up from the stairwell like a hissed whisper. 'Why be hindered by a dead man. Leave him, otherwise you'll never escape us. We don't want you, Bishop; just him.'

As Bishop stared down into the blackness, he knew the Dark was all around them, carried in the night air like some invisible parasite. He could feel its coldness caressing his skin, freezing the beads of perspiration into tiny globules of ice. He saw pale blurs that were faces in the black pit below.

'Leave him. Leave him,' other voices inside his head told him. 'He's no use to you. An encumbrance. A dead weight. You'll die if you keep him with you.'

His grip tightened on the rail. He could make it without Kulek. He could get on the roof. They wouldn't be able to reach him there. He could hold them off.

A rough hand snapped his head around. 'Don't listen, Chris.' The torchlight stung his eyes as Edith Metlock spoke sharply to him. 'I can hear the voices. They want me to help them, too. Don't you see? It's the Dark – the voices are trying to confuse us. We must go on, Chris.'

'I hear them,' said Jessica. 'They want me to shoot you, Chris. They keep telling me you're leading my father into worse danger.'

'BISHOP, IT'S NOT TOO LATE - YOU CAN JOIN US!' the tall woman screamed. 'YOU CAN BE PART OF US!'

'Take the light out of my eyes, Edith,' he said, turning away from the stairwell.

Both women sighed with relief and, once more, they resumed their arduous climb. The footsteps below grew louder, became more hurried. Through sheer willpower, Bishop increased his own speed, almost lifting the injured man clear of the steps and dragging him upwards. They reached the next floor, turned the bend, began the next flight upwards. But the footsteps were drawing closer, running, scrabbling up the staircase, other sounds accompanying them, noises that could have come from frenzied animals. They were now below the floor Bishop and the others had just left, scurrying up from the darkness like creatures climbing out from hell.

Jessica felt weak with fear. She pushed her back against the wall, her legs still climbing, but her movement slow. She held her arm out rigid, pointing the gun towards the terrible scuffling noises that were drawing closer and closer.

A light appeared at a point between her and those approaching, growing stronger, beginning to fill the darkness in the bend of the stairs. Cold air blew in from the landing as the swing-doors were pushed open, and suddenly there were voices, more lights adding to the brightness of the first.

'Who's down there?' a gruff voice demanded to know.

'Look, Harry, there's someone up there on the stairs,' another voice said.

Jessica was suddenly bathed in bright light.

'Christ, she's got a gun!' the same voice exclaimed.

Edith, who had been concealed around the bend halfway up to the next floor, quickly descended a few steps and shone her torch towards the voices.

A group of men and women stood in the entrance to that particular landing staring up at Jessica and now her. They were obviously neighbours who had banded together for safety when the power had been cut.

625

'Go back!' Edith called out to them. 'For your own safety, go back into your homes and lock yourselves in!'

Someone pushed past the first man in the doorway. 'You tell us what's goin on first, lady.' His flashlight was powerful and threw out a wide, undefined beam. 'What's this girl got a gun for?'

'They must've had something to do with the crash downstairs,' another voice murmured.

Bishop was close to Edith, but still out of sight of the people below. 'Shine the torch down the stairs, Edith,' he whispered. 'Show them the mob coming up.'

The medium leaned over the rail and did as he said. The figures crouching below were suddenly lit up.

'There's more of em down there!' All the lights were pointed downwards and the people on the stairs covered their eyes, moaning in pain.

'Jesus, look at that lot. They're all the way down the stairs.'

One of the men cowering under the glare began to creep upwards, keeping his head tucked down. Another man followed, moving in similiar fashion.

'They're coming up!' a woman's voice screamed out.

The man carrying the flashlight stepped forward, descending a few steps and bringing a heavy boot down hard on the creeping figure, sending it reeling backwards. 'I've had enough of this,' was his only comment.

All hell seemed to break loose at that point. Other men and women who had come to a halt on the stairs suddenly surged forward, shielding their eyes from the light, shrieking their demented cries, and swamping the man who had been foolhardy enough to defy them. His friends ran forward to help and more lights appeared on the floors below and above, almost as though a signal had been given for many of the residents to venture out from their separate flats, curiosity overcoming their previous caution. Many rushed back indoors as soon as they saw the people on the stairs, while others decided enough was enough: if the Law wouldn't do anything about intruders, then they, the residents would. Perhaps they would have stood more chance in the confused and brutal battle that ensued if a number of their own neighbours had not already succumbed to the Dark as they had waited in the blackout. The residents of the tower block had no way of telling who was friend and who was foe.

The swingdoors on the floor above Bishop opened and lights were flashed through it. He grabbed Edith's arm and said, 'Get Jessica – we're going on.'

The medium did not bother to protest, for she saw his logic: the roof – if they could get on to it – was still the safest place to be. She reached Jessica and pulled her upwards, leading her around the bend in the stairs, catching up with Bishop and Kulek. They reached the next floor and the people waiting there watched them curiously.

'You'd better lock yourselves in until the police get here,' Bishop told them. 'Don't try to fight those people downstairs – there are too many.'

They looked at him as though it were he who was mad, then peered down into the confusion of sounds and flashing lights below. He didn't bother to see if they had taken his advice, but kept onwards, the cool air that was rushing in through the open doors helping to revive him. Kulek was trying to help their ascent, his legs moving haltingly over each step, his thin frame trembling with the exertion.

'We're nearly there, Jacob. Just a little further.' Bishop could almost feel the remaining dregs of strength draining from the blind man. Kulek's left arm was tightly clamped against his stomach.

Jessica cried out in relief when she saw that the stairs ran out on the floor above: they had nearly reached the top of the building. Her arm encircled her father's waist and she pulled and lifted with Bishop, urging her father on to the last flight of stairs. Edith's steps were heavy, her breathing laboured. It had been a long climb and her body was in no condition for such stern exercise. One plump hand grasped the stair rail and dragged the rest of her body forward, the movement slow, the effort exhausting. Not far, she kept telling herself, not far now, a few more steps, just a few.

The man who waited for them at the top was the caretaker of the flats. He lived, in fact, on the ground floor, but earlier that evening had gone up to the tenth floor of the building to give a warning to the elderly couple who lived there. He had warned them before – or at least, he had warned the old man. The Council did not, *absolutely* did not allow urinating in the lifts. The old man had always denied it had been him, blaming it on the kids who roamed the estate, vandalising property, making the lives of

627

the residents miserable. The little bastards broke windows, scribbled graffiti four-foot high on walls, and generally created pandemonium up and down the stairs. The lifts were a particular source of joy to them and the all-too-frequent breakdowns were due to the kids tampering with the buttons, blocking the closing doors, opening the doors between floors, or jumping up and down while the lifts were in motion. Certainly, they messed in the lifts, but they were not the main culprits of this misdemeanour. Oh no, the old man had a lot to answer for in this respect. Why they put elderly people at the top of these flats, God only knew. When the lifts were out, either through the misdoings of vandals, the normal and not infrequent mechanical malfunctions, or – as was the case tonight – general power failures, these old folk were stranded. Another problem – and this was the relevant one – the two lifts had been engineered to move slowly, for too swift ascents and descents scared the life out of the residents. If you were aged, and if you liked to drink a lot, and if your bladder was no longer the sturdy water carrier it used to be, then a trip up in the lift could take a lifetime. Unfortunately, the old man was well past his prime, and had a weak bladder. Other residents had complained more than once that the lift doors had opened revealing the old boy standing in a puddle of liquid. The way in which he always doffed his hat and bid them a pleasant good day or evening could never disguise the fouls smell of piss as he swayed past them. The caretaker had warned him three times so far, ignoring the protested denials, and now he would warn the old lady as well. Either she kept reign on him, or they were out, O.U.T. No nonsense. No more pissing in the lift. Putting up with the other tenants with their carping complaints about the heating, the plumbing, the vandalism, the rent, the lifts, the refuse collectors, the noise and their neighbours, was bad enough, but having to mop up the mess left by some incontinent old imbecile was too much. Sometimes the caretaker fantasised about planting a time bomb in one corner of the tower block, setting it for one-thirty and retreating to the pub further down the road, sitting there with his pint of bitter, checking the second hand of his watch as it crept up to the thirty minute mark, chomping on his veal-and-ham pie, studying the building through the pub window, ordering a fresh pint, having a joke with the landlord as the fatal seconds ticked away; then the lovely bang, the floors of the tower block crumbling like playing cards

628

or like those films you saw of industrial chimneys being demolished, blown up at the base so the bricks tumbled down in a straight line, the structure resembling a telescope closing in on itself. All those tenants off his back once and for all, no more complaints, no more running around after them. All crushed, all dead. Lovely.

The caretaker had been halfway up when the lights went out and the lift came to a shuddering halt. He had groped around in total darkness, cursing loudly as his index finger finally found the alarm button. He hoped his silly mare of a wife would hear it in their ground-floor flat, but after ten minutes of constantly stabbing at the button and banging on the metal walls of the lift, he decided the breakdown was probably due to something other than just mechanical failure in the drive motor. Bloody power cut, he told himself.

It had been creepy sitting there in the dark, sightless and unseen. Yet it was strangely comforting, like being back inside the womb, still unborn and still untouched. *Or like being dead, nothing for companionship but nothingness.* Soon, though, he had found he was not completely alone in the darkness.

After a while, the caretaker had forced open the lift door and, feeling with his hands, had discovered he was almost on the next floor, the step-up no more than three feet. Opening the shaft door which would let him out into the hallway beyond was a little more difficult, but he persisted, summoning up the reserves of strength the voices inside his head told him he had. The strange thing was that once you knew you could do something, it became easier to do.

He had continued his journey to the top of the building, using the stairs, no longer bothered by the blackness around him. The wind had howled around him when he had pulled open the swing-doors to the tenth floor landing, but he was grinning as he walked the length of the short hallway, then round to his right to the old couple's flat. They hadn't wanted to open the door at first, and he'd had to insist, telling them it was official business. The old lady had been the first to go and for her he had made use of the broom she kept in the hall of the flat, knocking her down, then forcing the broomhandle into her throat as far as it would go, blocking it so she could not draw in air. He had taken his time with the old man who had not tried to help his wife, but had cowered in his bedroom beneath his bed. The caretaker had merely laughed as he splashed through the foul-smelling puddle that was spreading out from under the bed, and had dragged the old boy out, enjoying the croaking screams as he hauled him back down the hallway and into the kitchen where so many innocent implements of death were waiting. Unfortunately, his victim's heart had given out before he could finish the job, but at least it had been pleasurable up until that final moment. No more pissing in the lifts for the old boy any more. No more pissing.

The caretaker had sat on the floor next to the warm corpse and continued to enjoy himself, free now to do whatever he pleased, free to indulge in new, forbidden experiences. The freedom tasted good. The sound of the crashing lorry came not long after and the sky outside briefly flared orange. The caretaker selected one of the bloodied kitchen tools he had been using and walked out on to the landing. He stood at the top of the stairs and waited.

Edith Metlock sensed his presence before she saw him. She was nearly at the top of the stairs when she stopped, her mind abruptly cutting out the screams, shouts and sounds of struggle below, to direct itself towards what lay ahead. One hand still gripping the iron stair rail and one knee resting on a step, she slowly shone the torch upwards – slowly because she dreaded what the beam would reveal, an inner sense fearing the worst – and found the man's legs, his knees, his waist. He was dressed in the blue overalls of a workman and, as the torch beam came higher, she saw he was holding a stained, short-bladed chopper across his chest, the kind used in a kitchen for chopping meat; and as the beam reached higher still, she saw he was grinning, only his teeth were red, and his mouth was red, and the redness ran down his chin and she now noticed it had splashed on to his overalls. She knew he was insane, for what normal person would eat raw meat. He came down a step and she screamed.

The first swing of the small chopper missed because he was blinded by the light, but the second scythed across the arm she had put up to protect herself. The whole of her arm went numb, as though it had been struck with a hammer and not a sharp instrument; she tumbled backwards, the torch in her other hand, sending its beam careering upwards, then around the walls as she fell. Bishop used his body to block her descent, gripping the handrail tight and still maintaining his hold on Kulek. His legs nearly went from beneath him with the medium's weight, but he

630

managed to steady them. She had collapsed sideways on the stairs, her stout legs sprawled across one step, her body against the uprights of the stair rail; mercifully, she had not released the torch. Sure she would fall no further and sure he had regained his own balance, Bishop quickly snatched the torch from her grasp and pointed it upwards again. The man was slowly walking down, his grin made even more obscene by the sticky blood around his lips and on his teeth. The weapon was held high over his head, poised to strike.

Bishop tried to back away, but encumbered by Kulek's limp body, movement was awkward. Edith clawed at the man's legs, grabbing his overalls and tugging, trying to overbalance him. It was no use; the man was too strong.

The chopper was already swinging downwards when the bullet shattered his breastbone, the blast from the .38 made even more thunderous by the concrete walls around them. The caretaker screamed and fell backwards, the chopper dropping from his hand and slithering harmlessly off Edith Metlock's sprawled body. He turned over and tried to crawl away from them, but his legs kicked out spasmodically before he reached the top step and he slid back down, bumping Jessica as he passed her on the stairs. The gun was still pointing at the empty space where the caretaker had stood when she shot him, smoke curling from the barrel, the smell of cordite heavy in the air. The noises below had ceased as though the single, reverberating blast had stopped all action. Bishop knew the silence wouldn't last.

With one hand, he helped Edith to her feet, catching a glimpse of the cut in her lower arm as he did so. It was a long wound just below her elbow, stretching from one side to the other, apparently not too deep, for she seemed to have no trouble in using her arm. He pushed her in the direction of the landing above and followed, almost lifting Kulek with him. He gently sat the blind man down with his back against the swingdoors. The stairs ended on a small landing, separated from the short hallway leading to the other side of the building by the yellow swingdoors. The iron stair rail ran off to the left making the small landing Bishop was on a balcony overlooking the steep stairwell. At the end was a door, which he assumed was the fire exit to the stairs for anyone living in the top flats on that side of the hallway. He saw what he was looking for when he shone the torch towards the ceiling: a large trapdoor was housed there, the metal ladder leading to it

631

running down the wall opposite the balcony railings. A wooden plank was chained and padlocked to the ladder, top and bottom, a simple device to prevent children or trespassers from climbing up to the roof.

The sounds of battle began again and he ran down the few steps to Jessica. He had to prise the gun away from her clenched fingers and forcibly drag her past the spot where the overalled man had been standing.

'See to your father, Jessica,' he said harshly, shoving her towards Kulek. He knew the killing had sent her into a state of shock and the only way to bring her out of it was to occupy her mind with other problems; after all they had been through, it would be too easy for her to crack completely. Jessica knelt beside her father and cradled him in her arms.

Bishop shone the torch on to the lower retaining chain on the ladder, tugging at it to feel its strength. He was surprised when it fell away in his hand; someone – kids probably – had already worked on one of the links, cutting through it, but leaving it in position until they had cut loose the chain near the top of the ladder. The second chain was just within reaching distance, too high for smaller children, but easy enough for the caretaker or maintenance men to get at. He gripped the chain and pulled. It held.

Bishop swore. Should they use the fire escape door and get into one of the flats beyond? No, they'd be trapped in there; a determined mob could easily force their way in. The roof had to be the best bet – an army could be held off from that position. He had to break the chain somehow, or bust the padlock; the gun he was holding would do it.

'Edith, get over by Jessica!'

The medium quickly did as she was told, realising his intent. Bishop moved around so his body was between the three crouching figures and the target he was aiming at. He half-turned his head, keeping his eyes narrowed, praying there would not be a ricochet. The sound of shattered metal was smothered in the blast and the deflected bullet spun onwards, thudding into the wall just above the fire escape door. The chain fell to the floor and the wooden plank toppled away from the ladder, bouncing against, then resting on, the railing opposite. Bishop wasted no time; he climbed the ladder and pushed at the trapdoor. It would not budge.

He slipped the gun into his pocket and used the torch to examine the trapdoor; a small hole was set into a metal square at a point near the ladder. The caretaker obviously had a special key to allow access for himself and any authorised person.

'Edith, quickly – hold the torch!'

She reached up and took the torch from him.

'Shine it on the lock,' he told her. His ears were still ringing from the previous gunshot, but he was sure he could hear footsteps mounting the stairs once more. He jammed the .38 up against the lock, having no other choice but to hope for the best. The recoil in the confined space jerked his arm downwards and scraps of metal and wood spat into his face. He clung to the ladder, his head tucked down, almost losing his grip on the rung he was holding. Then, the gun still clenched in his fist, he pushed at the trapdoor. For one dreadful moment, he thought it would not lift, but he exerted more pressure and grunted with relief when the door shifted. He climbed another rung and pushed even harder; the trapdoor swung open and came to rest against something behind it. Bishop jumped back down on to the landing.

'Up you go, Edith,' he said, once more taking the torch from her. He watched her climb, telling her to reach inside the opening for some kind of handhold. She had obviously found something, for soon she was pulling her plump body through the gap, her injured arm hardly impeding her progress. Bishop stepped up a few rungs and handed the light back to her.

'Keep it on us,' he said, then jumped down and went to Jessica and her father. 'We're going to get him up to the roof, Jessica.'

Kulek opened his eyes at the sound of Bishop's voice. 'I can make it, Chris,' he said, his words slightly slurred but still coherent. 'Just get me to my feet, will you?'

Bishop smiled grimly at the blind man's willpower. He and Jessica lifted the thin body and Kulek bit his lower lip in an effort to contain a cry of pain; something was wrong inside, something deep in his stomach had been twisted or torn. Yet he had to go on: he could not allow those creatures of the Dark to take him. Despite the weakness he felt and the pain he suffered, a thought was pounding in his brain, a thought that was struggling to surface, to sweep through his mind and . . . and what? Even as he tried to concentrate his head swam with a nauseating dizziness. The thought was close, but the barriers seemed impenetrable.

They helped him to the ladder and Bishop told Jessica to go

first. 'I'll support him from down below, you try and pull him through.'

She swiftly climbed the ladder and disappeared into the black hole above. Bishop guessed there was some kind of box room built on to the flat roof of the tower block, the kind that usually housed the lift motors and drive pulleys, or water tanks. Jessica leaned her body back through the hole and reached down.

Bishop guided Kulek's hands on to the ladder and immediately knew the blind man would never make it. Kulek clung to the metal frame but did not have the strength left to move his legs. And the footsteps closing in from behind told Bishop that time was running out.

The first man was nearly at the top of the stairs, his two companions almost halfway. In the wide angle of light from the opening above, Bishop saw that all three were in a dishevelled state, a condition that had come to be recognised as belonging to the longer-term victims, those who had been affected perhaps weeks before. Their faces were black, their hands and clothes filthy and torn; no one could be sure where these people hid during the daylight hours, but it had to be somewhere dark, some place beneath the ground where nothing clean existed. The first man lurched forward, his deeply-sunk eyes fixed on Bishop, but dead and expressionless. The festering sores and scabs that corrupted his skin became clearly visible as he drew nearer.

Bishop drew the gun and pointed it at the advancing man who ignored the weapon, fearless because inside he was already dead. Bishop squeezed the trigger and the hammer clicked against an empty chamber. In panic, he tried again, knowing the gun was empty, the bullets all used.

The man spread his arms open to take him in his embrace, his eyes mere slits against the light, and Bishop struck out with the pistol, using it as a club, the blow cracking against the bridge of the creature's nose. The man still staggered forward as though the pain meant nothing to him, blood pouring from his injury and adding to the grotesqueness of his appearance. Bishop ducked beneath the clawing arms and used his shoulder against the man's chest, sending him reeling back towards the stairs. The gun was useless to him and he let it drop when he saw the only other object on the landing that could be used as a weapon. He picked up the heavy wooden plank that had been resting against the balcony rail and hurried towards the sub-human teetering at

634

the top of the stairs, smashing it into him and pushing with all his strength. The man toppled backwards, falling on to his fellow victims, who were almost on to the landing, all three going down, their deteriorated bodies glancing off the concrete steps as they went, the heavy board following. They did not stop until they had reached the broader bend in the stairs where the tall woman stood gazing upwards.

Bishop saw her there in the gloom and hate surged through him. Again he wanted to rush down and kill her, not as punishment for what she had become, but for what she was and always had been; instead he hoisted Jacob Kulek over his shoulder and began the strenuous climb up the ladder. Just when he thought he would never make it, his last reserves of strength almost depleted, helping hands reached down and lightened his load. Jessica and Edith pulled together, grasping the blink man by his clothes, beneath his arms – anywhere they could get a grip. Bishop made one final effort and heaved upwards, almost willing the injured man into the opening, and the two women gained firmer grips, lifting Kulek's upper body through, pulling him to one side so he could not fall back. The relief to Bishop was shortlived, for other, hostile, arms were wrapping themselves around his legs and pulling him down. His feet slipped from the rungs and he fell, the people beneath him cushioning the blow. He flailed out at the bodies trying to smother him, using his arms and feet to clear some space for himself, hearing Jessica's scream from above, the sound somehow making him even more desperate.

He felt himself lifted and then knew what they were about to do; the railings of the balcony rushed to meet him and suddenly he was looking directly down into the terrifying black depths below.

Chapter Thirty

His body was slipping from them, going over the rail, beginning to slide forward; and the receding floors below were like a square-shaped whirlpool, its dark centre eager to suck him down. He started to scream, but his own instinctive reaction took over from his petrified mind. He grabbed at the handrail that was only inches away from his face just as they released him. His body went over the top, but he maintained his grip, falling back against the other side of the rail, feet dangling in empty air. He gasped at the pain as his shoulder socket was wrenched, his fingers almost opening at the shock. In one movement he swung round and grasped a metal upright, both hands now taking his full weight. He managed to get a foot on to the sill of the landing and there he clung, pausing for brief seconds to recover his strength and senses.

A hand smashed down against his and he looked up to see the tall woman standing over him. Bishop knew who it was even though her features were in shadows, and, despite his helpless position, the anger flared once more. A man was reaching over to grab at his hair, trying to push him down, away from the rail. Bishop twisted his head, in an attempt to break the grip, but the hand merely moved with him, pushing, forcing him away. Someone else had a foot through the metal supports and was kicking at his chest, trying to dislodge him; through the fury of the attack, Bishop was vaguely aware that this third person was a young girl, no more than a teenager. Another shadowy figure, unable to reach Bishop because of the others, stood at the rail and shouted encouragement.

Bishop felt his fingers becoming numb and he knew they could not resist the constant hammering for much longer. The tall woman changed her tactics and began to prise them open one by one. His body was well away from the rail, the girl's foot forcing

636

him outward, the man's vicious grip on his hair pushing his head backwards. The tall woman cried out in triumph as she finally broke his hold on the rail; only his grip on the upright prevented him from plunging downwards. He knew he had only seconds left.

And then Jessica was down among them, kicking and clawing, merciless in her desperation to help Bishop. She pulled the teenager away and thrust her hard against the wall, the impact stunning the girl. Then she was on the man who held Bishop's head, tearing into him and raking his face with her fingernails. He let go of Bishop and tried to grab her, but was powerless against her fierce onslaught; he fell back, his arms covering his face. Jessica had her back towards the man who had been watching and now he moved towards her, arms outstretched.

'No!' the tall woman screeched, knowing Bishop was the more dangerous. 'Help me!'

He stopped, then leaned over the rail and began to smash his fist down against the clinging man's head. the blows stunned Bishop and he did the only thing possible: he jumped.

Using his grip on the rail and his foothold to thrust himself sideways, he snaked out a hand to grab the descending stair rail to his right. He seemed to be suspended in open space for an eternity and Edith Metlock, in the hatchway overhead, closed her eyes, unable to watch the frightening leap. His fingers curled around the slanted rail as his body slammed into the uprights and the side of the concrete steps. His other hand found purchase and he pulled himself up instantly, tumbling over the stair rail with a speed that owed much to panic. Without pausing, he raced back up the stairs, reaching up for the collar of the man Jessica had been forcing backwards and who was now near the top stop. Bishop pulled hard, twisting sideways as he did so, and the man hurtled past, his body only striking concrete when it was three steps from the bottom. He screamed as he made contact, then was silent as he rolled down. He came to rest in a crumpled heap among the groaning bodies of those who had fallen earlier.

Still Bishop did not stop; he was on the landing, running past Jessica and slamming his shoulder into the other man standing next to the tall woman. They both went down, but Bishop's mind was his own and he was able to move quickly. His fist smashed down into the upturned face, knocking the man's head against the concrete. Bishop dug both hands into the man's hair, then lifted the head almost a foot off the floor and pushed it back, the sickening smack telling him the man would not be a problem for a while.

Hands closed over his eyes, digging into them, and he knew it was the tall woman who was trying to tear them from their sockets. He threw his head back and the pressure eased slightly. Then he was released and, as he staggered forward on his knees, he saw that Jessica was holding the tall woman from behind, one arm around her waist, the other around one shoulder. The tall woman was too strong, too cunning; she brought an elbow sharply back, driving it into Jessica's ribs. Jessica doubled up and the woman whirled around, aiming two swift punches to ber breasts. Jessica screamed and collapsed to the floor. The tall woman's eyes were hidden in the dark shadows, but Bishop could feel the hatred in them. She rushed at him like a thing possessed, her teeth bared in a snarl that was primitive, the sound ascending to a high-pitched screeching as she closed in on him.

He rose to meet her and failed to stop her clutching his throat, her strength no longer normal, her savagery no longer her own. But he remembered her evil, the horrible deaths of Agnes Kirkhope and her housekeeper, the near-killing of Jacob Kulek, the murder of the policeman. The burning of Lynn. She was the willing tool of the unclean force that was in every man, woman and child; she was its servant and its instigator, a creature who worshipped the dark side of the mind. He pushed her back against the rail, her eyes visible now, tiny black pools in muddy brown irises, shrunken apertures to something darker and boundless inside. She squeezed his throat, spittle from her open mouth splattering his face, her own neck straining forward in an attempt to tear his flesh with her bared teeth. His whole body quivered with the fury he felt and blood rushed through him, swelling veins and arteries with their torrent. Then he was lifting her, scooping her legs up in one mighty heave, the movement fast but drawn out in time so the action was slow and dreamlike. Higher, her back on the rail, her shriek becoming that of fear, her hold on him loosening. Higher until she was tilted over the black void as he had been earlier. Higher until the balance was drawing her down. Then her body slipped from his grasp and she was screaming and flailing at the air as she plummeted, bouncing against the sides of stairs, an arm snapping, a leg torn from the hip, her back breaking even before she disappeared from sight and squelched against the concrete below.

Bishop hung over the rail, the strength finally drained from him. He could no longer think, no longer reason; the urge to sink to the floor and lie there was almost overwhelming. But the shouts below grew louder and footsteps drummed on the stone steps. He saw faces peering up at him, disappearing, hands snaking up the stair rail, the crowd now ascending as one, the battle with the tenants of the tower block over. A hand pulled him away from the railing and towards the ladder reaching up into the roof. Jessica implored him to climb to safety, her face stained with tears of anxiety and exhaustion.

'You first,' he told her.

'Hurry!' came Edith's voice from the open hatchway. The mob were on the last flight of stairs, the strongest of them coming fast, the torchlight growing strangely weaker as though the darkness of night were approaching with them.

Without further hesitation, Jessica climbed the ladder and disappeared into the hole above. Bishop leapt upwards, forcing his weary legs to climb, knowing the desperation of the hunted. He felt a hand close around his ankle and he stamped down hard with his other foot, the heel scraping down his pursuer's face, causing the man to drop to the floor. And then Bishop was rolling over the side of the opening, the hatch slamming closed behind him. Edith and Jessica fell on to the covering as fists pounded against it. Fortunately the hatch was solidly made and they knew that no more than one person at a time could climb the ladder to push against it. They lay in the gloom, the torch on its side and pointing towards the machinery that operated the lift, Edith and Jessica slumped over the hatch, Bishop on his back panting for breath and totally spent, Kulek sprawled on one side near a wall. They listened to the muted howls of anger below, the drumming of fists against the hatch, and they were aware of the oppressive darkness that was there with them in the small box room on top of the ten-storey building. The wind tore round the corners outside as though it were an unseen force trying to enter and Edith Metlock rejected the probing she felt at the edges of her mind, refusing to hear the anguished voices that whispered their threats. She thought only of her three companions in the machine room, keeping an imagined wall of light between her and the Dark.

After a while the noise below faded away and there was no more pressure against the hatch. Bishop breathed more evenly as he raised himself on one elbow.

639

'Have they gone?' he asked, not daring to hope.

'I don't think so,' the medium said. 'I don't think they'll give up until they have Jacob.'

'But why do they want my father?' said Jessica. 'You said before that they feared him. Why should they? What can he do against them?'

'Because I'm close to the answer, Jessica.'

They swung their heads around at the sound of his weak, quavery voice. Edith picked up the torch and shone it towards where Jacob Kulek sat, his back propped up against the wall, his hands pressed down against the floor to keep his body erect. He seemed strangely shrunken, as though his body were slowly crumbling in upon itself, his cheeks collapsed inwards, eyes half-closed as though resisting sleep. Jessica quickly crawled towards him, not having the strength to rise, and Bishop followed.

Jessica took one of her father's hands and tenderly touched his cheek. The lids of his eyes briefly opened wider and he tried to smile at her. She pressed her face against his, afraid for him without knowing why; it had nothing to do with the physical danger they were in, and concern over his injuries was only part of it. He opened his mouth to speak again, but she softly placed her fingertips against his lips.

'Don't, Father. Save your strength. Help will be here soon, I'm sure of it.'

A trembling hand took hers away. 'No, Jessica . . . there will be . . . no help . . . for us this night.'

'We managed to get a message through to the police, Jacob,' Bishop said. 'They'll try to reach us.'

Kulek wearily turned to him. 'They have no . . . control over this . . . terrible thing, Chris. Only people as individuals . . . can fight against it. But it can be defeated.' Strength seemed to be returning to his words.

'How, Jacob?'

'Pryszlak . . . Pryszlak knew how to unleash the evil inside him. At the moment of death, he knew how to direct that evil. Don't you see, his death was like opening a box, releasing the contents. The content was his own psyche, and his will was strong enough – even in death – to control that psyche.'

'It isn't possible.'

'Years, Chris, years of conditioning his mind for that final moment.' Kulek sucked in a huge breath and began to cough, his body doubling over and shoulders jerking spasmodically. They lifted him upright when the seizure had passed, resting his back against the rough brickwork; they were alarmed to see the speckles of blood on his lips and chin. He breathed slowly for a few moments, then his eyes opened. 'Don't you see? He built up the power of evil around him over the years through his own practices and those of his followers, their minds communicating, joining as one, directing their separate forces so they merged; all that remained was the barrier of life.'

'And he knew he could go on even after his own death?'

Kulek's eyes closed again. 'He knew. He was an extraordinary man, his mental development stretched far beyond that of normal men. He could use areas of the brain that we know nothing of. The mind is a mystery to us; he had unravelled some of its secrets.'

Edith Metlock spoke from the darkness on the other side of the torch beam. 'Jacob is right. They fear him because he knows the truth.'

'But I do not have the answer!' Kulek said loudly, anger and frustration in his voice.

Edith was about to say more when she suddenly looked down at the hatch beneath her and listened. 'They're still there,' she said in a whisper. 'Something is being moved – I can hear a scraping noise.'

Jessica and Bishop moved towards the hatchway and listened, fighting to keep their own breathing as soundless as possible. They did not see the thin line of blood appear at the corner of Kulek's lips, running down his chin, forming a pool around his jawline before falling in spots on to his chest. The flow thickened and then ran from his chin in a steady stream.

The scraping noise below had stopped and for a moment there was only silence. All three jumped when something crashed against the hatch. It rose several inches before slamming shut again.

'Christ, they've found something to batter against the hatch!' Bishop said, his nerves beginning their frenetic dance once more.

The crash came again and both Bishop and Jessica combined their weights with Edith's to keep the hatch closed. It slowly began to rise beneath them.

'They must have got a table or something from one of the flats to stand on. There's more than one person pushing now.' Bishop

641

grabbed the torch from the medium and shone it quickly around the machine room, looking for a weapon of some kind, anything he could use to beat back someone climbing through. There were small windows set in the walls and a door leading out to the roof itself; the drive pulley and the lift motor were nearby, the opening to the shaft black and menacing. There were no tools lying around, nothing at all that could be used as a weapon. The hatch beneath them opened a few millimetres wider and a stout, metal bar was pushed through to keep it open. Bishop pulled at the bar, but it was jammed into the gap. Fingers curled around the edges of the hatch opening and the pressure below became even more intense. The gap widened and they heard another object being scraped through to be used as a lever by the person on the other side. They tried to prise away the fingers around the edges but they merely returned in another position. Their arms and shoulder muscles were taut with the effort of pressing down, yet they could feel the hatch rising higher each second. An arm came through the gap and Jesica screamed when the hand closed around her wrist.

It was at that point that the power came back on.

Light flooded in through the opening, blinding them with its suddenness. The lift machinery clanked into life and the pulley turned as the car resumed its interrupted journey. There were cries from below as the hatch dropped and came to rest on the objects that had been pushed through; the arm and the hands around the opening had already disappeared. They heard scuffling on the landing below, the sound of footsteps running down steps, screams as people fell in their haste to escape the dazzling lights.

The two women fell away from the hatch, both crying with relief, praying that it was finally over for them – for that night at least. Bishop cautiously swung the hatch open wider, the metal bars sliding away and bouncing off the table below before clanging down on to the concrete landing. The upper stairs were empty apart from the sprawled bodies of those who had been injured before. He could hear the others scurrying down, many moving fast, knocking aside those who had been victims for a longer period and who were totally blinded by the lights.

'They've gone,' he quietly told the two women. He shivered as the wind rushed into the machine room and turned to see the door was open wide. Jacob Kulek was no longer sitting against the wall.

The two women looked up when he dropped the hatch and rushed to the door. They, too, realised the blind man was missing.

The wind hit Bishop like a physical blow as he ran out on to the roof, tearing at his clothes and whipping at his face so that he had to half-close his eyes against its force.

The lights of the city spread out before him like a vast silver and orange constellation and, for a moment, he could only gaze at its manufactured beauty, for the first time truly understanding its potency. He panicked when he could not see Kulek; the roof was completely flat apart from the machine room and another similarly shaped building that he guessed housed the tower block's massive water-tank. Jessica and Edith joined him and all three apprehensively scanned the rooftop.

'Jacob!' Edith Metlock called out.

Jessica and Bishop followed her gaze and saw the blind man standing just ten yards away from the edge of the building; they could only make out his shape because of the lights blocked out behind him. He turned to look at them as they began to walk as one towards him.

'No,' he warned them, 'it's dangerous here. You must stay back.'

'Father, what are you doing?' Jessica cried against the noise of the wind, her arms reaching imploringly.

Kulek clutched at his stomach, but refused to bend to the pain. His face was just a vague whitish blur against the night sky, but they could see the blackness spreading down from his mouth on to his lower jaw. There was a thickness to his words as though the blood was filling his throat.

'They wanted me dead! They wanted to kill me before I found the answer . . . before I learned how I could use my own . . .' his words were lost as he stumbled towards the lip of the roof.

'No!' Jessica screamed, breaking away from Bishop and Edith Metlock and running towards the blind man. 'No!'

Kulek turned to look at Jessica and his words were whipped away by the wind. Then he plunged into the night.

Chapter Thirty-One

Jessica brought the car to a halt and once more Bishop leaned out the window and showed the special pass card to the soldier. The sergeant examined it then ducked his head to scrutinise Edith Metlock sitting in the back. Satisfied, he signalled to another soldier standing by the red and white striped barrier, which was then dragged to one side. It had been the third time their car had been stopped since entering the area around Willow Road. The group of soldiers idly standing around an army truck watched them as they drove through, their curiosity apparent, their weapons even more apparent. The military were taking no chances with this operation, not after the total disaster of three weeks before. Many men had been lost that night, police and civilians, as well as soldiers, their brains infected or affected by whatever chemicals the scientists said the Dark contained, turning on each other, damaging the lights that had been their ultimate protection. Their defence against the hordes who poured into the area had been hampered by the confusion within their own ranks. The battle that had taken place had been horrendous and only the swift arrival of reinforcements had prevented those unaffected from being completely overcome. A nightmare action, but one brought about by their own under-estimation of the unseen enemy. Tonight they would be better prepared.

Jessica swung the car out to the middle of the road, avoiding the lorry bearing the huge searchlight parked at the kerbside. They had passed many such machines on their journey, many of which had been in service for the past two weeks, others brought in for that night's particular operation. Most had been adapted so they did not throw directional and defined beams, but shed a broad and powerful area of light. Smaller lights had been fixed to roofs of houses or hung from their eaves; that area, which seemed to be the worst affected in London, had been literally flooded with lights. The curfew was still imposed throughout the city and lighting-up time had taken on a whole new meaning. Veterans of the wartime blitz thought it ironic that now it was unlawful not to show a light at night-time, whereas in the war years it had been a punishable offence to do so.

Bishop's uneasiness grew as they approached Willow Road and he looked across at Jessica to see her features were also strained, her hands clamped tightly around the steering-wheel. She felt his gaze on her and turned to give him a quick, nervous smile. Since the death of her father, they had grown close, the earlier attraction they had felt for each other developing into a strengthening bond of friendship – and something more. They were not yet lovers, but both knew that when their separate wounds had healed, their mutual stress subsided, then their intimacy of feeling would be matched by a physical intimacy. It was a desire in both of them, but one that could not – and would not – be hurriedly fulfilled.

She braked as a military vehicle carelessly turned the corner from Willow Road and swerved across their path, the driver obviously taking advantage of the empty streets. He waved an apology and sped on. Jessica took her foot off the brake and guided the car into Willow Road.

Bishop's eyes widened at the sight ahead, even though the details were not clear because of his slight short-sightedness. The road was filled with vehicles of all kinds, most of them military, others belonging to the Metropolitan Police, and also many civilian cars. Open-topped lorries bore more searchlights and armoured scout cars kept a watchful eye at each end of the road. There seemed to be uniformed figures everywhere, blue mingling with khaki, soldiers lining the pavements as though they were a guard of honour. Houses were being entered and searched for any hiding victims undiscovered in the earlier searches. He could just make out the bright red of fire tenders at the far end of the road, and the ominous white shapes of ambulances told him the authorities were prepared for the worst. But the sight that astonished Bishop most of all as Jessica eased the car past the parked vehicles and scurrying men was that of the strangely naked area halfway down. The houses on either side of the Beechwood debris had been completely demolished, leaving a wide, empty space. He had no clear view into the extended site because of the confusion of machinery and vehicles around its fringes, but he guessed what lay inside the boundary, for the intentions of that night's operation had been fully explained to him. The authorities had been forced to involve Edith Metlock and himself, albeit reluctantly, for they had unsuccessfully repeated their experiment for the past three nights and, as yet, the Dark had not returned to the site. Sicklemore, the Principal Private Secretary to the Home Office who had been fortunate to survive the disaster of three weeks before, had suggested that Bishop and Edith Metlock be called in to assist once more. There were protests, for the scientists and technicians involved claimed that the Dark had nothing to do with the paranormal, that it was merely the carrier of some unknown and, as yet, untraced chemical that in some way triggered a reaction in the hypothalamus region of the brain, creating electrical charges that manifested themselves in acts of extreme aggression. The Dark was a physical entity, a chemical catalyst, not some mystical and incorporeal leech, and therefore could be overcome by scientific means, not by spiritualistic mumbo-jumbo. Since Jacob Kulek's death, the uneasy alliance between scientist and parapsychologist had become a disdainful non-alliance. But Sicklemore had insisted. Three nights of failure and three days of the Home Secretary bellowing for results had made him desperate: Bishop and Metlock were thin straws to clutch at, but at least *something* had happened when they had last been present.

Edith Metlock stared out at the military and scientific paraphernalia from the darkness of the back seat and her heart sank into further depths of despair. Had it all been for nothing? Had Jacob died in vain? The Dark had only grown stronger after that night, nothing happening to dissipate its power. She had tried to make contact with him, but now it seemed her powers as a sensitive had left her, for nothing came to her any more, no visions, no voices. It was as though the thin veil between herself and the spirit world had become an impregnable barrier. Perhaps it was because she had lost her own beliefs.

Peck saw their car approaching and walked out into the middle of the road, waving his arm at them. He leaned in the window when Jessica brought the car to a stop.

'You'll find a space to park further down, Miss Kulek,' he said, then directed his attention towards Bishop. 'If you and Mrs Metlock could come with me?'

They stepped from the car and Jessica went on searching for a gap by the kerb in the congested street.

'How is she?' Peck asked, nodding towards the departing vehicle.

'She's come to believe her father's death was pointless. It's made it worse for her,' Bishop replied.

Peck mentally sighed. He remembered how he had found them on the tower block rooftop weeks before, almost frozen, physically exhausted. It had been dawn before he and a couple of squad cars had made their way to the high-rise building, only the persistence of one of the block's tenants alerting them to Kulek's whereabouts. The tenant had tried all night to get through to the Information Room, phoning in every hour but, because the lines had been flooded with emergency calls, his message had only been taken when daylight was approaching. Peck and his officers had been halfway to the top, checking each body on the stairs as they passed, not allowing themselves to spare time on the injured, when they had met Bishop coming down. He had looked dazed, his shoulders slumped in a weariness that was both physical and mental. He told them the two women were still on the roof, that Jacob Kulek was dead. It was only when they had all been brought down to the safety of the ground that he learned that Kulek had deliberately jumped; Edith Metlock had said that Kulek's death would provide the answer to the Dark. The medium hadn't appeared to be hysterical – she spoke softly, calmly – and Kulek's daughter seemed to see some sense in what she told them, although the girl's grief was apparent. When Peck had walked around to the side of the building and had found Jacob Kulek's smashed body, his rage burned inside. The blind man had been badly injured when the police car had crashed – from what Peck had gathered, Kulek had been busted up inside as well as concussed. He had obviously been delirious when he had jumped, they should have seen that. Now, the medium was making him out to be the new messiah, someone whose death was for the benefit of mankind. Peck had turned away from the misshapen body, barely disguising his anger when he returned to the waiting group. The blind man had been thrown through the windscreen of a car, dragged up ten flights of stairs, chased by a mob of zombies and madmen, and then had fallen from the roof; what glory could there be in such a death? Even Bishop had seemed to listen to the medium's crackpot assertions. But now three weeks had passed and nothing had happened to diminish the power of the Dark. They had been

647

wrong and Peck could only feel sorry for them.

'I'll take you over to the site,' he said to Bishop and Edith. 'The Private Secretary wanted to see you as soon as you arrived.'

They followed the detective, carefully stepping over the thick electric cables and avoiding the white-coated technicians who were making last-minute adjustments to various pieces of equipment. Dusk was not far away and already many of the smaller lights had been switched on. Bishop looked incredulously at Peck when he saw the newly expanded site. A huge pit had been dug out in the area that had once been Beechwood and its grounds, and seated within it were four massive light machines, each rectangular in shape, their Perspex surfaces pointed towards the sky. Similar machines, but smaller, more compact, were placed in positions around the pit. Further back, on the flattened land that Beechwood's neighbouring house had been built on, stood a pre-fabricated steel hut, a dark-tinted window stretching along its entire length and overlooking the site. On the opposite side stood the generator which would supply the power for all the apparatus.

'They're taking no chances this time,' Peck explained as he guided them towards the hut. 'They've got backup generators and lights, and enough guards to fight off an army. The power stations are heavily guarded too, by the way, so there's no chance of someone doing the same as that madman three weeks ago. He held out for hours before they finally got to him.'

They had just reached the squat, metal-walled building when Sicklemore emerged followed by a bespectacled man in shirt-sleeves, whom Bishop recognised as the chief scientific adviser to the government, and who, at the Birmingham Conference Centre, had openly rejected any paranormal connotations regarding the recent disasters.

'Mr Bishop, Mrs, uh, Metlock,' Sicklemore briskly acknowledged. 'Perhaps your presence tonight will bring us more luck.'

'I don't see why it should,' Bishop replied bluntly.

The Private Secretary regarded him speculatively, then said, 'Nor do I, Mr Bishop, but you seemed to last time. You remember Professor Marinker?'

The scientist gave them a grudging nod of his head.

'Perhaps you'll explain tonight's operation, Marinker?' Sicklemore said, having privately made it clear that he was no longer prepared to put up with petulance over the use of what the scientist termed as 'bloody cranks'.

648

'Your part is simple enough,' Marinker said gruffly. 'You just do the same as three weeks ago. I, personally, don't see why the Dark should return just because you're here – it makes no sense at all to me – but that's the decision of others.' He looked meaningfully at Sicklemore. 'Although the Dark seems to be an insubstantial thing, we have managed to detect a denser area at its centre – a nucleus, if you like. We believe the chemical which reacts on certain other chemicals present in the hypothalamus region of the brain is strongest within that centre. Our intensive tests on living victims have now made it clear that the disturbance is certainly in that region of the brain, and further tests have shown that minor radiation disperses those chemicals. Unfortunately, the radiation, slight though it is, damages brain cells to a degree where the victim can no longer function as a living person.'

Bishop shook his head, no humour in his smile. 'You mean your experiments kill them.'

Sicklemore hastily interjected. 'We have no choice but to be brutal in our tests. Those victims would not have lived long, anyway.'

Marinker continued as though there had been no interruption. 'It explains why the Dark can only exist at night, why the radiation in the sun's rays causes its disappearance. It goes to ground, if you like.'

'You said you believed it was a chemical. How could it react in such a way unless it were a living organism? Or something else?'

'I used the term loosely, Mr Bishop, to keep the conversation in layman's terms. Certain chemicals do have negative reactions to opposing properties, you know. We are sure it's the ultra-violet rays from the sun that are harmful to the chemical and further tests on victims bear this out. The tiniest exposure to ultra-violet light makes them try to hide, to cover their eyes. You've seen our light machines set beneath ground level, the others angled around the excavation. Unfortunately, the ultra-violet wavelength does not travel far, but our specially constructed machines are extremely powerful and, so that the area will be fully saturated, we will have several helicopters mounted with similar but obviously smaller lights overhead, their beams directed at the ground. Gravitation itself will give them a longer wavelength so the helicopters will be fairly high and in no danger. Of course, gamma rays or X-rays would have been even more

649

effective, we believe, but then, that would have been highly dangerous for everyone in the immediate area, too.'

'Lasers?'

'Too defined an area. They would penetrate, but not saturate.'

'But surely too much exposure to ultra-violet rays is harmful to us.'

'You will be protected and we will be inside the hut. Those outside will wear gloves and hoods and stand behind shields. Their normal clothing will give them added protection.

'How will we be protected?'

'Special suits with oxidised visors.'

'And if nothing happens? If we don't attract the Dark?'

'Let me speak plainly, Bishop: I don't expect you to. I think that what took place three weeks ago happened by mere chance. The fact that the victims seem to be drawn to this place each night indicates that there is a fundamental source of energy in this area; we have no idea what that source is nor have we been able to locate it specifically. But we know it's here, we're sure this thing that everyone calls the Dark will return to it. It's just a matter of time.'

'Which we don't have,' Sicklemore snapped. 'The point is this, Mr Bishop: your presence will not hinder the operation, and it might just do some good. I mean no offence, but I personally find the argument for psychic phenomena far from convincing, but at this particular moment, I'm ready to try anything if it will mean our success. In fact,' he said, turning his eye on the scientific adviser, 'I shall even indulge in a few prayers when I'm inside that hut.'

Marinker opened his mouth to speak, but thought better of it.

'Now,' Sicklemore continued. 'The light is fading fast. Can we please make our final arrangements?'

Marinker called through the hut's doorway and an agitated youngish man appeared, a sheaf of papers in his hands, a well-chewed pencil clenched between his teeth.

'Get these two kitted out, Brinkley,' Marinker said. 'Full gear, they'll be fully exposed to the light.'

Brinkley waved the papers in the air with one hand and grabbed at the pencil in his mouth, pointing it behind him into the hut. 'But I . . .' he began to protest.

'Just get on with it!' Marinker pushed past him and disappeared through the doorway. Brinkley stared after him, then turned to inspect his two charges.

650

'Right, I'll leave you to it,' Sicklemore said. 'Will you stay with them, Peck, see that they have all they need?'

'Yes, sir.'

'I'll see you both presently, then.' Sicklemore strode hurriedly away from them, his small, waspish figure soon swallowed up by the crowds of technicians and soldiers on the site.

'Gone to report to his superiors,' Peck said, enjoying the fact that the man he had to be servile to had to be servile to others. 'He's had his own little department set up in one of the nearby houses, with a direct line to the Home Secretary. Poor bastard's been popping in and out every half-hour all day.'

'Er, if you'll come along with me we'll find you a couple of suits to put on,' Brinkley said, eager to get back to his work. He led them through the site to the road. 'You're Bishop and Edith Metlock, I take it,' he said, forced to slow his brisk pace so the others could keep up. 'I heard what happened three weeks ago; sounds to me as if the whole operation was too hastily put together.'

Peck looked at Bishop and rolled his eyes upwards.

'Still,' the scientist went on brightly, 'that won't happen tonight. I think I can promise you we've found the answer. All very simple really, but then aren't most things if you approach them correctly?'

As Brinkley babbled on, Bishop looked around for Jessica and saw her making her way towards them along the pavement. He waved an arm and her pace quickened.

'Here we are then.' Brinkley had stopped beside a large, grey-coloured van. The back section was open and they could see the shelves inside were filled with white garments. Brinkley stepped in and checked the sizes marked on the shelves. He soon returned with the appropriate uniforms. 'They're pretty loose and very light – you can slip them on over your normal clothing. Helmets are separate, but they're not at all cumbersome. There we are, the light will just bounce off you.' He gave them a cheerful grin, then frowned at the medium. 'That's a nuisance – you're wearing a skirt. Never mind, you can change in one of the houses – they're all empty.'

Jessica had joined them by now and Peck noticed how close to Bishop she stood, almost leaning against him. It gave the detective some satisfaction, for he knew the ordeal both had been through; perhaps they could at least give a little comfort to each

651

other. He was worried about the medium, though: she seemed lost, confused.

'Are you all right, Mrs Metlock?' he asked. 'You look a little pale.'

'I . . . I don't know. I'm not sure that I can be of any help tonight.' She looked down at the pavement, avoiding their eyes. Jessica went to her.

'You must try, Edith,' she said gently. 'For my father's sake, you must try.'

There were tears in the medium's eyes when she looked up. 'But he's not there, Jessica. Don't you understand? He's gone, I can't reach him. There's nothing there any more.'

Brinkley appeared to be embarrassed. 'I'm afraid we don't have too much time. Could I, um, ask you to put the suits on now, please? I've rather a lot to cope with in the operations hut, so if you'll excuse me . . .?'

'Go ahead,' Peck told him. 'I'll bring them over when they're ready.' He turned to the medium and his voice was hard. 'I know you're frightened, Mrs Metlock, but they're only asking you to do what you've been doing professionally for years.'

'It isn't fear . . .'

'All right, maybe it's exhaustion. We're all bloody tired. I've lost some good men over the past few weeks – two of them trying to protect you – and I don't want to lose any more. Now, all this may be nonsense, I don't know – I don't have to judge – but they . . .' he waved his hand at the site in general '. . . see you as a last resort. I've seen things recently that I never thought possible, so there may be something in it. The point is, we've got to try anything, and both you and Bishop *are* our anything! So will you please help us and get into that ridiculous spaceman's outfit?'

Jessica took the medium by the arm. 'I'll help you, Edith.'

Edith Metlock looked at Bishop, her expression a mixture of helplessness and pleading, but he could only turn his head away. 'Go with Jessica, Edith,' he told her.

The two women left, Jessica leading the medium by the arm as if helping a very old, and very tired woman. Bishop struggled into the white suit, surprised at its toughness despite its flimsy appearance. The helmet itself, with its stiff, black visor, hung loosely over his back; it could be pulled forward like a hood, the visor snapped into position by two lips on either side. The arms

652

ended in close-fitting gloves, elasticated at the wrists, the feet made to the same principle. He zipped the suit up to a point just below his chest and looked up to see Peck watching him, his face grim.

'Bishop,' the detective said, then hesitated.

Bishop raised his eyebrows questioningly.

Peck looked uncomfortable. 'Just watch yourself in there.'

They sat side by side, the huge, square lights set out before them, lifeless yet threatening. Two lonely, white-clad figures, the centre-piece in an outward spreading array of technical equipment, weaponry and manpower. They were afraid, and those around them were afraid, for the tension among them was steadily increasing, feeding upon itself and touching them all as they watched. The sun had disappeared from the sky an hour before, its sinking hidden by dark clouds that had formed on the horizon, and now the site was lit only by subdued lights. The men around the perimeter were all shielded by metal screens and they wore special glasses already positioned over their eyes, making them look sinister and emotionless; a certain number were equipped with full protective headgear and gloves. They waited as they had waited for three previous consecutive nights; but this time they sensed it was different. This time, each man would occasionally look up at the sky, removing his dark glasses to study the black rolling clouds for long moments before turning his attention back to the two figures sitting in front of the open pit. Something would make each one shiver, but not outwardly; it was more like a sudden shudder of internal organs. It passed from man to man, mind to mind, an infection whose carrier was their own thoughts. Even the scientists and operatives inside the squat steel hut, surrounded by their own technology, felt particularly uneasy that night. Marinker's mouth was dry, the palms of his hands wet. Sicklemore kept clearing his throat and tapping one foot. Brinkley could not stop blinking.

Outside, behind a screen, Peck jangled the loose change in his trouser pocket, while Jessica, who stood by the detective's side, bit on her lower lip until her teeth left deep indents. The minutes passed and all casual chatter ceased; if anyone did speak, it was in a whisper just loud enough to be heard over the steady hum of the generators. The air seemed to be growing colder. And, of course, through their protective glasses, the night looked even darker than usual.

Bishop found it difficult to think clearly. He tried to remember, as he had done before, the first day he had come to Beechwood, the terrible sight that had confronted him. But it was all vague, all misty and remote, as though it had only been a dream which could not be brought into focus. He looked over at Edith sitting two feet away, but her features were barely visible through the darkened visors they both wore. Her hands were clasped across her lap and he could see them clinging tightly to each other.

'I can't think, Edith. It's all a blur to me for some reason.'

She said nothing for a few moments, then her visor turned in his direction. 'Don't try to think of it, Chris. Leave your mind blank. If the Dark really is what we believe it to be it will seek you out. It doesn't need your guidance.'

'Can you . . . can you sense anything?'

'I see Jacob's face, but I can't feel his presence. I feel nothing, Chris, only emptiness.'

'Did he really believe . . . ?'

The medium turned away. 'I don't know any more. Jacob's perception was stronger than any man's I've ever known; even stronger than Boris Pryszlak's.'

'You *knew* Pryszlak?'

The black visor made her inscrutable. 'I was once his mistress.'

For a few moments, Bishop was too stunned to speak. 'His mistress? I don't understand . . .'

'It was a long, long time ago. Twenty years, perhaps more. So long, it sometimes feels as if it never really happened, as if the woman who slept with him was someone I knew vaguely, but whose name or face I can no longer remember. Boris Pryszlak was an astonishing man, you see; his very wickedness made him attractive. Do you understand that, Chris, how a malignant thing can be attractive?'

Bishop did not answer.

'I found him fascinating. At first, I didn't see the deepness of his corruption, the depravity that was not just part of him, but *was* him, his very being. It was he who recognised my powers as a sensitive, who encouraged me to develop those powers; he thought he would be able to use me. It was Jacob who finally drew me away from Pryszlak's influence.' She smiled almost wistfully beneath the mask. 'Jacob and I were never lovers – he has always been faithful to the memory of his wife. You of all

654

people will realise that in our world, nobody dies; they merely pass on to something more enduring.'

'But why didn't Jacob tell me this at the beginning?'

'Because I asked him not to. Don't you see it wasn't important? It had nothing to do with what was happening. Boris Pryszlak's immorality was like an infectious disease – it tainted anyone close to him. For a while I wallowed in the filth he thrived on and it was only Jacob who tried to help me. Perhaps he saw I was being used, that I was a victim of evil rather than a perpetrator. Jacob once told me he had tried to lure away other followers of Pryszlak, but had come to see those people were as sick and twisted as the man they idolised, and it was my own desire to leave – to be saved, if you like – that made me different from them. Even so, Pryszlak hated Jacob for having taken away just one of his followers.'

'Yet he came to Jacob for help.'

'He needed him at that time. He wanted to combine his own extraordinary mental powers with Jacob's; that combination would have been formidable. But Jacob had no desire to become involved in the ultimate aims of such a man. Besides, he knew that involvement would mean eventual subjection. Jacob bitterly regretted not having tried to destroy Pryszlak's plans all those years ago before they had become fully formed; but then, he was a truly good man and failed to recognise the extent of Pryszlak's malignancy. Even I failed to see that and I had shared his bed for almost a year.'

Bishop drew in a deep breath. He was disturbed by Edith's revelation, but not shocked; too much had happened for his emotions to be jarred by any fresh disclosure. 'Is that why Jacob called you in at the beginning of all this – because you had some connection with Pryszlak?'

'Yes. He felt it would be easier for me to reach Pryszlak. I knew something of his mind, something of his intentions. I had never visited Beechwood before, but I felt his presence as soon as I entered the house. It was almost like walking into Pryszlak's mind, each room a different, dark cell. He used to experiment with his own telepathic powers when we were . . . together . . . using me as his receiver. He never failed to penetrate my mind with his evil thoughts. For him it was a new kind of eroticism, a fantasy of imagined deviant sexual acts yet, because of the strength of his mental powers, experienced as though physically performed.'

Bishop saw her white-clad figure shudder.

'Those thoughts are still with me, burned deep into my brain. Only Jacob could help me subdue them and now he's gone. That's why I'm so afraid, Chris.'

'I don't understand.'

'Jacob poured his strength into me. Here, when we first gathered at Beechwood and you saw the vision, I was the one who made contact, but Jacob was helping me resist Pryszlak, preventing him from dominating my mind completely. Even when you found me at my home in a trance state, Jacob, who was lying injured in hospital, was using his mental powers to keep Pryszlak from taking possession. He was my protector, the barrier between myself and the full force of Pryszlak's parasitical soul.'

'But the Dark *can* be resisted, Edith. The reaction is only against those who have some imbalance in the brain.'

'We *all* have that imbalance. We all feel hate, aggression, jealousy! As the Dark grows stronger – as Pryszlak gathers his spiritual army – it will seek out the evil inside all of us and use it to destroy! Those it can't overcome – and they will be few – will be killed by its still-living physical legions. There will be no escape for any of us!'

'Only if the Dark is what you say it is. The scientists claim otherwise; they'll destroy it with their machines.'

'And with all you've seen, all you've been through, can you believe the Dark is just a chemical reaction?'

Bishop's voice was firm. 'I don't know any more. I almost came to believe in what you and Jacob told me, but now . . .' He looked away from her, his gaze falling on the huge light machines before them. 'Now I hope you were both wrong.'

Edith's body seemed to slump further into itself. 'Perhaps we were, Chris,' she said slowly. 'Perhaps I hope so, too.'

'Bishop?' The call came from the tiny radio receiver fixed into Bishop's ear. The voice had a metallic sound to it, but he assumed it was Marinker from the control hut speaking. 'Our helicopters are in the air. Anything happened with you two out there?' The question had a cynical edge to it, but Bishop sensed the underlying tension.

'Nothing so far.' His reply was picked up by the small microphone clipped to his chest. Slight static in the receiver made the scientist's next words hard to grasp. 'I'm sorry, what was that?' Bishop asked.

'I said we've just had a report . . .' more static '. . . trouble

656

near here. Nothing for us to worry. . .' static '. . . being dealt with. More victims on the loose, that's all.'

Another voice came through the earpiece and Bishop guessed it was Sicklemore. 'You'll let us know the moment you feel anything, um, strange happening?'

Marinker spoke again. 'The build-up from the ultra-violet lights will be gradual, Bishop, so you needn't worry about any sudden flare. Just give us some warning. . .' more static, then, 'Can you hear us all right, Mrs Metlock? We seem to be getting interference from somewhere.'

There was no reply from the medium and Bishop anxiously turned towards her. Her body was rigid in the chair, her black visor facing straight ahead.

'Mrs Metlock?' the metallic voice came again.

'Be quiet, Marinker,' Bishop said harshly. Then, more softly, 'Edith? Can you sense something?'

She continued to look ahead and her voice sounded faint. 'It's here, Chris. It's . . . oh my God!' Her body shuddered. 'Can't you feel it? It's growing. It's all around us.'

Bishop tore his eyes away and quickly looked around the site. He felt nothing and the tinted glass he stared through made everything seem darker. He quickly unclipped the visor and lifted it back over his head.

The soldiers and technicians positioned around the site glanced uneasily at each other, sensing something was finally about to happen. Jessica felt a weakness spread through her, a weakness born of dread. A perception that was akin to intuition but stronger, more certain, told her that the menace was even greater than before, that they were all more vulnerable, their resistance against the Dark a fragile thing. She clutched at Peck, afraid she would sink to the ground. He turned in surprise, beads of perspiration on his forehead despite the coldness of the night. He supported her weight, then turned his attention back to the two figures sitting near the open pit. Bishop was looking around him as though searching for something, his visor pushed up from his head.

Inside the control hut, Marinker was speaking agitatedly to his radio operator. 'Can't you cut out this bloody static? I can't hear what they're saying out there.'

'I'm trying, sir, but there's not much I can do about it. I'm afraid it's atmospherics – it's interfering with our contact with the choppers, too.'

657

Marinker avoided Sicklemore's eyes, afraid he would give away the alarm he was strangely feeling. He cursed himself inwardly for being stupid and hoped no one noticed his hand trembling as he stabbed at the speaker button once more, 'Bishop, is something wrong out there? Can you hear me?' A constant crackle of static was his only reply.

Bishop tore the earpiece away, the interference becoming unbearable. His eyes narrowed as he searched the site. The general gloom was because only a few lights had been switched on, but was the air becoming heavier with something more than just nightfall? He blinked, but still he could not make out any definable difference in the lighting. He began to wonder if an hallucinatory tension had built up in the minds of everyone present on the side, a muted form of mass-hysteria that was creating a false fear.

'Edith, I can't see anything.'

'It's here, Chris, it's here.'

Something swirled in the corner of Bishop's vision and he snapped his head around to see what it was. Nothing there. Another movement, to his right this time. Nothing there . . .

Edith was pushing herself back against the chair, her hands tightly gripping the seat. Her breathing was heavy, laboured.

Bishop felt the coldness on his exposed face, a prickling sensation of closing pores, tightening skin. The coldness crept through to the rest of his body. More movement, and this time he caught sight of something shadowy. It flitted across his vision like a tenuous veil, gone when focused upon. A sound, the kind the wind makes when it suddenly sweeps around the corner of a house. Gone. Silence. Lights dimming.

Bishop spoke, hoping the microphone would pick up his words. 'It's beginning,' was all he said.

But in the control hut they only heard the irritating noise of static. All eyes watched the two white-uniformed figures through the long, shaded window until Marinker said, 'Check those lights – they seem to be fading.'

A technician turned a dial and the lights grew bright again. But slowly, almost imperceptibly, the brightness dulled.

A low moaning sound came from Edith and Bishop was about to reach out to her when his movement froze. Something was touching him. Something was running a hand over his body.

He looked down at himself and saw the loose folds of the white

658

suit becoming smooth, flattening out. But the material moved on its own; nothing pressed against it. The whiteness of the suit which had been subdued under the poor lighting now became a dark grey in colour. The coldness that was in his body began to creep into Bishop's mind, a numbing frost seeking corridors to chill, and the familiar welling up of fear encouraged its progress. He tried to speak, tried to warn the others of what was happening, but this throat was too constricted. The darkness was descending, a shadowy blackness that threatened to extinguish all light.

Bishop tried to stand, but felt a crushing weight pushing against him, the same cold hand that had explored his body and which had now grown into a giant, invisible claw holding him captive. He knew it was only his own confused mind lying to him, making him believe what was not possible, but the pressure existed as though it were real. Once more, he tried to reach Edith, and his arms were held down by his sides, too heavy to lift. He saw the medium begin to slide from the chair, her own moaning rising to a piteous wail. Then the figure began to appear.

Inside the control hut, Sicklemore was speaking urgently to Marinker, years of civil service breeding preventing his voice from rising to a shout. 'For God's sake, man, turn on the machines. Can't you see what's happening out there?'

Marinker seemed uncertain, his eyes switching from the array of controls before him to the barely visible figures outside. 'Bishop hasn't got his visor in position. I can't risk turning on the machines while he's exposed like that.'

'Don't be stupid, man! He'll use the mask as soon as the ultra-violet lights begin to come on. Do it now, that's an order!'

The figures were just dark, ethereal shapes, their forms having no clearly defined image. They drifted closer, converging on the two people by the pit, black shapes that were part of the blackness around them. They drew near, looming over Bishop and Edith, the man locked into his seat by an unseen force, the woman cowering on the ground. Bishop gasped for breath, feeling as though he were sinking into thick, slimy mud, his mouth and nostrils choked by the foul-smelling substance. He forced his arms up, slowly, tendons straining, fists clenched and trembling. He tried to grip the invisible thing that pushed against his chest and found nothing there, no shape, no substance. But the pressure still remained.

659

The soldiers around the site, those in the road, and those in the streets beyond the road, held their self-loading rifles and Sterling sub-machine guns at the ready, knowing the inactivity had come to an end and that the danger had finally presented itself. The policemen felt comforted to be under the protection of their weaponry. In the distance, they could hear shouts, the occasional burst of gunfire; elsewhere trouble had already started.

Jessica tried to dodge round the metal shield, wanting to reach Bishop and Edith, but Peck grabbed her wrist and held her back.

'Leave them,' he said gruffly. 'You can't help them! Look.'

She followed his gaze and saw the sudden white glow emerging from the pit. The ultra-violet lights had been switched on, their brilliant light slowly spreading upwards and out. Other lights around the site began to glimmer, growing stronger second by second. Overhead could be heard the whirring blades of helicopters and the sky itself began to glow with the spreading white light.

'Chris hasn't got his visor down!' Jessica cried, struggling to free herself once more.

'He soon will have, don't worry. Just keep still, will you, and watch!'

Jessica stopped and Peck released his grip. 'Good girl. Now keep behind the screen.'

Bishop was dazzled by the rising brightness. He closed his eyes against it and tried to reach the visor lying flat over his head. He forced his hands towards it, sucking air in wheezing gasps, the black slime clogging his throat. Suddenly the pressure on his chest was gone; his arms felt free. He snapped the visor down and opened his eyes. The glare was still strong, but the silver chloride in the photochromic glass of the visor steadily counteracted the brightness, enabling him to see around him. Edith was half-crouched, one arm on the seat of her chair, looking towards the pit, her other arm shielding her eyes even though her visor was down. Bishop thought he could see the dark shapes falling away from the light, the images disappearing as though swallowed by the brightness.

The intensity of the light grew, becoming bluish in colour, a red tinge tainting the hue as it became more powerful. Soon the whole site was flooded with the blinding glare, shadows dispersed completely because of the positioning of other lights. The glow merged with the lights from above, the Gazelles

660

maintaining their position, careful not to infringe on the air space of their fellow helicopters.

The area was completely bathed in the peculiar blue-violet light, every shadow quenched by it; even the man-made metal screens were lit from the back with less powerful lights so that no darkness could linger behind them.

Bishop felt his mind soaring, his fear leaving him. 'They've done it!' he cried to Edith. 'It's gone, they've destroyed it!' The scientists had been right all along: the Dark *was* a material thing, a physical property that could be obliterated as any other chemical, gas or solid matter could be. Jacob, poor Jacob, hadn't realised what it was; his mind had been too steeped in the paranormal to understand that the Dark was nothing more than an unexplained phenomenon and not a spiritual entity. Their own minds had fed the exaggeration, making them see things, imagine things, that did not exist. He, Bishop, had received the telepathic thoughts of Edith when he had had the 'visions' at Beechwood; she had known Pryszlak, had associated with his followers, known their cravings, their degeneracy, and he was receptive to her thoughts because he had discovered the dead and mutilated bodies. Everything else was the madness inflicted by the thing known as the Dark, and the earthly evil of those who had been followers of Pryszlak when he had been alive. The knowledge was overwhelming, for it was not just the answer to the terrible, catastrophic events that had recently passed but a reaffirmation of his beliefs over many years.

Bishop staggered towards Edith, his arms reaching out to help her. And it was as he was leaning forward over her, a hand beneath her shoulder to pull her upright, that the shadow fell across the glaring blueness of her clothing like a dark blemish on fresh-fallen snow.

He stumbled away from her and fell, going down on to his knees and staying there, the mask hiding the horror on his face. Edith was rising, looking down at the shadow spreading across her body, her arms outstretched, her legs wide. She lifted her head and screamed up at the skies.

Then the blue-violet glow began to dissolve under the swift-falling darkness.

The shapes came back with the shadows, like wisps of black smoke, twisting, spiralling above the light machines in their pit as though taunting their power. The lights could clearly be seen

661

receding back into their source as though forced by some invisible, descending wall. The generators on one side of the site began to whine, reaching a pitch, slowing, then rising again. Technicians leapt away from them as sparks began to shower outwards. Every glow, whether it was from floodlight, searchlight or handheld torch began to fade, bulbs popping and glass shattering. The instruments inside the control hut became erratic, needles bouncing across dials like metronomes, switches shutting themselves off as though operated by invisible fingers, noises booming from receivers and transmitters. The hut was plunged into darkness as all the lights failed.

Overhead, a helicopter had pulled sharply away from the confused scene below, its broad, ultra-violet beam of light fizzling out as had the others in the companion helicopters. The pilot felt the Gazelle dip suddenly and struggled to maintain height; but the power was no longer there. It hit the helicopter which was rising from below and had inadvertently crossed the former's flight path. The roar of the explosion was deafening, the swirling ball of flame blinding. The tangled machines plunged to the ground, the red flames trailing behind like the tail of a comet. Because both Gazelles had veered away from the site their death fall took them into the troop-filled road. The screams of the soldiers were drowned in the second explosion as the machines struck the ground. Scalding metal and burning petrols splattered towards the exposed men.

The third pilot was more fortunate, for he was able to direct his machine into a clear space two streets away as it lost power. It crashed to the ground, but neither the pilot nor his companion was badly hurt. As they climbed shakily from the damaged machine, they failed to notice the people who moved in the shadows towards them.

Bishop tore the mask from his face, the site now lit only by faint light from the machines in the pit and the red glow that came from the fire in the road beyond. His cheeks were wet from tears of rage and frustration – and newfound fear. Other small fires had started, caused by dropping flames when the helicopters had first made contact, their height spreading the fallout wide. Edith Metlock was silhouetted against the feeble light in the pit, her arms still held wide, the screams still bursting from her. He tried to push himself upright, but the oppressive weight was on him again, bearing him down, crushing his limbs. The black shapes swirled towards him, growing out of the darkness seeming to become solid as they approached. He felt something hit him and he fell to the ground, shocked rather than hurt. He raised himself on one elbow, but there was nothing near him. Another blow, glancing off his forehead, and the skin where he had been touched burned as though ice had been smeared across it. The man he knew had been Pryszlak was before him, his malicious features clear even though they were totally black. The head came forward and his breath was fetid as he revealed his black teeth in a grin that made Bishop cry out and try to cover his eyes. There were others with Pryszlak, familiar faces that had become distorted with their own corruption. The man who had tried to kill him with the shotgun. The bearded man he had seen in his visions at Beechwood. The tall woman, her eyes ablaze with triumphant hate. And her short companion, cackling derisively. Others he did not recognise. And one who could have been Lynn, but the distortion was too great to tell. They moved closer to him, touching his body, prodding him. Yet he could see through them; he could see Edith, still hear her screams; he could still see the dimming glow from the pit.

Then the glass from the lights was bursting upwards, sparks, then flames leaping from the machines as they exploded, destroyed by something that had come to know no limitations, something that could only become stronger. The glass spun in the air, the shards flashing redly as they turned and reflected the distant fire; huge sheets specially strengthened to protect the delicate but powerful filaments beneath them. He saw a piece flying towards Edith, its glistening surface the size of a door, saw it slice her body in half, and closed his eyes before her legs, standing on their own, slowly toppled over.

The hands that were smothering him clutched at his throat and it seemed that each figure had a grip, their faces swimming before him, the mass that was the mind of all of them sucking at his own mind, no longer probing, searching, instead drawing out what it desired, what it needed to exist, to propagate. Just before the blackness became total he saw that crowds had invaded the site, screeching maniacs who attacked anyone who was not of their kind. Jessica was running towards him, her face hardly visible in the darkness. The shroud descended and there was nothing more to see. He could only close his eyes against the Dark.

And then he opened them, wondering where the blinding white

light came from, the light that grew from nothing and washed the area on which the house called Beechwood had once stood with its vivid radiance, scouring out every rut and crevice with its brilliant intensity, making every brick and stone shadowless, casting out the darkness.

The light that burned into his eyes even though he had closed them once more.

. . . The dreams have left me; time has numbed the horror of those terrible days. Even Jessica is no longer afraid of the night. We're together now, not yet as man and wife, but that will come. We need to adjust more fully to our new existence; formal rituals can take their turn.

After two years, we still remember that night at Beechwood as though it were only yesterday. The events have been discussed, analysed, written about, but still no one can explain the phenomenon that took place. The Church tries, of course, and now the scientists are prepared to listen to us, to consider what we tell them, for it was they, the technologists, who were proved wrong, they who came to realise that evil is a spiritual power and not a biological malfunction of the brain. Jacob Kulek would have been pleased – is pleased – that a true bond has been struck between the scientist and the parapsychologist, a working relationship no longer grudging, the alliance opening new doors to our self-discovery. It's everything he worked for when he was alive, only his death achieving those aims. Jessica frequently communicates with him, and I am slowly learning to. Edith is helping, acting as my guide.

She has spoken to my daughter, Lucy, and has promised she will bring her to me soon. She tells me Lucy is very happy, and Edith, too, is content in her own death.

The Dark never returned after that night, but Jacob has warned us it has not been truly vanquished. He says that as long as there is evil in the minds of men, it will always exist. One day, I suppose it will manifest itself again.

There are many of us who are aware now. All those who were at Beechwood and saw the Light form and grow until its effulgence destroyed every dark shadow has gained this unique extra-sensory perception. Only those who could not cope with the new powers they found they possessed have suffered, for their minds have retreated from it, hidden within themselves so they can no longer function as people. The scientist, Marinker, was one such person. But they are being cared for, and have not suffered the same fate as the victims of the Dark, who were left empty and alone, their bodies becoming weak shells that no amount of medical attention could save from wasting away and eventually dying. Some who were present that night say the Light was like a ball of fire, a new sun rising from the earth itself; others claim it had no form, no visible shape, but was a tenuous gas, expanding in sudden flashes, filling the air with its charges. Several say it grew in the shape of a cross, losing its outline as the brightness became too intense. For myself, I remember seeing only the brightness, no shape, no structure, just a brilliant light that flooded my mind.

We've heard reports that the Light has been seen since, in different parts of the world where oppression is prevalent. Jessica tells me Jacob is strangely uncommunicative about this. She has also asked him what part God has played in all this, but again, Jacob will not answer the question. He has told her that our new perception is at too fragile a stage for us to know, that even in death we are still learning, no truth fully realised.

Jacob had known he was dying from internal injuries that night on the rooftop; but he also knew his own mind had to maintain control as death eclipsed his life. The Dark, with its growing power, had endeavoured to fill him as he died, to swamp his thoughts, to destroy his spiritual will; the swiftness of his death prevented that. These black, incorporeal beings knew that as the body died, so the will, the essence that is within everyone, faded too, only to be restored, reawakened, when the tenuous strands that tied it to its earthly shell were finally broken. A metamorphosis that, in our terms, took three days. But Jacob had not allowed his will to deteriorate with a slow death; he had controlled his spiritual power in his last fleeting moments, aware of and playing a wilful part in his own rebirth. As had Boris Pryszlak. Both had chosen different paths.

Jacob had found himself among an awesome realm of energies, a new dimension that was partly of this world, but ultimately a doorway to something greater, something that could be glimpsed, but not fully perceived. He had been confused, lost; and not alone. Others awaited him.

666

He had become part of them, joined the flow that never ceased growing, moving, yet which, again in our terms, had no reality; and eventually a part of that flow was allowed to return to its beginnings and combat an opposite energy that threatened its embryo. We are that embryo. The Dark is that opposite energy. The Light is the power we will become.

None of us who saw the Light resents the affliction it dealt us, for the blindness isn't a burden but a release from our lack of vision. Jessica is carrying our child and we both know that he – it will be a boy – will be blind, like us. The thought makes us happy, for we know he will be able to see as we do.